POMPEY

POMPEY

JONATHAN MEADES

F/382585

JONATHAN CAPE
LONDON

First published 1993
© Jonathan Meades 1993
Jonathan Cape, 20 Vauxhall Bridge Road, London sw1v 2sa

Jonathan Meades has asserted his right
under the Copyright, Designs and Patents Act, 1988,
to be identified as the author of this work

A CIP catalogue record for this book
is available from the British Library

ISBN 0–224–03293–3

Photoset by Deltatype Ltd, Ellesmere Port, Cheshire
Printed in Great Britain by
Clays Ltd, St Ives, plc

I know more than anyone about the firework maker's children, about their antic lives and special deaths.

The night is shrill with colour. It's bright enough to blind. Rubies change to white cascades. The man I saw becomes a bird. The man I saw becomes a bird. All the sky is filled with fountains. My head falls back so far it hurts. Their little mittened hands clutch mine. They gasp to see the flowers go dancing. Loud saltpetre fills our noses. Mineral light beats out the black. Darkness is defeated. That's when I remember that I know more than anyone about Bonny and Donald Tod (as they were from that day forward, for better surely and for richer, yes, till death did) and about Poor Eddie and his fearful gift, and about Jean-Marie's troubles with his work permit, and about Mrs Butt – all about her and her Daph and her Ray and her Ray's big boy Jonjon, who had double the muscles too. And there's nothing I can't tell you about the Old Man Dod who used to work in the print and whose hearing got so sharp with blindness. I can tell you about the teeth and diet of a six-year-old crocodile, and about the way that cancer does its stuff, how it moves like fires beneath the ground. I'll make you feel the noise of a skull being broken. I'll make you listen to the motor of obsession. I'll make you listen to another motor, the one that screeched at night in the dunes to free the wheels – there's the gun beside him, there's the panic in his eyes, there's his forehead slapping against the steering wheel (they found blood on it: AO–1, not much, but enough). I can show you the flaw in the stone in the ring on a stiff finger and you'll never want to eat another soggy biscuit the rest of your days. You'll never take the kiddies to see the fleet or to picnic in a wood. Here's a palm that bleeds to order. Here's another that bleeds because the bolt went through the line of life

5

and two arteries and a delta of tendons and through the median nerve and right into the wood.

I know these people. I lived around them. I've felt their breath and read their brains.

'Snooping?' Bonny's mother used to ask when she found me gaping into the fridge.

You bet.

I've looked on this lot as I did on the lactic profusion and dead animals that littered the racks of that humming coffin all those years ago: I can still inventory the stacked oblongs from the Commonwealth and the fatty fists of beef and the brand-new plastic tubs whose lids were the colour of surgical rubber. But what I liked, what I sought when I sidled off to that kitchen was the icy balm, the cold gust when the light came on. There was the excitement. It was the defiance of summer and the certain eternity of electric midwinter that pulled me to it. The chill was all artifice, sure. But it stabbed for real. Did I think thus then? I didn't. I didn't think of the plays that could be made on *frozen*. I didn't know the milestones to eternity were quarterly bills – and bankruptcy was a distant state of disgrace, akin to tuberculosis and divorce.

After using this book please wash your hands. Thank you.

It was me that pushed Poor Eddie in the river.

The Grieving Widow gasped and started from the prone willow, so ripping her tartan trews (McGuinness, yellow and black). I remember my father's glare in the mini-second before he waded in after the floundering boy: I was for it. I remember the ripple on the water, the weed billowing like the hair of a drowned Venusian, the weeping leaves that stroked the stream, the moored boat and the rod with a gyroscopic reel. A gingham Thermos spilt, the rug turned moss green, a thistle spiked my thigh, my mother held a sandwich as though it was a Schick. John Constable had stood just here thirteen decades before and now Poor Eddie was in The Grieving Widow's arms, soaking her, sobbing, trembling, his hair stuck down with temporary brilliantine. That was the end of that picnic.

We rowed round the point and up the dark stream away from the spire past the jungle and Old Morphill's jazz-modern palace and the great cedars and Douglas pines in the garden of The Garth (which Bonny's parents didn't buy till years later, when Saxon-Smith the dentist disgraced himself and Grace Saxon-Smith moved the family away). Poor Eddie sat swaddled between his mother and mine in the stern and I cowered in the bow; my father's arms had never looked so big, he feathered the oars with giant's ire, the rowlocks squeaked, his tattersall back glowered at me.

He moored the boat and had me drag the oars, one at a time, between the barren apple trees to the brick shed which had once been Twose's abattoir and whose stalls now housed the apiarist's tackle of Twose's deaf son, a reluctant butcher with a snail in his ear. I tripped over the slimy tiled duct down which the blood of countless beasts had flowed to the river, to the green pool where pike with massive memories still waited for the viscera of kine. The Grieving Widow led the ambulatory blanket to the Morris Minor whose muddied seats I would be blamed for; I hung back among the hives and lichenous trees of the orchard till my mother took me by the hand. No one spoke as the car jostled with the furrows; I sat in the back, in disgrace. I knew that what I had done would have been bad enough in any circumstances, no matter whom I had caused to ruffle the surface.

But with Eddie: it was a wicked thing to do to Poor Eddie, to say such things, to hurt him that way. Sure, he *did* invite it, all his life he invited it. His terrible passivity made ogres of us all, he was quarry.

Beside the willow where his mother sat an arterial leet, which fed the water meadows, joined the river. Mr Thick, the octogenarian drowner who worked the baby sluices, had properly succumbed to his trade disease (arthritis) and the channels were grown over with reeds. Poor Eddie gingered behind me as I stalked along the muddy bottom. I stopped where a rotten fence stake lay across my path; I had seen a viper here the previous autumn. It was in slough, it was the milky pink of antibiotic syrup. I kicked the reeds with my colander sandals and told Eddie that though it had been three feet long and broad as a cricket bat he was not to be scared because me, I had a father who would slay it (my very words) should it chase us. Poor Eddie's marmalade eyes seeped, he clambered from the leet and knock-kneed beside it towards his mother. When I caught up with him he was on the bank where the water-rats had sculpted model cliffs; the river was immediately impervious to scrutiny, it was all surface, its bed was invisible, John Constable coloured it shiny tar and it hadn't faded.

'There are', I said, tugging his aertex sleeve, 'crocodiles in there, lots.'

He cried mutely, he must have marvelled at the abomination of the world. And then he was in a different plane to me, quitting the solidity of kingcups and cowpats for an horizontal foxtrot through the elements.

It was the splash, the splashes, the collisions of water with water that made her gasp, that made The Child Bride (not yet The Grieving Widow, not quite) gasp and start, and the cries too, those screeches – the last sound she heard the man she loved make was an appalling one, in all his life he'd never uttered such a noise. Death isn't like what goes before it, it brings along its own props, makes you do things dignity forbade, we're all cowards at the last – the screams were those of a man telling the devil he'd made a pact, that he'd sacrifice the poor little boy, anything, to be spared. The Child Bride (just about The Grieving Widow – *now*) hauled herself from the back seat of the shooting-brake where she'd been napping and, with one foot shoed and with one shoe in her hand, ran between trees with scaley, leprous bark, obscene blooms and leaves whose fallen spines pierced her instep. She ran by the abandoned termitaries where her son and his father had stood for her Leica five minutes before, for the last photograph – l. to r.: Eddie shying from the sun; his father, dressy in bush hat, dashing kerchief, martial shirt, jodhpurs, leather and canvas boots (one, filled still with limb, was netted two miles downstream); his father's left arm gripping a bargain knobkerrie; the termitary which was a ruined gothic asylum tower. She ran past the site of this unrepeatable tableau. She stumbled and hobbled towards the great river. And there was Eddie. She called to him, swooped in embrace, and he turned from the sparkling caramel water which was also a grave and told her: 'Daddy gone in the river with a big fish.'

Now Eddie was not yet four years old or literate, but he'd been to the zoo, he owned a book of colour plates and avuncular prose called *Your Reptiles*, his sight was fine, his view had been unobscured. He knew what he had seen, he knew that a fourteen-foot-long crocodile (*Crocodylus cataphractus*, doubtless) is not a big fish; equally he knew he had to protect his mother from that terrible reality and thus discovered the comforting power of euphemism; and he was protecting himself too – an unspoken beast is a beast already in transit to oblivion. Shock possesses this apparatus of diversionary solace, shock is intoxicating, it invades your head, it's a benevolent trank (you can o.g.), it's a sensory tourniquet (you can tie it too tight). The

9

trouble is, it doesn't last; when its anaesthesia dissipates the hurt begins, the unbandaged wound begins to fester. The strength of shock is its aptness: it is a phenomenal reaction to a phenomenal circumstance. When it disappeared and you, Eddie, were returned to a mundane state, the memory of that circumstance refused to abate with it – the enemy was still there, and you were unprotected.

In the month following his father's death Eddie curled round his mother at night, cosseted her and hugged her as he had on the river bank. He stroked her while she keened, he clutched the hand that hadn't the cork-tip viced in it, he kissed her marvellous neck and her cheeks – which powder and light made like fruit, which tears made like brawn. He stood with her beside the aircraft when the box that brought back the bit was loaded. He nodded gravely when she cursed the man at the embassy whose desk had been so big it was like the incomprehensible continent itself. When she wept and wiped the pink moustache from the glass with her ever kneading fingers Eddie offered his hanky, said that he'd take care of her and of the little sister they had always promised him.

'He's quite the little man,' said a porky, floral-printed woman who boarded the plane at Lagos. The Grieving Widow believed, wrongly, that she was mocking Eddie and ignored her while she listed the variety artistes she knew (Sid Field, The Fabulous Dunstables, Ray Butt, Luton And Who?), but Eddie revelled in the compliment and enjoyed listening to her because her friends had exotic names and cars with rumble-seats. When, though, he sensed his mother's distaste for his new companion he feigned sleep. He was that loyal; shock gave him strength. And the funeral protracted the shock: ritual heightens grief, makes it momentous, enforces concentration on its object who is yet gone for so short a time that it is unimaginable that he will not come back – the conviction of death's certainty is founded on prolonged exposure to absence rather than on the presence of the meat in the coffin or on bearing witness to the agent (physical or chemical, alien or quisling, sudden or chronic) of that immeasurable change. Thus it wasn't for a while that Poor Eddie properly connected his father's infinite truancy (and the lack of stairs in the house where his mother took him to live) to what he had seen under the equatorial sun that ruddied afternoon.

In the morning they had, once again, driven through the mad streets of Léopoldville from the Hotel Troozlaan (one bed for three) to the house behind the white wall on rue C. Lemaire where flies lived in the moist, crateral sores on beggars' limbs and where soft-boned children bit on roots protruding from the unmade pavement. Once again Eddie had sat with his mother on the terrace of the house (cubistic, piebald – dazzling blanco and acacia shade) while the balloon-breasted servant brought them coffee and fruit pulp. And for the third day running Eddie had, whenever he turned towards the house, seen his father and the man who spoke funny English together in the room whose ceiling fan made slow parabolas: mostly the man sat on the edge of a teak table with verisimilar elephantine legs, mostly his father moved. He made scrolls in the muggy air with his hands, sometimes his hands were palmate claws, sometimes he pushed them across his huge forehead which Eddie thought was a sort of cheese. One time when Eddie looked his father was enacting a domestic calvary, his arms stretched along the window, the seat of his jodhpurs corrugated on the sill. Then he beat a pretend-drum and revolved to look out to the terrace: Eddie had never seen his face like that before, Eddie was frightened and delighted by his father's magical metamorphosis into pirate or giant or wicked gypsy. Eddie sensed (though he can hardly have articulated it to himself) that the intense actuality of panto and picture-books might shift into the everyday crawl – when you're that little time is a basket case in a broken chair, it moves with quadriplegia.

The man scratched his face which was made of roast, cracked pigskin and decorated with extra moustaches above his eyes, then he put a hand on Eddie's father's shoulder. Oh, Eddie was proud of the way his father scowled, of the way he spat words (jagged speech-bubble, exclamation marks), of the way he removed the chummy hand. You don't hear anything, the puzzling panes with massive boughs and a version of the sky on them preclude hearing, this is all mute-show. But there is sound

11

in this scene: beside the interminable loop of hoopoes, grey parrots, green monkeys etc., there is the violin of the man's son. This, too, is repetitious.

In an upstairs room, behind a window meshed against insects, he is, once more, playing Dvorak's Humoresque; his tone, his phrasing, the length of pause between reprises are invariable, as they were yesterday and the day before. Now and then he walks onto the sun roof beside his room and stares unsmilingly down at The Child Bride and Poor Eddie, all the while gripping the metal deckrails with hands too large for a boy of six years, too meaty for a violinist, so sprawlingly knuckled they promise willed asphyxia, paroxysmal ill, the fistic law. His eyes abet all this, they'll look indulgently on the wrong wrought by the hands. They track Eddie as he runs to greet his father who picks him up and holds him to his trunk; the little boy is soon astride his father's shoulders, complicating the silhouette. Then, before he knows it, they are back in the car. This time they have not bidden the man who spoke funny English goodbye, nor the boy. And this time they do not drive back to the hotel.

'Herman's Cross,' says Eddie's poor father, regretfully.

Poor Eddie's father drove to his death through the eastern suburbs of Léopoldville. Street goats fled nimbly from the shooting-brake's path, men in skirts on bicycles teetered as it passed. He held his hand on the horn and it cried like a fractious animal. Eddie sat on the rear seat gauging their progress into disorder: the houses got smaller; their white walls got dirtier; the walls stopped trying to be white; the houses stopped trying to be houses and became hutches, cardboard kennels, machines for subsisting in; a black face pressed itself to the window – it owned no teeth and had grey pus for lips; the king of Belgium's face was printed on a woman's bottom; Mr Macadam who lived near Bristol zoo and had visited every road before Eddie had not come here; Eddie felt car sick. And he was worried by the loudness of his father's voice and the way his father said the same things over and again: 'loose wallah [or loose walloon] . . . morals of a pig'. Eddie assumed that morals were contiguous with skin. Another thing his father repeated was 'every last penny'. Also: 'no ruddy redress . . . end up in the damned slammer . . . you know what the Frogs say about them . . . over a barrel . . .'

The Child Bride raced herself at smoking, chain-lighting Craven A in a serial Dutch fuck while the vehicle did jarring vaults from one furrow to the next. When Eddie's father wasn't shouting he was hissing oaths and mocking roadside women with enamel bowls and plaited mats: he responded to Eddie's complaint of car sickness with the phrase 'you wincey little driveller'. He accelerated and punched an insect. Eddie endured his oesophagal torture, the ball of socks in his gullet which jumped and distended as the hills became a switchback.

There was the river, there, across it, was Brazzaville with its sinuous attic of smoke. At Kallina Point Eddie's father stopped the shooting-brake and walked towards the cliff with a bottle of *alcool blanc*. The Child Bride was crying; she turned to Eddie and told him to go to his father. They looked down on the lake-like pool named after Stanley who first saw it the year Custer got his. Eddie's father stared at the bottle's label (gothic script and belfry), he didn't drink from it. He scraped the umber ground to reveal earth that was flowerpot red: 'Like Devon Eddie.' Eddie knew Devon was a sort of celestial chocolate that he was going to eat lots of when rationing ended; now, having seen the colour of the stuff, he wasn't so sure. He was even less sure when his father told him he had seen a calf born in Devon when he was the age Eddie was now. Eddie accepted that the mysteries of life and confectionery might be but one. Now, why was his father standing so still, so close to the edge of the cliff, what could he see in the river by coma-gaping at it? (River: pale chocolate and eight knots, cliff: 50 feet above it). And did the half gill of viscous liquor he distractedly and painfully swigged help him see? Unequivocal no – the label was a lie, it was a distillation of palms flavoured with mango skin, it promoted optical neuritis, coagulation of the tissues, melancholy, red noses in black people: it was good for camp-stoves and wounds. Eddie's father drank more; then he turned and took his little boy by the hand.

The next place they stopped was different because The Child Bride had quit weeping, just. She got out with the smaller of the two Leicas Eddie's father had given her the day after they met, and he followed her through the passenger door to avoid the cutting rushes he had parked against – they swayed like a chorus of hissing sibyls. The happy family snaps: perm eight from mother, father, son, tree, termitary, bargain knobkerrie; it's The Child Bride who holds the bottle; in the one that Eddie took his parents are at a mad angle – his father's falling from the frame, his mother is begrutten but still pretty. Then the film is expended, she puts the camera in its case and lobs the bottle to him: 'Shut eye – 't'll make me beautiful for you again Poppet.' She moued and went back to the shooting-brake.

On the river bank Eddie wondered at his father's thirst and capacity for stillness (only his right arm and his thyroid cartilage moved). He liked the look of a thin isthmus stretching into the river, it was on his scale. The sun overachieved that day; shadows were black, made pygmies of everything, made pygmies. In the river floated black bodies, logs maybe – Eddie peered and the sandbanks, which rose like the dorsal deformations of drowned beasts, hurt his eyes. Everything seemed derived from animals: the trees were totemic ruins of animals; their super-terrestrial roots were skeletal claws dug for ever into the earth; their trunks were trunks – thick skinned proboscides frozen for all time; all the puny bushes wanted to be trees but couldn't, so cowered. And from one to another swung monkeys, gymnastic prostitutes, screeching because they wanted to be men but couldn't: animals have much to resent, and they get their own back – check the bottom of your shoes, the joint of heel and instep. That's nothing; when men conspire with them in that revenge (for no matter what end) men cede primacy.

Eddie's father knew that, knew this was sure death. He threw the empty bottle in the river and beckoned Eddie and hugged him, squatting.

'I love you Eddie,' he said, and fell back on his bottom. He bothered to dust the seat of his jodhpurs; he wasn't good at getting to his feet, he was a temporary quadruped when he told the bemused boy: 'Never trust a Belgian Eddie, never ever trust . . .' He tried to become a man again but his hooves failed him. 'Trusht' would be a phonetic misrepresentation, in that last

14

stage he achieved emphatic consonantal precision. Then his elbows let him down. He shrugged and made a face that was all gums, and crawled towards the knobkerrie; he didn't turn to see Poor Eddie, who thought this was a game, crawling after him till his knees itched. The knobkerrie became a prosthesis for the already dying man. It just about supported him on his terminal stagger – wood alcohol, sun-glare and sweat turned that drip down the sandy isthmus (which was also a pirate's plank) into a babel for his eyes.

He conceived a formula for computing the number of grains of sand in the entire isthmus but forgot it before he could apply it.

He saw grains of sand the names of whose colours he knew he knew.

He forgot whether he was very hot or very cold. He saw a spur-winged plover grubbing on a little mudberg and his eyes told him the mudberg moved when the bird screeched, flew, became a mote. Then there was no mudberg. He was shagged by the strength he used, by the weakness that gave him strength, by his fear of the future that would never be the past, by his fear of the water that would quash oxygen, turn him eternally inert, fill him up till he overflowed. The finger of sand narrowed, water lapped up close by him either side, his short shadow rippled. He was with the river now, nearly. He took one last swing with the knobkerrie, at a pile of rotting branches and sun-stewed leaves and bark shards and something white.

Well, that did it. The mudberg showed its teeth and its terrifying grin with many folds too many like an evil Irishman, it slapped him with its tail, the knobkerrie skittled to nowhere, he screamed before the first teeth got him – he could not believe it.

He saw the churned water getting red, as he bucked in frozen time he saw the machine that had come to keep him from himself, he saw its awful eye (just one) and teeth like amber arrowheads and the special tooth which had already severed his right leg. Up and down he went, in and out the water – he might have died of drowning after all; he might have died of shock (just the sight of such a lizard from hell is enough to make my spine sing). This one smelled of rancid musk, its skin was crazed, cratered scale, self-distending scale.

15

This one dismembered Eddy's father without ever letting go of him – it had many mouths; the water crashed in cataract. There was pink spray, that's the pink you see when you die – you give your blood to the world now you no longer need it.

In less than a minute Poor Eddie's father was dead; in his time, in real time it took the beast (387 kg; two full grown impala, a black child and part of a sewing machine already in its stomach) forty-one years to do for him – each of those years was meant to crawl in front of him. Something ruptured his kidneys and spleen during the seventeenth year, and his cerebral cortex snapped in the mid thirties – so he never reached the end, never saw himself as he was in that last instant, mouth to mouth (the second mouth is a deadly weapon). Now he's in the full foul reptile. Now Eddie hears his mother behind him. Poor Eddie's poor father was shaken into sobriety before he died.

If you walk down Britford Lane . . .

No, walk with me down Britford Lane. Can you remember the whaler by the Sea Scouts' hut and the echoes under New Bridge and the slimy island water rats? (They're just rats, really.) And what about the sleek MGs in Furlong's showroom: they were all polish and clean oil – smell it still? Can you? Can you remember? Did you follow me the way I came, past Arms's corner shop and Sid the butcher's and through the car park of The Swan (you've got gravel in your shoes)? Arms is dead and his daft son too, both proof that shock-frizz hair does not mean genius; Sid must be 80, if he's still with us, bless his chops, bless his kidneys, he knew his Vernon's – he cried when Duncan Edwards died, was most upset anyway; The Swan is The Grey Fisher now (and that's a steak you're eating). With me? Were you with me then? There was a house whose thatch was poured honey, there was another in whose garden sat an old man with purple sporades on his pate watching tits and finches peck at rinds, at bricks of lard – he was pining for his wife and he never felt the cold.

It was always cold down Britford Lane. There was always sleet down there; the morse babble of heaven's waste blew across the edge of town. The horses wore blankets all the year, they stood forlorn among henges of hay. The fields flooded, the cricket hut was skew from rot, the midden gleamed with frost at noon, ice-panes glazed the puddles in the unmade road, trees groaned, little ducks died because spring didn't show when it should have: there were always cyclonic recidivists, isobarbarians, rolling in from the north, the east, one of those points, at it again despite their previous. Codeine mist rose from Navigation Straight to show its line across the fields.

It was always damp down Britford Lane. Broken willows, all black with fungus, sprawled like dead mendicants in the boggy meadows; it was bad for your chest, buggered your bronchioles, brought on lumbago.

When The Grieving Widow cycled back to this place where she'd brought her Eddie (*she had no choice*) she wheezed and coughed and the rubber grips didn't mitigate the jarring of her cold bones. All the bobbing dynamo-light picked out was the floury fog, the sauce that settled nightly round their little home, she never saw another man's sperm so long as she lived. She got saddle satisfaction instead: that's what the Tap Room Chaps at the White Jam Tart sniggered during their sessions. She cycled past houses with their own roof, past houses which shared a roof, past houses whose roof had (Eddie said) been put on too soon. Theirs was one of these: no topping windows (all talk of suicide was of course proscribed); eaves that an adult could reach with hardly a leap; no stairs – so, if a little boy enters the naphthalic darkness of his mother's wardrobe and revels in the disorienting forest of fur and crêpe de chine and then teeters back into the light high on the heels she never wears now there's no chance of a mortal tumble, he simply falls into his mother's arms as she comes in the front door rouged by the cold, puffed, shiny with droplets and love. She kneels on the scraped parquet by the door to her bedroom, by the front door, by the door to the living room – they're that close these doors. And the one to her room is the one to Eddie's too: that's his bed by the window, and every morning (after dreams where his father is throwing him high and not being there to catch him) he stumbles from the soaked sheets and wipes himself with the dry part of his pyjama trousers and lies beside his mother who's twice as warm as he is and ready to clutch him without waking.

She put the back of the bike inside the porch to keep the precious saddle dry for morning and opened the door. Eddie looked like his face had been food-mixed, and she gasped in the micromoment before she twigged – lipstick. Then she sighed and dropped to her knees, not far, either from the bathroom or kitchen doors – this was a very small dwelling: count the rooms on the fingers of a deformed hand. There was no room for a live-in, no money moreover (he died in debt, he left them bills and paper trouble). There was no money even for an orphan from a firebombed home on the Elbe, the sort of girl who'd cross Europe for the promise of a daily crust – they didn't come cheaper. They did, oh they did. The sort of girl there was money for was Stella who had abandoned her four-year-old charge half an hour before his mother returned in order to meet a bombadier in the scrumpy bar by the bus station. The Grieving Widow expected nothing but stupidity and negligence of the girl. She had born two illegits (not cognate with *git*, or get, a whore's whelp) by the age of seventeen.

The first died; Stella wasn't to know that the hospital door outside which she left the mewling boy in a pillow-case one February night was bolted, that the kitchen staff entered by a different wing. Probation.

The second, a girl, and the issue of her union with either a coalman or 'a fellow from out Grateley', was taken for adoption. None of this saddened Stella or quashed her eagerness to please; no doubt she pleased her bombadier before he caught the last bus to Larkhill – if she pleased him too long he'll have had to steal a car.

She had certainly pleased Eddie when she got him home from school. The Grieving Widow was kneeling again, dabbing at the boy's face with cold cream and cottonwool, when he leant ever so slightly forward with bulbous cheeks and bombed eyes and vomited onto her chest. No warning. The lumpy gut-mix stuck to her jersey, miraculously transformed oatmeal wool into steaming porridge. This was Stella's doing; Eddie was the agent, the gastric timebomb she had witlessly rigged.

Mother and son cried. The one provoked the other, the sotto sob precedes the howl. When routine's dam fractured she always did the same, she always cried, she was that tense, that brittle, she lacked elastic, was in servitude to her daily design, was fuelled by nicotine and scratching. And Eddie cried because he'd made her cry, because he was ashamed he'd done that. He tried to comfort her, the sick stuck to his shirt and so they both had to change – he didn't know all petticoats were not so frayed as hers. She made him eat plain toast for his tummy. The larder was a baby green baby coffin; she sought margarine to spread on her wedge of toast.

There was none, there was never much, this wasn't like the big cold coffin that the other Vallenders, the proper Vallenders had: the refrigerator of my dead husband's brother's wife purrs in endless plenitude while this cantilevered box with an airbrick in its back is mute with want and its flymesh is redundant. Still, there had been some marge there that morning, without question there had because a) it always lasted till Thursday when Arms's shopboy Vivian brought the order in a reeking carbolic box that she'd cut up to insulate the roof; b) she would otherwise have checked in her purse that she had enough to buy more at lunchtime, and then would have spent the morning worrying about her coming profligacy; c) she could picture the plate (Poole Pottery, chocolate and turquoise, cracked) and the greaseproof refolded over most of a half-pound block.

'Oh Eddie – where *is* the margarine?' An inch of detumescent ash fell from in front of her face, Eddie tried to pick it from the crazed lino and dispersed it, she rubbed her wedding ring against her chronically sore red finger.

Eddie said: 'I drank it Mumma.'

Stella had said: 'Not much milk there isn't Eddie – wan' tea?'

Eddie told her he wanted melted margarine because he liked the taste of it on his curly kale; so Stella put it in a saucepan, with the handle of course protruding at Eddie's head height, and when it began to boil poured it in a navvy mug that The Grieving Widow had found in the lane and used for Eddie's painting water (you'll be there the day that Eddie drinks his painting water, I was there). Stella watched Eddie ingest the variably dense oils – a section through the navvy mug shows strata of spectral sludge from window grey to grainy manilla. Then Eddie watched her stretch her lips till she was toothless and fellate a lipstick that she coaxed from its gold tin prepuce.

'I got', she said – and here she moues at the mirror, 'to meet this chap. 'E's gettin' 'is stripe soon. Like that did you?'

Eddie's lips were greasy too; he followed Stella down the twilit path to the old wicket gate that crumbled as he clung to it. The hinges bubbled with rust, the paint sloughed, the wood was halva.

'She'll be in in jus' a jiff, yer mum.'

Stella stumbled down the lane, between the ramparts of the hedges, cursing the puddles, huddled in her collar, hurrying after the place where the lamplight started, further down the lane. When she was inside it Eddie shivered and turned to face his little home, lit like a pumpkin. He went and dressed as Stella's ape, painted himself too.

The Grieving Widow sought the secret sore on her scalp that she had made by chronic scratching and scratched it again; it yielded blood-smeared scabs beneath her nails. She feared she would drive herself bald: the hairless clearing grew from tooth-size to sixpence-size during the first year of her widowhood, the skinflakes grew proportionately, dandruff to seborrhoea. And the more she worried the more it itched and the more care she took to dissemble this willed alopecia with hanks held against the current of her crown by grips that fell about her neck when she began to scratch again.

She scratched with her cigarette hand, said to Eddie: 'She, she'll have to go.' She kidded herself that she had the choice – she hadn't; and to say such a thing was to punish Eddie who loved Stella, revelled in the two hours he spent with her each afternoon (this day had, truly, been exceptional), and hoped that she would marry him. He hoped his lack of stripe would not disqualify him, consoled himself with the knowledge that it had many years to grow, and wondered if the proscription on sliding down banisters in Bonnie's parents' house, or in my parents' house, or in any house where he furtively compensated for his lack of domestic opportunity, was prompted by this practice's harm to the developing stripe. The rectitude of this notion became sure.

He asked my father: 'Do you ever slide down banisters?' No.

He asked me, in my father's presence. No, of course not.

He must have tried to picture his own father's back, to recapture the downs and downy mountains of begetting flesh above a series of stretched waistbands, to summon the image of the stripe that indeed proceeded with vertical authority up the middle, paler than the rest and lumpy with subcutaneous bumps. Thus he conceived an antipathy to banisters (and to

stairs, tree-houses, ladders, diving boards, double decker buses) that matched his fear of shoes and wallets made from reptiles' skins. And he became proud of the rented bungalow; he boasted about its exotic etymology and Bengali origins, though it lacked even a verandah.

He fixed my father's eye and told him: 'Bungalows don't *need* stairs.'

He even blamed Stella's accident on the stairs in her mother's house, on the single flight she mostly missed out on the way from up there to down here where she lay whining and bleeding and drunk. Everyone blamed the drink. Eddie knew everyone was wrong, drink didn't break bones and make haemorrhages. It was risers, treads, carpets, it was floors which accelerated towards you that did the damage, that got in their retaliation for the constant pedal assault made on them. Poor Eddie held Stella's hand and the woman in the next bed – was that ash smeared on her face? – tried to smile at him; the ward was full of women whose faces were wrong, and they were all turned towards him.

He mimicked his mother's action when he had dyspepsia and rubbed his palms on Stella's tummy: 'Ooh Eddie tha's so nice . . . so warm your hands are. Real hot they are.'

One of the women smirked. The Grieving Widow came back into the ward having nipped out for a gasper: 'We'd better be on our way Eddie . . . let Stella get some rest.' Eddie trailed beside his mother down the ranks of beds looking back at Stella whose tummy flushed with thermal balm long after he'd gone.

Eddie and his mother got off the bus at New Bridge Road near the allotments and Eddie wondered if it was there, among the hurdles and bean poles and giant-leafed rhubarb and tiny huts and corrals of compost and tufty causeways, that he might start to look for the baby that Stella had lost.

Douglas Vallender had a big voice, a martial stride, navvy's hands. His face was veal in winter, beef in summer; its lips were obese all the year through, the hair above it was scalped from a baby. His tummy bulged like a cyclopean teat. He was always laughing and quaffing (his sort of word) and slapping backs too young to suffer such strong hands. He liked big houses, big checks, big cars. He wore tweed woven to blind, drove cars with plenty of wood on them, with running boards and exhausts like exposed intestines. He ate with his hands, licked his lips, was kind to animals and good at knots. He swam, fished, sailed, picked up Bonny, sent her spinning to the sky and was there to field her before she hit the lawn. He rolled on the hard blond grass (water shortage) so his little girl might clamber over him. He drank long from his pewter tankardful of Guinness and White Shield. He threw a ball to Poor Eddie who was crouched beneath the yew prodding an exposed root with a stick; the ball bounced past him through the dusty shade and Douglas Vallender shook his head.

The Grieving Widow warned from her deckchair: 'You'd better fetch it Darling else Uncle Douglas won't play with you after lunch.' Eddie obeyed, and was still searching a border of shrubs and manure clods when Monica came from the house and called us to lunch. Douglas Vallender stuck out a hand to The Grieving Widow and to my mother: 'Come on girls. Rally, rally, rally.'

And to me: 'Get yer skates on Johnson old chap. Sirloin's already cooling. Do you know,' – he pirouetted with Bonnie horizontal and gurgling – 'Johnson, why it's called *sirloin*? 'Sbecawse Henry Eight, y'know, Good King Hal and all that, *knighted* it. Arise Sir Loin.'

I believed him. I went on believing him for years. I liked the way he addressed me as Johnson.

The judgment of children is invariably aberrant. Never think otherwise. A child is born into solipsism, is blessed with the confidence of the ignorant, is confided in by the ignorant, is importuned by children in adult bodies, i.e. the maquis of the inadequate and stunted and cerebrally fucked – the ones who want it all simple for ever, the model makers, the gricers logging locos on wintry platforms. (Never talk to a man with a vacuum flask and a duffle-bag.) The fact is, a mutual attraction exists between children and wrong 'uns; the wrong sort of wrong 'uns, the hairy shinned onanists who'll do their tronk solo, Rule 48, out of fear of reprisals, the ones whose probing fingers trespass beneath the elastic and have nails so long the skin is bound to break, the mucous membrane bound to bleed.

Douglas Vallender's fingers are not like this. They are smeared with his own excrement, water drips from them back into the bowl; it's no use pretending that his dislike of Eddie is qualified.

His timid nephew (5) enters the dining room having searched for the ball – it's impossible to remember whether he found it: Eddie's knees are grained with dirt, they're big fingertips. And his shirt's out, his socks are down, his parting's zigzagged with hanks and shocks. The beef is bleeding on the Spode, the Yorkshire leatherette, the veg are making the windows wet. Here's Mrs Gub the help, smelling of old age and boiled laundry, and carrying the gravy. The pannelling's rich, brown, bogus Stuart; above it are plates, a coach horn, mugs with monks' faces, beersteins with lids. Monica is strapping Bonny in her high chair, my mother's drinking pink gin with the angosturas in, The Grieving Widow's at the leaded window – there's much she might envy out there: the Allard, the Healey shooting-brake, Douglas's traction engine, the cedars and wellingtonias and acacias, the tile hanging, the brick paths, Russet the pony in his edible field, the white post and rail, the orderly gravel raked like plough. Her bungalow is smaller than Douglas's garage.

She told Eddie to wash. The dog beneath the table sighs. Eddie opened the heavy door with battered hinges and crossed the hall. The soles of his sandals squeaked on the tiles (the complexity of whose pattern was enhanced by lozenges of glass-stained light so rich he wanted to own them. And a chair was striped with purple, a chest was arced in green). The stair newel was carved into fructuous abundance, his fingers loitered in the deep dark incisions. The corridor beyond was dusk all day long, coats hung from contorted pegs and their bristly hems brushed his face, it all reeked of Uncle Douglas's rubber riding macs, skirted garments so stiff that they were headless men emitting bad breath from the sites of their truncation. Eddie turned the handle of the lavatory door.

Douglas Vallender crouched on the lavatory, his thighs spilled over its sides, and his lip jutted and his hands were clenched round his knees in excretory effort. His tiny penis (a clitoral apology for a cock, a cockette, a pork penknife) peeped out of its silky bush, which was itself obscured by creamy belly folds. He filled this small room. Eddie gaped at the vulnerable monster. Douglas roared. The smell was a grown-up one, one that Eddie (representing all children) hated; Eddie was going to say something like 'no lock Uncle', something like 'sorry Uncle'. Eddie said nothing. Douglas Vallender shifted himself, extended a freckled arm into the lavatory bowl, chose his missile with prompt deliberation, and hurled it at his nephew.

Now the average daily stool is about 140 grammes (5 oz for readers with pre-metric scales), representing 12.5% of food taken. Douglas Vallender ate much more than that. Moreover he was prone – fatally prone is near the mark – to constipation (he didn't get enough thiamine, suffered a lazy colon); he used violent aperients – senna, fig, desiccated plum, dry aloes, the resin called scammony. These are the agents of a rectal wash and brush up, of intra-colonic hoovering; thus what he threw at Poor Eddie was not sausage but stew (actually it was his breakfast).

'You pissy little orphan – bugger off! What are you bloody playing at . . .' This is what Eddie said he said. It doesn't make it better that Douglas missed – he didn't have much to aim at, a peeping face stuck between jamb and door, that's all, and he was throwing from a sitting position, he has that excuse too. No, it makes it worse: the little boy who creeps back into the dining

25

room and blubs into his mother's lap is physically unchanged. There are no faecal freckles to show you, there's no impasted stain on his shirt. There's just the eye that saw, the drawer of memory where it's in store, the shadow on him. Douglas wipes the door down, humming the starting bars of Tchaikovsky's first piano concerto, 'bom bom-bom bom-bom-bom-bom-bom bom-bom' – you know the one. He wipes in time to it.

He claps his hands as he enters to carve, his clean hands. The hands, anyway, do not necessarily touch the meat they carve. The Grieving Widow scrutinises him – Eddie's not usually a liar (he's been at her ear from close to, filling it with sibilant horrors). And he gets worse, his asthma plays up, his chest fills with short wave signals. Douglas beams at him as he saws the meat. And The Grieving Widow wonders, she doubts her son in the face of the brother-in-law who did her, stitched her, showed little mercy and no grace. How could she have doubted Eddie? (Something platinum crosses left to right at this point.) Yumyum, Douglas licks his fingers, passes a plateful of meat to my mother. He sharpens the knife on a horn-handled steel.

The carving of meat is for many men emblematic of strength, male assertion, sex; carving matters to these unfortunates (they can't all be as genitally wanting as Douglas, they can't all be compensating). Blade against steel is an aural analogue of the duel – shut your eyes, picture an épée, then another, then two men who don't need skeins of wool down the front of their tights. Now keep your eyes on the rolled, tightly-strung strata of quondam bull and see the golden shower of fat emitted by the vicious tines. Don't go – the knife now makes its first incision, shaves the brown bark from the hunk of amputee: how do we know, Douglas, that our amputee really was bull when it resembles and represents man? It's cannibalism, this hieratic surgery, isn't it? It's familial eucharist (which is the same thing) celebrated by the head man. It's auto-celebration of the head man's prowess as provider, hunter, killer. Castration, too – it's that as well: the offal chop, the chopper off. Come off it, it is. Own to it D.V. Whoever did you want to chop?

Certainly, Johnson, it was, yes, a limb of the vanquished. But, Johnson, I tell you – I spell it out – that meat, that Sirloin (you got that etymology from me, remember?), that beef was bull, wasn't my brother. Ask the croc. Ha! (How *are* things? Felt your Pa the other dusk – still offish, you know. I'd like some light, Johnson . . .)

Tosser, dead tosser.

The light made by garden beeches is fugitive. It worries children. Here's Eddie, Poor Eddie, postprandially pram-pushing – here he is, in the sort-of shade, heaving Bonny's hefty Pedigree Elizabethan. He's tired, can go no further. His baby cousin gurgles and bounces, she's a perfect model of a dappled being. Aren't her little hands just so? Cute as mini-bricks, curled like caterpillars.

Me, I'm the only witness there ever was. The house is almost out of sight, a flash of bargeboard beyond the fronds, bits of bricks, the dazzle of a sun-struck pane – this is all that's discernible from the Clump. And they can't see us. My mother's badered, slumped in an armchair, she's berating Douglas for his meanness to The Grieving Widow. Douglas is grinning. The Grieving Widow's contorted in embarrassment like a fretful foetus and she's at her scalp again, as ever. Monica's going, 'Oh pipe down Bunty and have another drink.' In the meadow beyond the Clump a Friesian calf has a complicated curved formation of flies round its head, a gyroscopically mutating hat that I'd like to touch, that I would touch were it not for the barbed wire, the thorn hedge, the hairy stingers, my fright. And I'm captivated by the fondant caramel that issues from the calf's eyes and dries crystalline across its soft hide.

I ignore Eddie till he calls: 'Jonerfin, it's that dog.' I turn to him: what I saw, what I see now (effortlessly, through the layers of the ages) is Eddie bent over the hooded pram so it lists on its contorted springs that are complicated as suspenders. The glossy black baby-hearse squeaks and its load purrs, for Eddie has his right hand in her nappy and is moving it as though to soothe an itch. He's too preoccupied to shoo the pooch, which scares him shitless, which is a machine for turning meat to turd, which is called Postman because it once bit one (its previous cynonym was Brack. Douglas soon got rid of that). Postman is part wolf, part jackal, wholly labrador, easily distracted. Throw the dog a cone and he's away. I don't believe I said anything to Eddie. I probably reckoned that this is what cousins did – though I was sentient and knew that my cousin Elinor (Hi, Lindy, how's osteopathy, how's Geo, how old's Davey now?) didn't entertain me so; but then she lived far away – it was twenty-three miles to So'ton in those days – and I saw her rarely, knew her less.

Eddie saw Bonny every Sunday; his mother and he set off regular as the calendar after church in the church where I was baptised. They waited twenty minutes for the no. 55 at the bus stop close by the entrance to the mess called The Cliff; young officers, the Grieving Widow's coevals, tooted their horns at her and double de-clutched (all roaring revs) as they took the corner with sporty braggadocio.

They got off the bus at the Canal – there was no canal, the tontine funded company had gone bust; all that remained, still remains, of the thwarted venture are the street so named, a docks building, Navigation Straight, the freakish mounds of excavation at Whaddon where it made the bankrupting cross from the valley of the Avon to that of the Dun. They walked from the Canal through the alley beside the Guildhall and across the Market Place to the bus station. Here they waited three quarters of an hour in infirmary gloom beside tarnished tea urns.

Hungover, awol soldiers heading back to camp and jankers fixed her from their benches; these were Stella's lovers, layers, impregnators. They came in squads, these bloodshot squaddies with their oily hair and glottal lingos and ready seed; they breathed each other's loutishness, fed on mob yobbery (team spirit with dropped aitches), they grunted sullen taunts, smoked Weights from behind their ears. The closer Eddie moved to his mother the more they called him Little Softy. Now one would make a circle with his left thumb and first finger and pump the second finger of his other hand through it and sing: 'If you don't get shagged on a Sat'rday night you'll never get shagged at all.' Now another would let his tongue descend his chin then moan: ' 'Slike a nun's minge in an effin' drought.'

The Grieving Widow was resolutely impassive. She stared through the metal-framed Daily Mail windows at the red buses and the green buses and the airbricks in the back wall of the scrumpy bar. A soldier vomited in the corner. The acne moon next to him split where the teeth were: 'Come on Softy, come 'nd lick i' up.' His tongue slapped about the split, he stretched his hand towards Poor Eddie, he was the first The Grieving Widow whispered about to the military policemen, the 'soddin crushers' whom he'd spotted as their Land Rover, showy in its sylvan camouflage, tiptyred from between buses. The first red-capped crusher beckoned the second while the third and fourth and fifth made with their nightsticks, prodded conscripted kidneys, looked dangerous. The second was the boss red cap (tidy ranker, lousy vowels). This second's lips were full, puckered, dry. He listened with officious courtesy.

'Nothing wrong with them that the usual methods won't rectify. Apart from laddie there.' He twitched to indicate the wriggling half-nelsoned tunic two crushers were scraping across the floor: 'He's in a fair spot of bother I'd say. His future's looking *gloomy*, I'd say so yes.' He turned to watch his men do their stuff, scrutinised the now empty waiting room.

'Rightyho then that's all taken care of – the cancer gouged out I'd say. Believe me, there's not many rotten apples. I trust you haven't been too inconvenienced Mrs. . . ?'

'Vallender,' said The Grieving Widow. 'No I haven't, it's just a little . . .'

'Vallender?' he murmured, did something dreadful with his lips. 'That's not a name you hear too often . . . Still, indubitably a coincidence, I'd say.'

The Grieving Widow said: 'It probably isn't . . . I mean, it'll be my brother-in-law that you know: Douglas. The firework manufacturer. At High Post.'

Eddie said: 'The family firm.'

The middle-aged red cap captain shook his head, 'I've observed the factory of course – can't hardly miss it . . . but no that's not the Vallender I, ah, had in mind. No, that would be a different Vallender – a certain Major Guy Vallender. But there you are . . . must be a more common name than I thought,' he staged a rictal smile.

The Grieving Widow sniffed and winced and gasped. Outside

a squaddie screamed, the sun jumped through the window sure as floodlight, Poor Eddie squeezed his mama's hand. 'He . . . was my husband,' she croaked.

'Ah! Your husb . . . well, blow me. *Was*? Did you say *was*? Was your husband . . . What, did a bunk did he? – that'd be his style. Well well well – so you know what laddie there's in for eh? Can't be much you don't know about courts martial . . . Well, what a turn up . . .' He clicked tongue and teeth and grinned in autocollusion. He looked down at Eddie: 'And this's *his* boy is it. Well I never – must be like being dealt one off the bottom of the pack . . .'

The door swung behind him. The Grieving Widow put a hand to her crown. Poor Eddie wondered about the man's twanging accent, tutting tongue, clacking strut. 'He didn't say bye bye,' said the indignant boy. His mother didn't hear, her ears were packed full of roaring blood, and she didn't hear the martinet's bark that pealed like gust-buckled sheet metal. The aggregate in the concrete out there was smooth tan pebbles.

The bus, a red Dennis in this green valley, drove away from the crossroads. Mother and son stood beside the signpost. Also: rookeries in the elms, banks of Queen Anne's lace, tyre marks on the bend, haze, clumps of trees in brain formations, jungly fecundity, grass up to here, a wall with thatch on top, cattle chafing against willows in the meadows, summer.

She took his hand and they walked first up the steep road stained by chalk and starred by flints. Their shadows wriggled round their ankles. Then the verge was cropped, springy, and the ball bearings were rabbit dung. After a five-bar gate, a sign proscribing fires and a cabin with broken windows there was a rutted road between conifers and birches. Eddie kept to the track of grass along its centre. The Grieving Widow started when pigeons and squirrels hurtled through the wood, fearing they were rangers out to catch her fag in hand. Hideous brooms made of twigs were strapped to poles set beside the road. The Grieving Widow panted. When he reached a boggy firebreak Eddie turned and ran back to her and cowered along beside her: this was the dorsal bayonnet, Eddie. This is what scared you best, this terrorscape your young mother dragged you through, it was built to make your shoulders chill. Is this what you see when you die, is this what they saw when they died?

It's like it still; I returned the other week (grid ref: 127352) and smelled the ghost of your boyhood, I felt the ghost of your mother's life. The anthills are slumped like sacks with moving threads. The twigs are bright with lichen. There are lichenous branches underfoot. The sloughed bark of silver birches is monumental swarf, it's curled like shavings from a giant's turbine. The firs are dead, their needles are bleached. This must be death itself, it's all built from bones. And between scrolls of bark and formic cities grow death-caps, death-caps, death-caps: enough amatoxin here to do the livers of very many unhappy families.

Now they're coming down the hill and I'm running out to meet them. 'Don't' – called my mother – 'go out on the road.' 'Wait at the gate Johnson – there's a good fellow. That way you'll still have your limbs for lunch. Mnhnhnar.' The Grieving Widow kissed me distractedly, then Eddie and I ran together to see the pony. I patted it, Eddie kept his distance.

One of those Sundays, there by the clean fence Russet nuzzled against Eddie asked: 'Jonerfin – what's courts martial?'.

Another of those Sundays, while he fondled baby Bonny and the first breeze of autumn slipped through the Clump, I told him: 'Court martial is when your daddy's naughty.' Eddie winced and I turned to kick a little puffball. He put his hand in Bonny's clothes and stroked her milk-smooth pudendum. I didn't see him; but he did stroke her, I'll bet he did, I can see him now, and Bonny, she's cooing at her coz.

In the foetid afterbirth of mass death men were making money. If you'd been fool enough to believe in the kitschy utopia which fell 988 years short of its proclaimed span you were certainly fool enough to swap your watch for forty cigarettes, your camera for twenty more, your girl for less.

This calvary of burnt trees represents a business opportunity. This charcoalscape lively with rags spells gelt, the rags rustled and danced like frayed banknotes. Here's a city whose cellars are filled with bits of the houses that once hid them, made them dark and covert: bombs made them quarries seamed with gilt. Here's an old soldier on the street where he might have lived when the great lie seemed true, but it might have been another street, and he isn't really old, just worn and maimed and attrited by famishment and by despair contracted in pursuit and service of the great lie. He's abandoned socialism for the elemental graft of survival: the first step towards the economic miracle is made on stumps where knees should be. Just watch them go. Watch them scurry down a pyritoid heap of stone, cisterns, lath, stucco, dust, dust, filth, wood, brick, this, rat, torso, china, blanket, that, bathtub, wrench. Watch the hands that hang down to them. Look at the nails attached to the hands. The nails are curled, long; black with yellow for chromatic relief; ridged for strength; they are emblems of their owner's state, of his nation's state, of the national trade: the eagle has claws in order that it may scratch about in imperial ruins.

'Hunbelievable,' wrote Guy Vallender, 'absolutely hunbeliev-able!' It was a catchphrase in all his letters, to Douglas and Douglas's young wife, to my mother, to men he had messed with, to Margot Case whom he'd messed about with during his last leave and whom he'd sort of promised to marry – he meant it, he always did: the day before he reported to Woolwich he had strapped her to her parents' bed with his Sam Browne and, while she gammed him, talked of the opportunities for converting belligerent explosives into fireworks that must exist in Germany.

His ten days at Woolwich were passed in martial oblivion.

One Thursday in June 1945 Guy Vallender sailed from Chatham to Antwerp ('steak the size of a plate, chips fried in Heaven, beer, wine, any amount of cognac'). He underwent a War Office Selection Board ('wozbee') near Dendermonde, at a former seminary whose gables stood like rearing horses against the sky which was vast, molten. He shared a room with two other substantive majors, one of whom, Tigger Dawkins, accompanied him to Brussels to see the ENSA production of Richard III, the title role taken by Laurence Olivier. Later, in the foyer of the Astoria on rue Royale, they saluted that actor, now dressed in his service uniform, and his drunken mufti'd Clarence. Two days later Guy Vallender was called to the office of a man he refers to as 'the Brig with the conk' and offered 'railways, newspapers or accommodation. Well I never wanted to be an engine driver and there are too many chaps with experience as journalists for me to exactly shine in that game. So I'm set to become a Town Major.' He spent a further week in Belgium billeted on a baker's family at Malines. He fished in a tributary of the Schelde and took two eels; he spent a day drawing the ruins of a belfry at Duffel; he borrowed a motorbike and visited the battlefield of Waterloo; he ate copiously; an outing to Spa to see the place where Dick Seaman had died during the Belgian Grand Prix the summer before the war was curtailed when a drizzle-soaked road caused the tyro motorcyclist to skid – he gave up having travelled no further than the Bruxellois suburb of Schaarbeek. The weather was otherwise fine. All this is recorded in his letters. He makes no mention of Alban Meyer-Decker. But then why would he?

The momentous comes all dressed in black; it arrives unseen like a germ in water; it disguises itself as the man whose bar stool in a dingy corner café in that brick suburb teeters parlously when he leans towards Guy to warn him in a public whisper that

'Elle, celle-là, elle était collabo – tu piges? Une collabo en collage: c'est bien bon, non? La collabo en collage.'

Here he begins to sing with a thump on the terminal syllable –

'La belle collabo en collage
Pompe dans une maison d'abattage
Elle jure "Si t'as gouté du boche
Le jus de tous les autres est moche
J'étais la collabo en collage." '

The man's stool lurches and he seizes the pression tap to steady himself, the stool's foot shrieks, a couple of men at a table (they're only props) ignore the now tearful singer, the crone perched behind the bar struggles with her numeracy problem and a column of figures, the child sweeping the floor makes her brush swerve round a suitcase and leaves a comma of ash and dust and stuff.

Guy Vallender looks about the bar for the song's subject, its singer clasps his shoulder.

The singer shakes his head: 'N'est pas là.' The man who sends Guy Vallender to his death, that man shakes his head in maudlin spasms and whines 'N'est plus là' and exhales ulcerous warmth onto Guy's face. This is Alban Meyer-Decker, those epaulettes of his are scurf, those eyebrows are to frighten children. And this was how they fell in together. There's danger in diffidence, it's not safe to be at a loose end, you may be hijacked by a bad hat. They went on a bender, the singer and the pyro-technician.

They agreed about women: Guy Vallender explained the difference between fuck and fuck up. 'You fuck them, they fuck you up.' No woman fucked up Guy Vallender the way his new friend Alban did.

There were smooth, dungsteaming cobbles outside, lots of rain on them, lots of shine, lots of glister in the drizzle. The air was like just-breathed-on glass. It held water particles in visible suspension. It obfuscated the carts (rotting wood, rusty metal) and the horses that heaved them, horses that were truly too weak to work and too thin to eat, horses with hardly the skin to cover their ribs, horses whose bones were highlit by their tight wet pelts. This air makes impressionists of us all. It gangs up with the sky that's like human ash to conquer detail, expunge colour, make it all the same then more. That mansarded barracks is a smudge of itself; that sooty 0–4–0 shunter is out of focus – it's already wrapped in its steam and smoke, and new commas of steam and new screamers of smoke punctuate the slug forward of this train from the wharf on the black canal. This clanking convoy of trucks that carried children to their death moved on rails down the centre of the street. Here's the café, there's the barracks, that's the train, this is no weather to go drinking in.

Did they hear me? I was born too late to tell them that alcohol works in concert with such weather. I was mere seed; but by the time I reached Guy Vallender's age then, thirty-five, I knew that drink brings down blinds, that it works from the inside out to build temporary cataracts, to custom-weave fine grimy nets (the filthiest curtains you ever peered through) that snugly cover your corneas; it turns day to dusk, drink does, it turns day to dust, and a day like that with a bent to dusk, with emulsified dust filling up all the gaps between matter, it turns a day like that to the ape of night, it counterfeits the dark. Now evening is here – the sort of evening that occasions electric light, clock evening – and Guy and Alban (who's cajoling, shouting at, pleading with a janitor) have not noticed. You don't lose time, you didn't lose time, did you? Can they hear me? Both dead, gone to dust, like that day went for them. You don't lose time. You win, you defeat the very idea, you vanquish chronal tyranny, you stuff the Switzers and the Nips, you know it's all an Helvetic business scam, you know that for a moment till you turn to tell Alban and misplace the hunch between brain and tongue so you tell him instead that the wrinkled cylinder he's putting a match to should be a cig not a cigarette because it is shorter than a cigar not longer.

Now, the fratchy rabbit chop of the air Alban Meyer-Decker does at this moment should have been warning enough – he's patently playing with a nine man team, he doesn't need to treat the frail old janitor thus. Guy has forgotten why they have come to this appartment building in the garden suburb of Joli Bois (aka Pins Noirs) where the dormers wink and the hedges come up to your knee. Three possibilities.

35

a) Alban Meyer-Decker, whose name he has yet to commit to memory, is here to prosecute one or other of the deals he has boasted of (obligingly translating anticipated profits into sterling and, with infantile cupidity, into cars, houses, horses and a future of willed sloth).

· b) Alban wishes to show off his mistress in person: so far all Guy has seen is a shadow of the lot. In the bistro where they ate a dish of pancreas and oxtail called *choesels* Alban leaned across the plates and asked: 'Tu veux que je te montre ma Cato?' And from his wallet (reptile skin, crenellated with bills and tickets and banknotes' corners) he pulled a photographic print, three inches square with a crinkly border; he laid the photo before Guy with smug ceremonial. She was naked. This is the first thing Guy notices. Guy looks up at Alban Meyer-Decker who exposes a wedge of palate (i.e. smiles). Cato (already referred to as ma Catherine, ma p'tite Trina) wears a kerchief tight about her neck, heavy Amara-work bracelets around her ankles. She sits on the arm of a Leopold II chair, one foot on its seat, the other's tense toes touching a swirling carpet. Her aureola are, in this monochrome copy of her, black puckered quoits; the wake of her bush trails back to her navel which is spelaean; her head hair is thick and falls in steps over the right eye; the visible eyebrow is as abundant as those of her lover, this lover who gloats: 'Pas mal hein?' Guy's distracted nod dissembles the spinal charge, the shiver in his shoulders, the testicular itch which the woman prompts. What Guy would like to do is to – oh he will, he will.

c) This building is in some way associated with, is maybe a former home of, Madaleine Van den Putte, the subject of the song Meyer-Decker first sang two pages back and which he has reprised in different versions since. It cannot be her last home for that burned with her and her infant son inside it on October 21 the previous autumn, 1944.

The incident is cited in Patricia Barnes: *Resistance, Reprisal, Revenge: The Phenomenology of Post-Liberation Belgian Public Punishments 1944–59. Vol. II Flanders, Brabant, Limburg* (New Haven 1969). It was also reported, so partially as to be incorrect, in the London *News Chronicle* of Monday October 23, 1944; the headline is The Wages of Treachery, the photograph shows the black, smoking ruins of the little bungalow near the beach at Saint-Idesbald, the presence of the little boy is disregarded as being irrelevant to the arson by petrol-soaked rags. Dr Barnes contends that the boy's presence, indeed his very existence, were crucial. Her book, an important influence on British proletarian youth coiffure in the years immediately subsequent to its publication, presumes that the boy was born of Mlle Van den Putte's union with a German officer commanding a coastal defence squadron and it suggests that had she enjoyed a fruitless relationship with this man (Sepp Kupp, now a widowed concrete technologist living in retirement near Regensburg) she would merely have been shaved and shoved through the streets. Dr Barnes further notes that Saturday October 21 was the day that Aachen became the first German city to capitulate to the Allies, and that the murder of Mlle Van den Putte may have been an instance of 'celebratory retribution'. Meyer-Decker believed that the boy was his, conceived before the woman left him for Kupp.

'C'était mon gosse – tu sais? Venait de moi . . . fabriqué avec ma semoule.'

He had met the woman at the Bar-Music O'Connor on Rue des Trois Mollettes, Lille, in the spring of 1938. He had topped the bill, he was then at the height of his brief fame; she was an artistic dancer. They lived together for three years (in a series of apartments whose increasing insalubrity was determined by the failure of his career, the proscription of his records, the forced closure of theatres and music-halls, the nazification of radio).

At Christmas 1942, just before the boy's first birthday, Meyer-Decker travelled by train to Ostende and thence by bicycle to Saint-Idesbald. He carried two parcels. One contained a wooden toy cart which he had painted in the black, yellow and red of the Belgian tricolour and to which he had attached a lanyard of those colours. The other had in it two Maredsous cheeses, combined weight 3 kilos; these were intended to induce Madaleine Van den Putte to allow him to present his gift to the child he had never seen, never would see. He was within sight of the pantiled, steep-roofed bungalow, standing to pedal against the wind and the wet sand of the unmade road, his heart chugging in excitement or exertion when a motorcycle combination that he hadn't heard (wind, ears full of blood) drew alongside him. The malnourished youth in the sidecar waved his rifle as though frightened of it. Alban Meyer-Decker's bicycle bucked and reared and threw him onto a bank of marram that grazed him, put sand beneath his nails. The Germans were skulls with helmets and threadbare greatcoats and bloody eyes. The one with the rifle prodded him and swore at him in a catarrhal voice. The other tore open the parcels. He threw the toy to the ground then he held one of the cheeses in the crook of his arm and sliced it with a dagger whose blade was chipped and smeared. The two soldiers ate with furtive desperation, noisily, rind and all, specks of curd stuck in their stubble, they smacked their lips. Meyer-Decker gripped the front wheel between his knees and straightened the handlebars. He picked up the little cart. When he looked towards the bungalow a curtain moved, he was sure of that. The way he stared at the place made the soldiers quit masticating a moment (they saw in his eyes what Guy Vallender was blind to). Then a full mouth shouted 'Raus', and he pushed his bicycle away up the soggy road between the wan gardens of other requisitioned villas where city doxies, who before the occupation would not have entered them save as maids, swanned in nicked silk and purloined pearls waiting for their German lovers, the harbingers of terror and scent. He heard the sea beyond the dunes and the twisted trees. He tied the lanyard to the centre of the salt-pitted handlebars and the cart bumped against the crossbar as he pedalled back to Ostende with the wind behind him.

Alban Meyer-Decker finds the right key the right way up and opens the door to the apartment. He turns to the janitor who has followed them up six flights of stairs: 'Ne pas entrer. Si? Restez là mon vioc.'

Meyer-Decker closes the door on him and pushes past Guy along the narrow hall that's lit by a wedge of light from the room at its end. Both men trip over unseen objects on the floor. Meyer-Decker swears and enters the lit room. Once it was a sitting room, now it is a chaotically improvised store room. There are boxes to the ceiling casting a cardboard dunness, there are shoeboxes and crates, labels, stamps, packing codes like brands, tea chests, bottles, packs of stockings, jerrycans and soupcans, enough cigarettes to last a five pack a day man the lifetimes of six non-smokers, twenty-four methuselahs of Pol Roger, three Sten guns, the keys to a feast of sardine tins, a pyramid of veterinary syringes, a damp bulgy sack, a kukri, a side of beef with ochreous seeping fat, jars of suppositories, a drum of spam, five Willis Jeep tyres. There is also a sofa over whose back Meyer-Decker stretches, his shiny bottom higher than the rest of him. When he rights himself he is clutching a bursting foolscap envelope into which he puts his right hand with gynaecologist's bravura and withdraws a quire of banknotes. He counts them with a spat-on finger, stumbles out of Guy's sight behind a column of packing cases, reappears with a bottle of Canadian Club. He gives the money and the whisky to the janitor, pats him on the back, shoos him away.

It is now 7 pm or 1.30 am and they are drinking manhattans chased by tepid Duvel beer. They are friends. They are going to keep in touch. They agree on so many things they forget what they are now. Their trains of thought have suffered multiple derailments. Meyer-Decker has shown Guy Vallender framed posters that are souvenirs of his former career, before he went into business. The name Albeau is rarely at the top, and when it is at the top the music-hall is in Namur or Lille or Toul or Léopoldville; in Paris and Brussels he is billed beneath, say, Baba et Bobbi et Leurs Chiens Vedettes and well after such stars as Jean Lumière, Andrex, Dranem and Bach, the Odeon lettering of whose names melds with their profiles by Ponty or Gus.

Because the gramophone is beneath two crates containing fire-extinguishers Albeau's records may not be played. So the singer sings his repertoire unaccompanied, stopping between songs or mid verse to mix more manhattans (Old Buck Kentucky Bourbon and Martini Rosso). Songs collide, slide into each other and from the elisions spring new verses, fresh lines that Alban struggles to write on a sheet of memorandum paper headed 'From the office of the Deputy Commander-in-Chief Allied Control Council'. There are many such sheets, littered with

39

graphitic scrawls that their maker can't read, piled on a table in the window bay.

Have you ever heard Albeau sing?

In 1983 Retrovox of Brussels issued a compilation to mark the seventy-fifth anniversary of his birth. Its title, derived from one of his songs, is a lie: 'On se souvient d'Albeau.' Not even the song it alludes to, 'On se souvient d'Anvers', is remembered. The photograph on the record cover is all retouching and cigarette smoke, and the central glabella is hairless. The biographical note states that 'le patriotisme et la fierté d'être Belge que l'on trouve dans ses paroles se réfléchissaient dans la valeur de sa résistance personnelle à l'occupation de son pays' – an assertion which is merely publicist's hyperbole; it goes on to say that following the war he did not attempt to revive his singing career but became a businessman in the Belgian Congo where he died in 1960.

His voice was a thrilling, leeringly lubricious baritone, a voice used to asking for sexual favours, used to pleading for them – this is a voice quite bereft of pride; it makes baser appeals, to the sodality of the self-pitying, to the wordling's certainty that everyone has his price, to schadenfreude and sentimentality. It's the sort of voice that I am ashamed to be touched by. The tyranny of tone over lyrics is total; even a potentially light song such as 'Kiekefretter, Sûrement' is turned into a hymn to aggrievement by the pitifulness of the line where the narrating child, a Walloon teased by Flemings, whines 'Et ils ont piqué mes speculoos.' ('And they've nicked my biscuits.')

Guy Vallender suggested that he should design a firework show to accompany a concert of Alban's, outdoors by the lake in the Bois de la Cambre where the sky would be mirrored. Alban sang further chapters in the story of La Belle Collabo – her death might have occurred only to be made a ballad of. 'Les pompiers ont laissé la pompeuse en panne.' Alban spoke the line, 'non. Non. Et les pompiers patriotes.'

Guy opened his eyes and the sun was shining through the metal-framed window and his mouth was full of prickly felt. His knees were momentarily immovable. He had slept in the chair where he had been sitting, his fist gripped about a cut-glass tumbler. Alban Meyer-Decker was on the sofa, his head partially covered by a cushion, snoring, a vulnerable beast with an exposed throat and each eye rendered impotent by its segmental prepuce. Guy climbed gingerly over a barbican of Hershey boxes and went into the kitchen, a vertical coffin with no oven, no cooking rings and a larder filled with scent bottles and three-inch mortar shells. The tap emitted nothing. Guy looked out of the window onto the matching windows of the apartments around the same dark lightwell. Then he made his way back past Alban Meyer-Decker into the hall. He craved water. His armpits, his eyes, his crutch, his mouth had been kneaded with grit, anointed with salt. Two doors faced each other. The one he opened revealed a rudimentary bathroom – a small bath tub with a rusting sprinkler above it, a w.c., a washbasin beneath whose working tap he cupped his hands and drank and drank. He drank so his tight spotted tie and his officer's-issue cotton shirt got soaked. He doffed the rest of his more or less mufti and stepped into the bath. The shower was droughty. He peed more than it did. He shivered beneath a dorsal trickle he moved to his belly by turning to face the wall (lousy grouting, oxidisation).

Thus he has his back to the door and to the naked woman who comes through it, bleary and bemused as the newborn.

He never saw Catherine with clothes on. She lived in his imagination in a state of eternal nudity (p. 130). She was with him for ever, for ever raw. They didn't make fig leaves of their hands. They laughed in mutual appreciation. And they didn't make love – that compound is inapt. They copulated, rubbed offal. She told him he had looked beautiful when he was asleep. Not like Alban; she had stayed out late, as she often did, because she didn't want to see him. He was mean. He was maudlin. He was too drunk to fuck, *always*; he was impotent.

She squeezed Guy's urethra, twisted his scrotum, reached over his shoulder for the soap and smothered her left forefinger with it and pushed up his arse. His glans grew and glowed like a shiny apple, she licked it till little beads of sap oozed out. His eyes rolled and he sobbed. She leaned forward over the washbasin and stretched between her legs with her right hand, pulled his penis into her and out and in as though it were a dildo

41

and she a mere merkin. Her nails dug into him, drew blood from the cushion between balls and anus; he bit her shoulder to keep himself from screaming. Chimneysweeps' trade disease is cancer of the scrotum, totem poles are tall and redwoods are taller, oh mercy me, oh you greedy gobbler, you darling cannibal, your cunt's as big as the gaping neck of a beheaded horse, you smell like tar and pears, you're going to feel this. She rubbed her clitoris with her other hand, with machinist's speed, with strumming abandon. She gasped and quivered and again and still he kept – there, done, come, spent. He's finished and something else has started no doubt. Some sperm flowed down the inside of her thigh, but not all of it. Guy Vallender sat on the lip of the bath.

'God, hangovers are good for sex,' he said.

Brussels woke. Alban Meyer-Decker snored on. In the red-brick streets the scents of waffles and coffee, chips and cheroots mixed to make the smell of the city.

Guy Vallender who could smell only her secretions strolled, weak-kneed and light-headed, back to the Café de Sedan where he had left his motorcycle in a yard. The doorstep was gleaming, the crone was still adding, the child was still sweeping. He drank a glass of genever. The day was going to be a hot one. A cream tram rattled along beside the barracks.

He had not even spoken her name.

He wasn't a bad man, your father. He wasn't wicked. He didn't mean it, he really didn't. Careless, rash, negligent, weak – he may have been all those, yes: but wicked, never, never by intent anyway. Default's a different k of f, another wormcan. He'd never have done a thing like that had he not . . . He'd never have done it of his own accord, he'd never have thought of it. That wasn't his way. It wasn't even his way to go along for the ride. If only he hadn't been so lax. If only he hadn't been so loaded with guilt. If only he hadn't sought redemption in abetment of a greater ill – two wrongs don't, they never do, they certainly didn't with him. Wherever you got your appetites from, it wasn't from him – that's not just you, Eddie, I'm talking to, son, but the other ones too. It wasn't by him that the gene labelled '-cide' was issued; that slipped in from somewhere else. Sure, he was all that you children had in common – not that he knew, not that he allowed himself to know. None the less that gene (the symbol on the label is a skull) was not Guy's, no matter how it might seem, no matter how chance boasts.

I promise, he was gentle as a wounded paw. He rammed the jack into the redcap's jaw; the fellow gurgled like he was learning to speak – he was, contrarily, that second, beginning to forget how to speak. The fellow fell with a plash that drowned the gurgle. The yard was rutted, puddled; he was on his knees in mud and moonlight. Guy bent over him, panicked; he wasn't a pretty sight but then he never had been. He made another noise, something like a faulty pipe, precisely like a faulty windpipe. Just then Alban came round the tailboard of the truck with the last crates in his arms. Guy tried to move the man, *his victim*, and out popped a dental plate bearing a peculiarly narrow incisor, a perfect replica of the original whose narrowness was likely due to inherited syph – gleet in the pudding, not in the sauce. (No wonder he wasn't a pretty sight.)

Alban Meyer-Decker said: 'Tant pis pour lui.' He hefted the crate into the lorry. Then he said: 'Et tant pis pour toi, hein?' He picked up the redcap's rifle and put it in the cab: 'On sait jamais.'

The fresh tyre spun as Guy reversed the vehicle and sprayed clay over the disarmed soldier who was fixed in a state of eternal genuflection. He wasn't, he wasn't fixed. They got him to the court martial to which he gave evidence – a nod here, a shake there: all that was fixed were his tongue and his brain and his memory of the frightened man with a jack in his hand (this was the memory with which his memory stopped).

Did he remember the night of Monday the third of December 1945? It was within the scope of the finite store he was bound to carry round so long as he lived, just within its scope. He was the prosecution's only witness. Had his injury been less severe he'd have made a better job of it. Guy Vallender's punishment was in inverse proportion to the gravity of the damage he'd done. Had the wretched aphasiac not persistently confused the accused's given name (at the mention of which his eyes dilated in recognition) with the make of lorry (ditto) that the accused was alleged to have been driving he would have made a better showing, would have seen to Major Vallender well and proper. But Guy's defence (a literally barrack-room lawyer whose qualified success in this and other cases persuaded him, on discharge, to read for the bar – he's now a retired silk with opinions and a gong) sensed, with alacrity, our single witness's inability to distinguish the two referents of the one signifier. So Guy, the lorry, the kind with a bust of a head-dressed Sioux atop its radiator, looked frightened.

'And how, pray,' – featherweight mockery – 'does a *lorry* indicate that it is frightened? Do its headlights betray fear like eyes? Do the metal bands of its radiator miraculously contort as an appalled mouth might? And, if so, do they equally miraculously bend themselves back to the impeccably longitudinal before the Guy is identified as the man in question?'

The witness didn't cry – he should have. That might have alerted the presiding officer, a brigadier exhausted by himbeergeist and the three Estonian dancers on his staff (interpreters), to the conduct of the case. No, this poor fellow, this Private Bright (yes, a misnomial handle) grunted obligingly and gaped at the so far unlooted painting of a swollen peacock that hung above the accused: why, he wondered, has it the head of a chicken and not that of a Red Indian? He must have wondered that.

Then there was this: had or had not the witness attended the firework display organised and designed by the accused at Bramsche four weeks to the night before the robbery at Ruhl Optik? He had. And he'd seen Guy put his torch, the theatre torch, to the luminescent wheels named for the fired martyr Catherine. He knew him from there, he'd seen him with that torch in his hand – it looked like a jack? Yes (nod). Not guilty. Not on this charge. Guy Vallender was none the less stripped of his rank, was dishonourably discharged from His Majesty's Service after offering no defence to the crushers' further charges of dishonestly handling 800 cigarettes and fraternising with eight (actually, eighteen) frowlines – that was all they could sew him for. They stitched him for what everyone did, for what *they* did – this was not a guiltfree land, everyone was *at it*. If Bright had been a Kraut, Jerry, Bosch, Hun, Swine your lives would have been different, sons. Your lives would not have been how they were at all. Wherever you are you blame the state, this one there or that. And blame the partiality of justice: he wasn't to know it wasn't a German brain he was damaging. Had it been, the crushers would have ignored it.

Do you remember – do you, Bright (are you receiving me in Pompey, Bright?) – do you remember the fifth of November 1945? You don't do you? Veg! It was as if the lights of the city were reflected in the sky. There were cheers and whoops, and when you lay back across the sidecar combination the world turned upside down and you were looking from an aeroplane at the lights of a city thousands of feet below you, and you gasped. Your white breath streaked across your eyes in a racing cloud effect. The cold stabbed your nostrils. The heads silhouetted against the artificial furnace are pollarded by caps and berets. A face that a moment back was green is violet now. The man I saw

45

becomes a bird. A stone horse, ruinous and riderless, is as white as the day it first reared above this park; then it's carmine then it's orange then it's gone, back into the night. Poor orphaned putti, wanting legs and noses and crowns, humpty beneath the smashed allegories that once clutched them. The blokes don't even bother to nick them: out there were real children, pokable ones, little suckers, visited by their fathers' sins, prone in atonement, plating to pay their nation's debt, and all at two for twenty Seniors: there were other children, too, who had worse things happen to them.

Do you remember, Bright, the man without the hat? The one in mufti? He stumbles down the steps from the terrace of this harshly rusticated, requisitioned house (c. 1810 and, 135 years later, a well-stocked mess) and stumbles about the pitted lawns. He pushes through the crowd. He's the only one whose gaze is not enskied. He stands on tiptoe, stretchnecked and peering, so long as his toes will support him; when he lands on his whole feet his head oscillates quicker. This is Alban Meyer-Decker, the smokkeler, the bof[1] just arrived from Aachen where he's been on business (bulk passports, meat, metal polish).

M'sieu Albeau wishes to renew the acquaintance of Major Guy; he had a proposition, his head is bursting with propositions, he breathes business opportunities: he was pleased to see his friend's name in the Allied Forces newspaper he glanced at in the station café at Aachen while he waited for the Brussels train, but the bond of one boozing jag was not enough to cause him to cross the tracks and head two hundred miles north (with changes and delays at Cologne, Oberhausen, Wesel and Munster) on a day when the sky was coloured with dental amalgam and when the claims of Cato, who is now starting to swell in fecund rotundity, were strong – he longed for her. No, what fostered his change of plan was the start of the second paragraph: 'Major R. G. Vallender, pre-war a professional pyrotechnician – that's firework-maker to you lot! – and now Town Major of Bramsche, ten miles north of Osnabruck . . .' It was Guy's gubernatorial grip on that town which made Alban

[1] Acronym: B.O.F. stands for 'beurre, oeufs, fromages' – items much traded on the black market.

Meyer-Decker change his plans, just on the off chance; in this game you never know. There, he's found him, beyond the rope barrier, there in the polychrome inferno where rainbows are made after dark. Guy Vallender's arms are extended either side of him, each hand holding wooden-handled tongs in which are clamped flaming tapers; night and myopia (poor Bright suffered that too) could indeed transform these tools into jacks, though not half so well as a buggered brain could. Guy Vallender's arms are extended as if awaiting deposition.

Bramsche! On the Mittellandkanal, eight miles north of Osnabruck (not ten, the Allied Forces paper had it wrong). Bramsche! Its predominantly flat surrounds, flat yet relieved to the south-east by the wooded outline of the Wiehengebirge Hills, to the south-west by the wooded outlines of the Teutoburger Wald. Bramsche! Its quay, its little harbour, its fleet of maintenance dredgers, its aqueduct over the river Hase (some fishing). Bramsche! At the junction of the north German and Westphalian plains (pig farming, horse breeding, peat bogs, genocide). Bramsche! Its optical instruments factory is celebrated wherever people gather together to wear glasses, take photographs, bimp with binoculars, discover the interesting world that microscopy reveals.

This town was associable with Ruhl Optik as Jena was with Zeiss or Torgau with Neurath. It was the only reason Meyer-Decker had ever heard of the place, it was the only reason anyone had ever heard of it. Guy Vallender had never heard of it.

'Where?' he had asked when given his posting two days after he had met Meyer-Decker for what he believed would be the one and only.

' "Where?" I asked – I'd never heard of it . . . Ah, je n'avais pas . . . ah . . .' Guy shook his head.

Alban Meyer-Decker said: 'I get you Bud.'

They both laughed at his weirdly inflected GI spiel. This is after the fireworks. This is the bar of the mess. Guy, receiving the congratulations of his fellow officers on the display with a courteous diffidence, greeted Meyer-Decker with a kindred neutrality, not a coolness but a manifest lack of surprise as though he didn't know what surprise was, hadn't learnt about it, as though the dandiacal singer turned businessman was as likely a figure to frequent this blue and ormolu room animated by yards of khaki as Tigger Dawkins there (who'd motored over from Herford in his Auto Union with two pigs, requisitioned at gun point and now spit-roasting in the basement kitchen). Dawkins was not the only soldier who regarded Alban Meyer-Decker with distaste – zoot splendour was no splendour in the eyes of aspirant gents who'd style themselves by their rank long after demobilisation; but the fellow's not a jerry or a commie – he *is* a white man, and he's a chum of Vallender: look, they've got an awful lot to jaw about. A jawful lot Tigger.

It was Guy Vallender who talked. He talked in the bar, he talked with his mouth full of crackling (something Meyer-Decker had never eaten before), he talked with a glass of Piesporter in his hand, he talked as they drove back to his quarters, they talked there in the dining room of that house in which Guy had billeted himself – 'sometimes,' he had written to Douglas 'I don't know whether to service the mother or the daughter.'

From such letters we know what he talked about. 'Hunbelievable. Or, would you adam and eve it? (As most of the Tommies are wont to exclaim every other minute.)' This, followed by inventories of sights and litanies of smells, was his invariable formula.

He listed, and told Meyer-Decker of: vagrant Germans blinded by vengeful allied troops; British arms sold to Germans in order that they might fight on in the Russian sector (Meyer-Decker seemed particularly interested in this); the victim of a multiple rape emerging in a somnambulatory daze, in shredded clothes, from a forest-green forest of pines near Recke; a stench 'like the end of the world' (he didn't specify the source); the men who had comprised the war machine turned by war into machines with improvised prostheses – a scooter-wheeled fruit box propelled by the hands of a trunk, crutches built from tripods, legs made from chairlegs, amputations bound with chicken wire, an amended mousetrap strapped to a handless wrist, a missing ear bunged with brocade, a metal mug at each shoulder stump to receive alms where arms once had been (none proffered of course), a billy can colostomy bucket; rust; craters; cities like the worst teeth you ever clocked – black and holed and broken; a helmeted skull with a pistol in its mouth; bones, more bones, the reek of burning bones emitting gamboge gases and iodine-brown jelly; the woman in the outdoor café (trellises, wind-up gramophone) who winks and sits down beside Guy Vallender and tells him she has a malformed ribcage which she'll show him for two cigs; the woman with pus-encrusted eyes who stopped the lift between floors of the Atlantic Hotel in Hamburg, lifted her skirt with that hand, pushed the wedding ring finger of this into her vagina and holds it beneath Guy Vallender's nose, pouting, pelvically, thrusting, insolently imploring; the razed city that teemed like a termitary, its inhabitants, crouched beneath the weight of the wardrobes on their backs and the chairs strung from their necks and the cardboard cases in the wardrobes, scurrying from one hell to the next, crisscrossing, clambering over the fallen; the men who, even though they have limbs enough to walk, crawl lest they miss a cigarette butt; the escaped slave labourers, Auvergnats and Lombards, who died in a Bielefeld cellar ignorant that their oppressors had surrendered on May 8 – three of them had lived till mid August on a diet of rodents; the German who admitted to having been a member of the National Socialist party; the cocky lorry driver who, when admonished by Guy Vallender for blocking the entrance to the mess at Bramsche in contravention of the two-metre-high instruction to Keep Clear, retorted with a grin that yes, he had seen the sign, but that we Germans don't like following orders; the resourceful couple in Cloppenburg with an attic room full of human meat and blow flies; the caves near here – Guy Vallender swings his cigarette hand north, checks, thinks, swivels, points south-east towards and beyond the lump of Biedemeier which Meyer-Decker turns to look at – the caves in the Teutoburger Wald have got people living in them, a racial memory of troglodytism has scummed up to the surface and they (a clutch of armed charmers in black uniforms) have retreated there. We'll starve them out. They did.

Guy Vallender told Alban Meyer-Decker all about all of this and more besides. Alban Meyer-Decker boasted to Guy Vallender that Cato, sa p'tite Trina, la belle Catherine was pregnant. In the club, up the spout, got one on her, puddinged. Who was the cook?

'Elle est pleine comme une vache.' He stood and extended his tummy. His hand described an arc beyond his tummy. He was hoping for a boy who'd excel at chanson and cycle racing, a real Belgian. Guy said a real Belgian would be a boy who'd excel at eating mayonnaise with chips, asked when the baby was due.

'C'est en mars, en mars, c'est en mars que je serai père, père encore une fois, bibi.'

Three from one year, six of the other; the sixth month is June.

'Wan' more?' asked Guy Vallender wishing he could count on his fingers but his fingers were wrapped round a bottle of schnapps flavoured with sloes, and one fist of fingers (the free one) makes a mute abacus. Alban replied in the affirmative to these questions Guy asked: are you pleased; are you sure you're pleased; and (more tentatively put) is she pleased? Alban was so pleased that he wept, he wept and shook his head and gasped at the prospect of his bliss. Guy watched him warily. He watched to determine whether this was a lachrymose act – he must have wondered at some point what Meyer-Decker was doing here, so far from home, so far from Catherine.

But: 'Je suis si fier . . . One 'ell of a proud guy you lookin' at.' And: 'I wish you 'ad met her – Catherine. Tu te souviens de sa photo? Eh? Quelle nana hein? Sewerm broad buddy yah. Moi, *papa*, uh?'

Well, *you*, no, not actually, no. It wasn't just that Guy retained a muscular memory of the way, last June, she'd drawn him in her by uterine suction; there was, too, her amazonian scorn at Alban's incapacity – 'Trop paf pour bourrer, trop bourré pour baiser.' Alban's pride at putative paternity was a gloat, it was a misplaced gloat, he was claiming a goal he hadn't scored: he didn't know he hadn't scored. The unwitting cuckold is no cuckold: he's still the strutting cock, up to here in bliss, loin-bragging, generatively potent. He doesn't know that his bull about his balls is balls. Shorn of brawn, and he doesn't know it.

This is an awful thing not to know. Guy Vallender was a softie, not the man to let on. The hierarchy of hurt was his to resolve. It was an awful thing for Alban not to know, but that knowledge was as unborn as the babe so long as Guy kept mum (which the mum would – the mum needed keeping, the mum'd keep mum). Keeping mum was awful for Guy. He wore a gag so long as he breathed. We know how long that was. Schtum, mum, dummy – there's a happy triptych of irresonance, of palatal no-go, of the tongue floundering like a beached dolphin (p. 434). Oh, Guy Vallender held back all right. His stoic reticence was founded in circumstantial necessity – that's what stoicism is: the avoidance of bother when bother's the other choice.

No wonder he weighed in with compensation, with full-set repentance. He owned up to not owning up by agreeing to it, by going along with this bad, rash scam. Which astonished Alban Meyer-Decker; he could hardly believe Guy's willingness to go along with it. It was only his greed that prevented him being wary of Guy's willingness, his greed vanquished his suspicion. He had entertained little hope when he had changed trains, he had arrived expecting rebuff (the Albion mix of hauteur and mocking incredulity), he had expected to get nowhere, to have to use cunning to get anywhere, to have to offer the Englishman the bulk of the cut. He had even feared arrest. That's why it was 2 am before he even broached the matter. Yet, by 4.12 am (neoclassical clock on the mantelpiece) when Major Guy went to wake the daughter of the house – it was her turn this week – to get her to fix a bed for me it was in the bag, the plan was cast. He couldn't believe how easy it all was. He wondered at that: it made me think.

He was stupid as well as weak, your father. What could be more self-regardingly stupid than to infer 'moral' blackmail, to see blackmail where there is none, to submit to that blackmail without challenge? The man was crippled by an incapacity to give offence, by the terminal Englishness whose highest virtues are found in unrocked boats, in what's beneath the carpet. He could of course not admit this self-deceit and masked it with a further programme that he may have believed in and which his brief believed in or used – which is the same thing in the moral vacuum of the law:

a) That the British policy of 'spite and dynamite', of destroying factories (eg Krupps Essen plant, Knesser gearboxes, Halle ball bearings, Voss shipyards, Bloehm shipyards, Nettl at Recklinghausen, Haensel rheostats) was self-defeating, liable to prompt civil unrest and to increase the dependence of the vanquished upon the victor.

b) That Bramsche, unbombed save by a parachute failure from a Wellington who burst all over a roof and seeped into two streets, would be destroyed 'in spirit' if its main employer, Ruhl Optik (the streets of whose jugendstil workers suburb were named in honour of German optical scientists – Eppenstein, von Rohr, Voit, Steinheil, Scheel etc.) was blown up rather than re-opened.

c) That the ocular policy of National Socialism – to prescribe unground, non-corrective lenses as placebos – had resulted in a collective myopia which was a traffic hazard, and that this policy might be undone by re-activating the Ruhl laboratories and factory.

d) That believing in all this it is hardly likely that Major Vallender would attempt to incapacitate the factory by carrying out an audacious robbery and assaulting a private soldier into the bargain.

Acting on information received, three Military Policemen, led by a Lieutenant Colonel despatched from Hamburg, arrested Guy Vallender before the dawn of Sunday the ninth of December (he was in bed with the mother when the sleepy daughter answered the door). They act – hammering on the door, entering the house bearing rifles, the half colonel coughing with embarrassment – on information received by telephone at the Regional Commission in Osnabruck and at the headquarters of the Military Governor of Celle.

Both had taken anonymous calls in unsure, slangy, heavily accented English during the afternoon of the previous Thursday, three days after the robbery. The truck, whose tyreprints corresponded with those found beside the Ruhl Optik warehouse, was thus discovered in a wood at Nordhorn near the Dutch border; the steering wheel, gear shift and driver's doorhandle bore Guy Vallender's fingerprints though this was of little moment since he often drove this very truck to the site of evictions: 'It seems good sense to take along a lorry that people can put their possessions on there and then – gets it all done snappier.' (This impressed the presiding drunk.) Guy Vallender could not understand why Alban Meyer-Decker had not set fire to the truck as they had arranged. He didn't know this was a truck Guy habitually requisitioned; indeed, Guy had foreborn to tell him so lest he worry about the connection. Guy just couldn't understand it. The very last thing he said when he got down from the cab near a level crossing outside Bramsche on the Uffoln road (the rails moongleamed to the treeless horizon) was: 'Make sure it really burns – we don't want anything left, nothing.'

Alban Meyer-Decker wriggled to accommodate himself on the driver's seat he had just occupied. 'Like fireworks, it'll be,' he said and winked and drove west with a jolt, with a cargo whose worth was estimated at £40,000, none of which the bastard Englishman was ever going to see, he'd see to that.

No, Guy Vallender had not been stupid, not in that regard he hadn't. He watched the light of the truck diminish and disappear then walked beside the railway so far as the bridge over the canal. He rattled down the steps to the path alongside it. There was slurred singing on a moored barge. The moon twisted in the water, contorted grinningly. Major Guy Vallender marched at a nippy double, shutting his eyes now and again – but not too long: mind the drink, it's deep and dangerous – to conjure patterns to impose on the night, fluid scrolls and mutating dreamscapes of a grandeur that only funny money was fit to afford. Easy come, Guy, easy go.

The doorstep was gleaming, the crone was still adding, the child is just now making her brush swerve round a suitcase. It's always this way at the Café de Sedan. They never know who he's talking about, they're ignorant of the man he's asking after, they can't even remember his asking before. When he sees his face in the mirror behind the crone he wonders if he saw it there the day before yesterday when he winced at the coffee heat and watched his lip get red and taut and asks if they know the man, you know the man, with eyebrows, who sings, who sits here (gapes at mirror showing the mirror behind him and his face, his face, and his dorsal vented jacket and his face and an infinite series of back and front his back, his front and no one else's), the one who sits and sings?

'Ce type, cet Alban, vous le connaissez. C'est là que je . . . pfaf [pshaw] c'est pas possible que vous connaissez pas ce mec.'

The crone sucks her lips and looks up at the Englishman and shakes her head. The child must be deaf: the rustle of her brush on dust is not loud yet she betrays no sign that she has heard him, she keeps sweeping, patterning the floor with stripes like dry plough.

It will always be this way at the Café de Sedan. It will always be this way in Brussels. In Brussels in March 1946 Mr Guy Vallender, a former officer without a greatcoat, shivered and stroked his badman stubble and watched the children (whose cheeks were distended like red cists) skating on the little rink in the middle of a ruddy brick square. Every day their breath wrapped itself around their heads like scarves, every day they shrieked and giggled and bawled when bruised. Every day he gripped the yellow barrier through his cuffs, every day he stood under the wintry pollards and watched these children who

54

weren't his, these bright-mittened children, these foreign children, these little Belgians – they're big Belgians now and it's a clever Belgian who knows his father. Those cries when the ice burns limbs, those skeletal trees – they're humour signs, emotional colour, correlatives of his grave bemusement: nothing is so tritely eloquent of desolation as a naked tree. It creaks in the wind that's fresh in from Germany, it shudders with that force; if it could feel it would shiver the way Guy Vallender shivers when he turns to the smiling mother beside him at the yellow barrier and asks: 'Madame, vous ne connaissez pas, par hasard, Alban Meyer-Decker, dit Albeau – le chanteur Albeau, Madame?' And she shrugs, this woman with her eyes on the apple of her eye (Quentin, five years old, precocious repertoire of axels and salchows), and moves into a new private space a yard away.

Guy Vallender repeats this question, addresses it to chip fryers, concierges, janitors, soldiers, a man with a chain of keys round his neck, barmen, tram conductors, waffle sellers. His interrogative manner is that of a pink-eyed paranoiac, casually mad, so spontaneously casual it is evident to the least tutored object of his question that this man with no razor or coat, with a crazed beam and a cracked beamer, asks this as others of his kind ask for money or rant their woes or wail or leech, the way the lonely always will, on the eyes of the sane and stolid. Oh, pity them. Every bar in this city of beer has a pression and every pression has a crone behind it and every crone lives in fear of being identified as a former collaborator: she turns to pull another measure then she turns to pull another measure, she won't be tricked by an allied spy in this city of reprisals sanctioned by the state of Belgium, this city of fear and informers.

He hardly slept. His attic bed in the Hotel 't Galjoen was uninviting. He sleeps in his clothes and walks in the morning to the Café de Sedan, tramping through the city of bricks and scrubbed doorsteps, stopping to watch the children skating, asking, asking. He breakfasts on coffee and genever. He leaves the Café de Sedan to retrace the route that Alban Meyer-Decker and he took to the apartment at Joli Bois, the apartment that

55

Meyer-Decker and sa p'tite Cato vacated the weekend of December eighth last. The fifth day that Guy hammers with chapped fists on the janitor's window frame the old boy phones the police station on the Chaussée de Stockel.

Over a period of twelve days the Commissariat Central collated fourteen complaints about an Englishman with a red nose: eight of them were made by members of the theatrical profession – music-hall managers, agents, stage-door keepers, the choreographer of Frou Frou Yah Yah at the Théâtre du Cirque etc.; the others by footsoldiers of the janitocracy, old greys, jobsworths, men and women with a predisposition to register such complaints, to grass on tenants, to make your business their business. The hospital made no complaint; it smelled of blood which smells like metal, its lugubrious corridors were heaped with swabs, swagged with lint, lined with bins within which rotted the bad bits of people, the bits with the wens and the perforations, the bits that make seeping meatcakes, sup-purating faggots of poison. The bins leaked, the floor was slimy-tiled, it was sticky with lung gravy, duodenum juice, awash with the lactic swill of a million mastectomies, the thwarted seed of castrations. Guy Vallender saw all this and he saw people madder than himself, people who pressed so hard against the walls they wanted to move through them, people who scratched, people whose bad bits were in those bins and who were looking for them, scraping about in their filthy nightshirts.

The bit of himself Guy Vallender sought in these long lugubrious corridors would be good, fresh and pink, burbling. The bit he sought is not this one with its turtle wrinkles, not this one screaming, not this with its lazy eyes. He walks between the cots, scrutinising their tiny caches, wondering at the swaddled potential, at the inevitable promise of each of these lately foetal, womb-curved, furless pups to overcome it all and become a being as sentient and desperate as he is, this man on the turn. Mostly they resemble him, but not enough, not so he can be sure – but who can? A nose, a wince, a grabbing of the air: they're all his and someone else's too, everyone else's. He grabbed the air, aping this pouty babe, watching his hand, never having seen his

56

hand before, never having conned its closeness to an articulate claw. He might as well have put his face against a lobster tank to find the child that may be his, only *may*, just may, mind. But he yearned for a release from his uncertainty. He longed for the shock of paternity, for the assurance that he had made something more complicated than a firework, a fountain, say, which anyone with meal gunpowder, potassium nitrate, red orpiment, aluminium dark pyro etc. can make. He wanted his baby which no one else could make, the baby that could never be replicated because no one knew the formula. Fourteen per cent antimony sulphide? A being is a different bag of beans. The nappy here is changing from hospital white (grey) to the same lawn green of the MG in Furlong's showroom that he was about to buy when his call-up papers were waved at him by Douglas (already porky, already medically discharged). That green was a red rag to him. He took it as a chromatic token, a spectral hint. This plump lump of meat must be his, his; was his till he clocks the face attached to the nappy – it's a scowling brown, ploughed-field face. Not his. This one's a boy, looked it to his untutored eye. He knows his is a girl because her mummy was a girl: conviction beats even-chance here. He surveys the ward for nurses. This scowler must be a boy; he slips two fingers into the creature's nappy and probes for confirmation. The thing that is wet with excrement is a tight tiny sac, hardly yet a scrotum. He distractedly wipes his fingers and shaking his head shuffles into the adjoining ward where the moulds that cast these babies, the mothers with distended post-parturition bellies, groan and snore. She was not among them; he moved between the beds – where were the nurses? He gaped at each face. He could recall her face too. And her smell which haunted his meatus like an olfactory shade, like a matutinal reminder of last night's eau de vie, vaporous and fugitive. She was not here.

She was there, far away, in a forest, in a lodge rented by the month, dandling her darling boy, cooing, gazing across the valley of the Meuse to where a spur of conifers came down the slope like a widow's peak, sipping a tisane, dreaming of Africa, warmth and servants, wondering what little gift her Alban will bring her when he returns. She holds in front of Jean-Marie's face a postcard of the house where they will soon be living – the postcard was made from a photograph taken upon the house's completion when it was the subject of an article in *Le Document: Revue Mensuelle de l'Association des Architectes et des Dessinateurs d'Art de Belgique*, Bruxelles (Octobre 1926) which thus commended its architect Paul Jacquemyns: 'Il a pratiquement créé un archétype de ce qu'il envisageait comme qualité de l'habitation dans cette nouvelle société de Léopoldville.' Cato may not have known that she was going to live the rest of her life in 'the first building genuinely of its age in the entire Belgian Congo' (*Architectural Review* May 1932) but she is proud of its size and sleekness, and grudgingly grateful that Alban's commercial guile has enabled them to escape the privations of their country.

She enjoyed the Congo. She loved the life. She felt no embarrassment about firing servants she had fucked; they got no favours, she was an impartial domestic martinet, egalitarian in her pique.

'Toutes les pines noires se ressemblent . . . quand on en a vu une on les a toutes vues. Il y en a toujours des tas qui attendent.' This is what she said at parties. When she said it before Alban had passed out he hit her in the mouth. When she said it after he had passed out he hit her in the mouth the next day. Jean-Marie was excited by these monthly assaults, by the fundamental physics of blow and bruise, by his mama's jaw's mutability, by the immutability of the ritual – the cowering, the crying, the cuffing was invariably ordered thus; all that was ever different was the site (breakfast table, sun roof, bedroom, verandah, shower). Alban then takes the little boy by the hand and leads him from the beaten, bleating dressing gown and tells him: 'Il faut être fort.'

Then he sits down and helps Jean-Marie with his scales, encouraging him with the promise that he will teach him songs from his repertoire, songs (he emphasises) that are unquestionably his: 'C'est moi tout seul qui les ai composées, parole et musique. Mais d'abord tu dois apprendre la gamme. Ensuite on pourra chanter: "Cornouaille, j'y suis trop souvent allé. Cornouaille, le comté des cocus." ' And he looks at his boy's large hands on the piano keys and wonders. He wonders if the article in that sentence is hideously wrong: should I have written '*the* boy's', is 'his' a lie? Nothing taxed him more than the comparative aptness of the definite and the possessive; the latter was the representative of paternity, the other was as un-equivocal a sign of cuckoldry as horns or Cornwall. He compen-sated for this awful uncertainty, tried to obliterate it by making the boy in his image. He modelled him with brutal nurture, railed at his innumeracy, dressed him in the music-hall check that he affected, had custom-built for him a series of bicycles. Mostly he made him musical, a musical mimic of himself. Jean-Marie was a dogged prodigy. By the time his mother died he was a proficient pianist and accordionist. By the time the Englishman in jodhpurs with his nervy wife and micturating cry-baby arrived at the house he was doing well with the violin. (It was guitar that, quarter of a century later, he was strumming for his Mrs Butt when the picture window cracked and the dreamhouse on the dunes turned into a site of nightmare. 'Like an abattoir it is in there – someone's been playing silly buggers,' said Smerdon.)

Poor Eddie couldn't play anything else. Give the boy a drum and he pees in it. Give him a bright tin fife and he punctures the drum whose skin is buttercup naugahyde and undams the urine so it makes a patch on the mat. But then his parents lacked musical accomplishment. Beside the mat that he's wet, in a corner of the sitting room, is a veneered radiogram the size of two cabin trunks. When his father holds the drill to the rotating circle of licorice the people inside the cabin trunks begin to complain of their confinement and his father taunts them, joining in their cry even though he is free:

'Coffee and tea and the java and me/ Chuck a chuck a chuck a chuck boy.'

And he glints across the room to the Child Bride who lowers her head a little coyly: this is the song they courted to, the song on the wind-up on top of the bonnet, the song whose terminal grunt repeated during the temporal infinity of their initial swooning coupling (her first ever, not his); the metal needle decelerated swervingly at the point where the matt, greying grooves of the record adjoined the gloss black of label's border.

The grunt grew protracted, heavier, as the motor reached the end of its sprung span and expired. Guy Vallender lay panting, crushing beneath him this girl who was almost twenty years his junior, printing her back on the blanched grass of the mammarial down. He was as vast and vital and elemental as the sky that surrounded him, that dazzled her with its essential, reduced blueness. He had turned her senses: the dainty scamper of fieldmice's feet through the grass became a clatter; the grass rasped, blade against tempered blade; microscopic insects grew and showed her their busy afternoon; she'd never seen how lovely a fissure in the soil could be; life had entered her, hadn't it just? This down was Odstock Down and when she sat up she saw a leveret spring across the track, pleased with what its legs could do; here, in a field bounded by wire on whose barbs flocculated spermatazoa of paste-white wool, was a cloud of sheep and a wisp of lambs. This was a fresh state she was in, she wondered at the immense newness, she gazed at the agent of initiation (supine, oblivious, distractedly threading an ear of grass between his teeth).

'You'll cut your tongue,' she murmured, 'it's like paper.' And she took the hand with the wet vegetable strand from his mouth and fixed hers to it and of course the gust that brushed her downy dorsum was unlike any that had been that way before. His smell was unlike any she had smelled – bay rum and tobacco, and the flagrant musk of sexual afflatus seeping from pore upon pore. She was a pretty girl whom men gazed at but none had made his body a machine or olfactory cocktail for her. She was massively flattered. When she woke the sun had moved and while it moved it had dried her thighs so the stuff had caked like rice paper, it tugged at her hairs when she rubbed it off. He wouldn't look at her, he looked at the crest on his cigarette, he looked at the Riley (pre-war, sporty) and the trail of clothes leading from its open door, he looked at his spatulate nails.

She stroked his chest and he started as though her fingers were a wasp: 'You d-didn't . . . mind . . . you're not b-b-browned off. With me?'

She laughed a laugh of reproving reassurance, 'Nohoho . . . Why ever. . . ?'

Guilt, that's why; and cowardice – devirgination doubtless prompts the notion of responsibility and responsibility presented itself to Guy Vallender as a bodily burden, built to fit like a suit of stone. And the older he grew – he was now nearly thirty-seven – the potentially tighter and more frighteningly debilitating the imaginable garment got.

'You're sure?' he asked, dissembling the gravity of this petition for absolution with another bit of business – tamping the tobacco into the unlit end of a cigarette, something like that.

Sure she was sure. That then was a green light to Guy. That August the earth was their bed, a warm one, baked the summer through, eerily hot at night – not that she got out much at night, the old man saw to that, he was a willing jailer, he pried; though what he suspected or feared was venial (scrumpy, friends with make-up). He never would have believed this. He didn't believe it till you had swelled to the size of a melon, Eddie.

She was only an Anglican's daughter but she could take a rood up her schism: that's what the Tap Room Chaps at the White Jam Tart sniggered during their sessions. Yes, she was only a vicar's daughter but she could take the whole host in her priest hole. Did they guffaw! Eddie never saw his grandfather, not even after his mother died did he see him. The old man – he wasn't in truth *that* old, a dozen years older than Guy – did not come to her funeral (that would be because of the way she died as well as their estrangement). He could have asked to see the boy, he might have helped. But he was an agent of the Fear of God, he wasn't good at love. And by the time he suffered the very last stroke and had perforce to discover whether he'd been right or wrong he had probably forgotten about the boy's existence, so adamantly had he denied it. He won't have known that Poor Eddie came to share his wrong ideas – they're bound to be wrong (virgin, cross, blood, stone). He won't have known that Eddie served his God. He won't have known that the boy was in the same line as he had been, sort of. You'll hear no more of this pi sky pilot.

His glorious daughter was not the first girlfriend Guy Vallender had after he returned, disgraced, from Germany; nor was she the second (that was Ruby, maybe) or the third. He had

61

been back a year when he met her. He had digs with a Mrs Scutt and her spruce front room up the Wilton Road past the Old Manor loony bin; she told him he was worse than a theatrical, he picked all the walnuts off the top of a cake, she told him they didn't grow on trees; he strapped Margot Case to his bed and Mrs Scutt came home early from her whist. She told him to leave. He rented the cottage, that one there with the wicket gate and blond thatch and buttercup shutters with hearts cut out of them: you wouldn't recognise it Eddie, that first place you ever lived in. In those days the thatch was bracken brown, it sprouted tufts of grass, it was balding. And the gate was lost and the windows were metal-framed, horizontal-barred, rusting after just ten years. The garden was all nettles and docks, the ditch at the end was dry in summer and flooded in winter, its trees bore rotten fruit, its toppling fences were of chicken wire entwined with goose grass and dog roses, it smelled of something sweet and dead (that would be the carcase of the cat by the back door). The pugged chalk walls were tumorous and flakey, it wasn't much of a home. Guy Vallender was rarely there. Six days a week he drove uphill past coppices and smallholdings and the metal watertower high above the pines at the edge of Sladen's land and across the downs where swifts rallied on a sou'westerly with such order that the wind's escarpment seemed discernible. The beeches here are iridiscent clumps, tuftily sculpted; the spectral range goes from pearl to troutskin, from mole to rhino when the clouds are down on the soft horizon. He loved his drive to work: every crow was a buzzard, every time he jammed the throttle to the floor he was Dick Seaman, all this was his, and speed and clouds fostered mnemonic oblivion.

He was his younger brother Douglas's partner, i.e. he was a grudgingly indulged employee: 'You're a luxury item Guy.' While Guy was at OCTU in Dunbar, with the RA in north Africa, with an ack-ack outfit at Spurn Head, with a gang of kindred khaki sloths in Cairo, Douglas transformed Vallender Phoenix Fireworks (est. 1858) into Vallender Light Ltd. In lieu of waterfalls, mines of serpents, goblin guns, golden gerbs, green men, screech owls, Bengal matches, devils among tailors, prismatic bezels, Mount Etnas, jack-in-the-boxes, girandoles,

Turkish umbrellas, snow cones, bangers, sparklers, fountains, saxons, comets, Roman candles etc. it manufactured Very cartridges, smokes, wing-tip flares, signals, fuses – objects of utile pyrotechny which Guy Vallender reckoned a traducement of the art of Ruggieri, Hoch, Brock, Miller, Muller, Milholland, Aoki, Clarmer, Siemienowitz and Vallender.

'A gibbon with a tub of magnesium could make those things,' Guy Vallender told them in the White Jam Tart.

Popeye, Gen, Old John, Mac, the Brig, Padre, Baker the Butcher, Stiffy and Pudge said, all together now, 'A gibbon, a tub of whatsit, that's rich Guy, what about a jar of wallop . . .'

He dropped in early every evening: noggin, arrows, chat, sandwich. One evening he didn't till late. At 6.53 pm on Thursday June 12 1947 Guy Vallender, sweating in aertex and drill, sloped across the metalled yard between the old factory (snowcem, wrap-round windows, jazz-modern phoenix) and the new (buttressed and concrete-clad Nissen huts veined with drainpipes – a War Office design adapted for munitions and explosives manufacture). He half hopes Ruby or one of the girls may have stayed; he doesn't wholly hope because none of the girls, not even Ruby, wholly attracts him – they're there, that's the point with them, laid on to be laid on, not far to go to get them, just these twenty yards. As he enters the building the telephone in Chance's glass partition rings. He ignores it. He passes the choked rockets hung to dry like cobs of corn in clusters. He passes fresh wood boxes, sappy and splintering and stencilled with the martial sans serif of his unobliterable past. The phone doesn't give up. The girls are gone. Thing, the first-shift night watch, is boiling a pan of water above a Bunsen burner, strictly against regs; Thing could yet get spattered all over the girls' pin-ups of Tyrone Power and Stewart Granger (surely this man could have afforded a shirt). He refuses Thing's offer of a roll-up and a mug of char, four sugars and brown as bark. He wanders back to the door and the bell gets louder. He'd still have left it had the furry cord curled about the bakelite box not been shorn ringlets which made him shiver a little. He wanted that changed.

This was when he first heard her voice.

The story is simple. Roy Chance, who lived just down from the rectory near the watercress beds, drove her in the lorry to school each morning, and each evening picked her up on the corner of Rampart Road, 6.20 pm, on the dot. Guy told her Roy had had to drive over Ludgershall way, urgent delivery.

She said, verbatim: 'He'll crucify me if I'm late. Honestly.' Her voice was an octave lower than a girl's is meant to be; panic incited vibrato; fear brought on hoarseness.

Guy Vallender willed the tyres to squeak as he braked beside the phone box on the corner of Greencroft and Rampart Road. They squealed. She sat on a low wall with satchel beside her and a boater over her brow: the shriek made her start – the drive had taken him seven minutes, the wait had taken her many more. She tried to gather her case, she tried with the same limbs to wave imploring him not to drive away, she tried with those hands to point to herself, signal that she was indeed the prospective passenger. He grinned and helped her in; just a hand on her forearm, that's all.

'I'm not much of a white knight,' he said – a falsely modest formulation which she should have accepted in its unwitting literality. She should have taken it that way, then there wouldn't have been all that trouble down the years (nor would there have been this book).

Do you see, Eddie, that it would have been better had you not been born?

Poor Eddie. The progress to your begettal now in motion, and what motion: he drove in the new style, with his full-stretched arms jolted by the power drill of the steering wheel that he wrestled and vanquished, and again. He drove to impress her. He double de-clutched (all roaring revs), he did it as he braked with heel and toe, he did it in simulation of synchromesh, he took corners with sporty braggadocio. They passed Furlong's showroom at a lick, the wind through the window made her hair horizontal, she didn't even notice the turn into Britford Lane – that drab, damp place was yet far in the future, it was unseeable beyond the downs where there would always be summer, beyond the macadam switchback, beyond the perfect postcard they were heading into: in the pond at Coombe Bissett willows wept and mallards swanned; the knapped flints of yeoman walls shone like mussels; four-square houses with rude, weathered warm brick faces grinned at them, egged them on to breed a new generation of staunch tenant.

'You should have turned – there, that roa . . . Stratford Tony, that way.' The car was airborn over the Ebble bridge.

'Too slow. Bound to get stuck behind a cart. You can really dice up here.' Up here among the grassy tetanic tumuli of the long dead and the barrows of their brothers and the field systems of the Loincloth Age they discovered a shared antipathy to Roy Chance's practice of dipping his little finger into a rotting, spelaean molar then shoving it in one nostril then the other then exhaling with an appreciative grunt then wiping crisp discs of snot on the steering column or (at work) the underside of his table which was thus stalactitic. Contempt linked them. The first foundation of the world that they didn't know they were building was a nose with a finger up it, both bits belonging to the body of an asthmatic with a capacity for errands and a name that was fate. It's not much, sure, but then the utopia for two called love is a freakish folly, and its foundations are often jerrybuilt – that anyway was what Jean-Marie would sing all those years later (these things are eternal). Other foundations:

1) Her vocabulary. The conjunction of her deep voice and her barrack-room borrowings delighted him. She said 'sweet FA' with a throwaway insouciance which belied its schoolgirl affectation. (She was a schoolgirl.) She swore twice with thrilling carelessness. She referred to Roy Chance's shag spots, then added, laughing: 'I don't suppose that's where he gets them from though.'

2) Her smell. The baked earth scent of girls in summer was cut by another scent that was womanly, grown-up, profound, metallic, ostreaceous, sudorific and quite different from any-thing a male can exude. The two combine to form an olfactory signal of sexual potentiality, of a piece in bloom, of life, of climactic ripeness. After which there follows withering attrition – that's what Guy Vallender helped on its way; after which, too, there is only the latter scent; and the stuff in bottles is needed. Not, note, as an agent of sexuality but as a mitigating mask of it:

65

the job of the stuff in bottles is to socialise the elemental reek which frightens man with its evidence of the generic potency of woman. She had yet to realise that she possessed this potency; ignorance of the gift characterises adolescence – that's why adult men thrive and prey on it, that's why adult men believe that when roses are red they're ready to pluck, that's why they act so rash, that's why they put their lives on the line for bootleg poontang, that's why they risk tronk. An adolescent girl is the only woman over whom a man can exercise the kind of power that a man craves – total, irresponsible, unresented, applauded: all this without pleading or paying or knives and threats or friable promises. Statutory rape is the right appelation for this act of carnal burglary, all the worse and all the more perfect because the body with a child mind does not know what she has to give, does not know what is being taken from her, does not know that this is a simulacrum of love, a one-way transaction. Oh, bring on the boppers, do!

3) Petrol: his access to it, his profligacy with it, his willingness to burn it for her. Even if he did obtain it by obscurely illegitimate means from the reef of beefy brick garrisons on the Plain and from the RAF bases at Old Sarum and Boscombe Down (to all of which Vallender Light was a contractor), even if he stole it he still perceived his generosity and was flattered by it. Petrol cost; you paid for its pearly finish, for that rainbow lustre, for its reek which was the reek of abandon – the nose can suss the threat of adventure, can make the spine prickle with excited fright. Motoring – the very word's a period piece – was lent glamour by the price of petrol, by its scarcity. It was not a recreational norm; it was even less of a norm than it had been when she was a little child, a real child. In those pre-war, pre-dug days there had been more cars than there were now, more cars moving that is: when she had yet to get breasts she might count three or four cars an hour beyond the crosses, over the wall of the graveyard. She knew most of them, it was always the same three or four: the Rolls-Royce owned by Trelawney Reed (who had shot at a low-flying Hurricane in an access of appeaser's rage) and driven by his unnaturally blond chauffeur Frederick; Our Lad Osmond in his black and maroon Austin; The Urchin Moody's three-

wheeler with a tail like a duck's. They all stood unused, 'on blocks' she had heard, for the duration and longer. Now there were more crosses in the graveyard – one for Our Lad Osmond's brother The Boy Wilf; one (no lichen, smooth as the day it went up, it seems like yesterday) for her mother. Now she had breasts, but no brassiere – she was frightened to ask her father for the money. Now she knew she should be necking in cars, letting men put their hand in her blouse as though searching for a wallet or heartbeat. Now she and the time were ripe. But there were no cars save those of spivs, reps, yanks and green boys in khaki who really were boys, one-pip shriekers who travelled in packs, heads out the windows. Guy Vallender's suede shoes were stained with petrol, they were shiny in patches, they treadled in the dark beneath the dash, they danced a functional dance, nimbly, with such pedal grace she couldn't help but gape.

There are many crosses here. Left foot down and the right at forty-five degrees to it on the brake: he brakes from 70 mph (slewing tyres, dust nimbus) at the crossroads called Airman's Cross where stands, still stands, a laurelled cross to the memory of a Royal Flying Corps pilot who died when he ditched there during what Guy Vallender, a child at the time, calls 'the last show'.

'Airman's cross,' he says, baby-talking as he turned the car towards Cow Down and Ox Drove, 'airman cross because airman know he going for burton, can see ground coming at him.' She giggles. They remember this, both of them, all their conjoined life – Airman's Cross was their covert lingo for big trouble. They had cause to utter it a lot, latterly, in the variation 'Herman's cross' – big trouble with foreigners, with Belgians, say, who are, *au fond*, Germans. He'd excited her, now he solaced her with the soothing wooing of a safe progress: through tunnels of hawthorn; through sunken lanes; through osier coppices where the dappling is extravagant, piebald, lozenged (that's the lowering sun for you) and where the rude woodsmen saluted the vicar's daughter with raised axes. He drove that slow they could see her, they worked that late, they were that in thrall to the sign of the cross – which is what those axes make when they're raised in ranks, at the hilt, from wrists, between the splayed, split willows. He touched that car, Guy Vallender did, made it his horse. He could judge a grey tractor's trajectory from a thousand yards: this one, a Massey-Fergusson, spitted through a field, waked by gulls that are inland and lost – they never learn. This one, driven by The Urchin Moody's cousin Bri, turned out the gate – without looking: that goes without saying – just the moment Guy Vallender's car should have reached it. There could have been a real prang. But Guy Vallender had halted before he reached the junction of track and road, into which Bri proceeded, oblivious to the Riley and to the fact that his drive-on role is fulfilled. The grey tractor, gator-like, comes through the hedge just a bit. The sight of it stops her asking – the words are aborted between eyes and tongue – stops her asking: 'Why *here*? Why've we stopped here?' The tractor comes through the hedge just a bit more, and Bri's jaw comes through followed by his face, and she finds herself gazing at Guy Vallender, warmed by his comforting prescience and his orthognathism, warmed by his very being – which astonished her, which made her ask him to drive on so she might get out of the car by the watercress beds, out of sight of the rectory, out of sight of her father.

She said to Guy Vallender (with a formality that she wanted to doff and rip but dared not, didn't know how to): 'That was so kind of you. Thank you very, very much.' She added, looking at the handle of her music case, not at him: 'I enjoyed that.' And then she hurried across the shallow arched bridge and through the bipartite gate (whose purpose, children, is to obstruct the ingress of animals to the hallowed patch – it didn't obstruct Poor Eddie's father). Between the yew and the chequered chancel – liturgically north of it, geographically east, and swooningly insouciant of both directional programmes – she skipped a pace or two, swinging her case with abandon, frisky as a stripper with a boa and an audience of one. In sight of her home she deported herself straight-backed through the lines of graves and crosses. Her father spoke an unusually long grace. The two of them sat down, as they had on Monday,

Tuesday and Wednesday, to a supper of cold mutton. Next week, pork (sword).

'Trifle young for shagging,' tittered tipsy Padre dribbling stout. He wiped his nicotine-stained 'tache and scratched at his homochromic dogcollar – it got that colour from the scorching smoothing-iron wielded by its tight wearer who, outside time with inebriation, habitually reckoned that six minutes would render it twice as spruce as three minutes but was unable to reckon that span so gave it twelve. It bore marmalade skidmarks between increasingly narrow white striations. 'Trifle young I'd say, Guyo m' boy, Guy m' boyo. Aaah – that's very generous of you.'

Guy Vallender sorted coins to buy himself his fourth two-rounds-pork-sandwich of the week – he was sick of the pickle: 'The usual?'

'That's very generous. The usual, yes. Soon be pork *sword* of an evening eh? Get the old warrior out. What's your fancy Flo – mutton dagger? Ha!'

Flo, hacking a hand of pork with a bone-handled carver, waved it at him, teeth naked.

'I say, I say. No offence meant and none taken I trust. Double top, triple legs,' he yelled at hardly standing Stiffy, mine host at forty-five degrees to floor and dartboard, squinting. The Brig held his drink and his darts better, just about.

'Sure?' asked Stiffy whose slight arithmetical gift had gone some time between his pancreas and his liver.

'As God's in 'is 'eaven,' answered Padre, chortling.

Guy Vallender panoptics the saloon of the White Jam Tart: hank of bread; that pickle; grey porkmeat; optics; beer handles; Flo; eastern pattern wall to wall that turns to writhing slipperies when you're some over the how ever many it is; Padre's neck's fight with that repulsive collar; Stiffy holding up the wall; the

70

Brig who can't bear to look at his wife since her blackmarket PX pressure cooker exploded and put scalding spinach all over her face; Pudge whose nightly nightmare is of April 15 two years back when he entered Belsen with the 63rd Anti Tank; fringed lamp; filthy ceiling. Guy Vallender wants out. This norm has ceased to be his: he is about to shift into another. But not before Padre takes him by the sleeve, not before Ruby takes him in.

What I said to him – this is Padre, 113 years old (but dead since he was 74, cirrhosis, the day Jimmy Meadows was carried off at Wembley and Milburn had scored within the minute) – what I told him was: I remember her father the way you remember a boil. Holier than – well, not just than thou – but than the whole ruddy Holy Family. Plus royal que le roi. Too bloody religious to be in the Church for a living. You know – keen amateur, crazed with zealotry. When I saw Maureen's whatsit for the first time, when her mother (God rest her – I suppose they haven't let me near her, got not the foggiest where she might be) brought her home from the nursing home and I changed her nappy I thought to myself, eight days old she was mind, that some fellow neither of us know and she, Maureen that is, not even knowing what a fellow is, some fellow, my fine girl, is going to have his way up here not so long hence, in just a twinkling – that being the way of the generations as they say. Sure enough, night follows day etcetera, grandad by the age of forty-two. See do you? – She might be my daughter but she's still going to become a woman, someone's woman . . . *Her* father – well, how he ever got to beget her's a mystery: abhorred the flesh, drove her mother to . . . I tell you, no one ever *drowned* in a watercress bed, 'less they wanted to. Got me? Can you imagine him, when he got her home, even . . stt, wouldn't have touched a nappy would he, all that bodily filth, of course, it's not filth when it's baby's, but to *him*. He'll have taken one gander at her cunt – can you call it a cunt when it's still bald? – one gander at the way it goes from pink to mauve in the crack and he'll have wished one thing for her. A nunnery. That's what he'll have wished. He was repulsed by life. It makes for a pretty thin sort of life if you're repulsed by life, scared of the world. That's not the way.

Nor is this. Guy Vallender bought Padre a third Guinness, the old soak's twelfth that night, and exited with a curt nightall with them all saying, together now: 'You're not leaving us, Guy, not yet you're not leaving us.'

Those nights that summer – that breeze, that balm. It is dark now outside the White Jam Tart. Gusts jump as if from open ovens, jump up to toy with his neck, caress it, tease him, bolas him with the ideal of such a night as this. The gap between ideal and actual rankles, it always did with him. The actual is his shadow, his alone, leaping from porch to sill to moonlit pediment, expanding to climb dark houses and vault like a giant over the great gate to the Close, playing hide and seek in a row of limes whose pelt of rustling leaves nocturns from this greenback to that. The actual is also the roistering of squaddies in a lit-up tap, the stink of brewery mash, the old streets no one recreates themselves on (this is England land of the hearth). The ideal has this, every bit of it save the squaddies – cut them; it has the breeze and all that, and it has another shadow, leaping where his does, joined to his, vaporising over the same roofs, arm in arm. Man and girl are arm in arm, his arm entangled with hers the way arms can't, wrapped together in rapt conjunction, leeched tight. It doesn't get beyond arms. This ideal that he dreams before him, conjured in the streets that he walks (that we all will know when we're born and sentient and on the page: Eddie, Bonny, me, Donald even), this ideal is a state that combines pre-sexual anticipation with post-sexual familiarity; the specificity of coition doesn't get a look-in.

It's the state of love not its expressive act that beguiles him, that this actuality makes him pervious to – drink must have helped too, here. And the stars which are as clear as in a child's map of heaven: plough, harrow, tractor, thank God for the tractor. He is enjoying this momentous amble, he is breathing deeply – a self-ministered placebo against inebriation which lets him smell the brewery that much keener. Past the brewery where he might turn left through this mediaeval street grid to reach his car he turns right towards the Greencroft. He finds himself sitting where she was sitting not much more than three hours back – he can't remember a single step he took between the maroon brewery and this low wall. He was there, now he's here, where she sat; and the quarter mile, the four-minute slope between her and there – it's obliterated, done a flit. A man humdrummed by on a bike, standing, his head over the light beside the wheel, stretching towards everything Guy Vallender had ever and again abjured: home, progeny, permanent skirt. He keeled this way as the saddle leaned that; and Guy Vallender took the presumed banality of the man's life as a reproach. He had much to feel guilty over. He tried to imagine the chronic practice of uxoriousness, he tried to remember what the appeals of humility and sobriety were alleged to be – but he must have abandoned these endeavours (he'll have blanked on them), for the next time we see him is after closing time.

That's more like it. He has a bag of chips in hand and he's well shelled from a few in the private at The Princes In The Tower – no obligation to sodality or chitchat there. He's on the pavement outside Ruby's near the goods yard. You can be sure that the shunting kept them awake long into the night. She was a black girl with a heart of gold and when Guy turned her inside out there were the red bits of Ruby-gleaming pink-mauve lozenges to lick and sup at, like nacreous sherbet.

'Good for one thing only your nigger,' Douglas Vallender said to Guy who said back: 'Ten things, at least ten Dougadougdoug. Pearl necklaces, gnawing the bone, bagpiping – '

Douglas struck the air: 'Put a plug on it can't you. You know bloody well what I'm talking about . . .'

Guy knew well enough, he knew the charges against her – carelessness, lack of concentration, unpunctuality. He looked at Douglas's big ebonised desk, at big Douglas behind it, at the hands of the faceless clock on the wall, two strips of tapering perspex which cast viscous shadows on the plaster and which were now spread like the legs of a girl showing she's pleased to see you, twenty to five in the afternoon, though it's a hundred to eight in Ruby's bed that he sees now, that he pictures without shutting his eyes whilst Douglas moves on to the familiar second phase: the possibility of an accident, nay the very considerable possibility of a fatal accident caused by her negligence, of fire, commercial extinction . . . Ruby's hair, straightened but not that straightened, scrapes his abdomen. That's the least of the pains she submits him to – does she sharpen her teeth? And if she does how does she? And how does she know where – how does she divine his rod, his staff, his sac?

'What can you expect – ' Douglas's palms are open in invocation of common sense, reasonableness, one of those drear programmes, ' – feavensake Guy, she's the issue of – what? – some tart in Pompey and some black jacktar. God 'lone knows why you can't find yourself a . . . None of my business, I'm sorry Bro. Some of Monica's chums are terrific pieces of homework . . . Anyway old son, as for Ruby. I'm aaafraid – she's for the Spanish Archer. She's going to have to go.'

She's going to come. She did, with ventriloquial croaking, with the rasp of a stick against railings. Guy Vallender licked his lips, looked with eyes in the top of their sockets from the burnt scrub here at Avonmouth through the dark hills of Bristol city and beyond, to where her head rested.

He said to Douglas: 'I'll talk to her. Give her a talking to . . .'

Douglas said: 'Very well. Make it clear to her this is her last chance. And tell her to cut her finger nails – even if that does mean sacrificing your pleasure, me old beast.'

Technical note: Ruby Gray (20) worked in the part of the factory (Number 3 Shed) where chlorate and perchlorate compositions were mixed through sieves. The conjunction of these materials, $KC10_3$ and $KC10_4$, with fine metal powders, e.g. lead oxide (Pb_3O_4), is potentially hazardous and the likelihood of flagration is increased by sieves unearthed against static electricity, which electricity is most ordinarily generated by a finger nail scratching the sieve's mesh. It is more costly to earth sieves than to ensure that those who operate them have short nails, which are right for work if not for play. God bless girls with short nails for no one else will.

Ruby cut and filed hers so they stopped short of the meat of her fingertips which then rolypolied over them. What squat fingers she wears now! She sweeps the crescentic clippings from the vanity top into the palm of her new-made hand and blows them out the window.

In the little garden her auntie's gentleman caller, Dapper Nat, is stripped to the waist, his braces over his naked torso. In his left hand he has by its scruff one of the rabbits from the hutch next to the waterbutt. In his right – the one with the tattoo of a dragon – he holds a rusting cleaver. He hears the window and grins up at her, waving the still quick beast. Then he puts it on the torn American cloth on the mossy table and most likely maims it with the weight he applies to prevent its escape. His hair is gummed to his skull and bootblack. Are you other bunnies watching? I'd shut my eyes and dream of lettuce. He brings down the blade with no backswing, crisp as a cuke. And not a spot of blood on him – once a butcher, as they always say in the Catering Corps, once a butcher. The one-time butcher – used to work for Twose in the days when there was meat that didn't come from whales – drains the rabbit's blood into an enamel bowl. That'll thicken the sauce. He knows his way round blood, Dapper Nat does; he treats it as precious even though it's no use, now, to the creature who owned it. He values it, its smell, its stickiness on his hands, the skin it makes over his. He still makes Twose's son's black puddings for the shop but there's not enough meat for him to go back there full time among the hands and faggots and chitter-lings.

He works nights, up the Wellworthy, chamfer machine operator. He'll put the rabbit to stew with onion and a nice spot of turnip and a splash of barley wine so it's ready for his breakfast. When she's gone out – it's Ruby's auntie's night for her night out with Dot – and before it's time for him to cycle by way of the causeway across the watermeadows to the Wellworthy, he'll feed Ruby a couple of glasses of So'ton gin, see if it makes her game. If she's not, amen: he's not that worried. She tells him he's a tradesman and has to use the tradesman's entrance round the back. The front door's for the posh toff with the Riley who sometimes brings her home. All he ever gets to do at the front door is to push black puddings in and pull them out with his teeth; if he breaks the skin he gives her 7/6d. Either way she keeps the sausages and takes them to work to sell to the other girls who grill them for lunch over Bunsen flames. She never lets Nat do anything else round the front. That's how she knew for sure it was Guy's. She was proud of that certainty. In the hierarchy of the club certainty outranks putativity.

No one dared tell the vicar. Roy Chance should have but didn't: mum was always the word with Roy. It took him a while to twig, to do two and two, to figure why she no longer needed a lift home, why she said to keep it under his hat, why she gave him a fleeting buss on the cheek when he said of course he would. He wondered if she'd have kissed his mouth had he not had a finger in his left nostril. He wondered what might have been had he had his finger in the right one, the far side from the passenger seat where she sat, and tushingly cursed his ill timing; with luck like his he was bound to live at home with mum for ever (he didn't say a word to *her*).

As Mr Guy was walking from his office to the car park late one afternoon Roy Chance approached him with a query about a delivery to the Green Jackets at Winchester. Guy said he was in too much of a hurry to deal with it, that he had to meet someone. Roy Chance winked. Guy supposed this was a wince in reaction to Roy's scraping a nasal polypus with the nail of the index finger which was in up to the knuckle.

The Urchin Moody didn't tell the vicar because:

a) He was embarrassed to say what he had seen the girl doing with a fellow in Bokerley Dyke on Martin Down, not thirty feet from the A-road.

b) Even had he not been embarrassed he wanted the vocabulary to describe what he'd seen in language other than that which the vicar castigated as 'farmyard'. Fellatio was the word you wanted, Moody; though you'd have had as little luck with it as you would have had with gamming (farmyard) or gobjobbing (midden). Your vicar may have been a classicist but he was an expurgated one. Even had he been able to recall that fellare means to suck he'd have been none the wiser for he was dangerously unworldly and ignorant of this fine old Roman recreation which is both pleasure and contraceptive (a bit late for that now). He'd have asked: 'Sucking what?'

c) He'd be right in it, up to here, if it were discovered why he'd been up on Martin Down. (Setting snares in the long grass.)

d) He had enjoyed bimping from his set on the bank high above them down there deep in the dyke (Roman, post-Roman, part of an agrarian defensive system); he lies prone, tumescent on the tumulus, the ungreen August grass teasing and tickling and threatening to reveal him by having him sneeze – that's why, as you'll note, his hand covers his nose and mouth which ought to be as open as hers, agape at Agape. His entire face is an eye, fringed by long lashes. He enjoys bimping, he hopes to bimp another day. He doesn't want to obviate the opportunity by causing the plating player to be withdrawn from the entertainment.

e) He locked his bedroom door. He scissored the headlines in one issue of the *Salisbury Times* and two of *Football Monthly*. The work was arduous, slow, fiddling. The words he needed were not to be found so he had to cut out each letter. He had glued down only two words, 'deaR RevD', when his mother called him down for tea and lardy-cake. He screwed up the newspaper, the magazines, the sheet of lined letter paper and put them beneath his bed. That evening he wrapped them in his jerkin and drove all the way to Odstock before dumping the lot in a wire wastebin next to the phone box. No regrets.

No one told the vicar, told on her. The summer days shortened, soon the days were no longer summer days – leaf effects please. Still no one told him, told on her. He was convinced that whatever was the matter with his daughter was dietary and so instructed Mrs Moody to cook beetroot and boiled onion for every meal during the last week of her school holiday. The beetroot so stained her urine that, sixteen days after her period had been due and three after she had told Guy Vallender she was pregnant, she looked into the lavatory where she had peed after supper and, for just as long as it took to work it out, believed that she wasn't pregnant. She sobbed, she sobbed, she wailed, it echoed all about the cool cul de sac where she sat, bounced about the sienna floor tiles and the white dado tiles.

That's what she did when she thought you weren't to be, Eddie: she howled. That's how much she wanted you. Your grandfather heard nothing: he was listening to Sibelius or Grieg. Your mother wiped her eyes with the skirt of her veg printed dress – so much softer than the harsh brown stuff of the christian wipe (Saint Izal the martyr was put to death by sandpaper). Then she hurried through that house of dark panels and fearsome spirits to her bedroom. She took the box from the wardrobe, she took the glove from the box, she took the ring from the glove. Now she slips it on the bride finger and skips a polka, all swirling skirts and smiles. She holds her abdomen as she whirls, cradles it tenderly – this mightily welcome, unknown, unknowable, perpetually crouched, benign parasite who's set up house within her, who's forever raiding the larder, who saps her, lifts her, fills and fulfills her. You gave her such strength Eddie. She was a lonely girl whose friendships, paternally proscribed, never endured, whose burgeoning hermeticism was rupturable only by a man so singleminded as Guy Vallender. Her father would discern fault on grounds of class, wealth, indigence, hygiene, morality, accent, occupation, means of transport, creed, piety.

I wanted what was correct for her. I loved her, I had nurtured her: I wonder at her capacity to conceive of sin as an elective abstraction, as something one can choose not to give credence to. That capacity is always frightening – had we not seen those past few years whither it might lead? Man in his frailty may choose to ignore The Law, to make of himself a moral ostrich, to pretend to himself that the absolutes are chimera or – worse – that Our Lord's way is one of many and not the imperative path from which there can be no divergence: Man may choose thus, and when he does so it will be noticed. And God – whose prerogative choice is – may resolve not to extend his blessing and protection to those who thus deny him. This is his wrath expressed through the withdrawal of succour. I shall never forget that night. That night divided my life.

She arrived home at seven o'clock on the evening of Friday September 28. Her father was in his study. Supper was on the table. She went to her room; changed into mufti. She packed her larger case with clothes, her photograph album, a George VI Coronation mug, two framed photos of her mother, three pairs of shoes, a certificate of proficiency in life-saving, a marbled plastic Waterman's pen her mother had owned, a Dresden shepherdess, all of the jewellery she had been left save the ring because that wouldn't have been right, a print of Millais's *Ophelia*, a coat fashioned from the fur of foetally ripped

Mongolian lambs, two books by the late Mrs Woolf, a collected G. M. Hopkins with a tooled and fringed tongue of leather marking 'The Wreck of the Deutschland', *First Steps in Water-scape* by N. W. Ord, crayons (Lakeland), water colours in a black metal box, a Flemish doll, a set of hairbrushes with azurine moiré backs, a humorous diptych made from butterfly wings and entitled 'Pike Meets Duck, Pike Eats Duck'. In the other case she packs things for her baby: the children's books that remained to her; a broderie anglaise bonnet she had found on the pavement near school, brought home, washed and hidden (it was still damp); a set of building blocks whose paint had faded and cracked; the card game Happy Families; a threadbare teddy called Horeb El Isha; a pink plastic doll, streaked with black (like an Old Spot pig), representing Little Tom the Chimney Sweep – the brush his ill-moulded hand gripped was snapped.

This scene is a series of tableaux vivants. It is lit only by the little lamp on his desk. He is motionless, the graphite spike of his pencil grows from his jaw and links it to his sleeve whose folds undulate with zealous overmodelling. The sculptor can turn black marble into cloth but can't make eyes even seem to see. His eyes died the moment she spoke her first words. She is fifteen feet away, hands folded over her uterus, close by the door to this room that she has never before dared enter without knocking, without awaiting his impatient beckoning, without fear. She is fifteen feet away from him and thirty-two years younger, six inches shorter, three and three quarters stone lighter. She is also spectral, unfamiliar, a new being.

Womanhood has struck the girl, moved in along with the child. His muteness is doubtless occasioned as much by her amended presence as by the terrible litany of shamelessness that the creature, formerly his daughter, gives breath to. She is bearing a child. She is leaving home, leaving him, leaving school. She is going to live with the man who sired the bastard.

His capacity for chastisement is voided – by shock certainly but also by volition. He didn't want to berate her. To do so would have been an admission of a lifetime's parental dereliction; not to do so was clerical dereliction. You can't win if you've taken vows and then procreated. The two don't fit. You were meant to be married to your superstition, not furthering the flesh. The ideal you punted at the flock was not achieved by your family. You did bad Rev – first your wife now your daughter. Those who preach shouldn't do – when they do do, no matter what they've preached, it always turns out wrong, things won't adhere to programmes (that's the only wisdom), there are always tears. She stares at her father with such a tear seeping from her eye – another vicar's daughter off the rails.

The dusk overwhelms them, the room's panelling colludes with it, everything's grainy, there's a lot of lack of light, the air has thickened. This parting is as still as sarcophagal statuary, as uncommunicative as a funeral (one or other might be dead, they *are* to each other). It's not a farewell, that's not the right word, benevolence does not infect the gesture he makes when, at last, he moves. He places the pencil on the desk and waves her away with casual petulance: it's a gesture of dismissal to a troublesome child, to a chatty char, a gesture so inappropriate to the circumstance (which requires something on a larger scale) that she wonders if he disbelieves her.

Indignant, she lifts her blouse and V-neck to reveal her full tummy – already swollen to her eyes though not to his. She patted you Eddie, she was proud and triumphant and defiant, her two ranks of teeth were joined to prove it. He repeated that gesture, his fingers fluttering, tranced. She slammed the door.

That wasn't the last they saw of each other – that was at a zebra crossing by the NAAFI: he saw a blooming beaming pregnant young woman, she saw an old man hunched at the wheel of a dusty Singer that had stopped for her. She was the best part of the way across the road before the mutually alien figures resolved themselves momentarily into eye-locked father and daughter. He didn't turn to watch her enter the chemist's shop. He had moved before you were born Eddie, out of the diocese, to Pompey, where they knew he was a widower but never heard about his daughter, believed him childless (which he was), didn't dream he was a grandfather, appreciated his interest in their nippers, were ever so sad when he got ill and had to go into the home. So that was the last time he saw her, your mother, and indeed you. I doubt that he ever knew your name.

I doubt that your father ever knew Madison's name, Eddie. That name would have meant nothing to him; it meant a lot to your grandfather though. He liked the lad, succoured him, taught him, showed him patience where others didn't – all to no good, mind. He never made the connection of course; Ruby was a proud girl who didn't talk about what had happened to her nor about who'd got her with him, Ruby was a shamed girl who was wretchedly mute about why Madison was the way Madison was. It was something she tried to make herself forget, and silence fosters obliteration, anaesthetises mnemosyne. It helps, it helps even when the child is hurling ornaments about the front room, even when he smears next door's washing with anthracite, even when he's going for you with upholsterer's shears, even when he's in court again and piddles in the dock – it really does help to forget why, to shunt the guilt. His brain, his behaviour, his bruised speech, his dazed eyes – these are reproaches in themselves.

It's not necessary to dwell on their genesis. That's what has to be excised, the inculpatory memory of an abortifacient strike that missed: this is a form of assault whose euphemism, termination, is not a fib. There are not meant to be any wounded in that one-sided war, no one should come limping home, the innocent must go to their mass graves and sad pyres. And the parents, straitened and compromised, rue their victory, conceal their triumph. There'll be no VF Day to celebrate the capitulation and surrender of Foetus. Ruby wouldn't have had a co-parent, an ally, a fellow aggressor to have celebrated with anyway.

Guy Vallender said: 'Get rid of it.' Then he said: 'I shouldn't have said that. I didn't mean it.'

Ruby said: 'Yes you bleeding did.'

She was right. They walked between the river and the poplars, the other bank from the gardens of pebbledash semis and little brick villas and peeling bungalows, the same bank as the boat-station – not far from where the cattle market and new abattoir are now but weren't then. So she won't have thought that even pigs get a better deal than whatever this within me is going to get: they get to come to market and Dapper Nat uses everything but the squeal. It's a finer fate to end as crackling or as a chop in a pan and to donate those kidneys to someone who values their rank smoothness over the crumbliness of lambs' than it is to be turned into soap. Had the cattle market been built it might have made her construct such a comparison, weigh the tiny seedling against a saddleback. It wasn't, she didn't. She shrugged, and again, and wrung her wrists. Guy Vallender glanced at his watch when he reckoned she wouldn't notice, falling behind her to hitch his cuff beneath it, gleying down his nose the way old steamers do. The river was low, this was said to have been a glorious summer, Compton's Summer, the best ever summer for men who put grease on their hair; one such man, a gunner with his beret on his shoulder and his sweetheart beside him, sat in the bows of a boat and grinned as he rubbed her thigh with the rudder's handle. She dangled her hand in the stream that carried the boat; seeing Ruby's face spoiled her afternoon, quite put her off the idea of the legs round his neck she'd promised him – she could tell that the poor nigger was that miserable because of the chap, and she could tell that the chap wanted nothing but to slither out of it, whatever it was. The oars trailed from the rowlocks incising the surface; a mallard crossed the prow; Guy Vallender said he'd pay whatever it cost.

Dapper Nat stroked his jaw, considered a bit, stared across the kitchen table at Ruby: 'Twenty-five quid. He could fork up that couldn't he? Old Ma Cropper'll do you for that. A pony to pull a rabbit as they say.' Dapper Nat reckoned: Old Ma Cropper (freelance midwife with a ginger moustache, obese cats to feed, a tumbledown down Britford Lane, a garden full of empties, nettles in the borders, breath like coal gas) would do the works for £20, leaving a fiver commission for yours truly.

Ruby went to Guy's office during the lunch hour; he was drinking bottled Bass, his beetroot sandwich stained his face, his hands were streaked with coloured chalks. The blackboard was low on its easel. Dots plotted a pyrotechnic ideal of volutes, fountains, javelins, masts; chemically formulaic notes to himself were scrawled in his Arabic boffin's hand; he picked up a board eraser, the beak's friend, with his big sandwich hand and crouched to make an amendment. The sun moved clockwise expressly in order to blanco the board, clean the slate, aggravate Guy Vallender who kicked at the easel to shift it into the shade and legibility. Now he turns to Ruby. Her eyes are no more swollen than is lately usual.

His tongue and teeth clipclop: she is the arbitrarily unchosen carrier of my child, of one of my children, the mere object of an inseminatory fortuity, of a fuck that was retrospectively (though is not prospectively) a fuckup. The fuckup's natural consequence can be excised for £50.

'Fifty pounds . . . *fifty*?' said Guy Vallender, 'Matthew, Mark and bloody John – you can get two new legs for less, proper metal jobs. Fifty nicker Rube . . .' He held a tiny hand to his burgeoning brow, swollen with trouble to render his hand tinier, tinier by the second.

'Legs,' Ruby, whose are unhosed, repeats, 'legs are legal. I know: leg, legal, L,E,G. One o' your effin' whatsits, your ruddy puns Mister Not So Clever Dick. This – it's bloody *illegal*.' Cries, Ruby cries. 'This isn't bloody legal at all. Know what you get for it? Three years Guy, three years stiff – with gwynns putting things up your whatsit mate. Fifty quid Guy or I'll blow the whistle so fuckin' loud it'll fuckin' fuck your ears Guy.' And, she added, sotto: 'So loud it'll bring your lovely brother in, faffin' and puffin' all over: "Is there something to be sorted out?" You think about that Guy.'

He dipped his fingers in the till. He gave her £50 plus five 'to spend on yourself, for *you*.' He passed her the notes in an envelope (sealed with a lick) in the beer garden of the High Post Hotel which in those days was pink and flat-roofed, a roadhouse for the RAF and fallen. He asked – God, he was ever hopeful: 'Lift into town Rube? Ruby?'

Ruby got a bus. She smiled all the way to the embankment at the bottom of Castle Road by the railway bridge and winked at a soldier as she got off. Can you imagine the shoes she bought with the excess? And the maroon dress – 'Burgundy so suits Madame's colouring,' said the posh bint in Madame Francesca of Bond Street in the Canal just along from the biggest pram showroom you ever saw; the other bint, the one with a cigarette holder and the hat on her ear, distinguishable from the plaster mannequins by her ability to saunter along a parquet catwalk, hurt her face by contorting it into a cartoon of disdain. Ruby paid four times that bint's weekly wage for the dress, in guineas. She wore it out of the shop and strode with a swagger; she so delighted in herself swaying beside herself in the big window down the street that she didn't notice beyond her reflection the liveried Pedigrees and the gloss-finished, chrome-sprung, two-hooded twin perambulator across which was stretched a banner printed with the legend 'Double Trouble!' Ruby likes this dress so much she wants another.

Everyone knows that on Saturdays when Pompey is playing at home Dapper Nat turns in as soon as he's back from his shift at twenty past six am and gets up at midday to be sure of catching the train to Fratton with some of them from the Wellworthy. (Meet: quarter to one at the South Western, the commercials' hotel by the station.) Everyone knows he takes his bath on the dot of twelve and that Ruby or her auntie has to have it run for him, all ready and steaming, with the loofah *in* the water to soften it a touch, not left on the side like a 'dry old donkey knob' (Nat's very epithet). Everyone knows he likes to lie in water that's scummed with factory grease and dense with his dead cells reading the team news and farting so that it bubbles and ripples like a hot well. The clock woke him, and as he lay stretching and scratching and hawking on the pillowcase the roar of the gas geyser welcomed him to the weekend. He wondered where his tea was; he had that steaming too, three spoonfuls, good dollop of condensed milk, pink mug with coaching scene. He pulled at his scrotum where it was sweat-glued to his leg, sniffed at his fingers, strutted out of the bedroom in his jama bottoms.

'Where's me tea?' he called down the stairs. 'And me paper – oi. 'Allo.' He grunted and a comma of steam wriggled from the crack at the top of the bathroom door as he turned towards it. He opened the door. The steam came at him from everywhere. It rose from round Ruby's body. There was so much water in the air he near gagged, the heat went for his eyes, a thousand thorns stuck in his skin, the air was hauled out of his lungs by the geyser which was so greedy for oxygen it wasn't fussy where it got it. He thought: so *that's* what black skin looks like when it's boiled, that's how it goes in drowning water. He thought: she's dead. He thought: she's had it away with my gin, the cheap little thief – and so she had, though she'd been out and bought the second bottle, the Gordon's, the auto-abortionist's preferred brand. It bobbled empty in the cataract of the tap. The other was on the floor, its label ('Juniper Bush' So'ton Naval Gin) was skew, drooping, ruched and ricked like a victim's skirt.

He thought: I'm going to miss the match and that water's going to overflow. He shut off the tap, scalding his hand. Her eyes orbited torpidly. He cursed in resignation at missing the match. Her groans, her vitality despite her hydrocalorific self-torture, her resilience, her reluctance to concede life (or child) all kept him from Fratton. He'd have had more fun that afternoon had she gone under. He hauled her from the bath, wrapped her in sheets, smothered her burns with pigs' blood from the white enamel bucket in the larder and with Brylcreem: the blisters still grew like snails beneath the skin.

When her auntie came home she called Ruby an inconsiderate biddy and poured herself a Mackeson to help with the shock. Ruby sobbed as her alcoholic anaesthesia abated: 'Only wanted to buy myself another frock Nat. That's all . . . thought I could do it m'self, save the money he give me, get m'self a nice frock, a lovely one, peach with crepe lace on the collar.'

She sat by the open window staring at the rabbit hutch in the garden. The mock-onyx mantel clock sounded kick-off time. Nat's damp jama bottoms stuck to the leather armchair. Ruby's auntie went to fetch another milkstout.

Nat whispered: 'You could 'ave got me in proper hot water with Old Ma Cropper. Poaching, that's what you been trying to do, poaching what's rightfully Ma's. You don't want to get on the wrong side of her mark my word. Nor o' me f' that matter. No bloody gratitude.' Ruby gaped at the hutch, the lean-to, the water butt. 'Wicked what you done. Ma'd give you an earful right 'n' proper I can tell you my girl. Rabbit rabbit rabbit – that's Ma. Whole warren you might say. If she heard you'd bin trying to pull your own rabbit . . .'

The rabbit in the hutch leered at Ruby, it grinned as it chomped, shreds of kale stem protruded from its mouth, the more it ate the bigger it grew, its face swelled to fill the hutch, diamonds of furry flesh pushed through the wire net.

Ruby vomited gin and bile onto the bloodstained sheets. Ruby's auntie and Nat played cribbage till it was time for the football results. Nat got the wireless set warmed up well in advance, he took the Vernon's coupon from behind the china Alsatian on the mantel, unscrewed the top of his smart Parker, gripped it tensely, listened hard, blamed one or other team in each fixture for the result's incompatibility with his prediction – 'Fuckin' Wolves; bugger the Gunners; shitfaced bleeding Rams.' Then the voice said: 'Portsmouth four, Sunderland two,' and he scowled at Ruby and told her: 'I missed six effin' goals because o' you.' He thought: I'll be damned if I miss my five quid from taking you to Ma Cropper.

He walked her there, pushing his bike so he wouldn't have to walk back. Did you ever push a bike down Britford Lane? Did you ever walk that way with someone you didn't know and couldn't see, someone who was on the way to death? I'll bet that if you did you minded not to wet your feet in the puddles – you know what they say about cold soles in autumn. Ruby didn't know. She dragged her feet, scuffed, sniffed the apples that were tan with rot and dotted with death-white spores – they lay in the orchard grass among broken crates. And see, there's the bungalow where Eddie (presently curled in another womb) would one day live. Eddie's half sibling moved towards its end. It moved unseen, unseeing past the sodden cricket hut, the midden, the glass-houses whose panes are opaque with dirt and mostly cracked, then the rickety gate, the path – concrete with ginger pebble aggregate, the grass up to here, the nettles too, the dead birds, the dead mice, the rags in the rosebeds, the tiles slipped from the roof, the psoric paint of the window frames, the leaded lights agape as cataractic eyes, the wet cardboard boxes stretched by empties and reverting to wood pulp, the red vulval porch (tiled and gleaming against the buff roughcast).

And here's Old Ma Cropper in the porch to welcome her patient, welcome her with a cough and a blast of gastric silage and a log of ash detumescing beneath the straggly ginger moustache. Old Ma's cardy has long since turned to felt and those things in it, where her waist once was, are her drooping dugs, stretched as an old sow's, as dry now as ever, jutting like pocketed fists. Her actual fists, the stone-age obstetrical instruments at the ends of her arms, are filled with cats. Her face is like anyone else's bottom. This is a woman who drew the short straw. When her lipped anus moves words barge their wheezy way past the fag butt: 'See she's a blacky didn't tell me that did you Nat my lad.'

Ruby smiles. Some of the cats hiss.

'Not', Old Ma says, 'that it makes a lot of difference – your parts are just the same as ordinary folks are my beauty.'

In the hall there's such a smell of cat it smells like a distillation of the smell, an essence, a reduction. The carpets, the curtains, the coverings are moist with competing pheromones. There are glinting eyes all up the stairs. These cats have plates every-where, chipped saucers that are crusty brown with blood, they're always hungry, they always need more to eat.

That's just what Old Ma says, she pats Ruby's belly and the buccal sphincter opens to wheeze: 'You'd better come on in my beauty and we'd better get down to our spot of business – the cats can't wait, they're always hungry, aren't oo bubbies, boobiewoobies. I've such a family to feed my beauty.'

Then Nat handed Old Ma the envelope and left. Then Old Ma took Ruby upstairs, sat her down on a reeking counterpane, had her roll up her sleeve, bound a ligature round her upper arm, broke the capsule's neck, filled the syringe, wiped the needle on her cuff hanky to make sure it was clean, dabbed at the arm with another hanky soaked in spirit, pushed the spike through Ruby's skin, depressed the plunger and said: 'You won't need to undress – just your smalls. You just lie there and think of the angels my beauty.' Ruby's blood began to show in the dropper's neck.

Old Ma Cropper withdrew the needle: 'How's that. All right? I tell you, I never wanted nippers myself either. Now just you lie there like I say and next thing you know all your troubles'll be over. Old Ma's a good fairy to bad girls. I bet you anything you like you'll find half a crown under your pillow when you wake up – better than sixpence from the tooth fairy eh?'

She was as good as her word, Old Ma. Ruby got her 2/6d and no sepsis. Old Ma got her £20 and while Ruby was still under popped down The Swan's jug and bottle. The cats got their treat, cooked up with lights. Ruby suffered a three-day hangover but that'll have been because Old Ma administered a veterinary anaesthetic. Her clothes were so covered with moulted hair she sneezed and itched, was still at it when, wearing the usual skirt and zippered jumper, she returned to work.

'Gesundheit!' cried Guy Vallender as Ruby jerked in time to her nose's bidding, clutching the flammable air of No. 3 Shed. She turned back to her bench. 'It's good to see you, you know,' said Guy. 'I'm glad it all went – '

'Bugger off will you. You'll never know what I been through.'

Nor did Ruby know; she had no idea Old Ma Cropper was as drunk as *that* when she picked up the scalpel and forceps, when she wiped her fist clean on her cardy. And Ruby couldn't remember the cats licking the blood from her thighs, was still in nod when one of them gave birth on the pillow beside her. And the combination of a particular suction noise with Old Ma's navvy curses would never mean anything to her. She was humbly grateful that she had escaped the hades-scape of dreamless darkness, was resentful that she had had to be subjected to it, told herself *never again Girl*. Every time she changed the blood-soaked napkin she winced at the thought of it and cried for that lost life, that unknowable being; she rued that her curiosity about it could never be satisfied, that it was too late, always would be too late. She used to wait for sleep weeping for what might have been. Now she switches on the little lamp beside the bed to expel the picture of the little girl who has her face and scowls at her and always runs away. And when she wakes she is sick: every morning she vomits, she stumbles in her nighty to the toilet and gags. Every morning. She genuflects before the Shanks and wonders what Old Ma Cropper has done to her to make her vomit day after day. She empties her tummy through her mouth, and Nat shouts: 'Pipe down will you. I'm eating.'

Back from work and he's tucking into lamb's testicles fried in rasher fat, and bubble and squeak. There's grease on his plate and grease on his lips, different grease on his head, yet another on his hands. 'Dip the knobbler,' he says to himself and wipes the plate-grease with a crust. 'You,' he addresses Ruby coming past the mangle to get a cup of char, 'you sound like a camel giving birth. Trying to eat I was. What's the matter with you this time?'

'Nothing', pronounced Doctor Stobo (three piece, chain, Morningside vowels, boozer's hooter), 'is precisely the *matter* with you. Matter would not be the word I'd choose. Your condition is morning sickness. You are pregnant.' Ruby didn't faint, but she gasped and sat down, held the edge of his big brown desk, stared at the net curtains, Stobo was right, she was pregnant. 'Like the Virgin bleedin Mary,' whispered Ruby. You'd never have thought there was so much to see in net curtains.

These things happen. Old Ma Cropper was not to blame. She didn't know there were two in there, no one knew. When Dapper Nat called by one cold evening to demand the money back Old Ma told him to run along. Her pride in her obstetric prowess was hurt, her failure to detect the second twin rankled; she thought she'd better have a drink. Had she known before Ruby arrived she'd have asked for at least ten pounds more. By the time she'd finished the bottle and was slumped on the lumpy sofa among the bolsters and cats and cat-blankets she had convinced herself that Dapper Nat – a rat to the marrow – was lying, that he had devised a base ruse to regain his pony. She punched a cushion and toasted her victory with gin dregs. These things happen.

The lucky twin, the twin that now had its mother to itself, stretched in the uterine balm, blissfully tumbled in an amniotic brine that was all its own; the need to fight for life's essentials was gone, they were delivered by the minute, tapped in express. This is the way that Foetus liked it. The way it grew when it was free of its mother's succour suggests that it might have, anyway, strangled its sibling in the womb had the work not been done for it. Of course Foetus may have turned out this way because of what Ruby did to it. She did this: she went to Guy Vallender again. He listened to Ruby from the other side of his desk. He listened as a disinterested employer might, he did not try to dissemble his impatience, he drummed on the desk; his face had changed, the parts made a whole she didn't know, there was no point in going on. As she left the office he said: 'I'll give you a tip – Barium Chlorate.'

The demeanour of the remaining twin – named Madison for his unknown grandfather (a black American sailor who hired Ruby's mother for half an hour and, as he got his money's worth, impressed on her, too, his memory of a boxing match he'd seen at Madison Square Garden) and nicknamed Mad Bantu because it's the name that fitted – is doubtless attributable to Ruby's self-application of an abortifacient which didn't work, which reveals itself as teratogenic – Barium Chlorate, girls, is one not to use, even if you do slave in a fireworks factory, and do see it beckoning beyond your infuriatingly jutting belly: it, literally, doesn't deliver; rather it will breed a geek within you, a Madison, a Mad Bantu.

It is to his protracted gestation that are due the rare attributes of Poor Eddie Vallender, delivered – a year to the day after his parents first met – at the stroke of noon, Saturday June 12 1948 and still with us all, I'd say. The Child Bride's pregnancy lasted eleven months. Thus Eddie could – had he wished, and it didn't occur to him – have claimed conception within wedlock. The Urchin Moody knew better, he let her know he knew better, he pressed beside her in the meat-ration queue at Twose's where she was captive and he sibbed in her ear:

'Down in the valley where the green grass grows, There lives a lady without any clothes, Along come a cowboy – clippetyclop, Down with his trousers and out with his cock.' The Urchin's pink, poison, penile tongue nearly moistens her helix – he's as close as that. 'Three months later all was well, Six months later baby began to swell – '

And here's where the story doesn't correspond to the only work of verse The Urchin ever got by heart: nine months later nothing happened. She carried him to term and past, leasing ever more of herself to the creature within whom she loved and loved more the more there was to love. She swelled everywhere, burgeoned in lactic abundance, grew a dewlap, split seams, mutated chronically, burst from her shoes. The ring Guy had bought her contracted so that she had to wear it on a chain about her neck – it left a weal on the finger where Reginald Guy Vallender, bachelor, company director and pyrotechnist (sic), had placed it on the afternoon of Wednesday October 8 1947 during the ceremony at the Registry Office on Bourne Hill. The Child Bride, unattended, is wearing a suit whose chromatic property – it is the colour of slate and thunder – renders it unsuitable as a sacrificial garment; hymeneal blood won't show on this unchaste cloth. White is for girls, she's a woman now. And her beauty is beyond question. Douglas Vallender, our groom's brother, sets up his plate-camera outside the built-to-last civic palace they've just emerged from and, while Monica goes up on tiptoe to ensure that the confetti spangles the couple's hair, composes a photograph that will petrify that beauty, fix it for ever. She smiles with such delight at the prospect of all that is to come; and Guy, for Guy, doesn't do badly. In the one where Mr and Mrs Guy Vallender are framed by Mr and Mrs Douglas Vallender Guy's smile is of course slight and wintry beside that which Douglas wraps about his chops and aims at the lens whose aperture he controls with the bulb in his fist (p. 248). It is Douglas who looks as though he is going to have a baby, his body never learnt how to live within his tummy; his feet are at quarter to three, his shoulders slope in capitulation to the weight beneath them, his chin juts up.

'Trifle young for shagging I said to Guy,' says Padre to Monica with a glass in each hand and a dipping nod at her sister-in-law of two hours. 'But what a cracker eh? Oh Guy's done well there I'd say. She'll make a fine mother – I can tell, you know.'

Monica Vallender wanted a child, wanted a ring (diamond and diamonds) as unshowily gaudy as that of The Child Bride – where *had* he found the money? I knew this woman when I was a child and in my teens. Her qualities were appetite and envy which are mutually nourishing, and her catchphrase – common enough, but she made it her own, invested it with the power of her particular reservoir of resentment – was 'All right for some – not that I'm . . .' Here followed a teensy moue, a smile indicative of stoically born suffering. Watch her now as Padre takes her by her unwilling arm and ushers her along the dun carpeted Adelaide Suite (a wall of canapés, a cluster of flunkies, The Cake) and out to this scrappy patch which The White Jam Tart calls its garden, there to witness the ephemeral commas and neon spermatazoa that Guy is relieving the dark with.

Watch her watch: all she sees is money turned to momentary colour. The other guests gasp and raise their glasses to The Couple; Padre grunts approbation as stars multiply, change, fade, fall; the Tap Room Chaps will tell you Guy was an artist, an artist in flame and fire. But all Monica saw in the begetter of that fleeting daub, that loud scrawl, that cackhandwriting on heaven's wall, was a prodigal brother-in-law who had too long lived on the edge, who too patently despised the arms that bailed him out (and again), whose behaviour at her own wedding had been unforgivable – drunk, incoherent and smutty speech; unbuttoned uniform that he had slept in; leering advances to her cousin even though he had a hoitytoity tart in tow; an inability to remember said tart's name; loud allegations of her father's stinginess. Had Douglas entrusted him with the ring he'd have lost it or pawned it. And he was no better a bridegroom than he was a best man – leaving his Child Bride, who was as much a dreamer as he, to his shambolic cronies (they weren't friends, Guy didn't have *friends* just a ragbag of flotsam he gathered as he drank and drifted) while he played with fireworks he hadn't paid for.

She didn't give it a chance, this shotgun marriage whose nature they hadn't the pride to dissemble; she gave it a few years at the most. She was right of course, she was right; wrong reasons, mind.

At this point, say, let Padre tell her an off-colour joke which he heard told by Ray Butt – 'Butt Of The Joke' – at a NAAFI show a few weeks thitherto; it concerns a woman, Port Said and a cigarette. She winces at the punchline – 'I'm just blowing an Abdullah' – and makes her way to Douglas whose comprehension of the brief-span beauties he manufactures is as partial as hers. We know this because he made photographs of moments of the spectacle. The very act of photographing fireworks evidences an ignorance of their essence.

Fountains – hydrokinetic analogues of fireworks – *are* susceptible to photographic representation. The ornamentally harnessed element, water, is as capable of being chemically frozen on film as it is of being climatically frozen in tiered stalactites (thus does a fountain become a temporary statue of itself). The two sorts of arrestation are disparate but both suggest a potential for motion. The camera's catholic, instantaneous gape is evidently unable to render the perpetual metamorphoses of liquid light, the marchpast of quick-change

93

acts that never repeat themselves, but it can trap this web or that lozenge, it does advertise water's eternal continuum (subject only to drought and the parky's whim). Decorative explosions are different; they are orgasmic and temporal, their very nature is to be so; they are light itself, not its mirror. They can be repeated, over and again till the world's chemicals are exhausted, but they can never attain spatial perpetuity. Fireworks thrill because they *disappoint* – there is but a second in which the eye can taste the dense intensity of colour, the swerve and the tumble. Then there's nothing but smoke marbling the dark with lacy weeping boughs and the postcoital perfume of spent forces. They don't last, these luminous blooms; and when they're forced to endure, in photos, they're reduced to celestial petit-point, fancily wrought, bereft of perspective. Douglas Vallender's photographs of his brother's wedding show patterns that might have been painted onto the prints, scaleless marks that transmit no urgency, no speed, and no sense of dizzy exhilaration succeeded by frustration. Douglas was incapable of understanding fireworks.

His brother was incapable of understanding little else – pyrotechnic fervour shaped Guy's life. Retrospect his years: it is evident that his actions insouciantly aspired to the states associable with the creation and combustion of fireworks. He'd throw away everything for a moment's intense pleasure. He'd make rash sacrifices to the same end. He was lured by reckless ostentation. The future was unseeable and so could not be mapped or provisioned. He believed in the primacy of the present, hardly realised that the future is the present's progeny, yet resented much of the past because it was the parent of the discomfiting present. His comprehension of life's seriality was imperfect. He knew that anticipation – i.e. prospective imagination – is stronger than the actuality it precurses, and that that actuality is bound to disappoint. He was bemusedly delighted by the idea of the child, treated himself to happy dappled dreams of prams and nurture, dreams in which the child smiled and never cried and always beamed like the mute moon. He'd hurl the shining child high (the way fathers will and his brother would) and he'd see the child turn to light and fire as it spun through this corner of heaven, he'd see it dance a reel for one, dance like all the other lights he'd made, he'd see it take the shape of a flower, of a bird, of Christ at Easter, of a penny bun with currant eyes and icing mouth falling to earth, to arms which never failed to take the gurgling catch. In those arms he takes Poor Eddie. The boy descends from heaven, his limbs spatch-cocked by gravity and panic, his screeches shrill with fright not mirth, his face hatched with frown lines: he pummels the arms that clasp him, his big eyes bulge, his face is a skew tuber and on the large side. This is a big baby, easily mistakable for a bald dwarf. This is the boy that sapped his mother, that supped too long inside her, that outstayed his welcome there, that outgrew the temporary home he loved more than the world, that first saw the world through the ragged red rent in the wall of his temporary home. The cut signalled his eviction, and the destruction of that home which he'd never forget, which he'd always long for. Here is one of the special things about Poor Eddie Vallender: his earliest memories predated the taste of his mother's nipples, the sight of her face. Could he really remember? He could. He owned manifold memories of life before life – muscular memories, olfactory ones, calorific, auditory (he knew his parents' voices like the back of the hand that he'd never seen). Most of all he remembered immersion without drowning, without death; an immersion that was, contrarily, the condition of that life. It was his all.

It's still dark, no light, no fireworks, no moon on the curtains (which are anyway still lined to blackout light, to blind). We can listen to the wind in the boughs outside. We can listen to Douglas Vallender snoring (churned air and fifes – the cries of the sty). We can see the bedclothes swell and fall. We can see his wife – there! Pick her out? Look for her eyes. We can tell from her eyes that it's been another of those nights – premature ejacula-tion, impotence, penile flaccidity, one of those things or something like them. She wonders if she'll ever have a child; she has wondered this so long that she's had her insides scrutinised by strangers – they're just dandy; the fault is what these doctors call bad luck or it's Douglas's sperm count which evidently matches the size of the penis he can't see beneath the ledge of his

95

tummy (he wears a courgette where a man wears a marrow). And he won't get said count read lest this question is raised –this question of dimensions, of the veg that fits the man. He wants to keep his sex a secret (so would you). His history of asthmatic and rhinitic illnesses obviated his having to suffer a bodily inspection in order to obtain his disqualification from military service and for this he was thankful. He was thankful too that Monica's modesty required them to make love with the lights out. They can't see each other but we can see them and the curt congress which preceded her supine ennui; huff-puff-come-done-nod-snore. It wasn't even as much pleasure as that for her. She resented Douglas's inability to act the good scout and make fire with his stick. She resented her sister-in-law. She resented most the child for having elected to be carried by that mere girl whose clothes buckled and stretched like sail in a wind of terror, whose bellyful of baby squeezed between buttons and clasps.

Monica foresaw herself cooing dutifully, clucking over the bastard; she resolved to keep mute. Poor Eddie pushes his head through the bloody rent of the meat of his mama's belly, gapes at the creatures of his kind and whimpers – he isn't to know that he shouldn't judge humankind by a grinning obstetrician with a pair of salad tongs in his hand. He doesn't bawl though till Padre tips him a over t and immerses him in God's name and holds him there so long – the font is deep and Padre's tight – that Monica (hat like a scalp) wonders if the boy will drown. And when he emerges from his initiatory ducking and screams a scream that fills this Anglican byre she knows there was a moment, just a little tick, when she wished his lungs would fill with water, that he'd flood from the inside, that the proxy Jordan from the tap would restore the balance by taking the child, making The Child Bride childless again, like her.

Poor Eddie continues to scream outside the church whose clerestory flares like zinc in the noon sun. He continues to scream not because of the shock of the wet and the cold but because the deep font recalled the place he was snatched from and the incomparable bliss he knew there and won't know again: he has been reminded of all that he has lost. That was a hot day. Steam rose from the baby and from his baptismal garb as from meat in muslin. The usual photos followed: the swaddled neophyte, whose day this is, occupies the foreground with his parents, and the rest of each picture is filled with the beds of the dead, signalled by crosses and more crosses, by cypresses and angels and crosses, by yews and crosses. The brand-new being will one day be brought to lie in such a bed, but not before he's suffered other, living deaths – which deaths are inflicted by, inter alia, Monica and Douglas into whose charge he shall fall, making parents of his godparents, fomenting wickedness in deed where it had remained before in thought alone (more or less).

It's no excuse, no defence (rather the contrary) but Mr and Mrs Douglas Vallender's conduct towards their nephew who was also their godson and ward was characteristic of the behaviour that the poor boy invited. Poor Eddie was put on earth to be picked on, he made ogres of us all, he was quarry. Why? And how did he transform the otherwise pacific into harbingers of belligerence? What was it with him that attracted actions that we cannot recall save with shame – and, of course, with indignation towards him for having compelled us to act thus and so be forced into recognising our shameful capacities for bullying, for boorishness, for badness? It'll always be Poor Eddie who gets the blame. He was a catalyst of the ignoble, culpable of revealing the frailty that we express through the strength that is no strength. He was that way from his very start.

At the very start the unnamed creature caesared reluctantly forth from the rip in its mother's abdomen. The anaesthetist Yon Gasbag watched, incredulous and gulping, thyroid cartilage jiving inside his neck, egg-eyed, fazed. What he saw was the biggest baby he'd ever seen, the hairiest baby he'd ever seen. What he heard was a fresh whimper full of ancient sorrow – Poor Eddie utters this in anticipation of the years to come.

What Yon Gasbag said was: 'Ye Gods – send this one back, eh?' (Poor Eddie couldn't have agreed more.) 'Jesus Christ, this is what incinerators were built for.' (Poor Eddie didn't concur this time.) 'It's a toilet job.'

Mr Burn, surgeon and hippocratic hypocrite, agreed; he was displeased to have delivered less than an oil painting, but he warned through the grin he was fighting off: 'Keep it to yourself Gasbag.'

Yon Gasbag knelt behind the cumbrous cylinders and gave himself a cocktail in the arm. Then he topped up The Child Bride with a dose that was a treat. Then they all – Gasbag, Burn, Old Ma Cropper (earning an honest crust in her XXL uniform in this nice nursing home), two nurses and Adriano the POW who stayed on to forge a career as a porter – crowd about the incredulous baby. Rum, they reckoned. It was Mr Burn who saved Eddie for this life – not that Eddie knew, not that Eddie would have thanked him had he known. When Burn turned away to do his blanket stitch on the mum's tummy Old Ma thought of her cats and Adriano thought of the salami enterprise he wanted to start and Yon Gasbag thought of his wasted training in eugenics and the two nurses thought of circuses. Mr Burn, however, thought of the K which might one day be his in recognition of his discreet solo work for a royal princess; he thought (and he was right) that a whisper of impropriety might bugger the Sir, well and good. Here are some of the things that made him think.

a) Poor Eddie's brow: This item comprises two hemi-segmental surfaces separated by a geometrically perfect widow's peak (a hirsute presage that would soon rightly belong to the still drugged mother); this peak – named after the horizontal section through a crevassed mountain where once a bride watched her groom fall – descended to Eddie's eyebrows which were also fully grown. The child, they saw, has hair on its back, its arms, its chest, its legs, its toes, its fingers. There must have been a moment when he seemed pre-human, inchoate as the first fish, a living fossil dredged from deep down, wrapped in kelp and laver strands, a water babe too terrible to write the story of.

b) Poor Eddie's nails: long as night, long as the peaceful night he's left, horrible as those nights he's yet to face. These nails are texturally normal – no problem there, ten out of ten. It's their shape and disposition that are worrying. They're wide as well as long. They spread round the sides of the fingers; there is no room for the border of decorative flesh. They are hoods on the tops of the fingers – surveyed from the right angle they're thimbles. They are very likely attributable to an excess of chalk in the mother's diet; she tilled as she gestated, preparing the cottage garden for her baby, and as she toiled she nibbled on lumps of chalk turned up from the dry summer earth by her fork and hoe. Also, the water in this country of chalk streams tries to calcify all it touches. Poor Eddie's nails come from earth and water, his big toe is like a penis.

c) Poor Eddie's penis. This is not like a big toe. Eddie's Uncle Douglas has taken three and a half decades (and five courses of treatment through the post) to grow a penis this size; Eddie's lolls on his furry thigh with its gormless puckered mouth on his knee, just about. Old Ma Cropper tugged at it with the familiar gesture of her trade and said to the two nurses: 'My my – that's a fine and dandy one he's got there and no mistake. Knowing what I do about the way girls are I'd back that beauty to keep the pot boiling for Old Ma in years to come, eh? Nneherheeh!' Old Ma who was usually right is, in this instance, wrong. She'd have been backing a loser, wouldn't she Eddie? You never got anyone into trouble – excepting, always, of course, yourself, son. (You were never to be a father, not even to cat food.)

Eddie lies on his back on the pale green rug (which turned moss green on p. 7) on the lovely lawn that his mother made, on a lovely summer's day. After a while they got used to the hair, the nails, the penis, the frowning muteness, the gravity of regard, the eyes that follow the fleecy flocks of clouds across the slow sky then focus on this ridged blade of grass with the worm worming round it, *this* one, here. Eddie's parents are so proud of him, of his singularity; they bounce him on an inflatable mattress and he never forgets the perfume of perishing rubber that has wintered in damp and that flakes beneath the sun. They stroke him and cuddle him and discern receptive smiles where others (e.g. Monica) see only the same blankness as yesterday and the day before that. His parents also detect a gradual bleaching of the all-over down; the Child Bride runs her hand against the current of the hair on her baby's belly and peers, pleased as punch and pie, and tells Guy: 'I think he's going to be a blond, Darling.' Guy Vallender, on the edge of a lichenous garden chair, tensely sketching the blooming elder bush beside the cottage, nods like a dog and hears those words conjoin with the choric reprise of the song 'En Stoemelings', an account of clandestine visits to a brothel ('le poepkot à St Gilles') which was part of Albeau's repertoire: hardly a day passed when Guy Vallender was not prompted (by his parlous finances, by the taste of So'ton gin, by the earth-stained bins of brussels outside Crouch's) to think of Alban Meyer-Decker whom he hated, whose records he had flung high as his might allowed and fired at with his service revolver (missing mostly – the black discs cracked on the concrete of the abandoned thistled farmyard where he prosecuted this vicarious execution). The tunes they had been incised with were harder to eradicate: 'He's going to be a blond, Darling, he's going to be a blond.'

Three years later Poor Eddie is blond, or blonder than he was, or blond to his mother's eyes; by the summer of 1951 Eddie was, let us say, blond. His mother, yet too young to vote and so alter her nation's affairs (which are not ours), is habitually taken for his big sister and her husband's daughter. Her husband has not prospered, not even modestly. As the boy gets blonder so he gets greyish, greyer, fairly grey; and by the time the temples are fairly grey the incipient sideburns to their south are white, unmitigatedly – he couldn't believe this would happen to him. Still, the thatch on the cottage hasn't gone that way: it's not blond, it's not grey, it's not lighter than it was. Thinner, certainly, but ever darker, wetter, more sodden – the descendants of the fledgling sparrows who flung themselves across Eddie's cloudscape a page and three summers ago have found better-tended roofs to nest in. This one is neglected; the scrumped fruits of Guy Vallender's peculations are clothes for his Child Bride, clothes for his son (Walter Raleighs, smocks, velvet collared and cuffed coats – all grown out of within months), drink for himself, hotels for them all.

'Off to town this weekend? Dunno how you manage it,' says Douglas, knowing quite well how Guy manages it but reluctant to stem the illegitimate flow, reluctant to challenge Guy about his persistent misappropriations which began, way back, with his guilt money for Ruby; the sums are often nugatory, but they add up and Douglas always knows the current aggregate. It gives him something over Guy, this covert knowledge of embezzlement (which is not the word he voices to himself save in vindictive humour). Guy's evident delusion that he is undetected amuses Douglas who keeps it to himself, keeps it even from Monica who would nag him to act towards recovery of the money. Douglas hopes that Guy, in a moment of inebriate candour, will not admit to his chronic crime (aggregate on Eddie's third birthday, the eve of the outing to see the *Victory*: £617-14s-11d). Douglas's reluctance is born of two fears:

a) That of his embarrassment at having to face his brother's bibulous shame and so be obliged to forgive him. Douglas is, after all, a fraternally sentimental chap.

b) That of having to reveal the only weapon with which he may strike his brother. It's a weapon whose potency depends on its concealment. Douglas Vallender *wills* his brother to keep his fingers, both hands indeed, in the till; every penny strengthens Douglas, though to what end Douglas has yet to discover. (That comes soon enough.) Once his knowledge is revealed to its subject it is spent, finished, like sperm and fireworks; unlike them, not renewable.

'Matter of fact, we're not,' replied Guy Vallender. (Not 'off to town'.) Guy and Douglas close behind them the door to the subterranean magazine which holds marine signals and walk up the steps. This field beside the factory bulges with the grassed, barrow-like roofs of six such bunkers containing potential death. It is Douglas who locked the door.

'No, we're off to Pompey, taking Eddie to the *Victory*.'

Douglas patted his brother's shirt-sleeved shoulder: 'Jolly good, *jolly* good. Expressed a desire to have a decko on account of my Death Of Nelson has he? 'Swhat uncles are for – and godparents; to educate and succour in those areas where the parents are wanting. Eh?' Douglas probably believed – though he'd have jocularly denied it – that his 'famous' party piece, groaning and writhing in a newspaper-tricorn, really was educative.

I guess that Poor Eddie, who must have witnessed it many more times than I, had no idea of what it was meant to represent;

but, yes, I did enjoy it, as I enjoyed Douglas's blowing a post-horn through my parents' neighbours' letter box when tight at midnight. He lurched with aspirant stealth into my bedroom from the party downstairs, shook me should I be asleep – I wasn't – and instructed me: 'Johnson – you go to the window old man and I'm – ' here he stumbled against my toy cupboard, 'whoopsdaisy, I'm going to create merry hell outside. Now just you watch.'

In flannelette pyjams and high excitement I gripped the sill and saw him pirouette to salute first me then some adult children watching him from downstairs. He crossed the road, opened the gate of the house opposite, knelt at the front door and made the horn emit a series of shrieks that were shocks to the unwary. This was after Guy's death; this was the way he behaved after Guy's death, this was the way he treated Poor Eddie too – hoaxes, japes, the violence with a grin called practical jokery; he behaved thus once free of the burden of your father whom he thralled (so far as he could) with priggish piety, by recourse to 'example', by the demonstrative maintenance of the chimera called standards. He self-deprecatingly bragged of the last as he did of regularly servicing his cars, rifles, cameras, Aga, walnut and flower-marquetry radiogram, fleet of commercial vehicles, works machinery, fly rods and reels, Evinrude outboard motor (but not his wife – even he had a limit to his boastfulness).

Guy Vallender never serviced anything. I know, I can hear you – the women. What about his women? *Service* is not apt. He loved them all, he made love to them. Ask them. Ask Ruby, seen here with Mad Bantu, her little boy Madison (not yet nick-named) dribbling and dribbling a red and yellow ball with his two left feet (literally – that's why he walked as he did). They cast their short, stepped, noon shadows on the plinth of the Royal Naval War Memorial on Clarence Esplanade; the white stone lions darken in their shade a moment. Ruby has ozone in her nose, a drab gab mac unbuttoned to bulge behind her in the Spithead Bite, her hair trails too, the boy kicks and screams when he misses. Ruby looks oh so haggard, old beyond her years, worn, bloomless.

Guy, between the cars parked facing out to Spithead and the pitted metal railings that are the foreground of this marine aspect, is carrying three vanilla cones to his family who are enjoying just that aspect from within the family Riley: The Child Bride is pointing to stiff wind-engorged flats, to bloated sails, to kites anchored to unseen hands, to gulls stonewalled by the big sou'westerly and marking time up there above the sea's undulating peaks. Eddie isn't interested. What he's watching is his father's progress back from the tar-painted ice-cream shack, watching to see which is the largest of the melting bouquets, clenching his milk teeth in subgastronomic anticipation of the sweet, cool, soothing grease. Eddie is also confused: Ride cows? Cows, plop-plop? Cows, paddle-steamers? Eddie understands the conjugation of cows, milk, cream, ice-cream (no one has told him about whales) – but plop-plop and paddle steamers? His Child Mother chatters on, filling his childhood with names that conjure spectres of what may be people or animals, places, biscuits.

Where *is* the seventeenth century?

Is England in the Ile de Ré?

Why is Albert?

On she chatters: Carisbrooke, Buckingham, Felton, Osborne, Swiss chalet. The vanilla cones are ever closer. Da is beside a Stamgar Bamgar;[1] Eddie knows that these cars are always angry, and that this one will be glaring at his father. Poor Eddie has had a miserable morning up and down stairs in the wooden carcass called *Victory* which can't be a ship because it floats on concrete; this bobbing ice-cream is going to make up for the trudging and climbing and darkness – and for the lie about the vessel's nature. Yum yum. And then, suddenly, the compensatory cones are no longer moving towards him: Poor Eddie watches as his father looks across the roof of the angry car to the other side of the road. Guy Vallender has turned towards the source of the screams, he's spotted Ruby and child, *his* child, his loinfruit whom he has dreamed of – the oneiric child is accusatory, wears battledress and warpaint, emerges from rodent holes, bleeds

[1] Standard Vanguard

copiously. The child beneath the columnar memorial to the drowned of the Great War (their names are carved in brass) is nothing like that. It is a boy, he's dressed in shorts to his shins, he wears a plastic holster with a plastic cap gun in it, he's black, blacker than Ruby, black so it shows, black as his grandfather – he is a pigmental dermal (as well as nominal) monument to the memory of the unknown sailor that sired Ruby. The sometime soldier that sired him is now crossing the road. Eddie has never felt so betrayed as he feels the moment when his father gives his ice-cream to the little black boy; it is *his* ice-cream, the one in his father's left fist, the one that's unquestionably rounder than the two held in the right, the one Poor Eddie has had his eye on. Eddie has gaped at his father moving between the cars then across the road towards the high white thing and all that grass. Eddie's father waves the three ice-creams at the black boy and the woman who jerks all of herself, especially her neck part, then pulls the boy towards the grass. Why is his father doing this? These people do not even want Eddie's ice-cream. Eddie has seen his father give money to men who smell like Primus stoves and ask for money but he has never seen him give food to people who haven't asked for it and aren't hungry. And the little black boy not only doesn't want Eddie's ice-cream he pushes it back at Eddie's father, striking at the proffered cone so that the melting white grease smothers the flies of Eddie's father's trousers and the cracked wafer biscuit falls on a pavement crack to make a meal for the bears.

Poor Eddie, hungrier than I can tell you, decides to intervene, to rescue one of the remaining ice-creams for himself. He clambers from the back of the car whence he has witnessed the above through the rear windscreen and arrives arms first on the driver's seat. He makes to open the door but his mother reaches out to take his hand from the handle, saying: 'The giraffe will come in Eddie darling.' And she continues her story – of which Eddie has not heard a word – about the man called Wilson who shot curlews and sold them as wild duck.

Poor Eddie gets back in the back and watches his father hurry across the grass beside the woman who has now picked up the black boy and is trying to run towards the trees holding him while he holds his red and yellow ball. The trees are, of course, pestering each other; they are not built for belligerence; with all the force they can muster they brush their neighbours with boughs (thus amputee poodles get petulant). The woman stumbles; she goes this way, her mac goes that like a spastic wing, the boy's black legs bicycle, his blacker daps paddle in the speedy air. Then she's sitting on the green clutching the boy to her, shaking her head metronomically and refusing to look up at Eddie's father who's on one leg then on the other even though this (and Poor Eddie is certain of it) isn't a game. Were it a game Eddie would have been asked to join in, he knows that. When the woman moves, edging across the grass with the boy, Eddie's father follows them. Soon they're all out of his sight on the landward side of the War Memorial and Poor Eddie fears that he will not see his father again, that his father (who knows so many people) may have chosen the woman and the black boy to live with instead of Eddie and the best mother in the world and that the two of them will have to make do with this car forevermore.

Then there's a tap on the window and Eddie turns to see his father, and not just his father but one, two, three ice-creams in his hands, the globes of emulsion beckoning. He gets into the driver seat, gives one to all the family. Eddie says nothing when his father says: 'Gosh sorry I was so long, had to hike miles. Place here was like a sewer – and we don't want to give Ed Ned a gyppy tumtum do we?'

Eddie, drawing the stuff by suction between his teeth so that it melts, as he has learnt to make it do, before it touches his tongue, stays stum; even had he a free mouth he'd have stayed that way for he wants to believe his father, wants to disbelieve his eyes. By the time he reaches the cone's sagging tip and his father is reversing the Riley onto the soggy asphalt of Clarence Esplanade Poor Eddie, Loyal Eddie, is sure his father must have a man who looks just like him, the way the Saxon-Smith twins are copies of each other, wear each other's clothes. A hank of Eddie's father's hair falls over his right eye while his head is turned to reverse the car; Poor Eddie hopes one day to have that very hank, to flick it with a shake of his head. They drive past the War Memorial towards the suede finish bowling green and the lighthouse striped like a barber's pole above West Battery. Eddie shivered with pride when his father leaned across to kiss his mother. He adores the way his father wrestles with the steering wheel. He adores his father's singing voice. He is as sure as can be that his father has a twin. The car slows to take the sharp left beside the clock you can't tell the time by because it's made of flowers. Eddie has never previously seen anything like the boatered, whiskered, toothy head that acknowledges his father with a music-hall salute and a cheeky wink. The head is attached to a body that is attached to a gaudy tricycle which has a frame for cones on its handlebars and a cubic boot on which are painted lollipops, choc-ices, tubs, wafers, cones. Poor Eddie, confused again – by the multiplicity of ice-cream's sources, by the mobility of this source that's wind-assisted along the front, by the wink that his father didn't see even though the conspiratorial eye was only inches from him. And Eddie, puzzled, is further puzzled when he spies, far off across the common, the woman in her dancing mac with the little black boy but his father's twin nowhere in sight, vanished in the green as though he never was.

That was Eddie's first trip to Pompey. He'll be back; for ever, you might say. And so will I. I'll be back like Hell's spider. Here's my web, its barbs harm so bad it's astonishing you don't see them till they enter you.

They drove from the flat waterbound city to picnic on the cliff called Portsdown. The roads were steep, steep as Eddie had ever seen, grew steeper still. Green trees rose from each other's upper boughs. Houses sat above their neighbours; roof conjoined roof in a cascade of tiles. Hedges led to the sky. Poor Eddie wondered if this was the way to heaven. The car roared when they got there, relieved. He looked down from heaven onto the model of the city whose name is his story. He saw the blinding water of the harbours, the sails, the cranes, the shiny marshes, the grey boats, the grey birds, the smoke, the streets, the streets of Pompey that go on forever, cross and recross streets that are copies of themselves, streets whose houses have packs of Omo in the front-room window, streets where tattooed tars lick tired tarts and fill them with seven weeks' stuff, streets where Poor Eddie's unknown sibling is just now crying for want of a father.

In Pompey all is bright. The sea is a million mirrors reflecting the sun. It's too much to look on for long. Up on Portsdown, on top of the chalk wall that commands the city and the sea, there stands a rank of fortresses, all unkempt and jungly. Here's one that rises on the horizon like a thorny crown.

There's a chink in the curtains. There's light through the jamb. There's an eye where the key should be. You see *such* things when you peep. Keyholes reveal the abominable. They're conduits of what's forbidden, what's clandestine. Pity the greedy beholder, the one outside, face against the pane; pity the one clutching the architrave; pity Eddie on tiptoe, squinting, seeing what he was never meant to see. Oh why didn't you stay in the garden? You'd have been a happier boy, a happier man too, had you stayed out there kicking gravel and clambering over the traction engine. It took only a second Eddie for you to see what you saw; that was enough to hurt so terribly.

'Off to town this weekend?' asked Douglas. This was an inquiry. The usual knowing declaration was made on a Friday.

This was a Thursday, the one after Guy Vallender had taken his family to see the *Victory*; he shook his head, continued making holes in a cigar tube with a marlin spike.

'Aah . . . Thought had you been we might have met for a noggin b'fore I came back. I'm popping up tomorrow for the afternoon.'

Guy Vallender said: 'Didn't you tell me Kippax was coming here?' (W. Clive Kippax MBE, Senior Scientific Officer, The War Office 1949–53).

'Is – but that's next week. No, I'm, uh, going to see a quack chap – Wimpole Street, very port out starboard home . . .'

Guy – gestural realism – scrutinised his brother's face for liver spots: 'Nothing serious is it Doug?'

'No no no. Check up – chap's going to look under the bonnet. Tha's all. But I thought well if you were about we might tool off to the Cri Bar, have a few wets, get quietly slaughtered. Still, nothing to stop me so doing on m' tod. Is there?'

There wasn't. There certainly wasn't. Eddie was woken when the sheep surrounding the thorny thicket where he was hiding banged instead of baaing; they banged till he ascended through the dark branches towards the light and then into the light which the dawn sun pushed into his bedroom. With his right forearm he rubbed his eyes to excise the light within them; with his left hand he clutched his penis that was damp and sore. All things floated in the beams. The sheep had gone, their banging hadn't. Eddie stumbled against a lump of birthday present beside his bed. He didn't know where the sheep were hiding, wondered if they could fit beneath the floorboards like mice. He scurried towards his parents' bedroom, struggled with the thumb-lever of their latch (for a boy with his gifts he was strangely maladroit), admitted himself to their warmth. His penis prods his naked mother, his all-over down tickles her, his nails scratch her. She exhales, murmurs, hums; she's lost in nod. Eddie wriggles beneath the covers where the strong smells are, in the dark – they disappear by day, they do not follow his parents the way the invisible sheep have followed him. The flock is banging around the big bed; he dares not look out, he loses himself in this blind playground, disorients himself among the limbs that made him, curls up like a whorly fossil, prays the sheep'll go and jump over gates so he can sleep again between the people he loves so much that they're not like people.

One, two, three – he wills them; he sees them lining up and hopping over gates which are one gate, the gate at Odstock Down where the sun is for ever (baked track, blanched grass, cloud of sheep p. 60). Off they go, and off goes Eddie's father to fight them.

Guy Vallander makes the serpentine movements men make when waking; he's derricked from his family sheets by the need to quell the noise, that banging we've heard. He's put onto the boards; he follows the dark grooves to the door, to the stairs – steady now – to the flagstones that chill in summer. Douglas!

It'd be wrong to say that Douglas was standing at the front door of the cottage; as the door moved from him, as the knocker was released from his grasp, he sloughed off obligations to verticality, fell in with gravity. Stuff that upright stuff. He slides across the threshold, dragged by the void of the doorless jamb, hoovered from out there, from the milk sky of a sleepless dawn, from the neuralgic goods train and the cab, the cabbie, the cabbie's nippers.

Douglas Vallender arrived on foot at Waterloo station from somewhere at 3.26 am whereupon he made best friends with Charlie from just outside Falkirk who offered him a choice of buggery in the gents, a service revolver for £6-15s-6d, twelve dozen eggs, a little mystery called Tina.

Douglas chose the train that carried newspapers. Paper packed that way, tied tight in compression, is returned to the virgin state of wood; it makes a bad bed, it makes a worse one when the van it's in runs on bogeys like bones, bogeys that expressly transmit every imperfection in the iron way. A bottle of Tanqueray gin made it softer now, tougher then. He counted the grooves on the van's floor and forgot a while why it was that he had drunk himself into forgetfulness. When he thought he was almost home he clambered on a pile of lies and innuendo and gaped from the slit window at the sodium lights of a suburban station carved from soap. The draft, the noise, the sway of the van, the night music of steam and pistons, the click of points, the guard's sweet shag and mug of char, the coupling of carriages in far-off yards whereby tomorrow's rolling stock is generated – he was subject to all these as he was hauled west-south-west. When he at last arrived a Merchant Navy class loco on the So'ton platform roared at him. His nostrils were desiccated by the stench of burning soot. He sat with his bottle beside the machine that punched letters onto strips of soft metal. He stood and pushed three pennies in its slit. Tongue between teeth and squinting he turned the arrow on the dial to I, leaned hard on the lever, then turned the arm to M, to P, to O.

The chirpy cabbie sat with the motor grumbling while Guy counted the fare from coins in a Geo VI Coronation mug.

'Don't often', he chirped through a roll-up, 'see them in quite such a state as that.'

The narrow black Lanchester Chaplins away down the rolling lane between floating banks of birthwort and verbena, raising puffs of dust in the pre-breakfast haze.

Guy had never seen his brother in quite such a state. 'Quietly slaughtered' habitually signified a couple of beers too many, high-spirited high jinks, bibulous bonhomie, backslapping chappery; it did not mean inebriation bordering on poisoning, brain so fucked it sends wrong messages, lurches of mood as of limbs, serious stuff. Douglas has evidently drunk for drunkenness – gin, unmediated and from the bottle-neck, connotes secrecy, the ride to oblivion, giddy ignominy, guilt. Guy, dressing-gowned, walked up the foxgloved path to the cottage.

Douglas was at a gate-leg table in the sitting room, sitting on a ladderback chair, balancing that chair on its front legs, leaning over the table aiming the tilted gin bottle at the prismatic tumbler, working on the angle needed to get the fluid from one to the other whilst maintaining aim supported by an elbow. This was just a practice for he hadn't pulled the cork from the bottle. When he did the sun grinned its congratulations through the chink in the still-drawn curtains. He grunted his thanks. Now he had a parallax problem because he'd moved to shift the cork. The spirit seeped down the far side of the tumbler, made a viscous pool; juniper tears dripped from the rim as from a post-pissing penis dropping droplets on the floor for the dog Postman to sniff. Douglas grabbed at the tumbler whose rainbows flashed at him, he winced like a man handling a red coal or a snake.

He raised his eyebrows and shook his head and said to Guy above him in lachrymal fury: 'Pour the bugger. Pour it won't you.'

Temporarily crippled, he relied on Guy who did his fraternal duty and got the reward of: 'Good man, 'sway eh? Have one. You have one, 'elshelf.' The bottle was empty. Douglas helped himself, stretched for the bevvy and made the chair slide from under him, keening as it went. The hatred he feels for the stuff that has made him its temporary addict does not however allow him to stay where he has spudsacked on the flagged floor; he tries to find the way to his feet but takes a duff route and looks up with the indignant surprise of an assassinated animal. He can't find the way.

The next time we see him sitting, then, is after Guy has hauled him by his oxters to another chair where he clutches another glass, the tumbler having splintered in the inevitable accident. Douglas has of course thrice offered to pay for the item whose price he has overestimated by four times. He also offers to pay for the inches of gin he swigs from the fresh bottle Guy has fetched him out. He puts down this bottle and fixes Guy (across the table, cup of tea and cigarette) as well as he can given the constant list of his trunk and neck with it.

'Show you thumb in.' He blinks as he tries his tongue against his teeth in an investigation of why the word miscarried. He forgets, anyway, what that something is. He grins a daft grin of self-reproach, shrugs a shrug that has him wincing (unused muscles). Then he remembered what it was he had to show his tolerant, succouring, gem of a brother in a million. He rummaged. He slapped his body as though chasing lice. He flapped with neuropathic inaccuracy. His wet, red face aped the portwine of the welts where his collar garrotted. He itched in wintry tweed. His tie knot, not to be unknotted, never to be untied (the scissors are that very moment waiting in The Child Bride's sewing basket), was a taut pimple on his chest. The lining of a waist pocket follows out his right hand that's invisibly gloved by a left glove: he knows no connection between the rolling coins on the flags and his cackhand but stared at the furthest progressing penny, idly arcing as though by wit, teetering before it horizontalled on the floor, pursued by kings with perfect partings and feeble Windsor chins, by kings who were bearded namechanged krauts. They all stuck on the floor: no respecters of monarchical might, these round blighters, but manifestations of royal ordinariness. They all stuck to the floor, unbudgable as shoved ha'pennies.

When Guy, dressed (brickbrown aertex, camel twill trews), returned, Douglas's glass was on the floor among the settled coins – and, by some interim miracle of reach – out of his reach so long as he kept his fat arse on the chair. The boughs of japonicas terminate, in the eastward morning, in the silhouette heads of dogs and of throttled aborigines, in fat glans escaping starved urethras. Douglas's trousered arse is a living thing. It may contain his famous anus (p. 25) but it keeps that discreet. What it shows are cheeks, what cheeks! Cheeks like the medicine balls of a tyrant gymnasium. They bulge, they stretch the fabric so the thread eels out, zigzags in hairy hairpins. They bulge so that they can show off through their density the terraces of Douglas's bottom, stepped here and there, moated by elastic, an odeon of flesh that's ziggurated to belch at ease. Easy now! – Here comes one! The tweed wrapped melons jig a bit whilst his bad gases pop. And Eddie, hanging about behind his father, nostrils at the oddness.

Eddie was fed, Guy was perked with ersatz coffee, The Child Bride was up and about and loving every deep breath of rhinitic air when Douglas's head lurched across the table and the face on the front of it said: 'Bath – tha's tickt. Wan' bath. Bring us roun'. Tum ee um tum. Don't you – pour it shelf. Don' worry I'm not so – '

He rubbed his greasy brow with the grazed bit of his right hand – the source of these abrasions is unknown. He stood up with the uncertainty of a quadruped going anthropoform for the first time. From his suit's breast pocket he took the metal strip he had incised at the railway station: 'Knew I'd find it. Tol' you I had sumpt show you.'

He handed it to Guy and fell out of the room. We hear his bass footfalls on the stairs, the grunt and subsequent roaring of the beast in the geyser, the metallic early gills of a filling bath, the collision of water and water. These are the noises off as Guy considers the piece of metal – three inches long, already bent, screwhold at each end, bearing eight low relief capitals that form the word IMPOTENT.

Guy makes gestures signifying his puzzlement, the usual ones – you do them. Douglas, on the landing stripping for his bath and darkening the stairwell, replied: 'Whadyou mean whassit mean whadyou dammwell think it means?'

The brass plate in this rectilinear labyrinth of brass plates (Wimpole, Wigmore, Welbeck), the fanlight, the ether in the air, nice Irish nurse, Mr —— (a doctor more than usually eminent thus no longer addressed as Doctor), Mr ——'s professionally concerned tone, his wintry smile, the fingers, the diagram sketched by gold cufflinks and gold topped pen, the smooth euphemisms, the shortfall in quality *and* quantity, the immutable truth, the immutable condition.

'And thass all there is to it.'

He stood at the top of the stairs in underpants like nappies, with a bottle against his chest.

He weeped: 'I suppose Monica'll wan' divorce. Got grounds. Got the grounds. Wants a' infant – sonnair, all that.' He clutched the bannister, nodded at Guy. Then he lurched back so light filled his space, and Guy went to the coffee on the hob. And that's where he was when he heard the scream. The Child Bride heard it too even though she was outside with trowel and trug. Poor Eddie was so frightened by it he stayed crouched beneath his father's roll-top desk.

Douglas, who couldn't fill his palm or his wife with the regulation 10cc, had stumbled back into the bathroom, removed his nappy and whaled into the bath which was full near to the rim with hot water. *He had forgotten the cold.* It was hot he got in, hot he screamed at, hot he was trapped by, hot he couldn't escape, hot that did its longpig braise with steaming alacrity, hot that hurt, hot that might have been ice, hot that peeled him when it had lobstered him, hot that Guy hauled him from.

Up the stairs three at a go Guy, on the brink of the steamy bathroom, thought: so *that's* what white skin looks like when it's boiled. Douglas churned the water. The enamel straitjacketed him, the hot was glue, his limbs were impotent, his impotence was confirmed, dotted, crossed. Have you ever pulled an 18-stone man with second-degree burns from a two feet deep bath of scalding water?

Douglas was hard prey, not like Ruby (pp. 84–5). He was worse burnt – this was a better class of home with a superior and more modern water heater, post-war, Potterton's latest but one. The blebs on his tummy rose like dream soufflés in the eight minutes it took the ambulance to arrive from Odstock Hospital. That site of Nissen huts and byresque sheds had yet to achieve its reputation for the treatment of burns, but the young James Elsworth Laing, future author of the standard practical study of the subject, was already working on it.

He treated Douglas: 'He was such an ugly so and so it didn't really matter where you took the stuff from to graft.'

Guy Vallender who had followed the ambulance in the Riley

paced a waiting room, listened to Sister, drove home. His Child Bride was fretting because she had been unable to reach Monica on the phone. She didn't know it was out of order, that the line was down, that Douglas had spent yesterday morning, before he entrained for London, swearing at or about GPO engineers.

Guy drove. Eddie sat in the back with a lollipop. Eddie's mother waved them goodbye from the garden gate. And off they go: along the valley, over the Ebble meadows, past the wall that goes on for ever goes on for ever, down the dip with the turning that Poor Eddie wants to buy a dog for because it's blind, past poor people's houses, past common people's houses, past the workhouse, past the sanitarium, past the nuns' house and The Swan, The White Jam Tart, The Christ On The Cross, The Dead Brother's Wife. Look at the porkers going to market, look at the porkers trotting to death, look how they hurry and scurry from their lorries to their pens. It's the cows we hear on market day but it's the pigs we see, it's the pretty saddlebacks, pink and black with a wobble when they walk – they're the ones that catch the eyes among the hurdles and the slutch and the fierce farmers' men. They were held up a while by this livestock business, then there were more bricks, more windows – the ones this side are happy windows, the ones that side are sad windows. Eddie adored this high road to his uncle's house just as he feared the way his mother would take him in later years when his darling father was dead (p. 31).

Up here, his father told him, was the roof of the world; this roof was thatched with golden thatch, swaying thatch. From it he could see, far far away, mere hills that weren't roofs, steeples, green clumps. Guy Vallender braked at the crossroads. They followed a cart laden with bales and drawn by a horse. When they overtook it Poor Eddie saws the flies on the beast's blinkers. The horrid wood is all around them now.

Now, here's the house that you surely recall: here are the Allard (the Healey shooting-brake is where Douglas left it at the station), the traction engine, the cedars and wellingtonias and acacias, the tile-hanging, the brick paths, the white post and rail, the orderly gravel raked like plough and disordered by Guy's halt. Russet the pony is not here yet, nor is Bonny – she's just nine months off, that's all. From the paddock where Russet will munch and Bonny with learn to ride three furtive magpies take wing, hauling themselves torpidly up; they've heard the muffled roll of crushed gravel, the scattered stones, the sounds of Guy's coming. Now Guy's face as he approaches the front door, to do his duty: does it wear a grim aspect, that of a messenger of ill tidings? I guess it does, well it would, certainly it did, yes it did wear the hippocratic mask, the extremely unctuous bedside face that is genetically formulaic, that we simply (simply!) find on our faces when we have to bring news of our brother's and your husband's second-degree burns received in a bathtime accident after a fifteen-hour bender. Guy's face is autoprogrammed thus as he approaches the front door.

Excited Eddie runs towards the traction engine over there in the shade of a cedar. (When, two weeks ago, I took my daughters to see this house – they having asked what I was writing about and being more inclined to visit the supposedly signified rather than read the representation – they looked from my car across the paddock towards the house, which is smaller now I am bigger, and Holly said: 'You said they were *cedars* Daddy. Can't you tell cedars? There aren't any cedars.' Where the cedars had stood, where they still stand in my picture of the place which remained unamended by this aberrant sylvan actuality, were a walnut tree and a Lombardy poplar, both as old as the century, no doubt. 'Your *memory*!' Rose reproached me. But I want cedars, so let's keep them.) Here are the cedar needles on the grass beneath the cedars; the grass beneath cedars is like no other grass, they must bring their own grass from the Levant; either that, or they transform that which surrounds them. There are even cedar needles on the metal seat of the traction engine where Eddie has clambered. The boughs of the wondrous trees kiss as they sway. It's a lovely morning, no question.

The front door opens as Guy approaches it, and out of the house, across the threshold she has shined with her spit and elbow, cheeries Mrs Gub, salt of the earth, daily help, grandma of fourteen, a real card (everyone says) with her dirty laugh and smell of the mangle, tra-la-la-ing All The Nice Girls Love A Sailor.

'Mr Guy you didn arf give us a fright.' She clutches her American cloth bagful of windfalls and nutritious kitchen scraps. 'You didn arf.'

Usual courtesies from Guy.

And off she trundles, cash in hand, singing the song Ray Butt signs off with: 'All the nice girls love a candle/ All the nice girls love a wick/ All the nice girls love a candle cos it feels just like a – / Soft 'n' greasy, goes in easy . . .' Off she trundles cackling as she rhymes; that Ray Butt tickles her, she never misses his shows for the troops, often she's the oldest there, cackling with our boys.

This is when Guy Vallender looks his best, when he's trying to abort a grin. It's the dilatation of his nostrils and the civil war of his lips that give him glamour, it's the manifest gulf between the mask that propriety deems apt and the one his humour wants him to don. What we're looking at is a physiognomic graphic of social versus individual written on an individual of the sort that usually wins such ties. So by the time he has shut the front door and is within the second of the dark, dark pannelled halls the war has spread from his lips to his cheeks and his eyes. He can hear the song singing itself, bereft of jollity; it's sung like Alban would sing it were he to sing English, accentless; it's a song of sexual violence; the r in greasy is rolled, the vowel is stretched, the s is a z; he can see the candle disappear. His fingers loiter in the deep incisions of the carved stair newel. The sun has yet to reach the stained glass, the lozenges are mute and murky. He calls Monica and can hear himself over the radio in his ears. The ground floor is deserted. He goes from room to room, re-composing his face for each door, wondering at the quantity of things his brother owns, wondering (hard) at his want of envy, at his want of things. People are different.

Let's place him now in the kitchen which is chock with things then rare: Bendix washing machine; Lavomatic dish-wash, pistachio, and streamlined for speed; Ekco television (one of two in the house); two metal sinks, one with a single mixer tap; cream food-mixer like a rudimentary animal hunched to vomit in a thick glass vessel. He clocks this lot, thinks: a) he should chase Mrs Gub and discover when Monica will be back; b) he should check that Eddie's safe.

He's about to go when his song is quelled by another – its space is taken by kindred rhymes (breeze/please) seeping from upstairs. This is a complicated house, built 1887, and added to twenty years later with decorative felicity and architectonic ineptitude. It's thus mazier than it ever was meant to be. The song (about breeze and please, about some other time but now if you try, about saying no and meaning yes) shouts out from here, where, this room, that, from the sky, the roof, the balcony. The balcony: this is part of the addition, eight by five feet, oblique to the garden (south-east) front of the house, above the 'French' windows to the Jekyll-ish terrace. Guy Vallender has never before been upstairs in his brother's house – what a lot of house he has! So many rooms! Here's a room containing twenty-four methuselahs of Pol Roger. Here's one containing five Willis Jeep tyres and a stack of crates stencilled with War Office markings. Here's another whose wallpaper is patterned with teddy bears and in whose centre are an expectant cot and a rocking horse. The curtains in the next one oscillate; they're the long ball-gowns of forbidden women: I mean the curtains in *this* room here which is different from the others because of its double bed with plateresque headboard and the single bed beside it on a metal frame. These curtains, close to where the music is loud, sway with the night breeze of the song, with the south breeze of that momentous morning when Guy arrived to tell Monica about her husband's, his brother's, accident and wounds.

She was on the balcony, saddlebacked in her black one-piece. She turned over with no thought of modesty because she knows that the voice which tentatively calls her name is her husband's. She never heard till then that that voice is also her husband's brother's. She's pink and black, then, with cherry aureola and wiry wisps at her black crutch when she rolls onto her back, rolls thus to forgive Douglas his night away and to show how pleased she is to see him. She wraps her knees behind her ears to show she's very pleased, and to show the basket pattern the straw mat has temporarily incised her thighs with. The sun she's bathed under has pinked bits here, browned bits down there, and it has

118

also made her dream of what might have been, it has lubrically primed her, it has summoned men whose faces meld into that of one unseeable man, a lithe ideal far from her husband. The curtains onto the balcony part to reveal Guy who may be momentarily astonished but who's as pleased to see her as she is, apparently, to look at him. Sun is aphrodisian – it's an agent of wantonness: butcher, baker – either of those, making house calls, is welcome. Or the candlestickmaker bearing a candle the better to show his wares, a hardly hidden candle, a covert candle in a twill pocket. Yes, he's pleased to see her, he's a West-dressed man.

Her first reaction when she pieces together the parts of the face to make Guy is one of attempted concealment. But she hadn't the hands for the job. She wriggled on the rug, one hand here, one hand there, pulling fabric, pushing a tit into a cup, flapping. Her desperation was, doubtless, an incitement: watch her wriggle like a grounded fish, she's kind of maladroit, laid out there. Guy – a pigeon conspired against to forget its news – smiles vastly. The metal needle of the wind-up beside her PX tanning-cream decelerates swervingly at the point where the matt, greying grooves of the record adjoined the gloss black of the label's border.

There's a chink in the curtains. There's light through the jamb. There's an eye where the key should be. Did Eddie see them from every angle? Can he have climbed onto the balcony to bimp between the curtains? He cannot, nor was his face ever against the pane of the other window, the one that rose thorns scrape against like nails on flesh. And the door (male) wasn't open; there was no light, no sightline between it and its frame (female); it had softly arced across the carpet to fill the cavity of that frame, propelled by the breeze admitted from the balcony by Monica as she steps past Guy, brushing against him and feigning not to notice, then making to remonstrate with her errant hand, chiding it with arch childishness: such coarse cuteness attracted him because he knew the hangover of such attraction was self loathing.

Uxorious love gave him no chance to betray himself, to smell self-abasement: he missed the sensations of shame, of his own worthlessness – it used to be thrilling to feel cheap. This gross creature – how Douglas deserved her! – prompted neither curiosity or tenderness, certainly not love. He despised her thus could be sure to despise himself. A woman is a machine for frigging in – that's what I thought; I missed feeling base. And, besides, it was a damn sight easier to give the dog a bone than to tell it what Doug had gone and done to himself and have her blubbing all over me, blaming me too I shouldn't wonder. I know: I gave Monica a sight more than the old bone – that'll be why they were going to call it Bonny if it was a girl. Was it? Was it a girl? Is it?

She is. Her poor cousin saw her dough shoved in the oven that very morning. Pity Poor Eddie, on tiptoe, squinting: he saw what he was never meant to see. Oh why didn't you stay in the garden, in the green where the sun shines just for children? You'd have been a happier boy, a happier man too, you'd have been a happier boy had you stayed out there doing boyish things instead of coming inside that hall which was dark as a cave and creeping up the stairs, there to achieve a too early taste of adulthood, there to turn your father's adultery into an adult exhibition for your prying eye: they were meant to be *in camera*, not a peep show circumscribed by a pawn-shaped aperture. It harmed you many ways: it made the private public – you were a public of one who shared their several betrayals; when the private is bundled across the border into the public it is transformed into the pornographic, its agents become actors. Your eye at that pawn-shaped hole forced you into an abeyant adulthood, made you quite a little man (cf. p. 10); if it had to happen this was not the way – the violation of the union that made you was not an exemplary sight for a first-timer, you never witnessed your parents' mutually expressed affection, only this transgression of it – which was also a cartoon of the elemental act: he hurts her just as he hurts you.

Hugh Richards, the 'father of Liberation Paedology', argued ('Bucket and Spade, G String and Lifeguard' in *The Invention of Childhood* ed. Austin and Pilch, London 1979) that it is beneficial for 'children' to witness adults coupling since it is a means of liberating them from:

the ghetto state of childhood, the western, Christian fiction called childhood which was occasioned by the separation of home from workplace (and thus of 'children' from adults) and seized upon by the church as a means of control . . . his (Loyola's) assumption being that the size of the teachable 'soul' is proportionate to that of the body – a position which is, in its determinism, profoundly anti-Augustinian. The western child's dialectic resides in its perception of the disunion between the ghetto state that it is culturally and familially forced to inhabit and the entirely alien free state of adulthood it will one day attain; and in that free state the primacy of sexual activity is acknowledged not only in its performance but in conversation, art, popular imagery etc. So such activity is denied to the child. That denial is part of the ghetto's curfew, it is part of the promotion of 'innocence'. Innocence is a quality that has to be *learned*. Innocence is a product of conditioning. It is achieved by the usual system of rewards and punishment. Innocence is an artifice . . .

That children are usually denied sexual activity is of course indisputable; this denial is founded in the fears of the parent for the child. Now, Richards was not a parent and he ignored or underestimated this characteristic fear. And there is more yet of his writing which is covertly empirical and coloured by his own vice. His inclusion of voyeurism among the forms of sexual activity that are 'stolen from the young' (the very words he uses in *Springboards to Precocity*, London 1975) no doubt demonstrates the truth of the traditional saw that 'paedology is the purest form of autobiography' – he died during the night of 15 September 1984 when he fell from the balcony of his flat at Powis Gardens, London W11. He had been leaning from it with a pair of Ruhl 7 × 50 B binoculars to his eyes attempting to watch the complicated coupling of his neighbour Ann and her friend Richard (not their real names). When they finished Richard removed his rabbit mask and they went to sleep. Neither had heard Hugh Richards fall.

It goes without saying that Poor Eddie was not harmed the way Hugh Richards was – he didn't end up naked and impaled on railings, did he? No he didn't, not on railings, no.

What proof have we that Eddie did harm himself?

We have Eddie's life. We have his absolute equation of sexual activity with exhibitionism, we have that too. But most of all we have his life: it wasn't all Chain Male and soggy biscuit, there was also his gift. Was his gift released by the trauma of what he saw on Saturday June 23 1951? Was his gift conditional on his having been so hurt? Was that the price he paid for his gift?

Eddie is downstairs in the kitchen with a biscuit barrel full of petticoat tails. Guy is stuck to his brother's sheets. Monica, who enjoyed that, is trying to coax Guy into repetition. His brain and his balls are ganged up against her: he anticipated right – the scrolls of postcoital smoke netcurtaining the ceiling are from hell's forges, not from Nottingham via his lungs; he's a sad animal all right, but more than that he's ashamed, so ashamed that every other betrayal he has conducted, and all the treacheries of the years, fade – they were mere rehearsals; he loathes this woman whose slimy puckered anus is aimed at his face, whose pudendal hair is gelled into plaits by his wicked issue, whose secret smells disgust him. He loathes her for abetting his frailty, he wants to spite her the way we all want to spite those who speak the criticisms that we make of ourselves, i.e. the uninvited conspirators in self-defamation, the ones who know too much. He spites her thus: he lets her have her way, he submits to her teeth and gothic fingernails, he lets her climb aboard, he lets her part the plaits with his remarrowed bone, he lets her trot – she canters, he lets her offal rub his so fast she belches from the womb.

Then he says: 'I, uh, didn't tell you, did I . . .'

Grunting like a pump she gasps: 'Tell me, tell me, *tell* me Guy . . .'

'I didn't tell you Doug's in hospital.'

She emergency-stopped – which hurt Guy more, much more (imagine!) than all her imprecations which hardly hurt at all. She forgot she was naked, she forgot she had him in her clasp, she ignored the drip of sweat from her breastbone to his abdomen, she obliterated that part of the past called *the last twenty minutes* and began to rewrite history.

The rewrites are, of course, contingent on the uniqueness of those minutes; on their special content; on the fact that Guy *got a result* (he got several). This first rewrite, composed whilst they were still conjoined, shows the alacrity with which she got back 'into character' (p. 92). In it she accuses Guy of *preying* on her, of *taking advantage* of her – fine, true, he was a preyer all right. This accusation is, however, predicated on her having known – when she submitted to or invited their furious congress – what she knows now. She comes on like the bereaved, like a traduced widow, a newly made widow in need of rough comfort. But of course she had no idea Douglas had got burnt. Still, what she admitted to her private mythology was the certitude that her brother-in-law had preyed on her. (I'm almost sure he hadn't.) And when she discovered that she was pregnant with the embryo that turned into the foetus that turned into the child called Bonny (thus named, *pace* the uncle who was her father, because of Monica's Scottish 'connections') she composed another rewrite of that day, one that obliterated Guy and restored Douglas's potency. She willed this new truth on herself with such resolve that she really believes what she is saying when she says: 'Doug darling – she's got your eyes, she has, look how she has!'

Douglas – still bandaged, still daily scrutinised by the burns boffin Jim Laing, still incarcerated by the cell bars of his hospital bed five weeks after he took his bad bath – stares at Guy between ribbons of obfuscating lint and pushes a beaker of bubbly at the bottom hole in his off-white mask. The bandage darkens with the ill-tipped liquid – the hand that holds it is a numb fist; but he doesn't care, the periphery of the hole is already stiff with the desiccated stuff of his baby diet and, besides, he's all joy and ire. Guy, on his daily visit which sometimes coincides with Laing's but never with Monica's, nods along with grave sympathy while Douglas promises himself: 'I'm going to sue that bastard, that ruddy quack . . . Bloody Harley Street quacks – 'smattrofac wasn't bloody Harley Street . . . *Wimpole* bloody Street. The bastards of Wimpole Street eh? I'm going to sue them – none o' this'd have happened, would it, if he hadn't got it so bloody wrapped? Can you imagine what it does, being told that? *Impotent*, oh, and infertile to boot – that's the icing on the ruddy

123

cake. I'm goina wipe the floor with the pompous clot. I've got the proof; no chance he can get round that is there? Proof of the pudding club eh? Chrissake don't repeat that to Monica. Little windfall to go with fatherhood eh? I've got Leo coming up tomorrow to take my instructions.' (G. Leopold Lush – partner in Whitehead, Vizard, Venn and Lush, solicitors of New Canal, Salisbury, and Wiltshire Coroner 1963–1979 – almost surely dissuaded Douglas Vallender from prosecuting so futile and potentially embarrassing a suit. In any case there is no record of such an action being entered.)

Nor did the subsequent action that Douglas Vallender entertained come to law; the plaintiff was to have been his brother. The prospect of fatherhood fuelled Douglas's avarice. He returned to work eight weeks after suffering what had been represented (by Guy) to his employees as an industrial accident – laboratory lucubrations that went tragically wrong and all that. He returned to flowers and bunting, he returned to scrutinise the awry accounts: during his absence Guy's peculations had amounted to approximately £240 – the total thus stood at £860, give or take a few nights at the Savoy, a few blow-outs at Rules, a few pairs of Walter Raleighs for the monstrous boy, a few dreams come true in Bond Street for the boy's mutely superior mother (it was, rather, timidity that kept her quiet – something outside Douglas's ken). Also, orders for this year's Guy Fawkes Night are down; *The Skylight*, the official newsletter of A.P.E. (Association of Pyrotechnical Engineers), would subsequently attribute the decline in sales to 'the honest shopkeeper's persuasion that the nation was glutted by the magnificence of the displays at the Festival [of Britain] and could not rationally be expected to accept displays of a lesser magnificence or no magnificence at all!' The late run on domestic fireworks, forecast by A.P.E. optimists, may or may not have occurred: the industrial disputes at British Road Services in the second and third weeks of October ensured that many shops were bereft of supplies by the end of the month and that November 5 1951 – it was, anyway, the wet evening of a wet day – would witness (*The Skylight* again): 'the drabbest island sky since old Adolf went up in flames!!'

Now; now that Douglas's indulgence of his brother is tempered by the intrusion of public phenomena, by the great events of the era, by the contamination of the specific by the general, he jumps on the flock and runs with the flow. Monica is with him – God! is she with him: she backed her man, she was behind him, the volume of her malice astonished him – and that of her remonstrance too, and her capacity for fulmination against his cowardice in not having already told her of Guy's easy fingers. It bucked him; even her slight fed his propriety. Further – and this, ultimately is what stitched Poor Guy, and Poor Eddie in his typically unwitting turn – they wanted to redecorate. They just knew the child, *their* child, was going to fuss about lamp sconces, carpet patterns, wall patterns, the gauge of cot rails, Teddy's dimensions, the quality of cloth in books that show red double-cubes and say 'brick' beneath, the stair-gates whose pendant beasts had better be fully 3D doggies not feline silhouettes, the paint on building blocks; they just knew the child would be their ape, share their tastes, mirror one or other parent. They were right of course. Douglas's sentimental faith in the power of heredity – 'like father . . .', 'chip off the old block', 'take after' etc. – was evidenced in the life of Bonny Vallender who was born the day her father died 4,463 miles away; she took after him, that's beyond doubt.

Whence else her appetite for recklessness, her witting wantonness, her flighty carelessness? Why else was she so chronic a mystery to Douglas? Why else was it her fate to grow into such a little mystery? (There are manifold answers indeed, but they don't obviate the weight of her genetic backpack.)

Gargantua's cornflakes spin in the wind, sink to ground to make brown middens. High up there late emigrants, tardy refugees from this climatic tyranny (the ones who refused to believe the worst), point themselves at Africa and are repulsed by the bullying gusts of the regime they must escape, or die in. Guy (fleece-collared flying jacket *and* Donegal overcoat) stares at the lunchtime river from the garden of The Two Ferrymen; the incessant wind patterns the river prettily, modestly, with a gentle violence that's to the English taste, that forms the English taste. The pattern is that of a monochrome combed bookend.

Here's Douglas who just a moment back trotted in in his teddybear coat, rubbing his hands and brrrring at the nip, to get refills: bottle of Guinness for his brother, bottle of rubber-stoppered dutch Courage for 'self.

He's not trotting now, nor is he the same sort of bear as the one who disappeared through the door beneath the painted legend 'I. Kilbrough, Licensed To Sell Alcholic and Intoxicating Liquors'. He marches the funeral march, a purposeful bear, treading with heavy stealth towards its quarry. It's a bright day, it brings forth additions, sums on a squared sheet of duncecap paper that he withdraws from his grizzly-bear coat and unfolds beside the bottle of stout. It was, Douglas told Monica who'd given him old-dutch courage that breakfast-time and again over the blower, *all too predictable*. Guy giggled feebly, drank from the bottle, nailscraped a knot shinier than most of the still dewy table, made light of it. That figures, that sounds apt; he made light of everything, he made light of his life. Ion Kilbrough (interviewed in 1989, the reddest of the many red noses at the Licensed Victualler's Benevolent Institution, Asylum Road, London SE15) recalled 'Colonel Guy – not that, I'd say, he ever quite cut the mustard . . . for *that* rank.' He recalled Colonel Guy throwing a Guinness bottle at a moorhen, 'but underarm, very halfhearted you might say'. This will be after Douglas leaves, leaving his brother to decide between:

    a) repayment of his debt to Vallender Light Ltd. by December 1 1951, i.e. within six weeks.

    b) face criminal prosecution for theft of same.

    c) relinquishment of his equity in that company in exchange of the sum of £2000 plus the wittily computed gratuity of £864-11s-10d. As we all know Guy chose c).

As we know too he didn't tell his Child Bride, he never told her. His morning routine is unchanged. He leaves for 'the works'. The car sounds the same, Poor Eddie's puppet-wave is just the same: the Child Bride clutches him by the elbow in the porch and two of them conjoin in a greeting-card greeting. The two of them together – you had, Eddie, going on a decade of that, of the two of you together. Your father leaves at twenty to nine. Do you remember all the different things you did with your mother: drawing, drawing Daddy's factory, cuddles, hiding, jumping like Roman Candles, whooshing, being a banger, telling a Friesian from a Jersey, watching a calf being born at Matrimony Farm – the puzzled face in the filmy, milky, stretched placenta never went away did it Eddie?

And all that winter your father leaves at twenty to nine, to be in plenty of time for his days of truancy on unrationed petrol. He travels with a .22 Winchester repeater and never fires at a target that's ambulatory or in the air: thus he bags three hares, a brace of hen pheasants and a pigeon. This is within the usual quota of game bought in public houses, it requires no explanation. (He had explanations planned – chaps at work, a driver from the Silver Star company that bused the Bourne Valley and accepted such meat in lieu of £sd. He didn't need to recourse to these explanations because he was a bad shot.) He drove, habitually, to towns were licensing hours were amended on market days – Wimborne, Blandford, Dorchester, Salisbury (that's the Tuesday market, not the Saturday one (p. 115) when he stayed home or took you somewhere, as ever was). He did a fair old bit of thinking; I don't know what about save that he thought about money as he burnt money, turning it to speckled silt in the air behind the Riley your mother had to sell. I don't know who he met, your sad father, in those hostelries for men with the gift for acquaintance not for friendship: I don't know who they were, those sodales of repdom, tall-tellers with smut in their tales; I don't know if they were the decent, sentimental, fifty-shilling topers that arrived at your father's funeral in Morris 8s and pre-war Vauxhalls.

I do know that most days he was in The White Jam Tart at lunchtime and that when he wasn't it was The Juniper Berry he was in, down by the old town walls at So'ton. Queers' pub, *even during the day*; bum to bum with tars and tarts *of every sex*; knives outside in the shadows of the old town walls, tars falling where lascars have fallen before them; a strut down to the Hythe Ferry is a walk through hell, or heaven – it's all french in French Street and you can guess the kind of pipe they blow in Bugle Street. It was not called The Juniper Berry for nothing: the licence extended beyond that merely to sell. S. M. Hope, like his forbears, was licensed to distil gin, So'ton Naval Gin (p. 85), viscous spirit flavoured with that berry that in turn fragrants that stratum of the bar which the navy shag has risen from and the minge and cheese can't stretch to. The barman commemorates his love who was lost on the *Hood* with a tattoo (anchor and heart) on his thick forearm, he can carry eight pint glasses in one hand, he's passionate about the lads and their boxing:

'Since Roy didn't come home the gymnasium's been the keystone of my life. You meet lads from all over there, from all over the globe. Lot of pent up energy they store up on board, helps 'em work it off – three rounds sparring and a good rub down. Then down here for a noggin and meet some of us natives.' Guy listened politely, picked his glass of gin and bitters from the bar and went to sit at a table vacated by two bovine francophone sailors.

The momentous comes all printed and torn, corrugated by its former folds; it disguises itself as the newspaper one of the sailors has left on an old brown chair. *La Lanterne* of six days before, vendredi 7 decembre 1951, the edition with the pin-up of the starlet Nicole Sarry ('native de Liège, elle tourne en ce moment le 'Hola Bola' de Jean-Yves Bouscat. J'adore les roles de femme méchante – avoue-t-elle'). The next page was carnage: Les Jeunes Marins Tragiques de Chatham dans le Kent – twenty-three cadets had been killed by a runaway bus, the photograph showed five of them, the bodies were recognisably those of human beings. The body in the photograph below was not; death was experimenting with non-representation here, the meat might not even have been meat, the amorphism's relationship to limbs was tenuous. That it was meat, that this lump of something had once been a living creature rather than, say, a nude bough stripped of its bark, was attested by the headline 'Victime d'un Crocodile Congolais'. He turned to a page of bloody comic-strips and obese-cuckold cartoons. He finished his drink, cursed the corned beef sandwich he had eaten earlier, and made for the lavatory; two paces towards its streaked, stained door (this was a bog to judge by looking at its cover) he leant to the table and took the paper, just in case.

It was a mortal afterthought, it gave fate a second bite. It was the right afterthought only in the short term – the one cubicle with a sit-down was habitually employed for (and by) recreational rather than defecatory ends and so indeed lacked Bronco. It also lacked a wooden seat (souvenir hunted); Guy squatted, his jacket bundled round his tummy, his trousers tight about his knees lest any more of them than their cuffs wallow in the smegmal ooze and brooks of piss. He squatted with his bottom clear of the encrusted porcelain, his outer vastus muscles ached, he cursed all corned beef, he effortfully turned *La Lanterne*'s pages, a ship hooted, light dribbled through a grimy pane high above him, his eyes idled across one column to another, he expelled the tainted meat which was bad mud now, he winced as it went, the bulldog clip migrated several yards from his jejunum to his transverse colon and clasped it with a cheery pinch, his special smell combined with the ghosts of many others, it rose like mist from the lake of foetid water, it overcame that of seamen's semen swimming for dear life in the brooks of piss – already condemned.

He distractedly tore the paper into rough squares: one, two, three sheets for a firm wipe. How his muscles pained him, they were going to snap. The paper scratched but did its work, he dropped it sullied in the well. He had torn one further sheet when a conjunction of letters on the second of the previous squares resolved itself before him, as though developed on his retina. This is a commonplace instance of a preoccupied brain's failure immediately to interpret visual data. The circumstance, however, was not commonplace, nor was the unhappy necessity to dredge the faecally streaked paper from the bowl, nor the awfulness of what he read thereon when he'd gingerly cleaned it with his sole, nor the grisly duplication it fostered. It is the name Meyer-Decker – the eleven letters, the two majuscules, the hyphen that's a bridge to grander things – which ambushes him, which jumps from its inky thicket and assails him at last.

Peep at him through the holes custom-drilled by Tom. Any Tom's eye will be fazed by what it clocks. The man is slumped and *reading*, reading *words*; not gaping at a photo of Peter and Dick, not squeezing the brains from the little bald man in his lap while he gapes. And his mood, his emotional temperature, is up

129

and down like a barmaid's knickers (not, as Padre would have it, that barmaids wear them nowadays) – weepy incredulity, horror, smirking menace, insane resolve. Insane enough to send the audience stealthing back to the bar. The victim of the crocodile was 'Catherine Meyer-Decker, 33 ans, femme d'Alban Meyer-Decker, grand homme d'affaires de Léopoldville, connu dans tout le monde francophone sous le nom d'Albeau – chanteur de music-hall, poète liégeois, héros de la résistance à Brabant. C'est au bord du Zaïre que Mme Meyer-Decker pêchait en compagnie de son fils, Jean-Marie, 5 ans . . .' Five years old, already five years old (he was nearly six when he met his father); a boy, another boy. Did his mother really look like that: she lived in his imagination in a state of eternal nudity. She was with him forever, forever raw.

Is that what your father looked like Eddie? Is *that* what the bit in the box looked like?

And was it the same beast, were they conjoined, again, in a different fury, to rot beside each other? Guy washed his hands with a wafer of gritty soap. That wasn't the last time Guy Vallender drank at The Juniper Berry. Seven weeks later, the night they sailed, he put The Child Bride and Poor Eddie to bed in their cabin on the George VI. When he leaves the pub he walks on springs down Bugle Street – the lights across So'ton Water are the lights of Léopoldville, not those of Hythe and Marchwood which he hopes never to see again.

Later, whilst they all sleep, they will slip down the black estuary, silently; this is the first line of the book of their new life – in which retribution is arrived on the dishonourable thief, in which the ogre Alban is bested.

It is also the last line of that book.

Alban Meyer-Decker was never quite the same after he ate the pygmy. Jean-Marie was different too (though he didn't know it), and so was the world.

Straight up, no bull, as the day is long: *the world*.

It began to change colour when the last jerry can was dry – the motor's jerks racked the vehicle; the spasms grew graver; Jean-Marie braced himself against the windscreen; the leather hat with a feather in its band somersaulted to the floor; Alban struck the steering wheel (but this was no mule); the Land Rover stalled; the body of the pygmy who was tragic Erich's trophy rolled against the FN magazines; a ratel scurried across the track; eyes of many shapes surveyed the lunchbox on wheels that had been delivered to the dark heart of the land that God forgot and had probably overlooked in the first place; the trees that are also animals moved in closer; the jabbering babble of the bad bedlam out there bounced about the van that was already a coffin for one and might easily be for three; insects obfuscated the windows; night hurried along; steam seeped between creepers and trees from the malignant engine of this equatorial hell; the monotony of vegetable luxuriance was total.

Let's count the dripping fronds, count the leaves, count the creepers that are the ropes in the devil's gymnasium, let's count the refulgent fungi that grow on the fruit bodies of dead fungi, count the boles like the swollen feet of pachyderms – they are beyond number. Look at the trunks that strive for the sky, look at their coupling and trebling and orgiastic pleaching, look at the mutual pimping of cat and leaf, reptile and root, ant and fruit, bird and bough.

This pimping is dignified as the forest's ecology: Alban and Jean-Marie Meyer-Decker don't fit into it, they've no place here, they should go home. If only they could go home!

In this jungle it's always dusk, it's always wet. Every beast that treads or slithers reforms the mud and depresses it to make a potential pool, a fresh font of disease and ill – elephants make wells, crocodiles commuting from one stream to another (of which they bear immemorial memories of plenty and flesh) make tomorrow's lakes with their bellies. So is this world ever remade.

But what remade *the* world, our world, was already aboard the vehicle: the blood from the mortal wound to his left breast had dried all down his tiny ribs and glued his arm to his trunk. Tragic Erich had despatched his quarry with just a single dum dum round – Erich abhorred the Englishman's use of a submachine-gun and had lectured him on sportsmanship. The volume of expelled blood was about 300 cl; that's less than half a pint, the other half was still in there, still to be drawn. They'd have done far far better to have sucked on ferns, to have gobbled fronds, to have masticated sticks. But the branches are serpents and the leaves are spiders in disguise and the bromeliads spike the water and the birds' bills are honed like blades and the killer minnow called Remon's Fleche swims against the current of urine in order to set up house in your urethra (you have to chop your chopper off). So you stick in your rusting carapace that was camouflaged for a continent of brumal browns not for this malevolent fairground, you stick with the wheel arches you know, you don't stick your head out. And you piss within, and shit, if you've anything to shift – and it still smells better than out there: the jungle is a big bush with giant crabs and a full house on top.

Jean-Marie was thirteen years old and, save for his hands, might have been taken for ten years old. The widower Alban, who had taught him to play the violin, the piano, the harmonica, the guitar, the accordian, stared at the windscreen, which was a mad lab slide getting madder. He stared at it for a long while after the Land Rover stalled. At last he turned to the under-developed boy who had become his son, who knew no better than to address him as Papa, who sat beside him stoically (or flinchingly) mute: 'En panne – eh? On va chanter?' Jean-Marie took his accordion from its sweating case and, here, four hundred miles from Stanleyville and four thousand from Brussels, played the introduction to 'Les Filles de Saint Gilles', Alban's punning paean to both the girls who inhabit that slum and to those whose fate it is to have Gilles as their patron saint – cripples, girls in leg irons, girls with humpbacks. He sang, and out there the poison pharmacopoeia hummed, the harbingers of venom sought apertures in the metal, the hungry gorillas danced. Whatever were the two of them doing in a place such as this? Whatever were they doing with a load such as little Matabwiki who had four wives with tattooed vaginal walls, a bridgeless nose that spread like twin testes across his face, a reddish tinge to his hair, sharpened teeth, no left breast, no breath left?

What Léopoldville thinks today Elisabethville will think tomorrow, and what Léopoldville eats and drinks today Elisabethville regards with gastric envy.

Until 1956 all of Alban's mercantile coups had occurred in the capital: he obtained the concession to import DDT which was nightly sprayed on the city by two helicopters (he obtained it with *matabish, graissage*, drinks, backhanders); he consequently obtained the concession to import the aerosol apparatus manufactured by Tuemouche S.A. (St Etienne) which obviated the use of the second helicopter (*pot de patte*, large drink); his was the majority holding in Frigoluxe Brabançon which supplied the means by which the *les trois quarts* (i.e. the 75,000 Belgian nationals domiciled at Léopoldville) got their thrice-weekly oysters, mussels, orchids. His cut was not on the gift but on the wrapping – the ice, the supply and maintenance of zinc-lined containers, the distribution from Ndjili Airport throughout Léopoldville's restaurants and retailers.

The records of the contract he entered into with the Union Minière du Haut Katanga (UMHK) in December 1956 were destroyed in the fire at the house on rue C. Lemaire in the Léopoldville suburb of Binza before Mass on July 10 1960 (p. 170). By the terms of this contract Alban Meyer-Decker was granted a monopoly on the supply to Elisabethville of shellfish, orchids, chocolates, beer (specified breweries only), witloof, pullets (sic) from Pajotennland. This contract occasioned the daily flight BR-EV 0958. Thus for three and a half years before 'Independence' Elisabethville's inhabitants were the best provisioned in the entire Congo. Sabena ran this direct line at a loss, the Union Minière (which effectively controlled Katanga) hardly profited. The Société Générale de Belgique which 'held' both airline and mining conglomerate refuses to divulge information relating to its commercial transactions during 'cette époque confuse'. Look – there was, there must have been, a *quid* for that *quo*. Put it this way: a clapped-out, middle-aged, energetically winsome, astonishingly well-connected quondam chanteur de varietés does not cop a gig like that without nuts on his chest and cock in his mouth – that's a figurative rig of course, an exemplary meat and two veg.

The Union Minière was many things – open cast and subterranean mining conglomerate, nanny, police force, army, hotelier, landlord, haulier, rail company, exploiter of uranium, slaver, contoller of Sogelec and Metalkat and Minsudkat, brewer of Simba La Bière du Lion, the world's major producer of cobalt, the 'indispensable base of the Congolese economy' and a vital prop of the Belgian one – it was all these and much more but what it was not was a charity. Alban Meyer-Decker was granted those generous concessions in exchange for the performance of certain discreet services in the interests of UMHK of which (we understand each other, we are men of the world, we are responsible to our shareholders, we are a commercial organisation not a political one) that commercial organisation *had no knowledge* and of which its surviving officers to this day profess a complete ignorance.

No one can remember M. Vanblanke's face – it was unmemorable, 'featureless', 'ordinary', white. And who was the cautious and prescient Pol Wollanders? These sober and industrious men visited Alban regularly; even the motherless child Jean-Marie could discern the difference between them and Alban's habitual associates – Vanblanke came from 'our country', Brussels, Wollanders from Elisabethville; they did not sing, they did not transform business meetings into impromptu parties, they invariably asked Alban to shut the door of the study whilst they talked. In *Tshombe ou La Négritude Blanche* (Brussels 1977), published eight years after its subject's death, the Marxist historian Pierre Normand restates the familiar charge that Tshombe was the creature of a variety of European masters and interests, chief among which was the UMHK; but he further asserts that the Katangese secession was first mooted by 'a high official' of the UMHK as early as 1956 in response to the foundation and swift growth of the nationalist organisations Abako and MNC (mine hosts, respectively, Joseph Kasavubu and Patrice Lumumba). Normand argues that through a series of 'agencies' the UMHK began to make provision to retain control of the mineral belt: one such agency was CAMEL (later Conakat) which was founded in 1956 by Tshombe, a three times bankrupted entrepreneur, with the covert but prodigal backing of UMHK; among Normand's 'countless lesser agencies' was Alban Meyer-Decker. He is not mentioned by name, indeed Normand seems to have been misled by the two separate roles he performed into assuming that he was two people:

Person 1 is clearly known by name to Normand who in an atypical access of tact (or wrongly believing him to have been still alive at the time of the book's composition and liable to take legal action) refers to him as an 'import/export agent with connections in the Brussels *milieu*, a suspected trafficker in hashish [who] through a part share in a Léopoldville nightclub, Le ——, came into frequent contact with a group of potentially politically active *évolués*. [He also] enjoyed a wide acquaintanceship with senior members of the administration, the police, the press.' Normand, whose faith in conspiracies is unshakeable, aspires to demonstrate that the UMHK in alliance with Rhodesia worked to 'undermine' the Léopoldville administration; this is probably balls, but there can be absolutely no doubt that the UMHK and its ramiform dependents mistrusted the Governor General Henri Cornelis and Van Acker's socialist-liberal coalition which had appointed him; there can be no doubt too that it sought to keep itself better informed than it was by 'official channels' – it wasn't the refined gen in the conduits that it valued but the raw, untreated stuff, the bubble.

What sort of spy, then, was Alban? He was a sedulously

inventive spy. If he was to be so generously rewarded for information then he must provide information. He learnt early in his clandestine career that the spy's only sin is that of omission; that a failure to glean intelligence is heinous, whilst transmission of inaccurate intelligence is barely venial. In one regard they had the right man in Alban. He was eagerly biddable, prone to minor treacheries, charmingly duplicitous. He was also, however, small fry and privy to nothing and the confidant of no one (precisely because his acquaintances habitually discovered, or suffered from, his chronic flakiness before they became his friends and he theirs); and those *évolués* (it is astonishing that Normand should use that word) who frequented Le Robinson were hustlers, businessmen, *petits rouleurs, macs* (con-artists, pimps).

Sure, these are the careers habitually followed by putative politicians, such career experiences help; but the Léopoldville hustlers and pimps with political ambitions frequented, according to faction or party, such clubs as Le Vendredi, La Boîte des Iles on Bd Albert, Bar Selkirk etc. Alban deceived both Pol Wollanders of the UMHK and Pierre Normand (a posthumous deception that delighted him, that delights him): he claimed to have known and to have enjoyed the trust of Patrice Lumumba, a brewery representative, for several years.

He had never met the man.

His partners in Le Robinson forbade him from dealing with reps because of his proneness to accept gratuities and poor produce; besides, Lumumba's business was with canteens, institutional caterers, factories in the city's suburbs. This did not deter Alban: he embellished newspaper reports; he fabricated stories of Antoine Gizenga's attempts to foment inter-tribal hatred in the area around Kitwit; he suggested (with fortuitous accuracy) that Abako and the MNC were unlikely ever to enter any alliance save one of expediency, acrimony, and potentially murderous antagonism; he asked for and received money to bribe Félicien Mukanda who was a protégé of Jerome Ananay (publicly executed July 2 1966) and liable to attain a position of influence in UGEC (Union Générale des Etudiants Congolais) – Félicien Mukanda was the two-year-old son of Alban's cook; he reported that the journalist Pascal Ngud had become addicted to morphine whilst a medical student at the University of Gent; he advised that meetings of a Leninist group took place on Friday evenings at an address on Av H. M. Stanley and that members of the group greeted each other with two fingers raised to form a V (for Vladimir) 'à la façon de Churchill'; he claimed that the daughter of Judge Léon Waede, infatuated with a pharmacist who was a member of the Baluba tribe, had incited her father to 'extreme and unprovoked leniency' in sentencing another of that tribe who had stolen from the boot of a Simca Aronde a 7-iron (mashie-niblick), an empty petrol can, a punctured water wing in the form of a mauve duck, a Jokari set whose elastic was perished and a piece of brown linoleum with two bullet holes in it to eighteen months penal servitude; he regularly submitted lists of Belgian nationals possessed of 'miscegenatory tendencies'; he knew for sure, from reliable sources, that the laboratory assistant J—— O—— (presently director of an institute of agrarian research) had hypodermically infected three cows with brucella abortus at Cominière's dairy farm so wilfully causing the eight cases of Undulant Fever that presented early in November 1958 and which were diagnosed at the Clinique Mercier – this outbreak of brucellosis went unreported in *Le Courrier d'Afrique*. Alban knew about it because one of the lab assistants bulked her salary by working at Le Robinson as a hostess and dance girl. It was reports such as this last one which persuaded Pol Wollanders that he was receiving intelligence fresh from the field and confirmed his belief in *cet individu rare et vantard*.

The greatest and basest act that Alban Meyer-Decker performed at Wollanders's behest was not, however, one of 'intelligence' or, indeed, intelligence; he didn't even perform it himself. When his debt to UMHK was called in it was merely as a middle man that he was required to act, as an intermediary between a faction of that consortium and the boy whom Wollanders took to be his son: it was Jean-Marie who did it, he was to blame too, he carried it in past the guards (p. 175). (It was the other thing that he carried everywhere, evermore.)

The identity of *Person 2* was never known by Pierre Normand.

There are certain matters no one will talk about. There are certain matters that the passing of time turns from bad to abominable. Time doesn't heal (never believe that), it makes men mute, bitter, memorious. We decree that yesterday's sport is today's crime. We can't help but judge the past by the present. *Now* is unfair to *then* – and wants to have revenge on *then*. *Then* they were fair game, *now* they're a protected species.

Take pygmies of the Bamba tribe – they eat raw monkeys, they eat their female dead, they are reincarnated as pigs whose flesh they venerate and whom they celebrate by eating raw, they hunt with arrows envenomed with the sera of the Gale Viper whose flesh they venerate and whom they celebrate by eating raw from the tattooed vaginas of their women; they would cook the victims of the Gale Viper (ninety minutes from bite to death, ninety minutes in which the afflicted limb turns the colour of a starless sky and swells like a quick pregnancy, ninety minutes in which you go blind and forget how to breathe, ninety minutes in which the Bambute dream of life as a pig) whose flesh they venerate, they would cook them if they knew how to make fire which they have seen but because they don't know how they celebrate them by eating them raw. No wonder they're so small with a diet like that.

They don't know how to blow their noses. The females are fertile at the age of nine years and nine months, female life expectancy is twenty years, male is forty-four. Children are caused by the female eating a dead child three days after it is buried smothered in tobacco – the exhumation must be attended by a (live) pig and must begin at sunrise; after the woman has eaten the child she is thanked on behalf of the entire tribe by means of the nine oldest men in the tribe penetrating her (youngest first: these guys like to play on a sticky wicket) whilst her husband burrows in the child's grave and eats the tobacco and the earth in order to obtain the child's spirit which he transmits to his wife by defecating into her mouth as the eldest of the tribe penetrates her. Should her tummy not swell up like a limb bitten by a Gale Viper she is shot with poisoned arrows and fed to the pig which attended the exhumation – this pig attends the next exhumation and should the woman swell it will be eaten. Usually it is the pig that gets eaten. The Bambute enjoy poor health. And they enjoy it protractedly, they enjoy it all their short lives, they enjoy it as they themselves get shorter – they wither as their lives get longer, towards the end of their lives the Bambute suffer persistent diarrhoea, they expel eight litres each day, they lose half their body weight, they are very small indeed, pig-size and so weak they walk on all fours grunting in resentment at having lost their rudimentary powers of speech – instead of whistled words their mouths emit thick, off-white sap (like sperm, like the 'white blood' of the mgania tree which flows when the bark is incised).

Now, the virus codenamed HoTLoVe or LAV – those boys at nosology certainly have a sense of humour – is a sly little fellow, a real card, for whom survival is 'the name of the game' (Antonio Rivera, *Plague Daze*, San Francisco 1989). Yes, this cunning little chap – a warrior germ who's so small you cannot imagine how small, so small you'll never ever see him even though he's got you in his sights, all of you: none of you is immune (pardon my slip) – knows a thing or two about survival, he knows for instance that it doesn't do to kill your host too quickly when there is so limited a supply of alternative hosts.

Just as HoTLoVe is smaller than you can possibly imagine so is he older than the continents, he's been around for ever, this smiler with the tricky ways; he knows things that his hosts can never know. And his *timing*! After 35 million years he is capable of getting it right to within half a century, of timing his final leap across the species with such epochal exactitude, of coming to roost with the Bambute and of squatting in their cells just when their hermeticism is about to be ruptured, just when they're going to make contact with the rest of the race.

Getting hunted, for sport, by men who are giants, by men who missed out on pigment and so being pale giants aren't pygmies, by men who ride *inside* animals with round feet and glaring faces and eyes that stop the night being night, who throw loud and invisible stones through long pipes – all this constitutes contact with a piece of the rest of the race. The Bambute may not like it but they understand it, they know at least what the giants' lark is.

HoTLoVe is smitten with desire for the giants' insides: there is so much more of them to work on, there are so many more of them too – he'll be able to work that much quicker, he'll have no stake in their survival, he can concentrate on the serious business of destruction. Every virus knows this – out in the boondocks it tends to take things quietly; it's when it gets to the cities that the pace races, that's when it gets to dance a bit because there are so many partners in Pompey, say. With all these new playthings you might reckon that HoTLoVe would forget all about the Bambute. You'd be wrong: he sticks in there too, slow as ever, he's made the Bambute the source of it all, the font of death, the godfathers of the new plague – and all because Alban Mayer-Decker boasted that they'd make good sport.

That was on a boar hunt in the Ardennes in March 1959.

Welcome to Comblain-La-Roche in the province of Namur, to its cheese and its church of the XIVème. Jean-Marie whiles away the days in this hostile country of pine and ice that he has learned to call *our country* – he knows that's a lie.

He kicks frost-crisped leaves; he watches the breath of the men with Alban leave their mouths as if to show that they've boilers within them, in their big Belgian bellies beneath lumps of oiled cloth and fur and tweed; he trails along behind the guns and the beaters who are qualified for the job by their gingivitic grins and matt eyes – these are the analogues of negritude, of blackness here in *our country*, these and the men's accents. The reckless dullards did not recognise the danger to them of the terrified quarry tusking through the forest. Nor did they recognise the greater danger to them of the men with guns, men for whom even a boar the size of a donkey was an inadequate stimulation, men who had hunted human quarry and had never lost the taste for it – human blood is junk: you can rid yourself of the appetite, but you don't want to, nothing matches it, man is a matchless quarry, the rushing elation cannot be faked.

Let me introduce the brothers Bruno and Erich Berg. Bruno's the (literal) haemophiliac; Erich's the one drinking from the flask that Alban offered him, the one with the cap whose fur earflaps flap about his jowls leaving his ears naked.

When Bruno was eighteen years old and Erich sixteen they

140

waited at dusk behind an allotment hut in the village of Frahan (woodsmoke and silence). Florence Deroose crept from the backdoor of her family's bakery on the other side of a grassy track; she carried, with both hands, a wicker shopping basket. The pale cloth across it was humped with a loaf. Erich (who until he'd gone to the *école moyenne* in Bertrix four years previously had every day travelled beside Florence to school since he was six) could see that with no trouble. He beckoned his brother. They followed her past the little saw mill; she halted at the corner of the corrugated iron office and when she was sure no one was in the road or at the window of Mme and Mlle Stockmar's house she scuttered across the road with a monstrous show of invisibility and made her way beside the tobacco fields where the rabbits lived, thence darker and darker to the river Semois whose southern bank squelched beneath her feet and beneath the Berg brothers, too, causing them to stay well back. The other bank rises steeply, rockily, swartly hedge-hogged with trees and more trees. They pursued her across the wooden footbridge.

Up and up between the gothic trees they played their gravest ever game of grandmother's footsteps. She turned less often now, clambered onwards, shifting the basket from one arm to the other, shaking her aching basketless arm as she stepped on ledges and twigs. A clearing caused by a patch of bog where a tumbling stream struck a plain. She continued till she got to the point of this item on the Bergs' c.v. – they could barely discern her now in this place where the trees compete to conspire with the crepuscle, each taking successively more light as the forest grows deeper as the evening grows older. Her destination, a woodman's hut overgrown years ago, elides chromatically with the trees and night. The brothers hear voices, they hear Florence replied to by a man; then another man speaks. The brothers crouch among sharp branches as Florence leaves the hut. The pale cloth across her basket is humped with a stone. Twenty minutes later Erich Berg threw three grenades into the hut through the dust-encrusted pane of the only window. It was Bruno who stood behind a tree, it is Bruno who fires repeatedly (what else is a .303 FN repeater for?) at the only man to exit from the hut. The only man to exit – staggering, grabbing at the shrapnel hole in his jaw – is Florence Deroose's brother Léon, a member of the Rexist SS Brigade Wallonie who retreated to Germany at the liberation and was part of the Sixth SS Panzer Army which re-invaded in von Rundstedt's offensive six days before Christmas 1944. When that offensive failed and their fellows in arms surrendered to *les ricains* Léon Deroose and Henri Destouches (another young Belgian who'd backed the wrong horse, had been seduced by the wrong uniform, *any* uniform – the others, those like the Bergs, had no uniform – had been contaminated by the foul dream even though the dream-time was almost over) had hidden by day and walked by night after night till they arrived at Léon's natal village beside the Semois. Deroose the baker feared for his son's safety and told him about the old hut in the woods.

It was Condrieu who betrayed the two teenage Nazis to the Berg brothers. He had been stealing cabbages from the moonlit allotments when he'd seen them leave the bakery by the back door. He thought that they had been escaping the district till two nights later when he saw Florence at the same place with her basket (it was turnips he was stealing that time).

That's all you need know about Bruno and Erich Berg save that Bruno and Léon Deroose were blood brothers – the immemorial rite was performed when they were eleven, in the bakery's basement, among sacks of floor which were dotted with Bruno's unstaunchable blood: he had to go to hospital.

And yes, you should know that twenty-four hours after they had executed her brother and his friend, Bruno and Erich waited for Florence Deroose beside the tobacco fields. They both raped her: Erich enjoyed it, Bruno would sooner have raped a man or a girl with smaller breasts. They cut off her hair with a kitchen knife. They stripped her and threw her clothes in the river. They marked swastikas on her body with the stalks of charred cabbages from an extinguished bonfire. Then, as she ran (wailing and keening and sobbing and crying the name of the Virgin), as she ran between the dark fronds towards the lights of Mme and Mlle Stockmar's mansarded house the Berg brothers squatted on the bank of the river to eat the loaf, dried sausage and Herve cheese that she had carried in her basket. They argued over the bottle of milk. They both belched. (I owe my account of this incident to Patricia Barnes: *Resistance, Reprisal, Revenge: The Phenomenology of Post-Liberation Belgian Public Punishments 1944–49. Vol. I Hainaut, Namur, Liège, (Belgian) Luxembourg* (New Haven 1966).)

In the twelve and a half years between getting the taste and failing to assuage it here at Comblain-La-Roche they've knocked about a bit – Indochine, Algérie (which they've not yet finished with: pp. 325ff.), Kenya. That's the Bergs, then; they've blood on their hands, in their minds, on their minds. Blood's their biz.

M. Vanblanke needs no introduction. His unmemorable, 'featureless', 'ordinary' face has a cheroot protruding from it: imagine a sheet of white paper with a black finger stuck through it and you've got his face, the sort of face you're sure to forget. He is the host of this shooting party; his other guests, with the exceptions of Alban and Jean-Marie, are men whom the Bergs recognise as their kin – soldiers, warriors, adventurers, men with ideals, principles, pride, men who put country (this country, that country) before self. These are the men (Belgian, French, one English) whom M. Vanblanke wants on his team: they will play with UMHK on their shirt breasts. He flatters them. How he shares their ideals! He lauds their loyalty – 'la loyauté est un trésor rare.' He probably believes it, they probably believe it – they are bound by the sentimentality of sodality which blinds them to the *neutrality* of this questionable attribute. The signal property of loyalty (of sincerity, too) is that it is indiscriminate. It can be harnessed to anything. It is a qualification, not a quality; it is a moral or, more likely, behavioural *adjective*; on its tod it's worthless; it attains worth only from the cause (or faction or country or movement or man) to whom it is shown. What are these men loyal to? They are loyal to the very notion of loyalty, they believe in it, they're faithful to it. Loyalty is the necessary delusory system of the professionally bellicose.

Alban's sycophancy towards these men was total: he offered his flask all round; he corpsed at their crude gags. At dinner at M. Vanblanke's large and extravagantly half-timbered house called Sandringham he alluded to acts of sabotage he had performed during the German occupation; but his timing was off and, besides, allusion was not a mode these men understood. Jean-Marie was embarrassed for him, he knew that Alban was being slighted by these brawny bullies whose affection for snow and frost was part of the same chromatic programme as their hatred of black people – although: 'Le bidasse bougnoul, c'est un type loyal.'[1] Bruno Berg allowed this when M. Vanblanke reminded him that the troops that he might – in certain circumstances, under particular conditions – command might (same provisos) be black. M. Meyer-Decker here, added M. Vanblanke, shares your opinion of black soldiers. Bruno Berg looked incredulously at M. Vanblanke.

Alban, sweatily anxious to impress, waved a forkful of the meal that some previous guests had shot and declared: 'C'est bien bon la chair du sanglier, ce goût . . . légèrement faisandé; mais je vous jure que le chair de pygmée est encore plus extraordinaire. Et la chasse au pygmée – ça va sans dire – est la plus chouette de toutes les chasses.'[2] M. Vanblanke, the Berg brothers, the Englishman (DSO and psychopath), the prettier of the serving girls who is just this moment spooning celeriac puree for the Frenchman called Houart – they, and everyone in the room, stop talking. Alban has touched a nerve, he has appealed to the collective base of the assembled men who wait on his next words, he's struck the core. He's done it, he has ingratiated himself.

He's done it by a lie, by a fabrication, by filching and adapting from J.-F. Desmarest's *Chez Les Anthropophages* (Paris 1927), an account of the Bondjo's chronic preying on the Mangetu, hunting them with stolen rifles, pumping palm oil into their carcasses as a subcutaneous marinade, acknowledging no taboo against eating any part of the body, valuing the thumb balls and intestines most highly in men and in women unborn foetuses and earlobes. The veracity of Desmarest's book was challenged

[1] 'The wog squaddie's a loyal sort.'
[2] 'No doubt about it, boar is good . . . this slightly gamey flavour; but I tell you pygmy meat is even more special. And hunting pygmies – it goes without saying – is the ultimate.'

by Jacques Wilson in 'Dissertation sur les éléphants qui volent' in *Revue Ethnologique* 1929 no. 3. Alban did not know this, and it hardly matters. Here he goes, piling detail on detail, it's like writing a song, one fib fathers another, his audience dares him chance another fictive recall – this time, a culinary counsel: how to crisp the skin. He paints the hunt, a verbal mural, a cracking tale and a *credible* one – he never lost the knack; say what you will of his songs they always incited belief, the self-pity seemed *real* just as the derring-do of the hunt sounded *real*.

And that is how Alban and Jean-Marie found themselves well and truly up the jungle with the pygmy as tiffin.

M. Vanblanke invited Alban to lead a hunt – it was a perquisite and a bribe, an inducement to the Bergs, to Houart, to the Englishman. What a sweetener! What a very large drink! M. Vanblanke congratulated himself on having recruited Alban, *cet individu rare et vantard*. This individual who cursed his facile prolixity, his eagerness to please; there was no way out, he was in a cul de sac of his own devising, corrupted by his vanity which was not narcissine mirror vanity – the terminally vain eschew looking glasses lest they mitigate the *idea* of self, lest they disclose the breadth of the gulf between notion and actuality. The face, the fact, that Alban would have seen in the device that should, with palindromic exactitude, be called a mirrim or a rorror did not correspond with the one he believed he had on the front of his head. You know that he used to dress in black (p. 33). But you don't know that he owns a terrifying grin with many folds, too many, like an evil Irishman (cf. p. 15); you don't know that his lips are obese all the year through and that his tummy bulged like a cyclopean teat (cf. p. 23). You don't know that his nose is maculate with mauve pores and grey comedos. You do now. Yet Alban still conceives of himself as Albeau, the Albeau of the posters – once he saw a hundred in a row on a wall in his native Liégeois suburb of Outremeuse, and that repetitive and inaccurate silhouette against a pale orange background fed him flatteringly, chronically.

He drove past that very wall on Rue Puits-en-Sock when he took Jean-Marie to Les Olivettes, the café-chantant near a bridge across the Meuse where as a boy of fourteen in the summer of twenty-five he had stood on a chair to sing Li Vin d'Payis.

'On dit qu' po les niers
C'e-st-on vin maheti;
Qu' ci qu' e beut tofer
A cint-ans deut mori'.

This was where he had first been drugged by applause: the audience of furnacemen bought him glass upon glass of the watered wine of Le Petit Bourgogne which he had celebrated with an apparent passion even though he'd never tasted it neat. A tram-driver and a boxer had helped him home across the Pont St Leonard after the oscillating room had tipped him to the floor; they told him that one day he would be famous. Thirty-four years later the face of the formerly famous Albeau was among those framed above the piano; none of the bluecollars in the silent bar that afternoon recognised the fat tanned man as the idol in the photograph among the dozens of photographs of those who had had their day, long ago, in another age. They may have seen him find the photograph, show it to the boy; they surely noticed that when the man left he was near to tears.

Alban directed M. Vanblanke's Panhard up and down the steep cobbles of this brick city of cliffs and drops where houses perch on top of their neighbours; here are *les corons*;[1] here are the villas of the rich steel millers; here in the park at Cointe is the dream-like memorial to the fallen of the nightmare called the Great War – Alban's father was among them; and here, at Sclessin, is Le Petit Bourgogne whose vines are barren, whose slopes are patchworked with allotments and little sheds. Dusk crept up the valley of the great river; lights were illumined to map the streets of the city beneath them. A train whistled as it approached the Guillemins station, trees chattered in the stiff wind, Alban puts his arm around Jean-Marie's shoulder and tells the boy that he believes he'll never see his native city again. Jean-Marie looks up at him; Alban says, quietly:

'Je n'y *crois* pas, j'en suis certain.'

---

1 The back-to-backs.

Then he reverses the car and they make off down the hill towards Spa and Comblain-La-Roche for their last night in *our country*.

Alban Meyer-Decker foretold right, his hunch was good. That was the last time he saw Liège. He knew – he was this prescient –that his sycophantic fiction was the worst lie of his life, that in a life of lies this one was the mortal lie, the own goal, the boomerang, the muzzle in the mouth. This was the lie that would just grow and grow, throw out tentacular limbs and consign its maker to a different state. He knew this, all he didn't know was *how*.

Here's how. Here's looking at you Alban, just listen to yourself back in Léopoldville.

All through that early summer of '59 you importuned strangers to Le Robinson. Anyone from out of town was your prey. Once you would have boasted to them of oyster shipments, of the size and freshness of mussels, of how it was you that kept the city's insects at bay – as the night got older you would claim that *no* insect could survive the evening spray. That summer you boasted of nothing; your eyes were ever on the *qui vive* for a lead; you accepted imaginary invitations to talk of pygmies. The words *petit* and *nain* were green lights, red rags. An overheard request for 'un tout petit pot' would send you scurrying bonhomously down the length of the bar to rejoin, to a bemused punter:

'Comme ceux que boivent les pygmées j'imagine.'

And you ruined that Sabena steward's braggadocian tale of the night (a nonce night he was so proud of) with a dwarf whore in Cairo. You ruined it too for his audience of sots by interrupting time and again to inquire whether:

'Cette pute, elle est pygmée? Et si elle l'est, elle vient d'où?'

The steward bangs his glass on the Kindaceda bar top, glares at Alban, huffs out. Thus the standing joke that had become a bore mutated into a threat to the establishment's survival: that, anyway, was the fear of Hervé the barman who – reckoning (rightly) that with a record like his he'd never get another job, let alone one so bibulously and peculatively rewarding – decided to act. He wired his recidivist cousin Xavier-Bob in Stanleyville.

147

This literal bush telegraph was effective: the double murderer Xavier-Bob called collect two nights later, 22.20 Friday June 19. Sure, there are Bamba pygmies in the Kivu forests south-east of Stanleyville towards the border with Ruanda-Urundi *and* who wants to know, what's the price? Xavier-Bob got his finder's fee, his *pot de vin*. He got much more too.

They arrived in Léopoldville during the first week of September. The Englishman (DSO and psychopath) and the Berg brothers landed at Njili 11.38 Tuesday September 1. They stayed the rest of the week at the house on rue C. Lemaire whilst they awaited Houart, Eugene Pommier, Jean-Christian 'Le Polonais' Slowik and 'Boule' (whose name I've been unable to find but who was certainly mad). This bunch was late in arriving because the sporadic fighting in and around Algiers had caused numerous flights to be suspended: so they had to travel from Algiers to Oran to Marseille to Paris to Brussels and thence to Léopoldville. Charlot came from Nancy, but he still had to get to Brussels.

The two days following the arrival of the Englishmen and the Bergs were the happiest of Jean-Marie's life until he met Mrs Butt (p. 320).

He was woken in the morning by the Englishman, who slept, despite contrary counsel, in a balcony hammock outside his bedroom. At daybreak he woke Jean-Marie with the boom:

'Rally, rally, rally.'

He marched through the house calling thus. Alban, Erich Berg and the Englishman (who etymologised marmalade according to the folkloric elision of 'Marie malade') left right after breakfast between 7.30 and 8 am. When he re-awakes Jean-Marie prepares coffee and buttered biscottes for Bruno Berg who sleeps in the room which, when he was a little boy, was his mother's. (Her clothes are there still, in the concealed wardrobe that stretches the length of a wall: so many clothes, and as clean now as the day she resolved to give up wearing them – Alban hoovers them when he believes the boy is asleep and he's alone with her. Oh Cato!)

Bruno Berg does not go hunting (for 'green pigeon', that's all) with the other men because he is sick. He grazed a finger. He's got blood trouble.

He suffers Neild's Syndrome (Morbus Neild), a delinquent strain of haemophilia associable with the rare blood group AO–1 – 98% of haemophiliacs of this blood group succumb to Neildism which is characterised by:

a) the initially intermittent and, from early middle age on, chronic resistance to the intravenous administration of the clotting agent Factor VIII and

b) the consequent need for frequent transfusions of AO–1 which has been treated with Factor VIII – this is the only circumstance under which the coagulant is effective in the treatment of Neildism; the volume of blood that has to be transfused is great because of the dilution (and diminution of potency) of Factor VIII. And sources of such blood are obviously scarce: AO–1 blood occurs in less than 0.1% of Europeans, it is not invariably on tap.

It is only within the last year – Bruno is now thirty-three – that his haemophilia has developed into Neildism; when he scratched his left forefinger (on the celluloid of a suitcase's name tag, at Njili airport) he assumed that the usual shot of coagulant would dam the flow. A doctor was called from the Clinique Mercier and administered it within an hour of Bruno's arrival at rue C. Lemaire. He continues, however, to bleed and thus elects to stay at the house rather than to shoot.

This man who wears nothing more than a Vietnamese silk dressing gown, a subfusc pullover knotted around his waist and old leather sandals grows weaker by the hour.

Wednesday morning: he lies in bed listening to the boy playing the piano in the room below; he attempts, with his unbandaged hand, to pick up his coffee cup and the plate, lets slip the latter so sowing crumbs across the bedclothes but is too feeble to bend to gather either the blue and white picture of a windmill or the myriad urticants; he descends the stairs one by one with the effortful deliberation of one who is *ascending* an infinite flight; he signals Jean-Marie to keep playing (a sonata by the typhoid victim Lekeu) with a tremor of the towel – head-sized and rusty with blood – that is wrapped about his right hand. He lies, wan as a white cell, on a low sofa whilst the sounds bounce about the room that is uncarpeted and uncurtained. Jean-Marie shyly asks him what he would like to hear. Throughout the morning the boy plays, seeks scores from the unruly pile beneath the instrument, accepts Bruno's praise and his invitations to continue. The houseboy brings Bruno a bowl of bouillon, toasted bread and stewed chicken: Jean-Marie eats his jambon beurre as quickly as he can and embarks on a piece by Franck.

This is when Bruno Berg whimpers: 'S'il te plaît Jean-Marie . . .'

The boy kneels beside the man, gingerly kneads the cushions behind his head, holds the bowl to his lips. He spoonfeeds him chicken sinews, cuts the toast as for a baby. Bruno's eyes swell and redden. This is because he pities himself; it's because he despises his plight; it's because of his gratitude for the boy's solemn tenderness and for the way the boy tilts the spoon so that murky, particulate chicken stock doesn't dribble on his chin. He reaches out with the towel that is moist and sticky with blood to touch Jean-Marie's shoulder. The boy knows this is a warrior's gesture borrowed from the battlefield. Later, when Bruno wishes to go outside into the garden, he supports him as well as he can to the glass door then has him sit on a metal bench whilst he fetches the wheelbarrow from the garage. He lines it with cushions and a blanket, parks it on the terrace so that Bruno can roll into it, clutches the smooth, sweat-shined handles with his big hands, lifts vehicle and load, pushes it along the concrete path that stretches to the very end of the high walled garden, then back again. All afternoon Jean-Marie works for his invalid guest who repeatedly expresses his fear of falling asleep and his determination not to. He drinks coffee against the coma he foresees. He holds a muslin cloth full of ice blocks to his forehead. Now Jean-Marie is fanning him; now Jean-Marie is helping him, holding his good arm (the bad arm and its globular ensanguined fist is the bad meat brushing the bannister), guiding him up the stairs' modest slope. At five o'clock Alban and the other men have not returned. Jean-Marie telephones the Clinique Mercier and asks to speak to M. Cembrowicz who left his card beside the fat lacquer vase on the hall console-table.

The ambulance is a dented Peugeot, the seat Jean-Marie sits

on is limp canvas across a metal frame, the vehicle smells of putrefaction, Bruno Berg clasps his hand, the driver describes a crocodile victim's limbs, Jean-Marie bites his lips because he is ashamed of his mother, Bruno Berg is afflicted by the solipsism of the sick.

He says: 'Ne t'inquiète pas Jean-Marie, tout ce qu'il me faut c'est du bon sang, un coup de fouet.' He says this faintly, with his eyes nearly closed and sleep postponed only by the jolting and the stench in his nostrils. When they arrived at the clinic (white stucco, hederic stubble) Bruno made a big brave smile.

They soon wiped that off: AO–1 was not on the menu. It does not occur other than in 'caucasians'; black blood, the red stuff that fuels hundreds of millions of African bodies and which was sold by the litre to the clinic belongs, mainly, to the same groups as that of whites though the proportional division between groups is different – 30% of blacks are AB as opposed to 2% of whites, and O occurs with only one fifth of the frequency that it does in whites (8% rather than 43%). The vats at the Clinique Mercier which could have transfused an army of Bs or As had nothing to offer the lone mercenary soldier AO–1.

Bruno Berg lay in his dressing gown on a bed in a glass-walled cubicle. Jean-Marie, seated beside him, watched as M. Cembrowicz spoke with increasing agitation to two other men, fellow doctors, in the corridor. When M. Cembrowicz, having scolded his wrist watch, hurried away the two men surveyed the patient through the glass; made mute mouth movements then beckoned Jean-Marie.

'You speak English son?' asked the younger of the pair.

The boy replied: 'At school I speak.'

The older man, bespectacled, crew-cut, button-downed, shut the door to the cubicle. He turned to Jean-Marie: 'We gotta problem here simply on account of your dad belonging to what we call a haemotypical minority. Y'understand? It's like a replacement clutch say. You take a Packard in a garage some place where they got no Packards and you're not going to find the spares. So we're wiring everywhere to see who's got the clutch that fits. You follow me son?'

Jean-Marie, who had discerned the words Packard and

garage, and who had understood that the last sentence was a question, nodded in the hope that the doctor might take him for a ride in his Packard. Jean-Marie found himself ushered along the corridor by the younger man whilst the other, stepping over pus buckets and limbs and bloodied swabs, continued:

'I have every confidence that we'll find a crock of the right blood sooner or later – but later could, frankly, be . . . a problem. So what we're going to do is to check you out, check out if your blood's compatible with your dad's and – if it is – we'll pump some out of you, mix it about a piece (a kinda cocktail) them pump it into him. Easy as pie – eh Kent?'

'You got it Doctor.'

'So what d'you say son? I'd say it was the least you could give in return for the gift of life. Eh Kent?'

'I'd say so Doctor.'

'We're looking at a long shot – you gotta realise that – but not such a long shot as pulling in Joe Doake off the street and testing him: there's about a one in a thousand chance of finding the right Joe Doake.'

'Twelve hundred,' corrected Kent, guiding Jean-Marie into a little room with no windows.

The older man, sweating, unshaven, tennis-shoed, shut the door to the cubicle. He told Jean-Marie: 'You just sit there a moment.' The boy obeyed; it was in Kent's left hand that he saw the spike; he understood what was about to happen but his fugitive movement was impeded by Doctor (saw the magnified irises, saw the swab of spirit, saw the red rubber tourniquet). Jean-Marie saw his brachial artery bulge, saw Kent wink. Jean-Marie saw the syringe fill with his blood and hoped he wouldn't ever suffer razor-rash so bad as the Doctor's; the skin beneath his bristle was ploughed meat.

No one was surprised that Jean-Marie's blood was AO–1. Hippocratic relief obviated astonishment. Kent and the Doctor ascribed it to heredity (we don't know much about AO–1 but we do know that, like noses and handwriting, it can be passed down), and Jean-Marie, uncomprehending of what he'd been told, had no idea of the odds against his being AO–1. He didn't realise how special he was: there were only 65 or 70 of them in Léopoldville.

None of them knew then or for many years to come that Jean-Marie's haemic compatability with Bruno Berg would contaminate Pompey, kill the race, that it was the first act of a torpid genocide – in September 1959 the Clinique Mercier's place in the epidemiology of HoTLoVe was unknown. There *was* no virus called HoTLoVe then, certainly no name for it. Jean-Marie's blood would make Bruno Berg a slow murderer; it's not for nothing that HoTLoVe's called a *lenti*virus.

Kent stole as much of the boy's blood as he dared; it was still good blood, unsullied by nasty dietary habits. Jean-Marie was so proud to have helped his friend Bruno that, despite his post-leech feebleness and nausea, he wanted to help him more. It was Bruno's bad luck that the boy got the chance; Bruno should have remembered what had happened to his blood-brother Léon Deroose (p. 142), remembered what he had done to that young man – shared blood is bad blood, in the end it is.

When the Doctor learned that Jean-Marie was not Bruno Berg's son he said to Alban: 'I guess it shows God's one of the good guys.'

Each day of that week Jean-Marie cycled to the clinic to visit Bruno; the bike's brakeblocks were worn to wedges; the metal tubes were exposed like the skin of a bald dog; the handlebar tape was unravelled; two of the five derailleur gears (Benelux, no doubt) failed to engage the chain; the spokes were rust-pocked. He rode it with shame; his schoolfriends mocked him for it. But his compulsion to see Bruno, to listen to his tales of guerrilladom and belligerent fellowship, was such that he resolved to ignore the slights of anyone who might see him standing to pedal (it was the low gears that were crocked). No one he knew saw him – his friends had not yet returned from their holidays in *our country* and at Cape Town and at – a fashionable destination that last summer of the old life – Bela Vista in southern Mozambique. Bruno promised him what Alban had refused him – a new bicycle, not a hand-me-down acquired in a meagre deal. When Houart, Eugene Pommier, Le Polonais, Charlot and Boule (whose name I've been unable to find but who was certainly bad) arrived on the evening of Sunday September 6, Jean-Marie told Bruno that he wanted to stay in Léopoldville and to continue to visit him at the clinic. (Prognosis: M. Berg will be fit to leave hospital in four or five days.) Bruno was touched, he admired the boy's loyalty; but he instructed him that he should participate in the hunt –

'Ce rite éternel de la communion: c'est grâce à l'acte d'homicide que l'homme se découvre, c'est par le sang des autres que l'homme se renouvelle. Mon enfant, tu seras homme lorsque tu reviendras: rends-moi fier de toi.'

It was Jean-Marie's disappointment that Bruno considered him a child that persuaded him. He shook Bruno's hand, gripped it with a manly grip, glove size 10: that was when Bruno noted (slyly, greedily), just how big the boy's hands were (p. 12). As Jean-Marie mounted his bicycle outside the clinic on the swooning asphalt Kent loafered by, laughing with a pretty nurse:

'Hey, how you doing Bloodbank?'

Jean-Marie smiled, not understanding; he scooted beside the bike, right foot on the pedal, left leg cocked.

'That kid's got gold dust in his veins. Ought to sell the stuff, buy himself a real smart cycle.'

The armed convoy of three long-wheel-base Land Rovers left Léopoldville at dawn on Tuesday September 8. They travelled three to a vehicle, averaged thirty mph, occasionally slowing so that one or other of them might take a shot at a monkey or buck. As they passed a hut built of car panels and bark beside the river Kwilu the Englishman fired at a water butt and a goat, puncturing the former and maiming the tethered animal which genuflected in its blood. Eugene Pommier and Boule who had not stopped drinking genever since they embarked on the plane at Brussels-Zaventem three days previously pulled a framed photograph of Patrice Lumumba from a wall of the Bar Waterloo in the village of Kasemshi. Boule broke a full-up Simba bottle to hold to the throat of the jittery, protesting barman whom he addressed as 'espèce de bougnoul' – Boule's thumb-ball cut from the green glass went unnoticed by his pain centre but not by Jean-Marie who wrapped lint round it. Their clothes turned darker with sweat and darker yet. Houart reversed, one hand on the wheel and the other round his Scotch bottle, to crush a pregnant basking viper whose rabble burst from the belly and stuck to the herpetocidal tyre like a black girl's pearl-necklace. A fly as big as a bee stung Charlot's glans when he urinated in long grass near Bulungu – he tore the flag of St George from the aerial, soaked it with rubbing spirit and held it to his penis, causing the Englishman to stumble from the Land Rover and repossess it, hurtfully, noisily, patriotically. Although Charlot lived on a street in Nancy whose name was a programme in itself, rue André Berri Fusillé Par Les Allemands le 19 Août 1943, he none the less taunted the Englishman throughout the early afternoon with his chant of:

'Dunkerque, Dunkerque – ces Messieurs-les-salopards d'Angliches ont trahi la France!'

Houart threatened to leave him by the roadside if he persisted, which provoked a second chant of 'connard Anglophile, mac des perfides'. At three o'clock Houart signalled the other vehicles to stop in the shade of what the Mangbetu call a 'meat tree', and Charlot was transferred to the one which Eugene Pommier was driving, the mute Slowik taking his place on the hard seat behind the Englishman.

The former Antwerp madame who owned the hotel at Idiofa where they stopped for the night clutched her rosary beneath the visitors' register and prayed to Julian, patron saint of innkeepers, that the nine men and a boy in their stained fatigues and soiled shorts would not undo her diligent work of thirteen years (she also had a side bet on a prayer to The Seven Sleepers of Ephesus, patrons of those seeking the state which they enjoyed for two hundred years, in the hope that this farouche gang might soon be kidnapped by Old Morph). Her prayers were for two hours heeded, then unheeded at table when the near naked room (bare boards, Baudouin iconolatry and Rubens nudes, tinted photos of the sometime house of assignation in the jugendstil suburb of Cogels-Osylei, no boas) echoed with Charlot's repetitive, deprecative equation of the food and the English, with Pommier's litanic complaint about the temperature of the genever, with Alban Meyer-Decker's frail calls to order, with Erich Berg's proclamation that if his brother was here soldiers would have to behave like soldiers, with the crunch of broken glasses trodden by jungle boots. The old whore uttered oaths, threatened to call the civil police, offered to procure some girls from la maison de tolérance.

They strutted in at half past nine, three half-cast half-sisters who had been apprenticed to their mother in their early teens, Flo and Bébé and Belle (who wasn't – she was a sad, malnourished creature, hardly older than Jean-Marie). These *filles de joie* gave the lie to that *man*-made euphemism as they were manhandled, scrutinised, commented on, jocularly abused in gastronomic similes (boudin, morue), unflirted with, despised despite the desire they made rise in our men here. Alban, quitting the table with Jean-Marie, stage-whispered to Erich Berg:

'Méfie-toi des vérolées!'

He should have remembered that four days later.

No one slept much. The drink got them, sent them off like bairns then shook them into worried consciousness before dawn.

Charlot's scream when Flo squeezed the site of the fly sting filled the building. Slowik, sober, thrashed Bébé with a belt till she bled from the buttocks. Bébé – the pick of the sisters because her skin was lightest, her hair straightest – smoked *marjie* whilst Eugene Pommier buggered her. Bébé – the pick of the sisters because her teeth were cleanest, her smile widest – tried patiently to coax Houart to engorgement but the blood wouldn't flow, the marrow wouldn't turn to bone, the owner sobbed beneath the skin. She was the last girl he could have had. Bébé la cocotte-minute.

Look at Xavier-Bob, two names to his account, two murders too, a ring on every finger, one lazy eye, that suit – *zut! quel costar*: not zoot, mind, no no, this badhat's is *dernier cri* OK, tight little jacket, three buttons covered in the fabric of the garment which is silk and mohair and shines like petrol in a puddle. Look at him, point-toed feet at a table in the shaded garden of the Hotel Terminus at Kindu, gin fizz and Camels, porkpie hat over his eyes, waiting, waiting since last night when he stepped off the river boat *Barbara* after the 72-hour voyage upstream from Ponthierville south of Stanleyville, during which he had got up the noses of two (black) surveyors from the regional department of forestry. Why, they asked the purser of the floating juke box, has this piece of filth been allotted the queen of cabins?

UMHK was the purser's unanswerable answer.

They asked the same question at the hotel, received the same answer; and when they returned from a hard day's dendrology were miffed to find Xavier-Bob with his feet up, drinking, belching when he wasn't whistling. Their distaste turned to loathing when the men he was waiting for made their loud entry.

'M'sieu Xavier-Bob?'

'M'sieu Alban! Ça me fait vachement plaisir . . .'

The surveyors picked up their beer glasses and made their way between the white blackguards into the hotel whose lobby was piled with the blackguards' martial effects – canvas hillocks and camouflage tumuli and sharp shapes that might be guns. They were guns. And the ceiling fan wobbles, wheezes, gets up a local zephyr. During the next hour Xavier-Bob and Alban talk – out there in the garden, at the bar, around the square where Xavier-Bob hangs his arm about Alban's shoulders. The man's asking for more money, he apologises for asking for more money but there's more to this gig than first met his eye; Xavier-Bob's on the ball, he *knows* why this ad hoc platoon is seeking pygmies, he knows they would be lost without him. Oh, they will be lost without him (p. 163).

Xavier-Bob has never felt so important in his life, he's puffed with greed, he can sense Alban Meyer-Decker's desperation – this man needs him; he's never been so needed and it's his unwontedness that inflates his greed, he doesn't know when to stop, he doesn't understand the limits of avarice (it has them). And he doesn't understand why the moon grins like that when Alban pauses in his protestations, shrugs, smiles such a cute smile as though he's lost a battle with himself, pulls from the pocket of his bush jacket as thick a missal of sweated-on notes as Xavier-Bob's seen since his first (and only successful) bank job; then he had to kill for such reward, now he had only to talk for it – his triumph, then, was one of moral (or methodical) progress as well as of pecuniary gain. He'd come on a bit. They stand

157

beside the memorial to the fallen of Mons, to men who gave their blood and bones as fertiliser in *our country*. Through the meshed windows of the Hotel Terminus we can see the pawn shape of Houart's head's silhouette, there's Pommier with a bottle to his mouth. Alban held the notes in front of Xavier-Bob then knelt at the base of the memorial. He placed the deck of money on the very plinth beneath the analphabetic recession of dead men's names, took a switchblade from a patch pocket and doggedly sawed it in two. One half of the notes to Xavier-Bob, the other in the pocket with the knife. The blackman strummed the pack, sucked at a cheek ulcer, stuck out his hand which Alban, brushing his knees with his right, stood up to take with his right rather than with the more proximate left: Alban clasped Xavier-Bob real firm. They put their arms around one another.

'Allons prendre un pot d'ac? Un Lillet par exemple?' suggests Alban reckoning it's the sort of drink black widesters drink because

a) it's French

b) it reminds them of the bark they pulled off trees and chewed as jungle kids.

As they walk through the glaring, peeling, bare-boarded, fungal-walled hotel foyer Alban rubs (for luck) with his foot (for slyness and convenience) one of the gun cases piled beneath the reception counter. His outer instep feels a raised sight at a barrel's end. His foot is down there, his eyes are up here and he gazes at Xavier-Bob, tightens his clasp on the fellow's elbow, grins. Use that gun Alban!

Alban uses it. Later. He waits in the driver's seat, humming a new tune, watching in the wing mirror till Xavier-Bob has unzipped his fly to unload his kidneys. Then he steps down from the Land Rover, speaks Xavier-Bob's name with gentleness and deliberation (so that the owner won't ever forget it) and, as the owner's face turns to him from the steaming stream, fires the old Browning service revolver straight at his nose which just then stops being a nose; see how it becomes a fountain; it's now no fountain and no nose but a red and pink crater with white highlights: noses can be fountains just the once. And the last time Alban looked at it, the front of the late Xavier-Bob's face was black with flies on a free feed.

That was after Alban had dragged the body by its oxters from the roadside across tussocks and broken branches that turned to dust and across earth cracked like an old toilet bowl, after he had taken the book of elastic-banded money from within the meat-speckled jacket, after he had started back towards the vehicle which was invisibled by the grass arras walling Xavier-Bob's personal cemetery. He turned expectantly because the idea came to him that Xavier-Bob might have only been pretending – an idea born, no doubt, of Alban's unwillingness to admit to himself his new state, to tell himself he was a murderer. He turned expecting to see Xavier-Bob grinning, full-face on. But no, there wasn't much mouth left to grin with, and there'd be even less left when the flies and termites and cats and birds had left the bloody table. Alban shook his head in astonishment, drove back to camp; and it wasn't till the fires were lit around the tents, till the spirit stoves blued the faces of the crouching men, till Xavier-Bob's head had had countless thousand eggs laid in it, till Alban was licking fat from his fingers, that Jean-Marie asked:

'Alors, il se trouve où, le Noir?'

There was silence in front of the tents, there was silence by the tight-parked vehicles, then Eugene Pommier cacklingly rejoined that you couldn't expect to see him in the dark. Erich Berg, buddha-legged on an oilskin, addressed Alban: 'Je crois qu'il a disparu.'

And all the men tittered while Jean-Marie felt, for the first time in a week, that he was a boy, unbearded and uncomprehending amongst the now fiercely stubbled men whom he longed to emulate, longed to smell like – so he laughed too, just a little, and Slowik nodded:

'Ouais! Il est *extra*, ton père. Adieu Monsieur Bob hein? Impec!'

Out there the beasts of Africa slept; here, in the compound of metal, canvas, flame and hatred, Jean-Marie begins to cotton on.

Now, let's have some pygmies. The place the murdered boogy (*le bougnou*, for you lex guys) has brought us to is high above them – everything is high above the pygmies. This is savannah's end, it's like a lateral moraine, it's a table and there's the floor, a thousand feet beneath us. That's the floor where midgets do their savage stuff, act like animals – down in the deep green valley whose trees push together like they've got no room, cuddle up to make a floor above the floor. It looks soft as moss. But we know better, we know it's rough down there. Those nude dwarfs don't know better: they hide, not from shyness, not from shame (one of the manifold states they haven't learned – they'd major in it if they had). They hide out of fright, out of the one exterior knowledge they own, that of *scale*. Forest gorillas are big, savannah elephants are bigger; forest horizons are close enough to reach in eighteen paces, savannah horizons are where the world stops and where god lives. This people's god is necessarily far off, otherwise he'd redcard them (*they* don't believe this, *they* believe he watches over them from up there, *they* believe he flees to hide when he sees them coming, flees to the world's edge and clings from it by his toenails, head in hands lest they track him and try to witness his face). They hide, too, out of fright at the exposure of the dead on the savannah – if the sleeping want to burrow, the dead must want to burrow more. They are frightened by untusked elephants, skinned zebras, giraffes on their sides which only reveal themselves as giraffes when the Bambute climb trees to survey the disposition of the bones. Add Xavier-Bob whose clothes are reduced to the worm threads they were before he wore them, and to the goat coat they were too (they now buttress termitaries, cosset nests). Add Xavier-Bob and they're looking at an augmented intra-specific bonescape. And it's all above ground – that's what terrifies the Bambute – the prodigality of the dead's kin terrifies them. The absence of burial is unholy and unwholesome, it's insanct and insanitary. These pygmies don't come up to the savannah, not often. Another reason they don't come up is that they haven't the strength (always ill, always tired).

Our hunters have to go down there to get them. They had to descend to the Bambute's level. At dawn the day after Xavier-Bob's disappearance they stood at the savannah's edge gazing over the verdant eternity of treetops. The wind flattened the grass, gave their hair false crowns, filled the map so it crackled and billowed. It ripped when Alban fought its flight from the bonnet. He finger-stabbed the plate that Xavier-Bob had identified as the quarry's likely location, the confluence of the Bili river with one of its (unnamed) affluents: there are, he said, caves here, shelter during the rain season which was less than a month away, the Bambute crowd together in the spelaean dark, to hide themselves from the sky-water. Alban oriented the map – the slave-built road they had to follow was there, look – *there*! Erich Berg pointed at the tree-peaks, moved his hand latitudinally through the wind: he might have been indicating a cloud or a hidden palace.

Cartographic encodement is, necessarily, neat. The world it reduces to symbolic abstraction is not. Further, this map, surveyed and drawn on behalf of the Ministry for the Colonies by the geography department of the University of Louvain in 1951 was boastful. It classified tracks as roads, it took no account of the jungle's fecund self-renewal nor, specifically, of the failure and closure of the gold mines that had occasioned the road's building. It told fibs about bridges – it forgot about wood ants and rot and rust and floods. It believed rivers have limits. It was out of date when it was published. Eight years later it was the representation of a labyrinth that had been succeeded by another. But whatever misgivings these men might have had were quite overcome by their closeness to their sport, by their sufferance of such discomfort to get here, by their optimistic anticipation of blood and trophies.

Here they come now, jolting down and down again, down the sandstone road from the savannah's lip – it snakes and zigzags between rocks as big as houses, columnar rocks, rocks with ragged nests on them, rocks that are warnings not to enter (rolled away, driven over). All the rocks glint with mineral promises. The sun sees to that. When the sun goes out it does so with such alacrity that Boule, at the wheel of the leading Land Rover, brakes and sends it skidding across scree and breccial detritus – it stops with a jolt that unseats Slowik and with a noise that is bad news. Swearing, recriminations, the usual jaw – but the vehicle restarts. So off they go into the dark, dark forest, headlights at noon, eyes scanning the sheer, vegetable walls for targets – it was all target, everything moved, the noise of the forest was audible above the engines that screamed in the mud of the road that was now a marsh, now terraces of fronds, here tree-trunks and there a lake. They were equipped for all of this; they carried a floating pontoon and two two-stroke motor saws, adzes and axes, chains for towing, winches and hoist-tackle, explosives and detonators, a petrol-fuelled flame-thrower, a spade per man, machetes, scythes. Alban was a diligent quartermaster.

Even so he had provisioned no weapon against the literate malevolence of the creepers that turned into letters, that conjoined to spell oaths and warnings and mortal taunts, that mocked tired eyes in the dirty light, that profited from the day-long dusk – these orthographic delusions are momentary, finite; their bright afterglows are retinally adhesive, they're persistent and polyglot. The Englishman swore he read *dead dog* when he looked up from chopping flora at 14.23 hrs; the francophones started seeing for themselves at 2° 886′ S,27° 103′ E when Charlot grasped Erich Berg's arm and tried to make him see the terrible calligraphy that he had seen, still saw. He saw the one word *charlmort* – but Erich Berg searched for it as he had for the crones' heads in the puzzles his big brother had shown him as a child. They drove and they drove, and it was Houart's turn next: the veg sibyls told him *t'es dindon* (you're a mug). It was as if the crimson creepers had been charged with neon, illumined with carmine bulbs, as if they could do HAZCHEM at will or at the beckoning of the forest gods who aren't the pygmy gods but their enemies and prey. The veg syllables said *mortibus* to Slowik. Also, they transcend lingo, these sky creepers. They transcend it graphically, diagrammatically – the ease, the aplomb with which a creeper becomes a death's head! There's no equivocation here – it's not like reading tea leaves or entrails or mucus. The message is unmistakable, these creepers are telling this hunter of his impending death, they're telling this one too. These men's time is running out.

But, surely, now, they were the ones who were meant to do the killing, that's why they'd come all this way. It looks like they've got into the wrong part of the sentence, moved from subject to object, active to passive; they're condemned by the shift of a letter, r to d, the shift that turns killer to killed. They're condemned, too, by Alban Meyer-Decker's ignorance and homicidal optimism. They're soldiers, they have an infantile faith in their leader there, sweating at the head of the convoy which, on the morning of their third day in the foul forest, is racing down a natural avenue. Its lights are beaming to blind, its roofs are high with racked canvas and crated victuals, its windows bristle with small-arms. It's the beaming lights of the first Land Rover that blind the wounded pig, that make it cease its terminal progress, that illumine the arrow shaft protruding limply from its left haunch. The incision is shallow, cutaneous. The arrow has little purchase. Yet the creature is exhausted, near expiry. And the circumference of its wound is distended and black, like there's a sac of boiling blood waiting to soufflé through the hole. The beast forgets its genetic programme. It doesn't tusk-bite the bipeds that surround it. It merely stares at their boots, butts, muzzles, magazines. It stares, and there seep from its shivering mouth viscous worms of piss-green pus. Erich Berg pulls the arrow from the wound, raises it like a standard, its pike-tooth head to the unseeable sky and proclaims:

'On est ar-ri-vé!'

The men whoop and jig and kick the pig which duly lies on its flank, resigned to fatigue and abuse. They stumble back to the Land Rovers, a jolly sodality of backslappers. The last wheel of the last vehicle crushes the pig's snout as it passes. But maybe it was gone already. Who knows? Who's been watching from the trees?

The place where they died. This is the place where they died. This is the terrain that became a battlefield, this is where the rivers meet, greet each other with a fluvial shove, where the affluent turns the mainstream to rust with copper particles. Later it will get red with Franco-Belgian blood. This was the place where they died, the world capital of HoTLoVe, a clearing by a confluence, a jungle slum, a charnel-patch for the living, a foul smell, an abattoir and a crèche, a crude arsenal, a casual ossuary – where there's not mud there are bones, bones to which desiccating tissue still adheres, white bones, jaundiced bones, big brown bones, skulls on wicket poles a foot above the ruffled mud. These are the skulls of children and pigs and hinds and cats – they make an egalitarian display. They show the exhibitors' indiscrimination between pygmy and pig, between self and other. The huts aren't tall but then nor are their inhabitants; and the caves between the rivers where they go when the rain comes are little more than burrows, warren. The Bambute hut – bent branches, leaves, a mortar of mud – is habitually constructed by the old men of the tribe. They're doubled or crouching or crawling (poor health, p. 138); they build for the height they are not, not the height they were and that their children are, but the height their grandchildren are. So the big men (everything is relative) begin to bend before HoTLoVe makes them bend. Thus children crawl in imitation of their elders, find their feet (the back ones, yes), grow, attain full height, are forced again onto all fours by their shelter. Between their deterministic kennels the Bambute come and go, do whatever it is they do. A man struggles to remain a biped. His knotted body is supported by two poles that keep his hands from the ground; the poles might equally support skulls – have, shall. They are standard measure, arrow-length and thicker girth. The man wears nothing but mud and bones. Save on his wet feet and shins where it shines in imitation of boots the mud is matt, crazed, aged. A child's ribcage is tied round his neck, hangs by his chest; his glans is pierced by a rodent's fibula; skeletal feet dangle from his wrists. He looks easy meat, sitting meat, soft target – and so do the girls with the swollen bellies of perpetual pregnancy. From the ledge of forest above the rivers it looks like No Contest. The Bambute move slowly, purposelessly, crisscrossing each other's paths between huts and bones, chewing leaves, excreting liquid, eating mud, shivering, chattering at the ground. There are perhaps thirty of them, all moving, all in pain. Babies wriggle in the mud which is the cot that suffocates, the infirm slither like creatures in the wrong element, even the hale are halting in their walk. What's that pit?

The first thing that goes wrong is this: the hunters have checked their arms, loaded them, prayed to the Virgin, stamped, headbutted air, cursed, chanted, rited silently for luck, smeared their faces with dirt and leafmould; they've done all this when Erich Berg, squatting on top of a roof load to fasten it hard, spots little Matabwiki less than a hundred yards off. He's preparing to descend the cliff from which his murderers survey the village. Mud, bones, bow, arrows, dead monkey, slow progress – that's Matabwiki.

Erich Berg leans over the passenger window and, although the forest's loud as a juke, whispers to Jean-Marie lest the struggling pygmy hear him: 'File-moi mon flingot – fais fissa!'

He lifted the .303 by its webbing strap, proned himself on bumpy waterproofing, fired. An aviary fled to heaven. The pygmy somersaulted. His breast went that way, the rest this. The bar after the shot is mute, then the volume is turned up so it hurts. Erich Berg grips his rifle by its stock, stands high, salutes himself. First blood! First fault too – that noise, that crack, that advertisement of bad devils in the jungle. Erich Berg dragged his catch to the Land Rover, watched by unseen all-seeing eyes. The body stunk, the teeth might have been sharpened but they hadn't been cleaned. Everyone crowded round, prodded it. They didn't hang about, like with the pig. They smelled blood. So they got into the vehicles.

That was their second mistake. This cliff is made for pedal descent, nature's way: rocks, roots, unsteady earth – it's these rather than the gradient which make it so unfriendly to wheels. But the cliff is no big problem. What comes after the cliff is the big problem. With Houart at the wheel, the first Land Rover metals downwards; the Englishman clings to the outside, he's a monkey with a submachinegun, screaming, all gums, all murder, all – whoops, there he goes. And there they go, all of them, jolted about the inside of the metal box as though they're on some insane ride at a pain-park. The Englishman retrieves his weapon, slides and runs and rolls after the Land Rover, leaps aboard again.

Now they're on the flat, speeding towards the Bambute and the bones. Lights full on, plenty of roar from the power-horses, from the hidden hippic might – oh, would that they had been mightier, then, why, well, well they might, had those fictive ponies owned mightier might, have roared *across* the ditch-trench-ha-ha that they roared into.

They never saw it coming. The Englishman was firing at the cripples and the huts, Erich Berg was looking for another target, Slowik had his trunk through a window and a Mauser revolver in his grip, Houart was busting the gears to get adhesion. The Bambute must have thought it was The Dream, The Death, The End. They certainly thought that when they saw the second truck, with Pommier firing in the air, and Charlot's howls. The fast animals with blinding eyes are coming to the bones and the huts. And like the lions and tigers – no, not tigers, *no tigers in Africa* – like the lions and rhinos and elephants, like the lions and beasts and elephants they'll never ever reach the bones, the huts, this mud, us.

They'll never reach us because of the covert ditch, the camouflaged ha-ha, the tricksy trench, the moat the eye doesn't behold, the dry moat that's deep as two full-size Bambute in the pink (say, eight feet deep). See, it's hidden, webbed with branches, fronds, a mud crust. See – well, no, you don't see. They didn't see.

They *felt*. Oh they felt! The two Land Rovers are alongside each other – four eyes, two mouths, double the noise, double the flashes, so much smoke and spray. The Bambute could hardly hear themselves scream, they didn't quit screaming when the loud animals hit the trench, they screamed more, a frightful sound, hawking and asthmatic, a vomited whistle through bad teeth, an echo of something bad in the back of the head. The Land Rovers hit that trench together, not a billisecond between them. Down they go.

I didn't tell you – it's at the bottom of that hidden trench that Gale Vipers live. That's where the Bambute keep them: this is a defence, and it's also an arsenal. The most poisonous of equatorial snakes can . . . But I don't need to remind you (p. 138). Then there were the other men from the band little Matabwiki had been hunting with. They reached the camp in time to crouch above the trench and fire envenomed arrows at the pigmentless animals from within the other, mud colour, animals. I'd say that the Englishman and Jean-Christian 'Le

Polonais' Slowik were the lucky ones. They died in the collision. They didn't live to see death wriggling towards them. They never saw the army that marched on its belly and took revenge on Houart. Poor Houart, his leg turned into a telegraph pole, then into an unchamfered trunk. Those Gale Vipers slither in everywhere; two arrows missed Pommier but a viper clung by its fangs to the back of his neck and shake as he might it wouldn't let go. He wanted to tunnel through the broken windscreen which is *above him* but Erich Berg was in the way and Erich had been to see an ear specialist who'd stuck a rod in the side of his head. Pommier, Charlot and Boule took a long while to die. They were trapped inside; they had to wait. They knew what was going to befall them. I'll bet they argued till the end. Those men wept.

So that's how Alban and Jean-Marie Meyer-Decker got marooned, landwrecked. The way Jean-Marie told it to Bruno Berg they were behind the other Land Rovers and braked in time, arrows struck the pannelling, Alban hung 180 degrees, no chance to assist the others.

Believe that if you will. They were far from the Bambute when their supply of diesel ended. The forest is nightmare: count the creepers that are the ropes in the devil's gymnasium – they are invitations to a dream topping, to a d-i-y release. A noose, a bough, a leap from the vehicle's roof. There's a way, now. Here's another: look at the scavenging animals, feed yourself to them before it's too late, while there's still some meat on your bones. Or snakes – you saw the Gale Vipers in the pit. From the cliff, binocularly magnified, they were black and silver maggots twined like flax, hemp, moving hawser. They are out there in the nightmare forest too, solo serpents – Gale Vipers, banded kraits, four sorts of puff adder, and all the unclassified killers: the ones that specialise in paralysis, in immeasurable dorsal amps, the ones that are pumps of ill, the ones that bite the taxonomic hand and so evade the books.

Nightmare which had broken its bounds, and burst through its sac to contaminate day, checked in longterm – this sort of limitless nightmare, the seeping sort that doesn't play by the rules, this tyrant coloniser of consciousness, *demands* suicide.

That's the only alley left to you. After two days their rations were consumed. After five days Alban was thinking of nothing but suicide – he didn't want to die but more than that he didn't want to die slowly. He put the revolver to his mouth while Jean-Marie slept, he savoured the metal (blood-favour ice-cream), he held it to the boy's temple.

When the boy woke Alban told him that he wasn't his father, that he loved him like he was, that his father would not have loved him thus, that the tragic destiny of their family would be fulfilled were they to die together.

It was Jean-Marie who suggested they eat the pygmy – anything to allay the end. The boy didn't want to die: he had hope, he was that age. He had strength. That was a fortuity, that hadn't come by way of his parents or the man who was revealed as his adoptive father – he realised now why he had despised him. So as the gorillas watched from without they cut through the mud, through the skin of tragic Erich's trophy, and drank from arteries, chewed on muscle, feasted on pipes that were speckled, on fibrous flesh and ligaments like leather. It didn't taste like suicide, but then it wasn't. They didn't *know*, so it wasn't. It saved them and condemned the world, that meat, that bad bad meat. The blood became glue, it turned brown on their clothes. They crouched over their long meal, the dish of the day – toxin stew for two. It smothered their faces, made them vomit, pushed Alban into delirium. His hallucinations were of *our country*: he saw a gothic spire built of giants' bones and, within it, a bell which was a heart; he saw a little boy in burning clothes pressing his face to a window pane; he saw pantiles mutate into the scales of a monster's humpback and he heard the monster groan as it collapsed; he saw two trees playing grandma's footsteps, now they move, now they're stone, and now they're aiming auxiliary boughs at him.

Jean-Marie saw them too, the soldier-saviours, armed and camouflaged for the exercise codenamed Jaspar. They were two rookies, unwilling boy soldiers, scared of what the vehicle might contain. They were right – they were scared, now they're scarred. They didn't forget what they saw – imagine! Imagine the print it left on their sprog brains: the two male humans, *fellow*

Belgians, our compatriots, like miners – stained with blood not coal, stained where they'd plunged their faces into the split trunk and peeled belly and quivering liver. And their hair was knotted with blood, teased and pompadoured with dull gell. We never want to look on eyes like theirs again, not in this life and I doubt that we shall. The two boy soldiers suffered the horror of witness – often worse (it is said) than the horror of being, doing, acting. That, anyway, as I say, is what they say and it's what they, the two boy soldiers, say to this day – they're men now, past fifty, and memorious.

There were questions asked. Pol Wollanders asked them of Alban Meyer-Decker, in anger. He also bought the silence of the boy soldiers, but he didn't buy enough of it; UMHK should have paid more, and because it didn't, because Pol Wollanders was a tightwad who pulled rank and made threats too, one of them, Wim Deceuninck, blabbed in Antwerp, in a bar, and so ignited myth's motor. The tale spread, mutated, squatted in the brains of those who heard it, permeated the collective conscious of Belgium, became one more weapon in the armoury of jibes that the French employ against their northernmost neighbours. Certainly, by the mid 1960s the epithet *jaffeur de nains* (dwarf-eater) was current among French teenagers and would be yelled indiscriminately at Belgian cars. It was probably the very ubiquity of the by now folkloric epic (versions of which included slavery, recipes, the canning of meat for the home market, secret gastronomic societies etc.) that prevented Pierre Normand establishing its source, the identity of its protagonist.

He got close. In *Tshombe ou La Négritude Blanche* he quotes, without naming him, a quondam OAS member, a Corsican, who was in Algiers from 1958 till '62.

The Corsican recalled a group of Belgian and French mercenaries who boasted of their connections within UMHK and left Algeria shortly before de Gaulle's announcement of a referendum (Wednesday September 16 1959). Only one of them returned, and though no one ever dared ask him what had happened to his fellows a number of rumours circulated that they had gone to hunt pygmies and that, addicted to their meat, they had stayed on in the equatorial forests.

Bruno Berg listened with dumb incredulity to Jean-Marie's account of Erich Berg's death. He sat on his bed in the house on rue C. Lemaire. He nodded awhile after Jean-Marie had finished talking, pulled his dressing gown tight about him and shrugged:

'Ce n'était pas un bleu, mon p'tit Erich . . . les autres non plus.'

That was the last Jean-Marie saw of him for two years; in the morning he was gone. Jean-Marie cycled about Léopoldville hoping to find him. He wanted to leave with Bruno – for Algiers, for *our country*, for no matter where. When he returned to the house that he was going to have to continue to call his home he pushed his bicycle into the garden and there found M. Pol Wollanders addressing Alban with irate intensity. When M. Wollanders came to leave Alban didn't see him to the door. M. Pol Wollanders passed Jean-Marie who sat drinking a herb infusion in the hall. He stopped, glared at the boy and said:

'Ton père nous a bien eus.'

And before Jean-Marie could correct him he opened the door and strode from the house. That was the last Jean-Marie saw of *him* for two years.

Monday November 30 1959. Alban Meyer-Decker attends the Clinique Mercier, submitting himself for investigation. For six weeks he has been suffering respiratory difficulties, persistent headaches and dizziness. The blood sample taken from him by Dr Arno Motulsky of the University of Washington will become known in the HoTLoVe business as Blood One. Dr Motulsky asks Meyer-Decker if he was a singer in 'the Perry Como mould'. The reply is curt and negative – that's all that he ever knew about the donor of Blood One. It still tests good after all these years, that first drop of HoTLoVe in the viral museum, the archetypical bad blood bottle; it still stands up.

Sunday July 10 1960. Alban Meyer-Decker, thinner than he's ever been, listens to the gunfire, listens to the churchbells that imitate clarions, listens to the radio. The news bulletins are infrequent, inaccurate and interrupted by recordings of Lumumba's speech the night before in which he informed the friable new nation that he had cabled the UN Security Council. They are interrupted too by an American song that Alban sings along with: 'Timin', ticka, ticka, ticka, timin' . . .' Hervé, the barman from Le Robinson, up on the deck-like roof with a beer, a rifle and a pipeful of grass, dances to the song. He clicks his fingers, spins, pumps the air with his rifle. That, that was his mistake. An hour previously, the last time that record had played, it wasn't a mistake. Alban had stationed him on the roof with a rifle precisely because he was thus visible from the street. Alban reckoned, rightly, that the sight of a black man with a rifle might persuade other black men with rifles – those who had pillaged several villas in Binza, attacked and/or raped their inhabitants – that this house had already been liberated, looted, turned over. It was a simple ploy, and an effective one. Lusty, gun-toting, cock-heavy uniformed mutineers of the former Force Publique had twice exchanged greetings with Hervé, a black white who was happy to take Alban's money, drink, drugs, happy to act the part, insouciant of his treachery.

He acted it well. (Type-cast; like his cousin Xavier-Bob he wore the air of a casual killer.) He acted it too well; three Jeeps turned into rue C. Lemaire at 10.18 while Jimmy Jones sang and the churchbells rang and Hervé (apparently) war-danced on the roof beside the glass conning-tower called the 'sun room'. To the Belgian paras in those Jeeps Hervé looked the very picture of a looter, a rapist, a wicked boogy, one to teach a lesson to. They could have taken him out with a single shot. They could have. What they used was a mortar. 'The first building genuinely of its age in the entire Belgian Congo' was now just like any other building genuinely of its age in the twelve-day-old Democratic Republic of the Congo, i.e. a smouldering remnant of its former self. The explosion took out Hervé OK, it turned him into bird food, rat food, monkey food, it spread him about with largesse, a feast for all creatures. There! – a chunk of him hangs from a bough, like an abraded sloth. The house, till that moment orthogonal, goes topsy, shows its bones, flaunts the bits beneath its skin. It looks like it's been hit by a bomb. It had been. Well hit: Alban Meyer-Decker's office is on fire when the paratroopers break down the gates and weave towards the house, where Alban cowers in the ground-floor toilet and Jean-Marie sits at the dining-table clutching a revolver in his big left hand.

Sunday September 17 1961. They didn't recognise Alban. Pol Wollanders and Bruno Berg banged on the front door of the partially demolished house for three minutes before they heard the bolts being pulled. The creature that greeted them was crouched, almost on all fours. Its hair was missing from parts of its head as though it had suffered random tonsures. Its skin drooped in pendulous folds, it was a garment too large for the body that wore it. Its skin was brightly piebald, polka-dotted with beetroot patches. It smelled of double diarrhoea, anal and buccal, tail and head. There was a white crust round its mouth. Alban was so sick he was no longer Alban. He smiled at them with teeth that were bruised fingernails. His mouth moved to greet them but all it emitted was a shrill cough that sent his hands to the floor. Pol Wollanders and Bruno Berg looked at each other very anxiously. When Alban spoke he was no longer Alban – his body, his eyes, his voice had been borrowed by HoTLoVe. It borrows and it doesn't return, it welches, it borrows and wrecks, vandalises what isn't its – it lives by trashing. It has trashed bits of Alban he didn't know he owned. Most of him itched – he could scratch outside, but he couldn't scratch within: his ridged and crumbling nails, each one informally crenellated, couldn't get within, there was no way inside. A hand can reach only so far into a throat, it can't haul out the ball of brain-white fungus which squats and grows and wants to choke. A hand can wipe the noxious yoghurt from the lips but it cannot stem the well. Nor can a hand creep inside bones where the marrow lives, nor can it push through visible ribs to cheer a heart, nor can it chase HoTLoVe through the arteries. Really, defence is pointless. There is no defence.

Is that a nappy Alban wears beneath his pyjamas? It is, it needs changing, the blood is drying, the faeces are seeping. But it's no defence; it's a courtesy, that's all – to himself, and to the boy who tends him and who is less a boy each day. They didn't recognise Jean-Marie. He heard the voices when he got out of the bath, he stood at the top of the stairs and listened:

'Le milord anglais . . . Godefroid . . . Ndola . . .'

Then he heard what was unmistakably the voice of Bruno Berg.

Jean-Marie smiled, he found himself smiling, his face moved in a way it hadn't moved for months. He pulled the white towel tight around his buttocks and descended the stairs as Bruno continued: 'Il paraît que notre grand ami Moïse s'est dégonflé encore une fois – c'est grave. Il va, sans doute, *caler*. Au fond il est lâche – il va tout céder à *ce dieu suédois* . . . Je te jure, Alban, que notre pays remerciera celui qui empêchera cette réunion d'avoir lieu . . . En fait ce n'est pas seulement *notre* pays qui le remerciera – les Francais, la Grande Bretagne aussi . . .'

They didn't recognise Jean-Marie. Bruno Berg stopped talking, looked on the young man greedily: he was pleased to meet him, here was meat to please him, here was meat to beat. He exhaled through his teeth. Water dripped onto the herringbone parquet, made puddles as though to draw attention from the festering brooks of waste that were Alban's mortal wake, to draw attention too from the bucking cock beneath the towelling. But puddles couldn't detract from that, it was coming out of hiding, out of bathtime hibernation, stretching itself for a new spring. Bruno Berg took it in. He would take it all in.

He said to Jean-Marie: 'T'as l'air bien beau Jean-Marie. T'as envie d'une nouvelle bicyclette?'

Jean-Marie feigned mishearing and Bruno Berg smiled flirtatiously at him. Alban vomited from his rectum.

Jean-Marie would have done it without the bribe of the bike. He'd have done anything for Bruno. (He did for Bruno.)

Pol Wollanders pressed on the doorbell of the apartment above Pneus Van Handen. A fat black whom no bike would support leaned from an upper window. When he told them to go away Wollanders simply held up a loaf of folding bread. Chap was down in a flash. Spokes, chrome, leather, metal *bidons*, Simplex sprocket boxes, tape, rubber, hard saddles, handlebars and caliper-brakes that are ever-charging horns, oil, oil, gleamy clean chains, silver pumps and patterned tread, pedals by the man that thought of mantraps – Jean-Marie wandered through the showroom. He was unmoved, he was bored. The smells, sights, bikes and brakes that would have held him, oh, only a year before meant nothing to him now. Another source of embarrassment, that's what this place was. It tried to drag him back into childhood. He shaved, he shaved now. And he walked. Bicycles belonged to his boyhood which was uncomfortably close. Pol Wollanders tapped his wristwatch.

Bruno put his arm around Jean-Marie: 'Vas-y – il faut choisir.'

He chose a Bobet-Vedette, cobalt blue and black. Pol Wollanders paid for it, shook Jean-Marie's hand, threw the keys of the van to Bruno, saluted him, turned smartly and brisked it across the street. Jean-Marie and Bruno then forced the bicycle (an animal unwilling to exploit its double-jointedness) into the back of the van. Bruno taps his teeth and distractedly surveys Jean-Marie. Then he clicks his fingers. Our salesman is re-summoned. And Jean-Marie is taken back into the shop where Bruno buys a pair of shorts for him and orders him to wear them instead of the black jeans with green stitching.

They drove to make death, they drove to fix his death, *that* death which was more than one man's death. Street goats fled nimbly from the van's path; men in skirts on old bicycles teetered as it passed. The houses got smaller; their white walls got dirtier; the walls stopped trying to be white. The road rose above itself in the heat, the cars and trees are by impressionists and myopes, are seen through moiré cloth. The houses stopped trying to be houses and became cardboard hutches, machines for subsisting in. The houses stopped altogether, and there was only the tar black of the road and the tan of the scrubby bush and the blinding blue of the deadly sky.

Jean-Marie was dazed with love (though he didn't own to it). He suffered the limpid delirium of high happiness.

He didn't ask Bruno where they were going; no, he just basked and tingled. He didn't ask Bruno why he had been made to wear shorts – which also dragged him back into the childhood he had escaped. He would not have worn them for anyone else. They drove beside the airport at Njili, they drove the length of its perimeter fence.

Bruno Berg slowed the vehicle to a walk and said softly: 'La voilà.'

Jean-Marie looked across the hotplate of the runway to the terminal building whose parapet still had a bite out of it where it had been shelled during last year's battle. 'La voilà!' Bruno Berg

174

swerved from the treacly road onto the hard earth curb. He hardly knew he had swerved, he was that rapt. It wasn't, Jean-Marie realised, the building that Bruno Berg was looking at with purse-mouth, ploughed-brow concentration.

It was a plane. It was a big plane, a big white plane that he was looking at. *Looking at* – it was more than that. He stared so hard he owned it in his gaze, he held it. He was doing much more than look at that big white plane (with its profile of an avian dolt). The reefs of muscle in his forehead knotted above his eyes; possession was his intent. It was so big, so white, so pure, so gleaming with cosmic beneficence – this was a transport of goodwill. Bruno Berg willed it otherwise; he wanted to see it broken-backed, black with smoke, shattered – not a plane at all but random shards of sheered metal, scattered, say, around an anthill. He wanted to see the ants that marched across the bust-up bloody body of the Swede.

He put his hand on Jean-Marie's shoulder and said: 'Il m'a dragué une fois, tu sais, notre bon dieu suédois, notre Saint Onus – c'était à Strasbourg. C'est bizarre, non?'

It was about now that Jean-Marie twigged.

Some things that Bruno Berg had in the van: a rucksack containing a bottle of mineral water, a gruyère and ham sandwich, and a bomb; an 'exploded' drawing of a DC-6B torn from an anglophone boys' annual – what other sort of drawing could be used at such a briefing? They sat in the van, in the partial shade of eucalypti, in a stony depression east of the airport. Jean-Marie listened, Bruno Berg spoke; neither demurred. It was all technical, mechanical, logistical. They did not allow the possibility of failure.

When the two blond mechanics who had been repairing the plane's exhaust pipes knocked off for lunch Bruno pulled the brand new bike from the van's back and Jean-Marie, strapped about with the rucksack, cycled all the way back beside the thick-gauge wire mesh perimeter fence, past the blue-bereted UN soldiers at the main gate. One of them waved to him, to this child in shorts out for a day's plane-spotting; the other went on excavating his nose. Jean-Marie felt no fear. It seemed ridiculously, playfully easy. He cycled across the baked ground, across the wide runway – all the while the big plane grew bigger. Its whiteness radiated heat. Its shadows were heavy on the metalled surface, crisply bordered. The mechanics had left two short ladders leaning against the outer starboard engine. Jean-Marie needed neither, they weren't props to murder, he could reach inside the nose wheel doors without a ladder. It was enough to climb on the rib-tread Goodyear tyre, cling onto the actuating arm, gain a few inches by standing on the torque links. That was all it needed. The correspondence of Transair Douglas DC-6B Albertina to the popular representation in an exploded drawing of any craft of its type was uncanny. The terrain conformed to the map. The bomb was an adapted *crottin* (turd – it was named for its shape) of the type developed in Indo-China and Algeria from the elemental magnetic mine (not so named) that maquisards had affixed to the bottom of Wehrmacht tanks. Herr Doktor Boffin devised a defence in the form of an anti-magnetic emulsion called *zimmermit* which – too late to save the great tyranny – was liberally pasted onto those tanks and other armoured vehicles.

This defence was not adopted by Algerian school buses.

Nor was it by our big white Albertina. The *crottin* gripped the metal. Jean-Marie had to position it to within three inches of the point where, when the wheel was retracted, the top of the wheel fork would rest. The trigger worked thus: from the *crottin* there protruded a longitudinal metal 'frame' fashioned from a hacksaw; in lieu of a blade there was stretched along one side of the frame a strip of sprung metal and a catch which might only be opened by pressure on the sprung metal from without the frame; the retracted fork pushed against the sprung metal which, once the wheel is fully retracted, springs back thus clamping the metal frame about the fork; when the wheel is actuated for landing the fork hauls the frame with it, and the frame, attached to the *crottin*'s firing pin, removes that pin thus occasioning the explosion of the device.

Not a very big device, but powerful enough to take out the cockpit, to murder the pilot and his co, to give them cock burns through their joysticks.

Jean-Marie did not consider the consequences of his

handiwork, but the way the Phillips' screws gaped at him with retards' eyes made him fretful, nervy – and those accusing rivets, those bolts that scold! When he clambered down from the wrong named tyre – it was the agent of a bad millisecond and of terrifying nothingness thereafter – he cycled, one hand on the handlebar, eating the sandwich, towards the gate. He cycles beside the fence and, when he looked up at, when he looked along it – it was high, it was long – he saw to his horror that it was now a solid wall, that the wire had fused into grey sheerness. The scene of his crime was also his prison . . . It was. Although, as we know, he cycled unchallenged from Njili airport and back to the sweating Bruno; it was his prison, he never forgot that hot airplane, nor the smell of oil thinned by heat, nor his panic when the fence turned into a wall. He remembered the stiffness of the new bike's brake-blocks, he remembered the way Bruno jumped from the van on his return – he had been gone less than eight minutes; he remembered the way Bruno jumped to hug him and grazed his arm on the doorlock.

They drove to the Clinique Mercier where the boy who had just turned man gave Bruno his blood. Later, at dusk, when the Albertina was still in the sky, they drove to the house on rue C. Lemaire. Jean-Marie ran up to his bedroom, packed a few clothes, and a book by an American. That was all he took with him save his old guitar, his accordion and his violin. He placed them in the back of the van in the spaces where the bicycle wasn't. And while Bruno Berg, flush with fresh blood, hummed in the car outside Jean-Marie went to say goodbye to the man he used to believe was his father.

Alban Meyer-Decker was on the floor in the sitting room trying to put a 78 rpm record of his song 'La Fin de l'Amour' on the gramophone. He could not lift himself from the pool of his own waste in which he lay. Jean-Marie took the record from his claws and lowered the needle onto its circumferential slick. The band struck up – this is the song with a clarinet that weeps for all lost loves, for every love that was ever lost. Jean-Marie kissed the top of Alban's punctured skull, watched while he tried to move his lips to the words, while he tried to lift his open palm in the stage-gesture he'd made a thousand times on the line 'Pas

177

toi; dis moi – pas toi.' Jean-Marie switched off the light, and that's the last you'll hear of Alban Meyer-Decker. By the time Jean-Marie is out of the house the clarinet is playing alone and the voice has gone forever. Alban had never been quite the same after he ate the pygmy: I doubt that he ever noticed Jean-Marie had gone. He dreamed his presence, that was enough.

And Jean-Marie rode off, side by side with Bruno Berg whose blood was his. They were side by side when the Albertina exploded, they were side by side in a bed, in Brazzaville, when, at six o'clock the next morning they listened to the news broadcast which began 'nous regrettons . . .' They tore the good of the earth from the sky and gave the earth HoTLoVe in exchange. Rattle your bones like the Belsen clowns, cheer the way the world blows.

We can all remember where we were the day we heard that Dag Hammarskjold had died.

'Soggy biscuit soggy biscuit soggy biscuit. Soggy biscuit Vallender!' Poor Eddie – he always lost, he always came last, he always took the biscuit.

We can all remember where we were when we heard that Dag Hammarskjold had died. Surely we can . . .

Can you remember where *you* were when you first heard that name – Ndola? Where were you, what were you doing? Think!

You weren't with us. You weren't with Eddie and me and Toddy and Arse and Pits.

We were beside the river, down Navigation Straight, beneath the willows, near the sluice, the sluice where we found the dead duck that time when we were only twelve. You weren't there. And you wouldn't admit it had you been. Pits wouldn't admit it either, and nor would he admit to that nickname of his early adolescence – he's *so* pompous now, on 350K near enough, Haslemere, golf, a tax brief, a QC. That summer it was briefs and QT. You and Pits wouldn't admit you even know what *soggy biscuit* is let alone that you once played it.

That summer we were fourteen, we bought Nelsons in tens from Noyce's on the high pavement near the bridge and the station; this is where Dapper Nat got his snout, he was grey by now, still spruce as a tree of course, had changed haircream brand in '56 the day the Russians went into Budapest and moved to Keg with Bay Rum. He was often to be seen across the road outside the public of the South Western catching the sun late lunchtime with a pint, a fag and the sports page in one hand, and his steel comb in the other keeping him ever dapper. I knew his name but of course I didn't know the link with Eddie, I'd

179

forgotten all about Eddie's poor father who seemed to have died a lifetime ago.

How did I know Dapper Nat's name? Forget – but I certainly didn't have it from Noyce. All that Noyce (three-strand pate, cardigan, year-round cough) ever said to us was: 'No reading. Three and sixpence Sonny Jim.'

But we weren't reading; we were *looking*. We lurked, furtive and engorged. We lurked, we looked; thumbing fumblingly through *Pose, Foto, Slik, Silk, Kiss, Klik, Klit, Kitten, Kiosk, Kamera, QT*, we looked. We lurked in the back of that dusty shop which smelled of old sweets and sweet tobacco and fresh shiny paper, oh that paper! Its sheets ever so slightly adhered to each other; they had to be peeled apart, *peeled* – those bad girls' clothes were forever getting peeled from them, they peeled their skirts before they started work, they peeled their stockings at work; they peeled so much, so often, that they lacked the tiresome shell, the thick thick pith. What you got with these girls – oh why couldn't we meet some of their kind? – was the heart of the fruit, the dirty kernel, the forbidden essence, the distillation. It was so dim in Noyce's you had to edge towards the dusty beams that ran through the window where mags were hung like panties on a washing line; you had to move that way to get a proper fix on Lorna's liver-dark and wicked nipples, on Janette's cloven G-string; you had to move close to the door through which you might be seen from the street by your mother just off the train after a morning's shopping in So'ton. Then Noyce snuffles: 'That'll be three and sixpence Sonny Jim.' So you put your hand in your pocket and hold the notched edge of a halfcrown to your glans which is in there too.

Then we are off on our bikes to Navigation Straight, with Lorna and Janette contrabanded in my saddlebag. I ride the Bluestreak with drops and derailleur; Eddie, he's got my old Space-rider – £11 to The Grieving Widow out of charity, Daddy says it was worth £14. Not a bad bike *for a boy* – three-speed Sturmey Archer, American tan grips, white wall tyres; none the less, Eddie has to really work to keep up with me. I just ease away from him. But he didn't mind. That was Eddie for you, he always struggled to keep up, took it all in good heart, showed bags of pluck.

Look at the way he always lost at soggy biscuit. He accepted it. He accepted that he was a loser. And we knew it, we all knew it, even if we didn't realise it. He must have wanted to be that way, mustn't he? That's right, his pathological pathos was dissembled aggression, he used his chronic humiliations as a means of attack, he invited suffering the more to make *us* suffer. He made ogres of us all, he was quarry. He hurt us by releasing the poison of shame within us, he could divine shame's source, he had a mainline to it. It was a facet of his gift.

He learned it early – he was not yet five when he drank the painting water. It wasn't that he couldn't paint *a fish in the river* but that he didn't want to try, he wanted nothing to do with fishes. The big fish which had stolen his father often came to grin at him while he slept; no one else saw its stained teeth, no one else had seen them apart from his father. Fish are wicked, fish have this potential to steal fathers. He knew it was a crocodile, he knew that it had eaten as well as stolen his father. But he knew too the comforting power of euphemism – an unspoken beast is a beast already in transit to oblivion.

There is a catch though. Terror doesn't let you off so easily. Terror attaches itself to the euphemism and finds you that way – thus the word *fish* acquired an abominable significance for Poor Eddie, it connoted horror and loss and the worst thing he'd ever seen. And it wasn't only the word, it was the creatures themselves; even tiddlers and tadpoles and minnows and dace were agents of fright – who knows what size they might grow to. Here are some things that terrorised him: taxidermally mounted perch in glass cases; the speckled, iridescent scales of the wares on the marble slabs in Green's; the smell of that shop and of The New Neptune ('Guarantee beef lard – We Do Not Use OIL') where Young Neptune smarmed lard on his hair and his four-inch sideburns, and fried tonight and every night, with balletic bravura, in a vat; the smell of evaporating vinegar on hot 'n' flaccid prick-thick chips; a china trout set on a pyritoid fist of crystal that Monica had bought in Brittany; the salmon leaping in the Test, leaping against the rush of white water at Romsey Mill; the salmon my father lifted triumphantly from the car boot the week before the Queen was crowned – he'd taken it (not caught it: *caught* was for coarse fish) at Ibsley and it weighed 47 lb, measured taller than either Eddie or me; my father's elaborate boxes with celluloid-windowed compartments showing flies and plugs and spinners and Mep spoons; cod on Friday; Douglas Vallender's waders which were stockings for the really bent; nets, no matter what their purpose; glue; sou'wester'd bo'suns stoically sucking lozenges to springclean their sea-rotted bronchi; the bludgeon called a *priest*, but not thence the clergy – there were limits to his fear, there were places terror's tentacles didn't stretch to; the sinuous illustrations to the edition of *The Water Babies* his mother found at Laverstock W.I.'s Bumper Jumble Fair; the tales of Jonah and Pinnochio; the feeding of the five thousand – he sobbed so loudly in Sunday school when he heard this whopper that he had to be led outside even though it was just bucketing through the porch roof; the Clyde and Scotland outside left Harry Haddock; Fisherton Street; the aquarium in the gas-scented waiting-room of the dental surgery of R. Lawrence Saxon-Smith, L.D.S., R.C.S. (Eng), C.P.S. – he wished that he liked that aquarium and the neon butterfly fish in it because the Saxon-Smith twins were so kind to him, as he would be to them when the time came, when they needed something other than taunts to the tune of Connie Francis's hit; the pike that basks there, where the sun dapples the water, makes the water opaque, makes it a mask for the beast in the weeds, the beast that preys on baby ducks, that grows to prey on babies, that grows more so that its hideous prognathism is emphasised, that grows more so that it can accommodate larger prey in its death chambers – it needs larger prey if it is to grow more so that it can accommodate yet larger prey, prey such as a father: *that* is a fish in the river.

The desks were semi-detached, light wood, splintering along the desiccated grain. The desks were tables with two of us at each. While we wet our brushes and tried to wipe the rat-brown crust from the lozenges of paint so that they might disclose their traffic-light spectrum Eddie sat beside me with his paintbox closed. I paint. I pull the loaded brush across the coarse paper. I smudge the paint. I repeat these actions to achieve a rat-brown diarrhoeal blob which is anything but ichthyomorphic. When

Eddie looks at it he begins to cry; it is a fish to Eddie as it is to no one else save its begetter. And all around him fish are being created from water by crude hands, fish that are fish rather than trees or cats (who like fish) because Mrs McG has said they are.

She says, too, as she moves behind the desks: 'That's a lovely fish, Priscilla . . . that's a, now, that's a *very* good fish, a lovely fish . . . that's a big fish Jonathan why Eddie you haven't painted a fish – a fish in the river Eddie. Come along dear you can paint a fish in the river . . .'

Eddie's face is contorted, begrutten, red, a beetroot that has been branded. He looks up at Mrs McG and she opens his paintbox and smiles as she tells her little class in the sunbeamed room: 'Eddie's going to paint a big fish in the river for all of us.'

And all the little children laughed. Eddie picked up the former jamjar of murky water from my end of the table and drank it, gulpingly, guzzlingly. There were shrieks, shrieks, shrieks: Priscilla who always pinched Eddie shrieked best. Mrs McG hurried from the room and returned with Miss Ellaby and with Miss Ellaby's lopsided hair, transparent skin, marmalade tan walking-stick, oldness. With those; without Miss Ellaby's lips because she had none. Miss Ellaby's lipless mouth told Eddie that he was going to die; it told him that stupid little boys who drink the painting water die, like stupid little boys who lick the bitter aloes from their bitten fingernails.

You could definitely tell that Poor Eddie was going to die – the eyes in the beetroot face gasped, and Mrs McG hung a rat-brown travel rug round him to warm him as he died. And then she helped cowled Eddie from the class which was silent, and so sorry for him, so sorry that it hurt our tummies, made our throats fur with sickness: we knew that dying was a sad thing to happen to a child, to one of us. He was doing the suffering for us, teaching us guilt, teaching it us more efficiently than Mrs McG taught us painting, teaching us through our throats and gullets (the receptive parts). We learned too that dying was connected to brown shrouds, probably because God wore one. He humbled us: would we have asked Mrs McG the question Eddie asked?

He asked her: 'Who will look after Mummy after I have died?' Poor Eddie, he so wished his mother not to be deprived of another beloved. He wished that more than he wished not to die. He waited in the hall, trembling; he waited, hoping that his mother would arrive before he died. The rear wheel of her bicycle was segmentally enclosed by black umbrella material to prevent mud spatting her back; she was smoking, breathless, kneeling beside him. I drank my breaktime cocoa and watched on tiptoe through the window-panelled door of the classroom. I never stopped watching him. I watched as The Grieving Widow lifted her little boy into the flimsy pillion behind her saddle, her satisfying saddle (p. 18); she lifted him into the precarious structure of thin-gauge metal and butterfly nuts, swaddled him tight, stood astride the crossbarless bike and shakily carried him off to die, wrestling with her sit-up-and-beg between trees brightened by green apples (cf. brown shrouds). I never stopped watching him but I couldn't be everywhere. I wasn't there when he didn't die that afternoon; he sat beside his mother whilst she smoked and scratched her crown.

He twice asked her: 'Am I dead yet Mumma? Have I died?' When it grew suddenly dark at quarter to one he gripped her hand and she looked up to see a tractor's trailer skypiled with straw bales passing funereally along Britford Lane. When the ever-sodden wicket gate from the lane squeaked and groaned, and when a single decisive beat of the door knocker filled the bungalow with a thunderous tumble, then Eddie knew his time had come. His mother sighed, she patted him and made a big big smile which he, Poor Thing, mistook for a sign of glee at his end – and that made him long to die, that maternal betrayal. She stood up, leaving him on the sofa, and went to the door to welcome Death. Poor Eddie clamped his arms about his knees and buried his head in his dark lap, the better not to witness His face.

The doctor, Dr Cunningham-Kelso, suggested that The Grieving Widow should remonstrate with 'the old witch Ellaby'; the gate squeaked and groaned, and Eddie was saved.

He didn't understand how he had been saved; and it wasn't till teatime, when he and his mother and Stella sat down to toast and marge and Marmite with a spoonful of Virol for afters, that he believed he was properly alive again. His mother was docked a half day's pay and Eddie was apprised of the closeness of death, of its imminence, of its ability to track him wherever he might go, of its presence in water – which is where big fishes live, and where his dead father lives.

When the box that brought back the bit of his father (the carnal token) was unloaded from the airplane it was hidden from Uncomprehending Eddie for five days. It reappeared one afternoon in the back of a black urrse, a lacquered cabinet gay with waxy hyacinths and bursting with men whose faces were hewn from soap, a cabinet with wheels and a bad engine that wouldn't go fast. Nor would the engine of the hardly smaller car they followed in; he sat between his mother and Uncle Douglas (who wasn't crying) and behind two more soap men, this pair fashioned from hyacinth scented soap and supplied with auxiliary neck folds. And off they went: along the valley, over the Ebble meadows, past the wall that goes on forever goes on forever, down the dip with the turning that Eddie used to want to buy a dog for because it was (still is) blind, past poor people's houses, past common people's houses, past people who stop to lift their hats and press them to their breasts, past the red house where he went inside to see his newborn cousin Bonny, the only cousin he has, the only cousin he's seen, a cousin who can sleep but can't speak. They followed the urrse through an arch like a whale's jawbone, an arch with a flint-built whale still stuck to it. This blueblack whale might devour them all: Poor Eddie clutched his Mumma's arm. Uncle Douglas belched behind his hanky (which smelled of grown-ups as surely as did The White Jam Tart and The Dead Brother's Wife which Eddie had put his face round the doors of even though he was meant to be in his father's car outside with his crisps, waiting).

Why did they bring the box of his father to this garden inside a whale? Why is the garden spoiled by hunchbacked stones and dirty crosses and green pebbles like big bath-salts? Why has that angel no head? Why did they bring him to such a little church? And did his friends dress in black (mostly) so he couldn't see them? Did they sing so loud in the hope that he would hear?

185

Didn't they know he wouldn't see, that he couldn't hear? Poor Eddie was so scared. Why did they bring the box to this site of lichen, cypresses, bird-droppings? They talked to it, sang to it, kept it in the cold of a stained-glass larder. And then they burnt it. They rolled it on rollers which were invisible to grown-ups but not to Poor Eddie who was only up to here on the door jamb (height check every month on the twelfth). Eddie saw the circles, and the oily, fluffed chain that turned the black circles into wheels. He watched them roll the box of his father through the satin curtains. Why did they bring the box for exhibition, sing to it when it couldn't hear, then hide it behind these panto curtains? Why did they bring it all this way from the hot river where big fish live and kill, why did they bring it all this way if they weren't going to open it?

It was when the box didn't come back from behind the satin curtains that Eddie began to worry. His mother chewed her hand. When the singing stopped she led him between the ranks of dark trousers. She stood in the sun and shade of the dusty doorway, dappled and grieving, and she thanked the trousers who gathered together to laugh, to emit man noises, man-breath (pipes, beer, dirty sofas). Poor Eddie wanted to go back inside, he wanted to recover the box. *They were leaving the box*. They were abandoning it, they were rendering it an orphan box. Poor Eddie worried so much about the box that he refused to get into the car that his mother was tugging him towards.

The Tap Room Chaps in the car, the Brig's Alvis, needed their wets, needed them so much they forgot themselves – they referred to the boy, in front of his distraught mother, as 'the little perisher'; thirst had got the better of their tongues, and she cried, The Grieving Widow howled. Only Padre knew what to do. He had a flask to her mouth quicker than you could say *Crocodylus cataphractus*. He toddled after the boy. He waddled back from where he'd found him, at the sharp end of the chapel with a hassock beneath his feet to give him height, gaping at the void beyond the curtains. (Beyond the satin curtains is the inferno – but Eddie didn't see it, the door of the oven was shut, bolted against prying eyes and heat loss. The door was no more than the tunnel's end. Poor Eddie would never wear satin trousers, even when they were dernier cri.) Eddie knelt on the back seat of the Brig's big Alvis, between his mother and Padre. It smelled of must, of leather, of men. He stares through the box-shaped rear window at the receding church, littler and littler by the second. They are through the jawbone, out of the whale, when he sees the smoke.

Guy Vallender's last pyrotechnic exhibition: we can so call it for there's no smoke without fireworks. This exhibition, the posthumous addition to the oeuvre that had gone up in smoke, should have been the *summum*, the ultimate auto-epitaph. There is not a firework maker alive who does not hope that, when dead, he will be a firework himself, that his body will be barded with sulphur and potassium, that his skin will be rubbed with nitrate of barium, that his cavities will be keenly stuffed with shellac, hemp coal, strontium carbonate and ammonium perchlorate in an act of beneficent necrophilia. Every firework maker alive hopes for this temporary taxidermy and wills that he be placed upon a night pyre, on a high hill above a city, thence to lighten the sky of the living below (p. 472). Guy Vallender didn't get his will. There wasn't enough of him to stuff. He was burnt as waste. His son saw the smoke. It was nothing like fireworks – it was a scrap of voile in the nippy wind; it was an old maiden's minge mane; it was meagre, thin, horizontal. It was a smoke signal that conceded frailty, defeat, surrender. It hardly stood out from the bright albino sky. It wasn't much of a show. It was enough of a show to worry Eddie. Why did they bring it all this way and then burn it? (He never doubted the link between box and smoke. He knew what was what and where it came from, the source.) And why did they burn it and then throw the grey remains in the river?

One of the soap-faced men knocked on the door, early afternoon. Then they walked together across the Ebble meadows, The Grieving Eddie and The Poor Widow and the soap man in his satin hat. They walked across foot bridges, through tufty grass and tyred mud; the leets were filled with spring, everything was green, the perky flowers smiled their hullos. When they reached the main river, which was fuller than the leets even, plump with shiny water, The Grieving Widow hesitated. Her feet squelched and she read the water, sought directions. Then she walked downstream towards a wire fence on whose barbs flocculated spermatazoa of paste-white wool (p. 60). (She never saw another man's sperm so long as she lived (p. 18)). She stood beside this fence, beside its last post. (Sound taps for my dead husband, my only ever husband.) The last post was sunk into the river bed; it stood proud of the eroded bank (mocha topped with pistachio – there's always more mocha in summer). The Grieving Widow (brawn-faced, blotchy, lost) nodded to satan hat/soap face. She clenches her face and nods to the stream by the last post. Poor Eddie wondered what it was that the man had been carrying: it is a vessel of a kind. An ornamental vase? A cooking pot? A helmet? A trap for water rats? Mother clutches son, pulls him to her hip. Soap face clears his soap throat, delicately. He extends both arms out over the water hieratically, holds the vessel as though he's about to perform an act of legerdemain. He is: the urn is turned in Greek style, lathed like a finial. Now, its tip is a lever. When he pulls the lever the bottom opens. And from the aperture there fall, with no urgency, the ashes of the box of Poor Eddie's father. They fall and fall to the full spring bourn which will carry them away, which will bear them to the sea. We're made of water. The ashes fall to the water, slowly, they take all this time to get there, they're held in suspension by cruel draughts, by the wind's low blows (the elements are on a jolly, on a vandal-crack; deep down all elements are voys). The ashes fall to water that is as evil as the painting water, as the water in the Congo, as the water in Navigation Straight. This water's spite-special was a foetal whirlpool. It didn't flow straight. When it reached the last post it deviated, it reeled, it danced round and round the rotting pole, ploddingly – so when the funereally directed ash met it it, too, went round and round, unabsorbed, refusing to drown, shining the nacreous sheen of the flammable agent which had been generously poured to fuel the mortal flames. The oily ashes formed a little pile, a token pyre. The Grieving Widow could not believe that this was it, that this was all there was, that the man she loved whose life had been hers was reduced to a mound of slate-blue sludge that (now it was too late) wouldn't sink or clear off. Ashes clung like wrack to the post, they glinted like an electric sky – that was all they did right. It was one of those days. Poor Eddie grew used to them. If it wasn't water it was fire. Fire: now, there is a one hundred per cent no-good element, so far as poor Eddie was concerned.

It was fire that got Eddie into trouble the first time. They blamed the home, the background, the familial circumstances (generally agreed to be tragic), they always do. I know better, Eddie knew better – but he knew, equally, that no one would believe him. This is the story, no embellishments, *just as it was*, the whole and nothing but, straight up, kid you not, on Guy's grave. Same personae as p. 179, just about. Pits wasn't with us. There was Eddie, Toddy, Arse and me. This was two summers after Dag Hammarskjold died. It was the last summer we rode bicycles which were thereafter reckoned unbecomingly boyish. But we still rode them then. I'm on the Bluestreak, Arse has got his Palm Beach, Toddy's out front on the hand-built Claude Butler that's the envy of us all – light alloy, 12-speed Simplex, brown-walled racing tyres, pick it up with one finger. Eddie? Poor Eddie's way behind, still on my old Spacerider; he's outgrown it – the saddle is at maximum height, it protrudes from its socket like an ostrich, but even thence gives him inadequate purchase on the pedals. Good for his muscles though, he really has to bullwork, build his sinews, fortify the body-piston – it will all come in handy, later, when he works. (He needs muscles for his kind of work.) The dry gorse just whizzes by. We've a sou'westerly just about behind us up on the heights near Bramshaw Telegraph. The road shines ahead. Motors make their own mirages, our shadows are 45 degrees left of us, it's two o'clock – you can figure which way we're heading. The wooden fire tower is unmanned, for lunch no doubt.

Our lunch is in bottles, in my saddlebag and Arse's panniers and Toddy's tartan duffel bag and Eddie's tattered rucksack (he was strapped up by it, bound around by dun webbing – he was wearing a hand-me-down prosthesis of unfathomable effect, fetish-gear for outdoorsy porn, just what Jorgen the Hiker – he has hose in his lederhosen – will be wearing when he espies Renate, Naked Cowherd of the Oberland). Today Eddie's

189

wearing unseasonal clothes, the clothes he wears the year round because they're the only ones he owns – they won't buy him any more. That's another reason he is at the back – those flannels are midwinter weave, they're leg blankets, they're black with sweat, with all the salts that he can give them, and he gives them a river when we turn off towards Nomansland and no longer have the putto-wind puffing to push us. Eddie's the one puffing when he drops from his bike beside us in the beech light of this Forest nave. He unstraps himself. He coughs for life on his first ever Kensitas.

Now you hear him speak for the first ever time: 'This is that place I told you about. You know – where I came on scout camp and that girl asked to look at my tool.'

Collective: 'Oh *yeh*!' But yes, it had occurred. Eddie had gone with four of the Mowgli troop to buy lard to fry their breakfast. But the tin-leg who owned the shop pretended not to hear them and wouldn't open. They knocked on a few doors and were unanswered. They knocked on the door of a complicated shack built of corrugated iron, asbestos tiles, wood, breezeblocks, broken bricks (each allowed to express itself with truth-to-materials probity). A ragged girl came to the door, listened to their request and returned with a chipped mug filled with greasy white dripping (only a few hairs in it). The girl smelled. Eddie thanked her. Eddie, Poor Eddie was the one who had done the talking and was thus the one who was set upon by the entire camp when our dozen scouts gagged on their fry-up because it had been fried in Brylcreem.

Eddie was alone and bruised, lying tearful and crouched, hiding from his assailants in Four Mile Enclosure when he heard her voice. He knew without looking it was the ragged smelly girl, there was death in her voice. She looked at his bruises, the grazes on his cheek, the fist abrasions. She told him he ought to dress them, at least wash them in a stream because he didn't want them septic. He shook his head violently at the mention of the stream. Then she lay down beside him trembling like a shocked animal and licked his hand. Poor Eddie started, he sat up on the twiggy leafmat, he looked aghast as she clasped his wrist and ran her tongue across his red-hatched knuckle. She smelled of damp and cabbage and road conkers. Her hair was long, the cakecrumbs in it were kept there by the grease and dirt, ditto the hardly discernible filaments of horsehair and grass blades. She excavated a mop of moss and pressed it to his cheek which flushed with cool balm, which was nice but not so nice that he didn't still wish to escape. He wished thus even more when she slid her fingers into the button-fly of his flannel trousers (he owned only half of a scout-outfit – his mother couldn't afford the whole set. 'You've got the Baden but not the Powell,' observed Douglas).

She scratched his penis with gnawed nails and said: 'Let's have a look then – it feels tha' much bigger than me Da's.'

Eddie ran, oh he ran and ran. He ran back to the Forest nave where we are today, where he tells his tale in earnest wonderment and causes us to exclaim: 'So you *didn't* then?'

He shakes his head, without rue.

Collective: 'Well, I'd have done.'

Toddy took his scrumpy bottle from his mouth and told Eddie: 'You're spaz Vallender, you know that? Spaz and wet.'

Poor Eddie, he shrugged and looked at his round toe-capped shoes. I had chisels and Toddy had cuban-heeled boots from Anello and Davide (but not for cycling). We all had scrumpy; in the matter of apple turned to tractor fuel we were equal, save that Toddy had had the florid lowbrow at the Brewery Tap next to the bus station fill *two* litre bottles for him, against our one. Manners: Arse and Toddy and I drink the clouded, particulated intoxicant from the bottle; Eddie drinks from a skyblue plastic picnic beaker. A little goes a long way with him. He can't hold it, not the way a man can, not the way we can, not the way that Toddy can.

Toddy (Donald Rollo Hogg-Tod, b. 27 June 1948, m. Charlotte Jane 'Bonny' Vallender 24 July 1971 (pp. 290ff.), d. 21 Jan 1975 (p. 433)) can really hold it, he has twice as much as the rest of us to hold. Each mouthful is a nanodose of cyanide, it's there in the pips in the mash – but I didn't die, I'm still here, evidently, and so is Arse, somewhere. No, it wasn't that (that killed him, I mean). The last thing we think about that day is the last thing, or last things. Scatology, not eschatology, is the form.

Toddy is into his second bottle, badered as only a boy aspiring to be a man can be, when he does it. He feels it coming on. He does most of a backward roll – leaves are dorsally crunched beneath him (sound effect: a distant forest fire). Now, Toddy is a looker – he and Bonny will make a beautiful couple (p. 295). We judge looks by faces. His is winningly sallow, with the right cheekbones, with an orthognathism so right it might be a face job (it isn't, he never met James Elsworth Laing for a professional chip 'n' chisel). We envy his face the way we envy his bike and (we must have known this) his facility to ride all the bikes he rode before he rode Bonny. But his arse, the cotton-jeaned hemispheres he presents to Arse and Eddie and me, is a fat apple, a macro-scrotum, cleaved by a red stitched seam. This is his bad end, the end the oil-painter flunked. He doesn't care for this end the way he does for the other, he doesn't look at it the way he looks at the other – catch him at the mirror and he shows no embarrassment, he merely continues to gorge on his face. But he treats the bad end otherwise.

He lights it: a hand creeps round the spread arseflesh. The lighter is streamlined, gleamy, its flame is pale in the partial sunlight. And so is the flame that, on the rasp of the fart, follows the methane fuse from a point on the arc of the red stitched seam across the spread of his southpaw buttock. And it is so pale that we shriekers ('You gross-er . . . you digusting fox . . . poo-eee . . .') don't catch it all, we don't see it extend. We rollick with our bottles of bad apple, we cat-call and hiss, we don't see the flame grab the dry lichen and crisp grey moss and desiccated leafmeal.

It's not till a twig leaps with pain and a broken branch creaks with fright that Arse observes: 'Youhouyou've you've s-set the fuck . . . fucking thing . . . whatsit – look, fire.' We all gaped, we all heard the meek crackle, we all saw the dwarf flames bounce about the forest floor. 'Oh pissanus,' mumbled Toddy and rose to stamp the flames. He rises, he kicks out with a foot that, the last time he used it, was not chemically impaired. Now he's back on his back and the flames are procreating, grinning gleefully, furcating, jiving with joy, leaping like loonies on furlough. These are bluecollar flames, they wear the yellow hoods of klansmen and penitents. These are bluecollar flames that love their work. They're not deterred by Toddy pouring the remnants of his scrumpy on them, they're all-weather flames. Toddy's feet won't hold him, and those heels don't help. But he's doing better than Eddie. 'Lesh go, 'mon,' advises Arse, crawling. This is when Eddie vomits. He genuflects against his will and leans ever so slightly forward with bulbous cheeks and bombed eyes. A cataract rushes from him, there's a pump within him – that's what accounts for the force, for the volume of gaily speckled tummy mud (ambient colour: luncheon meat). Watch it steam, watch him add to the gleamy pool. Now the flames are ganging up on some ferns, and they're swelling by the second. Flames never stay still, never – and their progression is (in a wood, in late summer) exponential; flames' progression scorns the unitary plod of bones' growth, and trees'; flames live for the moment (forget eternity – the eternal flame is the flame denatured). Eddie knelt over his excremental reservoir, wracked by abdominal spasms, retching abominable spam, the victim of thoracic tomfoolery. He was unable to move. He watched the flames become a fire, he watched the freeform pyrotechny with something like rapture, his watching eyes blocked his ears. Sight sat on sound. He doesn't hear us. His eyes deafen him to our calls. We didn't mean to leave him. Honest as the cross was wood; we didn't mean to leave him. Cider – blame it, blame apples, blame cider. It's the christian way, to blame the apple. As we ran for our bicycles, as we staggered towards them, we were embracing that tradition.

He appeared before the Juvenile Court two weeks later. He did OK, considering. The name Vallender meant something to the rotarian scum on the bench. The scum bubbles and wriggles and comes to a verdict. Poor Eddie got off lightly, with a magisterial kiss: two years probation, suspended. Had it been me or Arse . . . we'd have felt a different kiss. Toddy wouldn't have, of course. Donald Rollo Hogg-Tod could have burnt down the entire Forest (he tried) and been congratulated on his youthful prank. Does that tell you what the Hogg-Tods were like? It should. It really should. It was Toddy who set fire to Four Mile Enclosure, who caused £—'s worth of damage for every day of Eddie's probation, who never stopped to see the flames, the sedulous bluecollars that outgrew the trees and scraped the bluesky as they sought chromatic congress. (By the time they got there they weren't blue but yellow. And the fleece-white billows had attained an innocent beauty; they were climbing too, adding to the show, snowing the wrong way.)

Heavens! Was Eddie's life always like this? Was he always the one who copped it? You know very well he was. You know that he can outdo you in hurt, in suffering casual negligence and wanton neglect. Eternal shame is not like eternal flame: there's nothing denatured about it. It's the shoulder parrot that forever squawks the unsaid in the earhole that tunnels to the place where oblivion cannot be arranged. Eternal shame – that's what Eddie's life was for; he was put on earth to shame us. When we think of Eddie we think of how we wronged him, we wonder why, oh, why did we treat him thus. And the answer's always the same – we treated him that way because we were meant to. It meant that he always won in the end – the moral battle, that one.

Even someone like Iremonger must have known that he had lost to Eddie. Not because of her yet more emphatic spurning of him, not because of the obloquy she made him endure, but because the pathetically patient stoicism of Poor Eddie himself was sufficient to let him know he had lost. The boy's refusal to complain, his acceptance of bullying, affected even Iremonger.

Iremonger was so desperate for a job, such unpromising material, that he was able to take up Mr Redmond's position as senior geography and mathematics teacher only two days after Mr Redmond had been relieved of it for 'kissing Reed'. Iremonger's proclivities were otherwise. He did not want to kiss small boys. Even had he wanted to he was too tensely withdrawn. Iremonger had a piece of metal in his head from Korea. No wonder he was so good at geography – he'd been to Korea to get the metal for his head. It made him angry, that piece of metal. What kind of metal makes you angriest? Tin, iron, zinc, lead, copper? I used to ponder that matter as Iremonger assaulted the blackboard, covered it with spiky disjoined strokes that were (he deluded himself) now numerals, now letters, always illegible, always accelerating down a 1 in 5 slope. And where was the piece of metal? Was it buried in his forehead's corrugations? Is that what those folds were for – the fat lateral ones, and the ruddy rogue fold that extended his nose into his brain? His face was carrot and pebbledash. His face told us that there was a man behind him with a club, a blade, a throatwire, a gun. Even on the pillion of his sagegreen Matchless? Was the man there too? He was. Iremonger was always haunted, always on the edge. He didn't want to kiss little boys, he wanted to hit them because they conspired with the man behind him. Look at me when I dropped an eraser – he pulled me from my desk by my ear, took me into the dark corridor. From the exercise-book store he withdrew a cane (thick as a fuck-star's working-tackle and much, much harder) and hurt himself more than he hurt me, did me a power of good, did me so well that my bottom was stung, numb, *burnt*. What he did to Eddie was worse. The sadism he visited on me was commonplace; in the case of Eddie he excelled himself. Poor Eddie's crime was not to have conspired with Iremonger's eternal foe but merely to be his mother's son. Oh, yes, Iremonger went a-courting.

It takes one to spot one (actually anyone could have spotted either of them); the metal in his head rang in recognition when he met The Grieving Widow. Wrecked, fraught, timid – they were both of them those OK, but whilst she was placid Iremonger was seething. What a gorgon got for hair he got for the inside, for a brain: his brain was a pit of white snakes. He rode the road of unrequited love (it's a cul-de-sac). He rode down Britford Lane with Eddie on the pillion – Eddie was the only boy thus treated; we all pleaded with Iremonger but we didn't have mothers who were widows buckled with grief, dumped on by life. Eddie was the key, the poor unwitting clue to his mother's heart. I've told you: she never saw another man's sperm so long as she lived, her widowhood was immutable, she was married, she was faithful to the shade of the crocodile's lunch. It would never have occurred to her to break her faith. It never occurred to her that Iremonger's intent was suasive. The man was so gauche, so liable to stare for half an hour at the crumbs on a plate, so mute, so periphrastic when he opened his mouth (see the tongue – it's tied with metal ropes). He had no small talk and no big talk – he was forbidden by his brain to talk big, to enunciate the perfectly shaped declarations of this and that that coursed about his heart and back. He just sat at the attention in his British Warm, clasping his helmet (a fat yarmulke, an infant cloche), nibbling his Marie biscuit and his top lip. When he talked he talked of Eddie, the poor unwitting clew whom he hadn't the nerve or nous to use; he failed to bend Poor Eddie (their only link) into an agency of intimacy. He spoke of the boy in the formulae of a school-report. It wasn't as though he didn't appreciate his shortcomings – he did, and he tried to compensate for them. Poor Eddie, poor innumerate Eddie had Iremonger leaning over his shoulder as he blanked on algebraic abstractions. He continued to blank on them but Iremonger gave him good marks (for trying, for neatness).

Poor Eddie, poor gawky Eddie possessed no eye for a moving ball, no sporty appetite, no taste for the huggermugger of rough scrums, no turn of speed. Yet Iremonger, in a monstrance of his love, in his capacity as beak i.c. rugby football, promoted the boy to the first team, to lock-forward. This gesture touched The Grieving Widow's pocket but not her heart; she had to buy Eddie a pair of studded boots – he'd previously made do with daps. Eddie's potential prowess as a lineout jumper was a new subject for Iremonger to woo her with. *Still* she didn't suss. It was Douglas Vallender who told her what everyone knew. Those Vallenders, the proper Vallenders, had by then moved to The Garth, bought at a knockdown sum from Saxon-Smith's shame-crazed wife, the woman who dared not show her shame-face, soon after the trial. It was while Douglas was showing off that house (the size of an hotel or a sunset home – it's eight flats now) to The Grieving Widow, his sister-in-law, and to my mother that he made, with boorish nonchalance, a remark that included the phrase (my mother recalls) 'Your beau's scrummaging stratagem'. The Grieving Widow was staring from a window towards a frost-crisp lawn where Eddie and I were punting a ball between us. Rather, I was punting a ball to Eddie who failed to catch it, picked it up, threw it in the air, followed it with his crooked leg, didn't connect – and so on and on.

'My *what*'s *what*?' she asked.

No one save Iremonger and she knew what she said to him when she went outside the bungalow as the Matchless pu-putted to a vespertine halt. He already had his helmet off and had it under his Warm's fog-cold elbow when she halted him on the threshold, ushered Eddie indoors, shut the door. Whatever she said was enough.

I heard the crack – it was late afternoon, I heard the rooks, I saw them in the elms. The sky was pink, the sun was saying goodbye again, the cathedral bell told the hour, it was time we finished, it was time we took our shower. It was time we finished – but Iremonger didn't hear the bell, he never heard it, he coached us as if we were pros, he flattered us thus. We'd won Saturday's match – The Grieving Widow had been at Chaffyn to see us win. She stood with Douglas and my father, she shivered in a sheepskin coat (mail order from Fort William) and a Jaeger headscarf (jumble), she cheered when Douglas did, she was proud that Eddie did his bit. But Iremonger had not been satisfied. His methodically designed lineout gambits, based on those of the French XV of the previous season and signalled in that language ('Uhn . . . Der . . . Twah . . . Katra . . . Sank') had failed. They had failed because Eddie, the tallest boy in the line, had persistently dropped the ball, had persistently failed to adopt the correct place in the line, had persistently failed to remember when he was supposed to be decoy.

Iremonger had it in for Poor Eddie. He berates the boy throughout the afternoon – for his muddy shirt (no washing machine), for his handling (no co-ordination), his inertia (no will). Iremonger is coach and ref and player. He plays for both sides. He lets himself be tackled if the tackler is in his good books (Shute, Innes, Masters). If the tackler is in his bad books (anyone else) he strides through the tackle, generally deprecating its feebleness. Now, as the horizon blushes and as the crows go spinning like burnt paper, and as tiredness creeps over our unfinished limbs he blows for another lineout. Up goes Eddie, up so that there is a gap between his boots and the stud-furrowed mire, up he goes with the gawky awkwardness of a gauchely mastered puppet. He pedals, he kicks, he flays with synchronous imbalance. And as he fingertips the matt and sodden ball Iremonger mutates from ref to rampager. His whistle, the buccal prop of impartiality, is pocketed: he charges, his thirteen stones of sinew and ire head-on into Eddie as the boy buckles back in a gesture of aspirant retrieval. I saw the crack. I heard it and I saw it. Shoulder to rib, boot to shin, elbow to trunk. And the ball slithered off. Iremonger scooped it with one hand and raced for the try-line, unchallenged. He scored; oh, he'd scored all right, he'd settled that one. His victim writhed near the twenty-five, he converted his try, his whistle shrilled for time.

I said to him: 'I think Vallender's really hurt, Sir.'

I thought he was going to cuff me; then he smiled – man-to-man, collusive – and hoarsed: 'Shamming.'

Two of Poor Eddie's ribs were broken, which we understood, and a cartilage was ruptured, which we didn't. We were too young to understand why they had been broken, why it had been ruptured. Whilst Iremonger shadowboxed towards wherever it was that he changed and bathed Toddy, Pits and I carried Eddie across the field to Matron's room (iodine, lint, verruca cream). It was getting dark outside and she had to turn the light on.

Was that the worst thing that ever happened to Eddie? You know it wasn't. You know that with Eddie there's always worse to come. It's bad for all of us – every morning we are aborted from sleep into diurnal terror. It's bad for us but it was always worse for Eddie, he was magnet, honeypot, bull's eye, fly strip. Bad Luck stuck to this half-orphan; Ill Fortune could always find its way to him. These are protean items, quick-change artistes, malevolent mutants. One day Bad Luck's disguised as water, the next he's transformed into Iremonger. Sometimes Ill Fortune's a dog, others he's Father Christmas. Of course Poor Hapless Eddie often sought his own Ill Fortune, worked at unearthing it, enticed it into the toilet with him.

That's what he did with Postman (part wolf, part jackal, wholly labrador); he whistled and clucked at the mutt-psycho till it followed him into the very toilet where five years previously Douglas had – he claimed – thrown faeces at him (p. 25). Eddie didn't know why he exposed himself to the dog; it wasn't on-site revenge against Douglas's best friend for he believed that he might even please the beast whose glyceric icicles of slobber stretched from jaw to floor, he believed his already prodigiously sized cock might be a dog's delight. And he desired what every sexual adventurer, prepubertal or not, desires – the corporeal thrill of foreign contact coupled with the shiver of guilt. Dog, milkbottle, inkbottle, a requisitioned mouth, a stolen bracelet – all as utile as one another, as foreign as one another when you're ten: they all do the business, they're all nuts for a boy's bolt. (A boy's nuts need no tightener. A boy's nuts are unfallen, they're the unfallen parts of the fallen boy.)

Freefalling Eddie – down, down little boy, there is no bottom before the blackness – got the dog in the bog. There is sun on the frosted sash, and somewhere in the garden he can hear Bonny; he can hear his mother too, and Monica – but it's Bonny's mouth that is open widest, most often, most beautifully. Whatever else that girl did she always sounded delicious, her mouth was two fruits with a music-box between them. It was also a box, but not for Eddie, not for Poor Eddie. Postman bit Poor Eddie's veal meat. Slobby poochums smells and licks then bites. Here is Eager Eddie one moment, the one-eyed cavalier, laughing. And here he is the next, screaming because Postman has growled and nipped like a pike at a fly. Oh dear, locked in the lavatory. Eddie bestrides the bowl, feet on the precipices, buttoning his shorts while the creature barks and he bleeds from his secret wound: the cock-blood he's used to is that which flows at the summation of cock-fights in the swimming pool changing room. Cann keeps watch whilst Vallender and Ford duel, then it's Vallender on watch, then Ford (names changed here). That sanguinary ejaculate is one thing, this fang-drawn stuff is the same but different. Same blood, different source. It doesn't come from within. Those are love-wounds, the things comedons with guitars sing about; this is the battle blood of the sex-warrior. This is a mistake. This is all pain, no pleasure. This is life, Poor Eddie's life: pain and pleasure are meant to be mixed in equal measures but we all know Fate is a bad barman.

Most of us don't pick on biters such as Postman; most of us

don't have Douglas for an uncle nor Bonny for a cousin; most of us know better than to hang around rotten actors in red, rep-rotters who are too bad for panto, so bad they're Santas. Stella – it would be Stella – Stella fumbled the florin into the paw of the woman at the tunnel's mouth then pulled her charge around papier-mâché'd, tinselled, trash-bright bends into the heart of Santa's lair. Red, and here's more red.

'Oh sod the bleeding moon,' cried Stella. ' 'Ere,' she said to the rotten rep-actor, non-acting for Yule, ' 'ere, 'smee time o'the month. Mus' go to the powder room.'

And away she scurried, oohing at her cramps, abandoning Eddie beside a plywood reindeer whose rednosed muzzle was attached to the red rep-actor by red real reins, not plywood ones. Poor Eddie gaped at the forever resting nose (it's bar rest that reddens a nose) and at the forever resting eyes (it's insomnia and cigs that do the eyes); Poor Eddie gaped and turned to scuttle after redblooded Stella but Santa was nimble, Santa's matching eyes and nose (OK, fairly matching, salmon and salami) were on the job, spotting and sniffing. Poor Eddie was prey. Out of the sled slid Santa, Red Ridinghood in the true tale, the suppressed tale – the wolf *did* eat the girl, then he dressed in her clothes and lived happily e.a. – out of the sled he slides and has his red felt arm and redhaired hand round Cowering Eddie quick as a flasher.

Have you seen Santa's finger nails? They're ever so long, two are Capstanned brown as well as long, they're all of them thick and ridged and sharp enough to scrape your skin. Bad nails, bad man – and what's that he thrusts into Eddie's hands. That's a cricket bat. The handle's rubber is red.

'What does that remind you of?' asks Santa, nail toying inside the rubber, distending it to make a foul proboscis, 'what's that then my little fellow?' Kneeling he is, breathing grown-up breath that's scented for the occasion, breathing Empire Oloroso and Bristol shag out of his insides, through his holey molars, his plate, his unsteradentures, his thick split lips, through what he, the actor, calls his instrument (he was an ENSA Clarence once (p. 33)), then through his mask that's fluffy white (save for where it's been Capstanned), through the mask that's trade-mark and failure mark.

'My little matey's going to play a leg stroke,' proclaims he, actorishly acting – he's no lithping thethp, he's a bellowing man's man, a wolf fit for a boy. Poor Eddie can't stand his smell. Poor Eddie drops the bat and tries to wriggle from the Klaus-clasp.

'Let the side down eh would you little man, would you, surrender your wicket, would you?'

And while his foul mouth utters the gross pieties of team spirit his endless hands obey the stage direction to clutch the boy and to catch the bat before it strikes the greengrocer's grass on the floor. The store's P.A. obeys its direction to direct a frantic mother to her bleeting child. Eddie wants his. Our Santa actor pushes the rude red rubber past the cuff of the Poor Boy's shorts. Poor Eddie's worry is for his snake-belt (rubberised canvas, blue and white stripe, serpentine clasp); that's his fresh present, the pre-Christmas gift that he's so proud of. The teeth attached to Santa's hand climb beside the hard red rubber. What greedy seeking teeth they are! Crocodile teeth, big fish's teeth. They wanted their element. Frightened Eddie gave it them. He gave them water, he made it for them, expressed his fear, warmly wet his leg and those big fishes' teeth so they turned back into fingers, fugitive fingers.

Santa wipes his hand and mocks Eddie, he asks the cowering, damp-flannelled captive: 'Are you a boy or a baby little man . . . Come on, boy or baby?' This is the point at which the potential for a graver offence is revealed. Poor Eddie is no longer Santa's friend, no longer passive prey – he has a new contract with Santa now. That was the closest Eddie ever came to death. That was the one time (previous to the other time) when he brushed up against it, heard it, saw it in the red eyes. Stella thought something funny had been going on, she thought to herself – she was, she often boasted, Ray Butt's number one fan – she thought to herself: 'Sniff, sniff, there's something fishy round here. Is that fish I can sniff?' Panting Eddie's new contract with Santa concerned his windpipe; Santa's purpose-built nails stroke and fondle the boy's soft neck. Eddie shuts his eyes and sees that they are red too.

'You're such a baby – what naughties have you been up to?

You've been up to naughties haven't you? That's why you're still a baby, that's why you haven't grown up.'

Then, in the red dark, in the bloody blindness of his covert eyespace Poor Eddie hears saviour Stella: 'Wass goan on then?' The hands dash from his neck. He opens his eyes; he clings to Stella; all the baubles wink the message of Christmas good; happy dolls smile.

Santa booms: 'The old chap got so excited he excused himself on me sleeve. It might – ' and here he reached to ruffle the escapee's hair ' – it might be a spot of kidney trouble.'

Lucky Eddie, the escapee. That Xmas, 1953, there were reported in England and Wales sixteen cases of in-store child assault by Father Christmas. (In Scotland such assaults are traditionally undifferentiated from other seasonal crimes of violence.) And Lucky Santa too: Stella didn't tell, dared not tell lest she reveal her abandonment of the boy. Eddie was luckier (was he?) than Jean-Marie whose first English song went:

'Hey Little Boy, d'you wanna make bargain
Come for a ride in my Volkswagen
I am forty six and you are only eight
But you could make a really special date
I am forty six and you are maybe ten
But I'm the kind of man that likes you kind of men.'

His previous composition, his last in his native, non-paternal tongue had been his last in the commonplace idiom of his coevals. It was the one that began:

'Autrefois, sur cette belle plage, il y avait des palmiers
A l'aube d'enfer, sur cette belle plage, les Ricains sont venus,
La plage n'est plus,
Les palmiers sont des napalmiers.'

It was – it goes without saying – in his non-native, paternal tongue that he found his true voice, his peculiar subject – the killer he'd known and his life as that assassin's strumpet (pp. 325ff.).

Lucky Eddie. Eddie lucky? Not really, no, not at all. Eddie struggled with Bad Santa – not with that one in that store, but with the whole idea of the Man In Red. He struggled within. He knew that Christ had been born in the old days when they wore funny clothes, when they all wore bedclothes. He knew too – but could not articulate it thus – that Christ was the product of the troilist union of Mary, God and Joseph (poor sod, poor chippy, cuckolded from above (p. 316)). He didn't know about gestation's protractedness, he didn't even know about his own's super-protractedness. He assumed that God had first shown up when Christ was born, at Christmas in that sartorially strange age. He mistook God the Father – it's easy to do – for Father Christmas (what a name, what tablets of paternal blame are built into it). 'God' – we are all apprised of this now, we have all read Baptist and Buttist posters – 'is a Good Guy.'

When I was young, and Eddie too, He was no friend; the old order reigned. God was Not Good. God was frightening, fearsome, maniacal; He wore brown bedclothes and a beard. His annual disguise as Father Christmas was chromatic, nothing more. He wore the same dress in another colour, slapped chalk on His beard, made no further concessions. God's wrath, His wrath, was seasonally manifest in the attacks He made on wicked children. Stella told Eddie, Wide-eared, Harrowed Eddie, that:

A little boy at a parish hall Christmas party thought he recognised Santa/God as the local policeman who had arrested his father. PC/Santa/God had taken his father away to a place with more bricks than anyone could count. The little boy punched God in His lap. God retaliated with a truncheon.

That made Inquisitive Eddie wonder about God's lap. He wondered aloud to Stella. He told her about Santa/God in ——'s store in So'ton. He told her how he'd seen the pouty lady from Make-Up go into Santa's den even though there was a tasselled rope across the entrance hung with a 'Closed' sign. When The Grieving Widow went to the toilet, instructing him on no account to move, Inquisitive Eddie gingered into the den. Santa, The Wrath-God, roared and threw a woolly lamb (of God) at the boy, He threw it over the bent back of the kneeling lady who must have wanted to go to the toilet too (skirt round waist) but had taken the wrong turning and was crying in Santa/God's lap because she was lost. Stella giggled, 'Ooh croipes, almos' forgot – the pork butcher's.'

Poor Eddie. He could have done with God on his side. Even as just a sub, sprinting on in the last five minutes. (Actually He'd be *super*sub, well useful.) But because God – whose nickname, Old Nick-name, is Luck – had been disobeyed and betrayed by Hapless Eddie, He was not there, not when He was needed. Eddie hadn't paid the premium so Eddie didn't get the cover – that's what it comes down to. The Man From Heaven was elsewhere in Pompey that night (p. 472).

He was foreseeing all. He had begun foreseeing it Only He Knows How Long Before. The North Sea crude – the refinery at Grangemouth – the sludge – the tanker to Humberside (yes, He was the one who put the *cunt* in Scunthorpe) – the adhesive – the carry-out bag factory (where the adhesive meets the trees) – the nationwide distribution service – the dodgy lorry drivers (hardshoulder rapists) – the wholesaler at Fratton – the take-away order of two mutton vindaloos, one Madras chicken, four nans, three Basmatis, eighteen popadums, one Bombay duck – the collapsing sagging bag (bad glue? iffy wood? toxic meat juices?) – the seepage of spiced and steaming abattoir gravy from the bag resting on the front nearside seat of Escort 2000 RSL reg JTM 147J onto the grey suedette of the seat itself – that vehicle's emergency stop – the somnambulistic six-year-old who has wandered in Snoopy pyjamas to the middle of the Fratton road sixty yards from where, oathing, God-cursing, 120 mph Derrick has got out to wipe the dog food from his pride and joy's deluxe interior. Who knows at which stage God intervened? All we can be sure of is that the little boy (recovered by his Godthanking mum) was a believer. And Eddie wasn't.

He never even considered the possibility that He was the source of the Gift. When Chubb asked him he said no, with no ado. When Chubb repeats the question he shrugs at Chubb. He shrugs and says 'Butt' even though he knows that isn't so, even though he knows Chubb knows this isn't so – the Gift predates his first meeting with Butt by a decade (p. 361). And he can't, surely, have believed that Butt visited him with it, the culpable and repenting Butt whom he had heard of but who didn't reciprocate, who was unaware of his existence in the same patch of planet? This, believe it or not, is just what Credulous Eddie might have believed, had he *bothered* to believe. But believing (anything) is not merely the opposite of not-believing. Belief is built on thought, inquiry, tension, research. As Eddie grew so he grew idler. His cerebral couth flew. He was ignorant of his Gift's source – of course he was. We, none of us, know anything of our faculties' provenances; we have no one to ask, there's no one with the answer. Me? I can try, I have already, I shall again. But wait . . . Later. Listen: it wasn't simply that the question of *where-It-came-from* was unanswerable, unanswered. It was that Eddie wasn't interested, he was incurious about its source. And about its nature, its potential for good, its application: that is, its application to any end other than that of bashful self-advertisement. *There* was the witting end to which he directed his unwilled Gift – he demeaned it, reduced it to a trick, a turn; he made himself a virtuoso without virtue. He built himself a neon halo, pimped off his hump, lent his burden gaudy wings. He sailed in a ketch of clay.

The Gift was the one thing which, in his own estimate, made him special: it was not the fact of having witnessed his father's death, nor – more or less – his mother's (p. 219). Those may have singled him out, but not the way his hands did. It was his hands that made him special to himself. He had heat in his hands. No one else had such heat. His fingers spoke to truant muscles, recidivist nerves; they yelled through body-walls to organs on the blink, to iffy kidneys, lifeless livers, bilious spleens, to gall bladders pursuing industrial inaction. They admonished cancers, they banished migraines, they colour-corrected corpuscles, they made hearts fast again. They were magical – whitely, blankly, magical. I felt them, I thanked him, he shrugged – there wasn't an audience, save this audience of one who doubled as patient and was thus, to Manual Eddie, no audience at all. He yearned for a throng, for its approbation and clap (he could heal that too – well, help NSU on its way, apparently). Later, much later, he needed that throng. It became the sine qua non of his turn: no audience no Gift.

He so wanted to be liked.

'Do you like me?' he'd ask, imploring the affirmative.

'Do you like me?' he'd whine, *did* whine (hourly) when our mothers took us to Ruan Sands in August. Which August? The August of the summer when Hydrophobic Eddie flinched at the vertical breakers and scrolly rollers – they were tympanic majuscules rising above the lower-case plane of the silent briny. The August of the summer when the Tests were versus the South African team of Cheetham, McGlew (Danny/Jacky), Hugh 'Tapfoot' Tayfield. We ran down sandy rabbit-runs between crewcut tufts of greygreen dune grass, we ducked past tamarisks, we hared after the stronger, sprintier Saxon-Smith twins who were with us at the pointy white house (behind us, up there, Atlantic-pink at dusk). Grace Saxon-Smith had sewed full-volume shorts for her boys, aggrandised them, trousered them outside the khaki norm: emerald for Nigel, royal blue for Giles, the elder by eighteen minutes. Nigel aped Tayfield, he thrice tapped his plimsole on the sand (a colour called *bedge* according to Eddie) and bowled over the rotting beer crate of a wicket that our Poor Batsman gawkily defended. Giles took a run-up twice the length of our stride-measured pitch and flung the tennis ball at Eddie's head.

'Don't you like me?' he asked as, red templed, he picked the ball from the sand where it had stuck after it had struck (good aim Giles!).

'Spaz,' jeered Nigel, wicketkeeping (in pads), then addressed the same word – an observation now, not a taunt – to me, at first slip. The other fielders, the ones in non-glamour positions that involved retrieval from dunes or wet sand, were batless urchins we'd met on the beach. They were poorer, by far, than Poor Eddie. Them, they never even got to bat. Poor Eddie's wretchedness was – in that regard – relative. Nigel and Giles saw to that. They protected him from the batless council-house boys with drizzle-thick Bristol accents and subfusc hand-me-downs. They protected him because he was *their* punchbag, their whipping boy, theirs alone. They bought him ice-creams (smaller cones than theirs, but ice-cream none the less); they made sure he got turns on the dodgems at the little fair; they let him paddle their inflatable on rough days. Eddie's poor wretchedness was relative. Compare it to that which they were to suffer.

Dad's prick on her molar
Told a tale on him
Dad's prick on her molar . . .

That was as far as the choric amendment of Connie Francis's big hit went – but that was far enough to wound. I heard it before I reached the corridor where we lined up for tea (marge and aereated bread bricks). The corridor was bedge, gloomy, un-daylit. Its ceiling was rogered by pipes and bolts. The pipes were lagged like trenchwar limbs, they shook like invalid shanks, they were dropsical with water. That was where I first saw Nigel and Giles Saxon-Smith cower. Cowering became their necessary forte. For as long as they remained at that school they cowered. That is, until after their father's County Court trial when Grace Saxon-Smith sold The Garth and they moved, did a shame-flit; she shed the Saxon barrel (it must have been a wrench to lose it), she took her Smith sons far away to start anew, we never heard from them again. All that term they cowered. When I turned into the corridor they were cowering and the crocodile queuing for tea was singing those lines (author: Anon) with the easy malice we're born to and which school is meant to rid us of. The school wasn't doing its work, schools don't.

'Your pa gave her the sort of filling she didn't want.'

And the grey-jumpered, grey-flannelled crocodile grinned. Its teeth shine with the power of the pack, its incisors and malign canines are hatefully gleaming in the gloom. R. Lawrence Saxon-Smith, L.D.S., R.C.S. (Eng), C.P.S. had tended these teeth, these second teeth, he had viced them with alloy braces that made mouths radiators, he had drilled them, filled them, scraped them (the repeated 'tartar sauce' joke). His maggot-white hands were freckled the way toilet bowls are diarrhoea'd; he prodded with them, we knew them too well, we scrutinised their pores and the gravel brown hairs that enbrossed from them to make nests on his knuckles. These hands had hurt us, they had gassed us. They had mined roots in tender jaws. Me, I'd smelt death and smouldering bone in the charnel house of my mouth. His silver drill had mined the fibrils of every tooth it had touched. He was a duff anaesthetist, prone to undercooking (that's why the girl woke). He must have learnt to extract at the same school as Old Ma Cropper. Never trust a dentist who collects (and laughs at) ancient dental cartoons, who longs for the age of tongs and brandy. He was a buccal bully (and much more too). Splinters of dentine and enamel in young gums? Amalgam tamped into still carious cavities? He could do both, with torpid aplomb. Dentistry deals in thousandths of inches, he was fit to work in feet – at least. He ruffled our hair as we bled and wept. When Poor Eddie was gassed he dreamed of a pike sloughing its skin and sliding towards him across sodden grass, luminous flesh led by ranks of needle teeth. R. Lawrence Saxon-Smith was a moustached myope with Dimple lenses and a mouth like a vat. Oh, we all wanted revenge, and if we didn't know it our teeth did; our brief molar memories were bitter.

The twins were picked on, and on; they were often off sick; they reverted to the exclusive idiolect of their infancy (which was not merely a private, parallel vocabulary. It was, rather, a system of sensory and volitional expressions occasioned by their specific patterns of play, by the topography of The Garth's great garden, by their observations of their parents and everchanging nannies). Their whole infantile world was contained in a gamut of shrieks, grunts, cowshed noises. The idea that 'we should not crawl beneath the laburnums because they are poisonous at this time of year' was rendered in a bi-syllable, and the qualification that 'we will get into trouble' by a further hiss. Their re-adoption at the age of twelve of this idiolect, which they thought they had forgotten, is characteristic of the 'trauma-led' regressions cited in George Leigh's *Jumellingo: The Covert Codes of Yoked Yolks* whose premise is that twins communicate *in utero*, and that private languages are post-natal transformations, extensions of those rude chats, that any return to the idiolect of early childhood is a sign of 'a yearning for foetal recovery, a form of amniotic nostalgia, a desire for a soft and double suicide'.

They held hands. Iremonger cuffed them. They were picked on. They suffered toothaches. Arse and Pits are said to have forced Giles to push his glans into a bottle of indelible Quink (Blue Black for the bigger bruise). Arse and Pits 'are said to . . .' They *did*. I was there, keeping *cave*, keeping my distance. What distance? How do you measure pusillanimous collaboration?

How do you forget the glans that creeps from its prepuce like a terrapin's head from its carapace? You don't. I haven't. I'll never forget the collar of the bottle neck closing over the bonsai cyclops. He shook with sobs.

The attacks the twins suffer: these are also internal. The genes that they were loaded with by their father respond to their father's fate. Nigel began to rasp with asthma. Asthma's attack was internal and invisible, novel. It was the work of a pulmonary quisling. He didn't know how to fight back. He knew how to fight back in defence of his father's name (which his father had made up), in defence of the name he would not much longer bear, which he'd never pass on to a son. (How could he make a son after what his father had done to his sons?) He'd fought back and had grazes to show for it, and cinders deep in his thumb-balls, coalface grey. One or other eye was ever bright as a bird, blue and jet and mustard: children whose parents hate them often have such eyes, darlings. Asthma's a prowler. It stealths in, then it groans. That's the first you know: you hear it before you feel it. It announces itself then it gets to work viceing bronchioles. This prowler practises ventriloquy. It squats in your chest, makes bad music with the pipes in there. It uses your body to a frivolous end, abuses it – no respect; it doesn't give a toss about your body's purpose in life. Your well of breath is its playground.

Eddie's arm was balm. His face was enraptured, he loved you as he rubbed you with his left palm, as he pressed your hairless chest, hand-heated it, thermally banished the prowler, saw him off without a tiff. He loved you Nigel – wherever you are, Nigel Smith – he loved you with his hands as you lay on the mock battlefield of Twose's floor, gasping, fighting the prowler.

The inner organs of kine reminded Nigel of his father's crime (twenty-seven similar offences to be taken into consideration – oh, the mouths of the girls of the town). The organ meat and the victims' gums, the bleeding beef and their fat red lips – Nigel dared not admit their congruity to his mother who continued to have him run errands to Twose's where the reluctant butcher hung hanks from hooks, mounted medical secrets on marble slabs, brim-filled bowls with the eelish insides of cows, hid bone shrapnel in the sawdust, coloured that sawdust with blood, scented the air with warm death and fermented pasture, whispered names with furtive relish as though they signified the covert parts of humans not the cheap bits of animal. (The man linked meat with meat, you see what he did to Nigel. Twose, reluctant butcher and apiarist, was a virgin, also a vegetarian: vegetarians don't eat meat.) You see what he suggested to Nigel. His shop was a rare instance of retail irony. It flaunted its grossness, emphasised the meatness of beef (.o scale model bulls) and the beefiness of meat ('Beef!!' on signs, in Twose's hand); it connected pretty baa-lamb to scrap of scragend, pastoral scene to sawn limb; it yelled out about the creature on its feet becoming the creature that we eat, about the meta- morphosis wrought on brutes by humans – meat had feet once, it was not meat a day and a half ago.

Lucky for Nigel that Poor Eddie was there, beside The Grieving Widow, in the queue, waiting her turn, waiting to issue her order so sotto that its meagreness might go unnoticed. Nigel exhaled as though he was playing a game of trains. The queue stretched from the shop behind him. The old bags in it began to twitch. Eddie had an audience here, he had a quorum, he acted. Nigel crumpled, deflated, to the sawdust and bloody muslin and marrow grease. His fingers tic-tack like they belong to another organism. The old bags deary-me'd, retreated inside their dun headscarves, clacked their store-boughts, wondered about boys who turn into trains, raised their subfusc shopping bags like shields, tut-tutted when the boy kicks out. Poor Eddie acts. Purpose defines itself. Its end (the answer to *why?*) is on hold. His very alacrity, his sureness, prompts the old bags to gasp, to pop their eyes and drop their jaws and forget their defencelessness against the train who was a boy, who is swallowing, who is now a fish on the bank, who's getting sawdust when he wants air, who's fighting privately against an invisible antagonist.

All their curiosity, all their wonder, all the easy benefaction of their washing-line lives conduct themselves through Poor Eddie's hands. The bags want Eddie to win, to reveal his purpose. Poor Eddie: his gift is all he has to share (and that's why it's conditional on being witnessed). Oh, of course he won, he raised Nigel from the floor to the gasps and awe of the bags. And his Mama was so proud of him she moved her cig to the corner of her mouth and laid the rest of her mouth, her dry and sexless mouth that swallowed only smoke (for her brain) and cheap meatfeed (for her body), she laid it on his cheek while he held Nigel like a twin, like the brother he never had, the brother who flees, meatless, from the shop past the bags, past my ken, out of frame. He was here to demonstrate the indiscriminacy with which Eddie would apply his gift – forget him unless you've met him, unless you've married Nigel Smith.

No one ever married Eddie, Poor Eddie always wanted a girl. He wanted a girl like Bonny – no, not *like* Bonny, but Bonny herself, the sweet meat eater, his darling cousin, the girl he'd die for, he'd go as far as that for her, he really would, he loved her, he doted on her (always had), he dreamed of marrying her and saw the swan-white dress, the garland, the rapturous smile like the sun that shone for him only (p. 290).

He thought of Bonny. We thought of the bad girls, the girls who peeled their clothes for us, whose tiny monochrome shadows illumined the adhesive pages of *Fast, Hussy, Popsy Hots*. He closed his eyes and thought of Bonny; we were stared back at by the insolent eyes of the bad girls. That was the difference. We kneel in a ring, Eddie, me, Toddy, Arse, Pits. What Noyce calls our 'books' are in front of us on the thick sheaves of meadow grass that won't be flattened, that seek tumescence, that stand vertical *as though bidden by the strumpet breeze*,[1] that regain their natural posture, that now turn the page from Jaqui ('enjoys riding', wears a rubberised mac and stilettos like spurs, carries a crop) to Martine ('she's a beach-girl', and to prove it she covers her cunt with a segmentally coloured beach-ball whose swollen valve protrudes proud of the plastic). And now the bolshie grass shuts the book, the books, and we hastily break their feeble spines, flatten the wort, lose impetus. In the centre of the ring there lies the biscuit, a circle of cooked meal, a digestive – four times the size of Lorna's face and wrongly

[1] © Jean-Marie Meyer-Decker 1969. This line, which I've used with no regard for its original context, is from 'My Mind and That Hedge'.

named. It's dry as can be given the dampness of the grass near Navigation Straight: these meadows are not called water-meadows for nothing. If you walk down Britford Lane you'll get here, you'll even find the place where Pits was kneeling when he reached for the biscuit and held it to his lap, if you walk down Britford Lane to Navigation Straight . . . Water, ducks, willows, boys. The immemorial rites of boys: there are blood rites (p. 142), there are these rites which are seed rites, late summer spore. This is an immemorial rite of boys, unlearned, not passed down by example but genetically inscribed. Our fathers did this, our furthest forbears did this too but must have used unleavened bread because they lived in the pre-biscuit age, there was no one in Reading then to bake and pack the abusable sweetmeat, there was no Reading, just this urge of competitive intimacy, this show of – so we would later learn – the wrong prowess. Pits was first, as usual; he whooped in triumphant relief as he held the biscuit to his glans and watched the drops of ejaculate ice the mealy surface. Then he put the biscuit back in the centre of the circle and lay prone whilst we continued to masturbate, continued to will relief, continued to concentrate on the bad girls' meaty lips and engineered corsetry. Our cocks were raw, red and sore that summer. That was the price of Poor Eddie's humiliation. Poor Eddie – he always lost, he always came last, he always took the biscuit last, he always had to eat it. With Eddie participating one didn't have to hurry; indeed when I felt the first fire of urethral heat I slowed down, enjoyed it, toyed with Brenda, teased her rotten, didn't give her what I knew she wanted, toyed so long that Toddy and Arse finished before me. So when I loaded the biscuit there were already 30 c.c. of sperm on it.

'Soggy biscuit soggy biscuit soggy biscuit Vallender!' Poor Eddie was frotting dourly, eyes half shut, summoning Bonny, summoning her scent of fresh bread and gentle spice (mace, cinnamon). Bad girls smelled of fish, empty fishcans, Shippams fish paste, we *knew* that – we had heard that, we had heard of hunting the anchovy and were prepared to suffer the smell when the time came.

'Eat it!' I'll bet that when you played soggy biscuit the one who lost and had to eat the biscuit tried to get away. Not Eddie; he spoiled it for us by not minding, he was resigned to this mouthful of seedcake, this open sandwich of wasted future planning and aborted genetic programmes. The varying viscosities and densities of adolescent semen; the comparative absorptive properties of Huntley and Palmers, of Jacobs, of Crawfords, McVities, Peek Freans; the peppery, yeasty flavour; the textural disparity of biscuit and topping – Poor Eddie was expert, (apparently) willingly expert, in the endgame of soggy biscuit.

Toddy, wiping his shrivelled cock on a rag from his saddlebag, says: 'I think you're probably a queer Vallender. Round-heads twice as likely to become queers as cavaliers, they say – they are. One for four and four for one – the foreskin cavaliers.'

Chorus: 'One for four and four for one – the foreskin cavaliers.'

Poor Eddie was trying to swallow, having oyster trouble.

Toddy hurled his copy of *Slit* at a tansy clump. 'Damn sluts,' he says. 'Munch munch munch. Haven't you finished yet Vallender. You *like* it don' you.'

Takes tranny from saddlebag, tries to tune into Lux. Snatch of crackle. French cover of 'Runaround Sue' – 'Volage' by Les Chaussettes Noires. Dance band. Dutch. Eddie isn't choking, no. Fluting ululation. A shriek near Hilversum. Pips, time pips. We can all remember where we were when we heard that Dag Hammarskjold had died. We can all remember the smell of Nelsons in tens, the fuel tank stench of scrumpy, the reek of silage, the mustiness of fungal early autumn. We can all remember the seedy drowsiness of teenage summers coming to their end. Water, ducks, willows, boys stretched in the meadow grass failing to form smoke rings, watching the disobedient smoke trail into the thin haze. Regret tempers lazy bliss – the end of another holidays, all that: the swapping of jeans (I wore a pale green, stain-free pair that year) for school flannels, etcetera.

Reception was clean: 'It has been confirmed that Mr Dag Hammarskjold, Secretary General of the United Nations, died early today when the aeroplane on which he was a passenger crashed just prior to landing at Ndola in Northern Rhodesia . . .'

Toddy said: 'My pa says he's a queer.'

'*Was*,' said Pits, quick as a brief, 'was a queer. He isn't queer any longer.'

'You don't stop being queer because you're dead,' said Toddy. 'He's a dead queer.'

'He was a good man,' Eddie speaks, again.

'So effing pi you are Vallender,' says Toddy. 'He might have been good but he was a good queer.'

'Good Swedish queer,' says Pits.

So it went, something like that. There was no sudden chill in the meadow, the organism might be extinct, but the name wasn't, isn't; the ducks, the willows, the boys who are now men if they're not dead, the announcer's voice, the voice that tells us:

'The comedian Ray Butt – Butt Of The Joke – is this afternoon fighting for his life in a Pompey hospital after a motor accident which claimed the life of his wife Heidi. Butt's Allard Palm Beach was involved in a head-on collision with a Foden lorry on the A27 at Titchfield, Hampshire as he was returning to his home in Littlehampton after the conclusion of his sell-out summer season in Bournemouth. Butt's sons – The Three Little Surprises, Jonjon, Sonny and Laddy – are being cared for by their grandmother May Butt at her home on Hayling Island. We wish them all the very best. Now here's Bobby Dee – no, that's Bobby Vee, but there's not much difference between Vee and Dee is there, hurjchhurjch . . .' You must have heard Butt's one about Titch Field and Little Hampton.

I doubt that Poor Eddie had heard it: when The Grieving Widow's Ekco valve set (the bakelite one her husband left her) went on the blink in the winter of 59/60 she couldn't afford to have it repaired and when it went mute in the early spring there was certainly no money to replace it. She was out of work again. She was behind with the rent, the gas, the grocery bill – Arms demanded cash now, didn't deliver now. Eddie's trousers didn't reach his ankles. The front door was bare of paint and pervious to the seasons; when there was rain it swelled to fill the jamb and couldn't be opened. She coughed, she smoked, she scratched her scalp, she couldn't get another job. Before she was thirty she looked fifty. She lost her looks ('and didn't know where to find them' – Douglas). She was cold the whole year round. She shivered, she coughed, she smoked, she scratched her scalp so it bled, so her tonsure grew as big and round as a jamjar's lid and could not be hidden by her hair: those were among the reasons she could not get another job.

Here are some of the jobs she did have: companion to the Misses Turnbull (one drunk, the other daft) – sacked by their niece who feared for her inheritance; deputy assistant matron at La Retraite Convent – sacked for persistent lateness; counter assistant at Miss Wanda's Wool – lease expired, became The Two Bare Feet coffee bar; teacher of geography and scripture at Mrs Bundy's Pre-preparatory School – left as a result of 'Major' Bundy's importunity; showroom receptionist at Scutt's (Agricultural) Ltd. – asked to leave following complaints from the Massey-Ferguson rep; secretary to the Land Agent, Southern Command – the bus service was discontinued, disenabling her from getting to work by 0815 hours; office assistant to the Diocesan Registrar – was discovered not to be a communicant member of the Church of England; visitor's guide at Wilton Royal Carpet factory – invisible particulates caused eczema and asthma; part-time area organiser for the League of Pity, a children's charity which dispensed collecting boxes and enamel bluebirds – unpaid, and her son ought surely to have been the *recipient* of charity, of pity at least; secretarial assistant to the Cathedral School bursar – his baldness worried her. There is no viciousness like the viciousness of the genteel.

There was only so much she could take. Her hair went grey. Her skin went grey. Her hair went orange from fags. Her skin went whiter from them. She thought of her husband. She made him an idol, made him an example to her son. She sits down, she feels his hands round her breasts. She lies in bed at night and his tongue worries her. He never went away (who's that hawking in the hall?). Crocodile or no crocodile, he is ever with her – so far. Memory is ink, it fades. Support it with photos, with Guy in Aertex, with Guy beside the car, with Guy clutching Eddie like a ball – death happens to the beloveds too. Suffer? They grieve. The Grieving Widow. The knock on the door, the shadow on the convent wall; that silhouette – New Bridge in July; the man on the end of the platform who incites the arrival of the eight fifty-four to So'ton and Pompey by glaring at his wrist. She felt him, she saw him, she conjured him – she met her want: every now and again he walked down Britford Lane beyond the tattered curtain, beyond the porch and path and the wretched garden hedge. And she runs through the porch, she scurries down the path, she wrestles the gate in the wretched garden hedge, she doesn't worry about the puddle. There's no one except Mr Sweet drudging to and fro the allotments beside Navigation Straight, and there's the Barratt boy – my, how he's grown! If she stands beside the wicket gate in the wretched hedge down Britford Lane she sees the living, she sees her boy pushing his bike back to her veinous arms, to her secure self. Doormat to the world, she was his hearth, the home of his heart. She was a woman without vision, without the capacity for seeing past the next bill. She'd never borrow, debt was the greatest disgrace, the kind of thing she cared about. She needed the small pride of paying her way; she needed the prison of circumstance although it bowed her. To have escaped the trap she'd have had to make herself a different woman, not Guy's wife, not Poor Eddie's mother, but a different woman, she'd have had to shed her widowhood and that would have been a sort of divorce, a different disgrace, like tuberculosis, a living hell, a treble betrayal (of herself, and of the dead husband and the damaged boy she pathetically dignified as 'the family', 'our family', 'our little family').

Verdict: death by misadventure. How could the Coroner, Q. M. Sexton (G. Leopold Lush's predecessor), have found otherwise? That death by water was a family habit, getting on for a tradition, was neither here nor there; inadmissible coincidence, no more or less; Sexton had presided over the inquest into her mother's death (p. 71); he knew what had happened to her husband. But it's not evidence is it? The law represents a reality that is as straitened, as conventionalised as that of 'realism'. Sexton knew that. You know that don't you Quinton? Facts: sometime that afternoon she admitted to herself that her grief had maddened her . . . No, that won't do, will it? Nor will this: she resolves, staring into the mirror at the face she's appalled to own, to make her boy an orphan. That's not evidence. Moreover it's wrong. She didn't even think of him, of his future that she wouldn't witness.

Had she thought of him – of the being she had born and milk-fed, had carried to the Congo (her one journey abroad), had slaved for, gone grey for – had she thought of him she wouldn't have. Would she? Would she?

She saw a face in Eddie's face, in its new pubescent contours; she saw her father in his face, discerned a shadow in the boy's glabella (it was something to do with the eyebrows failing to follow the escarpment of his forehead), she worried about the generational leap of those cheekbones. She must have wondered what else she had transmitted. He was not like Guy – oh where are you darling, let's meet soon – was not like his father, was hatefully facially akin to hers (let's not meet). Would she have been this way, this grey, had Guy not . . . Ask the men who are griffed up on cell structure, know it like the backs of their lab hands. Ask the pigment gurus, the genetic cartographers. Suicide goes in families too, but we can't *prove* it – inadmissable. It's a quasi-fact. Inherited disposition? Maybe. More likely the begetter's act gives licence to the offspring, sanctions it as an OK refuge, sanitises the dirty hermitage. It's an example, a standard set – that's the inheritance. Would Eddie? Will Eddie? Wait! Don't turn – read, wait, see. Don't turn to the bottom of the right-hand pile. Don't cheat yourself. That's what suicides do: cheat themselves, ape fate, usurp God. You can take self-determination too far . . . Suicide is beyond the limit, it breaks the great rule, ruptures the contract we have with everything that isn't ourselves, with otherness. It denies the opportunity to the animal fats in our arteries, to the tar in our bronchioles, to the falling stone, to the dead drunk's car. It's not a sin of despair, it's a sin of presumption. So, since she presumed so little, since she was double humble, can *we* not then presume that she didn't do it, that it *was* an accident?

Me, I'd say that she got presumptuous just the one time, the time it mattered, some time about 5 pm on that deathly Sunday all those years ago. She is feeding on a cigarette and she doesn't close the wicket gate behind her when she leaves the bungalow behind her to walk down Britford Lane. Mr Sweet with his barrowful of horse manure (we put custard on ours); the Barratt boy; a nipper crouching to count paper-round money behind the cricket hut and creaking with autumnal asthma – they all saw her, even the wretched hedges have eyes down Britford Lane. The nipper recognised her, he'd seen her disputing twopence on a bill at Arms's and had admired that. She was smoking a cigarette, he remembered, and she held her elbows to her ribs as though there was a wind (there wasn't). Q. M. Sexton praised his observational acuity. He was the last person to see her as a living being. No one knows how fast Navigation Straight flows. No one knows if she could swim. There's a photo of her in a swimsuit in one of my mother's albums: 1956, Hengistbury Head, a demure one-piece, demurer than Guy would have liked; but by then she'd been a widow longer than she'd been a wife, her grief obviated display. Eddie is behind her, the belly he once swam in is shrouded with pleats, folds, tucks. No one saw her swim in this wittingly disfiguring garment. Of course she could have slipped – the poplars that line Navigation Straight's north end render the banks dark, dank, moist; the accretion of leaves is shiny, like brown ice, like pre-Euclidian parquet elbow-greased for mirror gloss. The creepily straight cut is sunless. Of course she could have leaned too far. Vertigo's most potent agent is depth, incalculable depth; the water's high-polish veneer hides its interior, gives no hint of its extent; you have to lean too far to see how deep down it goes, you have to stretch, you have to test your balance; water plays havoc with the middle ear.

Must it be Poor Eddie who finds her? It must. It *was*. He took the shortcut, wheeled his bike along the bank, kept it between him and the water. Poor Eddie – pity him, for he was not surprised; and without surprise there is no shock, no grief. He saw the luminous tonsure floating towards him. Only he could have recognised it from such a distance. (His mother's baldness was a mute secret they shared.) He saw it coming, a white saucer in that dark avenue. She still had a fag end in her mouth. That was how he remembered where he was the day he heard Dag Hammarskjold had died – he saw his mother's leaf-print dress stretched about her belly; he saw the unsalvageable, un-dimpable cigarette unravelling to flotsam a moustache above her newly blue lip. He must have known that he'd see her floating towards him, her pate gaping to greet him; he must have known, he'd never taken that shortcut before – too scared of the water where his mother now floated like a broken vessel, a riverlogged capsize shrouded by its soaked sail.

I think that recognition was immediate: he'd have known that headlight anywhere, even in the (obviously) unprecedented setting of a wet tunnel whose sylvan walls were reaching to whisper to each other. Eddie had continued to spit, to try and expel the wooden spoon. All the way from where we'd left him he'd spat. He worried about shame, about being found out – now there was no one to find him out. He must have been relieved. What he saw floating towards him was his release. He leans his bicycle against a tree trunk crabbed with creeper's vines. He dips his hand in the water first – 48° Fahrenheit. Then he folded his clothes.

The freshly minted orphan moves in with Douglas Vallender's family. Douglas calls him 'Our Barnado Boy, Our Burden Boy'. They take him in. The Unfortunate. 'Didn't know when to put the seat down.' (That's Douglas: irrepressible!)

The Lodger. There was a floor between Poor Eddie Vallender and The Proper Vallenders. Some of it wasn't carpeted. Some of the rooms were locked. Eddie's bedroom was in the attic storey.

The girl whose blood, whose rare blood, whose special blood he licked from a finger wound (p. 241), whose tidal blood he could smell across the dining room, whose pants he stole and stored in a tartan duffel bag (McGuinness plaid, in remembrance of p. 7), whose diary he read daily, the rhythm of whose breath in sleep he peeped on by the light of the moon and the stairs – this girl, this cousin Bonny was stored two floors down from him. He doesn't bother about his own breath. Snug, snug, tucked up under duck down, that's My Bonny, my bug in a rug. He does without his own breath whilst he stealths downstairs, now bare wood, now not. Bonny REMs and rolls, dreams with a pillow in her mouth, dreams already of galloping boys, bite bite the pillow's scalloped edge – the galloping boys are never Eddie, they're not at all like Orphan Eddie. With his scared animal stare. With his furtive scurries – does he believe he's invisible?

'Did he? You tell me, Johnson!' bellows dead (and invisible) Douglas Vallender. 'Comes into the room, *half* comes into it, takes a dekko, creeps off as though he reckons no one's seen him poking his effing head round the door. Whasis? Thinks we're what – blind or something?'

These voices. These voices – I can conjure my father's, can make it play again, can hear it echo down the years. Listen to him tell me: 'Guy was a bit of a chulaka, Jonathan, a loose wallah – and Eddie . . .'

And Eddie's a night spy. The Burden's a peeper. The Blood Relative knows how the moon rules the moods of the growing girl, and how (clouds allowing) moonlight seeps certain nights each month between the curtain and the sash. Those nights he closes the door behind him; closes his eyes tight; opens them, conditioned, onto the now qualified darkness of the room which, in sleep, she fills with warmth and murmurs. But when the moon's no more than a neon scythe he lights her with stairlight, leaves the door ajar, spreads a broad wedge of Osram onto the bed so sleepyhead stirs and wriggles, so the folds and creases resolve themselves into mouth, counterpane, blond hair, pillow, fist, teddy, nose. Eddie – invisible in nod, and unwanted there – strokes her hair, it streams across the pillow. He lays his hands gently on the bellows of her trunk, pro-phylactically no doubt. And he prays for her. He prays for the day when they will be married: wreaths of oak leaves, doves that make white scrolls against the trees, that fall and tumble in our honour Bonny (p. 290); we'll have a family, Bonny, we'll engender mewling security, an emotional bastion that wakes three times each night. Because Eddie was so different he wanted the most ordinary things for himself.

The watcher slips back to his hardly carpeted room where he'll conjure his cousin in his sleeplessness and sorrow, womb-curled in memory of better days, safer nights; he longs for the time when he's no longer the adoptee, the orphan in the attic where the window whistles when it admits the giraffe. Freezing Eddie soaked paper in water and wedged it in the cracks so that the room got to smell *like a rabid kennel* (Douglas). Douglas opened the window, told Eddie the room smelled like a *suppurating gorgonzola* and Eddie drew Bonny a blue-marbled gorgon with maggots for hair. When Eddie put plasticine in the cracks Douglas called him Bodger The Lodger, told him he'd die of asphyxiation, told him the room smelled like *old earwax, the marmlade coloured paste that comes out last*. Douglas opened the window, raging, throwing vermicules of dun plasticine (the bright spots are the unmixed primaries) at Poor Eddie. Yet:

a) Douglas always owns a dog, always calls it Postman – by the time Eddie goes to live/lodge at The Garth it is Postman III; the cynonominal continuity emphasises the generic dogginess of the dogs and mitigates their peculiarities; each Postman smells as bad as the others, permeates soft furnishings and clothes with its reek, moults generously, belches halitotic gusts of cow slurry, fouls the ground with fat wursts that grey with age, barks, bites (the bite is always worse); Douglas feeds them from his plate and they thank him by making him smell of them, it is Douglas that smells like a kennel; in Douglex *smell like a kennel* should be a term of approbation (*rabid* is redundant in this construction; that disease has no specific olfactory property).

b) The sort of cheese Douglas eats, but which Postman declines, *is* suppurating cheese – he calls gorgonzola 'gorgon' and demands that it be seething (look no further for the inspiration for Eddie's drawing); crust – should be iodine brown and should assault with the stench of ammonia; Stilton is second best and is accompanied by aperient 'digestive' biscuits and the story (inaccurate) of why it is so called (cf. his wrong etymology of 'sirloin', p. 23) – he doesn't know that Gorgonzola is an outer suburb of Milan.

c) When he is not heavy petting Postman I, II or III, and isn't filling his face with blue cheese from beyond the grave, Douglas is mining his ears – the bit may be a matchstick, a tight spiral of handkerchief, a spoon handle, a biro, a sprue stalk, a limb of his reading-glasses; whatever it is, he scrutinises the trove from his aural enema, sniffs it, rolls it on his thumb and forefinger, wipes it on his dog-haired jacket, feels more like a man, or manjack – which he considers a manlier form of man: this is a hypermale who doesn't like the look of Big Eddie's cock; rather, he resents its being appended to The Blubbing Orphan. You shouldn't have worried – at least not on *this* score, Douglas, we all fucked Bonny, all of us, save Eddie. The Burden never rode the bike.

Besides, your penile envy was not prompted by paternal concern – the Barnado's Boy and the Apple of Your Eye! Unimaginable – to everyone save Eddie. Your special sort of penile envy was prompted by paternal longing, paternal want. A son. Bonny asked for a brother. You wanted a son, son and heir – teach him to shoot like a real manjack. You mistook length for strength: the lack of spice in your trousersauce was not why there was no boy to hand, to hand the business on to. And you had a daughter. You believed you had a daughter; you had a daughter. If you ever questioned Bonny's provenance you never asked aloud – although my mother's benignly made observation that Bonny and Eddie were 'like brother and sister' prompted your fulminatory rage; but maybe that was simply because of your despisal of the boy, because of your indignation at my mother's linking them thus. Even had she suspected it she would not have inkled at Bonny's paternity that way. Mumless Eddie kept mum, of course: not because he knew how to keep a roof over his head; not because he had failed to make the equation between p. 120 and Bonny – though he almost certainly had (he was only three and a half years old on p. 120); not even because Douglas frightened him every day he was under that roof; nor because Monica is staring at him, almost squinting to glean what he remembers, as though tightening those gelatinous muscles may admit her to his interior album. He keeps mum because he is embittered by my mother's traduce-ment of his intended relationship to Bonny, his *de jure* cousin who will one day be his wife. She won't, but he hopes, how he hopes, and plans. He will do anything for her to make his dream come true, anything. Here is where this story starts.

I know more than I can tell about the firework maker's children, about their dress, coughs, bodies, schools, wants, hair, songs, trips, colds, faces, bodices, shoes, habits (bad), habits (good – few), skirts, toes (and verrucas between), allergies, gerontophilia, cars, guns, hobbies, sores, obsessions, digs, friends, accidents, loves, their loves.

It's not true that Eddie pimped for chestnut-bronze Bonny. She was an alluring girl, she was a goer, she was sexually precocious, erotically manipulative. She grew up overnight – she went to sleep in flanellette and woke in a babydoll; she sloughed childhood one vernal midnight; she came down to breakfast ready for the adventures of womanhood. Only Eddie could see this. Bonny Vallender was now just thirteen and a half years old. Poor Eddie, he longed for her. She was his heart's joy.

He was her beard. He put her on a plinth. She used him as a gofer. Princess. Flunky and punch bag, but not pimp, no – it was ugly of Douglas to use that word that ugly day.

Douglas picks up the phone in his study (wet suits and flippers, hunting prints and carnagescapes, stuffed animals and mounted fish); Eddie is on the kitchen extension, munching – 'D'you know what it cost to feed that orphan?' – as he talks.

The coarse, hoarse, just broken voice says: 'Wawas that?'

Masticating Eddie, deafened by nut-brittle from a Tupper box beside the cream and chrome Kenwood anteater, had not heard the click of another handpiece: rocks are tumbling to a eustachian moraine. 'What, what was what?'

'Noise. Look. Bring her over Rufus's tonight. Yeh?' Douglas has the earpiece to his ear and the mouthpiece to his eye, as though it's a sight: he's aiming at a mallard flatfooting up the lawn for a handout – as though one cuckoo wasn't enough.

Cuckoo Eddie: 'Come on Reds . . . *told* you . . .'

Reds: 'Softee.'

Douglas grins, finger on the trigger – there's a stretched spiral of chord between his thumb and his big finger: the coarse voice has got the Burden's measure, good on him whoever he is, chap's got spunk, which one was he? Douglas lived, and died, and is dead, in a confusion of adolescent faces, voices, names. They change their faces and their voices; OK, they're changed for them, programmed that way – the thin ginger infant turns into the buxom chestnut mare, understood; but they have about five names each, each month another name (if only they were like Postman). This month's Fats was last month's Dodders (probably). Douglas, who was always Douglas – except to Guy, a nominfactoral menace, but dead, doesn't he know it – Douglas, né Douglas, listens with growing glee as Reds (formerly Arse) sorts out Eddie, gives the Burden his desert. 'Spaz . . . wet . . . creep' etc.

'If,' says Eddie, Poor Eddie, Spaz Vallender – and Douglas is now aiming at a swan coasting left to right, downstream, on the khaki, rain-pocked Nadder at the bottom of The Garth's garden – 'if, Reds, you *really* want me to try and get her to come that's going to cost you.'

'Tosser,' said Reds, 'don't be such a haemorrhoid.'

Douglas nods in absolute accord and good as takes out the swan which disappears behind a clumb of reeds – he has asked Eddie to cut those reeds, but what do you expect?

Neither Eddie nor sharp-eared Reds hears the bungpull plosive as Douglas fires; Doug-A-Doug-Doug cannot resist popgun noises, big-arsed bullies never can – offer one the chance to utter an onomatopoeic grunt and he just gobbles it. Do they *all* belong to H.R.H. The Queen? Roast it? Braise it? Is it legal? Hang it? And for how long? Pheasant recipies? Duck ones? Cranberries? Bacon rolls? Apple and prune . . . The anticipatory apparatus of Douglas's palate is activated, his moist mouth catches up with his greedy brain, his overweight lips fondle each other. Liver dumplings?

And then his hand bangs down the phone as though he wants to hurt it. His heavy veldschoen dent the carpet. He rages through the parquet house, quarter-irons clacking.

What Eddie said was this: 'Look, we're not talking about Smeggy Beggy[1] – Bonny wants seventeen and six, OK? And – ' This is when the eavesdropper reveals himself. 'Oh Cripes,' said Eddie, knowing what was coming next, knowing what was coming through the kitchen door – hear its handle percuss the tiled wall.

'Pimp.' Douglas swells to fill the frame, red in nicotine tweeds: 'You disgusting little pimp.'

Cowering Eddie. Those clothes are weapons. They bristle. They can graze – a glance from that deafening arm is like being scratched by a sugar cube, by emery.

'You're a pimp, d'you hear.'

Eddie twists his mouth by the fitted units. Rain on the windows. Douglas advances among the hobs and blenders, animated by three years' resentment:

'Blasted pissing little orphan pimp.' Three years' resentment

---

[1] Nicola Begley, b. 7.1.50. E.: S. Wilts Girls Grammar and LSE (LLB, LLM). Lawyer and cause-whore: represented the Modenese bomber Giovanna Scalapi in her application against extradition from the UK; author of *The Forensic Lie* (1981) and *The Rights of Mammal* (1986).

of supporting the ingrate orphan (food, clothes, board, especially board – it adds up).

'There's a name for poncing pimps like you.' A lifetime's resentment of his dead brother, of his dead brother's line, of his dead brother's posthumous presence in the Burden – cut him and he'll bleed Guy's bad blood. He wants to cut.

'You little bastard.' Douglas has been waiting years to say that. He's rehearsed it because it means something: 'When you were started your parents weren't even spliced.'

The plates on the table he pushes with his loin are willow-patterned save where bacon grease occludes parts of that sad avian tale. The cutlery is likewise frosted. It chinks against the plates. Douglas, the pig, advances on Fretting Eddie, all teeth and nosehair, each nostril a separate anus, each one dilated in prefaecal aggression, each one tooled up with the wires of the chippie's fascinum (p. 408). The blue ghost of a bacon breakfast hangs like a reeking sloth to the ceiling and Douglas fills the rest of the room with wrath: crown to floor, sole to light-rose, arm to wall and back again. Swelling, hatred. Cutlery is for cutting with. Douglas sees that even the handles are testimony to the putative victim's filthy kitchen ways, his prodigality with Trex, his coarse smearing of ketchup, his cackhanded fidgeting. Even when he ate alone Eddie covered his back, wolfed lest his pig uncle should steal from his plate. It was Eddie's lifelong habit to eat like that – a burger inside his turned-up collar beside the dodgems' generator; a hot dog round the back where Sonny and Laddy wouldn't find him; a pack of Golden Wonder crushed hidden in an inside pocket; his back to the curtain of condensation on a grease-caff window with his plate jammed against the wall – like a dog. He'd eaten his last meal at The Garth, the pimp. Out – for ever.

Douglas didn't believe this: he didn't believe that his thirteen-and-a-half-year-old 'daughter' had told her 'cousin', the sixteen-year-old lodger, that she would only go to Rufus Turnbull's party on receipt of seventeen shillings and sixpence; if Nicky Begley was worth twelve bob . . . Brunette Bonny knew her price. Boys could keep their eyes open with her. All Eddie said was: 'That's what Bonny said to say.' Douglas didn't believe him. Trust Eddie to get the blame. We all fucked Bonny, all of us, save Eddie.

'You can fuck my bum. Or you can fuck my mouth. But I'm saving number one till when I get married.' This is what Bonny said. She said it so often she often said to those to whom she had said it before. *Number one*. Bonny's number one was all of our cynosure. A bull's full-browed conjunctival eye. But no – though she was a goer she was strict, she meant what she often said, there were anatomically fixed boundaries, limits to the sites of her abandon. So no one really tried, for that would have been to try her generosity. Later she added: 'Or you can fuck my tits.' Generous girl, and a happy one – she revelled in the gynolatry she received. She was (obviously) never in the club, she was no trouble in that regard, she was an exemplary pupil. She was touchingly proud of her hymeneal maidenhood; she believed in her intactness, she boasted about it. To everyone else Bonny was a great ad for sexual plenitude, chronic polygamy – and things hardly changed when she went straight, when she cleaned up her act, when she went against her nature, when she married Toddy: they were Bonny and Toddy behind their backs, Bonny and Toddy in holy monogamy, a specialised monogamy, adulterated, yes, but anything but loveless. There is love, there is love. Douglas loved her too – and that is why he expelled Poor Eddie, sent the orphan into the world of foundlings.

He hadn't had much of a childhood, he didn't get much of a youth; but each was a piece of cush besides his adulthood, those brief years when he worked with his hands. Eddie loved Bonny, he always did her bidding. She made him follow her mother; she wanted to know the name of her mother's lover; who's to say whether Monica's example encouraged Bonny? It excited her, it was useful to her. Bonny could smell it when her mother was going to meet him; she could smell the scent with her nose (an excess of Eglantier de L'Avenir); she could smell the clothes and slap and rushed preening with her eyes; she could smell the tension and the blustery bold mendacity, smell it with the small of her back. She sent Eddie after the nippy yellow drophead: by the time the boy had pedalled against the drifts of gravel to the end of The Garth's drive Monica and her car had disappeared;

he listened to the voices calling scores on the invisible tennis courts. It excited Bonny, the way her mother was lit by illicit love, the way it sharpened her face (the slap helped here, of course).

Oh, The Garth on a summer morning, late summer, late morning. The serpentine curl of the drive. The warm terracotta trunks of wellingtonias. Baubles of amber sap. Black shadows. Bee noise. Distant lawnmower. Drone. The wantonly, haphazardly, asymetrical house – roughcast, brick, half-timbers, candle-snuffer tower, bargeboards, gables, roofs and more roofs, another gable, and the windows, all those windows: circles and diamonds and sashes and mullions; oeil de boeuf dormers, arrowhead dormers; a bay of curved panes which are sections from the giant's poison bottle, a horizontally barred anachronism by Crittall (*c.* 1937); French windows; windows with Flemish mouldings and faience reveals; windows with rotting frames; sellotaped panes. But it is still a dark house within, despite all this glass. The glass is rippling black patent. The boughs of the trees are suspended in it, wavy in the heat. The boughs of the trees are repeated, distorted, truncated; so is jingo Douglas's St George's flag, dangling flaccid in the windless shimmer, a red-stained sheet with – there, in the trapeziform window of the stairwell – Bonny's face printed on it. She is watching. The mirrors of the ground floor are splashed with yellow: Monica's drophead, waiting spick and garish for its adulterous driver. Here she is, slingbacks, shantung and rictal Revlon, hurrying – infidelity shortens hours. Bonny is watching. What she can't see, what the windows don't show, is Eddie.

He's in the boot. The night spy is a blind spy for Bonny. He always did her bidding, always. When she smelled her mother's anticipation that drowsy day she upstaired to his room. He was miming to Billy J. whilst training his feet in quasi-manual articulation, attempting to open a pen-knife with his toes. (Eddie was a diligent student of Dr Clark W. Grover's *Our Forgotten Bodies: A Forty Point Programme For Maximal Potential*. A papercover copy of it was open on the bed. Bonny sat on it.)

So here he is, blind, hands round his head, knees to his chest, inhaling a jerry can, shunted, bumped, drills through his bones, hurting. Not deprived. There's an *excess* of senses in here. Blindness finetunes the rest. The octaves of the differential; the polygonality of wheels (circles? – a lie); tyres made of stone; smooth surfaces' sharpness – he suffered all these for Bonny. Boots are for the dead; at the very least they're for D.O.A.s who, often as not, get that way because of being in boots. Heat: yes, yes it fills every bit of the boot, clingwraps the goofy adventurer, burgles every cove of his body. Nonetheless Eddie enjoys the primal excitement, the fairground thrill. And the risk of discovery. This is hide and seek with an adult purpose. Monica drives in lurches and surges; she brakes to bruise him. His orientation was shot within minutes, his inner clock stopped. Corners, speed, horn, the gruff notes of low gears, a different ground – gravel? cinders? Eddie shivers, as though touching baize or flour. Handbrake, door, diminishing feetfalls. Eddie counted to ten before he tried to prise the springloaded lock. Ten. Maximal Potential was not yet realised.

When the grease monkeys found him he was faint from heat, his hands were bleeding, his face was apached with blood and oil, he was any body in a boot. Between them Bern and Trev had twenty-three years' greasemonkeyhood, five H.N.C.s, four BMC Proficiency Certificates, nineteen fingers (Trev had an amputation up Odstock after a jack accident, all part of the job and no hard feelings); they had all this and so many tits on the walls that it was like a dairy (said Bern's Bev) but they'd never seen anything like this. Hoity-toity, lardy-dardy, nose in the air – but you still don't expect her to have a wounded boy in the boot, not in a Vitesse, not Mrs Vallender, not in this heat, not her nephew. They gave Eddie tea and a fig roll. He was dizzy, stiff, sick, dry-mouthed. The nipples gaped at him like a flock's dark eyes; move, and they follow you. The comfort of an enamel mug; a gas ring's succour; Swarfega, and plenty of it. Bern and Trev were salt of. They ratted on Monica, Her Ladyship. They ratted without knowing it. They bickered about how long Eddie had been in his temporary coffin: this was important to them, precision (and service) was their business. Eddie could hear 'Bad To Me' on the burgundy skivitex tranny over there, that's what he wanted to listen to, not:

'Ten to twelve, it were, she left it.' (Behind the corrugated iron garage, next to the rotting fence.)

'No! After the news, it were.'

'Bern!' Trev waggles his quiff like he's dealing with a thick (which he wasn't – it was Bern that had the lion's share of the H.N.C.s) 'the news were already on when' – and here Trev fails to ape Monica's accent – '*my associate* bin and shown up.'

'Yarhh you . . . that were the alf-past news. She were waitin a good alf hour.'

Agent Eddie forgot about *the birds in the sky* and asked who My Associate was.

'An' it's twenty-five past two now. That makes – what – goin on two hour and twenny minute you was in there.' Plus the fifteen-minute drive from The Garth. Precision.

Livened by tea-tannin Eddie asks again: 'Who's this My Associate?' Greasemonkeys are fishwives, another gender, Castrol not hake. But they blab.

The File on My Associate: Male. (We may presume 'caucasian'.) Thirty years old (Bern); forty, forty-five (Trev). Brown hair, hook nose. Black hair, swarthy. Check shirt. Sort of pinkish shirt, cravat. Unanimity: he drives an Austin-Healey. A 3000. A 100/6. Tomato red and cream – which makes it a 3000 (Bern). Wire wheels.

This was all the gen Bonny needed. She wasn't greedy. She wasn't going to overdo it. She was not greedy; she was, rather, fastidious – 'you picky little sausage' (Douglas). Wanton yes, promiscuous no – she exercised choice. Now, look at the way she licked a strawberry cone. She clacks back to the lichened terrace where her mother lies in a deckchair, pondering. One cone in each hand, one for each of them. The swans are stately on the river, the rooks swarm in the elms, the birdbath throws a shadow for Bonny to trip through, the wasps are slowing with summer's passing. Monica's iced coffee (last word in soft drinks at The Garth) is tepid now; she likes a livener of Lamb's Navy in it. Her plucked, porous legs are getting a toney top-up of real sun. Ooh, that's a nasty bruise there.

'Mmmm thanks love,' Monica murmurs, distracted by the questionnaire in her mag. *Can you hear the words paella and sangria without dreaming of romance?* Monica gives five-star thought to this one, her Bic flitters from Yes box to No box, she moues and sighs and tuts a little too. The borders of her bush push out of her one-piece's tight vee, capillary invertebrates craving air.

'Mum? I saw this outfit in Early Bird.' Bonnie sits on the edge of her deckchair so she can feel the lateral strut across her bottom; she runs her tongue round the cone's roughish rim. 'Well not an outfit really – an *ensemble.*' Today she's in a striped T-shirt, *style matelot*, short shorts, sandals with a three-inch heel; today her hair is silver roan (that's what the bottle says) and straight – she ironed it damp and then she gave herself a further three inches on top with a steel comb, a pro brush and a megaspray of Dreem-Hold; this afternoon her legs are orange, her lips white, her cheeks mauve, her eyes blueblack. This is her ensemble and she wants another: any thirteen-year-old would want another. The pink ice-cream is spherically moulded: the Proper Vallenders boast, already, in this present, a kitchen of the future. In the future all kitchens will possess an Italian ice-cream scoop, as used in the trade. Bonny and her ice-cream, a potter and his clay; her goal is the simultaneous disposal, in a single ingest, of the remaining gout of pink and the terminal shard of the cone. She gnaws the cone's seam, she scratches it with her incisors, she traps drips with her tongue tip, she works the sphere into a helical helterskelter which beads of itself slide down; her chubby fingers are chaste, maculated neither by animal fats and colorant G8 nor by crumbs. She takes risks, she attrites the holster, termites the foundations; the ice-cream must surely slip, fall away to the lichen and lavender. Just in time, just in time – who'd have believed her tongue could stretch so far. It's a tensed runnel. Her mother has not replied. Bonny licks her lips. 'Seventeen pounds twelve and six – that does include a bolero thing. A bit gypsy.' One night years later (pp. 446ff.), one smack and brandy night, Bonny will write, with her *still* chubby forefinger, in inebriate letters, in the fat on Boumphrey's wall: *Fellatio – for pleasure. And profit?*

Despite Eddie The Pimp's efforts she is, presently, still pecuniarily reliant on her parents: handouts, subs, allowance – she is not a child, she can't bear to hear the notes and (more usually) coins referred to as *pocket money*. Whatever they're called there aren't enough of them, that's why Eddie has to thieve for her. Only little things, only things that won't be noticed, that no one minds about: moral and practical limits – what's OK and what fits in a pocket – are in felicitous coincidence. Eyelashes, the very can of Man Tan Bonny has smeared today, lip gloss, panstick, 45s, anything turquoise then anything mauve till it's anything pale grey, an Amara-work bracelet from a myope's junkshop that Bonny clasps around her ankle, *style pute*.

Living Wage Lewis, pestling a potion in the pharmacy at Treadgold's glanced between eye-high bottles to catch Eddie emptying a display box of Young World Egg Shampoo sachets into his windcheater but because, as an irregular at The White Jam Tart in those happier times (when he was, actually, paid even less – hence his sobriquet, hence his irregularity), Living Wage knows the boy's sad history and so takes pity; and because he hates the Treadgolds, father and son, for having put him to a life of pill-drudgery, he lets it pass, grinning as he guesses at the relative proportions – he disdained all scales, Living Wage did. Bonny doesn't use Young World Egg Shampoo on her hair, it guarantees brittle. She loves to squeeze the transparent plastic sachets of petrolic joke-yolk, she loves to vice them to the point of rupture then to shoot them with her Webley Junior; Eddie has clothespegged them to a willow's boughs on the riverbank. She is a good shot, her breath and hand and eye combined fine; she was a good girl, too, who never shot a living thing. Just see how good a shot. Squint, aim, and there they are – like the abandoned skins of tree insects, burst pouches curling in the heat, getting yellow, but not so purely, so keenly yellow as they were before the pellet struck and sent gobbets and droplets cartwheeling, cossacking in little death over leaves and lawn. (This is a scion of a firework dynasty at the trigger.) Now, squint again: ten o'clock of the shaggy dog's wig of willow and its desiccating sacs – *there*, the middle of the river.

This is a sight that so alarms Poor Eddie that his gut panic stretches to his testes; it's a mental aperient which havocs his colonic sluices. Custom doesn't lessen the terror when the river's perfect surface is burst, when spray catches the sun and parabolic pearlstrings lead brief decorative lives before pattering back to riverine anonymity.

Black, shining, webbed with weed, Douglas rises from the water, a rubber triton, lofting a harpoon gun to greet his proud wife and doting daughter, to proclaim his piscatory triumph: impaled on it is an eel that wraps itself about his wrist. He pushes his mask onto his smooth black forehead, detaches his breathing apparatus; this is a grown and swollen man who backpacks oxygen in a river four feet deep.

'Oof – he looks like a whatdyoucallit,' says Monica to Bonny, clenching her face – she can taste it – 'a black pudding.'

'Mum! He doesn't. I'm going to tell him you said that.'

'You dare.'

Eddie, at his high dormer, does not see a black pudding. He sees nothing comical in this monocular cuckold who knows he hurts when he tells Eddie: 'Being in the river is like being inside an animal.' Eddie sees the janitor of his parents' ghosts coming back from checking on them. He sees a bestial amphibian whose claim that the river bed is *my new hobby* he knows to be a lie. He knows the depth of Douglas's attachment to the second skin he polishes and strokes. He knows the extent of Douglas's relevant ignorances: Douglas can't tell a perch from a roach; he boasts that a cow's skull dredged from downstream of the old abattoir (p. 7) is *prehistoric probably*; he ascribes a Victorian stoneware pot to the Beaker Folk; he is pleased to have learned the word liverwort.

'Mum. That ensemble. I was thinking . . .'

Monica pantomimes incredulity. Postman (III) with ears for wings flies down the wavy slope of the lawn to his master whose best friend he is – really. Douglas, waddling, would look like a little boy if he wasn't so big.

Monica's mag sunshields her eyes, her voice swoops: 'Se-ven-teen powunds!'

'If' – Bonny's swift – 'you buy me it, won't tell Dad 'bout your young friend with the Austin-Healey.'

Douglas is pounding in flippers, shouting, waving, grinning, petting Postman, licking and getting licked, getting close, big and ever bigger.

There's such sureness, such casual malice in Bonny's voice. Monica stares at the daughter she does not know.

'Promise.' Bonny grins, cheery, chirpy, pert as a carmened flickup.

You little bastard is what Monica stops herself saying because that is a truth she hates to admit. She stares instead.

'That bruise Mum!' Bonny glances towards Monica's inner thigh. She giggles. 'Looks ever so like a lovebite.'

'God almighty!' And she rolls onto her tummy wasting her daughter with her eyes. 'All right, you . . .'

Bite me, more, more, now lick: she can remember the wires under the dash to a tee.

'That's right stay like that Mum – Dad won't see a thing. You don't mind really do you?'

It wasn't till the evening of the day when Eddie was thrown out, the day when Eddie broke the windows on the south side, the day when Eddie poisoned Postman that Bonny asked her father for money – to buy a powder blue suede jacket. By then she'd found the photographs that made her laugh to start with then made her feel sicker than she did already once she'd deciphered the labyrinth of tubes and buckles and the things like lab things.

Not that Bonny stopped demanding money from her mother – who wanted to call her *you little bastard* more and more and desisted not just to shield herself from what she had good as buried, and certainly not – God no, no longer – to hide from Bonny the knowledge of her bad genes' provenance, but to protect Douglas's and her *marriage*, that was the thing, her marriage. Which was her history, her foundation, her being, her comfort. Which, now the Burdensome Usurper had gone, might turn the corner, enter a new chapter of mature friendship based in mutual respect and the sharing of everything secret and special to you two alone. So she paid up, and the leech's clothes colonised room after room.

Thank God Douglas has no eye for domestic detail. Thank God Monica's such a ruddy lazy mare that she never checks Bonny's rooms. They gave mute, cursing thanks for each other's apparent deficiency, there was relief in their despite.

They dream their secret dreams in different beds, separate rooms. Snore and you toss alone, grope your own, mumble to a deaf bolster. The headlights' beam waxwanes on Monica's ceiling, it silhouettes Douglas's mullions. Slow tyres on the ghostly gravel trouble Douglas when he's dreaming – their sound is that of damp bangers, faulty firecrackers, wholesale returns, balance-sheets from hell, commercial nightmare. The front door's gloved thud. Do they hear Bonny tut when she snags a hosed tiptoe on the hardwood hall floor?

She's home again at half past three, she's been out late again, again. It's getting to be normal. Not of course that there's anything she can do at two she can't do six hours earlier and does do, don't you know; but they, her individual parents, they don't know. And they don't know that at two abandon takes its second wind, that satiety is merely a means of working up an appetite, that she speeds on fatigue, that there *are* things she didn't do earlier; the long night lights the light of beneficence in her. She thinks: why the hell not? She was no trouble really, a paragon in a way, good as gold, diligent, A-stream, top in divinity and above average in every subject (save Latin – ugh, those gerunds, Mum), she was helpful, she was a collector with a slot-top tin and cardboard tray on flagday in the market square – not like Eddie who falsified his Bob-a-Job sheet. And she communed with Our Lord, on her knees, in the cold perp sternness of St Pelagia's,[1] drinking His blood which had been bottled in Devon, gustatorily famous too as a sort or source of chocolate (p. 13). If the wafer stuck to her tongue she waited – no matter how great the discomfort, no matter how close to choking she came – until she was back at her pew before she peeled it and glued it to a dusty hassock.

She was a good girl but that's not why her parents so indulged her: neither guessed why the other, *the other half* of the

---

[1] There are three saints called Pelagia and which one this rare but not unique dedication is made to is unknown. Between them the three Pelagias lived at Antioch and Tarsus; two were virgin martyrs, one was a licentious dancer; one dressed as a man, retired to a hermitage (the dancer, repentant); Virgin A jumped to death from a housetop; Virgin B was roasted inside a red-hot bull; the cross-dresser died of natural causes on the Mount of Olives.

conjugation, should also have gotten suddenly tolerant of their one and only's mores and movements. Nor do they suspect that this weekly mutating girl, the chromatically adaptive apple-of, is gnawing the bough of the Vallender family tree they all three perch on – a stout bough, please, here, for the Proper Vallenders, the only ones left. But no matter how stout, Bonny still gets through it. She has such teeth that girl.

And doesn't he know it, doesn't 'Cary' Grant know it. 'Cary' Grant is Monica's Associate, tracked, before he left – the car was a giveaway – by Dogged Eddie, ever loyal, to inside a sheepskin coat, inside a paraffin-heated breezeblock lean-to where he sells seeds, bedding plants, Xmas trees etc. The man is a pro seedsman and amateur swordsman with the fearful eyes of a chancer on the point of being found out. His boring furrows stretch down downland to where grass starts and there's surface chalk like year-round snow. Look at the poles, the spruce toshed huts. Go-ahead? In the fields on the south side of the B-road he will pioneer PYO. That takes vision.

He never knew whose daughter she was, this girl with the magic laughing tackle, this little mystery in Greenhouse 3 where, for the sake of a longer cyclamen season, the heat thugs your throat. She was lost – it seemed – among the scarlet poinsettia and show pelargonia; she wasn't a regular. Oy-oy, he said to himself and to the RAF grey heater that wobbles the Ullswater on the wall. Oy-oy: that's what he thought. He needn't have. She sobstories him into giving her a lift in his 3000 (you was right, Bern). In drizzle when tarpaulins glister at mustardy dusk, in his Mille Miglia driving gloves (which tighten climactically round the wooden rim), in his sheepskin, in a Foden's lee, in the lay-by at Pepperbox by the steamy windowed caff where silhouettes swill char and chomp wad, in the driver's seat, in mean November, in a minute near enough – she was that good, he was that excited, the lights are wobbly in the puddles in the mud.

She smiles, now, a secret smile at her mother who never knew why, just fretted more, just hated that much more, just cursed the little bastard oftener beneath her breath. Thus Bonny gnawed their parlous perch. She bit her way out of childhood,

236

keeping mum about her mum's seedsman's seed she'd swallowed, saving it (the secret, the threat) for when she might need to use it. She lived by secrets, they were her power, the condition of her freedom, her weapons, her corrupt currency. And the more secrets she had . . . she'd observed, for instance, the way 'Cary' Grant kept money folded in a cigarette case. She was sent to earth to pry.

She fostered Monica's paranoia, fed her guilt – no wonder the woman was so touchy (p. 6), no wonder she skulked, haunted, through that house of hostile tiles and belligerent cornices fearing there were spies behind the chesterfields, contorted in the davenport. There was always something, someone, blocking the path to total fulfilment and truer happiness, the kind of happiness you can (it says here) test like it's pulse and comes through A1 every time, 70 per min, no question mark, clean bill – *whole* happiness; the someone in the way isn't meant to be your daughter though. It doesn't say anything about a daughter's casual blackmail. Nor about that law of the familial jungle which states that the void occasioned by the clearance/culling/natural wastage/taking out of one Burden is invariably filled by another whose characteristics may be contrary to those of the predecessor but who, according to Hugh Richards,[1] 'nevertheless focalises resentive aggression and targets the animosities of the parental units, including self-animosities typically prompted by the reluctance to recognise that the organs of sexual pleasure may also have generative consequences'. Or, as in Douglas's case, not; but he didn't know that. And though he learnt to fear Bonny he never resented her; he loved having given her life, loved her through all the humiliation she wrought. And he did understand, he could see the way it shocked her, that's why it was his secret (though obviously not by its very nature his alone); so long as it was secret there was no shame, but he kept it secret because he knew the potential for shame that was there. He should never have brought the photographs home. He kept the buckram albums of his vital joy in his office safe at Vallender Light and they would

[1] In *Succoured Slaves and the Chains of Nurture* (London 1977).

never have left there had Bollock-Features Last from Telegraph Insurance not threatened another sodding premium raise if the safe were not replaced 'by yesterday, by one made this century'.

The weekend the locksmiths from Chandler's Ford were installing the new Banham was the weekend Douglas called his nephew pimp and the order of the house, of their lives, was changed for ever. There was new light in The Garth that day. Bonny's itineraries about the house were unfamiliar to her and she approached doors from angles different enough to make the mouldings, the lintels, the recessed panels like ones she had never seen before. The stairs were shallower. The sun unfurled beams that stretched into places it had never bothered with before, which Bonny had never seen: she didn't know there were initials carved in the capital of a pilaster in the panelled hall; they'd been there almost a century. The house was silent. Poor Eddie packed. Bilked by life again. Monica drove to So'ton, to the fabric department at Tyrell and Green. Poor Eddie was incredulous: he knew Douglas meant it when Douglas handed him an uncrossed cheque for thirty-two pounds, eighteen shillings only. By what formula did he compute that sum? What are its components? The recipient's presumed loss, the donor's guilt, two pounds for each year of the former's life?

Douglas said to Eddie: 'I'll be back at five.'

Eddie said nothing, he knew what that meant, he wondered where the matching comb that slotted into his tortoiseshell-handled hairbrush was and wished he could think of something else like where is he going to spend the night if he can't stay at Rufus's after the party, and the night after, and the nights stretching to the infinity of his seventeenth birthday almost two hundred nights away, and who will want him now that he is unwanted more than ever, and if he walks into the cold river and holds himself down to die by drowning the way his genes must be urging him to will he meet his people again, and what is he going to do now?

But he finds himself fretting about the torn babyblue-white striped sleeve of 'Only The Lonely' which his mother bought and *listened to* as though it might tell her something; she scraped her crown and listened still when the needle scratched the circular song's mute core, over and over, in the ghost bungalow down Britford Lane. The sleeve was faded, frayed, a bit unstuck. Little things: shock has a talent for minute detail, for deflecting attention from its cause and its consequence. It faces the grave with frivolity; the shocked lack application, cannot concentrate. Poor Eddie knew what he should be thinking about, but those silk Flags Of The World, that cap badge, and here's the letter from the boy in Lorraine with whom the exchange trip had to be aborted. He packed methodically, he ran up and down stairs, inventing reasons as he went. Even the preface to an adventure is an adventure. He fought his helplessness by folding clothes, by rearranging his chattels. This was reduction – the only child of two dead parents filled just two suitcases and a dufflebag with all their possessions.

Bonny studied the little piles he made and remade, taxonomically almost, before he packed: 'Can I have that?' she asked of four or five things, and he nodded each time. She skipped away to see how a scarf of his mother's did as a cummerbund – it didn't; she abandoned it over the edge of a wash basin.

She was excited. After Douglas had foot-prodded Postman into the car and gone to inspect the locksmiths' progress she went down to his study, poured herself a double-double Mirabelle, winced at its buccal punch and idly inspected the contents of his desk whilst keeping half an eye on the televised rally-cross. She thinks about telling Eddie how sorry she is but puts it off and refills the glass with Cinzano bianco, plus Benedictine for extra warmth; she thinks about telling him how easy it is to cope out there, in the world beyond this world of The Garth and the warders who chanced to have them in their charge. She is convinced *she* could cope; she will see.

There's no question that, at sixteen, Eddie was still a child. None of them was less fitted to fend for himself.

Bonny opened a window to relieve the heat and then the rooms were filled by curtains buckling and doubling and looping like ampersands in the nor'wester's rush. Bonny giggled, a table lamp's shade caught the wind, became a sail. Eddie heard the crash as he opened the door to the top terrace but didn't let it deflect him from his purpose: shock might obviate purposeful thought but it didn't inhibit action. He acted; he may be dazedly incurious about life ('the brumous forest in front of me' sang Jean-Marie translating his father's famous line), about the puzzle of how it all moves and how what comes to be comes to be, about gaining entry to the mysteries, but he can still *do* something.

Douglas had expelled the wrong one of his brother's children; he had expelled him with a gleeful hunch about how ill he might fare. None of them was less fitted to fend for himself. Douglas had picked on the pigeon not on the princess, Bonny, who is now groping in a deep drawer for money. Douglas had picked on the pigeon who was also a cuckoo and made him a hawk for an afternoon.

'Deary me there's a spill an' an 'alf that's an upset for the Nuneaton lad, goin' so well he was,' says the commentator to Bonny who withdraws her arm from the drawer like a vet from a cow and peeks over the desk in anticipation of mangled limbs in monochrome, is disappointed, is struck by a gust that lifts the curtains' skirts to show a glimpse of black gladstone against the wainscot, is surprised to see Eddie coming from the direction of the outhouses with a can of Mickey-Take held at arm's length in front of him with just two fingers, gingerly. He treads like he's on a tightrope.

When Bonny goes to the kitchen to fetch ice for her Fire In Limehouse (mixed according to the book but with treble measures) and for something to force the gladstone's lock with, Eddie is genuflecting before Postman's big bowl, an enamel former pie dish crusted with crenellations of desiccated minced mare and with a pyramid of same – but juicily, deliciously, temptingly moist – in the middle on a bed of Sprat's finest.

'There's a chicken here,' says Bonny squirting ice oblongs from a rubber tray. 'Be nicer. Stth ooh.' She wipes moult and grime from two ice bits then displaces drink onto her wrist with them.

Eddie attempts, ineptly, to conceal between his thighs the copyright-infringing can of Cuban rodent poison whose packaging design is of Mickey Mouse (© The Walt Disney Company)

240

clutching his throat in his death throes. (Ah, those Cubans and their wacky humour!) This is how Eddie did for Postman, who would soon be replaced by Postman (IV). He mixed enough of the rotenone-rich powder into the dog's mince to take out approx eighteen mice or ten black rats (*Rattus rattus*, so bad they named it twice). This was the first stage of his tripartite revenge on the man who had killed his mother (he'd decided). Bonny giggled, told him she'd tell on him, giggled again, vomited on the gingham-printed plastic worktop, reached for the kitchen-roll roller, lost her balance, pulled it off the wall with rawlplugs, gouts of plaster too, ends up all ends up splayed, giggling. Eddie broke the Havana'd plastic spoon and stuffed it in waste-disposal, switched that on, buggered it, hadn't meant to, but was pleased he had, it sounded like a big-end going, he looks down at Bonny.

'Bonny? Can. . . ? Can I. . . ?'

'Eddie!' All motherly. 'Tdbe *incest*.' Too right, Darl. 'Don't be silly.'

Oh that necessarily practised grimace he wears – of cosmic pathos, of sorrows, infinite past sorrows exhumed by every slight.

'Respect me as a friend yeh?'

She sucks at a cut hand, a carmine incision he has to touch now he's seen it, wants to taste so much because he may never taste her again, who knows. He squats beside her, licks the little wound that has been lent him to play with, out of pity, for a while, feels the ferrous spritz on his tongue, adores it because it's *her* blood which he may taste over and again, who knows, when they're more than friends as inevitably they will be, later on, bonded by love that is latent in her now but *is* there, deep down, definitely, that's his faith – it is the very condition of faith that its subject have no foundation in evidential certitude; we have faith in what we cannot know; faith creates expectation and feeds off it; it's solipsism with a collar and tie, an exclusive order of solace through delusion. No wonder faith is such a comfort, such a source of strength. Poor Eddie had so many faiths because he had so little else; he believed for the sake of believing, his capacity for credulity was to be measured in jeroboams, imperials. He didn't have faith in the power of his hands, he didn't need to because he *knew* about that power that visited him when they all willed it, when all the retinal rods and warm hearts of the congregation focused their analeptic favour on the hands that, by chance, were attached to his body. But it was faith – so he would insist to Chubb – that did for the windows just as surely as it was Mickey-Take that did for Postman (who was the only other creature he ever killed, ever, in the course of his life which was a life devoted to life). That's what he claimed, what he stuck to: faith.

Of course, no one saw him. Bonny had by now forced the gladstone's lock with a barding needle and was engrossed. Eddie finishes in the kitchen. He secretes the poison in Mrs Gub's cupboard of fermenting mops and felt-lagged pipes where the floorcloths are stiff as stockfish. He eats: a peanut butter and Sandwich Spread sandwich, toasted; a chocolate spread sandwich; spongecake dipped in Lucozade; a tin of white peaches in heavy syrup. He carries Douglas's big jar of birthday gift Stilton up the half flight from the larder. What an animated cheese! It seethes with vermicular life, it blast-reeks toxins, its veins are rush-houred by an off-white army, it's granular where it should be smooth, fudge-brown where it should be cream. Maggots? Cheese lice? Lactic crabs? No microscope needed. The scooped centre is a pond of port with a meniscal film of teat fats. This is where Eddie pisses. This is the first time he does anything of the sort (character development). It didn't occur to him that Douglas would probably consider the flavour enhanced. The lamb's liver, sliced special nice and thick by Twose so Douglas can eat it burnt outside and raw within, lies in a bowl in the fridge growing a skin of blood. Eddie closes the larder door behind him, sits on the half flight, spends eight and a half sore and boring minutes masturbating (picture a spectral Bonny) before he ejaculates onto the liver. He mixes his twelve c.c. of emission with the hepatic blood of the lamb.

At 4.14 he puts his head round the door of Douglas's study and asks Bonny: 'Are you going to come to Rufus's tonight?' She does her best to stand, creases some of the photographic prints on the floor, shrugs.

Then she looks down at the photographs: 'Yes, I'll be able to come.'

At 4.19 Eddie, holding all his possessions, went out of The Garth's front door for the last time and broke the windows. The version according to Chubb (pp. 360ff.) is that the newfound foundling stands on the gravel in the dusk with his bags floored beside him and the house in front of him. In this light the house aims to scare – why does a tourelle spell terror, why is a hipped gable a device of tectonic fright? Eddie stares at the house for a while then *wills the windows to burst*, to implode. He stares and he stares, with a gaze the far side of concentration, with unalloyed confidence in his power to amend molecular composition, to do the glass actual physical harm, aggravated damage, extra ill. He knew he could do it. He knew he could achieve Maximal Potential. Was Poor Eddie Vallender a witch? No one saw him do it. He was his only witness. There were no special effects of light or sound or wind, save those occasioned by the very act of rupture. There was nothing peripheral.

I am merely repeating here what Eddie told Chubb and what Chubb duly recorded: 'I wanted, I wanted, I wanted. You know? There was an instant when I wasn't there, more than an instant. Like when you go from A to B and when you reach B you can't remember the bits in between, you know? You might as well have sleepwalked it. Well it was like that but . . . even though I wasn't there I was seeing it. I was very – I was going to say very cold but that's not – right. It was like I was temperatureless, like temperature didn't count, you know? And it took a long time. I mean it doesn't usually take long for the glass to fall out of a window frame does it? But it was all crackled, crazy paving, the panes, it was all like that and still in the frame – I could see it like that in all the different windows, waiting to fall out and I had to make more . . . I had to *want* more to get it to come out the frames. It was just waiting. I was like halfway there, you know? I'd broken it but I hadn't . . . budged it. It was on the brink. The process wasn't whole. D'you see? So I made it happen . . . It's like creating your own storm. It's like being a generator. A power station, yeh?'

Chubb's investigations of Eddie's gift were curtailed before he had done anything other than tape record eleven hours of (mostly) repetitive recollection and fantastical boasts. He was prevented from proceeding to the stage of interrogation and of, specifically, challenging Eddie's accounts of unobserved phenomena such as the breaking of The Garth's windows. There is no question that most (though not all) of the windows of the entrance front *were* smashed; but those that weren't were on the second and third storeys and inaccessible from roofs, balconies, other windows etc. There is, equally, no question that Eddie *believed* that he had effected the multiple breakage by will; he wasn't lying, not wittingly, anyway. But rage is a drug, as liable as alcohol to promote amnesia. Moreover, as Chubb discovered and admits with understandable reticence: 'The validation of certain acts of healing (and "harming") is not susceptible to the usual proofs.'[1]

Bonny heard nothing. She was at the back of the house. The televised ice-hockey international – 'the battle of Brno', as it's still called by those in ice-hockey who can pronounce it – was on at full vol. And her ears were filled by the ululating groans of senses rearranged by a bottle-bashed brain. But her eyes can still see – oh, yes; alcohol's obfuscating gauze can't stop these messages getting through, can't stop them fazing her like a phone breather who's guessed correct. Douglas's photographs are of several sorts, none of them to be trusted to the GPO (what would the sorters think?), none of them to be greeded by eyes other than his – furtive guilt heightens the excitement of stolen moments with stimuli that are private as dreams: Bonny has trespassed into a secret garden of oneiric analogues, a forbidden site, a place where base and fantastical imaginings are made plastic. Some of the photographs are gummed to the pages of two 'family' albums with marbled covers and leather spines; Bonny may be badered but her mnemonic capacity is not so shot-up that she can't recognise one of these albums as the pair of that in which her own (and often similarly naked) progress from birth to toddling is recorded, sometimes with Eddie beside her pram, sometimes with Eddie cropped by pinking shears so

[1] Letter to the author 12.12.91. The 'certain acts' are, without exception, those unwitnessed by a third party.

244

that whilst one side of the snap may be borderless it is still wavy edged.

Dirty, dirtier, dirtier still, disgusting – but fun, mind, and funny. How funny is proportionate to how complicated. Bonny is unusually sexually practised for a girl of her age, in that age/place/milieu; but by the absolute standards of congressional invention she is a tyro; she may be keen to please (herself, too) but she has much to learn – she sees that. What novelty in numbers! Whose is that? This flesh exists in an extra dimension. It's choreographed with imaginative ingenuity for a future audience: Bonny is delighted that these, one, two, five, five people should, a long time ago to go by their stockings, stays and hairdos (and there's little else to go by), have made themselves into a baroque knot for her on this special afternoon; and these three, more recently no doubt – what guileful gyno-gymnastics they've perfected in their attempt to become one cephalopod. Watch them go in frozen show-rapture. And her father looks too, peeps, pores on them and on all the other actors in the meat carnival, the carnal pageant – these special actors who are their roles, who are propless and beyond the code of pretence, who are different from their audience in never being alone. Who has comprised this sodality of the genitally articulate down the years? Where are they now? The rest of the race is recognised by name, by face. Bonny replaces the albums in the gladstone and picks up a manilla folder, opens it.

Oh God no that hurts it's ill. This exhibit is made up of seventeen burns photographs; this is Bonny's father's souvenir of the injuries suffered by the four female workers (another died, and two were male) in the explosion and consequent fire in the bunkered priming workshop at Vallender Light early in the afternoon of Monday May 14 1956 just after the end of That Little Ray Of Human Mirth Starring Butt Of The Joke, Ray Butt, on the Light Programme. Poor reception because of the quasi-subterranean disposition of the building even though the aerial is on the asbestos roof; but good enough to hear.

'Gaw 'e'll make me split moy britches one o' thum days,' phoneticised Shirley Fletcher the very moment before half her head was blown onto the ceiling.

There is no photograph of her here; that's a different taste. There's no necro not because of a moral boundary but because it wasn't to Douglas's taste. His taste is for these *things*: you must take my word for it, they *are* faces, mainly, but also hands, thighs, other parts shown in close-up that obviates a reading of the body's geography. This is skin. It may look like fondue, glue, failed crackling (which is skin too), putty, icing, plasticine, melted latex, bubbly rubber: but it *is* skin, cooked, roasted on the hoof – each of these women has a crisp chop for a jaw, a drumstick stuck to her cheekbone. Each would wear an expression of shame on the face that is the cause of the shame if that face could be thus contorted but it can't, it is set, dead as steak, mute about its own disfigurement. Only the eyes signal anything, and that is the further fear that the camera recording them may explode, may hurl its lens at theirs.

These photographs are not purpose-built fetishes; they are perverted to that end, given new meaning by the more orthodox material they are stashed with. In the doctor's Nissen office at Odstock Hospital they are medical tools set out on a scratched table; they are the pre-surgical complements to those which will be taken later, after James Elsworth Laing has rebuilt the faces and limbs with an eye to beauty rather than verisimilitude: 'No point in putting them back together as they were if they looked like neeps.' (It is from Laing's office that Douglas Vallender stole the photographs, the day he visited their subjects, who still sued Vallender Light.)

Bonny drank a White and Mackay's, then another with a precautionary Alka Seltzer stirred in. She felt guilty, repulsed, betrayed, powerful, older. She was going to kiss Eddie's cheek but he was in and out the room so quickly. She did kiss his cheek that evening at Rufus's, just before she went upstairs, there to ape in the playground of her host's parents' bed some of the specialist contortions she'd conned that afternoon.

Not these though: again, it took her six neck angles and several spins of the first photo before she *saw*. She strewed them on her father's brothelish ottoman daybed, all across the floor. Here *was* her father! Shit. He was in the photographs, in the frame, in rubber but no longer a rubber triton, no longer hoisting a triumphal eel, no longer in the river but in a room which Bonny thought looked like the upstairs of a pub (it wasn't), a room with darkness in it and a carpet woven for poor people in the days when carpets had flowers and borders and now so thin, so greasy, it coalesced with blistered lino, a room with a picture of a horse at plough hung skew, with a scorched lamp shade and alpine sheets on a big bed and shadows and a person. This person is in the room of sad wallpaper with her father who is flipperless. This person is not so fat as he is but the bulk is still there and it's *quasi-male* despite the lips, the breasts, the genitals which, together with the puckered winking anal iris, are the only exposed parts of this man-woman. Head to toe rubber. Shiny, lumpy, like a piece of something else, like something with a piece missing, like something from before scales existed when fins were far in the future, when creatures were at one with mud, when slime might go either way, when animal was vegetable and vice versa. The apertures are metal ringed. The breasts that gape through them have nipples that photograph dark as black rubber. The unshy bush is a coarse puff of sofa-stuffing seeping from a split. This person has lips but no face, no eyes. This person is a machine. A tool of torture and solace, a fantastical toy. This person is the game, Douglas is its player. Look at this tableau, look at it through his daughter's disbelieving eyes: this person – who is not a person but a reduction of a person, a self-made merkin, penetrable mineral, a porn pawn whose sex organs are pleasure pits – this person in this photograph with her father has its halma head to his glans. Bonny never knew her father had such a shortfall of tackle: that was another thing to appal her – it's a snack not a lunchpack even though this person is gripping its root with pliers and there is a bulldog clip clamped to his scrotum: one clip suffices for two balls. His rubber all-in-one has holes the same as the person's. Now he's hooded, now he isn't. But even had he been masked in every frame she'd still have known him by the black downlands of his belly, by the contours of his arse which, in the one we're looking at, has grown a tail. A tail made of hose. A tail that stretches to his mouth. A tail he sucks at like an autofellationist. But that's not it; Bonny knows he's no Nijinsky, that he's trying something else. This person's teeth are sharpened, its fingers are tipped by steel plectrums, prosthetic claws. Bonny wonders at her father's appetite for danger. She wonders who took the photographs (p. 70). She wonders who this person is. She wonders where this person's stained room is.

The answer to the last is Pompey, Military Road in Hilsea, a house with a history, the house where Commander Crabb – Lionel to his proud old mum, Buster to the wardroom – passed part of his last afternoon out of water, on earth, the house behind the Territorial Hall.

See that curtain? The one Douglas is kneeling by whilst he eats from the dogbowl and this person pushes a spike heel in him where his tail should be? Pull the curtain and there's a picture window that's the envy of one and all, a feature: the picture is the cliff of Portsdown, Fort Widley on top. (One and all agree, too, that lovely as it is the view might be a teensy bit enhanced by a bolder eyecatcher, a stronger accent up there on the escarpment.) Military Service: that's what this person calls it and Douglas is proud to share a taste with old Buster who was topped for freedom: 'My favourite caller when I was getting started in the profession.' This person gives Douglas the can of Mickey-Take that Eddie so abuses.

A sailor had suffered persistent nightmares of Mañuel The Hand Pirate who severed sailors' hands with a kukri and attached them with wire loops to his belt and his ears where they swung like sticky pygmy gloves as he walked the furzy cliffs whistling hand shanties. This person listened with sympathy to the sailor's tale.

The solution to oneiric woe, to fear of amputation? Blindfold the sailor so he enters dreamspace; tongue-wet his fingers, stick them in orifices filled with honey; and, whilst his hands are primary instruments of pleasure, scrape his penis with talons till beads of blood ruby the urethral ridge, then rub the glans with chilli paste. The sailor thanks this person for efficacious therapy with the gift of his can of Mickey-Take, a souvenir of old Havana, of Batista days, of when they had a real sense of humour and the whores' painted labia grinned at passers-by from the seats of Buicks and Fleetwoods. He no longer dreams of that pirate, of those amputations.

And this person passes it on to Douglas, on a whim, because he's that kind of gentleman caller, because he has that same sense of humour as the sailor has (and Cubans had), because he's the only other one with an appetite for chilli. Douglas doesn't suffer bad hand dreams. He craves chilli for its own sake, for its special accomplishments: chilli burns, chilli is fructose heat, chilli is fire without combustion. There's no flame to photograph, the ointment's big property is not thus transmitted, the camera lies by omission, it obscures, Bonny is in the dark, in her father's room and in her father's distant dreamroom which is gymnasium, lavatory, theatre, lab and parrot's deathtrap – the dull and backward who dailies for this person finds two bell chillis in the tiny bloodstained kitchen.

Whilst she's hoovering the mess off of the carpet Joey squawks: 'Famished for lack of nourishment, famished for lack of nourishment, famished for lack of nourishment.' On and on he went. The dull and backward couldn't very well disturb her employer who was entertaining a gent. So she went to the kitchen, chopped the funny tomatoes, broke up a crust, smothered the lot with salad cream, shoved it into Joey's cage. Did he squawk! Lawks. When Douglas arrived there was no chilli to anoint him with. 'They don't grow on trees . . . least they didn't, then. Wasn't a Patel on every corner . . . course you can't tell Pompey from Madras now, all Halals and whatsitcalled – galangal.' Douglas lost his rag that day – all dudgeon and dander. He was a dangerous man in such circumstances. You should have seen him when he returned to The Garth the afternoon that Eddie left.

The house looked like it had been bombed. While Postman hurried inside to eat the Last Supper Douglas stood, stupefied, he about-turned to check he hadn't driven into the wrong drive (even though there was no other drive that resembled The Garth's). Then, very slowly, because time (dependent on his mentation, and out to prove it's not an absolute) was hardly ticking over, he counted the wounded panes. Was there solace in numbers? Was the act of inventory an aid to belief? Does shock foster need for detail? And did he get it right? Or did he count the same one twice and mistotal? He could have done, for he looked back at a window in the tourelle three times and each time saw Bonny's silhouette pass across it *in the same direction*. He shook his head. He bellowed. He found Bonny coming downstairs gripping an ungrippable rail smiling a smile that was not the smile of a Dada's Little Sausage but a smile *about* his little sausage, *inter alia*; this was a smug and cunning smile, a codecracker's smile. He didn't see it. He growled, he stamped, he slapped panels, he kicked wainscot. He didn't see what Bonny's smile said. He didn't read that the familial rules were about to be changed, that the end was beginning (with the biggest glazing bill he'd ever paid).

Bonny short and curlied him, the balance of bullydom shifted. Whirling his arms, cursing the Burden, computing the damage, he was locked inside himself listening to rage's generator, blind to the new order, to the filial tyranny he was now to be subject to.

'I'm not going to have to show them to Mum am I Dad – don't want to upset her, do *we* Dad?' Coercion in a pronoun. The girl's learning. Top of the form again, albeit in a specialist study. Where did she hide the sample photos? Douglas's wintry veal face is beef-red, his nose is glans-claret, for a moment there's a ring in it, for a moment she fears he'll charge. This is a bad day for him, she understands that. The house is inside out, out of control, there are random slammings, the elements love to colonise places previously denied them, gusts and currents shove like gatecrashers looking for the action. The house might as well have been burgled. He doesn't take his eyes off her when he throws a crinkly roll of notes to the floor, petulant as a baby.

'You little bastard,' he murmurs; him, he's free to say that, uninhibited by literality. In the kitchen Postman is beginning to die, victim of a revenge killing (p. 199). He's never seen this girl before. She is new. She has created herself to fill the void occasioned by The Burden's expulsion. It has taken only hours for that space to be squatted by this cocky painted tartlette. Butter wouldn't, wouldn't seep so easily into a mould.

And Monica is broody for another. God forbid – you build them, then they rebuild themselves out of ingratitude. That's the partial, the parental diagnosis – commonplace but not inevitable, just as parenthood itself is commonplace but not inevitable. Childhood is, it's a mandatory stretch which Bonny has now completed. She's out, and blooming, all over life, with her mum in one pocket and her dad in the other, lapping it up, cynosure and honey pot, loved, longed for, loving it, believing that *she's her own*, that she owns herself.

That night Douglas sat in the blowy kitchen eating Stilton with a spoon, thankful for gustatory solace, thankful for Postman's moans of sympathy even though the dog is overdoing his solicitude. He wishes he had given his daughter a pituitary drug to stunt her, to fix her forever at four years when she was such a joy: he had doted on a fantasy, on a person who is past, who lacks a dog's constancy and incapacity for change – so *that*'s why they're man's best friend; well, some men's, those men who would embalm their daughters, commit them to an eternal kindergarten, to stasis in a smock. He wanted a daughter who wouldn't give her old toys to cause-vultures scavenging to ease their consciences and someone else's famine, who didn't thus dispose of part of his life too – you remember them by their dolls and their garages, as well as by their smiles and their credulous dependence; those objects are the links when they've flown, grown different faces, betrayed you by owning bones that expand, expand, expand. He wanted a daughter who didn't have a cousin who was his burden and her rogue varlet, her knave, her witch. The pimp. He wanted a daughter who wasn't *his* daughter. Why couldn't someone else have had this daughter?

Oh, but someone else did, Doug-A-Doug-Doug, someone else did. And then there was —— too. And 'Peter', 'Dick' and 'Rod'. The Toxins – that is Douglas's word for them, for all of them: Toxin of the Month, Spotty Toxin, Damned Noxious Toxin Hopping From One Leg To The Other. Etc. It wasn't a word Bonny minded, she indulged her father by acknowledging it, even using it, collusively sycophantic. But she adored the poison, it was beneficent as an opiate. She didn't think of it the way her father did. Here are Bonny's Top Toxins Winter 64/65:

Micky Izzard. Pro: Really nice voice, looks like the one in The

Raiders who wears the dark glasses and plays mouth harp and tambourine. Con: skint; says his father, a ranker major, won't give him dosh, always bumming fags, 'borrows' money for cinema/booze/taxi home to the army estate where he lives and where Bonny is never invited, *I'm not*. Bonny wanks him in the Regal, Endless Street whilst they're watching *The System* starring Oliver Reed, Jane Merrow, David Hemmings (dir: Michael Winner, 1964); Smeggy Beggy, sitting two seats away and escorting the present writer, demands loudly: 'Where did it go. Where's the wet patch?' Present whereabouts unknown, last heard of working as a boat nigger in Antigua (*c.* 1972).

Tim Dudley. Mature, crackshot at adult conversation, shares risqué jokes with Douglas, drops names of shoots, fishing flies etc. Mature but thick: claims that his father, a colonel, a martinet who is decidedly not a ranker, has traced family history back to one King Duddo of Northumbria. Pro: *great* sense of humour (e.g. filling the gin bottles with water at one of his parents' parties), makes a girl feel special (never a slouch with flowers), own car. Con: Duddotoxin (Douglas has a great sense of humour too) enjoys a reputation – he jinked out of a paternity suit by persuading four of his friends to say that they too had slept with the luckless mother of his first child; he overturned a carful of his muckers, some of whom would still lie on his behalf; his liaison with the daughter of a bearded, bonhomous doctor prompts that doctor to phone his daughter's friends' parents with warnings about Duddo, Potential Vector of Veedee. He and Bonny are longterm, going on two months at least. He buys her two Zombies singles and The Lancastrians' cover of Gale Garnett's 'We'll Sing In The Sunshine'. Love nest? A beach hut at Hengistbury Head owned by Roeskin's parents and not used by them during the week. Now a PR executive in Tamworth, Staffs.

Jimmy Roe, aka Roeskins. Aka thus because *either* someone made a crummy pun on foreskin which stuck (the pun, that is, not the prepuce (which didn't)) *or* because someone picked up on his habitual cry of 'Gor any skins?' Con: wimp (a word unknown then – *wet* will do), liable to whine, dress sense of a Daltonist (goose-shit green with claret, mauve shirt and brown trousers). Pro: nothing much. Bonny sucked him off in the back of a Mini-van on the A338 on the way to a party at Avon Castle, the kitsch-integral housing development south of Ringwood; she spat it out, her way, then she lit Vallender Light bangers and pushed them through the skylight in the roof of the tiny vehicle I was driving. Issigonis provided for such diversions and for a reflective view of the interior and the road behind where the Classics and Cambridges braked and swerved, reflexively. James Craig Roe, 'The Time Share King', now lives in Sintra, Portugal.

'Cary' Grant. Once a seedsman . . .

Lewis Brian Hopkin-Jones. Pro: good looking, world famous hairdo. Con: unreliable, itinerant, alcoholic, sadistic. Bonny certainly went to see The Rolling Stones play at Longleat on Sunday 30 August 1964. She may have made up the rest. Stone dead July 1 1969.

Gavin Mungo-Geddes. As sexually precocious as Bonny though less discreet. Pro: the oleaginous manner of a small-town gigolo (which is what he aspired to be); this appealed to Bonny who considered him sophisticated as well as charming, handsome etc. Con: the same. His manners didn't invariably cut the mustard. He flirted with Monica who called him The Greaseball. Bonny was exceptional among his paramours in being younger than him. Property developer and bobsleigh international, currently serving 21 months for fraudulent conversion (Ford Open).

Me, the author, the present writer, Meades. Mea(des) Culpa. Downstairs there was shouting, laughter, *Concrete and Clay*, *Blue Turns To Grey* by the Mighty Avengers, something by The Kingston Trio, *Go Now*. Bonny and I had ascended to a dark room in this house neither of us knew where coats were piled on a double bed, and mufflers and scarves and handbags and hats – a freezing March it was. I greased her arse with vanishing cream. I stood, untrousered. She bent over the bed. Her skirt was round her waist. She wore off-white knitted stockings. She was silent. I couldn't really see her face. I could see that as I fucked her arse she was going through the pockets of the coats her head was buried in, she was searching purses, nicking lipsticks, clutching folding money in her fist, tutting when she fumbled coins. I guess I should have been insulted by such lack of attention, but I was, in truth, grateful for the loan of that aperture. Thus we bugger our characters.

M̶eet Ray Butt!
But which Butt?

Butt of the Joke?

Butt the Buttist?

Butt the drunk they cut from the wreck, in a coma, with the inside of his wife's face all down his dinner suit? (He was a pioneer of the shawl collar look too.)

Butt the loyal widower of loyal Heidi?

Butt the father (to the triplets Jonjon, Sonny and Laddy – the Three Little Surprises, the Voys)?

Butt the son (to May and Harry: 'My dad, drunk so much gin he did, they dressed him in his coffin like a beefeater!')?

Butt the brother of Daph, a living legend in G & G?

Butt the employer and patron of Poor Eddie Vallender?

Reg Voice's Ray Butt?

Ray Butt, medical curiosity and prosthetic bodge?

Butt the putative stepson of a man young enough to be his son ('You Voys are going to have to look into this, well and thorough.')?

The dreamer, the penitent visionary, God's toolkit?

Hayling's most favoured child?

Meet Ray Butt, who's all these, and more besides. Man of contrasts, man of parts – some of them titanium steel, some plastic, some Gortex, some Dacron, some porcine, some he came with.

That purring whirr, those thuds against the wainscot, that crack, the curse that follows and the muffled oaths of self-contempt – these are the sounds of Ray Butt coming to greet us. Respect. Show it. This is a star, *is*.

'Once a star,' opines Reg Voice, The Man The Stars Confide

In, 'once a star, always a star. A star, a true star, never loses that indefinable something, that special je ne sais quoi.' Not even when that true star is only just over half a star, when so much has been cut away, replaced, replicated?

No, because 'stardom comes from the very soul'.

The soul, then, is not to be found in the kidneys, the legs, the colon, the hair, the teeth.

'It comes from the very heart.'

Parts of Ray Butt's heart are, admittedly, his own; indeed, since no one else claims them, he owns even the parts he didn't grow, the spare parts, they're his own too.

'Oo'd want em? Tell you what, you tell me the name of the geezer who'll buy a used pacemaker with fifteen thou on the clock. No, tell you what – I'll tell you 'is name: *Cunt*. Hrraghcrr! Eh? Beg pardon. Pardon my swahili. That's Mister C. 'Unt. My mistake.'

That purring whir. Another onomatopoeia. A splintering falsetto: that's the blue bohemian off the occasional table. You'd have thought that he'd have learnt by now to steer it better – Butt of the Aim.

But then you remember it was bad driving that got him started at this; bad driving and all those bevvies and the row with Heidi she began as they crossed the Hamble bridge at Bursledon, a row about an imaginary popsy, about some transgression he'd never have made, not in a million years, on his mother's eyes, swear, family and that – but you got to be friendly to the hired helps even if they are in fishnets, with legs up to their oxters. Silly thing to spat about, but then she'd had a few too. Foden. A sort of furnace, its headlights which were eyes became a consuming mouth. The lorry ate Heidi. And – do you know? – the driver (who was a fan) never drove again, not after what he'd done to That Little Ray Of Human Mirth.

Of course he was a fan, who wasn't? And of course he blamed himself, who wouldn't have? The man who drove the lorry that crippled Ray Butt. It was an accident. God bless, it wasn't his fault. But none the less – Ray Butt! It's not like gimping a nobody. By chance 'Ray's earliest ambition, he confesses, "Was not to be a nobody" ', writes Reg Voice. 'Fiercely determined to be a somebody, he's achieved it in spades, but not, he admits with his usual modesty, "Without a lot of luck along the way and some terrific sorts giving me a hand up on the way!" '

Here he comes. Here it comes, through the door. Solid grey rubber tyres, iridescent metal tubing, upholstered armrests (bespoke, those), rods and levers, spherical black knobs. And there's a piece of a man in it, the leftovers of a life, a little bit of body and a lot of car rug (Dress Stewart); this, though, is no car, you can't call it a car, no. Cripple trolley, Baderbus, Delanomobile, spazwheels, gimp-pram, yes. This is a vehicular prosthesis with its own prostheses: a battery like a cubist bum beneath the seat, tensile rails, screws, wingnuts, folding tackle – these are the supports of the chair which is his support. Life's like that: we need props to sustain it. Ray Butt's life is more like that than most. The more life he tucks under his belt, the less of him there is, the greater the store of props he needs. Consider how much the truncated original bit of Butt must carry in order to be. He's a refurbished ruin. From the north: toop, bifocals on a cord, hearing aid on the blink, clackers, pacemaker, some clerk's kidney, colostomy, hip custom-built from petroleum by-products.

Every time he's aped, every time a car crashes and a life goes out inside it there is a surgical opportunity, the possibility of further bricolage – a gland, a spleen, a lung. Butt is an orphanage for organs, for yards of blood and freshish flesh. Is this the Butt we want? Not yet.

'The trees that line the Avenue of Life we all must walk down cast everchanging shadows on us: we are inconstant creatures.'

The Butt we want is the one way back there, glowing in dapple, lit through spring's leaf etc. Literally lit through smoke and breath at the Cardiff Palace, the Burslem Rex, the Hippodrome in New Cross. This is not the Butt that talks about the Avenue of Life; this is the Butt that leers, cocky and Brylcreemed, that struts the stage, that lifts his middle finger and runs it under his nostrils which dilate as he says:

'Sniff sniff. What's that? Smells like fish to me.'

His wink is lewd. He repeatedly crooks the finger, a slim sexual limb exposed to the guffawing gorblimeys, the chars and mops, the rookies with berets on their shoulders, the broken-teethed demobs – they howl when he says 'Anchovy.' They know he's going to say it and they still howl. Butt never died, not even at the Glasgow Empire. Timing, that was it. It must have been, it wasn't the material, certainly not the material that Reg Voice records e.g.: 'My mother-in-law's a gem, she is, a treasure, honest, the crown jewels she is. So why hasn't anyone tried to steal her then, you tell me, why hasn't anyone tried to nick her?' Brings the house down (apparently).

The lone heckler, the bird man? Butt fixes him with mock glare: 'Hello. Got the runs out our face have we? Looking for Butt On Your Lip eh?' The man felt the gape of the fishwifery fixing him; Butt had an unerring eye, a sure ear. He told Reg Voice: 'There might be a thousand of them out there – but they're never a crowd. I see their faces, I can hear them whisper. I take them all in. They're individuals, hundreds of individuals and I speak to them as individuals.'

Down there, end of a stage-left aisle, twelve rows back, seats J12 and J11 – a girl with a peek-a-boo flicks away a squaddy's hand from her thigh. Butt: 'These long engagements play havoc with the genito-urinary tract.'

Two women get up, their seats slap, they push along their row. Butt: 'Here, look, if you want something that's really dirty, tell you what, you going the right way Mum – there's a bus outside, you can go and sniff its exhaust pipe. Sniff sniff, what's that – smells like filth to me!' And Butt bows. His right wrist describes decreasing circles. His right foot slides forward. Once upon a time, in the twilight of the Empires, he was an elegant man, quite a dish, lithe, he cut a figure.

Look at him now. Now, at last, he has what it takes to be a great comic; he's a geek, a teratologist's treat, a gargoyle on wheels, a grotesque, a piece of pathos, misshapen as a Fool. Now he has the physical attributes he lacked then; he has a lack of physical attributes. A handsome comic is not a true comic. The people, 'his people', might have adored him – but, *adoration*: it's inapt. Adoration! He thrived on it as sure as children did on Sunpat. His prettiness bred vanity which is a mask which occludes nakedness which is the s.q.n. of the echt comic. Got it?

This has nothing to do with the clown's desire to play the prince, a piety which Reg Voice subscribed to: 'Ray has a feeling that the old Ty Power roles will come his way one of these fine days.' (They didn't, they hadn't.) This has all to do with his unwillingness to bend his looks, twist his face, foster hyperbolic jowls, turn his lips inside out.

He was no more than a vehicle – a well tuned vehicle, certainly – for gags and patter that enlivened a filthy England of smog and peasoupers, of subfusc and reticence, of backs to the wall bonhomie, of everything-under-the-carpet-*quick*, of an England whose national dread of colour was only temporarily alleviated by late career routines such as:

'Got on a bus I did yesterday – Butt on a bus, put my butt on the seat, I did, upstairs – and I sit there, looking out the window, very pretty, magnolias and what have you, forsythia – don't laugh – nice piece of homework down there – I bent me neck, thought I'd like to be coming up the stairs behind *you* dear, upstairs downstairs bit of a stare, just a peek love – very lovely it is out there: dogs in spring – a young man's fancy now spring is here: that'd be Geisha Lady in the three o'clock at Haydock[1] – very lovely. But what's that smell. Sniff sniff sniff sniff – what's that? Smells, smells – it smells nasty to me, it does, J. Arthur nasty. An' I hear the clippie cloppin' up the stairs: "Ave dem right change pleese." Well I'm goin fru me change when I takes a dekko at the seat across, the one opposite – And there's this effing great dog turd on it, steaming, all shiny and coiled like. Sniff sniff – you know wher'the smell's comin' from. So I says to this nigger clippie, big bastard he is – unja, umja, unja, umja – ' Ray Butt's hands reach for his armpits, 'I says to him: there's a doggy-do on the seat there Rastus, what you goin' to do about it? And he says, know what he says, he says "I know dere is man – and I'm a going to take it home for my suppah." Eh? Take it home for is supper!! Wouldn't want to kiss 'im even if I was that way, duckies.'

The night he drove his Allard into the front of a Foden and

<hr />

[1] Or: Kempton Park, Chepstow, Market Rasen *et alia*. The name of the racecourse altered in accord with where he was playing. The recording I reproduce was made at the Alhambra, Toxteth.

killed his wife he had brought the house down with that one; oh, the encores, and after the encores another bottle of Johnny Walker, and then a few trebles for the road, just to steady him. The night he drove his Allard into the front of a Foden and killed his wife he was eight times over the limit (that would subsequently be prescribed by the Road Safety Act of 1967); one of the firemen reckoned it was his intoxication that saved him (how is not recorded); the degree and consequent duration of his intoxication obviated the administration of anaesthetic – the surgeons at St Mary's, Pompey had to wait to chop, and because they had to wait they had to chop more. Five hours is too long for legs that have been through a mincer. 'Gangrene's like a boy scout – always prepared.' That wait made Ray Butt a double amputee; he'd have kept the left had he not been so pissed.

He lost his legs, his car, his licence, his wife. It was the last that mattered. It was her not being that hurt. And the space vacated by his legs, his *scotches* – though that was a synonym he was necessarily shy of. Early on, before he faced his eternal culpability, before penitence raged in him, before contrition squatted his face and thrashed it and left it looking like a worn scrotum, before his first go at suicide (the only help he should have cried for was the right recipe for dream topping – he flunked on the barbs, got the gin right though); early on, before despair struck and promoted a second, a complementary paralysis, a mental one, all the inconveniences merely irked him. Even though bits of it had maculated him like red paint and white braiding, he had not actually seen Heidi's body and she might as well have been away on a long, selfishly long, holiday; she might come in with a Spanish tan and rope-soled shoes to wake him, take him for a spin.

Why had it been necessary to ban him from driving when he had no legs to reach the pedals with? That was adding insult. It wasn't the bereavement of his legs, his car, his licence, his wife that undid him, unzipped him so much that the insides went out of tune; rather, it wasn't *precisely* that bereavement. It was the comprehension of irrecoverableness that toppled him. It was a long while coming. Shock delays everything. And then he had a store of delusions to exhaust: delusions about the impermanence of his lot, about Heidi's whereabouts – for a while he convinced himself that she was in the house, leaving rooms as he entered, spying on him from behind swaying curtains he couldn't reach, *he could smell her*, he felt her presence, she was forever creeping out from the onyx urn that held her ashes: that swift shadow was her shadow.

That his career was finished did not occur to him. Celebrity-cripples ascribe their celebrity to their feats not their impairment. The spring and summer of '63 he talked every Thursday to Reg Voice and to Reg's fat Grundig, and he talked as though the last show had been last night, as though the new Light Programme series 'Mind My Butting In?' would be in production next month.

Reg Voice colluded. *Butt Joking Aside* (Javelin Books, 1964) is tirelessly anachronistic. Its subject's brain is on hold, he retrospects from the point where the finite past stopped, he is locked in a life that died with Heidi and his legs; but the present is in continuous production, it's pumped into his room like off-white wadding that is going to fill it, that's already hit the cornice, that will one day smother him. Reg Voice wrote – or, as he would and did have it, *penned* – an unwitting study of elective amnesia.

'Mind My Butting In?' had been cancelled ten weeks after the accident, when Ray Butt was still in hospital, when the whisper was *veg for keeps*, when he was unable to recognise Jonjon, Sonny and Laddy, when his hand lay limp in his mother's and she told the man from *The Echo* that 'We're not a religious family but I'm praying to Him on the hour every hour, regular as clockwork.'

It was his agent Nat Lewis and the scriptwriter Johnny Peabody who devised a solution 'where the sawbones had failed', where even Daph (who was in that game, sort of) had come up with nothing.

'Made me see red,' said Johnny Peabody, 'when you heard them referring to Ray like he was dead: you know, "Ray *was* one of the best . . ." Made me see red.' They knew their man, Nat and Johnny.

Nat: 'I never known a man love the sound of his self, his own voice, the way Ray does. Loves it.' Stroke of g. They came down the A3 like the wind, stopping only for a bite at Hindhead ('Loved that Macon, the one Ray does'). Ray Butt was his own best audience. They played him tape recordings of his shows – radio shows, the odd panto, the summer show here and there, Prestatyn, Clacton: they were all taken down for comical posterity. They played them and soon he was fighting fit, literally, he was punching the air. Well, of course – he'd been born into the profession hadn't he? A true professional – there's an epithet Reg Voice uses 63 times in the 159 pages of *Butt Joking Aside*. The true professional responded to the song of the true pro that was himself. That cure entered showbiz lore: the man who rescued himself from a coma; the power of laughter etc.; all the sentiment of the profession was invested in its propagation; mind over something or other; trouper's grit; was it 'The Day I Forgot Me Trousers' or was it 'That Frigging Nancy With Her Alsatian'?

The latter had aroused the Watch Committee in Great Yarmouth in 1958, which body was not satisfied by Butt's apology: 'Well I'm the last fellow who'd want to offend anyone, believe me. I'm not your angry young man or anything. Frankly though, if anyone was offended they had a funny way of showing it. They was rolling in the aisles at that one, falling about they was.' This gag is *not* about bestiality (p. 454), it goes like this, this is what brought Ray Butt out of his *ripvankip*, this is a gag with medical properties, tastes nicer than codeine and doesn't have letters after it:

'There's this queer, ain't there, this frigging nancy boy goes in a pub – you know, with her pink shirt and her trousers all cut tight over her cheeky little bottom. And she'd got this Alsatian with her. Big bastard. And she says to the barman – he's a big bastard too, she says, "I'd like a Martini and a Crème de Menthe if you pleathe dear." And the barman looks her up and down he does, and he says, "We don't serve your sort in here, you'd better hop it double quick." Well, she flaps her wrist against the bar this iron does and she says to the barman, "Look ducky you'd better therve me or I'll thet my Althathian on you." So the barman just laughs and he looks over the bar at the dog and he says to the dog who's just standing there looking a bit hungry the way them big bastards always do with his tongue lolling out, he says to the dog, "Get on, you wouldn't do what this nance tells you – you wouldn't harm me would you Rover?" Eh? Looks the dog straight in the eye, he does. And the dog, the dog, this big bastard of an Alsatian, he goes: "Bowsie wowsie." Eh? "Bowsie wowsie." Only – *thank you*, thank you very much you're a truly discerning audience if I may say so, and I may, thank you – only goes to show, only goes to show – thank you – that you never can tell one just by looking, you never can. Now, don't all turn round now, will you. Don't have a sniff. Sniff sniff what's that gent wearing, smells like perfume eh? Little dab on the limp wrist . . .'

They played it to him over and again, bad sound balance notwithstanding, till it broke through, seeped inside his skull. Ray Butt believed, initially, that the leery coarse rasp was something other than what it was:

'It took some time to sink in. I promise you this: I wondered if I was hearing God, I thought that's what God sounds like, that's His voice. Then I realised it was me.' Remember this. Ray Butt did. He built half a life on that delusion from a coma's edge. Not immediately of course, not till after the third failed suicide.

The wheelchair tumbled down the rough grass towards the edge of chalk pit's cliff. He could hear the drills of hell and the death rattle of hoppers three hundred feet below, he was that close. The ground was rutted, the bobbling vehicle overturned with only this much to go. He lay with his prosthesis shackling him, that close, listening to the drills and the rattle of hoppers with stalks of rue and wort tickling his ear and a lump of clunch denting his cheek, he lay helpless just six feet from the sheer drop to sheer salvation on a bright day with a scallywag nor'easter that gave him a headcold for his trouble, ticked him off the way God's wind will: he read His warning, even if he did curse the messenger.

Jonjon (provisional licence) had driven his crippled, widowed father up here, high up on the downs where the landbirds meet the gulls and they dogfight on the meaningful nor'easter. He and Sonny had returned to the car after a quick smoke (£4 per oz in The Kiss Me Hardy from a fat bullshitter called Quean Danny who scored from the sailors he pulled). No dad. They'd parked him beside the Super Snipe hearse with his rug over him and he'd rolled away. They ran down the mansard slope of the escarpment; the south and the sea before them, and the city, too. They saw the distant sampler of greens and greys and local colours. They saw pylons Indian-filing across the faraway, and the eezeefoam of cement works smoke. They didn't see their dad till they almost tripped on him.

He was smiling. He lay flattening the grass. He was smiling. They'd all but forgotten his smile. They could only have been boys when they last saw it. He'd forgotten how to move his face that way, he'd had nothing to move it for, no reason, no one. He was smiling and he smiled at them as though he had a secret to share – oh he would, he shared it. The brothers glance at each other as they upright the wheelchair. And their timid smiles – the whole family's smiling – their timid smiles are mutual acknowledgement that the Old Man's smiling the smile of the sane, the smile of contentment, and not the other. 'You're good Voys you are . . . could have been a gonner there I could, nasty slope, deceptive.'

Jonjon and Sonny ascribed it to bad driving: it was too private, insufficiently exhibitionistic to be another suicide attempt. Jonjon carried his father and Sonny carried the folded wheels. Ray Butt smiled at his sons. Jonjon comes over the grass towards the hearse like a young ventriloquist clutching an old dummy whose unfilled trousers make shorthand as they flap and twist. He had so little pride, this self-made widower, this uxoricide, that he neglected in those days to strap on his legs, he preferred the comfort of his big boy's arms. His limblessness was like a lachrymatory, a manifest of his guilt, of his penitence, of his grief. Not of his redemption though, that was not to be had by abandoning the articulated prostheses on a Parker Knoll in the corner of the bungalow's sun-lounge. They'd moved by then: Ray Butt had come home to Hayling, to his own, and to stairlessness (p. 22). Convenience of course; also, the beamed house at Littlehampton, The Jokesmithy, had been too pervious to Heidi's shade.

Ray and the Voys had been in the bungalow less than a month when she tracked them down, moved in with them. He was parked under the white lilac eating a rollmop for his tea, really savouring it, when he heard her, behind him, saying:

'It's the onions. It's whoever thought of adding the onions that you've got to thank.'

He spun himself through 180 degrees, but too slowly – it's not a cinch with a plate in one hand. She had gone, she was hiding. He had once asked her why she (née Marion) had taken Heidi as her stage name. She replied, with atypical obfuscation: 'You'll find out – one day.'

The lilac blooms swung gently and the poison laburnum shuddered and Heidi was hiding from him as she ever would. He could hear her voice though. And he'd heard his voice which was His voice. And he'd been spared each time he'd sought to finish his life. The foundations were laying themselves. He didn't suffer visions but he had vision. God is a surveyor, God is a nurse, God is a navvy, God is a caution, God is a lawman – these are conceits familiar to those practised in the treatment of theomorphic delusion. But God as a stand-up? God as a stand-up with a blue routine, a foul-mouthed misanthropic smug unfunny stand-up? A stand-up who is forced to sit down for ever?

A stand-up who never had a partner – no Warris, no Wise, no Allen – because no partner would have him even though the notional partner could have pimped off the name Ray Butt had made from the age of fourteen with his uke (The Ukelele Sprog made his debut at Chatham in 1941). Respected in his profession, but not *liked*. Too aloof, hoity toity, his own man and didn't he let you know it, a loner. Ray Butt knew what was said about him.

He wheels himself to the fridge in the sun-lounge, mixes himself another Martini: it's named for a barman, Stupid – they say *for* – and if you want my special recipe (as told to Reg Voice) it's ten measures, give or take half a doz, of Beefeater in a cold glass, no ice *in*, then the Noilly which only a mug takes the cork out of. Hold the Noilly nearby: sniff sniff – what's that? Smells like vermouth to me Mr Butt. Well don't you fuckin' put it in then. Eh? Twist or olive? Don't give a monkey's frankly. A loner:

the man who cannot stoop to retrieve the herring from the lawn. Look at the forsythia; it's disgusting, the way it turns to twigs. Typical. Blooms too early – someone got that wrong, the timing. God. Again. And magnolias, don't talk about *them*: in and out like a flasher's prick, gone before you can say *you pretty little purplish thing*. The garden's lovely though. And the bungalow. What you call them? Pantiles. Old mellow red; and the rough-cast plaster, very Spanish style – like a cloister down the short bit of the L, arches with tub plants and coils of green hosepipe. With benefit of mature garden. That's because they demolished the heap that was here before, kept the garden, stuffed the pile, mutatis mutandis – whoever they may be: did they ever play the Gateshead Ionic? New house, new God. Mutability's His trick: surveyor, geometer, nurse, quisling. He's in all of us – even sky pilots. Eh? Misses a lot, mind. Blooms for instance. A loner: the foundations are laying themselves, *themselves* (don't let Butt hear that – he's got enough wank gags to dry out a nickload of scrotums. And dyke gags? He'd drain the fens).

The foundations of what will come to be known as Buttism.

There are Buttists alive today who have never seen Ray Butt, The Founder, The First Redemptor. They know The Story – which is partial, omissive, fictive. They may even know that those are among The Story's qualities. They still fill the unmade road outside the bungalow called The Realm, Rest-A-Wyle Avenue, Hayling Island, PO 11. They still take the train to Pompey and the D7 (an apple green Dennis) to Eastney and the ferry to Hayling. They still, they still buoy along the road in their happy family flocks, passing the word to their little 'uns, their very own Voys, their Jonjons and their Sonnys and their Laddys (a stickler for education and spelling, The Founder, he'd raise an eyebrow or three at a proper name taking *ie* in its plural).

Flocks, I say: past the real golf and its nineteenth (p. 302), past Sinah Common and the Health Club shacks and the beached boats painted pink and garish to stand out from the mud which you're going to get to know. Here they come in their pastel track gear and platform trainers, and here are the oldsters in their zippered cardies who remember Ray when he was Butt Of The Joke – they're as young as he is. Where do they buy them?

Mail Order: no retail needed, not for velour nor for redemption. There's the mini-golf: that dad's burnt arms are around his putting boy and he's never going to look up, not so long as this crew is on the road. Nutters. Pilgrims. Sniff 'em a mile off. Plague, ague. The land's so flat they see the groynes. The land's so flat they smell the smell of rotting sea where it has struck the Hayling shore and fermented bubbly white, off white, brown now: sniff, sniff – what's that? They saw the scum on the bathers' shins from the ferry, and still they smiled, like Ray Butt. Trudge, trudge – further than it looks. (There was a cardiac in '86.) A map, a scaled fold-out analogue, may mislead by precision. A Buttish Map Of Life never does that. First left, second left, third . . . You didn't see, you concentrated so hard that you missed it. Now you've gone too far.

It was over there, on the dunes, beyond the coarse grass that shimmies on the sand, off out there towards the bleached marine horizon: all that's left now are rotted timbers, the skeleton, the silhouetted corpse of the house on the dunes, a bleached beached wreck. They don't know, they don't want to know. It's not in The Story thus it's not a landmark, not a Devotional Stop. Forget I mentioned it. Forget that Poor Eddie Vallender ever met the geek on wheels, let alone his mother.

Meet May Butt (née Marie Josephine Devreker, b. Ixelles, Belgium 30.6.09). She is the one who is not ugly in old photos. A proper corker in all the photos.

'Cor, I'll cork 'er all right,' would have said Ray Butt, but he wouldn't say that of his ma, no.

She was a refugee, a brave little Belgian, a foundling in the sylvan So'ton suburb of Portswood, taken in by a family called Baird who subsequently claimed kinship with John Logie of that ilk. She danced, she sang: her prospective fortune was in her throat not her feet, a modest fortune. Novelty dancer.

She was sixteen and pregnant when Harry Butt did the decent thing. He was a bad baritone, a bevvy man who aped McCormack: 'Oh the lilt of the Kerry dancers.' He'd have called himself Count had he had the nerve. He didn't; he had the scared, bang-to-rights gape of the eternal loser, the covert boozer. They scraped a living on the halls. It was down to her spunk. She made him dance. He never sussed that they were laughing *at* him. She abandoned her gift for him, they were lowest common dancers, so far down the bill you needed a microscope. Ray is their one and only son. Daph's a girl.

Every time May (née Marie) attempts to teach the nappy to speak French she gets a walloping, a proper black and blue from Harry. She believed – no, she knew – that it all went on Beefeater, Gordon's, Booth's, So'ton, Plymouth; he never blew a breath that had not juniper on it those twenty years. Yet when he died in 1951 with a liver the size of a suitcase in him and with a son receiving (on av.) five marriage offers per day, with a son of whom the Incomparable Max (Miller) said, grudgingly, 'he's minge but he's tasty minge, mind', he left his widow the freehold of seven houses: houses won in card games, snooker games, spoof jags, dog bets, bets on anything – the size of that biddy's bristols, who can piss furthest/highest/most, the wind's velocity, what the parrot will say next, the name of the copper on the white horse at Wembley (PC George Storey), the sex of the next person to come through the door, anything. They were not houses that those who had the choice would have wanted to live in; Harry hadn't even bothered with the rents from some of them; there was a family in Havant that hadn't paid a penny since the outbreak of war.

May changed all that: May Butt, Belgian of property, woman of means, mum of a star, gran at 38, a doter, well liked on Hayling, pillar of this and that, discreet, closer to her Daph than to her Ray but what a boon to him after his tragedy, what an oak, what patience, what a burden he was to her, what a way to be treated after all the hours and months of love she'd put in cooking, swaddling, bathing, rinsing the catheter, wiping him.

'Oo's my baby boy then?' she asks bravefacing it, trying to cheer him, not letting him see her wince as she crumples a soiled tissue at arm's length. He was her prisoner; he resented that as he resented his mongrel inheritance of her Brabançon blood: it contaminated him, mitigated his Englishness. He resented his dependence on her, longed each day for the Voys' return from school, longed each week for Reg Voice's visit, perked a little even when Daph dropped in for a moan about the senile vegetables who were her bread and butter and a nice cuppa. Daph's tip – warm the pot and *dry it*, thoroughly. He thought: these people she feeds off of, I'm one of them, I've achieved all they've achieved at half their age, it took me only thirty-four years to get where they've got with natural wear and tear in seventy; what spendthrift precocity. He hadn't a grey hair on his head, yet his face was an aerial view of sidings. May and her Daph plotted her Ray's prospects: Daph's expertise was in gerontology, her collection of thank-you letters from relatives of the lovingly cared for yet sadly passed on weighed 6 lb, her sunset home was Hayling's finest. See its curtain of grimy laurels, see its spirited repointing: the bricks were like bricks in a kindergarten illustration. That suited the senile vegetables. They knew where they were. Brick walls, slate roof, metal fretwork round the lantern. They knew where they were with Daph. She understood them; a good sort, Daph. She understood her brother too; *she* didn't believe he was mad.

That was their mother's conviction when Ray started to feel the pressure that was God's presence in him, when Butt of the Joke pronounced himself Butt the Buttist and began to talk about the Avenue of Life, when that became a catchphrase, the first catchphrase of the new Butt who was not so different from the old that he would abandon catchphrases which are instruments of solace and recognition – the words *sniff sniff* had been Butt's badge; they became a shibboleth, they were uttered by young shavers and old drabs who thus pronounced their adherence to the society of Butt even though they didn't know it. Ray Butt knew it though. The liturgic collusion of performer and audience; the litany of shared words (bereavement of meaning is no barrier); the church of comedy and God's palace of varieties – the same power shall drive them both.

He was a couple of wafers short of a communion (if you ask me, May Butt).

He'd been famous since he was twenty, fame was his norm, he treated it like I treat air (Daphne, pensive), it was more than a drug, he couldn't compensate for its loss, he had to regain it, he needed an audience, I've never known anyone who so much wanted to be the centre of attention let alone anyone who so much was, he spoke to them individually that's his magic, The Church Of The Best Ever Redemption and The Ministry On Wheels were his way of supplying himself with the fame he had to have, they were more of the same, the next trees on the Avenue of Life – there, he got me saying it even though I never believed a word, it would be like believing in the characters in a joke, they're not much different – jokes and the Avenue of Life, he peddled them both, I loved to listen even though I never believed a word, not that he ever saw it like that.

Daph Butt SRN, SEN, FRCM, was more starstruck than she'll admit; she was lit by reflected glory, by being his sister, by being the (literally) maiden aunt of The Three Little Surprises, the nation's favourite triplets who became the nation's most tragic triplets; she was more in awe of her brother than of any other man which may be why she was a proud victim of virginity and her hymen's closest chum. Equally that state may be ascribable to her antipathy to hands-on midwifery, to bearing such persistent witness to the bloody mess men make of women's insides that she opted for the other end of the Avenue of Life, the other g, and severed all but administrative links with the gyno side of the business, put in a manager, concentrated on the geriatrics who knew where they were with Daph – her brother's sister, a woman surely touched by him, his grace and name and blood, his faith, his vision. Daphne, sister of Ray, witness of his vision's conception.

She was there, at the very moment, a few feet behind him, at the very edge of the carpark whose cinders are separated from the cliff's skin of grass by a dotted line of squat stakes. Each afternoon the Voys took him for a drive in the Humber hearse, they always made the effort. Despite their differing characters they all loved dad at heart. Watch them manifest that love. Despite their differing characters they push him up the planks into the back of the hearse and bolt fast his wheels. They shove the two 6 × 2s in beside him. Daph nattered in the front. Sonny drove, slowly. Sometimes he drove to the hard at Bosham or to the ruined palace at Bishop's Waltham or to the cool chlorophyllous beech woods at Rowland's Castle. Ray enjoyed staring at duck ponds and old lichenous walls.

That day Sonny drove slowly up to Portsdown, up and up, up trim roads of villas conjoined like Siamese twins, up roads that zigzag towards the sky, up gradients that grow so the engine wails with pain at the load and the slope, up to the chalk rampart and the serial fortresses on it, monuments to martial might and Palmerstonian paranoia and old salts' fear of Boney Frog. The world seen from Portsdown. Did you ever look down from Portsdown on a summer day when the rain was on its way? Ray Butt wasn't mad – stand where he sat, and look down: awe *will* strike, sooner or later. The coastal plain is a map of itself, full scale, *grandeur nature* and natural grandeur; The Solent, the three great (natural) harbours, the horizontal sea, the many greys of sea and land, the strata of refulgence, the solidity of haze, the density of water, the shimmer of the skyscrapers – all the buildings bend. And you are made to understand the *necessity* of water colour – the weather arrives in vast washes of every pastel Dulux would shudder at: pewters and gamboges, the colours of mould and charnel, of the seepage from dirty bandages. Now and again the sky *is* blue, or blueish, sky-blue even – but it's already reverting, showing off its protean spectrum of nameless shades, never-to-be-repeated hues (grasp it now, fix it retinally, it'll never come back so long as you live, this is your one chance ever).

Ray Butt had been here before of course, he couldn't remember a time when he didn't know the view from Portsdown; he'd looked before, he'd gaped, but he'd never *seen*, never seen what he saw now. He forgot Daph was there, over his shoulder in her floral print and her caramel pea-jacket; he forgot that, and he forgot to hear the Voys' grunts as they flung their day-glo flying saucer between them, he forgot everything because what he had looked down over throughout his life was now articulating something, it was telling him it was itself, and a map, and an exemplar, and a model of the totality of this earth. The grey birds ride the swirling thermals like the fishes they used to be, they bounce on unseen waves, they make the air seem liquid. And in the dockyard the cranes that perch beside the rectilinear basins of graphite water are the skeletons of giant waders, orthogonal predators who feast on sea cargo and are never apart from their

271

own reflection. When a cloud – that is, an aloes- and coal-stained bladder parked low over the port – is split like a dirked haggis and it spews out its innards they pock the harbours, they pucker the basins and the serpentine creeks and the channels whose courses are marked by the blinding bleached sails of unseeable craft, they artex the little lakes that the spring tides fill and that the neaps let die, they give all the water (fresh, briny, deep, undrowning, oily, pure, bright, brown) an homogenous texture, that of a plucked bird's skin. One bird: Ray Butt's initial delusion is monoavian; one bird, larger even than those whose skeletons are now cranes and thus plucked by an infinite butcher, seethes beneath Pompey and beneath Hayling and all round Wight, seethes and pushes, and breathes in and out according to the moon to make tides. Ray Butt wasn't mad – stand where he sat, and look down through the steam when the city wears the high-gloss shine that only rain and distance can lend it, when the full scale map is polished, stand there and see the sea seeth and breathe and you will believe, as he believed, that the sea is a featherless fowl, an unfathomable fowl that founds the world, whose limbs push up against Darwin, Bombay, Montevideo etc. One world, one fowl. The fowl in Buttism is metaphor for and symbol of the integer. It was so from then on, from when the system revealed itself to him in The Infinite Moment. He said: 'We'll be eating lots of chicken then. And turkey. Duck . . .'

He sounded serene, keen, calm. Daph heard him, wondered about his tummy and his red meat lunch; he shared his chronic dyspepsia with all his loved ones, broadcast it with groans and halitosis. Lack of exercise. Daph moved towards him, then halted. Ray Butt had raised his arms horizontally, full stretched, oddly untensed, so they dangled there, floating on a zephyr, like the armatures of wings, like a man on a cross. He had once had a routine which comprised that same gesture, held for half a minute; then he would drop his arms to his sides with a sigh of fatigue: 'Uncomfortable way to spend Easter.' But here on Portsdown during the afternoon of the fifth anniversary of his wife's death (known, according to mood and circumstance, as The Founder's Tragedy, The Lord's Harsh Lesson, The Greatest

272

Sacrifice, The Dark At The Start Of The Tunnel, The Price I Paid) he maintained that position with ease, as though on the point of addressing the unseeable people with newspapers roofing their crowns in the gleaming city below. Sure, he had read ('studied') Dr Clark W. Grover's *Our Forgotten Bodies: A Forty Point Programme For Maximal Potential* and, yes, the cream of Havant and Hayling's physiotherapists had treated him, had coaxed his extant limbs to life as a whore might a john's shy cock. But *they* hadn't tranced him, *they* hadn't lent him extra-power, *they* hadn't rsj'd his pecs. He did it himself. He cantilevered his own limbs, solo. He generated the strength by will. Or he was invested with it: the power of passion; a gift granted in reward for his seeing; a physical manifest of supra-understanding; the vim of his lost legs augmented that of his arms; what he had conned in The Infinite Moment enabled him to transcend the shell which is a cell which is the blood and water fortuity called a body; in The Infinite Moment he had learnt how to hold his arms thus – and was giving thanks for that revelation and these:

a) The true eucharist is celebrated with the flesh of fowl, its blood, its egg. The fowl must be killed by the celebrant, by strangulation or asphyxiation, within such a period before its ingestion that the blood is warm.

When a plastic bag is placed over the head of a chicken the chicken will often peck through it.

'I thought, the first time, what a bloomin mess. Then of course it was shown to me and I saw, I knew and can tell you, that the chicken – *which is* – was a willing participant, that it was celebrating in advance, celebrating its glorious destiny, its fulfilment as a chosen chicken.' (It's astonishing, the number of people who swallowed Butt's guff.) 'And as it celebrates, the chosen chicken makes integral confetti for its wedding with death and its entry into the eternal marriage.'

In making integral confetti the chicken misadventures to admit air into the plastic bag. This necessitates resort to smothering by pillow, in Ray Butt's lap. The infrequent success of *this* method necessitates twisting the chosen chicken's neck, which action may cause the wheelchair to turn on its axis and the

273

chicken to evacuate itself and so leave a thin cloacal trail all across the walls and the ceiling etc.

Geese are worse. Two pairs of hands have to hold them whilst a third party punches the creature's neck. The Three Little Surprises surprise a goose by tethering it in the indoor pool where the stump called Ray Butt likes to lie on a Lilo, lapped by raw chlorine, thinking a bit. None of them wants the goose to die. But it must. It does. The smell of burning feathers and burning integral confetti ill befits worship and the practice is abandoned save between Whitsun and Yom Kippur (services outdoors). The use of geese and turkeys is abandoned on practical grounds. Duck egg is too rich for Pompey palates. And blood, uncooked, is less appealing to the faithful than is fried blood which is a rubbery moleskin omelette. They prefer, too, that the fowl's flesh should be cooked not raw. Thus is an elemental rite amended; the effects on a faith and its adherents of such liturgical excisions are moot.

b) The ingestion of the flesh of wingless creatures (oxen, dogs, pachyderms, foxes, horses, rodents etc.) is a denial of unity, a deprecation of the integer, a spit in God's face – for the consumption of a beast is a celebration of that beast, and of its species: and it is a blasphemy to celebrate those species which have failed, which are God's unsuccessful experiments, which show him to have been fallible, which disprove his prognostic prowess. He didn't know who was going to win the race of the species so he hedged his bets. There's no need to remind Him that, say, bears don't use toilets or that martens have never heard of calculus. The anthropomorphism of cartoons in which otters speak, of gags about homosexual Alsatians, of tableaux of monkeys dressed as men are all sops to God, improvements of his duff creations, means of disguising from him some of his mistakes. *Bambi* is a work of protective piety and devotion.

It is an invariable condition of enduring faiths that their dogmas should include dietary proscriptions. Indeed, a faith's success is in direct proportion to its complement of such proscriptions, to their comprehensiveness and to the stringency of their application. The tendency of Christianity 'to fall down the kazi and carry on round the U' (Ray Butt's phrase) can be attributed to its laxity in this regard. With the exception of Copts (very picky eaters, a hostess's nightmare) Christian sects can offer only Lent and fish on Fridays. It's not much. These perpetually bifurcating sects are fundamentally omnivorous. They eschew the practice of denial – and, thence, rigour, earnestness, commitment. A shared taboo is bond and badge. Ray Butt knew this without having to articulate it to himself.

Look how well Islam's doing, and Hinduism, Buddhism, Judaism: packing them in, all of them. Successful faiths, because if the punter is denying himself something for God then of course he believes that God will, in return, listen; especially if the punter isn't embarrassing God by munchingly drawing attention to duff species. Quid pro quo. Whoever's going to have faith in a faith where there's no price to pay, where redemption is free? The eternal peace has to be *won*. Hit them where it hurts – their stomachs, their plates and palates. Those are the agencies that speak to their minds. 'The Redemption through pain.'

Ray Butt never omitted the definite article: 'The Redemption' was Buttist style, as in: 'It's where the Roman gets it wrapped – in The Redemption. A few Hail Marys, a lifetime of peccavis – peck, peck, like the pigeon, eh? Peck. Peck. Peck. It's a habit. Don't tell me that's repentance. Pull the other one, Monseegnaw, eh? You don't see off sin by whispering through the grill to the self-abuser in a frock. Sin stains. Stains forever. There's no dry-cleaning of the soul. The Roman'll tell you he can get the stain out. He's a fibber, the Roman is. Like the dry cleaner with the stain he knows he's got no chance with. You've got to live with them. You have. With the stains of sin. The self-abuser in a frock's a dry cleaner, the blaspheming fibber. I'm not against tradition per se, history and that – but if there's one thing I know as well as the wheels of this chair, it's that the damned, and I use that word advisedly mind, the damned Pope has less legs than I got to stand on when he gets up there and pontificates like some pontiff, eh! What right? What right's he got? Lot of *wrong*, more like. It was shown to me and I saw, I know and can tell you that it's not just his clothes he's got wrong, it's the diet too. Look at what they'll eat, the Romans. Anything. Tripe. Tripe and onions. Where does that come from? I'll tell you – Lancashire: where they're all Romans. You look up your history books. Look in the index under R. Not R for Roman. R for Recusant – all from Lancs. Point proven, eh? Anyone here from Bury, Bolton, Preston? . . . No? Point proven. I went to Rome, I did, *once*. Just the once. Very important chap in films, took me to this swank ristorante – very posh, no mistake. I got the menu. Disgusting in its size it was. And of course they don't write it in English because they don't want you to know what you're eating. I said 'What's that mean then?' And this very important chap in films says: 'Zha eyes zheea spoinala chorda zee leetle bull.' Really! And it was shown to me and I saw, I know and can tell you that if you're eating the spinal chord of the calf you're eating not just the calf but that very bit of the calf which didn't get the message through to its rear legs that if it wanted to get on and not be a failure as a species it would have to walk on those two legs alone. And they eat it, the Romans – the ristorante is full of self-abusers in frocks, go sweat out sane. They eat it and they mock God with their mouths full of it. I'll vouchsafe to you that they've got the same chance of attaining The Redemption as a carthorse has in the Oaks.'

The question of Ray Butt's adherence to his own dicta. The problem is twofold: bacon and ham. Uncured pork was not a problem. Tenderloin, scratchings, crackling, chops, kidneys – he could take or leave them. But thick-cut, breadcrumbed ham between two wedges of heavily buttered bread with a smear of Coleman's – that was different. And blue tattooed rashers crisping and curling and emitting their perfume (green or smoked) – there was nothing to match it, there was nothing to match inhaling the reek outside Sam's Cafe or The South Hayling Luncheonette or The Man Friday (pedal decor, un-washed layabouts). Sometimes he'd smell it on the wind blown across the fields from the caravans at Higworth Farm, he'd smell it in his own garden, it crept through the hedge, vaulted the bungalow's roof. Back, streaky, collar. His nose puckers, salivation begins: he's a drunk, he's a junky, once more, once again, seeking an excuse: his mind moves to pondering the kinship of pigs and fowl, fowl and pigs.

The pig was a freak, the cross of an Old Spot with a Saddleback, an accident. It lived its pig life with seventy other pigs in a mud field that abutted on the mud flats at Tye, in a shared sty fashioned from reinforced concrete outfall pipe – such sties littered the field like hemi-cylindrical sarsens. Sonny haggles on the phone with Geoff Dickinson, the retard farmer the Voys call Pigfucker, though not usually to his pigface. For an extra thirty bob he agrees to deliver it to them at Mary's flat in Sir Bernard de Gomme Tower, over at Baffins, with a leash (a piece of string, it turns out: mean sod, Pigfucker); Sonny wants it delivered because Ray Butt won't have it in the hearse, not a pig, even if it does have special properties.

The hearse's silhouette crept along Eastern Road which rises as a causeway above reclaimed land and the slobbering persistent lapping of Langstone Harbour's high tide. Mallard Sands and Sword Sands are swallowed by water that's pocked as a plucked drumstick, and anchored craft perform their inebriate leaden jig of release from low-water mud, and South Binness Island is a subfusc streak of wind-dried mud and dog lichen (God can see that it's shaped like a section through a crab, like a bad try at a foetus). The hearse creeps across the site of the former airport and Ray Butt regards that as a happy auspice. It turns away from the blowy harbour with spray vitiating the nearside windows, blanking them with salt. Today's greys in Pompey are battleship and fresh asphalt. The reclaimed land round Tangiers Road looks unused to being land; transformed fowl, thought Ray Butt casting a withering eye over bum fluff grass and ill-laid pavement and adolescent poplars in wire sheaths.

Pigfucker was leaning against his van with a roll-up on the corner of Algiers Road where the wind whirls and eddies. Abandoned plastic bags zip through the air like predatory seabirds. Predatory seabirds swoop on marge wrappers. A ruff of foil round a gull's neck is commonplace. The wind whirls and eddies, the wind is bent and concentrated by the tall blocks, the towering dystopias, the vertical slums, the back streets in the sky, the affronts to God (they're not bungalows), the exhortations to suicide – which is not a sin of despair but of presumption, of presuming to usurp God's calling the terminal shot. Pigfucker got the pig out the back of his rustfucked Commer pig sty where it had been gnawing on a bacon side hanging from the roof – quite a feat when Pigfucker prosts every corner, for your piggy trotters keep sliding from you in the bath of pig blood, pig shit and Dettol that makes Pigfucker's van smell the special way it does. The Voys recoil from it as Pigfucker hauls the pig down the liquid sewer of the tailgate dragging behind it, caught on its trotter, a coil of barbed wire which it frees itself from before it is pulled to the hearse.

Ray Butt stares at it through the maculate window, tries to fix its eye but fails because a pig's idea of eye contact is with a half-eaten Miller's Pork Pie (its cellophane wrapper entire) that is rotting at the grass's edge. Ray Butt still stares, then he tells them: 'That's it. Take him up then.'

Jonjon, Sonny and Laddy pull the pig across the grass to the door of Sir Bernard de Gomme Tower, fifteen storeys, system-built with an OMO[1] pack on every balcony. Pigfucker counts his money with bewildered deliberation; he finds getting the tip of his tongue halfway to his ear helps him determine which are the forged notes and which the pinchbeck florins.

He pokes his pig face through the hearsedriver's window and says to Ray: 'That's it. That's all right . . . Interest's sake – what they want that pig for?'

Ray Butt doesn't look at him and replies: 'Proof.'

And Pigfucker's off down The Jenkin's Ear for a pint of wallop and a pork banger.

The Voys coax the pig into the lift, beat it into the lift, it shits in the lift which doubles as a urinal and has anatomically ambitious primitive frescoes to prove it. On the top floor the pig bolts. They kick it along the trashed echoing hall and into the flat whose front door Mary opens for them, smoking a joint of Congo grass.

---

[1] OMO: a washing powder manufactured by Unilever. The acronymic properties of the name were first exploited in Pompey in 1960. The display of a packet in a window signifies Old Man Out, and that the woman of the house is sexually available. Prices vary.

Mary doesn't mind them bringing a pig in. The flat belongs to the absent sailor and the sailor's wife whom Mary rents a room from and, besides, it's such an album of fire-scorched walls, smashed empties, soiled clothes, undulating lino tiles, jissom-stiff sheets and pyramids of Rimmel tipped filter tips that, as Mary has it, 'a pig won't notice'. Mary gets back to strumming a guitar, singing a song with French lyrics. The balcony: the OMO pack attached to the rails by a bent wire coathanger; the cleaning rags that have never cleaned the filthy flat yet are themselves filthy and hang like bats; the view of land and sea, mud and sky, the block opposite and the hearse below. They wave to the hearse below.

It took the three of them, and Sonny sustained a nasty bite on the ball of his thumb.

It took the three of them, and even then they only just managed to lift the squirming, self-soiled pig over the three feet eight inches high rails. They certainly did not *throw* the pig. It struggled on the heat-warped plastic covered bar along the top of the rails, and fell, fell, fell the hundred and eighty feet. Its legs flail as it squeals as it falls. Its legs do flail. It *is* trying – that is evidenced by the superporcine way it articulates its ears, as though they have a part to play, as though they are memorious of having once been wings.

'Did you see,' demands Ray Butt, 'did you see them? It was *trying* to fly, it *wanted* to – but you effin' prats, you scared it didn't you? You scared it shitless. I saw you getting it in the lift there. Kicking, prodding. No wonder. What d'you expect? If you took a pigeon up there after you'd kicked it around like that *it* wouldn't have been able to fly either, it'd be upset too. It wanted to, that pig, it wanted to . . . Here, switch that off,' he says to Laddy who has turned the ignition. 'Switch it off and go fetch. We're going to salt it and cure it. I got the proof, haven't I. It would have flown if it hadn't been for you prats. You go and fetch it here.'

Morosely, silently, the Voys open the hearse's doors and slope-shoulder across the grass to where the untwitching pig, which bounced off the eighth-storey wall and a Vauxhall Velox's bonnet, lies on asphalt that was never meant to be an abattoir, bleeding from its eyes and nose, making a crimson lake for the wind to ripple and for litter to stick in.

So may Buttists eat pork.

So may, according to Ray Butt, Jews – provided it is believed to be King Rabbit: the moniker amends the meat source, euphemises it, literally speaks happily about it. As we all know, representations of the pig – unlike those of chickens, guinea hens, pea hens, ducks etc. – are eschewed in the iconography of The Church Of The Best Ever Redemption. Pigs: eating bacon and ham is eating left-handed; they're tolerated as putatives of fowldom, not encouraged. For The Church Of The Best Ever Redemption does not wish to offend; in some regards it doesn't. Ray Butt, in twenty-five years as a comic, never cracked a Jewish joke. That's allowed only to Jews, that's sacred. He'd have loved to rip off gags from the compilations entitled 'The Other Parts of the Matzo' and 'Fishing for Gefilte' but most of his best friends were – that's showbiz. Ray Butt admired family – but as an idea only.

Look at his. Dead wife, those sons. They're called the Voys because on the beach on the last family holiday, at Nat Lewis's villa at Beaulieu Sur Mer (Av. Blundell-Maple), in 1960, Sonny and Laddy wounded a dog in the surf. Ray and Heidi watched, approvingly, and held hands between their stretch-out sun-sofas. The dog is a big bastard (p. 262), it's *un berger allemand*; they blame their dogs on the Krauts, just as they blame their Frenchies on us even though they've got a town called Condom (to whom do the Netherlanders ascribe their funtime caps?). A tearful Frenchwoman – a tart or a waitress, they all are – approaches Ray and Heidi. She holds a frightened beige poodle in her arms; her too tight swimsuit shows (when it's all added up) at least an eighth of a meridional beaver. She holds the poodle in one hand, waves the other.

'Sont des voyous,' she says, emphatically; she's pointing at the triplets, the bathing-trunk-boys with lofted metal chairs against the pure blue that stretches from Metropolitan France to far-off Algiers where the bad brothers Berg work. Ray Butt mistakes her tears for tears of gratitude. He believes that she's crying out of relief at the triplets' rescue of her yappy lap dog from the big bastard. Ray and Heidi are so proud when this Frenchwoman with a crutchful of vermicular hairs reiterates her debt to the triplets: 'Voyous, voyous . . .'

Ray Butt nods with a stage-size smile, gives her a thumbs up, points to his mouth: 'No parlay.' He mimes writing, hands her a Biro and a postcard (a pin-up with a beachball), gesturing.

She writes the word *voyou*, turns on her calloused heel, disappears among the gaily coloured parasols. Ray and Heidi conclude that this word must mean *hero*. So its anglophone truncation becomes the new collective nickname – they're growing up so fast that The Three Little Surprises is no longer apt. And it embarrasses them. So does the way he kisses them. Nothing can untie the knots of blood says Ray Butt; that's what makes family special, like it or not. That's one to remember.

His kissing is mere mimicry of most of his best friends. So was the trip to Waddesdon, the Rothschild palace where London Jewry takes its children in order to show what can be achieved: the Three Little Surprises are unimpressed by the gloom, the gilt, the stern and lumpy Frenchness; why should anyone wish to emulate *this*? And are the families gawping at the ormolu carpets and Limoges bedspreads and Aubusson clocks really Jewish? They don't look rich. They don't slip banknotes into the triplets' hands. Their noses are not smeared with sun-block the way they invariably are at home, at Littlehamptom, in the Jokesmithy's garden: *that* is what's special about Jewish noses, the glistening white emulsion, the stripe (p. 20). Without their stripes Jews are no longer exotic and they're certainly not as generous.

c) Christ was killed by Romans; if Jews had any part in the most momentous of all deaths they played it unwillingly or unwittingly, forced by Romans or duped by Romans.

d) Christ was not bearded. Would anyone who so believed in the creative prowess of mankind eschew an instrument as ingenious as the razor? There is further evidence yet, a further reason why The Church Of The Best Ever Redemption prohibits the wearing of a beard[1] – Barabbas was bearded; obviously, he

[1] The French Foreign Legion also proscribes facial hair, doubtless for different reasons.

was – with that name, which means *bearded* (so speaks The Founder). Christ is habitually represented as wearing a beard for no reason other than that 'the painter's boyfriend was growing his first at the time.' Ray Butt considers *all* portrayals of a bearded Christ to be: 'buggers' blasphemies, putting bumboys on a pedestal to mock believers. They don't celebrate the light of the world, they flaunt the objects of perverse lust, catamites and homowhores, brawnhawkers. Oh they nail them to the cross all right. I've seen the stigmata on the hands of boy prostitutes. I've felt the weals on those foul palms that have been for hire, that have roughly fondled the serpent of depravity and concupiscence, the many serpents.' Beards are masks, disguises, fronts. Ray Butt was no more afraid of tired notions than he was of bigger thefts. The Church Of The Best Ever Redemption 'borrows from everywhere. We take the best of the each of the rest. The *best* only is good enough.'

Butt's vision was born on Portsdown Hill, on The Founder's Day. It was conceived in his life. Run-on. Continuum. Buttism's dogmas are analogues of The Joke's life. The second half of his life is a metaphor for the first. ('Metaphors are mirrors / That distort for shape's sake.') Conceived in his life and in his affection for the only language he speaks (obviously).

Why's He called The Son of God? Because He blinds like the *sun*. This knowledge is granted only to the English (and the Gibraltarians, the Americans, the New Zealanders etc.). You don't get this griff if you're Italian; maybe that's why you're a Roman, Luigi – figlio/sol. You don't get it if you're a Frog with a wrong-named capote anglais in your pocket – fils/soleil. Son/ sun: it proves the closeness of anglophones to the source. That's why we're conquering the world. God's chosen.

The clichéd consolation (is it consoling?) is that the awful thing about death, in this instance Heidi's, is that there are so many things you wanted to say (to Heidi). Ray Butt thought hard, and again, and couldn't think of a single thing. If marriage is a lie that two people agree to tell, and to tell each other, then theirs was a silent lie, a longlasting lie transmitted and fortified by gestures, habits, tics, the depressing soft sounds of make-up being removed at night. No, there wasn't a single thing he had wanted to *say* to her. Certainly not a single gag. Not one. Not that she was that keen on his later material – the race jokes (he was a pioneer in this field), the genitalia jokes, the queer jokes, the religious jokes: 'The Devil would be doing a lot better ladies and gents, he'd be converting a lot more of you if he could spare the time to get out the house, but he's a homebody, he really is, he spends so much time frigging his family, shagging his little daughters, that he's too whacked to do his work . . .' All these jokes. The jokes for the pay-so-well Rotarians in Roundhay, the Round Table in Moseley, The Lions in Alderley Edge. Presence: they bathed in each other's presence, Ray and Heidi did, in a realm beyond words – believe that and you'll believe that words can jump from a page – beyond the necessity of words. He had had nothing to say to her.

This form of consolation consoles the consoler, not the consolee. It allows the former to make a semblance of entering the portals of the latter's grief, to make a semblance of sharing that grief. It's a long shot that will bullseye only once in ten times. Ray Butt understood this. (A plumber of the human soul as well as a colony of God.) He understood when he'd been hit by the earnest chitchat of deepfeltness, by duty rites. He thought about it. He put spin on it. He reversed the idea. There may have been nothing special he had to say to Heidi but there was plenty that she wished to say to him, she wished to tell him, and has told him, plenty – about grace, about the best ever redemption (hence the name), about swimming through the light. She talks to him. She has so much to say. The Founder listens. He moves the ashes around the bungalow. He loves her in her onyx urn, he loves her all around him. He doesn't envy other, completer men their wives. When 'Butt Joking Aside' was deprecated by the showbiz press corps' finest he thus consoled Reg Voice: '*Critics*. They've got no taste. Look at their wives. Critics' wives . . . blimey!' Reg Voice's wife had long since bolted with a curtain fabrics rep. He agreed with Ray. He always agreed with Ray. Founding a church was no problem for a star like Ray, with his chutzpah and his something extra, his charisma. For every little piece the surgeons excised and preserved in display bottles he gained an extra something: his power was in inverse proportion to his body's integrity. The less of him there was the more of him there was. There's Heidi in her urn, there's a nugget of his spleen in the jar beside her.

At any given moment – now, for example – there is someone in a Pompey bar (The Maritime or The Semaphore or The Albert R.N.) talking about Ray Butt, about how he lost his wife, and the terrible thing that happened to his mother, and what a shame it was about The Cross after all that effort, and the flotsam and bin people and starey brain-victims who came to him. All of them had imaginary animals clinging to them which they could never brush away. They were the joiners because they were the needy: madness is the belief that there are answers, that there are absolutes. A capacity for one faith means a capacity for any faith. The great division is not between Prods and Romans, not between Buddha and Mohammed, but between those possessed of an appetite for belief and those who lack it or despise it. And believers are wont to work their way through the menu.

Some were bound to try out Buttism, to place their hope there, however briefly, en route from, say, the New Cyrenian (Reformed) to Hubbard, crossing the path of others moving from Elected Adventism to the Embracement Love Of Kei Ji-Ha. The joiners, the believers, the faithful pursue topographies as set and signposted as those of gypsies or commercials. Butt, The Founder, was a stop, a fixed point then a cardinal point – that was after Poor Eddie Vallender had joined him and after The Voys had jacked in the band to promote their father. It was now the family business. And while no one much liked what Ragged Cathy Dodson did – everyone came over squeamish, in fact, especially Laddy with his weak stomach – it *was* A1 publicity, *what* an advert, all were agreed. Agreed that if it was managed right – tweaked a little, twisted a bit, perverted, tipped on its head – that it was *some testimony* to The Founder's Power. At the worst it drew attention to his name.

Ragged Cathy had what is called a history of what is called drug abuse (it wasn't, it never is *abuse* – it's just use, *use*, that's all). She had dropped acid tabs like there was no tomorrow, which there wasn't because days ran into other days and Sunday followed Monday, night is lit bright as the sun. The moon was a dazzling bulb indistinguishable from the sun which is also the son of God and can only be truly worshipped by staring at it till it goes out. She learnt fast. She believed in Butt, believed him whirling on his chair with his mike lead bound round him, screaming at the roof of the old drill hall by Fratton goodsyard, screaming at the eighty faithful, shutting out the sounds of shunting, tugging at the lead bound too round the wheels and axle, jabbering in tongues, all glossolalial abandon and jet eyes, jabbering a language that might have been spoken at the very root of the world, a gamut of ululations, shrieks, clicks, deep-visceral exhalations from the first farmyard. Ragged Cathy had a history, too, of self mutilation, self incineration. She got her own back on herself with scalpels and blowlamps. She got her own back on her parents and their parents and the special teachers and the wardens and the visitors and the day nurses and everyone who had been kind and everyone who had been unkind. Scalpels and blowlamps, pinking shears and lighters, razor blades, sewing needles, light bulbs. Especially those who had been kind – because they presume, they understand (they don't), they're seeking ownership, they're trying to trespass. She tramps Pompey streets, clutching a gingham spongebag. She tramps the relentless grid, the ranks and ranks of brick houses. She chews her tongue and bites her lips. Her mouth is a meal for itself. The desiccating leftovers stick to her chin. She tramps and tramps with chicken feathers glued in her hair for The Founder whom she'll listen to tonight as she has every night since she arrived at this brick city set on mud which is fowl. The first night she missed was the night of the day when she had followed the sun from her no-toilet, smashed pane, half-roof squat past the ranks and ranks of brick houses with OMO packs in the windows, past the people who were made of mud (*she* knew where they had come from), past the Halals on their haunches, past corners, street corners, house corners, wall corners, kerb corners, brick corners, past streets of houses that dash to vanish on the distant horizon, past streets indistinguishable from the street at the last corner and the corner before that, past bricks, past streets whose cast-metal signs she bends to stare at from so close that she cannot read the whole name without shifting her neck (vonsh, egina, ssie, wersc, lepho), past privet – in every privet is a sooty plastic bag, filled with the remains of something, a meal, a liaison, a life. Privets are secret museums.

Dutifully she pursued the sun, south to Southsea Esplanade. She tramped across half past the hour and noon itself on the floral clock. She observed the oscillations of a sprinkler, the temporary animals the jets created, the darkness of the wet grass, the plucked-skin surface of the perpetually disturbed pools of water. She clutched her spongebag which contained important items. She clutched it with both hands to her tummy. At the playground she ignored the prohibition of adults unaccompanied by a child. What is age? She put down the spongebag at the base of the metal frame that supported the swings. She could smell the metal. The concrete was crazed, it wasn't meant to be, the sun had got to it, done this to it. She licked the metal tubing. The hepatic tingle, the spinach taste, the boundless vitamins in metal. She clung to a chain that attached a swing to the frame. She sat on a swing, she jerked herself into motion, not high. Effortful kicks. Irrhythmic kicks so the chains buckle, joltjolt, jigjig. She grips tight. The total concentration, the centripetal vigour, the willed oblivion that precurse sexual release. When she finishes she crosses the road to the sea wall, to the stairs to the beach. Ragged Cathy knows the place when she reaches it. Blind to Wight, blind to the black bastion in Spithead, blind to the big ships on the bluegreen that seems higher than the land, blind to it all, she lies and wriggles and rolls and parts the pebbles to form a set. She covers herself in shingle. She lies alive in a self-built barrow. She blends with the beach, with the tarred stones and desiccated kelp. The shore's the end. The tumulus weighs some. Her breaths are short, curtailed by that weight, by the load on her. The luxury of pulmonic liberty is denied her – that's good, that's the ticket, that's how she wants it.

She stared at the sun all day long, all that sunny day, stared at the sun in a sky unstained by clouds and Spithead vapours, stared at it – omniluminous idol, world light, the son, the sun! (Metaphors are fairy tales. Don't believe everything you hear in

286

drill halls.) She stared at the sun till there were many suns, weeping suns, suns that sidle from behind the suns, bullseye suns, suns ringed with jet, with ruby, with tooth enamel. There are colours in the sun shown only to those who worship the light of the earth, whose blinkless eyes fill with motes big as swimming commas, swirling commas that grow and conjoin and generate further same till they obfuscate the sun in complete eclipse.

Ragged Cathy learnt that once she had seen the light of the world she was never to see it again. Once only, that's all that's granted.

Then it's dog-and-stick time. That's the price. She felt the wet sea on her undirected insteps, the invisible tide.

Simon Mavro had no insteps, the train had had them. Butt is a model, a lesson, an example. Butt's faithful were apes, sheep. Followers follow. They mime the mindcast of The Founder. They abjure facial hair. They believe. They borrow an imagination. They ask for and receive a map, the streetplan of the Avenue of Life, the routemarker to the best ever redemption etc. Deep-Worship demands: 'identification'; thraldom; trance; the willingness to practise 'mental terrorism for Christ's rebirth'; the untempered acceptance of all knowledge channelled through The Founder – that includes nuclear theology and the conception of God as an *attainable*, visitable, androgynous ancient. Its white-feathered body emits the beatific heat of heaven and bleeds dazzling blood onto pellucid white sheets that absorb it without stain. (It is very close to death, always has been: that's the special condition of immortality.) Simon Mavro tattooed his brain with Buttist precepts, slogans, dogmas. He followed, as close as he might. But there was still a gulf. He was not Ray Butt. Simon Mavro could not forgive himself for not being Ray Butt.

He suffered a stammer, eczema, seborrhoea, myopia, virginity; he coped with them, was resigned to them, they were irritants. Not being Ray Butt was a jape of fate that he couldn't come to terms with. He walked – to tempt himself to change his mind, to emphasise to himself the gravity of his prospective sacrifice. He walked for hours through the dark. It was already dusk when he disembarked from the ferry at Gosport on the tenth anniversary of The Founder's Tragedy, The Greatest Sacrifice, The Lord's Harsh Lesson – Saturday 18 September 1971. He kept his head down to obviate eye contact with tars, tarts, tabloids, trash-yous; he kept his head down to watch his pedal progress, the facile consumption of pavement stones, of cracks between them. He monitored the robotic responses of the tools at the ends of his legs; he despised the grinning plimsolls, the primitive rhythm; the invariable repetition, left right, the lack of versatility, the straitened gamut of his feet's repertoire. He hopped, he proceeded with one foot on the kerb and the other in the sodium-lit gutter, he scuffed. The feet of the species are underachievers, low level creations, God's inspiration was flagging by the time the southern extremities were got to. They are, *pace* Dr Clark W. Grover, of limited utility. Ray Butt had none and he was The Founder, The Truth: he got along without them.

At some time after ten o'clock Simon Mavro climbed over the stakes and wire of the fence beside the bridge in Gudge Heath Lane, three quarters of a mile from where Ray Butt's foot had depressed the accelerator and effected the collision that changed his life. Simon Mavro tried to walk down the cutting's black bank but his feet were predictably useless on such an incline, inadequate. He slid down to the cinders on ground elder. If you put your ear to the rail, which shines under even the dullest sky, you can hear the vibrations, feel the faraway train. A train can turn a ha'penny into a whole penny. A train is a surgical instrument, if the patient so elects. The driver of the 22.13 So'ton St Denys to Fratton goods knew nothing about it. A linesman in a dayglo safety jacket discovered him at dawn, on his belly, like a seal, moving very slowly beside sleepers, inching along, no more than a body's length from the separated shins and plimsolled feet, moaning, calling to God not, as the linesman believed, in agonised despair or amputational delirium but to attract His admiring attention to the sacrifice, to the achievement of Buttist normalisation.

Simon Mavro and Ragged Cathy were among Butt's people. They were Buttists. And so was Poor Eddie Vallender, after a fashion. But Mary never was, not Mary. Mary never took to Ray, and vice versa. It was May Butt that Mary liked; loved is not too strong a word. Though, yes, sure, love is not the first thing you'd associate with Mary, who played in the Voys' band and had shiny black hair that was iridescent like mineral, nacreous like sevruga coal.

Bonny Vallender gasped when she saw it: she thought it the most beautiful hair she had ever seen, and she thought Mary's the most beautiful face she had ever seen bar one (if you omit her own).

Two marriages, one death.

Donald Rollo Hogg-Tod to Charlotte Jane Vallender (Toddy to Bonny), Salisbury Cathedral, Saturday 24 July 1971. All around Bonny's place there were doves that drew white scrolls against the trees. They were out for her wedding. They were swooning at her wedding. They were falling and tumbling as they'd never dared before. They were dolphins in the air for you Bonny, for you Toddy. The marquee was almost a big top. Its guys were like sinew in steroid-porn – so taut they might snap. The overwhite canvas was distended. The acacias, the Scots pines, the cedar, the wellingtonias were such a green they might have been cleaned for that day, that special day when Douglas lost his little girl. Sky: blue as a flag. Everyone: drunk, cheerful as a halfwit, hot, just loving the breeze when it shows. Eddie: sad as war.

Try seeing Bonny all swan-white against the canvas with her sacrificial garland of leaves, the green and white laurel that'll be dumped when the hymen's ruptured. Oh look at her and her flowers and her rapturous smile, her smile of consummatory anticipation, her twinkly grins to her friends who were parties to the conspiracy of purity (Smeggy Beggy, Chrissie Wasserman, Gayle Tingay). She had her arms around Douglas whom she hated everyday but that day. Monica breathed gin and quinine, her face was stiff in a representation of learnt joy, she wore a moustache of violet lipgloss, she wore it on her teeth too like bad blood from gingivitic gums. Her suit was the colour of the buddleias that lolled with brewer's droop: *too bright*, that's what the mondaine glances of the Hogg-Tod's side said, and three years too short. They were smart people, their London friends.

The division between the two families who united that day,

till death did (and it did) and not, yet, pecuniary; not even of accent or, crudely, of class but topographical. The Hogg-Tods were quasi-metropolitan, weekdays in town, weekends at the estate (2,700 acres of mixed use farmland; house ascribed to the Bastard brothers; parkland; stables; cottages, a ha-ha; two farmhouses). They dropped the names of world-class decorators, hairdresser friends of royalty, wits from chatshows, theatrical producers, sartorially adventurous antique dealers, faces famous from magazines – people whom, surely, no one actually *knew*. But they did know them and here they were, gossiping, drinking, yawning, stretching. Exhibits, exotics from a distant zoo, fielding the awed, dowdy, all-right-for-some questions of Douglas and Monica's exhibits, mundanes from the local zoo. Monica had never believed that anyone *really* wore Nehru collars; she had never believed that women of her age *really* wore dresses made of Moroccan cushions; she had never seen so many queers before let alone allowed them in her garden – and so many of the queers weren't queer but just had the Jules family voice, the clothes, the wrists: she could tell they weren't queer from the way they homed in on Nicola Begley (of whose sobriquet she, like its bearer, was innocent) – they could smell her, sense her aptitude and lubricious ambition; they could tell. Well, so could anyone have done. Smeggy Beggy was dressed in silver and black: four-inch black platforms with silver sequins, silver satin hotpants, black blazerette, nothing else, save a black fedora with a silver band.

Toddy had complained all week of stomach cramps, of duodenal fire, of such pain when passing motions that he had quit eating. Butterflies, was the unanimous opinion of the Vallender side; and the boondocks doctor, Bailles Barker, whom his mother had called to the farm, had, in his incompetent commonsensical way, agreed. Butterflies. They fluttered by, from buddleia to mahonia, lighting on lillies, clumping through the thick thick air on that special day. All afternoon, men from Vallender Light bent hunchbacked in the meadow on the far side of the river, trowelling divots, fashioning holes for the night's display. Beside the leet where I'd seen a viper and had so scared Eddie (p. 8) and beyond the molehills that their co-

291

workers were creating, others of Douglas's employees were erecting a lance-work frame as high as a house, built of thick stays, buttressed with same, hatched with laths, carpentered with swiftness, bolted with ferrous rods, covered with wire, leaned on by ladders, hung with conjoined shells of blue paper, a hoarding for the advertisement of a marriage.

Poor Eddie sat on the lawn's last terrace. I hadn't seen him in seven years. He had been back to The Garth once, late on an October night in 1968 when he had spoken twenty or so words and had stayed for half an hour: 'Hullo, just going by, thought I'd see how you were . . . Well, thanks for the tea, have to get along.' In between he had said nothing. His demeanour had precluded the expectation of replies to the embarrassed, banal, earnestly inquisitive questions Monica and Bonny had asked him. (Douglas was *away on business*, thanks be.) Eddie nodded in the kitchen, he shrugged, a bit. He squeezed a tea bag between his right thumb and that hand's little finger. He stared – mother and daughter subsequently realised – at his reflection in the window, he hung over the garden with broken nails and hands grained with oil. He refused to stay the night and scratched the crown of his scalp, his head down over the table so they saw the sore where, evidently, his damaged fingers had done damage, balded him.

He was there at the wedding, uninvited by either side, silent, teetotal, apprised of its occurrence, perhaps, but not of its date by a newspaper announcement. He didn't say. But he was there. He had grown tall and his suit was a short man's, a short dead man's, bumfreezing, north of the ankles, tight, buttoned, old, subfusc. His head was near shaven. He might have been on day release. There were dandelions around him (Douglas never found a gardener diligent enough to tackle the steep parts of the lawn); the diuretic leaves flanked him, framed his legs which were institution-white between his Maclary Easy socks and cuffless trouser ends, up near his knees, bermudaishly. I kept meaning to go across, to hug him or something. But Chrissie Wasserman. And besides, he was a statue of himself. He was forbidding, not part of the party, apart. It's shaming to admit to such negligence, to acknowledge it after all these years, after all the poison that has flowed under the bridge. His very presence was an embarrassment. We wanted him to have prospered, not to have conformed to all expectations, not to have crept into sad adulthood, not to have been sunk by life, not to have been dressed by charity, not to have had his scalp randomly shivved so that there remained tufts, missed bits, capillary islands, isthmi of razorlessness. His crown was gnawed, scarred. He was grown up now; he had grown up into covertness, resigned quietude. He was a man now. His being was as scarred as his crown. He was a veteran of solitude, a victim of friendlessness, of lovelessness: this was discernible even before the figure was recognisable as Eddie's. His body broadcast his plight. He was asocial of necessity for he lacked both the elemental nous and the will to make contact. And such bereavements foment a brittle carapace, a deterrent to others. He had handed Bonny a small cubic box wrapped in magenta paper: he leaned towards her, clutching it with two hands as though unused to such a manoeuvre, as though figuring the way to do it. He ignored Douglas in a manner which suggested that he might not even have recognised him. Then he had gone to sit alone, to talk only if talked to.

The sun in the west blessed our beautiful couple with a display of a million pinks striped with baby blue. (Who knew what that portended? Eddie? Eddie.) It was dark and dancing had started by the time that I sat down beside him on a riverside bench. In the marquee animated silhouettes kicked each other, threw their fists high in pain. Anthracite Entropy electrified the night with douce sighing guitars, electric violin and keening voices; facile predictability, that's the thing. The audience must always be ahead of the band. Eddie seemed untouched by the amplified balm, the formulaic thrills. He never once looked at me. He made no greeting. He spoke like he was taking up a conversation recently interrupted. He leaned forward on the bench as though uncomfortable in his own body, as if it didn't fit him right.

He said: 'We're going to build one like that . . . something like that – high, really high.'

I gazed across the river and the meadows to where the floodlit spire rose from black clouds of bough.

'You are? Who's we?'

'Maybe not quite like that, but very high. I like the red.[1] The red's important, very important. The red is the blood.' His voice was light, croaky, dry as old paper.

'Just *who* is going to do this?'

He ignored my incredulity: 'Oh our church . . . the people I work besides. The Founder. It'll be one of the wonders of the world. Do you believe she loves him?' Eddie was watching the ripply lanterns in the water, his face was hardly lit, his hand was soothing his trashed crown. 'She loves him. She loves him not. *Him – Toddy*: what does someone like that have within. Born with the lights out. And he's never tried to put them on. That's what's so . . . Sniff sniff – I smell emptiness. When they opened him there was a fridge where his soul should have been. Do you know that song? . . . I forget how it goes on.'

I was sitting beside a man who talked to me as if he was talking to himself which was who he habitually talked to. His concessions to *dia*logue were effortfully courteous, unpractised.

'She loves him. He loves her,' I murmured, apologetically.

'He's got the cheek of the devil.' Eddie spoke in such a way to strip the phrase of figurative frivolity. Eddie spoke as the unhappily dead speak in dreams. 'I don't hate him Jont –' Did he address me thus? He did, a nonce appellation, and a swan shone on the bottlegreen black. And the band played a roller coaster riff, a swooping sex ride from tension to release. I thought of Chrissie Wasserman.

'Coming in?' I asked Eddie.

He surprised me. 'Sure,' he said, and he followed me up the stepped terraces of The Garth's blue lawn. It lifts your step, that kind of lawn. I felt him beside me then I didn't and turned to see him walking backwards, his head high at last, fixed on the red light which now, with floodlights cut and nothing beneath it, was hung alone in the sky – a low rogue star going to the bad. He walked backwards with rehearsed facility, step by certain step, fluently, with full knowledge of where the serial slopes were.

---

[1] 'The red.' The spire of Salisbury Cathedral which is 403 feet and, Mae, 9 inches tall is surmounted by a red aircraft warning light.

'That's Mary's band,' he said as we entered the marquee, 'good friend, Mary.'

The girl singer was wailing, her unmiked hand clutched her ear in the approved manner. She was sweaty, coarsely pretty, pudgy.

Toddy didn't fall. When they danced with Bonny's arms all about him and his about her, enraptured, engrossed, they turned into one sinuously leaping creature, a reeling conjunction of desire and understanding. His concentrated tenderness, her unmitigated smile, their shared secret, their tight womb of mutual satisfaction – they displayed all the magical banalities of love. How it heightens everything! During that state's reign just doing the washing up together (she with brush and Fairy, he with towel) is a fulfilling duet, going to a petrol station is an adventure, nothing seems commonplace, selflessness is no chore. An island of love for two where everyone is equal. (This is theory: there was a dishwasher in the desolate farmhouse on the high downs that Alasdair and Jill Hogg-Tod gave their son as a wedding present. There was a Shell pump at the farm two miles away. Mrs Bohigas, the live-in at the Hogg-Tods' house near Marble Arch, took a 12 or an 88 to Holland Park three times a week to clean the flat Toddy peppercorn-rented from his parents.) As they danced that night they *were* cynosural, they radiated absolute conviction in their union: it seemed the aptest thing on earth, you could believe it might last for ever. They shone, they were more themselves than they had ever been, they had extra edge, they were super-defined. Everyone of the four hundred celebrants knew it. This wasn't an illusion prompted by the profligacy of the occasion. ('Johnson: she put the screw on me. She blackmailed me into bankruptcy. That dance floor – d'you know what they stitched me for? And those longhairs, *they* should have paid *me*. Ever think about going into *ice*? It's only frozen water! And I tell you, the capacity of the human bladder is infinite . . .') Toddy didn't fall. He succumbed to an invisible punch, to a silenced shot. The band had finished its first act. Toddy held Bonny's hand and was craning over his shoulder, laughing, when he folded. The armature of his trunk collapses. For a half second that has lasted all my life he gasps in shocked and dopey wonderment, his face is that of an abattoired nag, not yet indignant at the wrong visited on the attached body, still acquainting itself with incredulity. Then his teeth locked in high pain. Whole decades; prospective wrinkles; a future physiognomy that will never be – I know what Toddy would have looked like had he lived till now, beyond now. (He's finite, fixed, *as was*, full stopped. So are they all.) Fall, no; felled, yes. The temporary nave is mute. The sound has gone. The cynosure is supine. The tableau is still and terrible: tilted glasses, united focus, Bonny's scrabbling genuflection (which tears a seam). Toddy has sullied his own wedding, punctured the fizz-powered illusion we all subscribe to. He has stained nuptial fantasy with illness, with corporeal imperfection. He has deviated from his *role*: he was The Bridegroom, the archetype whose procreative virility was that day sanctioned, the ritual initiate and harbour of felicity. Now he is mere man; blood and bone on the blink. Grimacing, gasping, clutching at the recycled breath of his disappointed audience. He has let us down, made ghouls of us all, turned us to embarrassed stone. His hair is spread across the expensive floor, he's twisted, internally snared, good as naked, defenceless as a newborn. When we move we move in slomo, fighting the thick air, submitting each other to ocular interrogation; we move forward and stand back. Exceptions: Bonny whose love is manifest in her cradling of her damaged future, in her pleading glances; and Poor Eddie who soars down from the band's scaffold waking a moulting mat of grocer's grass behind his cheap daps.

Eddie had an audience here, a quorum to act to (p. 210). Grocer's grass haloed him. He was the mechanical. Donald Rollo Hogg-Tod was the breakdown. Poor Eddie is here to mend it. Lucky for Toddy that Eddie was there, with Mary and the band, chatting. Toddy didn't even writhe. (Wolfe, Nelson, Chatterton are the precursors.) His hands feebled about his trunk, as if to effect a cure, as if to indicate hurt's locus for someone else to cure. Poor Eddie, whose very alacrity makes the world-class hairdressers, the decorators, the languids unite with the bright dowds and the boondockers in a collective gasp that steals air as surely as fire might. Rhooss. Poor Eddie – a comic strip saint in mufti: willed to resurrect the leading man, to salvage the masque, save our day, deliver us from embarrassment.

All the tense reflexive benefaction of four hundred lives conducts itself through Eddie's hands, through his balmy arm. It's these limbs that he defines himself with, limbs that are now practised, hotter than ever. Does the temperature rise with experience or according to the size of the audience? This is a question that Chubb will address. Eddie's audience in the marquee is not that much smaller than those he plays to at The Church Of The Best Ever Redemption in its spooky new premises on Portsdown; those audiences believe, this one merely wishes. Debility, other people's pain, strangers' tumours, the unseeable sores inside bodies owned by men he despises or envies or has been slighted by – these, together with witnesses, are the elemental conditions of Eddie Vallender's animation. The credulity of the witnesses is probably not pertinent; besides, it will increase during the performance of the act of healing which is an act of persuasion, of shamanic theatre, of magical assertion, of balsamic promiscuity, of Power Cure (Ray Butt's epithet). Eddie's gratification is the awe in which he's held. The gift he is host to is as dissociate from him as are Mithracin and Vepesid from Daph's starched auxiliaries who administer them. But he has a greater incentive than they have in achieving an immediate and conspicuous amelioration of the patient's condition. Is it possible that he might overdose one in his eagerness for applause? *Can* he overdose with manual heat? Can he transmit too much? Is his charge measurable? These are more for Chubb. Eddie wasn't Butt's child (p. 204) but he was Butt's creature and he healed to convert not because he had faith in Butt, Buttism, The Church Of The Best Ever Redemption but because in that one and trinity was the source of his subjects. They came to Butt. Thus they fed Eddie's addictive need for wens, rashes, dorsal messes, friable bones, fungi in the tender parts, capillary crustacea, acne, nosological freaks, one-off debilities of the trachea, spots in the box, boffin-foxing bacteria, wounds, itches, Munchhausens, baldies, euphemisms, protein lacks, viral mysteries, HoTLoVE. He used them. He used Butt.

He owned a selective competitiveness, had grown it as a defence; he exploited his antic misfortune: no one could match *his* parents' deaths. He always won there. He would win here. Everyone needs him to: the Magreb dresses, the Rotary frocks, both sides, and Bonny, still in white. She's bent forward, her flared sleeves spread to suppress crowd proximity. Eddie plays deaf piano. His genual movements are hardly perceptible, yet soon he has set himself in purposeful profile – so far as majority regard goes. Some dumb doctor (Bailles Barker) rolls up too late to get on the case. The society abortionists on the groomside have forgotten this bit of medicine if they knew it and are too badered to move, anyway. Anyway, Bonny won't let; her arms are up, her cousin's are down on her beloved whose are still here and there. The one pointing to the spot, the other waving, still, for help. He was so insentient that he didn't know when help had arrived, he didn't know the form it took.

Smell them watching: canapés on their abated breath, the sweat of expectation, synthesised scent and alcohol, sex on hold.

Hear them: it's the strain of the day, of the preparations, of stag overload, of achieving the novel state of husband, of being the main player.

Eddie heard nothing. He floated on his knees. It rushed through him. Salt seeped from his pores till he shone. He was more than a mechanical, he was a machine, an agent ministering to a patient denied the choice of belief or disbelief: the faith was all Eddie's. Whether the patient be credulous or sceptical or mockingly dismissive is, again, of no moment: all that is demanded is that he or she submit passively and statically to The Epiphanic Hands (Ray Butt's coinage again). Toddy fulfilled this condition. Time trickled, seconds stretched: the will, the power, the need – and, at last, the relief.

When Toddy sat up it was as if from a planned nap, from stolen minutes with Morph.

And the silent statuary regained the electricity it had lent to Eddie, used it to cheer and clap. Noise up, please. Colours mixed again under the canvas top, among the flowers. Bonny hugged and cuddled and nuzzled the man who had been

298

returned to her; she swung about, showing him off. Then she moved to Poor Eddie. He was keenly scraping his crown, standing stoop-shouldered, disacknowledging the wonderment he had craved and fed: such ignoral gives him power, collusion with his audience would lessen it. He had his space which no one impinged on. (Respect? Fear? Repulsion?) Physical space, his circus ring. The only person in that vast pavilion, in that throng, who was separate from every other person.

Bonny's face is a practised simper. She holds Eddie's hands. Can he not discern the falseness in the face's set? She whispers with brazen intimacy: something like 'It's so great to see you. I'm so glad you came.' Words such as those, no doubt. Toddy stands ready to take his turn at orthodontal patronage. Bonny leans forward to kiss Poor Eddie's chronically unkissed cheek, in gratitude; the disposition of Eddie's trunk suggests that in his society (whatever that is) the social kiss is unknown. It's charmingly awkward: two worlds collide in one brushing buss, in a peck so light it's underweight. Her dry lips, his bad skin. Does he mistake this conventional gesture (made in that arena, before those eyes, on her wedding day with her husband beside her) for a sex kiss? Does he believe that it's an invitation to buccal potholing, to tongue fencing? Me, I'd say that he made no mistake, that he simply went for it.

Keen Eddie's hot hands clasp his poor coz's shoulder blades, his crosshatched knuckles and granite-crescent nails are matt on white taffeta's pure lustre, they ruche the dress of intactness's pretence. Lubric Eddie's famished mouth limpets hers: push-push for maximal entry. Eight hundred eyes bear witness to lingual rape. A lesser offence yet an offence none the less. Poor Bonny bends back broken backed. And he follows – he always followed; he was always with her – no matter how long it was since he'd clocked her. She was always at the front of his mind. His dirty grey suit (so dirty that the cloth's colour may be graphite, may be thunder, may be ocean) sullies as it envelops. It swallows the silken folds. His mouth wolfs the folds of hers. Limpet, leech, bad clam, wicked barnacle: his rooted oyster tickles her, a joyful prick touching the base, tasting. There's tenseness at the edges, muscular astonishment, mealy mucus slimes between them. What on earth? Toddy makes to wrest him from her; that's all it needs. Bonny's forearm is across her mouth, wiping. Poor Eddie, hands dangling tight beside his rosined strides, scurries from the stage of his triumph, furtive in his chastisement, twitchy, slighted. He bid no adieus. He knew all eyes were on him as he sought the shelter of the dark garden, of cosseting night, of disappearance and invisibility.

When the night is shrill with colour, when it's bright enough to blind, when rupees split in succeeding quarters and change to dazzling annas, when the man I saw becomes a bird, when the sky is filled with fountains and my head falls back so far it hurts – that's when I remember the duplicating river on 24 July 1971 and the thrilled silhouettes on the bank, that's when I remember the firework maker's children:

Eddie, who had vanished again, who had gone to the mattresses again, to pig it on loneliness, to build a cross.

Bonny, in whose honour the sky shone and crackled, whose dress was shaded now coral, now eau de nil, serial pastels according to the empyreal festoons, to the plumes and cataracts, to light's temporary geometry. There was a fairground in the heavens for you Bonny – freeform dippers, jewelled waltzers on their sides, Ferris segments rushing to oblivion. Chemical fire lit you. You were the show too. No one noticed that your husband clawed his tummy, that he could hardly raise his head. If he saw the synthetic spectrum with which his father-in-law had extravagantly countered nature, he saw it in the river, in ripply ellipses: the flow and totality of that trade-boast passed him by. He hurts that bad. The pain had returned as soon as Eddie disappeared. He imagined that his intestines were eels – they were cannibalising each other in the privacy of him, biting blindly, making meat of his milt. Across the river pyrotechnic auxiliaries moved between shells and mortars, rocket frames, candle batteries, lattice poles, spoked wheels. The fireworkers were dwarfed by their momentary monuments, by the vastness of their gay battlefield, by the bigness of the neon blitz. The penultimate set piece, a cross of burning wheels, made day of night. The last one made this bank gasp. The hoarding's lancework was ignited and there appeared, seriatim, from the meadow's blackness, the profile faces of Bonny and of Toddy, an arrowed heart, and their names conjoined in loopy fizzing script. 'Like a durbar in Blackpool,' snided a world-class wit.

Mad Bantu: where is he?

Jean-Marie Meyer-Decker: ditto.

The band was on again. Chrissie Wasserman beamed a beam of milky promise. Toddy sat this one out, sipping at brandy to settle him. During the first number the girl singer merely leaned against an amp, sluttishly becoming, smoking. The violinist sang in her lieu. He wore all black: stove pipes, cuban heeled cowpokes, a frock coat, a curly brimmed hat with a pheasant feather petrolling its band and sweaty webs of black hair filigreeing his nape. He sang incomprehensibly, slurred the words; the tyranny of tone over lyrics was total. The tone was a leeringly lubricious baritone, the voice was one used to asking for sexual favours, used to pleading for them. It was thrilling. It is the sort of voice I am ashamed to be touched by. Chrissie Wasserman's breath, her scent, her liquid mocking eyes. She was touched too by this aphrodisial agent who stared un-smilingly down as he played violin with sprawlingly knuckled hands. Meaty hands to coax such plaintive wailing from a fiddle, to make strings sing such mournful notes – notes which resolved themselves as the number petered into a lentissimo dirge based on Dvorak's Humoresque. 'Hail Mary,' cried the drummer, and the girl singer sashayed to the mike again, shaking her insect hair from her face. The violinist scowled. He suspended his instrument by its pegs. It hung from a bulbous thumb and a sausage finger. It dangled there a sec, the bow across it, an arrow through a heart. These hands: they're trout-skin, maculate, hepatically freckled. Is this guy a drinker? There are no other dermal signs – no Bardolph, no Rudolph, no red vein skein. These hands are old, otherworldly, primal, down from another race. They're hands for neckjobs, not hands for bands.

The singer screeched the night away. We danced and drank till dawn: kedgeree, shepherd's pie, shepherd's warning. I woke, late afternoon, beside Chrissie Wasserman. Lorry driver's crutch, and it was raining outside. I woke beside her for years to come: the morning after the night Toddy died; the day we heard what Eddie had done; the day of the fire at the desolate farmhouse (p. 431).

John Nat Butt to Susan Sheila Bannister (Jonjon to Hankey), The Church Of The Best Ever Redemption, c/o Fort Widley, Portsdown Hill, Pompey PO6, Wednesday 5 April 1972. (Poor Eddie was there, and so was Mary. The casts were otherwise different.)

Hankey swelled with baby, Jonjon swelled with prepaternal pride: he had double the muscles too, and half the brain, he was the Voy with the muscles to carry Ray Butt; he hadn't the brain to get his brothers to take their turns in hefting the geek. He was loyal. He would call the baby Ray; he did call the baby Ray; Ray is Jonjon's big boy now; he never was his little boy really – Jonjon was away all those years, in the echoing daddy-zoo they visited every third Sunday.

Jonjon was practical, on the soft side, a donkey. Not the man to sit at The Founder's right hand but diligent with building suppliers. The nuances of Buttist soteriology might baffle him but he regarded The Cross Of The World as a job of work, to be carried out to the best of his ability, for his dad's sake. You couldn't send Sonny and Laddy, looking the way they did, to the nineteenth at Sinah and expect planning officials and elected representatives to talk to them colleague-to-colleague, accept big drinks from them, get matey with them. Jonjon had no problems here nor in the matters of the aggregate in concrete, of discounted rheostats, of keeping the welders sweet: his man management skills! Lift a jar to them! Firm but fair. Feet on the ground. At one with hoddies; indeed he speaks their language rather than his father's. Buttism demands a capacity for fantasy (not imagination); it demands credulity, desperation, un-appeasable soul-hunger. Dogged Jonjon lacks all these. Yet he'll still square up to a saloon barrister in The Salty Dog whom he overhears using the expression 'Mumbo-Butto'. Blood's thicker. Butts stick by each other. The tattooist beneath the rail arches on The Hard at Portsea knows that. He burned 'The Founder' and a representation of Calvary into each of The Voys' right forearm.

Jonjon could have done without but familial unity told, and triplet pressure. He bore the scorching with fortitude. The melded reek of spirit, ink and his own broiled skin reached the furthest olfactory filaments, the ones near his brain – that helped him remember it.

Hankey's father Arth bravefaced it, stood in his corner shop up North End in his white grocer's coat with his ginger grocer's stripe across his freckled grocer's pate and made the best of it: 'She's marrying into the celebrity.'

He was a one for smut, but not when his own daughter was in the frame. He dealt Omo: 'For washing or display would that be Missus?'

But he wasn't happy, not when it was his own daughter on the fast and loose. 'They're nuts them Butts,' he told Mother over his luncheon meat and piccalilli, then repeated that rhyme which he had worked on all morning. They had used to sit there in the elbow-greased dining room of the flat above the shop, tune into Butt Of The Joke on the walnut Ekco, grin, knit (her), polish (him), fall about so that she dropped one pearl, so that he smeared the marble base with Brasso, fall about. Such a caution. 'Chas Pothecary met him. Natural as weather, he said,' said Arth, weekly, over the fullfruit credits. That was when Hankey was still in smock and Startrites, was still Susan. They wanted a proper wedding for her, uterine expansion notwithstanding: she was their only one. They wanted the pealing bells of Old England, a Rolls with a harness of ribbons, a lovely, lovely service so they could smear Vaseline on memory's lens and retrospect the day's soft edges in their dotage.

They did not want nutty Butt ranting from the ramparts of Fort Widley, holding their only one under water, rubbing roosterdown in her titian pageboy, cracking no jokes, inciting his tribe (the Nut Buttalion). They wanted none of it. Ask Arth. Pop into the Done Our Bit Club where he whiles away his resentful widowhood among Pel chairs and full ashtrays playing doms and drinking lemon tops with a grudge of ex-servicemen who laid down their lives at Anzio for nippers who've never shown any gratitude.

He was rash to make his feelings known. He questioned the propriety of a marriage ceremony conducted by Ray Butt, he had no doubts about its illegality, he insisted on a registry office, he wasn't having any grandchild of his a bastard and he said so.

The Founder fulminated against the pagan grocer, spun in his chair, crushed a leucous roll of plans of The Cross Of The World, beat his braced steel corset with a Coke can: 'Me . . . I . . . I . . . You two – ' Jonjon and Hankey emeried the floor of the subterranean office with their twitchy sheep feet.

'I didn't build this, all this, so I could be mocked by you two lovebirds and some pipsqueak registrar. Where does he get *his* authority from? You tell me that. Who from? Does he touch otherness? Does he shit! Who does he listen to? He doesn't even listen does he, doesn't *know* to listen. It's just a job with registrars. A registrar's soul – ha! Deskpilots. What sort – look at me Jonjon – what sort of marriage are you two after? D'you know what secular means? It means profane, two fingers to God. Here: registrar's language – the marriage *contract*. What is it – buying a plot of land, taking on a summer season? . . . Our Church – me – we unite you, we weld you in the water of the fowl and the sea. Protection through immersion. Permanence through the element. I give you my all, not just as a father but as a vector of things so far unnamed, of the mysteries. You mean so much to me you two. You shall share. I shall transmit it to you in the moment of your union.'

Ray Butt's high-performance longplay Nagra recorded every word: day, night, dreams, musings, false starts, rehearsals, planet solutions, oaths, maxims, snores, prayers, business meets, liturgical wheezes, phone chats, quarrels, supper banter, succour. He always took it to the toilet, just in case.

He said: 'Get your certificate. You go and get it. But don't you ever believe for a second that it's worth anything: a union sanctioned by the civil service, by the mayor and council. And you make sure you get it on a different day. I don't want the day dirtied by temporal . . . frivolity.' (Thus do prophets compromise.) 'I don't want my church kowtowing. You read me? My church is the best church because *me*, I've suffered more, I've pushed myself so deep I've had the bends. This is what you need to cotton to Son. I've been there![1] . . . Closer *to the centre* than any fat guru wallah, than anyone since . . .' It went without saying. Modesty forbade.

He glared to make his big boy Jonjon understand. Oh and where had all the girl's gorm gone? She was shy of this irate stomach in a 'FOUNDER' T-shirt. His navel's a nipple and he's not got his legs on; even without them there's an excess of metal – the corset that corrugates his flesh, the reeling chair, and then the M.O.D. surplus he lived in, that he fitted in with. File cabinets, file trolleys, boxes, tables, desks, radiators, lamps. No chairs. Everyone but Butt was made to stand in this mildewed, strip-lit room, two storeys down in the Portsdown chalk. The Founder-Bunker. So it was derided by the HGVs and palette-loaders and stock clerks of Flamebryte (Paints and Specialist Varnishes) Ltd., which rented most of the former fortress for storage. Its brick-vaulted tunnels and mycodermal chambers were lined with shelves bearing volatile cans of proprietary hues: Oslo, Pudding Yellow, Monument Grey, Windsor, Forest Red, Hampton Court, Log, Dragon, Beacon, Uppark, Marriott Black, Stresa 313, Beau Romeo etc.

Jonjon and Hankey were blessed, they got a registrar's cancellation.

A couple, unpressed by the imminence of Napisan and rusks, had been fazed by the fatidic date, 1 April; they didn't want their wedding to be a conventionalised prank, they put it back a fortnight, Sam and Ursula did.

Sam was a pram mechanic, Ursula was a nurse, an employee of Jonjon's Aunt Daph (coincidence), a G&G operative at the poles of The Life Spectrum (Butt). Sam and Ursula both had a pro interest in kiddies. But no matter how they tried they couldn't cook a little one of their own. There was no bundle of joy to fill a Pedigree, fasten in a Maclaren, to bounce on sprung rubber suspension, drool on the lacquered carriage work, practise motor skills on the line of plastic heads stretched between those chrome wingnuts that Dad Sam had buffed till

---

[1] Cf. 'I am the finest comedian in Britain today. I am the best comedian I know. I am the comedian I am because I have slept in waiting rooms and had nothing to eat.' *Titbits* 8.5.59.

his wrist ached. There was no cute mite for Ursula to coo over, stuff her nipples into, no baby botty to Eeeziwipe and sprinkle with icing sugar, no tiny mitt whose model perfection might be clasped in her worn delivery hands. Their little home in Telephone Road was haunted by lack, it was a site of bereavement. Other children's voices, other grown-ups' stentorian warnings, all the mewling and playcries can be heard from afar in their little home – they bounce off the bloody brick in Pompey's straight streets. There are always echoes in the glaring brick grid, in the unyielding grid of Pompey's straight streets which are canyon-conductors of sound from unseeable sources. It moves and it lasts, long after the last slapped brat has wept away to bed. Then there's no more noise to taunt the regretfully childless; they may sink into sexual union, willing it to be more than recreational. Sam and Ursula were not the sort to gamble on an April Fool's wedding, on the possibility of a hexed future, on doing anything which might dissuade the generational god of their earnest. Who would ever run the risk of making themselves equinoctial gowks? Jonjon and Hankey, that's who.

Afterwards they stand in the municipally floral square outside the registry office; Jonjon grinned, the photos show him slow and bovine. Hankey holds a vernal posy, she's plump as butter in her milk-white maxi-suit. Mother clamps her hat against the crisp wester off Wight. Arth wears his medals and ribbons as for Remembrance. Two of the Anzio dead cup fags in their palms like they're still on watch. Ray Butt: of course he absented himself. Daph *is* there, out of the kindness of her heart, gracious in roseprint, radiant as a royal, auntly proud, joining in, feigning frustration when her cash-and-carry confetti is lifted by the wind. It spins like polychrome motes, it swarms like a map of the breeze, collides with the wrought stones of civic pomp. Then its moment is over and there are drifts of pastel litter on the stylobate.

What are Sonny and Laddy up to, exactly? Shuffling, whispering, fingering their tie knots (fist-size, auxiliary adam's apples). Conspiring, glancing about, backslapping with pinchbeck bonhomie. All around the square there are pigeons that draw grey scrawls against the grey stone; they mistake confetti for crumb; they swoop on the drifts (they should have learnt by now – that's why they're still only pigeons); they scatter when the black bike's bell rasps and rings. Sonny prods Laddy. The photographer has finished. The secularly conjoined couple are crossing the street to the ribboned Rolls; yes, the Done Our Bit beckons.

The sweep's face is impasted with soot. His black brushes are strapped to the black crossbar, they protract the bike, give it a stiff little tail. Even his black bike's chrome is blackened. Sonny chases after him, pushing through the party. See Arth beckon him. Oh the joy of Mother – she's scratching in her handbag for a florin. Daph claps. The sweep's bike squeaks as it halts. Sonny has him by the elbow. He raises his stoker's black cap to beaming Arth. Now, isn't this a lucky stroke! Especially lucky given the diminution in the number of chimey sweeps in UK from 5,562 (25 of them women) in 1921 to 917 (two women) in 1971. But here is one, in the blowy Pompey square where Hankey has just pledged herself: the very fortuity smacks of a best ever marriage.[1] Arth, leading the sweep to his daughter at the Silver Ghost's door, swells too at last – here's confirmation of his conviction's probity, here's proof, clopping beside him in stud-

[1] In *Myth Routes (7): From The Burren to Brum* (Institute of Folkloric Advancement, London, 1986) Dr Roisin Bush suggests that: 'The sweep's role in a peat-fired society is magically exorcismal. He extends or *erects* his brush (which has connotative correspondences too with a tail). He inserts it in order to re-purify the originally pale stone chimney flue. This is an act of penetrative irony. When the sweep kisses the bride he is alluding to this process. He is confirming her purity or, tacitly, reinstating that purity, reinstalling her intactness. He is making her clean for her husband who will "stoke the fire" for the first time on the wedding night; the sweep removes traces of illegitimate entry into the "virgin" chattel. The sweep's magic is to effect hymenal repair and *make a clean sweep*.' The practice is first recorded (according to Bush) in Pierre-Henri Cazaud's *Une Voyage dans la Region des Lacs du Connemara* (1775): 'The prices of their labour are one flagon of apple cider at Ballyvaughan, two flagons at Carrowmoreknock.' Samson Doorly, son and grandson of chimney sweeps, migrated from Ballyvaughan to Birmingham in 1822 aboard *The Fair Amarylis*, putting in at Barry and Bristol before reaching Sharpness. Doorly's ledger (Warwickshire County Records Office) lists thirty-six weddings that he attended in 1825 and forty-eight in 1826. His payments ranged from 'two pennies and small beer' to 'two and a half pennies, porter and prune cake'. Bush's contention is that a custom exclusive to the environs of Galway Bay was thus adopted by 'pan-Hibernian' communities in Birmingham and the Black Country and swiftly copied by a materially wanting autochthonous population which regarded the Irish as 'lucky' and their superstitions as efficacious.

soled boots. Arth's ginger swagger adverts bulk hubris. The sweep slaps his black hands together, rubs them: the artisan prepares. Hankey's delight: Buccal 1): A slit like a fresh-incised wound, a greedy vulval bivalve. Buccal 2): A nude gum show, lips superstretched. Pedal: Twinkly steps of excitement or micturition. Her delight infects the party and its attendants. The Anzio dead wheeze blokeish gorblimeys. The photographer scurries into place with his tripod, the kidnapper of a witch and her broomstick. Everyone smiles. The sweep smiles. His teeth and gums are black, black as his bike, black as his cap, black as his overall, his teeth and gums are black, like he's carved from coal, like he eats soot.

The bride Hankey, clutching her posy, yields her cheek to him. The sweep's meat-pink tongue darts from its hiding place. He fixes his mouth to hers (there is now already grey saliva on her chin). His black hands are on her milk white suit, grubbing the lactic distension of her breasts; he's feeling her up with his knee, groining her femora. Oh her suit of stains. A black hand parts her bottom. He bites her neck. The muffled gags of suffocation are succeeded by a yelp. It's all so swift and they're all so slow. It occurs to them, tardily, that this is not the way sweeps are meant to cast their beneficent spells. But by then it's too late. The big day's big light has been extinguished, the suit sullied – it now carries the partial cast of a stranger. The bride is blackened, magicked by darkness, contaminated by the very charm that was meant to bless her.

No it wasn't. That was no sweep. That was Mad Bantu, paid to prank by Sonny there, and Laddy; they're hardly able to straightface it through the tears and the incredulity. Slip him a foal and he'll do your bidding, enforce your will, instruct, educate by jape/rupture/lisped oath/chummy wink (less fun). Do not bilk him. He does it for love, sure; he loves his work. But he doesn't work for love alone, he works for equine multiples – foals, ponies, dobbins, bleedin' dogs, that's-my-boys. A concertina'd roll in the palm, thickness dependent on risk and likely satisfaction; this was good satisfaction and no risk – away on the bike before they closed in (tho' he'd have sorted them).

He asked for more four days on. He was on bail, looking at a sending away. Sonny and Laddy showed in a Hillman, nicked for an hour from one of the guests at their brother's genuine (Buttist) wedding. 'Oi'm lookin at a sendin' away,' Mad Bantu told them.

'No nono no. Dolt simple, it'll be,' said Laddy.

'An' I'll guarantee that,' guaranteed Sonny, 'I will. They got a flat tyre, saw to it. Tight bastards. What kinda fuckin dowry d'you call that – second-hand fridge and thirty nicker. Tell you what I call it – a tightwad's dowry. Disgrace.'

'Worse than a fucking disgrace,' said Laddy, 'a fuckin insult to Jonjon, an' us, an' – well you name it. Now you hop in Madison. We just goin' down the wog for a vinnerloo, get shaped up.'

Mad Bantu phased his Haslar Nurse[1] across the corrugations of the rusty fence he stood beside, he played an iron shot with it, striking a macadam prune towards the slipway. Tipner Lake was putty mud; it was also gull-blue sea; it was, further, a feathering of down white wavelets, pretty pitched roofs on an Xmas card. The orange, oxidised conning towers of two scrapped submarines (one 'M' class, one 'X.1' class – Bantu knew the taxonomy of belligerence, it was about all he did know) rose from the water, pitted monuments to deep ocean death. He sniffed the spritzy gust, searching for a sign on it, rubbed the crutch of his camouflage trousers, *thought*, panorama'd the water, the hulks, the pyres of smouldering marine detritus (keels; hunks of funnel; vertical decks that are landborne and pointing to the sky before they curl with casual smelting; the Brunel chains of cosmic bondage; anchors whose saintly significance the Old Rev had lectured him in). Lucky omens, he remembered. Or were they the other way?

Sonny hit the halfring horn, leaned across Laddy, neck-stretched: 'Get your fuckin anus on the seat Mad. We gotta move.'

Mad Bantu moved only his head, and then only a vertebra,

---

[1] A metal stake, up to four feet long, used to contain inmates of the isolation and lunatic wards of the Royal Naval Hospital Haslar – an institution from which derived the euphemism, current among naval officers' wives as recently as 1954, 'gone to Haslar' i.e. mad. Cf. doolally from the Deolali transit camp near Bombay. A Haslar Nurse is, of course, correspondent to a Penang Lawyer.

just to show where he was staring, what he was mulling: 'Still goin on then, yeh? You sure?'

Across the water shine the cruet of hoppers and silos, and the formic conveyor carts. And sheer above them is Fort Widley, The Church Of The Best Ever Redemption. And above that the girders and reinforcing rods that form the armature of the base of The Cross Of The World, which climbs higher to heaven and closer to Boss God aka The Empyrean Emperor aka The Good Guy In The Sky with every passing day, with every cannily invested donation to The Church Of The Best Ever Redemption. (Cheques payable to COW Fund, COTBER, PO Box 66, Pompey PO6).

'Still boogyin' then up there are they? Yeh? Your dad givin some chickens a seeing to is he? Yeh? I want an upfront.'

'Piss off Bantu. Come on . . . All you gotta do is help us in. Then you can split.'

'A stud upfront. And I want the cream of the souvenirs.'

'Whatever you fancy matey. Take your pick. We're not thieving, we're just teaching the bastards a lesson, telling them not to show diss. Thirty quid and a 'lectroluck with previous!'

'You can thieve to your heart's content. Indeed I'd say – wouldn't you say Sonny – I'd say you can have the lot. But no upfront. You in?'

Mad Bantu hurled his nurse at a sharktoothed van panel bearing the cackograph NON ENTRY TO DOG STADIUM TRESPASSER'S WILL BE: it teetered then wheeled over onto a skein of wire and ground elder.

'It's an offensive. Don't want to be seen with an offensive,' he said, bouncing on the back seat. They drove slow but not extra slow; that, too, would interest any uncle, give him an excuse to wave them down. There were four uniformed uncles, parked up in a Panda car on a blasted forecourt, each one forcing down a pint of cow milk to settle his piss lunch. Mad Bantu kept his head low, didn't raise it till they were passing his alma mater, Meadowsweet Comp (formerly Bulwer's Industrial and Ragged School). They turned into Kipling, slothed past the end of Madeira, crossed Battenburg – the cakes are disparate, the streets are the same street, ruddy blocks in the labyrinth of brick and RN surplus painted window frames and Omo invitations and thus-spawned problem kiddies. (You might say that Mad Bantu was one such, expanded.)

In Anwar's Dodgy Tikka the Voys eat a vindaloo apiece, drink two large Vats apiece, on the house: 'Anwar knows how to frighten off the taste of the Kit E Kat. Don't you mate. Ought to be Hankey Bannister, mind. Still, tell you what Anwar – you're one generous Halal, mate.' Mad Bantu fasts, peers inside a plastic .oo scale Taj Mahal, lobs a flap of nan in the fish tank, asks the only other customer, a sexagenarian Victory tourist, if she wants to buy a comb.

They obtained entry to Arth's corner shop through a tunnel between two houses in the middle of the terrace, along a lapfenced alley behind it (mind the stingers, mind the shrubs' boughs, mind the bow-wows – invisible in their gardens), over the locked gate, through a store's door that Mad Bantu shoulder punched. They eradicated system, order, propriety, the very quiddity of a life-in-retail founded on the immutable presence of Lifebuoy in the corner, Fray Bentos fourth shelf up, Crawford's here, Carr's there, Johnson's Hardgloss Glocoat For Composition Floors in the little bay, Cardinal Red (ever in big demand in doorstep-proud Pompey) handy by the door to the shop itself. They turned rectilinearity into hazardous cardboard alps. They bunged the plug in the stoneware sink and turned on the tap. They made sludge of Winalot, stamped on Special K cartons, had Uncle Ben fuck Sarah Lee. The greengage-green blinds were tight over the windows of the shop itself. They were thin and the sun was obfuscated by the dark legends imprinted on them: ƧᴎOIƧIVOЯꟼ ЯƎTƧIᴎᴎAᗺ and lower down, crescentic: ИWAЯᗺ. МАꟼƧ. МАН. 'The bastard's a Commie . . . Ruskie bastard,' said Sonny. 'And he doesn't sell maps. Dishonest bastard.' It would take a man like the old man Dod to read it (p. 446).

Mad Bantu understood none of this. He pocketed four jars Shippam's anchovy paste and two bloater, a bottle of Camp Coffee, two tins of Meloids, a family can of Unox, hairslides and combs and Kirby grips. Laddy unplugged the deep freeze. Sonny sprinkled D-RAT-U on the bacon slicer. A fat man's profile, dorsally inclined (leash? lunch?), hitchcocked l. to r. across the blind to the dainty tap of quarter-irons. Sonny held a sentry finger to his lips, ushered them from the shop and up the stairs to the flat, the home their sister-in-law had now left, her parents' treasure, the gallery of the three of them, their monument to circumscription and petty virtue. Spruce? Not a speck. 'On moi muvver's minge,' proclaimed Mad Bantu, 'slike a funeral parlour.' Ship shape's not the Pompey fashion. Shit shape is how the Voys left it: they excreted vindaloo 'meat' on the twin beds' sheets then remade them, hospital corners and all, Bristol fashion.

'You said you wasn't thieving,' complained Mad Bantu when he caught Sonny pouring Hankey's mother's paste cameos into his satin bomber. Sonny mimed a wristshandy. Laddy stuffed £117 into his underpants while Mad Bantu was thus occupied. They prowled about the crowded rooms, trashing, plundering, pissing (a hyperbolic arc from Mad Bantu makes an old gold sofa gamboge). It was theirs to mar, a manor to lord by desecration. The Voys gorged on revenge, ate it hot. Mad Bantu had Arth's medals but not their frame, he tore a ribbon, he pinned them on his combat jacket. Satisfied.

3.48 it was when the Voys reparked the Hillman so tight to a vergeside hawthorn that they both had to exit by the driver's door. It was near enough where they'd found it. No one would notice that it had been moved. No one could oath to the Voys' not having been there the entire afternoon. Their attention had been on the ceremony, the Buttist nuptial theatre, the rites and ranting.

The congregation of a hundred people had assembled in the fortress's bailey among Flamebryte's prefabs and stacked palettes. Building work on The Cross Of The World which rose high above the fortress on the far side of the dry moat stopped at 2.20 though some workmen remained on the scaffolding for the view. The Founder had worked on this one, plotted it, choreographed it. Now he was on the rampart above the barbican flanked by two women with cymbals. Now he was among the host below, in the bailey. There was breeze and singing and smiling – oh there was smiling. Rictal collectivism. The bailey, which was also an arena, echoed. Hankey contact-hugged everyone present. She moved among the people – her people, Jonjon's people, Butt's people; most of them were Butt's people, smiling. She wore feathers in her hair. Her long dress was impasted with them. Manual feathers, pedal feathers. From the scaffolding she looked like a vertical caterpillar. Eddie Vallender took her arm and led her to an unplumbed bath filled with seawater, taps attached, enamel stained, The Founder beside it. The people crowded round. Arth held Mother by the wrist, furtively. Eddie Vallender held a hand to their daughter's occiput and a hand to her lumbar. He might have been a cracksman, a vet, a dowser. The engrossed virtuoso played to his familiars. He touched the feathered bride so that she would feel no cold during her immersion. Nor did she. She slipped into the water so that it lapped the rim and splashed the oily, crazed concrete of the bailey. The Founder leaned forward in his chair. She closes her eyes against the sacramental salt. What strong arms he has in the wet darkness, in the liquid warmth. She trusts his sinews, she believes that this gentle pressure marks her rebirth, she is blind as a kitten on the brink of life, she is closer than she has ever been to the child within her whose dependent bliss is briefly hers, closer than she has ever been to those immemorial forbears whose names she doesn't know but who were fishes. And when she is drawn up from the briny, she opens her eyes on her groom wreathed in seaweed. She's never seen him that way before. Ray's big boy will do anything for his father, dress as a figure from a carnival float, dress for his wedding as a besuited Poseidon, anything. He is within Buttist limits; he is greeted by the faithful on his father's terms, with sympathetic awe. The couple stand side by side facing The Founder. (She begins to shiver now.) The crowd crowds, basket cases to the fore for they are manifestly – through faith in mutilation – the most devout, the apes of Butt, the brides and grooms of The Good Guy; also they can't see if they're at the back.

Jonjon and Hankey might have been dredged from a wreck, saved from drowning in the gooseflesh of the harbour below. Those at the back hear Butt on the PA: 'I wed you. I weld you. I meld you . . . Hankey who was Susan has joined up, she's joined the world. By immersion, by the sucking of the planet's past into her, she has gleaned the entry to the mysteries of knowledge. She is blessed with the possibility. I wed you, I bind you, I lock you in eternal love – not forgetting mutual respect. It was shown to me and I saw, I knew and can tell you that He will smile on you because he's a good guy, THE BEST OF THE LOT –' Loud at this point, and all the crowd cheers and an echoic *best of the lot* rises in a speech balloon to the gratified eavesdropper in the nimbus. 'Your union is forged by me through Him with His mandate – that's his personal sanction of you. You've got a chit from Him so to speak – clean bill of health.' Hankey, soaked, shivered. But, yes, she was warm within. 'I cleared it with Him. Through the power of prayer. And you know what prayer is, you know what prayer is, you-know-what-prayer-is. It's – '

'Volition fuelled by faith,' rang the roar of the faithful rising on a Beaufort four round the fort's newly holy bailey and its ramparts and its custom-blessed airspace. 'That's right. Volition fuelled by faith. Yes! I forge one from two – and from that, one will spring – another one – who will link with yet another – unknown to us, yes, maybe unknown to the two who'll make that one, think about it, but not to Him – to make a further one. The movement of the generations is two-one-one, two-one-one. The eternal rhythm isn't it? Like one of them dances that never goes out of fashion. The waltz, your folk dances . . . Ever watched a bird on the wing? Two-one-one. That's how it flaps,' he asserted, avianly ignorant, neglecting to check with the inspirational kittiwakes.

'The miracle of flight, eh? But they've got other tricks, birds. There're other lessons we can learn from them. I'd say – and this is my personal view, mind, this is observation not creed – I'd say that any husband has a lot to learn from the fulmar, fulmarus glace . . . glacioro whatever it is. Latin word. *Roman* word. Used by self-abusers in frocks. The bird can get along without *that* handle then, can't it? What Jonjon here should inwardly digest if you'll excuse the gag, *the gag*, is that when Mrs Fulmar is threatened, when someone comes messing, sniffing round – sniff sniff smells like fish to me – when that someone gets

314

offensive, steps over the mark, you know, *come up to my nest and inspect my fetchings*, Mr Fulmar acts. He squirts this reeking oil; he's got it secreted in his tummy. Right over them. Bull's eye every time. And you know why: because he understands the sanctity of union. And he'll fight to preserve it. And Jonjon'll fight for Hankey not just because he loves her. Not just because he's protective. Not just because he's jealous. Not just because he's proud. But because she's half of him and he's half of her. Limbs of the same creature. They are one. They are wholly one – that's wholly with a double u and holy with an aitch. It's in union that we are made complete. That we are plucked and trussed and baked. So to speak. That we fulfil our greater destiny, that we enter the realm of holiness. Before, on the Avenue of Life, you get double-parking, you get the milkfloats of painful experience, you get reds and you get ambers. But with this union it's green light, green light upon green light. Green all the way right up the Avenue's length, right on till you look around and you're no longer on the Avenue: still green though – it's bright smooth green all up the hills on either side of you. It's a valley. Sunlit. And as you approach its end, the valley's end, and there are steep slopes all around you and you can go no further, the light dims, double quick. You'd believe a cloud had just passed across the sun; its shadow darkens that valley – and you may shiver but you also smile. Sheer exhilaration. You realise *you* are in the valley of the shadow of death. And you have departed the Avenue of Life, but you're just beginning – and you're just going to yell with joy because you've walked on the right side down that long Avenue and you're due The Best Ever Redemption. That's true. You've walked in union. Two as one. As sure as hydrogen and oxygen make water. That's marriage . . . Marriage. We've all had those fretful little worries haven't we? About the marriage at the root of our faith. Let's own up to it, shall we, to our weakness. We've heard the tittle tattle. The poison voices over the denominational fences. The sectarian fishwives. The gossips in purdah. The polygamous strumpets of Mormon. All the hypocrites in the cosmos whisper it. *They weren't married*. The Holy Ghost crept up on the blind side and cuckolded poor Joseph. Jesus Our Lord Christ

Almighty was born on the wrong side of the sheet. We demean ourselves by worshipping a bastard. I'll own up. Yes, I have heard the rumours, they've made me wonder . . . And I've sought guidance here. I've had to steel myself to ask Him some hard questions. Of a frankly personal nature. Look: I got nothing against bastards; some of my best friends . . . I'm a bit of a mongrel myself. Aren't I Mum? Nothing to be ashamed of. Listen and you'll hear. It was told to me and I listened, I heard; I know and can tell you that He is no adulterer. He sullied no marriage bed. He did not make a scarlet woman of Mary. He put no horns on Joseph [p. 58]. And He acted with Joseph's full knowledge. You ask – what sort of a husband can this Joseph have been then? Not Mr Fulmar, that's for sure. Suspicion of poncing sounds near the mark. But you'd be wrong there too. What I'll say to you – and what you may find hard to believe – is that there were three cousins: Elizabeth, mother of John The Baptist; Mary, mother of Jesus; and the little known one Naomi, who was, if you take my meaning, not as other women. Petitpoint and cake baking weren't to her taste. Her interests lay elsewhere: building walls, watching the farrier shoe donkeys, hanging around the joinery shop in Megiddo. Tomboy. Good with her hands. Less good with her glands – pardon me, but I'm being candid. She had a moustache by the time she was fifteen. Didn't get too many of the chaps after her as you can imagine, our Naomi. No oil painting, I'm afraid. Muscly, hairy, deep voice . . . She was shunned. If they'd had sideshows then they'd have put her in one. If they'd had Russia then she'd have been an athlete. But there is a place for all of us. No matter how small, how maimed – look at me – no matter how far we diverge from secular norms, from profane convention, The Good Guy's job-hunting for us, computing our place in the jigsaw of time. Naomi's role was to cross dress for Jesus, for her cousin Mary, for Him . . . Joseph was a woman. When Mary was pregnant The Good Guy provided her with a beard, a holy walker, a companion. He knew what she'd suffer if she had no husband but He also knew what she might suffer from a husband. Mysterious ways eh? Mysterious ways. Those three cousins were touched, blessed in their blood. Tell you what I'll say to the doubters: why did Joseph take his family to Nazareth? Saint Matthew says they went there because it "was spoken by the prophets: He shall be called a Nazarene". You can scour The Bible however many years you want and you'll never find any prophet speaking such a thing, I guarantee that . . . The truth is they went to Nazareth because no one knew them there. No one knew that Mary's child was The Good Guy's. No one knew that Joseph was Naomi. And I tell you what: when Naomi began to get the hump with her cross dressing and looked like kicking up He had to give her an early bath. Wasn't going to let her spoil the show, was He? He had to destabilise her glands – nothing modern medicine couldn't have coped with, I'm glad to say; but they didn't have endocrinology in Galilee Health District did they?'

The phrases underlined were repeated by the congregation. Hankey might have contracted pneumonia but didn't. She might have caught a nasty chill but didn't. Eddie's manual balm guarantees internal heat. The congregation killed chickens for the eucharist which was also the celebratory feast – 'A ceremony that feeds, a feast that has an added dimension of meaning. It's not just stuffing your gut. And it's not just some 'orrible wafer that's only a symbol. Two birds with one stone if you'll excuse the whamercallit.'

The down and feathers of expiring chickens fill the air. It's as though a pillow fight has developed into war. Feathers stick to the chicken shit. 'Fowl is fair and fair is fowl,' chants The Founder, wheeling himself among his plucking people who know to repeat his words which are holy, wise, persuasively incantatory. His people are the colour of mud. They jostle. They gabble. They cluck. The integral confetti of plastic bags shredded by chickens as they approach translucent death blizzards the bailey. Here's a chicken that is being kneeled on. Here's one whose head is staved by a size twelve shoe. Watch that pullet run; watch it flee Wide Eyes there with a billowing bag in her hand. Smell the blood and shit. Slip on the skid-rink: the boy with the Super-8 does.

Look at Adonis Evans who supplied the six dozen birds and has a further two doz back-up in his old Commer outside; he

317

should be laughing all the way to the bank but the bungling saddens him – a neck well wrung is a neck well wrung: these godly losers don't have what it takes, there are only about four among them who'd have a chance of earning a crust at strangulation. All that fish meal and abattoir slurry for this!

Look at Arth and Mother who only came because Hankey begged them; look at them and the Anzio dead. They're suffering the waking nightmare of having their one and only stolen before their very eyes. Worse, she consents to being stolen.

Yet by the time Sonny and Laddy return Ray Butt has charmed them, reassured them. Once a star. Remember Reg Voice. Butt of The Joke hasn't died, he's there for The Founder to summon when needed: jocular, salty, bonhomous. Cripple patter at his own expense, cancer patter at his own expense – he can take the pain because he knows The Good Guy's going to see him right: 'Doesn't stop the plastic in me sphincter nipping like a Jack Russell though.' And he's quick to flash the ash. Not to mention his jovial flask which is necessarily not a hip flask, which is brim with Oban. Yes, you bet he can recall the very show at Catterick when one of the Anzio dead laughed till he almost wet himself, sincerely he can: 'That sergeant . . .'

'What, that bugger with the missing teeth?'

'That's the one . . . Missing teeth. Yup.'

Ray Butt's their sort. Sonny and Laddy are astonished to see him sitting next to Arth with his arm round him, hooting.

'Here, you Voys,' he calls. And they slope over, shifty, between the ad hoc barbecues and red hot braziers, they shameface through the smoke. 'Here – you know what. A most generous gesture Arth here has made. To be announced over the PA. In his pocket he's got two tickets and an hotel reservation for our lovebirds. In guess where? Madeira. That's where. That's a handsome gift. Eh? Fancy keeping that a secret – you're a dark horse Arth.'

Sonny and Laddy were close to contrite till vinous anaesthesia took out their consciences and they remembered that at that precise juncture, that acting on the information then available, they had acted in the prosecution of natural justice: vengeance was theirs, they told each other, presumptuously. Strange how potent cheap drink is. Later they too had their arms round Arth's shoulder and brought tears to his rheumy eyes with the tale of how they'd shot seagulls and sold them to Dave Ring, the Fratton fishmonger, claiming they were pigeons. 'That was before gulls were sacred, mind,' cautioned Laddy.

How was Poor Eddie? Was he sad as war again? Is that how weddings took him? Almost invariably yes; each one provoked a specific sadness beyond the generic emphasis of his solitude, beyond – Buttist weddings only – his abhorrence of charred chicken and his antipathy to communal ingestion. (He eats in private – crisps in the pocket; or in the qualified privacy of off-peak cafes where he can crouch over his ketchuped plate, slices and Tizer in a quiet formica corner.) 5 April 1972, Jonjon to Hankey: the specific sadness was ascribable to Mary. Mary didn't actually laugh when Poor Eddie said: 'I think if I . . . I *conduct* myself correctly, if I judge it right, if I channel my powers, you know . . . I'll be in line for canonisation.' Mary didn't actually laugh, but a quizzical stare, a murmured 'saint', an indulgent shrug were as hurtful. Eddie expected more of Mary whom he regarded as a special friend, the nearest thing he had to a spiritual ally among those around Ray Butt.

Mary's only connection with The Founder was that of having played with The Voys in a series of bands (Rider, Raider, Zee Red Dares, Readers Wives); that was Mary's only connection till this afternoon.

Poor Eddie had even considered the possibility that he loved Mary; he lacked an intuitive amometer whose needle might have swung into the red to signify *this is The Real Thing*. And his shyness disinclined him to ask the only person he could have asked, i.e. Mary. He compared his affection for Mary with that for Bonny. He scraped his scalp scabs, listed their qualities.

Bonny: married, fickle, disloyal, cunning, manipulative, insincere.

Mary: earnest, fluent French, prone to nosebleeds, secretive, (can be) frightening, (usually) steadfast, oblique, orphan, orphan, orphan. Eddie wondered if it was this fortuity that bound them in extra-familial void, forced them to cling to each other as they freefell down The Liftshaft Of Life. But no, their circumstances were so different; Mary's material recollections were few and this was a matter on which silence was observed, inquiries deflected. And then there was the question of Mary's 'father' not having been Mary's natural father, and the consequent matter of 'identity' which worried Poor Eddie more than it did Mary who was, after all, used to generative insouciance and was bored rather than upset by Eddie's preoccupation with it. Mary was sufficiently vain to be flattered by Eddie's crinkled brow, by his intense speculations on the balance of genetic legacy and learned self. Mary enjoyed the attention, listened as attentively to Eddie as to the stereo that scragged the damp and fungal walls of Sir Bernard de Gomme Tower, rolled another J on an LP. Eddie mistook Mary's toleration of him for fondness. He was so proud of this friendship that he was unable to discern the habitually low-grade reciprocation, its onesidedness. A veteran of a lifetime of slights may a) discern emotionally injurious intent in a handshake's pressure, in overheard phrases, in a stranger's fractious glance (it's the weather – *isn't it*?) or b) be grateful for soft knocks, think sunrise, look brightside, exaggerate the up angles. Poor Eddie had much to be paranoiac about but weighted his delusion the other way. Hope was fuel. It kickstarted each bright day for him. Every petty courtesy paid him will be zealously inflated: the deep-fryer with a half smile will be raised to his personal pantheon of putative chums. But all this protective machinery could not dissemble Mary's offhandedness.

There was dancing and drinking and eating. Sonny (a chicken leg, a pint glass and a cigarette grasped in his right hand) dragged his grandmother May towards Mary and said between two quaking belches: 'Mary. My grandma. May. She's a jewel. Aren't you love? Got a lot in common you two. Gran. Mary. You take care of each other I'm goin to the kazi. What they call the tool shed down the Cloudesley Shovell. Be good.'

They talked. Eddie loitered by now and again but they talked. They talked in French. Eddie skulked. Mary didn't go so far as to affect not to see him loitering, skulking, smiling his eager-to-please; but nor, equally, was a series of unlit glances an invitation to join them. May talked excitedly about the Bruxellois suburb of Ixelles, took delight in Mary's informed interest, prayed that Mary would not yawn. She talked about her childhood (reconstructed from photographs), about happiness and skating before the Germans came. When she spoke her native language she was aphasiac, self-chiding, solecistic, lost; Mary corrected her, tactfully. They talked in English about Mary's work-permit problems. (Mr Rippon – Surbiton's youngest ever mayor! – had hurried to Brussels four months previously for a feed at Comme Chez Soi and to sit beside Mr Heath – a sometime editor of *Church Times* – whilst the latter signed a piece of paper at the Egmont Palace. The UK's membership of the EEC would not take effect till 1 Jan 1973, however – which meant that Mary still received regular visits from jobsworths in the immigration.) Eddie had heard all this before: the accusations of institutionalised xenophobia; the phrase 'ces salauds d'Angliches'. May said to Mary: 'What you need to do is get married. Easy as a log. Find a native who isn't embarrassed. I'm sure you wouldn't have any trouble.'

Later Eddie stood among the carcasses and snapped wishbones watching May and Mary who stood backlit by the cassata sunset on the rampart beneath The Cross Of The World. The wheels of The Best Ever Redemptor's chair snapped bones, ground them to meal on the metalled ground. He squeezed Poor Eddie's brachial artery: 'OK Doc? Letting your hair down again? Tell you what Eddie – I know that that Mary's a . . . buddy of yours, but I always get this funny feeling – sniff sniff – like there's something . . . weell, ship short of a fleet – shall we say? We shall. And my mum proves it. They been nattering for *hours*, haven't they. That proves it. My mum is *not* what you'd call a people person. Very short on discernment. Guaranteed to pick the rotten apple. I mean, look at my dad. Stt – fancy marrying that. You'd have never believed it to have looked at him but they used to fight over him. But fancy *actually marrying* him. Ah well . . . Suppose that's Belgians for you.' He looked at Eddie: 'I shouldn't talk like that about them that gave me life.' Then he hurried away, the whirring motor driving the wheels at a lick.

Eddie always knew when Butt was going to wrap barbed wire

around himself, around what was left of him, around the trunk and stumps, wrap coils of it around him then roll about the concrete floor moaning, screaming, bellowing oaths of self chastisement, smearing the concrete like the scene of a sacrifice, staining it with purgation, marking his own route to The Best Ever Redemption.

Douglas Esmond Vallender dies on Boxing Day 1973. An awkward time to die. A messy way to die. The most distasteful inquest G. Leopold Lush ever conducted: misadventure. Low-tech suicide? A special treat? The best present he ever got? A gift from himself to himself? (It was that, literally.) Disturbed balance? Could have been.

a) Vallender Light on the point of receivership, had been bailed out (humiliatingly) by his daughter's husband's father. And for every quid there was a quo.

b) His daughter (whose husband's father etc . . .) was facing charges of heroin and barbiturate possession. 'God, that tosser. Johnson – you hearing? That tosser didn't have anything better to . . . Howd'you like it if *your* daughter married a tosser? Eh? Needle in the trousseau? Bastards.' Dead Douglas speaks. Years after Monica screamed in the bathroom, he speaks.

c) His wife has already told him that she is going to seek a divorce, but 'we were still living under the one, trying to stitch it together – fat chance . . .' They didn't.

It was Monica who found him; early on Boxing evening.

They had eaten Christmas lunch in silence. Bonny hadn't phoned. Monica was repulsed by her soon-to-be-ex's boundless appetite, his method of ingestion and masticatory abandon. She left the table for twenty minutes and when she returned he was still at it, turning a 14 lb turkey to carcass; grease and gravy up to his elbows; a red and gold paper hat matted to his crown by sweat, toning with his nose. Monica smoked, and picked at a jar of brandy butter with a teaspoon. She watched the machine that destroyed flesh moistening a mouthful with a draught of heady red Rhone. He ate: sausages; bacon rolls with prune stuffing; sage, thyme and parsley stuffing – he liked it soggy; roast potatoes; the bird's mashed liver on fried bread; gravy with a layer of fat puckering its surface; sprouts lacquered with butter; mashed parsnips; cranberry jelly. Before he ate those he had eaten two dozen oysters, fines de claire, each one of them briny, fresh and fleshy: eating these labia in their crinkly shells gave him a hard-on: from cocktail sausage to chipolata. After his turkey he had Christmas pudding with that brandy butter from Cumberland, clotted cream from Devon and flammable spirit from Charentes. Monica left the table again when he began to excavate an earthenware jar of Stilton with old Taylor's huing it rose. Many life forms entered his mouth on a waterbiscuit. And there were dates, Sauternes, Armagnac, champagne to toast HRH, candied fruits and angelica to pick at, a Monte Christo to fellate. He dozed. He heard Monica say that she was going for a walk. He heard the common voices of light entertainers. He dozed in the cosy, half lit study: there was rain on the panes, out there boughs groaned, he felt swaddled by satiety, nursed from within, cosseted by eupepsia. He was happy in his heaviness, comfortable as a doughnut, drowsy before the twin flickerings of fire and telly. All his troubles seemed evanescent. When he woke it was getting on for midnight; he had the makings of a hangover. He drank three pints of water whose flavour disgusted him. He drank a pint of black coffee. Monica appeared in a dressing gown and turbaned towel. She blew him a kiss, said that she was going to bed, that she had been soaked to the skin and wanted to avert a cold. She reminded him that she was lunching tomorrow with the Rumballs at Avon Castle. He nodded; he was eating, of course – a fist of stuffing. That was her last sight of him alive, with his mouth full. His mouth was full in death too.

Monica returned from her lunch party at six-fifteen on Boxing evening. She had a nasty headcold. The house was unlit, apparently deserted. Snuffling, searching for what, never having read the packet, she believed was called a Lemon Sip, she opened the door to Douglas's bathroom and turned on the light. She screamed.

She screamed before she worked out the mechanics. Shock preceded comprehension. And comprehension intensified shock. She resented him. He disgusted her.

He had put up a struggle. He had grappled with the hose. He had tried to free himself, tried to abate the supply, he had struggled to remove the fully plumbed mask. Which surely suggests that this was not suicide. Maybe. Equally he might have intended to prosecute the act but had discovered that the means was untenable, that it is the process of extinction that renders life precious. He looked like a sea creature – a mutilated ray, an octopus of grotesque dimensions. He wore his rubber skin. The black downlands of his belly were unmistakable. This was the man she had married when they were young and different. She had (she supposed) once loved the contours of that polished black arse which has grown a fatal tail. A tail that stretches to his mask, to the place approximate to his mouth in the smooth head which is a generic capital, an abstracted bonce. The screwdriver that he had used to tighten the brass joint of hose and mouth and with which he had subsequently attempted to effect release and then, in climactic fear, to pierce the offending tube, was stiffed in his fist. The sour smell was no worse than that of any lavatory he had ever used: there was no seepage. Douglas had, down the years, administered himself innumerable suction enemas, self service meals, auto-hoovers.[1] But he had always done it under strict and expensive super-vision (p. 247). And he had been warned against eating alone. He had been told that he would be punished. In the dark of his eyeless mask, as he was asphyxiated by his own excrement, he may at last have rued his cheapskate ways, may have promised never to welsh again. Too late. (This is one he'll never speak about.)

[1] See *Enema Digest* No. 18 (undated) for further synonyms, e.g. end to end, self-felch, Hershey in a straw, an-or, liquid lunch.

A blood bank gets to travel. Jean-Marie Meyer-Decker was a nurse, cook, gofer, singer of lullabies, alibi, driver, bike, catamite. Most of all he was Bruno Berg's blood bank. The customised reservoir of AO–1.

Wherever Bruno Berg went he took his ambulatory vial of top-up. Jean-Marie waited on Bruno Berg. He waited for him. He sat in rented villas in towns whose names he didn't know. He rehearsed chords in gardens he had never seen beyond, in houses he had arrived at by night, whose exteriors he could only guess at. He sat demurely in many brothels whilst Bruno Berg pumped semen imprinted with HoTLoVe, into hired mouths, into wombs by the hour, into the mothers of gits who grow up to be SIDA drinkers, bibbers of the bad apple. Sometimes he knew the name of the town, sometimes a girl would tell him: Evian, Oran. He wasn't used to knowing. Sometimes a maid would tell him: Colomb-Bechar, Toulon. Sometimes a maid would tell him how beautiful his hair was.

At the age of sixteen be owned a Steyr. 455 pistol, two Belgian passports (in the names Jean-Marie Houart and Jean-Marie Meyer-Decker), one French passport (as Berg), suits that he had never worn, four collarless Cardin jackets, a cigarette lighter shaped like a pebble, two Rolex Oysters, a pair of cufflinks decorated with trout flies, a suitcase full of records *et al*. Whether Bruno Berg was away for a day or three hours he always had a present for Jean-Marie when he returned. A Lambretta: not to be ridden. A knuckleduster. A hairdryer.

Twice they escaped over roofs.

One rainy dawn, early summer of 1963, the phone in a bungalow in the Lyonnais suburb of Champagne au Mont-D'Or woke Berg. He ran along the little corridor, pulled Jean-Marie from his bed, hustled him through a window, across the tiny garden and over a prefabricated concrete wall. They were less than three hundred yards away when they heard the explosion, saw the hail of reformed familiar objects and the rolling boles of smoke.

Berg supervised Jean-Marie's diet. He proscribed, at one time or another, milk, eggs, sugar, smoked fish, aniseed, tea, most cereals (thus pastry, biscuits, bread, pasta), tomatoes (save unripe ones), nuts and nut oils, fruits with stones, rice,[1] pumpkin and squash, mace. His valetudinarian appetite for magazine articles on food and fitness was unflagging. He always had faith in the last one he had read; he amended Jean-Marie's regime accordingly. He demanded blood of the highest quality, blood free from the impurities associated with, say, 'cooked' cheeses such as gruyère. He demanded (the next month) blood *boosted* by ingestion of 'cooked' cheeses such as gruyère. He overturned his orders with such alacrity that Jean-Marie often forgot what he should and should not eat. When the boy got it wrong Berg would weep or scream or accuse him of plotting slow murder. The boot of Berg's Panhard was filled with false numberplates and clipped dietetic articles whose inevitably contradictory counsel worried him because he believed in all of them as another genus of sucker might believe in variant horoscopes. Jean Marie's permitted staples were liver, spinach, endive.[2] From October 1962 till April 1963 he was forbidden to eat anything other than ewe's milk yoghurt.

Bruno Berg believed he ran on blood of the highest quality – 'super sang, extra sang, mon Marie'; he needed such blood (top octane, haemin rich) in his line of work. Such blood has to be *made*, and nurtured; it is no more a fortuity than is wine. Wine's aptness as transubstantive is thorough and inviolable. No wonder Jean-Marie despised wayward eucharists. He was proud of his blood; his blood defined him; you are what you bleed. You march on your blood. It's corporeal current. It's currency: early on Jean-Marie rejoiced in the strangeness and uniqueness of his relationship with Bruno Berg whose very life

1 Berg objected to rice on the grounds that it was 'the habitual food of the Viet Minh'.
2 Endive is nutritionally worthless. It is, however, Belgian.

326

depended on his. He did not give his blood. He was no mere *donor* of corpuscular rectitude. He sold it, bartered it for goods, for a series of roofs, for money. He was kept. He rarely slept with Bruno Berg; there was little enthusiasm on either side. It was Jean-Marie's blood that attracted Berg; not his body; not his potential for belligerence; not his eagerness to further assert his coming manhood with explosives and hidden bombs; not even his loyalty – Berg never deluded himself that it was anything but bought. He never took a chance with it, hence the incessant stream of presents, treats, carrots. Loyalty is like love; those afflicted with a capacity for either are not invariably constant in their choice of objects (p. 143). Bruno understood loyalty. It is temporal. He had once been loyal to his other blood brother, Léon Deroose, but that had changed. He was loyal to every dietician whose secrets he read. He was loyal to every mineral water whose label analysis he read. Certainly nostalgia and patriotism did incline him towards Spa – but if Contrexéville was to come up with the right price, then he'd be loyal to that small town in the Vosges, he'd swear to the nephrological certainties invested in its water, to every one of its hepatic boasts. Bruno Berg understands loyalty: and Jean-Marie is still shaking off the infirmity called childhood, he is (interminably) at an age when the world reshapes itself. New idols. New nous. He looks at this boy who is his saviour, this sanguinary coincidence whose fingers spread over an entire keyboard, and he wonders: *how long*?

Whenever he rents another flat (Annecy, Bab el Oued) he is as concerned about Jean-Marie's preoccupations (the view, shower pressure, TV reception, bed comfort, complement of ashtrays etc.) as he is about the usual things – access, security, closed-off chimneys, triple locks, neighbours, covert exits, previous occupiers. His inspection procedure is thorough: Jean-Marie climbs on his shoulders to scrutinise the tops of wardrobes and cupboards. He unscrews floorboards, prises up parquet, jemmies wainscot, peeks, overturns mattresses, reaches behind boilers, never trusts a loft, never trusts a concierge: Berg follows them to cafés, taps their phones. He sits all day in the car logging the comings and goings at his new apartment block; at night he smothers boot polish on his face and hands, scales fire escapes, drainpipes, ascends to attic storeys in order to spy on the neighbours at his new apartment block.

Paranoia is a full-time occupation which requires organisation, administration, planning if it is to be done well; like any job it gives shape to a life, purpose too, and it has its satisfactions (a hunch proved right; the discernment of pattern in a street's behaviour; a duplicated gesture; the moustache and homburg who spends too long by a news-stand; an overexercised dog – no poodle demands six trips round a block; the pair of furtive plumbers; the headlights of a parked car that flash dip-dip-full; gloves in summer; a workman's clean hands; the streetwalker who turns away a john). The greater Berg's zeal, the more justifiable appear his fears. And he does have much to fear. He has not been forgotten. Bruno Berg understands loyalty and so understands that he will not be forgotten. Bruno Berg will pay with his borrowed blood. Bruno Berg, *la balance* (the grass, the canary). Sing or you die, squeal or you bleed – there will be no blood bank in gaol, you'll expire in a puddle on the cell floor, you'll measure the life left to you in litres per hour, you'll watch the mortal spillage and wail at your impotence to stem it.

So he sang. He was less than a line in someone else's song, a makeweight in a chorus. But add that to his fingerprints on the washer; he was detained on the morning of Sunday 22 December 1963. One sunny moment he is rubbing his gloved hands together and crossing rue Oberkampf, Paris 11 ème towards the little bakery where Jean-Marie is waiting to buy pain azyme (unleavened – yeast is off this month), the next he's being strongarmed into the back of a black DS which has turned the corner into rue de la Folie Mericourt and disappeared by the time that Jean-Marie has pushed his way out of the shop.

Jean-Marie did not go back to their apartment down the street. Indeed he walked past the peeling building without any acknowledgement of it. And he kept walking, never looking behind him, clutching the loaf, across Avenue de la République, uphill towards Ménilmontant; he is walking quicker now, and on the far side of the Boulevard de Belleville he turns from the pavement beside a cigarette booth and runs down a flight of steps into the Cour du Labyrinthe. Apt name. He does not know where he is running to. He rushes along alleys so that cobbles snap at his insteps, so that walls barge him, corners jostle him with brickbats. He finds his way barred by a metal gate whose scrolled top may represent a pelican, in its piety, plucking its breast to feed blood to its offspring. He ran winded, in terror of invisible possibilities. Here's a church. Here's a leaning tower of crates. Here are two bullnecked men who remove themselves from his path: there is danger in his panic, savagery in his face. At Place Gambetta he ran into the metro. He inhaled ozonic must. He skulked at the far end of the deserted platform reading, re-reading an advertisement for Denicotea cigarette holders, willing the train to arrive.

Three people descended to the platform in quick succession: a man of indefinable age, indistinct appearance, unmemorable features, a man who might blend in to any crowd, unnoticeably, and was thus an object of high suspicion; a bespectacled woman with a flick-up hairdo, check stirrup-cuff trousers and a wicker animal basket which, going by the ease with which she swung it, contained no cat, no yappy little *griffon* – so why carry it?; a gangly youth, hardly older than Jean-Marie, with big problem skin, a bronze mac (very 1962), a book and a bandage tied tight around his head so that his dirty blond hair rose from it in tufty fascicles. The youth is stooped, consumed by his book, blind to the world beyond words. The man stares at a circus poster. The woman clutches her basket, cradles it, as though cosseting the ghost of the creature that once inhabited it. One of them, all of them? Two? If so, which?

The woman gets off at Parmentier.

Jean-Marie walks through the tunnels at République to the Charenton-Ecoles line.

Nondescript man: whereabouts unknown.

The youth, bandaged head in book and now displaying myopia, walks the same tunnels, waits for the same train – reasonably, given the multiplicity of correspondences at République, there is a seven to one chance of his doing so. They do not travel in the same carriage. At each station – Filles du Calvaire, Chemin Vert, Bastille, Ledru-Rollin, Faidherbe

329

Chaligny, Michel Bizot, Porte Dorée, Liberté etc. – Jean-Marie opens the doors to see if he has disembarked. He has not. He disembarks at the end of the line, at Charenton, still reading, turning a page to prove it, following Jean-Marie across Place de l'Eglise (wrought metal, a lupine dog barking on a roof, visible breath, shutters against the wan winter sun, the distant raucity of a bal musette, old Flanoche gesticulating in Le Petit Caporal – all the usual). He moves like an automaton, finding Jean-Marie's path in the book from which he doesn't divert his eyes. Jean-Marie has suffered two years' tutelage in paranoia, in the tireless mutation of neutral tropes into imagined threats, in ascribing hostile meaning where none is due. This circumstance is without the confines of that discipline which is also a full-time occupation. No mutation required. Unequivocal meaning. Pursuer and quarry cast long enfeebled shadows across the square. Tired walls are buttressed by bare forests of stanchions: they're tired, too – they have to lean. The archaeology of poster art may be studied on Vernier's shop's side. No time: Jean-Marie hurries towards his destination, proceeds according to Bruno's instructions in response to Contingency iii.

He arrives at the embanked road beside the confluence: barges' milty wake; damp nip; stove-pipe smoke; river mist; the power station's big plumbing that lustres across the wide water. It is at the bridge that he thinks like a soldier, like the soldier he is (a uniquely important member of the secret army, the blood warrior of the Eighth (Paris) Cell); he is among his people; signs of his tribe have been daubed with increasing frequency the further east he has ridden and walked. At Liberté, for example, when he craned out the carriage, he saw no bronze mac but renewed scrawls of the three vital letters. He takes his decision, *the* decision, to act alone whilst standing beside a wall which the traitorous agents of traitorous government have failed to clean. Instead of crossing the bridge towards Kermarrec's place, instead of inculpating Kermarrec and his wife (40 stone the pair), he walks east towards Joinville. They look at him, the girls do, at his round loaf and corvine hair, as they make their way from church to café. It is on a mud road to a riverside café that Jean-Marie aboutfaces. The Marne is a river that men fish in;

fishermen require metal stakes to support their rods whilst they drink *un pot de rouge, un coup de calva*, whilst they munch their *jambon beurre* all which help them think of lunch. They are now taking lunch, talking pike, at Le Buffet Sur L'Eau (Chez Didier), a gastroshack. The road has become a path. Cars are parked on a terrace higher up the bank. Jean-Marie curses the mud on his shoes, and its cause. From where he stands with a metal stake in one hand and his loaf in the other he could jump onto Didier's corrugated roof whose pagodal chimneys reek of eel bound with pig's blood, Ile de France speciality no doubt. Jean-Marie saunters towards his pursuer, stake as staff. The youth's smile is wide and welcoming.

'Par là?' he smiles, wide and welcoming, indicating the wooden staircase down the bank to Didier's. He is armed? He has chosen the place of execution? Jean-Marie advances on him – one of his eyes has been recently bruised, it's taken the yellow road to recovery. He is still smiling when Jean-Marie drops the loaf[1] and takes the stake in both hands, hoofs the mud with it, points it like a halberd, swishes it through prenatal December. The Bronze arm lifts the yellow covered book, wide and welcoming: *Soeur Jésus*[2] (by) Edouard Manneret. Jean-Marie believes the book is a gun/grenade/bomb. He throws the stake, he ducks. The youth's bemusement is such that he doesn't move till he's made to move by the metal that strikes his thigh. Side down in the mud he smiles and recovers his book. He waves it with that same smile, with an arm that iridesced and now

[1] The approximately circular *pain azyme* carried in the left hand was, between *c.* 1961 and 1966 (when it was superseded by apple-green corduroy Newmans and left dress) *the* standard sign of an anally active circumcised homosexual male in eastern Paris; a baguette held vertically signalled a willingness to perform fellatio etc. 'Le Baragouin des Pains' (The Bread Code) was so named after an article in *L'Express* 23 October 1964 which drew attention to the phenomenon whose centre was the cemetery of Père Lachaise. Eight specific homosexual practices were allied to the same number of bread and brioche types. The article also reported the complaint of a cemetery attendant that abandoned loaves intensified the problem of pigeon excrement on gravestones and monuments.

[2] Published by Editions Terre Jaune, 1962. 'Edouard Manneret' was the pseudonym of Georges Marchat (b. Brest 1922), agronomist and poet. This novel, his only exercise in the medium, described in ritualistic form and quasi-scientific language 44 anonymous homosexual liaisons of between four and nine minutes' duration, one hundred words per minute, precisely, down to the second and *even* to the broken syllable.

doesn't, that reaches from the mud. He points (towards the loaf). Jean-Marie Meyer-Decker picks up the stake and crushes his ribs with it. The youth grunts after he has exhaled and has the time and the instinct to cover his head: 'T'as pas lu?' He holds up the book. Jean-Marie strikes his femora. Puzzled. He tries to get up, tries to run. When Jean-Marie hits his head the bandage unfurls, his hair flops and his chin drops. When Jean-Marie pushes him down the bank into the river he protests, truthfully: 'J'sais pas nager.'

Big fish, but the fishermen's eyes are elsewhere. Jean-Marie hurls the stake into the river so that it may or may not descend on its victim who already has enough to cope with in these difficult moments; bubbles, brownness, the flavour of mortality. When Jean-Marie crosses the bridge into Alfortville and his immediate future, he recalls a page in *France Soir*, the B-side of a diet programme, which claimed that the majority of Seine suicides are, in fact, Marne suicides – but owing to the latter's strength of current at Conflans . . .

He got the keys from Jaci Kermarrec at Pourquoi Pas Chez Les Kermarrec. He refused anything to eat or drink, save a glass of Cacolac in order to regularise the transaction in the eyes of the customers. The wall abutting this bistrot à vin had had its archaic graffito restored – OAS TOUJOURS. The inscription is painted over the top of a municipally removed one. The car, a twelve-year-old Panhard (unnoticeable) was in a garage in a lane of workshops that were all rust and rot. It starts first go – Yves Kermarrec has earned his exalted fee. He backed it out, checked the boot (t'es un vrai pote, Yves), drove east-south-east for six hours, stopping for petrol at Bar sur Aube, spitting as he passed the sign welcoming him to Colombey-les-Deux-Eglises. He turned off the N19 at Chaumont and drove through the dark, along unknown roads, past signs to mineral water towns, past signs to cheese towns, up and down hills of increasing gradient, round hairpins. There are the lights of a village in the sky; there are the lights of another a thousand feet beneath him. Arboreal canyons, pine naves, birch's pinchbeck bark in the orange beam, mossy banks, a stoat, a rabbit, a broken wooden sign nailed to a trunk: 'Etang de Pr . . .' He stopped, reversed, took this track.

For four nights he slept in the old Panhard. He daubed it with mud. He stuck leafmeal and twigs to it. He covered it with boughs. When he awoke the first morning he discovered that he had parked across the source of a stream, in a crevasse beneath bluffs of lichened rock. The sun shone on frost-stiffened leaves, the sun made chiaroscuro of the profound forest, there was no mean between dazzle and obfuscation, there was an excess of silhouette, the noises were more horrible than those of the dangerous city. Jean-Marie locked himself in the car for hours at a stretch. His breath froze on the windscreen. The radio received aerial flotsam. From within fifty yards of the car he could look down on two lakes: Pr . . . and one of whose name he was even more ignorant. He dared not walk to them lest he fail to find his way back.

The jar of fat and fibrous meat stew had evidently been in the car for weeks. The Kermarrecs were paid to ensure that the vehicle was fit for a self-imposed siege. They had failed. (T'es un vrai saligaud, Yves.) Jean-Marie was sick. He picked some purple berries and ate them. He was sick again. He missed clothes, mirrors, warmth, presents, comics, musical instruments – he missed those most of all, even more than comfort and gangster films on TV and Bruno Berg – whom he hardly missed at all though he did miss what he unfailingly provided. Jean-Marie had never been anything other than kept.

He was more than a *kept boy*. He'd met *them*. Some of Bruno's friends (not really friends, inevitable victims of acquaintanceship in their covert milieu) did have kept boys. Jean-Marie was Bruno's twin, the chance winner in a chemical lottery, a blood date, his life line.

He half woke the fourth day from dreams of drowning and transfusion. He writhed in the snug sleeping bag (victoire, Yves). He regretted that he had all this within him and only one person to give it to, and that that person wasn't with him, wasn't prepared to die with him in the gloom of this crystalline translucent cell which belonged to dreamtime till he realised it belonged to a different, external genus of terror and that he was about to be admitted to the mysteries of submersion and suffocation.

The car has been moved was his terrified thought – how easy he had been to track down. *The car has been buried* was his next: tracked down and interred in his sleep by unseen hands. The cunning, the expertise, the deft resourcefulness. He turned his head on the back seat and found that it was covered by fine white powder. Every window was entirely obscured, the car's eyes were blinded. The segmental back window, the wind-screen, the four windable windows and the two quarter-lights. The windable window whose handle his crown had wrestled with and lost every night was no longer movable. The door would not budge. Glue? Weld? Bolts? His nose bled, from fright or something. He lifted his legs in the sleeping bag that was a straitjacket and kicked the other door. He kicked till his heels ached. The silence of this grave made him long for the rustle of the little stream that had at first dogged him but which he had grown fond of as it spilled into his dreams. He wriggled out of the sleeping bag. His nose bled again. The car's ignition was dead. None of the other windows would open, nor the doors. The cold was excessive. *It is unnecessarily cold* he told himself: they didn't have to add that, but he was so deep down that the world's heat could not reach him to comfort him in his terminal prison.

He stared in the rearview mirror at his face which he had smeared with mud the first day. He was a secret soldier of the secret army. He was a daubed warrior. He would resist death with martial rigour and succumb with martial grace if resistance was not enough. He stared in the mirror. He looked at the speedometer, at the biscuit packets, at the litter in his coffin. He could see them all. He was a soldier, he thought like a soldier. Since there was a vestige of light in the car he deduced that he had not been buried in earth. Snow! He had never in his life seen snow. It was as strange to him as was adobe to an eskimo: Snow! According to *The Universal Fount Of Likenesses* (J. Greenford, ed., London, 1985) snow's usual similes are 'blithely disregarding of its treacherousness, its dangers, its potential for chaos; they portray snow in terms of cosiness, as the climate's contribution to the cult of the picturesque, as a sort of eiderdown that the world tucks itself up in. Germans dote on snow.'

Jean-Marie had of course seen pictures, icing sugar representations, glitter on Christmas cards from 'our country', films with ski chases and cablecar drama. But he had not witnessed it without such mediations; he had not been in snow's presence. He had not been *within* it, had not been surrounded by millions of hexagonal crystals. When he broke the windscreen with a jack the fine powder poured into the car, stung him; its malevolence fazed him.

The blizzard in the southern Vosges that began on the evening of Christmas Day resulted in snow falls of up to 1.06 metres with drifts of up to 6 metres at Gérardmer. Jean-Marie's Panhard lay beneath approximately 300 kg[1] of snow and the volume increased all day, it blew into the east-facing crevasse, powered by a wind that owned the voice of an animal. White-out, trial by blankness. The transformation of the plot of land that he had familiarised himself with during the previous three days was entire. Nothing remained. He didn't know till then how much snow hurt, nor that it made the world mute, that it rid the world of accents: the homogenisation was a wicked marvel, a tyranny of uniform, a climatic joke about purity.

Did you ever push through a drift that came up to your chest? You know then the way dry snow reforms around you, you know there's always more waiting to blow into your nose and make it bleed again, you know how it has its revenge for every drop of septal blood that stains it, how it sends for reinforcements that arrive quick as the wind and how they just want to spread the word, share the party with their friends back home who'll call in sure enough, gatecrashing on a blinder, the locusts of the north. It hurts his eyes, his ears, his chest – he's dressed wrong, he's dressed for crossing a Paris street to buy a loaf, he's dressed for cursing Bruno Berg's Contingency iii. Mishaps don't run according to plan. Two scared roes startle him.

Scott with his head down, Hudson floating inexorably towards his death, Pym in a clipper among marine Matterhorns, children burnt by rink ice (p. 55) – the gulf between actuality and representation (even photographic representation) in-

---

1 Dry snow has a density of no more than 0.1 grammes per cubic centimetre.

creases the lower the temperature goes. Thermal deprivation is unusually resistant to evocation. Jean-Marie might list the ills the weather did him (purple ears, broken skin, nosebleeds, gripless red fingers, sinus percussion, iced eyebrows, bully on his chest, communication problem with his feet); but the parts could never suggest the whole which is dulling, desensitising. Gangrene is painless – though Jean-Marie's frostbite, which didn't go that far (his teetotalism was a boon here), stung a bit. He trudged, he fought for each step, he fell repetitively, he fell before he had got up from the last fall, he fell down a gully. He had no idea where he was going save that it was sure to be white when he got there. He slid down a slope with a child's glee at the discovery of such means of motion; he didn't exactly smile but no doubt came closer to it then than at any other moment since Sunday morning. He had, indeed, very little to smile about. The hostility of trees and people; this new element that stored up bad surprises; his dislocation; his multiple uncertainties; his realisation that Contingency iii was specious, a plan devised for its own sake, a martial fantasy that took no heed of weather nor of his lack of woodcraft and his signal unsuitability. But Bruno Berg was not an imaginative bleeder; he didn't understand that Jean-Marie's pulse beat to rhythms different from his own, that he might have no appetite for starry solitude, for crawling, for boiling moss, for purging slugs, for that rudimentary exploitation of nature that allows you to vanquish nature, to fox the old drab, to come through, to survive.

Jean-Marie's methods of survival repudiated the rules that Bruno had persistently and earnestly tried to inculcate, rules that were stubbornly professed creeds and soldiers' superstitions, rules founded under circumstances of war and occupation, rules which allowed Bruno to dignify criminal activities as political/patriotic/revolutionary/counter-revolutionary; as the exercise of natural justice; as adjustments to the cosmic machine, adjustments whose beneficent ramifications might not be felt for a generation or more.

The abduction and elimination of Ben Malek, the unhappily necessary 'suicide' of Ferniot, the lessons that had to be taught to judges Gutrin, Donnard and Wanecq: they might all – in the short term and in the myopic eyes of those unblessed with inspirational presentiment – possess certain regrettable attributes (harshness, wanton brutality, treasonable intent, antinomian arrogance). And there was too the regrettable ineptitude of civilians, spectators who stray onto the pitch, whose ignorance exposes them to the firing line, who lack the nous to keep out of men's way. Don't they know there's a (secret) war on?

Paramount among Bruno's rules was that which stipulated subterfuge, covert breathing, solitude, furtiveness, no trace, existence through non-existence. Lie low, live as in sewers, hide, head below, no third light because there's not been a first, watertight seclusion. You have no being. You are not. All actions should aspire to invisibility.

Example: the bicycle. Not the bicycle that Jean-Marie rode at Njili (p. 174). The bicycle Bruno Berg works on in a bungalow in Annecy in the summer of '63. He rides out into the mountains in his cycle rig of shorts and Anquetil cap worn widdershins. He is one of hundreds seeking saddle satisfaction on a Sunday, one of hundreds curving his spine, vex or cave according to the toss of the gradient and the cut of the breeze. Ah the blessed blue sky, the crisp air, the extreme green of happy fields! He is hidden among the hundreds, he is typical – really he is, he is not that old, he is typical of those with growing bellies who ride on Sundays and dream of taking a stage in in the *Tour* or the *Flèche Wallonne*: the capacity for sporting fantasy extends to those beyond the age at which such fantasies might reasonably be fulfilled just as the colonialist, *France-Intégral* fantasy extended long after Algeria's separation had been effected. The typicality of Berg the cyclist was not entire; his bicycle was also a .22 rifle – the crossbar was a barrel, the saddle was a butt, a Simplex gear lever an ad hoc trigger. It was an ingenious machine which might, with sufficient practice, be transformed to its covert ballistic function in half a minute. It was with this weapon that Bruno Berg shot and injured (shattered his right scapula) the former Capitaine Mousnier whose information had gained him exemption from prosecution and had occasioned sixteen arrests. The modern house in which Mousnier was living at Bout du Lac, at the southern end of the Lac d'Annecy and about eight miles from the town, was close to the round-the-lake route taken every Sunday by hundreds of saddle fantasists. Bruno Berg lay in a wood on the hill that rose behind the garden. When he shot at Mousnier the perfidious traitor moved to pick up a pair of secateurs resting on the rim of a tub of asters. He cried and fell down a flight of crazy paved steps leading to the back of the basement garage. The noise attracted his wife and one of the guards, who came round the corner of the house at a sprint, holding a hand gun. Berg cursed the crossed thread which slowed the re-assembly of the bicycle. Another guard appeared and opened fire with an automatic weapon. Berg pulled his bike along a ditch. It wasn't until he was half way back to Annecy, among a group of almost twenty cyclists, that he noticed play in the handlebars.

It was his prints on the missing washer that inculpated him, that led to his arrest six months later, that forced him to follow Mousnier's example. The bicycle was not, then, invisible – but it had come close; and had it not been for Mousnier's fatuous desire for secateurs, had he behaved as he was meant to behave, had he played his (unknowing) role without getting the moves wrong . . . Why, yes, the utility of Bruno's murderous vehicle would have matched its cunning.

Jean-Marie shuffled through the afternoon on feet that grew muter by the moment. When he saw the house at the far end of a blizzard – it was, unmistakably, a house, a tiny house *cloaked in a velvety mantle of deep and crisp*, no doubt the very house that gave snow a good name on postcards, enough of a house in its soft outlines to be instantly recognisable even if its every detail is blanked out – when he sees the house it is not merely his eagerness to spite Bruno and to deride his paramount rule that makes him approach it, find the front door and bang on it with the immemorial anxiety of stranded travellers, of babes lost in woods. It is also the need for warmth, shelter etc.; thermal sybaritism is as potent a force as self-determination, the longing for snugness matches the longing for independence. This house is a resort for body as well as for brain. It will be when someone answers. It was – after he forced open a metal roller shutter and window behind it. TV reception – poor. Heating – radiators in most rooms, but switched off; he placed two electric fires beside each other. Water – frozen pipes. Cooking – bottled gas ring. Provisions – the house was evidently not continuously occupied: a cupboard in the kitchen which was itself little more than a cupboard contained tins of sauerkraut, pork and beans (cassoulet), ham knuckle with peas etc. Furniture – uncomfortable, scuffed, neglected. Each of the four rooms had at least two beds in it. Beds to let? Or was the house not large enough for the family which occasionally used it? He lay weighted by blankets, dazed and sated by rich food and cocoa made with melted snow.

He planned his future in the spiral orange elements of the fires – not, perhaps, as conducive to truly deep thought as embers but an adequate substitute. There would be embers, on the last day, when the electric fires fused and he burnt the furniture in the hearth. He burnt it as much to signal his presence as to generate warmth. By then he had decided, if nothing else, that he no longer wished to participate in the grave game, he wanted to come out into the open, he wanted to discover the humility of a humdrum life, to abjure his exotic incarceration, to rupture the symbiotic contract, plumb the illusion called normality. Any vampire's well would harbour fantasies of the commonplace. What Jean-Marie discovered was that he was entrapped by his very enslavement, that he was institutionalised, that his wishfulness was no more than that. He was stunted by the weight of his dependence. When he was arrested (forced entry, theft, criminal damage – the smoke had been spotted by a prying neighbour) he was taken to a cell at Bains-les-Bains. He was obstinate in his refusal to give his name, address, date of birth etc. He declined to cooperate.

A fat policeman with a dewlap offered him a Craven A; he patted the box of 50: 'Cadeau de Noël. T'es pied noir?' The tutoyage was a gauged slight which had its effect and did make him feel a boy; and his accent did retain a vestige of guttural broadness. Jean-Marie had received no Christmas present. He was on the run – not from a penal institute, no; but, equally, he did not know who from. Only Bruno Berg and his captors could answer that. Only Bruno Berg could stand surety for him. Was Bruno Berg his next of kin? This was a matter hitherto unconsidered; a second policeman, hungover and rheumy, who had sought the name of his next of kin, shrugged sadly when he didn't reply.

Jean-Marie rued his failure to answer the civil questions put by these two civil men, resented his adherence to Berg's dicta among which was the vacuous apothegm that: 'Pourvu qu'il la boucle c'est le taulard qui boucle le taulier.' (So long as he keeps his mouth shut it's the con who's got the screw banged up.)

The next morning, in distant defiance of Berg, he asked for and was given the cigarette he had refused. He gave his real name, and the address on rue Oberkampf; he told them about the abandoned Panhard; shown on a 1 cm:1 km map where it was that he had been arrested he assisted and identified the car's probable position – equidistant from the hamlets of Moscou and Jerusalem (laughter). He did not mention that – how many days ago? – he had pushed a young man into the Marne. At noon the fat one brought him potato soup, chicken with rice, a Duralex beaker of red wine, a second cigarette, a paternal smile. At half past noon the other, hungover again and still rheumy, unlocked the cell to ask Jean-Marie the registration number of the Panhard. A few minutes on and the first returns.

His demeanour is different. He looks at Jean-Marie with contemptuous distaste, he picks up the metal tray, he says nothing, the light is extinguished from outside; the day is all dusk now till it's really dusk and then it's night.

Jean-Marie bangs on the door of the cell in the basement of the hôtel de ville in this small town where the snow stretches across streets with no disturbance by tyres or feet. A street lamp's adulterated lustre smears one wall by way of a window high on another. There is a holed pail in the corner. The cell's light is switched on soon after 5 am; there are voices outside; the sleepy dewlap, tousled as a boy, glares and gestures to him to follow; at the end of the corridor, by the door to the yard behind the hôtel de ville a hook-nosed man extinguishes a cigarette, grinding it into the snow.

He takes Jean-Marie by the arm, hardly acknowledges the

dewlap's flaccid salute. He opens the rear door of a Peugeot for Jean-Marie, gets in after him. The driver doesn't turn his head. The fulgent streets, the slithery ascent from the town, the silhouette of a chapel, the starry sky, the factory rhythm of chained tyres on snow. 'Bains-les-Bains,' says the man beside Jean-Marie. He smells of coffee and women. 'Bains-les-Bains,' agrees the driver, 'ouais – c'est pas demain la veille . . .' Neither of them speaks again until an hour later when the driver expresses his approval for the Dutch practice of eating cheese at breakfast. By now a murking dawn is seeping over the peaks across the valley; the snow is grey, the canal is black, the mist off the Moselle is white as steam, a train of high-sided wagons pulls alongside the car to shut out the local monochrome. Wipers smear the greasy screen. The north is where the lorries live, they loom out of slush fountains, bellowing and shining. Jean-Marie sleeps with his head on his forearm, dreaming of ghost ships in fog, wincing at their foghorns, wondering why there are pins beneath his eyelids. He tries to cling to dream when they wake him, abort him from sleep's solace.

Sleet. A steep hill, paved with cobbles, parlously perched terraces – the ubiquity of brick is total, the absence of trees is total. Jean-Marie recalls 'our country', the smell of Liège, iron in the air, coal smoke and penury. The cobbles are shining, there is no snow, the sleet is absorbed by the sheen. He gets out of the car and stretches, the damp cold percusses his forehead. The hook-nosed man rings the bell beside a door in a brick wall topped by cheveux de frise. Jean-Marie looks over mean roofs, meagre strands of household smoke and taped-up dormers towards forges, hoppers, chimneys, gas cylinders, the elemental geometry of manufacture. Incuriously, he asks the driver standing tight beside him: 'On se trouve où?'

'Pompey,' he replies, 'un beau coin, hein? Pompey.'

Pompey is where Jean-Marie fell in love for the second time. Pompey is where the Meurthe meets the Moselle, where both rivers conjoin the Marne-to-Rhine canal. This is the deep heart of France, France's deepest heart: Lorraine crosses, mysticism about the very earth, every grain of soil through your fingers is French. Pompey is Nancy's port: the rough-tough Nancy boys work here, and the stevedores and the drivers and the lock guys (with their patriotic tattoos)[1] whose mistrust of strangers . . . This is the heart of France precisely because it is so close to Germany: invasions foment nationalism.

They should have been all right here, they had been fighting for France, and they would have been all right had it not been for Jean-Marie's amorous rashness.

He walked up the chequer path to the house between beds of dead flowers. Hook-nose and the driver followed him, jocularly greeting *nôtre Hervé* who had admitted them. The front door is open. All three wave him on into the house, they seem to hang back, preoccupied with bonding through joshing.

He is no longer scared: he is a familiar of the unforseeable, used to freefalling through climatic novelties and loveless landscapes. Orientation is no longer a staple, but a luxury that he can do without. He enters the tessellated hall with its old, oxidised gasoliers and enfeebled pot plants and chipped jardinières. It is lit by an unprotected bulb that pushes like a lipoma through wrinkled, discoloured wallpaper. The bowel-brown paint on the dado and achitraves is crazed and matt. This hall, this whole house maybe, has aged no better than humans do. It wears its years like an infirmity. Heaped on a crumpled chaise longue there are clothes, boxes, suitcases, a guitar case, an accordion faced in plastic ruby. He scrutinises them for some moments before opening the guitar case, running his hand across the perpendicular instrument's neck; holding up (as though to ascertain its size) a collarless black corduroy jacket. These are *his* possessions. He turns to the three men who stand on the house's threshold.

Hervé points to a room off the hall: 'Par là. A gauche.' He is inured to spatial achronia, temporal dislocation; they are what happen to him; but they are meant to be serial, episodic. This is

[1] These include: Lorraine crosses, legends such as 'Pour le Patri'; invocations to Jeanne d'Arc whose natal village of Domremy is close by on the Meuse; mermaids – there are a variety of myths relating Jeanne's reincarnation as a *freshwater* mermaid; 'Verdun', which was also the predictable codename of the OAS's military leader in metropolitan France. (Tip to salauds d'Angliches visiting Domremy: inscribe the visitors book 'Elles brûlent bien, ces pucelles.')

cyclical. His instruments, his clothes, his pistol (?), his passports (??). The driver is attempting to make three fingers of his right hand stand whilst the little one crouches in shame. Jean-Marie's collection of horizontally-striped ties droops from a hidden hanger. His life has moved beside him, in parallel; material normality is waiting to greet him, in the wrong place; the solace of chattels is lessened by their transportation: and they are tainted with the house's drabness – they add up to no more than a pile of bribes. This is what he has been worth. His price. Bought by chrome and wood, plastic and metal, gewgaws and clothes whose moment has passed. He opened the door that Hervé had indicated.

A man who was a version of Bruno Berg sat at a table, gripping the chestnut velvet cloth with his bandaged hands; he sat as though he had been there for ever, as though he were part of the gloomy room; as though waiting for a meal that would never be served. He looked up at Jean-Marie. Pain. His gaze returned to his hands and to the mottled material they took comfort in. This new Bruno Berg can divine patterns in nap the way other philosophers can in electric fires, embers, clouds, running water. This new Bruno Berg is an older Bruno Berg.

Ten days ago, on 22 December 1963, when Jean-Marie last saw him, he was thirty-seven years and six months of age. Now he is the other side of fifty. He was darkhaired, the new Berg's hair is grey. His facial skin was lightly tanned. His complexion is now multicoloured – gamboge, gravy, yolk, mauve, many many crimsons – and it's freshly textured, resurfaced with lesions and welts and highgloss patches where the skin shines like buffed ochre. There are burn holes, blanket stitches, droops of withered tissue. One eye is partially closed, its lid is as swollen as an udder. Berg's body of boastful muscle and bonded sinew has been replaced by a flaccid apparatus hardly able to bear its diminished weight. Berg looked again at Jean-Marie with inextinguishable shame. The right eye, whose lachrymal organs were intact, poured a viscous and continual tear over the furrowed site of his cheekbone. When he attempted a smile (of greeting, recognition, regret that he was still alive) a bulb of blue tongue lolled between smashed incisors and blistered gums.

343

He spoke like an animal whose tongue is yet unadapted for language.

Jean-Marie winced: how could he now abandon his dependant who wrestled with his organs to overcome para-aphasia, to wring from them a hardly decipherable 'Mon Marie . . . mon Marie'?

How could he abandon this traducement of his familiar who tried to acknowledge him from the far side of the chasmic table which was the untrespassable boundary between life and dark.

Bruno was a caller from purgatory – which is an unshakable carapace the tortured are bound to carry all their days till they go beyond. Bruno might have had concrete (béton) brutally poured in his mouth.

They hadn't thought of that, the shadow servants of France charged with the extinction of the OAS who had seized on Bruno Berg as their Christmas treat. He had been tortured for six days by men whose offices, rank, agency, very existence was not acknowledged by governmental executive. Men who took their work seriously yet enjoyed its creative side, derived pleasure from their base inventions, from their ad hoc transformations of quotidian, pacific instruments: there is nothing, from pencils to soft furnishings, from books to perfume atomisers, that won't fit the bill. Shoes, shirts, ladders, bones. You name it. These men enjoyed double function items – the bottle they could first drink from, the cigarette they could smoke, the spiny crustacean whose meat they could suck, the belt that would again be holding up their trousers when they went home on Christmas Eve for Mass and boudin blanc, bearing gifts that had come in handy during the day (that was little Alain's new bicycle pump).

And the elements – how they loved the elements! Water and fire in their varieties excited them. And don't forget the wonder of electricity, its secret powers, its ubiquity, how it comes through the wall to the aid of the inquisitor who's just a little browned off by this evasion, by that silence, that exhausted silence which has lasted, oh, ten seconds too long. We can all avail ourselves of these gifts. We can all learn from the CRS's imaginative conversion of magnetos into instruments nick-named *les gégènes* (generals; these magnetos enjoy that degree of authority). Berg's genitals were burnt and bruised by this means, a live wire was inserted into his urethra by a cross-eyed man smoking a Royale Gout Maryland and humming as he laboured. Berg pleaded that he was Belgian. The other torturer (hair *en brosse*, horse face) put down his newspaper and performed a sight gag about a Belgian knotting his shoelaces. (He lifted one foot onto a chair, leaned forward and attempted to tie the laces of the shoe that rested on the floor.)

The cross-eyed torturer murmured: 'Le beau-frère de ma cousine est pharmacien à Ostende . . . J'espère que toi tu n'as pas la vérole mon Belgico.' He looked with worried pride at his handcraft, at the wire invading the bound man's shrivelled penis. He scrupulously washed his hands over a basin in the corner of the windlowless room before he flicked the switch and kicked Berg's very core.

In the late afternoon of 27 December the colonel commanding the barracks at Vincennes was informed of the interrogation that was being conducted, illegitimately, in the subterranean cells. He instructed the *adjudant-chef* that *ces espèces de barbouses*[1] should be immediately removed, with their prisoner, by force if necessary: Horse Face remarked to the adjudant-chef that the colonel was thus undoubtedly revealing OAS sympathies and that *they might be back for him*. Bruno Berg was driven, blindfolded (not necessary, he was unconscious), across Paris to an office block at Gennevilliers leased by the BEL[2] in the name of The Brazilian Yerbama Company of London SA (someone's little joke). The site determined and limited methods of interrogation; it was a steel-framed structure whose thin curtain walls were not soundproof. Screams could be heard in the adjacent blocks of flats. It encouraged a considered approach to torture; it was consequently avoided by the more eager agents who resented the time taken in taping and then un-taping the mouths of victims. The BEL's executive was consistently importuned by its operatives who claimed that work rate could only be improved by a move to a traditionally constructed building, one with loadbearing walls a metre or more thick: Vauban understood the

1 These damned spooks.
2 Bureau d'Etudes et de Liaisons.

exigencies of the interrogative art. The success of Berg's inquisitors at Gennevilliers served only to convince the executive that the majority of agents were blaming their habitual shortcomings on the building rather than themselves.

Berg talked: quality bubble, and lots of it. When he regained consciousness he found himself in a carpeted room, teak panelled, with spindly-legged ebonised furniture that was comfortable, despite its angularity. An uncurtained window led to a balcony. It was night. Horse Face and Cross Eyes had brought their kit with them or had obtained similar, but they had no recourse to it. They'd have liked to have used it as they'd have liked to use certain of the gifts they'd received: little Alain, a father's boy, understood paternal needs, longed to enter the forbidden and unmentioned family trade – his present had been a stapler so strong springed that it took a fist to deliver the twin tines. Sorry, son, he didn't need it, your dad. He talked instead. He persuaded Berg that the loyalty to be overcome was not to a cause already lost, nor to the organisation[1] that had professed that cause, but to the idea and practice of secrecy itself. He persuaded Berg that the only interest he shared with those whom he had fought alongside, bombed alongside, was *the habit* of covertness. He argued that were Berg to cooperate he would be freeing himself from the figurative sewers; that once he had crept out from behind the wainscot of history he would be *giving himself* the opportunity to spend he rest of his life (after, that is, a brief period in protection until all those named by him, who were thus potential assassins, had been apprehended) in the light, in the open, in the extra-pure air that is available only to those who are redeemed by confession. The grass's grass is greener.

The alternative to such exalted rehabilitation was crudely alluded to: 'Le destin tragique de Bastien-Thiry.[2] Ça fait réfléchir, non?' Whilst he was being tortured, cooked and aged Berg transcended fear of death. But now even the second of pain

---

1 In defeat the remnants of the OAS changed its name to CNR – Conseil National de la Résistance.

2 Lieutenant Colonel Jean-Marie Bastien-Thiry led at least two of the attempts on de Gaulle's life and was executed by firing squad.

that might accompany such a formalised release was too much to court: firing squads hurt, and Bruno Berg never wanted to be hurt again, so long as he lived, not even in the very passage of his extinction, not even were he to have no subsequent lifespan in which to suffer and recall the pain of the eight ventrical bullets whose simultaneity is impaired by the varying distances from him of the ranked muzzles and by the inconsistent speeds of reaction to the order to fire: the bullets from the centre of the line *should* strike first – but the advantages of proximity might be overcome by slow reflexes on the part of those guns. And had not Degueldre taken fifteen *minutes* to die? Had he not required five coups de grace? Bruno Berg gripped the soft covering fabric of the solacious chair he sat in; he never wanted to be uncomfortable again. Despite the damage to his speech organs he talked initially for six hours. Sulphurous dawn was creeping from beyond the distant roofs of St Denis by the time that he asked if he might be allowed to sleep. Over a period of twenty hours Berg told his inquisitors more than enough to gain them promotion. This information included:

The names of the three former soldiers who had executed fourteen bank robberies in Algeria and Metropolitan France between February 1961 and March 1963; their current where-abouts; the names of some of the personnel involved in eight further such robberies.

The precise locations in Metropolitan France of six caches of arms and explosives. The names of the men and women in charge of ten other caches.

The names in which OAS/CNR deposits were held in Madrid, Saragossa, Alicante, Bern, Freiburg.

The names of five companies registered in Jersey and Andorra which had been used for the purchase of arms, ammunition, explosives, vehicles, safe houses etc.

Details of two separate plans to purchase armoured vehicles from Italy.

The name of the CRS officer who had tipped him off that his bungalow on the outskirts of Lyons was to be raided (p. 326).

A scheme to persuade sympathetic Spanish army officers to supply armoured vehicles to an OAS cell in Perpignan.

347

A list of officers of the Gendarmerie Mobile who had accepted bribes in Algiers, Oran, Orléansville and Biskra.

A list of officers of that organisation who had served the OAS unpaid and had provided information, ammunition etc.

A list of officers of that organisation who had never betrayed it but against whom he held personal grudges (he knew that the scope and depth of his knowledge was such that a certain amount of playful misinformation could be safely included).

Four prospective plots to assassinate de Gaulle – their code names (Guépier, Stégosaurus, Cyprès, Mac Beth (sic)), their authors, the circumstances under which they might be prosecuted.

The names of two *pied noir* irrigation engineers now reduced to working as plumbers who had devised a means of poisoning the water supply of Colombey-Les-Deux-Eglises.

A list of forty-one foreign politicians, statesmen, journalists etc. whose proclamations in favour of Algerian independence had amounted to attempts to interfere with and to influence internal French matters and who were thus under sentence of death.

Berg admitted to four robberies, two abductions, two attempted murders in which he had himself played an 'integral' role. He admitted to supplying explosives, detonators, timing devices on fourteen occasions. He admitted to constructing six bombs, one of which failed to explode (Nevers 2.5.62). He admitted to having been 'quartermaster' for the attempt to release Lieutenant Roger Degueldre from La Santé three days before his messy execution. He admitted only to those crimes which he suspected he was suspected of. Thus he made no reference to the random shootings that he had carried out from the windows of stolen cars driven by Jean-Marie Meyer-Decker through the warren of Muslim streets north of Barbès Rochechouart (La Goutte d'Or); after all, there were so many patriots out there taking pots at the Halals that he had no idea whether he'd scored any hits let alone bull's eyes, and he wasn't going to boast even though he was affected those few days in that room by an unprecedented candour and confessional daring.

He talked profusely about his blood, about Neild's Syndrome, about the need to track down Jean-Marie, the blood he carried and the Panhard that probably carried him, reg 8928 ET 75. He told them about his dependence on the boy. He didn't tell them about his part in a bullion robbery in Lille because some local smalltimers had been arrested and convicted and who was he to tip the cart of justice?

He heard himself ask for a comb. He scourged his scalp. When, five days later, Jean-Marie entered the sombre room in the house where Berg had been brought for his own safety he had a metal comb in his pocket. He tugs at his newly grey hair, he combs it hard, renders his crown the furrowed site of a self inflicted punishment, a topological analogue of the capital punishment which the many men and women whom he had betrayed will inflict upon him if they have the chance – and they may have, for betrayal does not inevitably result in arrest; moreover, the betrayed have their allies, those (*spectral, peripheral*) third persons with vengeful arms who are destroying not a life but a mere name. A name whose face they may never have seen till it appears at the end of a sight, at the middle of a cross, a face that is nothing more than a target.

By the time that Berg was arrested and tortured the OAS/CNR had been reduced to a dis-organisation devoted to the extinction of its former members and associates who had betrayed it; that was its exclusive preoccupation. And as more were betrayed and arrested and tortured into talking so the number of potential targets grew; it should have been a golden age for assassins and freelance guns but, of course, the more who talked the fewer there were left to stalk and snipe at. So the average freelance was faced by an *embarras du choix*, and the chances of survival for those who had talked increased exponentially. And one blessed day everyone would have talked. There would be no one left to torture, no one left to hit, no one left to do the hits: a utopia will have been created by betrayal which is also a form of loyalty, a new start in loyalty to a different code/faith/gang.

Nonetheless Bruno Berg lived in fear in the gloomy house in Pompey where he poured a monocular tear, where he had tried to hug Jean-Marie but couldn't because every muscle in his body was tender to an embrace's pressure. Jean-Marie gave him a transfusion instead, a kiss in blood, vein to vein (via the mediation that would become habitual – a nurse from Nancy called Paul Hellman who never took longer than half an hour to arrive with his spikes, tubes, drips, phials of coagulant Factor VIII). Jean-Marie gave him that transfusion the morning they re-met even though he didn't need it. The boy's pity was that strong. His devotion was that deep, and sanguinary emission was its expression. Berg was uncheered by the rush of blood and by those that succeeded it. He rarely ventured into the garden. He combed his thin grey hair, he dabbed at his scalp with rubbing alcohol, he referred to himself as a coward unfit to share the earth's air with those whom he had informed against, he persistently accused the men who guarded him of using him as bait to entrap greater patriots still at large. Representatives of the government agency which did not exist assured him that he was free to leave whenever he wanted. He wept. He climbed to the attic storey and gazed through an oeil de boeuf window towards a scythe of silver river whose destination was Germany: he thought about it. He read dietetic articles and one book – *La Noblesse Des Salades* by Jules Lagrange, former salad critic of Sud-Ouest and author of *Du Vin, Du Vin Et Encore Du Vin*. He reread old articles that had been brought from rue Oberkampf; in the corner of the crepuscular room stood a pile of them, tall as a man at prayer; beside it were Bruno Berg's albums and mementoes of his martial and secret lives. A warrior remembers – with pride, more often with bitterness. He places objects on the velvet-covered table – a desiccated finger (Philippeville 1957); the kitchen knife with which he had scalped Florence Deroose (p. 142); a crinkle-edged photograph of an erect penis (Hannoy 1953); another photograph, of a naked, flat-chested girl who might be a boy with his genitals clutched by the cache-sex of his arse (Brussels 1960); book matches from Le Robinson, Léopoldville. It is septuagenarian warriors who are meant to look back, not those in early middle age. Madame Graber calls him to lunch. He is not strong enough to confront her. Mammilophobic, he despises this heavy-chested chatterer, this lactic animal whose incuriosity fazes him – who does she think

350

he is? He abhors her chirpy cheeriness in the face of a life which has tipped shit on her. He abhors her lack of gravity, her cosy diminution of evil's wonders to the naughtily commonplace. He abhors her breezy disregard for his dictates: he fears that she cooks pollutants for Jean-Marie – cream and onion flans, cured pork, brains. He warns Jean-Marie that ingestion of brains contaminates man with the memory of a slaughtered animal, that it abases man, makes him dream of meadows and of the terminal truck to the abattoir. Berg fears too that the meat she stews for him is *lapin sans tête* (butchers' euphemism for cat); he is convinced that she serves him donkey instead of horse (a noble animal). The men who guard him mock his remonstrations. He slumps slighted; fingers gripping the edge of the oilclothed kitchen table; he drags a comb through his old man's hair; his wounds don't heal; his polychrome face is here to stay; his sores are perpetual; caffeine fails to keep him awake; his vision is impaired. He even mistrusts Jean-Marie: he mistrusts his newfound fondness for the blues, which idiom the boy rehearses every morning; he especially mistrusts his daily sorties from the house (he has given up pleading with him to stay home play cards).

Most every afternoon Jean-Marie dresses in one of the suits he had never worn and bids him adieu, saying he's taking the bus into Nancy. Berg is too scared, too exhausted, to go along; he doesn't realise or doesn't acknowledge that the greater patriots (who must be out there on the streets and in the pissoirs, at café windows with guns packed beneath the table) would not recognise in this enfeebled frame the man who shopped them. He mutters something about slave music, jungle rhythms, the primitivism of twelve bar (though he doesn't call it that); he rants hoarsely about everything he fought against – the Nazis whose mythology was Indo-European, *not ours*; the Muslims, a few of whom even formed an SS brigade; the apologists for *négritude* who would undo everything that a pan-European such as Berg was heir to; the physiognomical affinity between the St Louis bluesman Laird-Moncrieff Brown and the ape they'd thrown poppers to in Basle zoo. Jean-Marie shrugged and left, this day and the day before, the day after. Some days he did go to Nancy,

351

to the cinema, to the gardens of La Pepinière (poetry of naked trees in Jan and Feb), to the streets west of the railway whose facades (wanting right-angles, stony, bonelike, a tectonic ossuary, a premonition of houses built from mass death) unlocked a key into toddler time when he'd held his mother's hand in Ixelles all those years ago, before there were hot reptilian rivers and fraudulent fathers and parish songs untouched by the nerve of need. He was still proud though to see one of Albeau's records on sale in Salut Les Disques, rue des Carmes. 'Je me souviens de . . .' – but his memory of cheapskate memoriousness would be broken by the wail of blues guitars from the shop's speakers: Laird-Moncrieff Brown's *sincerity* got to him. He was at an age when throat cancer plus steel strings equalled depth.

Some days Albeau's 'son' never took the bus into Nancy; he walked that way sure enough, towards the bus stop – out the metal gate and right, in case Bruno was watching (he was). Then, at the end of the road, he turned into a steep brick alley, made his secret way through terraced allotments then up a ragged track on the forest's edge to the asbestos roofed shack where Madame Graber lived with her washing-line of brassières like serial airsocks and with her son who worked foundry shifts, who had the big bones, blond crop and horrible choler of his father, a one-night bosch in Nancy in '44. Less than a night in fact, but Madame Graber sought to dignify the relationship by adding a few hours to its duration. And by giving him a name (Hansi) and a cv. She had never married. No one would have her.

It wasn't so much her disgrace: there were many such – a girl has to pay for the drinks bought her, that's understood. It was the form her disgrace took: Bernard. A Swabian-blooded child who grew into a violent, myopic man. He hated his mother. He despised his bottle-glass spectacles. He loved France, the country his mother had betrayed with her womb. He loved France so much it said so on his arms in skin pictures, cutaneous legends. He loved his patch. He could not see (literally, too) further than Pompey. Centre of Bernard's world. A world away from Frouard on the other side of the Moselle (they're different in Frouard), let alone from Nancy, Maxéville, Malzéville, Jarville-La-Malgrange – places up to ten kilometres away where they exhibited traits such as cunning, ostentation, *strangeness*. Not to be trusted, those from outside Pompey; not to be trusted, and to be treated with hostility, silent animosity (a speciality, that), to be frightened off with imbecilic stares, with the belligerent slab of Bernard's forehead which had been granted him as an instrument of assault, as compensation for its lack of contents. So Jean-Marie only visited Madame Graber when this creature was at work.

She made English tea for him, inducted him into the rites of (comparative) gerontophilia – she was fifty, she owned a brightside memory for every month of every year, she remembered Albeau, she tra-la'd the chorus of 'Plus Belle Que Toutes Les Aubes', she turned over half this shack which was an album of her life, of a half-century's crazes, before she found a photograph torn from a magazine: Alban Meyer-Decker's sharkteeth gleamed for the camera. She held it up for swivel-headed comparison. She nodded knowingly: 'Les joues, ouais, les joues.' He didn't disabuse her, he didn't want to mar her pleasure; of course she had faith in the transmission of bone structure, it was only through the twenty-year development of her son's face that she could recollect the panting father's. She never asked who Bruno Berg was or why Jean-Marie was with him. She pushed coke into the metal stove. She stroked the cats that left a hair mat all over. She showed him gewgaws and told the story of each (alarm clock with boxing hares, antimacassar poker-worked with a haloed saint, plastic bottle in the form of a cactus etc.); she recalled rubbish piles, gutters, markets, employers. There had been an Englishman (very nearly a *milord*, an eminent man in the import of agricultural machinery, lovely manners) who rented a stately apartment in Place de la Carrière in Nancy – so much wood to polish her arm was always numb. He had been tickled that she should live in Pompey. When he returned home he sent her souvenirs of the English city of that name and cuttings from newspapers about its famous soccer team. She sat beside Jean-Marie on the undulating sofa. She gave him a china man o' war to hold; two lead battleships; a beer mat printed 'Blighty's Best Does Pompey Proud'; out-of-register postcards of a war memorial, a sailor's hat, half-clothed people on a beach, a fairground that seemed to rise from the sea – the cheap exoticism heightened by the site. He told her he'd like to ride that roller coaster above the briny. She nodded: 'Luna Parc-sur-mer.' She placed her hand on his penis the way she always did. Whilst he inspected a 1954 calendar photograph of seated footballers whose faces spoke of the famous English diet, whose hair gleamed with cooking grease, whose shirt badges (star, crescent moon) suggested sodales of a cabbalistic society, she kneaded and squeezed his balls. He was used to it, but still shocked. Her procedure was invariable. She unzips his trousers, compares him to Bernard: 'T'es bien monté, tu sais. Ca, c'est une grosse bite. Très jolie . . . Mon pauvre Bernard, il n'a que ça.' Here, with finger and thumb against his bulging urethra, she indicates the measure of her son's shortfall. 'Et sa jute – ç'est triste à dire. C'est pas du grand cru.' A brute in all departments save the one that matters. She does not let Jean-Marie touch her.

Froggatt, Dickinson, Harris, Henderson – the eyes of English-men with grotesque hair gaze into his as she rubs and slaps and grips and strokes. She does not let him lie on the familial bed (there in the corner) that she shares with her son. The cats watch too. She stokes the internal fire. He closes his eyes: the red labia of that far-off foreign Pompey greet dicks home from sea; they plough the sea like conning towers, they're enveloped on the shore by vulval waltzers, by carmine octopi, big wick dippers, pleasure-flesh rides; the tars, the tarts, oily hair, red tongues; the screams of bed and fairground. Madame Graber pushes his hand from her breast. Hot hydrant, intolerable pleasure. She insists that he take away the sodden handkerchief. They drink more tea, she takes a shot of rum in hers, savours it, makes no further allusion to the few minutes' friction, his meat treat. She is reverently enthusiastic about Bernard's appetite for pork stew and cider. She tells Jean-Marie that tomorrow will be a wonderful day because she can feel it. She warns him that if he washes his hair too often it will lose its lustre.

It was Estevenin who saw him. The dribbling old drunk was digging celeriac from his allotment plot the first time he saw

Jean-Marie, in the lane, at dusk, beyond the leafless hedge. Four days later Estevenin was hacking a frost-bitten cabbage from his patch of God-given, dung-rich, patrimonial, sacred soil. He hawked an orb of phlegm, noticed that the boy started at the sound, wondered at the way he scampered down the crisp rutted track between the precipitous terraces.

Bernard, staring into the irremediable opacity of his cider[1] at the bar in the irremediable gloom of Le Pommier De Pompey, listened to Estevenin then took him by the throat. The first man he'd taken by the throat since leaving work that day. Estevenin swore on *his* mother's stove, bought Bernard more cider, repeated what he said with full complement of placatory hand signals, left the bar.

Next morning, before daybreak, Bernard accompanies his mother to her work. The two guards nod. They know him: the four-eyed moron who hefts the veg, the veg who hefts the crates. They hardly notice that this morning he carries nothing. They do notice that Madam Graber's jaw is bruised and that her lower lip is lacerated but they think nothing of it. The guards are twitchy; Berg's suspicion that he is bait is indubitably correct. The guns are jumpy. Word of Berg's whereabouts has almost certainly been leaked, almost certainly by design: if police agencies know where he has gone to the mattresses then it follows that his putative assassins know too – the information had only to be imparted to, say, Captain —— of the CRS at Chaville for it to be sure to find its way to a desired destination. The guards hardly notice that the moron pushes his mother up the path to the house, that he prods her flank, snatches at her coat sleeve, that he manhandles her through the front door as though she's a bulbous parcel, that he kicks it shut so that the glass panes rattle in their frozen frames.

Two minutes pass before they hear the screams, the oaths, the

---

1 Apples are chiefly cultivated in Lorraine for the distillation of eau de vie de pomme, colourless in contrast to Calvados. Rough cider is also produced at numerous farms in the areas of Commercy, Toul and Nancy. Typically pips are left in the mash. Every pip of every apple contains a secretion of cyanide. Cyanide attacks the retinal nerve. A man who drinks between 7 and 10 litres of rough cider every day of his life for 20 years is liable to lose his sight. Bernard Graber lives today in a home for the blind near Metz.

visceral moans, the repeated thuds. They run inside. Bernard Graber had taken the wrong man. Jean-Marie was asleep in his attic room, he heard nothing. Bernard had dragged Bruno Berg cowering from his bed, kicked him, picked him up, butted him, banged his head against a marble washstand, filled the curtained room with northern violence, with dull might like smog and cold, his fists were boulders, he hurt, he maimed, he was double himself with cuckold's fury. He broke Berg. There was blood on the ceiling, bone on the chandelier. The wrong blood, the wrong bone, the wrong man, the wrong death – which was itself the wrong result. Bernard Graber's intentions (hardly self-articulated) had been less ambitious. He merely sought to deter his mother's lover, speak to him in manual esperanto, teach him a crash course. Had, that dark dawn, he taken the right one he would not have had a life on his hands: Jean-Marie was swift, fit, cunning. Bruno Berg was an invalid, stripped of all will to fight mortality by children's toys and signals magnetos. He had not, sure, expected to die this way: this brute's was not the last face that he had anticipated, this was not the means of execution that he was meant to suffer, this was unfitting, improper, this was a bad joke. He had thought about death every day since he arrived in Pompey at this house which was to be his last. His betrayals had bought him an extra two months and five days. Were they worth the posthumous opprobrium? They weren't good times. They were the worst of times, in Pompey, in captivity. And at the end of it, a prank, an indignity, a despatch unworthy of a soldier.

Bernard Graber made no mistake, and he was not the victim of either his myopia or his alcoholism. Estevenin's account had included no description of the man he had seen. As she cowered among the papers and trashed vases and uprooted souvenirs and blasphemed bondieuserie that her ranting cider-driven son had swept from the shack's shelves Madame Graber had the wit to realise that she could achieve two in one by protecting Jean-Marie, inculpating the misogynist with the comb and resolving the problem of her son the bosch. It was Madame Graber that did for Bruno Berg, that took away Jean-Marie's dependent buttress.

The boy was to be an orphan for a second time: during the eleven days that Bruno lay in a coma Jean-Marie hardly left his room. He gave blood, he gave thanks in blood to the insentient man who'd given him purpose, suits, the lost Lambretta, guitars, adventure.

When Bruno died they removed his body in a burlap sack. He was buried two days after Jean-Marie's eighteenth birthday, across the river, beside the steel mills at Bouxières-Aux-Dames (yellow sky, ragged horses). Jean-Marie's nose bled that cold afternoon. Madame Graber stood beside him. No one else attended.

Bernard Graber was charged with the murder of Bruno Berg and with membership of an illegal organisation; later he would be charged with the murder the previous autumn of another informer; he didn't understand what was happening to him.

Jean-Marie was allowed to take his genuine passport and his possessions. He carried them in a wheelbarrow to Madame Graber's shack. He greeted Estevenin whenever he saw him. Madame Graber cuddled him, cooked for him, addressed him as 'mon fils'. Her expression of sexual intimacy never varied. The nurse Paul Hellman arranged for him to sell his rare blood once a week at the Clinique Lallement-Gaudry. He had troubles with his work permit. He loaded barges, swept stairwells, shot animals at the abattoir on Boulevard d'Austrasie. The trusting eyes of kine! They trusted him not to do them harm, and he smiles into the bullock's stupid slow eyes the second before he makes its head erupt. He joined a rock band called Les Corvairs. He left. He joined another called Les Wisconsins. The first song he wrote was 'Luna Parc-sur-Mer'. The first line of the first song he wrote is: 'Le port de Pompey est très bizarre.' Les Wisconsins became Nos Cheveux Verts. They made a kind of living. They toured. He sold his blood all over France. He always returned to the shack above the allotments at Pompey, he always had a souvenir for Madame Graber – something from Angoulême, Narbonne, from distant Alicante where they played to an audience of *pieds noirs* who demanded a reprise of 'Mais Où Sont Les Plages d'Antan?', a hymn of resentment towards the *bicots* and *bougnouls* occupying 'our' beaches, cafés and houses around

Oran. In the general amnesty of 1968 Bernard Graber was released since his crime(s) were 'act(s) of war'.

Jean-Marie had all his things out of the shack before the myope arrived home from Mulhouse. He feared that Lorraine was no longer safe for him. He tried to persuade the rest of the band to leave with him for Paris. They were loyal to their soil.

He played a few gigs in Brussels with Le Jardin Biologique. The longer his hair grew the more it shone. He tried to trade on Albeau's name, get a recording contract that way. Albeau was forgotten – and, besides, these songs, well . . .

He followed an Irish band to London. But it was unsatisfactory. It lasted three weeks. He missed Madame Graber, the security, the bulk, the heavy-breasted warmth.

He was queuing with his guitar and grip at Victoria Station for a boat ticket, a ticket back to a misery where he at least spoke the language, when he noticed a poster showing a man o'war, a battleship, a fairground rising from the sea.

That rain-shiny autumn night he strolled along the front at Pompey; there were lights across the water. He leaned against a lamp-post outside the deserted fairground, felt the kiss of the Spithead Bite, liked it, decided to stick around a few days: this might be England's deep south but it felt like the quintessence of the north to him. He grinned at Nelson's statue. He was on his way to find a cheap hotel when he heard an an electric band at work. A stencilled notice beside the door to the Remember The Hood's public bar announced 'TONITE – RIDER'. The pub's back room was all hash smoke and kohl, sexual menace and swollen pupils, violet irises and mauve velvet. He felt unaccountably happy: he breathed deeply, joined the congregation, drank a glass of rum. The band played protracted and amorphous improvisations on a riff they'd long forgotten. When they stopped the bassist grunted: 'Back in ten minutes. See you.'

As he came down the three steps from the stage clutching a sleever of Guinness Jean-Marie approached him. He looked surprised, he glanced at the big hands and plectrum nails, he shrugged: 'Why not?' He led Jean-Marie, his guitar and grip onto the scuffed boards.

'What's your name man?'

'Jean-Marie Meyer-Decker.'
'Come again.'
'?'
'Say it again, your name.'
'Jean . . . Marie – '
'OK. People. People. *People*. We got a guest artist,' yelled Sonny Butt into the microphone. 'He's called Mary.'

'I didn't ask for it, any more than I asked for life. I wasn't around to ask for life. I wasn't given the choice. It's not as if your parents-to-be say to you: *do you want some of this?* before they go ahead. It's not like that is it? And even if it was, what would *this* mean? It's the unknown, the unmappable; you got wheat futures and barley futures, tin futures what-have-you . . . Well you got embryo futures too, to gamble on. Pre-embryo. Egg and seed. Sounds like a sandwich doesn't it? You ask yourself: what is it that they're offering to someone who isn't there to have an offer made to him? I'll tell you what it is. It's a version of their loveydovey, their rosetinted. It's two people going mad together isn't it – love? That's what love is. Even if it's only for as long as it takes to do the deed, it's still madness. The madness of optimism. You know: everything's going to work out right, et cetera. Best of all possible. And it's not just mutts who think it. It's a fault that runs right through all of us. Built-in problem like not being able to articulate our feet.[1] Like having one hand that can't write, like having an entire half that's hardly used – that we've forgotten how to explore, maybe never knew how to explore. I used to think that if I'd been given the choice I'd have told them: no, don't do it; I'd have said, on no account, because you'll regret it, he'll regret it, we'll all regret it . . . My father didn't live long enough to regret it. But I believe that if I'd known what I know now, if I'd known it then – well, I won't say that I can alter the course . . . Actually, I will. In a way I'm working on altering, ah, potentialities. Ray's got this phrase – A Curriculum of Dredgable Possibility. We've got to mine it, sift it, dredge it what-have-you, discover an *internal* wherewithal. Sniff sniff!

[1] 'Pedal Utility' is a chapter title in *Our Forgotten Bodies: A Forty Point Plan for Maximal Potential*, Dr Clark W. Grover (Chicago 1961, London 1962). *Op cit* pp. 228, 273, 288.

Now, I'd tell them: go ahead, I can cope, I can help untold others not to regret *their* birth, not to be angry about being. I can touch them, touch them . . . Of course I can heal them, I've known that since I was a kid – though it comes from Butt really, that's where the drive comes from, the organisation, how to direct it. Look – I've thought about this, it's *me*, you know. And it's like he's got the grand plan and I'm the one who knows how to carry it out; but he wouldn't have had the grand plan without me, would he? He's blessed because he needed to be . . . necessity, real yearning, his guilt, all that. I'm blessed because I can't help but be. Couldn't have happened to a nicer guy eh? Yeh, tell them to go ahead with it, in all its horror because I'll be there at the end, *me*! I'm the outcome. Abnormal gestation and they get me. They were given separate packs and then both drew the joker, or is it the knave – whatever. That's symbolism or something isn't it, I don't understand canasta. What I've been telling Butt is that Dredgable Possibility is here, in my hands. They're not here just for cures. I'm working on this system which isn't psycho but's physical. Right? I can make the right side of your brain work. I can get the left side of your body working. Ambidextrous, two-footed, a cue in either wrist. I can show the other half how to perform to peak capability. And do you understand what that could mean? I'm talking about prolonging life. Not, *not* rejuvenation – that's just quacks and monkey glands. Vanity. Cosmetics. Magical elixirs. It's a load of bull. You know they tried bull's balls, back – I dunno – the twenties, some time like that. *This* – I tell you – will revolutionise human expectation. No elixirs, no powdered gold, nothing like that. It's simply a question of putting people in touch with a resource that's already there. It's from with*in*. People go through life using only a tiny fraction of themselves. They get to seventy and they peg out. Why? What's old age? It's tiredness. They've put such a strain on those few parts of themselves that they *do* use that they wear them out – while all the time they've got these untapped resources there, just sitting there on the shelf, untouched. It's like a shirt: the collar and cuffs go but the rest of the fabric's fine. Spread the load – that's the thing. Dredge the possibilities. Use all of you. We must all use all of us. I'm not claiming immortality's just around the corner, it's not even under consideration. What is – is longevity. And better health. Start with ambidexterity: God didn't give us two hands for nothing. That's why he's got such a down on Islam because all they do with their left hand is wipe their behinds with it, that is if they haven't had it cut off and stuck on a post. I'm working on a way of unlocking the left side –the right side in left handers. Did you know the life expectancy of left handers is longer? You didn't did you? It's obvious when you think about it. They're made to use their right hands for so many things, you know – gadgets and all that, even if they aren't made to write with their right hands – they're forced into the beginnings of ambidexterity and so they *spread the load*. Now I'll tell you what they object to, all the old religions and the false prophets: they fear they can't control the ambidextrous. You know why don't you. You know why they fear they can't control people with articulate feet. I'll tell you – it's because to get in touch with the limbs that are, uh, in abeyance you have to open up parts of the brain that are normally permanently off duty. It's not *normal* at all as a matter of fact. It's not a case of *expanding* minds; it's all about stopping them from being contracted by society, allowing them to flower to full growth – without chemicals, without trepanning. They don't want me to do this. They don't want anyone to facilitate full growth. They think I'm going to upset the cart. Because I'm liberating people, that's what I'm going to do. I'm going to release them. Look, when I do things with my left hand I'm someone else. When I draw with my foot I draw as someone different from when I draw with my right hand. There's no such thing as my *self* – it's my *selves*. And each self expresses *its* self through a separate limb. See? So it's not just giving everyone the chance of a longer life but making it richer too. It's low-risk experiment with the probability of the most fantastic benefits. In fact it's *no* risk. I'm going to rewrite the race. Without jeopardy. Without genocide. Eugenics with a smile. I'm offering multiple fates. That's why they don't want me to do it, that's what they're scared of. They find it hard enough to keep a check on people as it is: think what it's going to be like when everyone can just switch into a new self at will, cast off personality, go exploring

. . . It's not going to happen overnight, I've got to teach one person at a time, but then they'll teach others and, you know, momentum, snowball effect. Eventually it'll become genetic. It'll be in the blood. Passed down. In a thousand years, ten thousand, who knows, maybe in a hundred, you can't tell, it'll be inherited. Every person will be more than one person *from birth*. That's what humans will be like then: choice of personality according to will, whim, need; longer lived; healthier. What I'm doing is planting a seed for the future. I'm not going to be around to see it. But I know, I know it. Dredgable Possibilities. A menu of selves.'

There are eleven hours of tape, recorded by Chubb during November and December 1973. Eddie's coherence is inconstant; his voices are several – which is ascribable to the different acoustic properties of the places where the recordings were made or to his multiple selves (more likely the former); he veers between prolixity and taciturnity, between revelatory nudity and covert evasion; he contradicts himself, and when Chubb reminds him of what he has previously said on a given subject he replies with silence or 'I was just saying that' or 'that was then and this is now' or 'that room was hostile' or 'you're talking to us, not just me; *me* is temporary'.

The weekend of 1 and 2 December Eddie has a cough; he strives to achieve symptomatic precision:

'It's ticklish but it's also tight. Like someone's tickling just there and they also've you know got my windpipe with tweezers. And also there's this sandpaper feeling. My throat is sandpaper – hasn't just been rubbed by it, it *is*. And it's very . . . here. I wouldn't call it chesty, exactly, but it is a bit. It makes it a problem you see because I'm not sure what linctus I should be taking – Throaty with phlegm? Dry? Expectorant? Sonny reckons there's this chemist in Gosport who still stocks Romola but he didn't get round to giving me a lift over there and the foot ferry gives me the heat, always gets pushed sideways. Too much water. So I've had some mentho, mentho . . . stuff – and this cherry which'd be OK but it's sort of a sedative. Bit of a down really, and it only works for a few – '

'Have you tried, by any chance, curing yourself?' asks Lalage

Chubb, faint (she's on the other side of the abundantly softly furnished hotel room, distant from the microphone) and impatient.

'I believe that what Lalage really means – ' begins Chubb, stretch-vowelled in embarrassment, mining monophthongs with his nervy tongue.

'I know what she means. I know what you mean [cough] . . . I thought you were meant to be experienced. How many books you written?'

'*Chubb* is the author of three very well received – '

'Four, Dear,' amended Chubb.

'Four mould-breaking case studies. All *his* own work. Little presses, not for the vulgar. I, Eddie, am merely his amanuensis. That's latin for typist. I don't have to be here Eddie. I could have gone shopping – not, I suppose, that I'd have come back with anything other than a model of the Victory and a Senior Service tea towel. But I didn't. I'm married to an obsession and I accept it. I knew what I was getting into, I accept it. When you grow up Eddie – '

'Dear!'

'You will find – then you probably won't – that the world is full of widowed consultant actuaries with one very difficult and resentful child and one obsessive hobby. Could be golf, could be stamps or coins or girls in frilly knicks, gofferbid. It's my lot to have married the widowed consultant actuary with the unbelievably problematic offspring who happens to spend all his spare time and an inordinate proportion of his admittedly outlandish income on chasing round the country after holy rollers, quacks, fruitcakes, maniacs who are in touch with the godhead – and that's to mention only the very cream of the scum . . . So I'm perfectly well aware when Chubb is being played along, having his time wasted – '

'I've got a *cough*,' cried Eddie. Then he coughs, then wheezes weepily: 'I really have. And your *name* . . .'

His name. Everyday Chubb fish-lunches alone at La Raie d'Or, London, W1. Doz. Colchester Natives, pike quenelles and Nantua sauce, black-buttered skate, a Manzanilla, a half bottle of '66 Domaine St Pierre Meursault, coffee, a pousse café, no pudding, no complaints, no colleagues, no Lalage, no secretary on the side. Devoted patronage is like paying into insider-tipped stock: he relishes the divvy-like treats, the bottomless well of liquorous troves that are omitted from the carte. They take his mind off his daughter who is a little mystery – often awol and invariably drugged (Lalage says, and he concurs, regretfully): she shows no interest in regulable serendipity or aleatory certainty or clever disease. He blames her mother. She does not accept the fundamental fairness of odds. On or against everything (just about), all the important things, certainly. Give Chubb your fit (age, sex, work, marital accomplishments, debt, eyes, ears, income, heart – pour it out, hide nothing) and Chubb will give you your death date, to the month. He told a boy who suffered two out-of-body experiences that he could expect to live till March 2020; he got that wrong, the boy died in October 1969 after stealing a fire extinguisher from an army lorry, smashing its cap against a tree in a glade and inhaling its contents. The boy's parents did not write to thank him for the copy of *The Network of Radiation* that he sent them.

He pondered an approach to long hair in men: when it was restricted to marginals (beats, hippies) the industry he served had ignored it; now that it was a widespread fashion afflicting even the middle-aged he was re-establishing his position as 'the most creative brain in the profession'[1] with a series of papers on the possible consequences. He had researched male life expectancy throughout the middle and late nineteenth century, had computed the liable endurance of the current craze, had drawn attention to the fears deriving from hair loss in a hirsute culture, and to spent testosterone, and to the increased likelihood of industrial injury (C2s, Cs and Ds). He had posited the existence of diseases specific to long-haired men.

He wondered why Eddie Vallender's hair was so short and made a note to ask him. He added it to a list that took up a dozen pages of his hardbound notebook. Eddie preoccupied him, trespassed into his dreams. He considered Butt a sort of pimp, an exploiter, an abusive steward. He acknowledged his own

---

[1] *Insurance World and Actuarial Digest*, January 1973

cupidity; but, then, he knew that were Eddie in his charge, his *possession*, he might be directed, his phenomenal power might be channelled towards beneficent ends. His phrase for Butt (and it was one he was pleased with) was 'a vulgar graduate of the Rank smarm school'. He despised brashness and bad vowels. He despised the way Butt used Eddie as a 'validation of a charlatanry which is both cynical and vacuous'. He regarded The Church Of The Best Ever Redemption as 'specious and slick' and The Cross Of The World as 'architectural blasphemy – if there is such a thing!' He guessed that Butt's inspiration was the 'grotesque, hypocritical cross that the genocidal Generalissimo Franco erected at the so called Valle de Los Caídos in Old Castile as a monument to – mark this! – the fallen of *both* sides in the civil war'. When he mentioned this structure to Butt 'the oily comedian disclaimed all knowledge of it. I am pretty damned certain that I hit the nail on the head though'.

When Chubb first drove along the escarpment of Portsdown Hill he was overcome by the sensation that it was a site of signs. That it was a 'visible shelf on which messages could be left'. The monument to Nelson is thus an incitement to marine belligerence. The fortresses – which are certainly real enough, martially efficacious against a landward assault on Pompey – are predominantly warnings, 'a way of saying to Froggy don't try it on *mon brave*'. Then there's the Royal Navy's telecommunications and radar establishment (no photography permitted). The leafless trees are *en brosse*, as though undergoing ECT. The kites[1] lend dragon colours to the all-grey sky 'like fireworks using another element'.

And bigger, brasher and 'more risibly self confident than all the others', The Cross Of The World.

The armature of its horizontal section was already finished; a crane hoisted prefab concrete slabs the way a rook does twigs for its nest; there are pyramids of sand and gravel, shuttering frames, mixers, plastic yoked donkey jackets with hard hats, rusty curls of reinforcing wire like brandy snaps for big

[1] The only Pompey pop band to have a hit during the period that Jean-Marie played in bands there was Simon Dupree and The Big Sound whose successful song was entitled 'Kites'. Jean-Marie had no connection with this outfit.

appetites. Small-scale men scaled the Cross, worker monkeys in dayglo harnesses, faithful volunteers trusting in The Founder to protect them from gravity's pull, to douse the wind that bent every tree; they reeled on platforms in the sky, buffeted and dancing, like mimes from the silents, never falling, never.

Ray Butt's wheels spin in the furrows of an HGV's tyres. He wears Fair Isle gloves, plaid blankets, ear muffs; slung round his neck are two scarves and a megaphone. Chubb knew the instant he saw him that the young man hurrying to free the wheelchair was Eddie.

'The quality of his co-ordination is [sic] that you almost expect him to topple over. He walks, not the precise word for so individual a kind of movement, as though he's pushing an unsteady wheelbarrow. His arms are not synchronised with his legs. Nor perhaps with each other. The legs appear to be experiencing what can only be described as torque. They give the unmistakable impression of being powered by the feet, not by the hip. His knees do not bend. I keep thinking of a VW doing the goose step. But the trunk is nothing like [sic]. He is very round shouldered. Is this Sikora's Syndrome? Psychogenically moulded limbs? In this case moulded by defensiveness, physical fear, terror?'

The preliminary interview was conducted over lunch in The King Of Spain's Beard, a jazz Andalusian roadhouse (with filling station) along Portsdown, walking distance and no strain on The Founder's batteries – he came too, and so did Sonny, 'to see fair play'. Eddie hardly spoke. He ate a cheese sandwich and left the crust.

Ray Butt said: 'Never met an actuary before. Not to my knowledge. I'd have expected you to look more like a bookie, frankly.'

Sonny said: 'We take care of Eddie, his interests, don't we Eddie? We don't want him getting in the wrong company.'

'I can assure you – ' began Chubb.

'*Course* you can – it's your business,' guffawed The Founder.

'We have to look to the boy's longterm,' explained Sonny. 'You get some very twisted people in the verbals game. There's some very bitter people out there. *Envies.*'

'They're not all like Reg, that's for sure,' rued The Founder.

'Reg?'

'Reg Voice.'

'Aaahh . . . Reg . . . *Voice*? I don't believe – '

'You never heard of Reg?' Sonny, genuinely surprised. '*Butt Joking Aside*? Dad's biographer.'

'I'm sorry but – '

'Thought all you book writers . . . you know . . . were . . . Dear oh dear – better keep stum to Reg on that one. He'd be mortified.'

'We've got some signed copies left haven't we,' stated the biographer's subject.

'Yeh. Discounts for friends,' smiled Sonny. 'Good read – and I'll tell you why. It's because Reg tells the truth. No acka-maracka. Nothing wobbly. Good man and true – which is more than can be said for some of the gents of the press we've had down here. You *talk* to them – they stitch you up. You *refuse* to talk to them – you got something to hide . . .' Et cetera.

Eddie picks at the cracked matt veneer of the table with bitten nails. Chubb gave Ray Butt a copy of *The Network of Radiation*, a copy of *The Frontiers of Somnambulism* and a photocopied review of the latter from the *Journal* of the British Association of Psychotherapists (Spring 1968). Butt pulled a pair of spectacles from within the rugs and scarves, spat on the lenses, wiped them so that a filament of blue wool caught in a hinge and trembled in the convected heat. He opened *The Frontiers Of Somnambulism* at the back. Sonny watched Chubb. Eddie rolled a beer mat between the knuckles of his left hand controlling it with conjuror's aplomb.

'An index', proclaimed Ray Butt, 'is a book's fingerprint. The hidden code. You remember that Sonny, Eddie. Never judge by the cover, always by the index. We're sitting here. With Mr Chubb. And we don't know a thing about him. Do we? We could go on sitting here, with him, all afternoon – and we'd still know nothing. *But* – I look at the index of this book of his . . . and it's shown to me, isn't it. His very being. His uniqueness. What it is that makes Mr Chubb Mr Chubb and not – if he'll pardon me – Mr Tench. This index is a window, pure crystal light into the depths of the man's mind, into his innermost. Sonny – you go and ask Doreen for a bottle of her sparkly there. We'll drink a toast. To index sniffing, eh? And get Eddie and me another ginger ale. This index, Mr Chubb – I like what I see. You'll do us proud.'

Twelve weeks later Sonny and Laddy will attempt to set fire to Chubb's house. All because of the tapes. They will fail. They chop up a William Kent console table, smash a Venetian mirror and a chair attributed to Juvarra, turn over bookcases, sweep china from shelves, rip Colefax curtains. They pyro-flunk because the volume of water from the taps they've turned on in a bathroom drowns the paraffin-steeped carpet in the study below. But they've tried. It's the thought that counts.

Before then: '. . . for instance I won't eat kidney. It makes me think of *my* kidneys. I'll do anything to stop myself urinating. I don't want my body to produce water. And I tell you I don't want to look at water when I have to produce it. I'd sooner go in a doorway. Side of the road. Anywhere. I'd sooner be thirsty. I had a room with a sink in it once: the drip drip drip of the septic prick/ and they call it gonorrhoea. Take-off. Can't remember the song it took off though. Mary might know, that's the kind of thing he knows. He's very academic about all that – outsider to it. If you speak French you *study* it, you don't take it for granted. There's a lot to be serious about . . . I think he's got it wrong . . . There are probably two people in England – what's that, OK Britain, fifty-five million – two people who've got parents who died the way ours did. You tell me what's the chance of us meeting. Of him playing in a band with my brothers? I'll tell you: it's beyond odds. Work it out. If I'd have bet on ever meeting someone like me . . . I'd be a rich man now. That's one way. The other is to say we're fated. Combined destiny. A marriage of hands. Look. Look at mine. Compare them with his – I'll get him round. If he'll deign to show up: he's picky nowadays. Very *fat* hands, big bones, long nails, every one a plectrum. We meet in the middle. D'you wanna know why he's never really made it? Just because of that, the size of his hands: they seem to be getting bigger, they're swelling I reckon. He's slow across the fret, too much weight in his fingers: those Chicago guitarists, they may weigh eighteen stone but their hands are bone. They could do *petit-point*. It's all in the hands – and I suppose you've also got to say he can't write catchy songs. But it's the hands mainly and the worse Mary's become the better mine have become. He's losing power, I'm gaining it. Sounds cruel doesn't it? Life's too cushy for him now. There is no dispute about what's in *these*. It doesn't matter how I feel *in myself*. I go up there with Butt and I know, I just know that I am the energy. I am the power. *My* music is my touch – I don't have to do sounds . . . You do realise that I can harm? Break windows . . . I mean, if I wanted to. I *feel* it.'

That is a distillation of 27.10.73 in Room 712 at The Raleigh International, PO5. From up here the lights along the front shine like a necklace of rubies and diamonds: the rubies are forever going away, the diamonds are forever approaching: oh, the front, at Pompey, at night, is a paste jewel. And the floodlights shine on the vessels of war and the grid of the city is mapped in twinkling orange and every window is a story of routine or boredom or paid passion (which is the routine of the OMO wives).

'Butt comes up to me: can you imagine this. This forehead on wheels – that's all I could see of him. There was Sonny beside him, coming down the pier, and Laddy. And Mary – this was before there was any bad feeling of course. Mary's hair is something else. He's like a raven. I tell you: they looked gang handed . . . That's when I was working the pier. I had this booth, this song on a tape loop – La Musica, sort of soft with a girly zest. I was doing nights too, at The Last Voyage of Henry Hudson. I was doing *sessions*. Wasn't really working out. Just about paid my way: you've got to be rich to be in debt. Shifts. I'd done every hotel in Southsea. Ever been to Caen? – I've been there about eighty times and I've never seen the town. St Malo likewise. That stewarding lark – no perks. I don't like docks any more. I never actually noticed the sea. I worked a mobile hot dog van one time but I left when they turned it over to fish and chips too. I did think seriously of moving to Birmingham – you know, landlocked. But then I read this book that called it England's Venice. Anyway I wouldn't understand a word they said – would I? I love Pompey. I can lose myself, really. You can walk into Fratton, walk round . . . and round, it's interminable. *You don't know it's by the sea.* Even when I was doing the rides, just down there – you can't see it, it's the other side of the building – it's almost over the water, like the pier. I worked on the Octopus. And the waltzer. I loved it. But it was seasonal. There were always fights. The squaddies would come down just to pick on the sailors. Then you'd get the redcaps, they're real bastards. Then there was this *incident* – that's what they always call them, incidents. We'd been warned: this chap Kenny who was the site manager had come round, told us so we'd be prepared, not that there's anything you can do. There was a US Navy aircraft carrier in port, and there was a Scottish regiment billeted down at Eastney. Well, you can imagine, can't you . . . I hate violence. I could never bring myself to strike someone. I don't even retaliate. I'd seen enough of it. Men wanting to revert to their animal state and all that. High as kites on risk: that's the real drug, that's what gets them going. Maim, or be maimed. Them or us. *Team spirit.* And of course all the jocks were roaring and the Yanks were blocked out their skulls on sulphate – chum of Sonny's called Bad Bugs had seen to that. There were running fights all afternoon. Guys in the gutter with head wounds. They got in the fairground about seven and by half past we'd been told to shut down the rides, let them get on with it. Police everywhere, and these American naval police built like sentry boxes swinging truncheons as long as hockey sticks. I wanted to run. I wasn't scared – you probably don't believe me but it's true. *I was aesthetically offended.* I can't think of any other way to put it. It was the way they were making *dis*-order out of order. There was this shoe, cherry red woman's shoes with a button strap, like a tap shoe, lying on the metal plate that goes round the perimeter of the dodgems. I've still got it. Right foot. I don't make a fetish of it. But I've still got it. It told me something. It went right to my heart. It was so pathetic and lonely, so useless – *one* shoe. A pointless object. It was so unnecessary that it should have met such a fate. It was a tiny thing. Compare it with men spitting out their teeth, and faces with so much blood stuck to them it might be caked make-up. It was nothing beside all the mess, nothing – the broken glass, and the screams, people running in directions they wouldn't normally go in. Normally there were patterns that the crowds in there followed. As if they were on rails. All that was upset. Panic is a quick-acting virus. I never went back, except to get my cards. It took me a while to figure out what it was about that shoe . . . I'm still not sure. Sniff sniff – there's a whiff of asymmetry, well more than a whiff. Imbalance. I wouldn't have felt the same if it had been two shoes. It got me thinking about my mother and me: that was imbalance. It was a lopsided life for both of us. If she'd gone when my father did . . . one parent does twice the damage. If there hadn't been anyone I'd have found myself – as it is I'm still looking, still groping about. I was too long in the womb, then I was too long in childhood. And now I'm twenty-five and it's all still with me. I can't kick it off. Me, I was born into defeat. My father, my mother – they were people who threw in the towel. By rights we should have been extinct years ago; the Vallender – a genetically unsuccessful animal. Dead as a Vallender. It lacked the common wherewithal. You pitch the Vallender against life and life'll win every time . . . The only chance I ever had of a reprieve was Bonny, that was the only way I could have stepped into . . . into your world, have got *inside*, have begun to feel whole rather than half. I crave everything that all Butt's people are trying to get away from. I just yearn for ordinariness, balance, symmetry, all the things I've been denied – I know *of* them, but I've never felt them. I'd love my everyday worries to be the same as the next chap's. That's what society is – common experiences, shared triviality, the small things people talk to each other about in pubs. I've got no common ground with society. I'd really love to have my little plot in it, my allotment in society's patchwork. I like how it is in murder stories before the murder's committed. Placid, everyone going about their business the same as they did yesterday and the day before that. The constancy . . . I get sick of them after that bit. When the disorder takes over. Throw the book away and go for a walk – street after street at dusk. When the lights are on and they haven't pulled the curtains. Every little house is a theatre of ordinariness, of routine. Silly rituals. Ribbing each other. Mile after mile, house after house. It never changes. Ordinary colours. And I think: that's what I want. I want some of what everyone else has got. I pray for banality . . . I suppose you think that's weird. Don't you. I got these, I've got a gift – and I want *that*. But the one of me who's got the gift doesn't exist outside of the liturgy. I tried it. I rented this booth on the pier. Between Madame Phillipina the fortune teller and the live bait. She was a bigamist ten times over, smoked roll-ups, must have been seventy. She used to go down the end to the landing stage and tell me what she'd seen over on Ryde Pier. She believed it. Courting couple in identical anoraks; man throwing sackful of cats into the briny (she always said 'briny'). This is four, five miles away. She could see through time and distance she said. Bit like you without the algebra. She'd get people coming back and complaining. There was this old bloke who'd given up the lease on his beach hut because she'd told him he was going to die in the winter – next summer came round, and there he was, fit as a fiddle but with nowhere to change into his cozzie. She'd made him believe *that*, that he was going to throw a seven; it's not what anyone *wants* to believe is it? She was that convincing. Triumph of credibility. She'd tell her punters they were ill so they'd come and see me. Nearly always the spleen. I didn't even know where the spleen is. And I appreciate it was well meant, but . . . it made me realise that I'm a charlatan. I felt very conscienced [sic] about it. Like I was conspiring on *them*, prostituting *my* hands. Still, what I did suss was that of all the people who came to see me the only ones who came back were the ones she'd sent me. They believed in me because of her credibility. Their faith in me came from her. Sometimes I'd energise ten people in a day – fifteen quid. Usually four or five: drunks, lads out for a lark, spinsters on a spree, desperate cases, lost causes, minor afflictions. And I know for certain that I fixed some of them. Don't ask me how – I'll come to that. But they hardly ever showed up again. They'd be doing chemicals as well if anything was really wrong. Or homeopathy – chemicals without the cap and gown. There was this trickle of regulars: you done my spleen, what about my liver/lung/abscess/goitre – you name it. They'd always mention Madame Phillipina, she was a charm. I still put flowers on her grave. Kingston Cemetery, up in Fratton, lovely stone, all her surviving husbands chipped in, they got the monumental masons to lie about her age. Flatter her in death. May Butt can remember her on the halls in 1914–18. I owe her a lot. I told her the only people who came back were hers. I came clean with her in the end. She just waved her hand. Next thing I know Butt is coming down the pier. She'd understood that what I needed was the sort of projection he could give me. Can we have some cheeselets?'

Here's a tape which begins unpromisingly. Eddie complains about Lalage's 'hostile aura', the 'unnecessary' way she clasps her hands, the 'funny angle' the room's curtains have fallen at. He blames Chubb for the taxi (to the motor hotel beside the mud flats at North Hayling) having smelled 'of live bait'. He reckons the weather augurs messily. He says the disused rail bridge across Langstone Harbour 'could go any time' and he 'doesn't want to be here to see it'.

They change rooms. Eddie says: 'This smells like live bait too.' He looks at Lalage. They decide not to change rooms again. Eddie addresses what follows to Lalage. He dares her to interrupt him in agreement.

'I am a fraud. I am a faker. I'm a trick. OK. . . ?' She doesn't interrupt. 'These hands can do things that no hands have ever done. Say I touched your womb – '

'Touch my womb . . . What a grotesque idea . . .' Lalage turns to her impassive husband.

'You're childless. I can tell. It's all over you. It's the root of your hostility. I have power over these things . . . Barenness . . . Infertility . . .'

'I can't believe I'm hearing this.'

'It's true . . . When I say I'm a fraud I mean to say I'm a mechanic. I don't *believe* in all the ritual, the pomp – but it's a sort of spur. I couldn't do it here, at least only with real difficulty. But if you come up to The Church I could have a go.'

'Hold on a minute. Hold on. Are you one of these sickos who's got a thing about gynaecology. D'you have a speculum tucked under your bed? Are you a peeper or something?'

'I'm just saying I could help you have children, that's all.'

'I do not want children. I am not parent material . . . Can you give me the keys Chubb? I'm going to Chichester.'

The recording continues in a bar or the hotel's dining room (from where The Cross Of The World is visible).

'Can we go back to what you were saying about being a mechanic. That's an interesting word. It's not how most healers would describe themselves. Nor do they call themselves frauds or fakers . . .'

'I know they don't. Maybe they aren't. I've read dozens of books about healers. I can't see that I've got anything to do with any of it – the spirit world, ESP, Christian miracles. Look, if someone's got a gift for pole-vaulting or for multiplying four-figure sums in their head you don't say that's because of *something else*; you say it's because they've got a particular gift for pole-vaulting or whatever. I've got a gift that's more unusual, that's all. It's real all right. And it may be God-given for all I know – some days I think it is, others I'm not so sure . . . When I'm ill I don't go to a healer. I go to the chemist. Or to a doctor. The body is a mechanism and I work on it the same as a doctor does. The doctor prescribes drugs, see. I *am* a drug. A conduit for chemical force. If fear has a chemistry of its own so does my love – or whatever it is. I'm proud of that. I do not work miracles. I perform *physical* cures. Material medicine. I'm not sure cures is quite the right word. That makes it seem like I'm claiming to do repairs. I've begun to think that maybe I don't actually *rehabilitate* the part that's gone wrong . . . I bring into play *a spare* – that's there, but dormant so to speak. I energise the entire organ or muscle . . . by-pass the malfunctioning part. So I may not cure it. The disease may still be there . . . the wound. Now . . . if I were to do the same to people who've got no disease, who – in everyday terms – are fully functioning . . . I don't need to spell it out. It'd be like giving them a supercharger . . . You'd make them double the person. All the energy that's in there'll be released. I'm just trying to give it a kick-start, see. That's why I'm a charlatan, whatever you like to call it. The punters believe in me because I'm indivisible from The Church and The Founder. I'm part of the Church's terrestrial trinity: there's The Founder, there's The Cross and there's me. They believe that it's *The Church*'s energy that comes through me. And I know it's not. It's mine. That's why I'm frauding them. I may be doing them

375

good – I often am, no question. It's not because of their sincere faith in The Church though – all The Church does is give me the platform and the audience. That's vital, the audience. (That's why I am so much better up there than I was down on the pier.) But it could be any audience. People who believe in toy soldiers. People who don't believe in anything. They *think* they've got to believe in me, believe in the Church, but frankly it's neither here nor there. That's the false pretences. It's not that I can't do what The Church claims. I can, obviously. But I don't do it *because of* The Church . . . though I am, like, facilitated by Butt. That's Ray Butt . . . not The Founder. They're different. There's the impresario, and there's the Man Of God. Multiple selves . . . I'd say one of *his* selves is a miracle worker. Or something like it. He can see further into the world than anyone . . . Patterns where you or I'd think it was chaos. The meaning of no-meaning. He sees the purpose in everything: The Infinite Moment occurred five years *to the day* after his wife's death, The Greatest Sacrifice, The Dark At The Start Of The Tunnel . . . He understands shapes. The numbers in the Avenue Of *his* Life. The symmetries. The signs in the tiniest thing. The lessons . . . there is nothing that isn't a lesson. I'd say he's got a point there. For instance: there was this uterus got washed up on the beach down near Gunner Point. Couple of children find it, think it's some sort of jelly fish and take it home . . . The Public Health visits Daph's clinic. Purely circumstantial mind, no proof. Then some journalist hears about it and comes to see Ray. Very offensive sort of man, asking what does he think about his sister throwing uteruses in the sea . . . Anyone else would have shown him the door . . . If *Sonny*'d been there there'd've been hell to pay. But Ray: he sits there. And he thinks. And he sniffs out the message . . . It's amazing. He tells this chap: If we used our bodies to their full potential, if women were taught how to use the *whole* womb, then they would continue to be fertile, they wouldn't have the change – so there'd be no need for hysterectomy. See? So, from that little acorn of an incident this oak of philosophy has sprung forth. The Avenue Of Life is a Golden Thread Of Opportunity – if you know how to look for it . . . He's been my university. *Has* been! He still is. He's taught me to think. I'm his heir in a way. The Voys are . . . they're brothers to me. But you'd never call them cerebral. I'm the one in the family who's most like him, the one with his curiosity. "The Thirst for knowledge can never be slaked." That's what he says. His cogs never stop. That's what I'm trying to emulate . . . Take ghosts. Everyone has a problem with ghosts . . . *They can be eliminated.* They will be eliminated. The longer we live the less likely we are to become ghosts. One day we'll be able to die in the knowledge that we won't cause distress to the living. Long life, happy death. See – ghosts are manifestations of minds that aren't ready to die along with their bodies . . . That's why they're so embittered, most of them . . . When we give our bodies a chance of a life as long as our minds . . . Hey presto. They die together. Simultaneous Extinction. There'll be no more dislocated minds wandering about, all twisted up inside, hoping to get their bodies back, knowing they can't . . . Mind you, I got to admit that I haven't come up with a way so far to eliminate the ghosts that are already there. But the other . . . People have been made saints for less, much less . . . Don't you reckon it's scandalous . . .'

Chubb counts 'extreme tolerance' uppermost among his assets as a researcher. He is willing to listen without comment, wearing an expression of concerned encouragement, nodding, jotting, never interrupting. His patience ensures that he is subjected to divergent loops, aberrant rants, material which he knows that he'll not use and which he'd curtail would such an act not impair the bond of confidence that his work is conditional upon. For instance:

a) 'Don't you reckon it's scandalous that they call a football team *the Saints*? It's a . . . debasement. I only got to grips with it just the other day. I've been praying, I've been willing them to be relegated to the second division.[1] That would be justice – and then the third. Spitting on sanctity in short trousers . . . Those gestures they make . . .'

b) 'The only thing I ever known Ray in a real quandary about is his mum . . . his mum and Mary – it's difficult . . . sensitive situation, see. There's the asymmetry to start with. Then there's

[1] So'ton F.C. *was* relegated from the First Division of the Football League at the end of the season 1973–4.

Daph: she's so loyal to Ray, she takes his side – and that makes it worse almost. His mum, she's a natural mocker, she doesn't mince words. That's what they're like in So'ton. Disrespectful, cut you down to size . . . she spent too long there, it polluted her. He can't help but love her, she's his mum, she looked after him after The Lord's Harsh Lesson. She gave him the will to live. But as she gives so she takes away . . . She doesn't have his wisdom. She hasn't got his humanity. She's sixty-four now and . . . I don't know what it is . . . Life's mysteries have never really affected her . . . She's happy never asking the questions. She's a woman of limited horizons. He loves her all the more for her failings. He calls her his big sister, "my delinquent big sister". It shows what a man he is that he never budges; constant in his duty. But the grief . . . the provocations. He's asked for guidance over and over. He's asked me to ask for guidance. It doesn't come through. It's a line The Good Guy doesn't answer. I'd tell him leave her to it, she's not worth the hassle . . . Let her get on with it. But he's not like that. He's a big man. He can't bear to see her being . . . used. It's the only word for it. Mary's got this side to him. I've seen him in a new light. I feel sort of let down by him. He's *betrayed* us . . . he's mercenary. Tentacles: he's a leech on her. She can't see it. If Ray says anything, she goes spare . . . You don't want to be around, not when she's in that mood. He said to me: "I have seen *murder* in my mother's eyes." Here's the measure of the man: he doesn't blame Mary. He won't have Sonny badmouthing Mary in front of him, no. Fact of the matter is – Mary's won the jackpot. D'you know what he was doing after the last band split up? He was selling his blood to all the private hospitals. He was selling his sperm to The Fecund Orchard – one of Daph's businesses, fertility clinic. He was complaining that for the money they gave him they ought to throw in a nurse to help him. Ray thought that was a hoot. Next thing you know he's off on a cruise with May Butt. Then they're going on holiday to Belgium. And she's bought him a sports car. And he's living rent free in this block she owns down by the Sally Port. He only has to click his fingers . . . fur coat, rings, guitars. He's her pet . . . The Kept Boy, we call him. She's infatuated. It does funny things to a woman at her time of life.

378

She's bypassed second childhood gone straight into second teenage. She wears these clothes which . . . well, they're unbecoming. Off the peg rejuvenation . . . Has the opposite effect. It makes her look like an old whore – an old whore trying to make a comeback down Palmerston Road. Slit skirts and halter necks. She's got all these wigs, funny sunglasses. *Hot pants*. Honest. You'd take her for a dockyard tart: three quid a go in the alley behind The Killick's Hook. Pitiful. Ray's embarrassed by her. For a man in his position . . .'

c) 'I failed my driving test twice: on the three-point-turn technique first time; then it was insufficient attention to rearview mirror. I've been practising in Daph's old car on the private road behind The Realm, the one that goes down to My Lord's Pond. It's a way of showing Him how important it is . . . You always got to keep The Good Guy in the picture. The Church'll buy me a car when I get the test. It's deductible, 'cause I need it for work . . . When we go on tour again I'll be able to do my share of the driving. It'll make a big difference to my life having a licence: guest appearances . . . all that. I get a lof requests. It's all potential revenue for The Cross. Laddy deals with them.'

d) 'I've written more than a hundred poems to Bonny. Sonnets, free verse, the word *us* one thousand times . . . I've sent her some of them . . . the best ones. She sent me a card last Christmas. Said she hadn't been in touch because Toddy had been ill. I think it's that he won't let her . . . He must know by now that in her heart of hearts it's only our being cousins that has . . . uh, inhibited her. That's a taboo which . . . Look, the Bible's littered with first cousins. Isn't it? It's the sort of thing that in a few years' time she'll realise that . . . it's a *social* convention. Hasn't got a basis in blood . . . See I can't believe he means anything to her, really. He's a meal ticket.'

e) 'I tell you who gives me the heat: that's Flamebryte bleedin' Paint Limited. Messrs Pharisee. Talk about cussed. The Church Of The Best Ever Redemption has offered to buy out their lease at more than twice what it's worth. We've found them new premises – up on the new trading park at Waterlooville; we offered to pay the removal costs *and* the first year's rent *and* to underwrite the trading deficit over the removal period . . . Will they listen? They will not. They don't need to be there. Wasn't decreed unto *them*, was it, that they should found a ministry on Portsdown: Ministry of Paint? Be a bit silly wouldn't it? So we're stuck with them. The Cross is on top of them – we got that freehold. The air rights are ours. But can you believe it? A paint warehouse getting in the way of our expansion. We need room . . .'

Why is it that all the streets are one street, that this street is not the one Eddie's looking for, not the one he once lived on? It may be a cartographer's dream but it flusters Eddie. He is flattered by Chubb; Eddie wants to help, he is conducting him round Pompey, showing him every place he ever lived since he arrived in the city with 'all my worldlies under one arm'. The hotels were the attraction then. A room with a job, a roof, a window to a light well. Every hotel, every flickering fascia, has a story whose victim is Poor Eddie. He directs Chubb left and right through the tyranny of rectilinearity. Every hotel is the same as the last: flickering fascia, precipitous fire escape, and the man in the doorway – he always cups a fag in his palm (p. 306).

Once upon a time Eddie lived in Tipner: domestics, OMO, tattoos, knives. Eddie points to a window no different to the other windows in Tipner, hardly different to all the other windows of this island city; he tells Chubb with inordinate pride: 'That was the first place I had of my own.' The mean houses; the streets that stretch to a low horizon; the Baby Bellings; the nylon sheets; the Sundays in the Maclary Easy; the carpet squares; the damp; the men with dogs who collect the rent; the other tenants (mad, senile, incontinent, criminal); the teakalike surfaces; the attic room with its history of suicides; the cracked shower curtain down the landing; the reek of gas; the meter someone else broke open (but we know who takes the blame); the window that'll never shut; soap so streaked it's like veneer; hollow doors; heating grunts; the partition walls that transmit the accelerating rhythms of onan's bedsprings; rogue fridges; the men who turn their faces to the anaglypta, whose eyes never catch another human's; the causeless enmities that turn to feud. Chubb begins to comprehend the pattern of domestic privation that Poor Eddie suffered.

On the spit at Eastney there are beached boats, hulks, winding gear, clinker sheds, shingle, a coastguard's conning tower, the Hayling ferry's landing stage, the persistent clicking of metal masts, the bruising breeze, the reeks of sea and diesel and mud, the jinking gulls, the statue gulls, the cloud of gulls that marks the sewage outfall. There is so much polished sky, so much water, so much gleaming mud. The Cross Of The World rises on the northern horizon. Eddie points to it as they get out of the car. Chubb follows Eddie along a boardwalk across mud and shingle; a rusting outboard lies beside it, and pitted paintcans, a skein of wire, metal pipes, two splintered oars, a cracked tarpaulin, coils of oily rope. The boardwalk leads to a tarred wooden hut built on stilts. More rope (etc.) protrudes from the space beneath the structure. Eddie stands beside the padlocked door.

'All mine, this is,' he says, fumbling with the key. 'My second residence . . . Ray gave it me. For the second anniversary of my ministry. His theory is that if I sleep here often enough it'll help with my hydrophobia . . . So I come down here in summer. I've managed a few nights. But I get these fears about floods and fishes getting onto the land. So I go home, usually. It's a crude sort of treatment isn't it?' Chubb felt such pity for Eddie. He wondered at the gulf between the grandiosity of his corporeal utopianism and his pride in this dusty dark beach hut which smells of creosote, the gaps between whose floorboards admit stripes of light. Later that day he saw Eddie's home – a one-room flat with a kitchenette and (Eddie made a point of this) its own *silent* toilet and bath. Eddie showed him photographs of his mother, his father and Bonny. He made instant coffee and offered Chubb a packet of crisps. With no tape recorder to speak to Eddie was silent. There were books (epiphanic memoirs, healing, self awareness, sci-fi), rock records, beer mats, Chubb was not at ease in the tiny, tidy room. He heard himself saying: 'You should come to us over the holiday . . . on Boxing Day – for a few nights, if you like . . . A bit of a change . . . If it suits you . . . You may have something fixed . . .'

'No. No engagements . . . Yes, yes – I should like that.'

Lalage to Chubb: 'What? *What?* Are you . . . Jesus! That geek

. . . on top of everything else. Has it completely escaped your memory – Camilla's here for the whole week – '

'She is my daughter Darling – '

'He's not though is he. Yet. Are you going to adopt him? You spend more time with him than you do with me.'

'Darling . . . It's just this once. I want to talk to him in a situation where he won't . . . where he won't be mentally referring everything back to Butt.'

'Do you? Well bully for you. I think what I'll do is go into a deep sulk . . . And make sure I keep the bedroom door locked. I won't have that geek snooping through my things.'

Sonny to Eddie: 'He's *pimping* off of you Old Love. You're writing his book for him. You could be writing your own book. We got a tape recorder haven't we. We got the secretarial. We could fix it up. An' I can guarantee that. Thing is Eddie, it's like Jonjon says: The Church is a holy enterprise and you're part of its capital – very vital part. So in a manner of speaking this Chubb is helping himself to what's ours. You with me?'

'Ray didn't . . . You were *there*. He gave Chubb his blessing. He hasn't said anything to me . . .'

'He's got a lot on his mind Dad has. You know that . . . All I'm saying, Eddie, is think about it. Eh? Think family on this one. There's a good love. We got to pull together aren't we . . . If you want to carry on with this Chubb he's going to have to come to some arrangement . . . Like Reg did with Dad. Dad give him fifty per cent. Honour satisfied both sides. Never undersell yourself – that's the mistake we made with the band. Well, that that cunt Mary made. What we'll do is *I'll* get on the dog to our chum Chubb . . . Familiarise him with the concept. So when you go up The Smoke he'll know what's what.'

Camilla Chubb's wrists are histories of her cries for help. She addresses Eddie as 'Boy Jesus'. She asks him if he can transform a bottle of VDQS Minervois Domaine Ventajou '71 (Peter Dominic £0.74p) into 'something a bit smoother. Like some of the gear we had yesterday.' She tells him she wants to see him 'prove himself'. She overturns a brimming bin of peelings, boiled giblets, stained tins, J cloths, brandy butter jars, spent crackers, torn packets onto the floor; she kneels to sort through the polychromatic scrape, bangs an empty magnum of Lynch-Bages '59 onto the kitchen table where Eddie is eating grease-frilled chipolatas, lumps of bready stuffing, congealed bacon rolls, gelatinous shards of gravy rubber. He peels skin from the turkey carcase in front of him. She rolls another empty across the table, Rauzan-Gassies '55. It clinks against the turkey's plate. Eddie keeps his head down, fearful that the scoff will be removed by his hostess. 'Hey – catch!' She lobs a d'Yquem empty. He takes it clumsily on his chest. He glances at her like she's a foaming bitch. She is a foaming bitch, he decides.

He's only been in the tall house – 166 Hamilton Terrace, London NW8 – for twelve minutes. He's already regretting having taken an early train.

'The Boy Jesus,' said the foaming bitch who was still Camilla when she opened the door. 'Welcome, Lord.' She held a hanky to her face. She proffered it to his: 'D'you do snap Jesus?' Now she leans across the table, across the bottles, towards the turkey's brittle breast bone, chin in hands above the starboard drumstick. Eddie looks at his watch.

'It's all right Jesus Pet – Daddy and Lal won't be back *for hours*. "We can play-yay-yay-yay/Make hay-yay-yay-yay." Whatever. You're early. Do you know what Lal says about you? . . . She . . . says . . . Look at that bottle: what's different about it?'

Eddie, tight shouldered, scrutinises the Sauternes bottle. He shrugs, eyes down, eyes on a dead parsnip.

'I thought you were meant to have the most phenomenal powers of observation . . . If Baby Jesus look closely wosely he'll spot that the bottle has no seam. It is manufactured as an entity. They don't make them like that any longer. Didn't know that did you? Other way round from stockings. They used to have seams. Now they don't. Does it get you going: S-t-r-a-n-g-e girls saying stockings? Does it? Lal says I've got to lock up my undies because you'll be at them. And – do you know – ' her mouth which is a wound protrudes over the tiller of the breast bone (her chin is hidden, her mind on day release), 'I think she's right. Arnold Layne.[1] Arncha Jeez? D'you want a toot – I'm going to

---

[1] Eponym. 'Arnold Layne' is the title and subject of a song by Syd Barrett (1946–). Layne's 'hobby' is stealing women's clothes from washing lines.

have a toot. You're *not* going to work a miracle on this piss – are you . . .' She refers to the uncorked Minervois. 'Toot and a beaker of piss, then. It'll have to be. He's got eight fucking thousand bottles of proper wine down there. And he double locks it every time he goes out. He doesn't trust me.' She pushes a glass of wine towards Eddie.

'I don't drink.'

'No – you wouldn't would you . . . You saint you.'

The Founder considers irony (and its underdeveloped sibling sarcasm) to be the real English disease. Poor Eddie agrees: he recognises its efficacy, the effrontery of the crude form. His is the victim's angle on it. It's dissemblance, which is a lie; it intends its opposite; it's treacherous; it's code – and he's not part of the club. (His jib is cut wrong.) It's a coward's device. Its ambiguity allows the ironist a way out: the ironist can always claim to have been talking straight. The Founder notes that it's 'for them that want to hedge their bets'. Its appeal to the English lies in its deceit, its dryness, its indirectness (there is a gulf between emotion and expression; indeed it facilitates the suppression of emotion). It's a device of the covert, the secretive. It's the slang of the professional classes. Twat judges, bastard barristers. It's for those who were born to sneer. It's their torn shirt, their rolled trouser leg. The Founder has told Eddie all this, but he has never told Eddie how to counter it. She's fixing him with a stare that's mocking, accusatory. He holds a wingbone with both hands.

He says, very softly: 'No. Not yet a saint. Not while I'm still alive . . .'

She whinnies incredulity. She watches him shut his eyes. The lids are thin. She wonders if he sees through them, if he sees in his sleep. He clasps his upper lip between his teeth. Then he smiles, surveys the room (fantasy farmhouse: big dresser, bucolic prints, Aga, Staffordshire). He gnaws the bone, scrapes at the table's grain.

He tells her, casually: 'My uncle's just died.'

'Oh God . . . Look I didn't mean to . . . I didn't know. Oh I'm sorry. Were you clo . . . I'm really really sorry.'

'You don't need to be. I loathed him . . . I'll ring later to make sure.'

'What?'

'To check – that he is dead.'

'I thought you . . . either – '

'I said he just died. Thirty seconds ago. He's still warm. I got a message. I never had one before. But I never wanted anyone to die so much. I never cursed anyone else. Not even Toddy – '

'What are you . . . You're trying to spook me. Aren't you. You are. Aren't you. Tell me you are for fuck's sake . . . Come on . . . I didn't mean to . . . Pax? Eh? Please? Yeh?'

'It's a letter's difference. That's all. That's the beauty of it. Tip it over with one letter. C-U-R-E . . . C-U-R-S-E . . . Easy if you know how.'

Camilla Chubb feels the horror, the cold stripe of dorsal rigor, the cosmic fright that numbs, the internal paralysis occasioned by fear's toxins – those that work quicker than a krait's bite. Her brain tingles – synapses in shock; someone's rubbing linament into the cells in there. Her tongue fills her throat. Her feet are fixed to the floor. Her hand won't shift her glass. This is the worst ever. This relegates ODs, stomach pumps, arterial incisions to paltry. This is unscreamable terror, this man whose mastications' din fills her ears with the echoes of hell's forge: bones devoured by industrial teeth, the wicked wet lapping, clicks, the grinding of ossific splinters, the ogreish cataracts of spittle, bungpull plosives, unnatural disaster. His gustatory absorption is massive. What species does he belong to? He's from outside, from further away than even her father knows. Even his dandruff is excessive – in net quantity *and* size of flake, each one a seborrhoeic almond. His eyes manifest a perpetual, profound hurt that a moment's quiet triumph cannot mitigate, a hurt redeemable only by infliction of a greater hurt, by the primitive alchemy of revenge. (Does she feel this? Yes – but gradually. The tight skein of synchronous sensation will unravel, reveal itself to her over suicidal hours and fraught years. There's such a galore of gen. Stored, awaiting the catalysis of Poor Eddie's futures: each of which she'll discover she has cognition of – they don't surprise her. Their seed/blueprint is with her from this moment which is unlike all other moments.) She dares not take her eyes off him. She computes putative dangers. She leaves the kitchen (he doesn't stop eating or acknowledge her departure); she hurries into the hall, grabs a coat and goes out into the wide avenue of grey, crazed pollards and stock brick. She runs to the corner, keeps running down the hill, around another corner.

Eddie alone in Chubb's vertical house. He has never been in such a house before: the stairs, the elegance, the well-mannered opulence. It is a museum, a gallery, a brainfood house, a meal for his eyes. He notices Camilla's absence and is grateful for it. There is so much to look at: ancestor (whose?) portraits on the countless stairflights; marble busts from whichever century it was when everyone had mumps; prints and masks and books and carpets. There are so many rooms to enter. Chairs to sit in. The quantity of material solaces astonishes him. His uncle's death has cheered him. He allows himself two liqueur chocolates, the hues of their gaudy foil are like those of baubles on the Christmas tree – there, fairy on the top, lights, tinsel. He wanders from room to room, sniffing scent, prodding cushions, opening cupboards, feeling brocades and velvets and silks. He bounces on beds and sofas; tentatively to begin with then with a keenness that borders abandon. There are fur coats for him to bury his face in. There are yellow rooms, powder blue rooms, gilt tables, ebonised tables, baroque chairs, rococo chairs, veneers like black ice, veneers like swirling oil. Surfaces, crannies, textures . . . He eats a further couple of chocolate liqueurs. He pops these in his mouth whole, doesn't even *consider* biting the 'bottles' at the neck. The cosy oesophagal warmth pleases him mightily. Oh, and there are nuts, elaborate crackers, glacé fruits, soft Spanish nougat, chunks of panforte and halva. Eddie succumbs to this saccharine exoticism, to drowsy sybaritism. Chubb's shelves hold hundreds of books on levitation, miracles, ghosts, table turning, mediums, hypnotism, magic, prophecy etc. But Eddie is on holiday.

He lies on a sofa in a darkening sitting room eating sweet-meats, watching a technicolour circus drama on television (glamorous trapeze artiste promises sexual favours to deformed clown on condition that he murder the bareback rider who is her rival for the lion tamer's hand). Incredulous and bored, he treats himself to more chocolate liqueurs. He switches channels: no luck. On a console table is a display of old metal animals with spring-driven motors. The entire zoo scurries across the polished floorboards, whirring, striking table legs and wainscots, overturning to reveal busy little wheels. Eddie crawls in pursuit of a porcupine, crushes a box of marzipan fruits. But he tires of these toys as any boy would, abandons them, prowls through the house seeking fresh pleasure, revelling in the safe mysteries of the twilit labyrinth, brushed by curtains and fronds, thrilled by squeaky joists, by fantastical shapes in the crepuscule, by silhouettes against the streetlit windows. He loses count of the rooms, of the past crazes they bear witness to. In Chubb's study notepads, folders, files and tapes bear witness to his current craze – Eddie. Eddie pries diligently – he owes it to himself. Transcribed tapes aside there is very little: lists of topics, lists of questions, arrows, illegible phrases. Eddie believes that Sonny was right, that he is writing Chubb's book for him.

He dials 0722 5004. The accent he practises whilst the phone rings is his idea of posh. A man answers.

'Hairlair,' booms Eddie. 'Can I spake to Deouglas Vallendah.' There is a void, then an intake of breath. 'Aah . . .'

'Probalem?' suggests Eddie.

'I think I'd better fetch – hang on a mo.' The police sergeant who came to the phone was all periphrasis and hawking.

'Is what you're trying to say is that Mr Vallendah is dead?'

'In, ughum, ehhm, a nutshell, urm, aah, Sir, it it *is* my my aarb sad duty to oooh issue an affirmative, yes, yes: the deceased, hmmm, *has* passed away . . .'

Eddie dances, shadow boxes, claps, stamps etc. This is how Chubb and Lalage find him. He cannot account for Camilla's whereabouts.

He whoops, punches the air. His glee fazes them. His triumph, he explains (and again) is tripartite: the efficacy of his (ten years old) curse is proven; his telecognitive faculty has developed through right-side exercises; and he is delighted that Douglas is dead – there was a man who didn't deserve to dredge his potentialities.

That evening Eddie hears Camilla and Chubb screaming at

each other. Later he hears Lalage and Chubb screaming at each other. He is deft in the distinction of the women's hysterogenic keening. He can recognise the source even if he doesn't know which room they're in now, now that it's each other they're wounding with their womb shrieks. He wonders if it's always like this, if the house is always loud with sounds of familial stramash, if there is always a tureen exploding against a wall, if there is always a door crashing against its jamb as a prelude to silence (bring up exterior sounds: internal combustion, wind through the pollards, Mr East against the panes). He wonders – but idly, for here is another box of crystallised ginger, here is a biblical film (risible dialogue, grandiose cumuli over Calvary), here is the chair that sloth built. And here is the chair whose edge Chubb sits on, demeaning himself with a fidgety grin the way he never has in hotel rooms at Pompey and Hayling, beating tattoos on its directoire arms, scraping a Kazak's tight pile with his heels. Here is the chair in which Chubb suffers his first disappointment, this man who is not at home at home.

'Oohff – I don't feel like it,' replies Eddie, curtly, unaverting his eyes from the U certificate crucifixion, when Chubb suggests that 'we may as well get started. Spot of lucubration out of the distaff's way?' Chubb tries nervily to smalltalk Eddie. He doesn't understand the inaptness of such triviality: it's a language Eddie doesn't speak – he doesn't see the signs, can't read the invitations. Moreover, even were Eddie appropriately kitted, there would be a wrongness in these two playing the pingpong of verbal vacuity – that is not the way they were meant to be, behave; that is not their proper bond in the jigsaw. Their contract is formalised in unilateral intimacy: it is Eddie who talks, it is Chubb who ignites the monologic motor and thereafter keeps mum. That's the way The Good Guy planned it: Chubb is an abstracted ear. There should be no role for him.

He is, then, further trespassing without the bounds of his propriety when, later, during an advert for power tools ('Give him what he *didn't* get on Christmas Day') he leans, host to guest, towards Curled Eddie: 'So. I hear you've . . . *met* Camilla . . . That's good, that's good . . .' he clears his throat – nerves, not phlegm: 'Harrrug . . . She's . . . she's had her problems – '

388

'Noticed.'

'Ah! Yes. She can be quite awk . . . *Tell me* – do you think that there's anything *you* can do – to help her . . . For her. You know . . . Which might, which might, which mi . . .'

Chubb isn't asking, he's pleading, there's desperation in his voice, there's paternal shame, guilt that the genetic load he transmitted may have been contaminated, guilt at the very fact of his procreation. This is a new Chubb, a naked Chubb; this Chubb has faith in Eddie. He *believes*. Eddie can discern it: his blindness to social nuance and conversational convention is compensated by his diagnostic sensibility towards humours and their beards. Chubb's face is rictal entreaty, beseeching eyes; he hopes for hope – in vain, for:

'You talked to Sonny then?' Eddie's tone is curt, his diversion cruel.

'*What*?' Chubb's perplexity raises his voice.

'Sonny. You talked to him didn't you? He said you did. He said he'd phoned you . . .'

Chubb slumps, crumpled, numb with incredulity.

'. . . To put you in the picture. So . . . you reached any conclusion? Decisions, like? Point is – I don't want to be unfair – but *they are my words*.' He has to wait for Chubb's reply.

'Your *friend* . . . has a most extraordinarily inflated idea of . . . of this modest project. I suppose I should be flattered.' Chubb explains the *ethics and economics* of private press publishing, the wrong flow of money, the abusive sobriquet 'vanity', the analogues with onan, the prop to *amour propre*, the recondite nature of his work, the retail problem, the retail void –

'So no one's going to be able to buy it then?'

'Financial gain is not my motive – '

'Just as well, if they're not going to be having it in the shops. Heyho . . . Who's going to read it?'

'Specialists, colleagues . . . my fellow researchers. All of the people you'll meet tomorrow.'

'This is . . . well, this puts a very different complexion . . . You know, you never told me . . . I mean, I thought it was a *proper* book . . . No offence, mind – but I've put in a lot of hours . . .'

They sat in silence, in television light. Choric surges accompany the deposition of the goyish Christ.

Eddie laughs at the actor's actorishly pained face, he turns to Chubb: 'We may not know what it was like but we know what it wasn't like. Don't you reckon? If I asked you for them would you give me the tapes?'

Chubb laughs. Not an easy laugh: think rather of embarrassment. 'Eddie . . . This is a delicate matter. Don't rush headlong into some . . . Look, don't be rash. I think really your friend Sonny is not – '

'Would you give them to me?'

'It's not as easy as that. The conception, the actual recordings – '

'Oh come on – yes or no.'

'You're being very . . . obstinate. We're *collaborators*. It's a joint ven – '

'You're saying no aren't you?'

'I suppose, frankly, I am.'

'Well we got that straight then haven't we? Know where I stand then I suppose . . . *What* was it you thought I could do for Camilla?'

The specialists, the colleagues, the fellow researchers: a coven of them gather in Chubb's house early in the afternoon of 27 December. Chubb's familiars, veterans of psychic campaigns. Men with twitches, men of military mien, a man with a wig he pushes back to scratch his scalp, a man with bugger's grips, a woman with a moustache, a siren with opaline earrings to her clavicle, the mousy misses of a certain age, a myopic hippy whose nipples are wrapped in cheesecloth, a diesel with a hearing aid that admits her to conversations of centuries ago – invariably such conversations are conducted by the noble, the martially powerful, the famous. She is at a loss to explain why – but then no one who suffered a previous life was a smith or dung seller. Posthumous travel of any sort is prohibited to the ordinary man in the grave. The after life is no more egalitarian than the before life; there exists a metempsychotic hierarchy. Pharoahs and courtesans most favoured. No one wants to believe he was a ditch digger. No specialist wants to talk to a low-caste beaker person.

Chubb fetches Eddie from the den where he has been talking to Camilla in apparent tranquillity. He introduces him one by one to the creatures who crowd the first floor sitting room, nibbling, sipping, boasting, clutching duffel bags and pasties. They crowd the space between their heads and ceiling with a brown nimus of arcanum: Claudine, Lambert Shepherd, Miss Walby and Miss Williams, Emma Zunz, Mister Honeybourne etc.

Eddie immediately forgets the names. He wearily notes the afflictions: squint, liver spots, stroke victim in vomit green tweed, Parkinsonism, nathty lithp, obesity, exophthalmic goitre. The usual. Eddie discovers that Chubb has an arm around his shoulder. The babble of competitive recollection: where they've been, what they've done. They are travellers spinning travellers' yarns, fishermen . . . They feign a disregard for Eddie, they hardly break off their narratives to greet him, they strive to outbrag each other: the states they've witnessed, the kilos of ectoplasm, levitational tours de force measured in metres and minutes, hemiplegia cured, paraplegia cured, the quadriplegic who now plays football, the footballer who learnt to talk, the ghost who posed for cameras, the girl who menstruated at seven, the girl who menstruated at four *and* spoke an ancient Assyrian tongue even though she'd never left Harpenden, Herts.

Eddie knew that they stole glances at him. He knew too that he was Chubb's trophy, that his presence obviates Chubb's participation in the contest of tongues, that he is indisputable in his physical presence, that he doesn't have to be recreated. He understands the kudos that Chubb gains: he has achieved an apogee of fandom. The hands are in Chubb's keeping.

The room is lit by floor-to-ceiling sashes. At two o'clock Chubb draws wooden shutters across them. The lights are turned on. He ushers the assembly to the end of the room further from the door. He momentarily exits from the door.

He returns followed by an African woman carrying a swaddled child whom, at Chubb's beckoning, she lays on a table.

'Godefroid', announces Chubb, 'is four years old. He weighs

less than one stone, less than he weighed when he was a year old. For a long time he has refused to eat. Mrs Ngoye has attempted every sort of treatment . . . No two diagnoses correspond. The child is dying . . . Eddie.'

Eddie has had no warning. He walks head down across the room to Chubb, speaks softly: 'What kind of stunt is this . . . You bring in some basket case . . . expect me to . . . to do a *turn*. I'm on holiday. Besides, I've got no authority here . . . haven't you taken that in? And who's paying . . . Are you? You're more of a pimp on me than Butt's ever been.'

The door to the room opened: Lalage, crying: 'It's Camilla! Chubb! She's done it again.'

Lalage holds up bloody hands.

Eddie grins. As Chubb bolts from the room he turns to them, to his audience, murmuring: 'She told me I was the devil . . . so I *was*. She asked me what the answer was. What could she do about life, about her life.'

Eddie hesitates then continues gravely: 'End it . . . Nothing else for it. That's what I told her. End it. That's the cure. I can cure anything.'

Camilla Chubb didn't die, that time. Indeed she was back from hospital by the time Sonny and Laddy broke in for the tapes (which Chubb had sagely deposited in his office).

Every time Toddy took a breath he lacked the breath to draw that breath within him. He could feel the air on his lips – the douce current from the linen cupboard carrying the smell of cuddly towels like fresh doughy bread. He could feel the jangly wind on his teeth; it knew where the bad fillings were, the sites of attrited enamel; the cold blows had him wincing; he held his jaw till the pain abated. And his tongue, it was a barometer, it knew the score, it tasted enough to know there was still air there, that there was plenty of vital fuel. The fault was elsewhere.

Jos, roasting goose, bitumen, hash, patchouli, Castrol R, Players No. 6, Chanel No. 5: there was enough air to vector them, enough air for smoke to make lassos in, enough air for a drizzle of particles to rest suspended in so they took the light like micropearls. The air teased him with its ubiquity, with its willingness to oblige his smell and touch.

And how else, by what other agency, could he hear the voice of the woman whom he loved (till death did, and it would, soon), how else could he see her, clutching the razor blade with a piece of card, chopping the powder, excising the granules, rendering it dust, cross hatching the junk on a foxed mirror on the knotted kitchen table in the farmhouse on the high downs? Then she makes lines of the powder, precise as buttered soldiers for a four-minute egg and just as comforting; she is absorbed in her deft craft. She holds a Bic crystal tube to the right nostril, nibless end to the westernmost line. And she breathes, she breathes a solace that is denied him, she breathes with relief and craving – not a coarse craving, not desperate (I swear to that, I witnessed it often enough): it would become those in time, later, when the going was not so good.

She savoured it as he savoured the air – what little air – he managed to draw with his pulmonary Hoovers. Air makes addicts of us all. That's what we realise when we don't get enough of the stuff. *You* are addicted to air. She looked fine on air and smack and brandy. She bloomed, as though in the early months of an easy pregnancy, a pregnancy that will result in a bouncing babe, an immaculate miniature, a child that's just bonny. Bonny is a junky. She's been busted. Toddy has cancer. He's been told.

If, in 1973, you spent midnight till four in The Last Resort, 294 Fulham Road, London SW10 and you huddled in a booth with Iffy Billy from Stadium Street and left with a folded envelope of Pure you were lucky. More likely you leave with a folded envelope of 50% Daz and a tap on the shoulder from Constable Constable, the nark's friend, the filth in Budgen's doorway. He nicked Bonny, shoved her in a J-reg Escort, charged her in the name Charlotte Jane Hogg-Tod, gave his lesbian Alsatian, Mufti II, a loose rein to her lap. Bail: £150. Bonny gave great head, greater headache. She protested that she wasn't a junky because she could afford whatever it was it took and, besides, look at her complexion, never better, look at its lustre and touch it – 'Touch my cheeks Johnson!': yes, she was a piece in bloom, at the table, in the house, up on the high downs. He came dogging everywhere behind her, Toddy did, paced out by the unnatural disequilibrium of their respective breaths.

He had cancer. No, no: that's too modest. Credit where it's due. He had cancers, plural, multiple wens. They spread like fires beneath the earth. They crop up. The crop grows far from where it's been planted. Cf. the mysteries of mycelium, fungal happenstance, where next year's ceps will show: what is the mycorrhizal circumstance? What is it that admits this beneficent parasite? And why does that one grow only on the heads of dead horses? Et cetera. Fungi don't talk. The bearers of cancers neither. To what combination of cells and weather are they due? Who decides? How far back? They were silent in his oxters. Donald Rollo 'Toddy' Hogg-Tod ascribed the stomach pains to chilli, to worry, to his wife: the woman he loved, the woman he hit. He hit her when she wouldn't go down – 'You're Bonny Vallender. *Darling.*'

Was it in revenge that his armpits stung? He hit her when he was drunk. He drank to obliterate it all; he drank for amnesia – so he could hardly recall the blows he delivered to her the night before, the blows to her face, to her ribs, to her conscience. He blamed her. He blamed her for his body's indiscriminacy, for its inability to bounce malignant gatecrashers. He blamed her because the initial pains, the inklings in his digestive tract, beset him the week of their wedding, the very night of their wedding (pp. 291, 295). That's not chance. Cancer came with her. She planted wens within him.

Up on the high downs where the owls hoot and clouds like moonlit brains scurry across the blueblack Bonny sobs in the garden. She tastes the blood from the lip he split with a swipe. The wind bends the elms (not yet clogged, but they'll go the way of all wood). She sobs, a flushed sack of opiates and fear, crouched on dewy grass. He staggers from the house. His legs confound each other. He shouts her name, the brandy bottle arcs with electric light. He calls repeatedly, pleadingly, there's always desperation in his voice. He needs her beside him, he needs spirits inside him. He collides with a sun-dial in the dark. He drinks for amnesia, to forget his body, to let himself damage hers so that they achieve communion in pain, in incompleteness: this is a conceit she despises. Nor does she wish to die with him.

He is envious of the years of breath and light that she'll have after him, so envious that certain nights she fears for her life and increases her dose in order that oblivion can have her, in order that he can effect her end without her knowledge. The apprisal of his mortality has embittered Toddy. He is, evidently, not too young to die; but he is too young to accept death's imminence.

'The pattern of expectation in our socio-medico culture does, I'm afraid, mean that we are unequipped for acceptance,' said Godwin the oncologist, 'In the Third World, in Africa, say, you wouldn't have this problem – '

'But I'm not fucking African am I you prat.'

Bonny drove him home, stopping at the off for bottles and

gaspers, glad of the peace in the shop though frustrated by its gloom – she wouldn't remove her shades lest her bruises be noted.

And he'd drink more, curse more, cry and strike her.

And they'd finish the day in the hours before dawn croodling in the dew on the lawn, clinging on for dear life, wishing his lack of future life on anyone else, as though release might be had by carcinomic transmission, by passing the parcel of malignancies to someone who deserved it, to someone who was *a cancer type*: a PORG,[1] a Fray Bentos,[2] a sclerry,[3] a spaz like Poor Eddie, an unter.[4] Someone who was already crocked, who wasn't going to last, who had nothing to enjoy, whose life was banality and drudge, whose life was missionary position and counting the pennies, whose life was bereft of the excitement that comes with pecuniary privilege, multiple residences, serial sinecures, boat (eight-berth Samson Orange-class berthed at Berthon Marina, Lymington), horses etc.

Toddy knew that the harried faces which emerged from the faïence pomp of the Underground station belonged to people condemned to move forever beneath the earth and that the portal was styled thus to give them face, to dignify their sordid mode of transport, to assist their self-delusion. Any one of them merited cancer more than he did. You there, you wage-hag, you with the facial skin like an eraser streaked with graphite, you, you've got nothing to live for save mole routes, routine, the daily dance on poverty's precipice, cheap food, condensation. You have it. You take it . . . The gusts of warm air which the lifts excavate and belch into the street with rattling and bellows: it reeks of poor lives, unchanged clothes, accreted sweat, socks and cock cheese. Toddy wonders *what use are their meagre lives?*

Suffering bravely borne is a valedictory fiction. In my book anyway. Toddy turned away from death, keen to make deals, to

---

1 Acronym: Person Of Restricted Growth. A euphemism abused.

2 Typhoid victim. A usage originating in a Hogg-Tod family joke about the Aberdeen typhoid outbreak of 1964 – this was attributed to corned beef, though *not* to the estimable Fray Bentos brand which takes its name from a town on Uruguay's Argentine border.

3 Abbreviation of sclerosis, substantive.

4 From untermensch.

enter pacts with whomsoever, the Other (where do you contact Him?). He yearned to buy time, to buy luck – but not to push it; thus he sent (anonymous) cash contributions to charities: the Imperial Cancer Research Fund, the British Association For Cancer Research, the Colostomy Trust (Patron HRH Queen Elizabeth the Queen Mother).

Electively jobless throughout his short adult life he was now employed full time, and over, achieving alcoholic oblivion, begging the fates and gods, begging for a change of plan. He was unequipped for acceptance.

He entered churches, genuflected, told silent lies that even he cannot have believed – lies about service, altruism etc. Then he'd look about him at the casualties naves attract, the disinherited meek, the wretchedly mackintoshed, and realise that he was petitioning the wrong mob.

But the Other owned no premises, no terrifying vaults, no carved bestiaries, no representations of elaborate torture and luxuriant suffering, no misericordous grotesques who sloth beneath seats pooning and quim-sniffing – no wonder they spring up like jacks in the box. The Other has no apparatus for the manufacture of magic, no sites of sonic trickery and incantatory fear. But the Lord's many houses have all these and Toddy's guess (which has been made over and again down the centuries though not, typically, by the terminally ill) is that the Other shares with the Lord, that He squats, that He's brought in His own gewgaws like a cuckoo with chattels. Toddy holds his hands across his eyes at prayer, peeps through the pinky keyhole at men en travesti, at their masoch collars, at their faces which are masks of themselves and impervious to the exaltation they speak of – which he ascribes not to the blocked boredom of repetition but to their being double agents hardly able to endure the perpetual dissemblance. Their mangled language and loony booming are crypto-lines from the Other. They're not what they pretend to be. Give the Other his due: He knows where to recruit: the domed heads in dresses speak for Him, they speak against the run of their texts. They're high ironists, these Anglicans. They're low ironists these Maynooths. They've all gone over to the Other, have been with Him all along. They may

397

be the bridegrooms of Christ, but they commit adultery with the Other. Thanks be to God.

The victim's parents, Alasdair and Jill Hogg-Tod, faff about. They blame each other. They blame *their* parents (Bridge of Allan and Stenhousemuir) and their parents before them. They split the blame with every generation: four, eight . . . arithmetical regression into culpability: *your* mutton shagger grampa in Alloa, *your* wheezer uncle in Dunblane. They can't decide. They send him to a clinic in Switzerland with the slut of a wife whom they warned him against, whose no-goodness is manifest in her tart clothes, and in her choice of head gear to cover the alopeciac effects of his chemotherapy; she has our son in bright berets that advertise his plight – Kangol has a subtler range.

It was her whom they blamed most of all. They'd always had it in for her. Their son's decline coincided with his meeting her, or the start of their liaison, or their marriage, some time like that.

His valetudinarian gaucheness embarrassed them. He'd stumble into the restaurants they frequented, flaunting his pain, drawing attention to the blood line of his infirmity, gasping for breath, removing his beret so the weightless strands of baby hair that still remained to him blew like cedillas in the door drafts. And her – beside him, in scrubber glitter, in a self-inflicted coma, it's a miracle that she's on her feet (and look at those shoes), look at her pupils, if you can find them – five-point full stops, heavily inked, inverted. She tried their compassion (they did not begin from a position of plenty). She turned their son, their only son, their fading son, against them.

They weren't equipped; they were self-made Scots, not Africans. Their impotence aged them. They owned tracts of land so great the eye could not see across. They had combined their names in an assonant mouthful whose sum was more than double its parts. They entertained ministers of state. They had dined with crowned heads (though they were not so boastful or self deceiving that they claimed intimacy), their name opened doors, glamour stuck to them, racing drivers borrowed their house at Cap Ferrat, the business pages loved them – here was colour without corruption, success without skeletons. A k was a certainty. Ermine and a place name a possibility. Neither was yet

398

fifty. They wore the unseasonal tan of the very rich (who *are* different – their skin's like leather). They delighted as much in each other now as they had as teenage sweethearts in Falkirk. Their lives were blightless, lit by love and luck. Their lives had been one life. Their life had been blightless, till that girl came into it. Soon she would be the only family left to them. And of course she wasn't family. Jill had been unable to have a second child; they had thought of adopting, briefly. But they weren't gamblers, they could never have learned to love a lottery prize – and they never learned to love a fortuity-in-law, the problem-in-law, the bad lot who'd taken their son and their name – duping the one, sullying the other. Her, she'd be their all. She was no swap for their son, to whom they'd given the best, given too much, given a birth under the sign of the crab called Cancer. She did not compare (they both believed), she was bereft of their blood, she'd never had that advantage.

She was a firework maker's daughter (so her box was full of rockets), an English firework maker's daughter. They were sentimentally Scottish when it suited, sufficiently Scottish to derive chauvinistic and scornful pleasure from England's annual pyrotechnical festival being a commemoration of a failure. English fireworks were uncelebrant as English air was, for their one son, non-functional, as English drugs were. Chemotherapy failed him.

Blenoxane, Alkeran, Platinol, Matulane, DTIC, Nolvadex, Depo-Provera, Velban, Orasone – the names are beguiling, panaceal, utopian; they might belong to planets, to garden cities in a far-off country. They made him nauseous, they made him vomit, they made him breathless, they made him bleed from his nose and his rectum. His blood didn't clot. He was tired. He was prone to colds, flu, coughs. His temperature was inconstant. His nude pubis excited Bonny who pretended it was that of a hairless boy child. His desire was slight, so slight that he rarely rose to die. He lay in bed like the corpse he was soon to be, bereft of appetite, a statue of himself.

Before he had begun to undergo drug treatment he had put samples of his sperm on ice (at −176° Celsius, mixed with protein and egg yolk, suspended in liquid nitrogen, yum). That had been when he believed, when they both believed, that it was going to be the cancers that were killed. He would recover, of course he would, but his fertility might be impaired and it was only prudent in that circumstance to have a future family in a jar, in a fridge, to cook at a later date, grandchild for Alasdair and Jill. Bonny loved Toddy; love was a habit like smack, she was used to loving him and longed to prolong his life, to delay the day when she would be denied his living presence, when she would have to face the future clean, sober, denied the drug of his being, his voice, his space in the world, his shape and tics. She feared that loss as much as opiate withdrawal. And the child in the vial was compensatory insurance, a little boy in his father's image, a Toddy doll to swaddle and coo to, to lullaby, to guide down the Avenue Of Life, to love in lieu of her dead man, her late husband.

I'm a widow, she could hear herself say; and she thought of Poor Eddie's poor mother, and of the appeal of a black mantilla. When she wasn't gliding serene on smack's white wings she was often angry at her love's forthcoming desertion of her, angry that he could ditch after he'd made her dependent on him, formed her to him in the mould of mutual sustenance. She was angry that she would have to reshape herself, that so many doggedly learned accommodations would have been in vain. The prospect of this loss afflicted her in a way Douglas's death hadn't. Oh, she had wept, she had grieved, she had hugged her mother, she had soared so high on shock that quotidian concerns had been obliterated by elemental things: death makes ontologists of us all. The anticipatory attrition of waiting for it to happen is harder to bear.

She wanted release through death or cure; Toddy was choosier, cure alone would do. But the Other neglected to deliver. He let Toddy down. Toddy tried to recall the selfless act that was evidently marring his record but could think of none. They must have been desperate to go to Poor Eddie. His only place in their world of two was as an eponym of cowering wretchedness: 'You *Eddie*!', 'He's such an Eddie'. Etc. As is habitually the case with such neologisms the meaning was inconstant. It also signified a whining sycophant, an enforced celibate, a gawky sap. They must have been desperate. It's a measure of their desperation, of their craving for life, of their shamelessness – even after Toddy had been diagnosed they would giggle at the poems Eddie sent. Heartfelt, pretentious, importunate – it made no difference, they were all items of contempt and ridicule which Bonny gleefully handed round to her friends, laughing, swaying.

She'd use him though, he was there to be used, that's what he was for. He was a monstrous magician who could pluck ills from a body as an ogre, having rent open a child's breast and plunged in a hand far as the wrist, might abort a heart to devour. What did Eddie do with the malignancies he hoovered? Where did the bad marrow go? Did the geek who shared her blood (more than she knew) really perform the acts ascribed to him? Bonny wanted to believe that he did. She needed her husband alive. She'd try anything. She talked about Eddie, talked him up – that was a self-delusory strategy. Talk. Laud. Invite concurrence. She talked one night at the house on the downs. She no longer bothered to quit the room when she needed a hit. She was naked in her appetites. Toddy moaned in a deep old chair whose stuffing pushed through parched leather, buboed the surface. A plaid pack of malt miniatures lay in his lap. He was bald and pudgy as a baby, as irritable too: his face was auto-caricatural, bum-smooth save where lined with lines incised like badland gullies. He was a baby made up to play old. He belted each bottle in a single shot: Highland Park, Strathisla, Ord. He replaced each empty in its set. It was the names he drank, it was the sentimental force he drank in (forbears, the personal past he'd never have the future to explore).

Catch him with a bottle in his hand on a Saturday at 4.57 when the permutable litany was weekly incanted and you'd see him cry for the places he knew he'd never go to, the places that had made his parents' parents' parents: Brechin, Forfar, Montrose, Arbroath. He'd always intended to go to them to allay their cheap poetry. He didn't follow football. Bonny would mention Pompey apropos of the Great Eddie and Toddy would murmur 'Pompey one Arsenal nil' in a display of divisional ignorance no one had the heart to correct.

He was suckling a lifesize bottle of Pictish spirit when he reached for my arm and said: 'You go there for me. Remember me in Elgin.'

There were glycerine tears on his baby cheeks, his fingers' skin was moss soft, he smelled of suffering and blankets. The big beaker of sentimentality bore me along and I said of course I would – and I did. And here's my plaid scarf from Johnson's of Elgin, discount Gordon, the tartan of the Tod sept: blue, green, and a yellow stripe like the one down my back when I was with them, with the couple in extremis.

They were frightening in their abandon. They were long gone, through the pane, tumbling on a different trampoline, subject to laws laid down by chemistry and mortal fear, moving out there, *limitless*. They'd believe anything. That Eddie could cause kidney stones to pass painlessly through the urethral tract. That the bad luck brought by elms beside a dew pond is deleted when a full moon shines into that pond. They sought signs, they found them: colours; the number of stakes in a wicket fence; cloud contours; the shapes of bales ranked in fields; the three-car, 60-mph crash they witnessed ahead of them on the Whiteparish side of Pepperbox – *that* was a happy portent. Two of the vehicles turned over, one having somer-saulted after contact; the third, a rusty Bedford packed with beergut and bum cleavage, flattened a hawthorn hedge. No one was hurt. Kiddies, mums, gramps – upside down families were intact. Not a graze. A sort of miracle – they both knew that. And they were fishing for a miracle, they were on their way to Pompey, on their way to Eddie – and here it was, a chance in thousands, the defiance of odds, the fluke Chubb craved as a hobbyist and denied as an actuary. Here was a miracle and it had paid its divvy to someone else, to labourers, to cheaply dressed people in old motors. They'd missed it by a couple of seconds, been rendered spectators rather than blessed actors in this 'Miracle Escape On A36'; they didn't need the *Southern Evening Echo*'s headline to tell them.

Toddy has twenty-eight and a half weeks left to him. Which time – its precise length unknown even to Eddie – his parents wish him to spend close by them, in the bosom. I.e. in London during the week, at the house on the downs weekends only. Bonny will fight with her in-laws over the death place, over the preparation for death; they'll scrap, as though contesting a chattel – and of course those will be contested too. At issue is ownership. Till death do . . . his wife's not of the blood; a temporary arrangement. *They* were the ones who gave him life, he is the stuff of their egg and seed, of their marriage – and their marriage has endured more than quarter of a century whereas their only son's rash espousal of (at best) a provincial sexpot can hardly be said to have stood the test. Three years. Against their twenty-eight. A half-numerate child of ten could tell you that each thus enjoys more than nine times as many rights in him as she does. Together that's about twenty times. And then there's the pecuniary investment as well as the temporal. What has the leech-in-law ever bunged in the kitty? She has squatted their property, besmirched their name. Now she intends to steal the corpse-to-be. She wants to deny him the anthumous dignity he deserves, wants to buoy him with false hope, submit him to a charlatan's clammy hands. They've seen the sordid orphan cousin (p. 296), watched him with incredulous distaste. They knew that his cheap suit covers a body whose blood is bad – it must be, he's a Vallender.

They are, perforce, students and casual historians of the Vallenders. They were, latterly, that benighted family's bankers and backers. They know more than anyone (save me) about the Vallenders' affairs (financial, amatory: there is a crossover), about the wretched wives, the luckless marriages, the self-inflicted damage, the hatred, the duplicity, the waste. They've seen photographs of Guy, of his frail good looks, his corruptible chin. They are themselves firework makers now. They own Pyrosouth (formerly Vallender Light). They own The Garth which they let back to Monica, for the moment. They know how Douglas Vallender died, they've read the post mortem, can tell you the weight of his liver, the contents of his lungs, what he ate for Christmas – which was, transformed, the contents of his lungs (p. 324). They have every cause not to wish to relinquish their expiring boy to the survivors of this bad blood-line.

Eddie was busy. Eddie was in demand. Eddie was the solution, the salvation, the balm before the storm of death, a hospice without walls.

There was HoTLoVe in Pompey. They had the sweats in Fratton. They vomited on The Front. Necks swelled. Men grew nipples on their backs. Pub people scratched. Hoban's Jump Disco bounced scratchers, most of them women. A ten-pint tar got badered on two. A gunnery instructor's balls grew like big red apples. The island city rasped with coughs. A garage receptionist's nails crumbled as she typed. A widower in his sixties emitted 'something white, like sour milk, Doctor, like curds that sting' from his nose.

The Founder could have done without the ones with chronic diarrhoea; even in the open air they were discernible; they did nothing for The Church and Eddie did nothing for them.

Faces grew prematurely old like those of professional sportsmen. Faces grew polka-dots – beetroot, rodent grey, mould green. The scratchers needed to scratch inside, to relieve their itching organs and scalded arteries: they couldn't, of course – so they wriggled in their ill-fitting skins, as though jolted by amps and dementia. A rare glaucoma manifested: rare in the speed of its development and in its impairment of vision, and in the age of its victims – a disease of middle and late life attacked three people in their twenties. There was hair so brittle it snapped. Teeth blackened overnight (almost).

HoTLoVe never lets on it's there, it spreads itself, wears masks. It has taken a leaf from syph's book, has learnt from that master. It mimics. It's a quick change artiste, protean (Sessions'll play it). It's so various no one notices that it's there. No one suspects. No one utters the word epidemic, let alone plague, because no one makes the link between a renal failure in Gosport and the part-timer in Jessie Road who can't get rid of the cold sores on her mouth not for love or money – it was love for money that got them there. On which subject:

An OMO wife, a stoker's missus, Denise G., refused to give a john French Gob followed by Full for the price of Hand. The john struck her. She ran from the door of her flat in her work clothes – a grubby basque and putty stockings that toned with her chubby sunless flesh. He followed her to the communal landing where he struck her again ('a right walloping belt it was'). He struck with such force that she tripped on her five inch working heels (this is truly an industrial injury) and fell backwards down a flight of concrete stairs. Denise G. received a life-saving blood transfusion at South Pompey General in the early hours of 12 March 1970. A Pompey Health District van was sent on what junior doctors called 'the vampire run' to a private clinic on Hayling which was found to have an abnormally large supply of blood of the patient's rare group AO-1. You can bet that she was the only OMO wife of that group in the whole of Pompey. She was back at work within a week. Because she had broken both hands in the fall she offered only French and Full and both of them at a celebratory discount price that was – irony – lower than that for Hand. This didn't endear her to the cartel of OMO wives in the reeking block at Landport – a minimum net price is a collectively agreed price and it's not to be undercut even by a supplier who suffers the temporary disadvantage of hands in plaster, a head turbanned by bandages, a face knitted with burgundy blanket stitches. Especially not when many gentleman customers are so literally blinded by strong liquor that they are incapable of noting such niceties which are, then, not disadvantages at all: the said gents are happy to empty themselves into the cheapest available vessel, happy in the prospect of matutinal amnesia. Denise G.'s business was never brisker. Never had she received – and given – such a volume of trade fluids. A bargain she was, a bloody bargain, and because she was a bargain there was a shortfall to make up which she made up by working through her bloody monthly which had, hitherto, been her week of rest, her week of housey and stout. She dared not take the time: Petty Officer Leading Stoker G. would never understand. When he arrived home from sea he expected money as well as *respect* as well as *minge on tap*. There was HoTLoVe in the navy, in messes, wardrooms, bunks, galleys. Let's sing the poison shanty of tars and tarts, of two ports in every boy: 'Fee fi fo fum yum yum yum let's all drink rum/ Fee fi fo fum yum yum yum let's come in yer bum . . .' Etc. P.O. Leading Stoker G. knew the words, knew the form. He sang home and away, on land and sea, and in between, at the shore establishments called stone frigates where he'd prowl and greet the boy matloes with a jocular 'that's a walloping pretty lunchpack you're carrying there my jack'. There was HoTLoVe in ships, HoTLoVe on decks. There was HoTLoVe on land, in port, in Landport, in dock pubs, in the knee-trembling realm of alleys and phone boxes, in the stained sheets which Omo had yet to wash the maps of Ireland from.

It was a foreign flu.[1] It was something nasty in the water. It was the Spithead Bite's revenge on an age which had dispensed with sail, rendered it redundant save at weekends. It was sailors overdoing the Nelson's Blood.[2] It was women got it most: the OMO wives, the once-a-week wives of adulterated marriages, the keen amateurs, the first timers, the competitive Wrens. Dr David Sadgrove – described in his *BMJ* obituary as a 'larger than life genito-urological legend' – was, by his own admission, *caught napping*. Like the rest he never thought virus, he never thought venus, he never thought pygmy. Of course he didn't; the only pygmies in Pompey are moral ones, they're not for eating. (Mock them, prod them, spy on them, yes. Eat, no.) Sadgrove was Blighty's man on Saigon Rose and Carcosa Fanny, Blonde Nonot, on gonorrhoeal strains out of Asia, on gleets with fancy names – yet HoTLoVe foxed him. He didn't see it (it wasn't *it*, it was them). He didn't discern the links which were causal, buried, way back – there was no commonality of symptom. There was not even HoTLoVe, not yet, not by name, there was just a gamut of afflictions, virulent and disparate. Women got it most – there were men too. Some of both were hardly sexually active. What they had in common was that mechanistic medicine had failed them. HoTLoVe was an ill wind and a fresh one too – new, without precedent. And thus initially incomprehensible, impervious to diagnosis since diagnostic practice is

---

[1] A pleonasm. *All* flus are foreign, all are attributed to elsewhere: China, Turkey, Russia, Asia; this is chauvinism in action.

[2] Rum. The sobriquet is evidently eucharistic; that is, cannibalistically celebratory. Strength is taken from the warrior's blood. His name is hallowed in the proof, it is *his* spirit that is imbibed. Hence 'Nelson's Courage', derived from and meaning the same as Dutch Courage (whose source is another spirit, Dutch gin or genever).

founded in comparison and comparison's posh sister simile. One diagnosis is, ideally, a synthesis of all previous diagnoses; it's dependent on former models; it builds a speculative present on yesterday's guesses.

The first insouciant victim to attend The Church Of The Best Ever Redemption was a shy nurse called Ronwen whose broken wrist wouldn't mend, whose hammerblow headaches had cost her her job. (Eddie had The Founder fix her up at Daph's where she tended vegetables in tartan rugs till presumed migraine again occasioned chronic absenteeism.) HoTLoVe was trade for Eddie. It drummed up business. He fed off the inexplicable, off Ronwen's perplexed anxiety, off hippocratic mendacity: what Doctor doesn't understand Doctor denies the existence of, or ascribes to psychogenic causes (where would Doctor be without them?) Poor Eddie was hope itself for the innocents, and they were all innocents, even Mary was an innocent. They came to him in hope, the sex gamblers who had lost, the hapless casuals who had sought the comfort of little death and found the big one thrown in for free.

'Those who live by the pork sword shall die by the pork sword,' preached The Founder, later, when the mystery ailments were shown to have the same father, so to speak, when HoTLoVe was known to have been behind all of them – by then HoTLoVe was an object of fear and awe. And Pompey was a quarantine island, an accidental lazaretto, it flew a yellow flag. A Pompey girl's prospects in the marriage market were dim. Folks believed a sneeze could kill, did folks. The ill were hunted down like Jews. There were beatings in alleys, drownings (now the water wasn't safe). The publican of The Fanny Adams[1] got a three-month stretch for serving beer in glasses washed at too low a temperature. Domestics were commonplace, so were false accusations, revenge castrations, poison pen letters about allegedly poison penises.

---

[1] Fanny Adams, 9, was murdered and dismembered by Frederick Baker in 1867. (He was hanged.) That same year Her Majesty's Navy began to include in its rations tinned meat, allegedly mutton but jocularly deemed to be child. Thus Sweet Fanny Adams fed the navy.

There was a chippie who blamed his fatal dose on a black veteran called Ruby. (The same? The same.) A divorcé, he sat alone in front of the telly fashioning a fascinum from soap; he carved diligently, for verisimilitude, and each evening stored the work in progress in the fridge. When it was finished he stuck it with a yard broom's stiff bristles. It was an exemplary instrument of torture: infantile and obscene (it was laughable; it was a sight-gag about a lubricious hedgehog; it was a porcupine sword). When he went to visit Ruby in Auckland Road East (she had not moved far from the War Memorial (p. 102)) he carried it in his dun canvas tool bag.

Ruby would not have died had it not been for the unwillingness of surgeons to operate to remove the bristles from the vagina and womb: there was too much bad blood; no Pompey doctor believed any more in the prophylactic efficacy of mask and gloves; she bled to a happy death on a stretcher; the Dead Beat squad that came to take her to the incinerator at Kingston Cemetery included her son, Mad Bantu. He felt nothing for her, they were estranged: it was the way he treated women she had abhorred. Now she was another job of work, another dead mother, another load to lift into the lorry. And, besides, there were rules that the Dead Beat worked to: no sentimentality, no blubbing, let's keep personalities out of this, any sign of emotion and you're off the case, it's just the usual bundle of poison so treat it that way please. No one got out of line, this was a growth opportunity, the best paid graft in Pompey, who'd blow it for the sake of a tear? HoTLoVe hardens hearts.

Eddie saw that. Even before HoTLoVe had a moniker of its own Prescient Eddie could feel it, could sense its presence in the eyes of the congregation. He began to sense it along about the time Sonny and Laddy were on bail for criminal damage and illegal entry (of Chubb's house). He sensed a bond between these people with their strange afflictions of wrist, liver, septum, colon, whatever; some suffered aphasia, some suffered lumbar catastrophes. All their complaints were chronic. Colds didn't go. Cuts didn't heal. Nails didn't grow. All their complaints revealed themselves, in time, as achronic. You – you will itch forever. You – you're going to have that black eye so long as you live, you're always going to carry the shiner the old man gave you when he discovered what you'd given him: it's a badge, you belong. Only Eddie discerned pandemic collectivity, unwitting union. He began to understand that there were people (whom he touched, whom he transmitted the might of his will to, whom he bathed in all his beneficence, whom he treated with the indiscriminate zeal that had informed his entire ministry, whom he tried to heal as he had tried to heal every soul who had ever submitted to him), certain people, a growing proportion, who were beyond cure, who *knew* they were beyond cure, who sought confirmation of their proximate mortality, who sought absolution in his body and hands, who believed that he was the vehicle of the Best Ever Redemption, who believed in him.

Ruby had believed in Poor Eddie; the name Vallender meant nothing to her after twenty-five years, her memory was shot, trade diseases and cider had taken out the meninges, oh, long ago. But no matter how ill she had been she'd always trusted that she'll pull through. This was different. HoTLoVe carries its prospectus with it, no matter how it manifests it tells its host *this is it, this is the one*, this is the last illness you'll have the chance to suffer, this is the real maladie d'amour. (The French acronym was MDA – which lacks the ring.) HoTLoVe was made for Eddie. HoTLoVe made Eddie. It lent him dignity, it gave him responsibility for terminal lives. There was nothing his hands and his heat could do to deliver the OMO wives and the competitive Wrens from aches, ruptures, sores, psoriasis, kettle scale on their teeth; but he, uniquely, could quell the fear, douse the panic. It was as though he'd looked round the corner at the end of The Avenue Of Life and could deliver an unreservedly affirmative report. He, uniquely, could solace the dying, prepare them for the move from one state into the next, could convince them that the move was an elision not a cut, that The Melody Field, The Good Guy's Garden Of Chums, The Buttercup Carpet, The Bounteous Fellowship Cloister, Serenity Meadow, The Village With A Song In Its Heart were as happily dappled and brightly buntinged as their names make out. Eddie was dragoman and proselytiser; he was The Founder's voice –

his vowels were softer though, and that was a boon for there was no suspicion of mockery, of a double edge. He was a comfort. He was sincere. He combined familiarity with inspiration, like carpet slippers with winged heels. He was The Founder's only True Son. He was held in awe. He was a parish god. He was revered because he had a purpose, he was a utility. The Good Guy's star had fallen, The Founder asserts, because the wrong people looked after His interests: all take and no give. They demand worship and reciprocate with bugger all. The dry-cleaner of souls has got to get the spots out or else the punters will do it themselves – the Dabitoff syndrome of 'personalised' beliefs, disorganised religion, anarchy.

Through Eddie The Good Guy was made to give value, to compete, to provide a pointful service in return for the adulation and idolatry: 'Working For His Worship' was the ambiguous legend on the postcards of Eddie that were for sale at The Church Of The Best Ever Redemption. Also available: The Founder, The Cross Of The World, The Cross Of The World (Floodlit). Best seller: Eddie. His face is humility itself. His famous hands are frozen in beseechment. He can be peeped at in the purses and the wallets of the afflicted, on their mantelpieces, on tables beside the beds they'll one day soon not wake in. He is their strength, he is their light, he is their guide. And they do not have to take his existence and his magic on trust: he's flesh and bone and blood – see, here's the photo of him; and they've felt his heat, heard the message from his hands. There can be no doubt. And Eddie was loyal to his cultists, loyal to the end, for they allowed him the licence to display a gamut of powers that were hieratic rather than merely remedial.

Sonny told The Founder: 'Eddie's taking over Dad. He's going top of the bill. It's like in a band when one guy becomes the man. All eyes on him.'

'You're thinking short term Sonny. The boy's bound to have his hour isn't he? It's the way they write the score . . . An hour doesn't last for ever.'

Bonny was made to wait.

'I'm his cousin,' she insisted.

The woman pushed a pamphlet into an envelope, licked,

410

sealed, added it to the pile. The skylit subterranean room is a trove of Buttist gewgaws: those postcards, stacks of *Butt Joking Aside*, models of The Cross Of The World, tracts, T-shirts, catalogues, badges, stickers, souvenir mugs, plates, plastic chickens, .oo scale wheelchairs, pottery pigs.

The woman's long-suffering smile: 'Cousin! I'm his sister – but *I* can't go barging in. You're welcome to . . . There's plenty to read.'

Bonny stumbles against a loaded table, she points to the door. A brown cloud fitted tight into the section of sky above Fort Widley's enceinte. It didn't flatter The Cross. The structure's grimy, the concrete's streaked, it's already aging gracelessly, it's pissed on by rain though never by public sector tabloids who may not fear The Good Guy's dander but know all about the Voys.

Around the base are the ad hoc crosses of Buttist disciples – devotion through mimicry: wooden stakes, fence posts, metal bed ends, string, electric flex, sawn crates, chopped tables, twisted wire, lino, brick, breezeblock. A bladder of cirrus seeps from the brown cloud like albumen haemorrhaging from a boiling egg. Rain polishes the ground, beads the car's windows but not so thoroughly that Toddy's turquoise beret, squashed against the nearside quarterlight, is obscured. It still adds colour to a dog of a day, to her dog of a life. Toddy's slumped against the glove compartment, coma'd by his bottle – bless Highland Park. Bless too the telltale fog of condensation – he's still alive (she never knows when he won't be), she's thrilled by the water from his broken lungs. She leans across the car, chin on the roof, breathes the squally wet warmth from the west. And that is how she is when Eddie sees her.

He emerges from The Founder Bunker, a healer with a briefcase, apprised of his cousin's presence but disbelieving, mystified; tremulous with excitement. He has not heard from her for a year and a half. She never even acknowledges receipt of his poems. Yet she has been thinking of him all the time! She has, she has. And here is the proof: her presence, her self in cowgirl suede and duster coat and western boots. Eddie stands in the doorway. She has never looked lovelier than she looks

411

today in the high romantic rain and poignant breeze. The Good Guy's got it right, He's laid on the very weather of mature reconciliation. They'll walk hand in hand along Pompey front oblivious to the bounding waves that are excited *for them*. Eddie creeps up behind Bonny and puts his arms around her so she starts, so she scowls at him with affront, so she pushes him off like he's a tiresome pooch. (She doesn't want this to move too fast, thinks Eddie.) He backs off with a placatory grin. A Flamebryte driver bangs his horn, leaves control of the wheel to elbow bend, utters a rogueish phoneme, mimes masturbation, revs the engine so it roars with lupine rapacity. Bonny pecks Eddie on the cheek, withdraws again. She's a petitioner, she has to watch it, she cannot let herself express the revulsion she feels (she's never forgotten the feel of his blind tongue fumbling inside her mouth, wetting itself from fear, from too long postponed excitement). But nor does she wish to feed the fantasies that Eddie's poems bear witness to. She has to court him for Toddy. She has to measure the encouragement she offers him: promise without delivery, that's the trick. Hints. Obliquity. Lies, lies, lies for the sake of the life that is more precious to her than any other. All the lies she has told before have, again, been mere rehearsals.

Eddie does not see the turquoise beret, he sees nothing but Bonny, he tells her: 'I always knew you'd come . . . I did. And I knew it would be raining . . .' And so on.

His rapture is mitigated when Toddy's sleeping form is shown him but he cheers up immensely when apprised of the cancers, of their gravity, of their extent. And if Bonny is only to be won by a show of solicitude to the bundle of malignancies she claims to love – well, so be it. Eddie can fake it. He can ask, simoniously, for donations towards The Cross's maintenance. He, too, can lie, with devilish imagination; he can offer the prospective excuse that when his dreams are *realistic*, when 'nothing dreamlike happens in them', his powers of cure and comfort are diminished. Such dreams are symptomatic of 'low levels in my psychic reservoir' which, implicitly, feeds his magic (his word). He warns her further that he is not a machine, that he can guarantee nothing, that reactions are incalculable, that dis appointments are inevitable and 'part of the job, regrettably'. He pretends to (a now atypical) modesty. He offers her small hope. He warns her not to expect a miracle. *But he will do all he can, his utmost.*

Poor Eddie can wait. He has waited all his life. He's waited since he stroked his cousin's pudendum beneath her nappies (p. 31). He did what, Johnson!? He could wait till the wens had joined hands and squeezed the last of life from Donald Hogg-Tod. That would not be so long coming, he can see to that, he can make the name fulfil its fate, live up to the meaning he relishes – dead pig.

'If you were a linguist, Eddie,' said The Founder the first time he'd heard this double barrel mentioned, 'you'd know that was a *very* unfortunate moniker. You're wasting your time with pigs. I've had up to here with pigs. Stupid animals. They take fright. They could fly if they wanted, if they tried. It was shown to me and I saw, I know and can tell you that they could – if they was built different . . . But look at them. Losers.'

Toddy the loser, Eddie the winner. He could wait to take the trophy.

He'd have to wait, for Toddy's health improved under his negligent care; he had not previously considered himself a placebo. He comes to believe he is the transmitter of Bonny's will, that Toddy's reprieve (Oh Lord make it brief) is a sign of her working through him. Their affinity! Not the way he'd have chosen to have it revealed to him, but nevertheless, what singular proof of their bond (he tells himself); The Good Guy's a prankster, a caution (he tells himself). What a wheeze, what a sense of humour. The more studied his indifference, the more Toddy thrives; the more Bonny wills her husband to cling to life, the closer she grows to her future lover (he tells himself); they are complementary parts of a life-support system. Poor Eddie buys her a 78 rpm recording of 'Nuts' by Pearl Dennis with Les Lesley's OCTU-Roons (Decca 1942):

> I'm the nut, you're the bolt.
> Finding you gave me such a jolt.
> I'm nuts about you honey.
> Don't you ever bolt, my honey.

413

Stoned and stumbling, Bonny drops it, smashes it before she has listened to it. But she didn't tell him, that would have been too cruel – he worked so hard for her, for them, so doggedly, so devotedly that Toddy was infected by hope.

OMO wives and their ilk (*passim*) were so done down by life (i.e. by the animals called men who rendered them tripartite receivers – of, in this order, fee then seed then HoTLoVe), were so contaminated by everyday transports that they knew it had to end. They weren't young; the clock had begun to tick anyway; they accepted the finiteness of what The Founder calls Avenue Span Time.

Toddy didn't accept: on his twenty-sixth birthday he stretched out his arms and said to Bonny, 'I feel today darling as though I can live for ever.'

They were on the beach at Alverstoke, 27 June 1974. Then he coughed, but only a little – not a Keats's last. There's a cute wooden house on the shingle, all the way across Pompey from Eddie's shack, a mirror sort-of, but make nothing of that – shacks aren't twinned. They could buy picnics from it, sandwiches and crisps; he'd wash down the salt and the chemical cheddar with purest malt then she'd hurl the bottle for him, to Spithead so it reeled on the way, light-played above the Wight horizon – the refractive poetry of empties, spent spirit etc.

They were there often. They were good attenders (Butt noted). They were necessary converts to The Church Of The Best Ever Redemption which is Pompey's Own. There was always another bottle in the car. Bonny drove. Toddy was even more clean-shaven now he was with Butt. They sang, they clapped. They tried to understand the primacy of fowl. They accepted The Founder's dictates in *The Reality Of Reality*. They felt The Good Guy's presence in all things. He's the genie in the Lagavulin; he's always there, too, in every grain, in every gram. Toddy's head shines, the biggest pebble on the beach that stretches to Lee; he glimmers with the prospect of Life's indefinite stretch. He plays ducks and drakes, he makes himself a kelp crown, and (when he isn't trying to breath, when he isn't trying to survive) he cockers about like a day-release and believes he's through it, that he's reborn, ready for the rest of his life. Magic Eddie. Spaz Vallender has come right. *I was going to live*. Poor Eddie, poor poor Eddie: Toddy loved you, then, in those months of happy triangular deceit.

Once upon a time there was Bonny and there was Toddy and there was Eddie and they lived in The Palace of Delusion: mutual manipulation, endemic dishonesty, stupid optimism – these were the shifting bases. But there was, through the summer, a kind of constancy. The lies they told themselves and each other were tonic, necessary crutches.

Which occurred first, 1) or a). And if it was 1) did it also precipitate a) rather than merely precede it.

a) On Tuesday 20 August 1974 Bonny Hogg-Tod signed a six-month tenancy agreement with Chasnev Properties Ltd for a furnished flat, £30 p.w., fifth floor, sea views, canoeing lake and putting green views, sloathlike Otis, garage parking, south-facing balcony with striped awning, lounge and two bedrooms, nice furniture considering, thin walls but no thinner than all the other jerry-builds of modern Pompey. She told Eddie she could no longer bear the drive from the house on the high downs – an hour at least each way, three times a week, Toddy car-sick like a child, the traffic jams at Fareham, the crawl through So'ton's suburbs (leafy and lovely as they are). She was blinded by oncoming headlights (she was apprised of The Founder's Tragedy). The sea air was good for Toddy, the more the better. She enjoyed the fellowship of The Church. Etc. It may all have been true.

Eddie believed he understood the covert truth that she dare not articulate. He was excited that she was going to live in Pompey, near him. She was coming close to him. But he wouldn't take advantage. He'd bide his time. She had to move carefully, he appreciated that. This decision, to take a flat by Esplanade Gardens – that close to him! – was an unequivocal gesture, he knew what it meant, she didn't have to say. He resolved to admire her inner strength, her loyalty to her expiring husband, her sense of duty, her self denial.

Alasdair Hogg-Tod bellowed down the phone at her. He didn't even attempt to check his anger. The earpiece was hostile, its grid a cage that could not contain him. He delivered a bosom-of-the-family tirade: he called her selfish, irresponsible, thoughtless. He asks who pays (though he knows that she knows that £780 is nothing to him).

'You've offended your mother-in-law,' he barks, erasing whatever intimacy there once was between Bonny and Jill, emphasising the latter's rank, abstracting her, depersonalising her – now she is a position, a title, a type. She is every mother-in-law there ever was, fighting with another woman for the son she bore and succoured, whom she gave the taste of tit to, who appeased the consequent appetite at the enemy's breast in the immemorial act of betrayal. (Every pearl necklace that a boy gives a girl is an arrow in his mother's flesh: happy the boy whose mother is as pierced as Sebastian.)

She is claiming her right to watch him die as she watched him born. That will be painful but at least symmetry will be served, the circle completed. The parenthetical parents – the idea of it makes her weep.

Alasdair addressed Bonny as a 'quack's dupe' and regretted it for she put the phone down. He rang back; the advantage had shifted to Bonny. She claimed that it was Toddy's idea that they took this flat, that Alasdair and Jill were putting their interests and convenience before his – which was true: the dying have no voice, their frailty is there to be exploited, their very disability makes them attractive quarry. The immediately anthumous period is rehearsal for the prospectively bereaved; they can practise their grief; they can gull the dying with declarations of love that they have not found the time to make these twenty-five years past; they can assure the terminal case of the regard in which he will be held; they can forget that *his name shall live forevermore* is a shoddy lie and tell it as though they believe it – besides which, what kind of comfort would there be in it were it true? They can take the opportunity to redeem themselves, to show The Good Guy whose side they're on. ('You can't fool him that way. He doesn't even have to sniff does he? Staring him in the face.') Bonny was adamant: 'It's where Donald wants to be. *Ask him* . . . It's what he wants. He hasn't given up . . . he's not prepared just to sit around and wait for it to happen. The difference is – ' tearful – 'you just want to get it over with don't you . . . You're just willing it to happen so you can get back to normal. Me – I'm never going to get back to normal. I want him to live . . . I'll do anything that . . . so he can. Anything . . . I'm sorry if it makes it difficult for you . . . But the quack, as you call him – he's the only person who's given Donald any sort of hope. That's why we're here.'

Her voice is thick with sobs, she whinnies, she emits strangulated staccato hoops, her consonants are approximate.

1) An afternoon, a Sunday no doubt, a sunny day for sure for every tabloid had his top off so that his body might be read, so that the sun might redden the trunk to match the arms. The Cross shone. Congers writhed on the pavement like mighty maggots (plenty of those too). There was flesh overlapping deckchairs. Tots with celluloid propellers. Tots with candy floss. A clock of flowers. A Sunday for play, for torpor and tag, you be he, let's chat the talent. Toddy loved the bright banality, the way neon's bleached by the sun, rendered puny by that might, the smell of abattoir waste fried with onions, the silly hats, the matey goosing that leads to HoTLoVe, to an unwanted pregnancy at best. They rode in their capsule through it and Toddy didn't once think that any of these people with their base tastes and coarseness and lolling guts deserved cancer. But then he didn't think he'd have it much longer either: it wouldn't be his to give. They were going to Eddie's for 'a drink and a sandwich'. They knew well enough that the hut at Eastney Spit (p. 381) was Eddie's retreat, that no one went there uninvited, that few were invited. At The Church it was spoken of with awe, as a holy place. Toddy was hot; he wore a midnight blue velvet suit that was unusually smart but, also, unseasonal. He wriggled. Bonny cursed pedestrians. When they reached the Spit it was worse. The sun had brought them out in their thousands. The road to the Hayling Ferry thronged with grockles and their dietary problems and unplanned families. The car snailed between high hulls and winding gear, lobster pots and outboards, between parked cars and oil-knuckled hobbyists fending the questions of snotty tots: 'It's called a rudder – now why don't you piss along off little man.' Dads glared at Bonny, they held a stop palm to her car and a restraining arm to their families – weekends, fatherhood and traffic make tyrants of the meek, generals of janitors.

A pick-up towing a boatless trailer forced her off the metalled road; the rear wheels spat freckled shingle, she sweated. 'That'll be it, that one,' she said to Toddy.

Eddie has toshed his hut with tar, under this sun it's fondant as liquorice, blazed with white paint on the window frames and the door above which is bolted the legend 'Haven On Earth'. There is nowhere to park. The road is reduced to a single track with cars on either side. Toddy gets out. He walks with his walking stick along the salt acne'd boardwalk to the hut; gulls miaow their greeting, a sail stands erect in salute, Bonny takes pride in the firm purpose of his steps. This is a man whose death sentence has been commuted: he may drag his left leg like it's been mantrapped but there is a hint of the spring in the right all right, that's obvious to anyone expert in his ambulatory manners. And when he breathes now it is with the *expectation* of air's influx. The air may not oblige. But he no longer denies himself the possibility of a full measure occurring, one of these days, today, who knows. He has been invested with hope – and that's a miracle in itself. He wears his hats with swagger not shame. A Hat Can Say Something Positive About You – Bonny had read that headline to a magazine article about Pimp Style velvet fedoras and bought him two. She read elsewhere that 'there is no ignominy today in a toupee or up to the minute hairweave' – she's going to look into that soon. She taps the horn, he grins, they wave. She turned and drove back, looking for a space for the car. The thermoses and beach bags may scowl but she is untouched, they can't quash her exhilaration. They are winning, the three of them, The Church too, the whole aviary. Her fancy was right. Her dream is coming true. Eddie can work miracles. She is beaming behind the wheel and hardly notices she is nearly at Fort Cumberland before she finds a gap long enough to fit into.

It must have taken her five minutes to walk to the Haven On Earth. She was brisk. The sun – The Good Guy's personal sun lamp[1] – was directed at her left flank, it warmed her heart. Masts

[1] 'Why did white man get where he is today? Because we wasn't greedy with The Good Guy's sun lamp. He favoured us because we wasn't greedy – not like some I could mention. We didn't borrow it without His say so. Look at the grief that came to them that did. Look at Africa.' *Butt What If?* (Pompey, 1973).

clanged and bright flags fluttered, tanned backs bent over saws and planes so that vertebrae pushed skin like stones in a stocking – she wanted to run her hand along these dorsal pennines, not from lust but from pleasure in their plasticity. Oh here's to creation! To the ozone, to the lapping wavelets, to white foals that go gently to and fro. Here's to the cirrus that beautifies the sky. The metalled road was sticky, shimmering, ripe for mirage. A child's ball bounced towards her, wobbling as it rolled, humptied by imperfect inflation, slowing with parabolic lurches till it rested at her feet. She stooped to retrieve it. Its colours made her two again – the creamy lapis, the crimson going on cerise, that white's tinged with clay. For just as long as it took to take them in she was a New Elizabethan again, in her pram again subject to a gentle hand that warmed her through. She held the doughy plastic with unwitting reverence, just for a moment. Then she carried the ball to a little boy whose hurrying father thanked her with a thumb up.

She turned towards the hut. She shivered. Its white door opens – and Toddy steps from it. A renewed Toddy, a fresh husband. She sees him blink at the sun's glare. She doesn't see him blink, she's too far away, she sees the hunching of his shoulders that used invariably to accompany that ocular tic. She gasps.

His hair has grown again, and when he moves there is no limp. (He's even discarded his walking stick; of course, he would, if he didn't need it. And the hat. He's left the hat with his healer so he can show off his new hair – darker than the old, tar black. That's a further miracle.)

Bonny ran, ran, ran; ran across the shingle, ran through it. It swallowed her feet, bit off her shoes. She screamed with exhilaration: 'Darling, Darling, Darling . . .' She sprung onto the boardwalk, she didn't feel the nail that punctured her instep. She yelled to him. She spread wide her arms. He hasn't heard her. He hasn't seen her. He is patting the pockets of his midnight blue suit, searching. She is only twenty feet from him with her arms spread wide, with her eyes lit, with her smile stretching to rip her face. She is closer than that when he looks up, alerted by the pounding feet, the reverberating planks, the voice above the metal halyards and gusts and gulls. He looks up and he is no longer Toddy.

She stops, a body length from Mary. Her facial contortion is so marked that he wonders if she's ill. She smiles feebly: 'I . . . I mistook . . .'

He points to the hut's door, decisively, making a pistol of his finger. His hair shines like petrol. She cannot take her eyes off him.

He says: 'You don't remember me? Your wedding? I was in the band. Yeh? I'm Mary – hullo.'

She shook his hand, not without hesitation. She shook his hand for longer than she might have done.

Mary's eyes are half shut against the sun. He does not reveal that he can read her. He knows how struck she is. She thinks his hair is the most beautiful she has ever seen (which of course is why she wanted it to belong to Toddy). And she thinks his face is the most beautiful she's ever seen, apart from Toddy's *as it was*, i.e. when Toddy was illumined by his delight in her and untouched by pain, despair, false hope.

Mary gestured to the white door: 'Here you are. I must hurry. I have to talk to a builder. See you again.' Bonny watched him run towards the ferry's landing stage. He sprung along with such ease, with such vital grace.

In Eddie's hut it was gloomy and airless. It smelled of sardines (which Eddie had mashed with vinegar to fill sandwiches). Toddy was already drinking whisky.

Bonny wanted to talk about Mary. Why was he so called? Who was he? Etc. It strikes like that. It's an immediately consuming force. It obliterates. It's greedy for attention. It's total. They sat in deckchairs in the half-dark. Bonny longed for the mention of his name, dared not speak it lest the extent and genus of her interest show in her face's improper bloom, in a too-delicate casualness, in a clumsy attempt to lead conversation in his direction. Conversation. Toddy was mute. He gazed at Eddie with pupillary goofiness, nodding in indiscriminate agreement. Eddie poured from a Thermos.

There was no conversation. Eddie outlined The Founder's forthcoming (and subsequently notorious) edict on hang-gliding.[1] He dog-eyed Bonny with sly prideless lust. Sun

[1] Hang-gliding is a sin of presumption because 'it was not given to man to be able to fly. It's nothing less than blasphemous. The Good Guy set His personal Sun Lamp on

420

squeezed through gaps in the walls, through knot-holes, through warped bleached Venetian blinds; motes swam like plankton in cuneiform rays. As Toddy drank more so Eddie moved his deckchair closer to Bonny's. His breath smelled of sardines. Bonny blurted: 'Who was that French guy? One who was here. Said he was in the band that played at our wedding? . . . I don't remember him.'

'Mary? The Traitor? . . . That's what we call him . . . He used to be an important, uh, *presence* in my life. But . . .' Poor Eddie shook his head and smiled wanly. 'He's not French, he's Belgian . . . It's very complicated – what I feel about Mary. He was a good friend . . . the best. You know, you think you've got a friend for life. Then he lets you down. Not by any specific action. Just . . . just gradually, he withdraws. There's no loyalty in him. He once told me he'd used it all up . . . Imagine that. He's a bit of a con man, is Mary. Ray sniffed him out a long while back . . . There are those that are taken in though. I was – and I count myself a good judge of character. May Butt still is, Ray's mum. She's having this house built for them, over Hayling there. Their dream house on the dunes.'

She thought of her dream house on the downs, of how it was soured by disease, of how its very fabric – every eave and lath – was contaminated. It was a nightmare house.

It must have been that day that she decided to move to Pompey. It must have been that day that she realised that all Eddie had given her broken man was hope. Hope had grown in direct proportion to the gravity of his illness. The more cancers the more hope. Hope apes cancer, it feeds on itself, it balloons and spreads. Toddy's face against striped canvas: he smiles a mad smile, his flesh is skate white, he must be rehearsing the ghost role, he is hopeful of success in it (of course).

While the nights were still warm, while the breeze across Esplanade Gardens was still the right side of autumn, while he could lean against a scrolled metal bench without its stinging his

Icarus to teach us a lesson. These heathens haven't heeded it.' This antipathy was occasioned by the sight of a hang-glider racing on a thermal above The Cross Of The World during a service. The Founder subsequently decreed that it was permissible to shoot at hang-gliders, but only when they are in the air, blaspheming.

kidneys Poor Eddie would sit there, hidden between the faded, papery roses and the indeciduous hedge around the model village. He would sit with his head inclined just so, with his hands clasped; the very picture of a thinker, a meditative solitary. Which was a picture he was happy to paint, for no one – not even a peeper – wants to be taken for a peeper, end up in the rag as a frotting Tom. He watched Bonny's flat, interpreted the paltry shadow play, saw her come and go, drive and park. He wondered at the hours she kept, at her destinations, but he couldn't follow, he had no car, no licence (because he was still unable to convince any of the examiners that, despite his ambidexterity and articulate feet, he had the eye/brain/hand/foot co-ordination to perform the base skill of car driving (p. 379)). Sometimes she returned within half an hour, hurrying from the forecourt into the bright, glass-fronted hall of the block, forgetting more than once to turn off the car's lights so red warnings shone throughout the night and only faded towards dawn: another day, another set of jump leads. Eddie guessed that those nights she had gone no further than The Hop Horse, to score – hence her alacrity. He could watch her ascend the stairs, two at a time. She was too jittery to await the lift. Other nights? He had no idea where she went. The flat was unlit and Toddy presumably asleep, presumably morphed on Fluorotext-rate and Highland Park (the wider neck gives greater access), presumably unaware of her absence; there was so much he was unaware of.

Toddy never found out for certain about Mary. She kept that from him. The walls in the flat were thin, and yes, the eternal soundtrack did pass through them, but Bonny and Mary only performed their drastic action when the deadish husband was comatose or drunk (which was often); and even then they gave priority to swiftness of prosecution, quality not quantity, passion not endurance; there were other times for marathons, longer ones in different beds. She locked Toddy's room of course, caged him in his cuckold's pen, had ready an excuse: 'But if you were to stagger out onto the balcony – and you know how unsteady you are sometimes. And the railing is so low . . .' But she never had to use it. She giggled lewdly into Mary's swollen ear that the noise was probably an additional soporific, a lullaby of adultery. She felt bad about it, sure. She felt she'd hit rock bottom and was now mining the rock to go further down. But her duplicity relieved her. She had forgotten the thrill of deceit, there's nothing to match the thrill of deceit. Duty doesn't excite like crime against the dying. She dared herself to take chances, scream her orgasms, teeter on the brink of discovery (but she never yelled *that* loud, never pitched it so the fantasy was likely to be ruptured by smashed doors, tears, recrimination). She lay in the arms of her future, the replacement model; his body was a wonder, he was brand new. The past snored. The other side of the wall, less than a foot away from the big hands that stroked and probed her, the past rumbled with dyspepsia, gabbled dream lingo, rolled so the bed fluted a puny solo in response to the bellowing duet from this side. Even when there was a trail of talc and blood from Bonny's bed Toddy suspected nothing. He may have attributed it to smack-driven carelessness, to clumsiness with her toilet, to overhaste with her works. He may even not have noticed it. Talc and blood were Mary's telltales. He left them beside beds as an otter leaves spraints, inevitably.

Bonny had tracked her man, tracked him in love's daze, singlemindedly. She damned the consequences. She acted with addict's possession. She was addicted to him too. He was a bottle, a line, a needle. She submitted without struggle. She could not resist the urge to find him, to incant his name, to scour crowds for him. She lost count of the times she thought she'd glimpsed him. She had sought him without recourse to Eddie.

She had, eventually, driven to Hayling from The Church. Late one afternoon she had found herself driving to Hayling, crossing the Langstone bridge, trailing behind a lorry loaded with bricks. She followed it along a shore road hardly proud of mud and spart grass. When it stopped the site workmen greeted her with whistles, bent elbows, immodest boasts, coarse suggestions. She was in love and thus uniquely focused, chaste in a way. She locked the car door and wound down the window by a single measure. 'C'm on darl what about some lip

423

service then . . . Does it look like dunes . . . Does it look like an 'ouse . . . You wanna try South Hayling.'

She crossed the flat land of piggeries and bungalows, mended hedges and thistle fields. Then there were waterwing shops and parades of chippies. A walnut face with a money satchel and a donkey stood beside a carousel at a children's fair. The beach was beyond him, then the platinum sea. He pointed west. The bushes are horizontal here. Scavenging dogs, wilder by the day, fight over bones and burger boxes. Half a crescent of urban houses gapes seawards, stranded, sand-buttressed, dream houses of another age, a fragment of the dreamed city that was to have risen, white as Brighton, on this gusty shore. Hayling Regis? Never. The marine prospect may still be there but the stucco's blown and the windows want panes. That's the fate of Hayling houses. The car bumped along a track with a central stripe of lanterns and tansies. The sea, over there to her left, is brim full, meniscal, ready to spill. It looms above the land – which is impervious to it, so dry it promises fire, so dry it crackles like flames beneath the tyres. Furze, gorse, a rusting trough, distant groynes that stand up like charred beams, a paintless metal shed all wrapped about with thorns. And then the dunes; they're downs in sand, mutating models of the downs, large scale models; their mammose smoothness is defiled by sharp grasses that cut, that iridesce like steel brooms as He switches down the Sun Lamp and tells us all to go to bed.

The dream house on the dunes was the dream foundations on the dunes, the dream armature above it, a silhouetted skeleton, an illegible timber frame upon which perch navvies and carpenters, uniformly shirtless. She hadn't expected him to be there. She had counted on no more than unwitting misinformation from workmen, the first thread of a clew. Had she even entertained the possibility of his being there she'd have stopped in a lay-by to make up, she'd have . . .

He wore all white. He was radiant as a bride. He patted a labourer's shoulder and sauntered towards her. He was apparently unsurprised by her presence. She said: 'Hullo . . . I was just passing – ' They laughed together, without embarrassment. She held her hand to her mouth, girlishly. But even that gesture was redundant, a flirty mitigation of her nakedness. She was wearing clothes – jeans and a jean jacket – but she might as well have not been: her posture, her teeth, her wet pebble eyes were those of a self-offering nude. He showed her the foundations, fleshed the skeleton. She thought of feigning a stumble, an excuse to take his arm but, emboldened by his suss, held it anyway, and it didn't tense, it gripped her wrist to his ribs, trustfully. He described a house he had lived in as a child (pp. 11, 58, 171). She granted supra-importance to 'light play', 'specially advanced', 'open shelter'; she adored these qualities because he adored them and was reproducing them. He flung forth his other arm. Amatory abandon? No, his watch was under his cuff. He had to go. He declined a lift so she made an exaggeratedly long face. He compensated by taking a biro from a passing ear and writing a number on her wrist; this was a token of intimacy, of possession. It was a functional tattoo he gave her, a Neapolitan brand.[1] The number was his phone number. He had spoken so many other numbers, prices, five-figure sums – the cost of the house, the daily cost of labour, the costs of gifts to a planning committee; he had a head full of figures. She prayed that he'd written the right one. Then he was away – he turns to blow her a kiss and then he's a head in the sandhills, tramping towards the Pompey ferry. She sits in the car, smiles secretively, ignites the engine. The wheels spin, the more throttle she gives them the deeper the trenches they dig for themselves. The engine screeches, she is helpless, swallowed by sand. Two workmen came towards her waving their arms, telling her to cut the engine. They tutted, shook their heads. It took all their strength to free her, she was in that deep. She stopped in a lay-by to transcribe the number, to spit and rub till it was a hardly discernible smudge, no cause for uxorial suspicion. She had it by memory before she'd written it in her address book. She put no name beside it, entered it under F, for future. She was thinking ahead.

The first time Mary undressed before her he counted the

---

[1] It is a male Neapolitan practice to scar women's faces as a mark of ownership, and to render them less attractive to rivals. See – Christian Schad, *Selbstbildnis mit Modell*, 1927.

change in his pockets. Curiosity and care rather than avarice. He talked about money. He often collected it for May Butt, whenever her regular rent-collector was hospitalised. Mary and Mad Bantu against the tenants. He had gig fees outstanding, always. He had Albeau's royalties to winkle out of offices in Uccle. He had related small claims to pursue in Anderlecht and Paris. She was naked, lotus-seated on a sofa in the flat in the block May Butt owned by the Sallyport, by the narrow harbour mouth which the big ships surged through, bursting with seamen eager for the crack, eager to spend their savings on an OMO wife, deposit them there. She was naked, droop lipped, a carnal oblation, a feast for him – and he was checking pennies. He stood behind her, stroking her hair, stroking her face, stroking her breasts. She felt his glans against the nape of her neck, she felt the moisture, she felt dorsal electricity. She turned her head so that she could rub it against her cheek. He moved back: 'No. Wait a moment.' She toyed with her penile analogue, counted herself lucky not to have a bouncing blood baton getting in the way of doors, counted herself equally lucky to have use of same, now and then. He came back clutching a photographic print wrapped in tissue paper and a tin of talcum powder. He kneeled in front of her, shook it onto her pubic bush, impatiently thumbed off the perforated colander top, filled his palm with the powder, worked it into the soft hair. He scrutinised his work. He told her to lean her head back as far as she could, so the occiput rested on top of the sofa back and her throat was stretched. He took the print from its tissue paper and told her to hold it to her throat, with both hands. The photo was of an open vagina magnified twice. Bonny sat quite still whilst Mary adjusted the photo's angle. He licked her vigorously, with his eyes on the giant pudendum beyond her breasts. He knelt to fuck her. She let go of the photograph in her rapture. He hurriedly replaced it over her face. When he turned her prone to bugger her he made her hold it to the back of her head. Did she enjoy it? It was different. It was always different. It is in the sexual act and its attendant rituals that you find out about your friends: you *mine* each other. Talcum powder and that photograph or a similar one were the invariable props of their offal rubbing. They were taken on every genital safari: he carried them in a briefcase. Talc was a means of ageing pubic hair, of rendering it grey; the practice is an evident admission of gerontophilia but entirely harmless (provided of course that the chosen talc does not prompt an allergic reaction). The photograph was one of many that Mary had taken of May Butt's sexual organs; Bonny got to know them well, if back to front – there was usually enough light to project the image through the thick paper. The blood Mary left behind was that which issued from his urethra at orgasm. The proportion of blood to semen had increased to the point where the latter was hardly visible. Blood streaked her thighs. When she gammed him he stood with the photo stuck to the wall in front of him, it might have represented the fatal wound in the flank of a wild boar. She swallowed his blood thus exaggerating the cannibalism of this practice. She was in deep with him. She watched the blood flow. She watched it squirt on to her tummy, onto the sheets and the carpet. He had nosebleeds too; they excited her less. That was not the blood she wished to taste: the site of the sanguinary source is as momentous as the particular side of the hill, the particular wells. She wanted his blood all for herself. She hated May Butt (whom she never met). She hated the gifts May Butt bought him; he knew the price of each one – the items of clothing, the MGB he'd not let Bonny ride in, the jewels and watches, the tins of foie gras terrine, the camera, the piano. Everything he owned she'd bought for him. He was her prisoner, her dependent. He was kept, she was kept young (she told the crones who were her cronies: money well spent). That's not what Ray thought, nor the Voys, and especially not Daph who'd had it up to here with The Fancy Boy.

'You're a sugar mummy,' Daph the maiden tells her. And May just crosses her old legs in their glitter tights, grins, nods: 'I *know* Daph love. I *know*. But I'm a hap-hap-happy sugar mummy. God don't you think I deserve . . . No. You don't, do you?' All the Butts watched as their inheritance was turned into Bourbon and frilly shirts.

'He's too young and too Belgian,' The Founder tells his mother who replies: 'And you're too mad and too crippled.' No,

427

she didn't cry as he wheeled about and whirred from The Realm's sitting room. He did, though his half of a body palpated with weeping as soon as he was through the door, he shook so the motor frame that was his legs threatened to buckle with stress. It wasn't just the money, in a way that didn't come into it: he loved his mother, loved her. She nursed him through the illness called childhood. She's nursed him again through the illness called widowhood. He loves her, they all love her. The Voys love their gran, love her more for her misfortune. The greater her misfortune, the stronger their love.

No misfortune is greater than the dream house on the dunes. Bourbon, frilly shirts, silly cars, a rentable property accruing no income – they're all minor league. A brand new house belongs elsewhere, it makes for much more love, £44k's worth of love. That was the estimated cost of the dream house on the dunes. It was a figure that Mary spoke with pride and wonder, over and again, a money mantra. A model of the house sat on a table: he often stroked it, named the cost of each part – the monopitch shingle roof, the totally glazed south front, the timber frame (British Columbian Douglas fir), the Western red cedar external boards, the cantilevering of the first floor balcony, the Afos duct-air oil-fired heating, the mixer taps, the Oneiros flame retardant, the cork insulation of the first wooden house to be built on Hayling for forty years. And May Butt was paying for all of it yet granting him joint ownership.

Mary didn't gloat – that would have been to acknowledge his parasitism. He wouldn't listen to a word against her. He was loyal to her if not faithful – though the photograph across Bonny's face did mitigate his infidelity. Bonny soon learned not to mention her, for he was thus reminded of his tempered infidelity, and that hurt. He told Bonny she had no right to intrude in such a way. She was not to speak her name, to do so was a violation of May. That's what he said. One post-coital p.m. Bonny was removing everything from her bag in the eternal search for the twist of smack *that must be there*. He picked up her address book and flicked through with an eye, less idly than anyone but a sort of spy might have. He saw his number. 'Why eff?' he asked with a crooked smile. She dared not admit to him that he was her future, that there was such a chasmic imbalance in their mutual affection.

'Eff', she murmured, convincingly mendacious and kneeling to rub her blood-smeared labia on his chest, 'is for fuck.'

She was prompted into pecuniary sensibility by him. That was one of Mary's gifts to Bonny – the lesson that it is vital to worry about money; another was the lesson that parasitism must not be lazily undertaken. It has to be worked at. He was zealous in his fealty. He said it with flowers, scent, chocolates, chocolate liqueurs, liqueurs etc. Bonny fretted about her torpor, her lack of groundwork. Her first husband, her primary host would soon be dead. He had little to leave her, they lived off his parents, off a monthly remittance and further begged subs. She had no parents to blackmail; once one was dead that was that – no leverage, no purchase. Besides, Monica was out of range, living a low-cost life of sun, fun and Fundador near Estepona; further she had nothing more to give, she had nothing to be parted from. Toddy's bank statements made dismaying reading. Bonny sold a canteen of Georgian cutlery to a gentleman antique dealer with a check shirt and a buttonhole who referred to the merchandise as 'flatware'. He stung her. Ignorant and thus undeterred she began to strip the house on the downs of its furniture, paintings, decorative objects. If it was portable it was saleable. She exchanged the car for a Transit. She would return ever more frequently, debasing the claim that it was too far to drive, that she couldn't drive at night. Eddie watched her go. Once when he came into the flat – which was a rare occurrence, the elemental trespass of audience onto stage – he sat with them laughing at a television film about insurance arson, mechuleh fire, Jewish lightning (Jimmy's lightning for viewers in STV and Grampian areas), Leopold Harris etc. He laughed because of the sheer ineptitude of most such arsonists, with their giveaway drums of petrol and kerosene; their methods were as crude as those of pyromaniacs; their execution was duff; their matches were damp; their getaway cars were out of petrol. Bonny's execution was perfect.

She suffered, rather, from ill luck. An oversight. An understandable lapse at the pre-preparatory stage. A planning failure.

When she had denuded the house on the downs of saleable items she set fire to it. The wiring was old, the plugs were inconsistent, two pins here, three there. Before Toddy and Bonny occupied it it had been let to a changing group of housemen from Odstock Hospital who (quasi-scientific training shows) had appended to certain sockets the once red, by then pink-inked notices on card 'NO ADAPTORS!!!', 'DO NOT USE THIS SOCKET IF THE ONE UNDER THE WINDOW IS IN USE', 'ONLY FOR RUBBER SOUL!!' There were sockets, too, masked with surgical tape (they'd always assumed that's what it was). They'd never removed the warnings, merely renewed the sellotape. Even paying heed to them they'd got the scent: it smelled like fish to them, they believed there was a dead rat behind the sitting room wainscot. When they'd jemmied off that ancient yew plank, so cracking it (they never bothered to replace it), they had found no rat, no fieldmouse, nothing but clunch white as the day it was laid. It took about six months of perpetual olfactory assault before they understood that it was the sound systems and the dishwasher and Bonny's sun lamp (lower case, that's right). Those sound systems, they ate the grid, they belted Zep five fields or more, they burnt sockets, they threatened fire. They'd even mentioned it to Alasdair and Jill the first of the two times they'd come to dinner (Bonny had burnt everything). Get this right: she did not *choose* the night of Tuesday 5 November 1974 for calendrical aptness, nor because she was a firework maker's girl and it was in the blood. She recognised, however, the appeal, the coincidence of her fatidic opportunity with familial tradition. She should have realised, then, that she would fail. She burnt the house all right. Everything worked out the way she had wanted it to. She was smug for days after. She gave herself a little treat, a skin-pop in the fireplace (whose artisan mantel had gone the way of the rest). She turned on every light in the house till it shone like a motorway in her lover's country. (Mary was proud of the claim that Belgium, whose motorways are lit, is visible at night from the moon. Nomdejeu.) She had sold the dishwasher, the fridge, the deepfreeze, the oven, the vacuum cleaner. So she had to scour outhouses for old electric fires, a valve radio, a hairdryer. She sat on the sitting-room floor playing Lego with adaptors, building a stepped cluster of rectilinear irregularity. It was so heavy that it had to be supported by cotton reels lest the initial pins slip from the promisingly scorched socket. She switched them on: record players, fires, an iron, the hairdryer, two standard lamps, a food mixer, a blow heater, three radios, a lawnmower. They stood on the carpetless boards in a tangle of wires, cacophonous, obliterating the furtive rustle of electricity on the move, obliterating too that rustle's succeeding crackle which is as dry and deadly as the rattle of *crotalus atrox*.[1] She didn't hear it, then, but she smelt it, the roasting bakelite, the glue that melts and fills the room with fish dock. Then came the flames. First a blueflash, a little chap who was to grow up into a big burly bully before long. He led the way, he procreated fast so his nippers were soon in line behind him, cocky as their dad, greedy for wood, keen on paint, omnivorously eating as they cooked. Bonny just loved the colours, the shapes, the apricot cowls, the ku-klux blues, the venusian phoenix. Oh look at them go: flames are gymnasts, vaulters, acrobats. They transfixed her. One raced up a curtain, took a bow at the top, jumped to a pelmet. They were a bright burnished army that grew in number and size. They pumped themselves up. They waved to her, their creator, they gave thanks for their life. She was proud of her pyrotechny, sorry to have to leave the show but all ups have their downs (withdrawals, hangovers) and flame has smoke which rolls in quiffs from within it. She hardly coughed. She was outside in time to see the pointed vanguard climbing from a window, beginning an exterior attack that the wind gave full support to. She danced. She ran to and fro the blackening walls and erupting paint. She leapt and span. She clapped when the first fall came. A wall collapsed with a groan that was audible above the busy kindling. It created a space for a draught to rush through. The flames whooshed, whistled, swished in the wind. They stuck out their tongues. They bucked and galloped. Bonny cartwheeled. There were new noises: popping, belching. The house glowed like a halloween pumpkin. It heated the garden,

[1] Literally 'the atrocious castanet'. The implicit simile suggests that the herpetologist on the case was hispanic and that the rattle snake is a Mexican invention.

launched debris into the sky. She laughed gaily. She rolled on the ground, scratched her face and muddied it.

Then she drove the Transit across the downs, away from the beacon, away from her past. She careered along estate roads and farm tracks. They were rutted, rough. She drove past the hulk of the Dutch barn and the water tower in the black firs. She drove between bald hedges and warrened banks.

It was 10.50, twenty minutes into drinking-up, when she silenced the bar at The Radnor Arms. She had never acted with such conviction. Hysteria, distress, fright – she did the lot. You could see fire in her eyes, they said.

'Fire,' she wailed, 'fire. Matrimony Farm. It's on fire . . .'

They wrapped her in blankets, fed her brandy, sat her on a settle. There was so much tragedy in her life. She did choose well. The fire brigade was having a night of it, they always do in the thatch counties, on Guy Fawkes. The first men to drive up to the farm were back within quarter of an hour, shaking their heads.

Girly Girling, electrician, murmured to mine host: 'I told Mr Hogg-Tod, I did. I said to him that 'ouse could go up any moment. And he said it's up to Donald . . . I didn't ought to say it but that'll teach him to ignore professional advice.' Mine host grimaced and Girly turned to see Bonny watching him. He put his sleeverless hand to his mouth.

She smiled weakly, forgivingly. Her heart thumped in orgulous satisfaction. She might need Girly's corroboration. She didn't. Arson was never suspected. The assessors were trusting men. They knew their client. He was a multi-millionaire. He was also one of their non-executive directors. He was colour without corruption, success without skeletons. Had he been just any farmer on the Wilts/Dorset/Hants border they might have delved into the flames' font, they might have brought in the boffins from IFLARS (Institute Of Insurers Flammability Research Station at Newport Pagnell), they might have conducted a covert search into his borrowings (they did: clean b of h). The man is kosher. Here's £50k structure. £22k furniture and art works.

Bonny had never thought to confirm that Toddy would be the

beneficiary of a claim on Matrimony Farm. She had sold the contents for less than 14% of their insured worth – she was lucky here for they got 44% of their real worth – they were insufficiently overinsured. She lost. By the time that Toddy died on 21 January 1975 she knew she'd get nothing. Matrimony Farm was a paternal loan, a favour.

The night before he died the three of them watched television – Bonny, Toddy, Eddie on the sofa. A serious man with a wig to his lobes told them that the Channel Tunnel was to be abandoned.

'Googly,' said Toddy, 'kinda. We don't get to the Belgians but the Belgians still get to us. Night.' He stumbled off to bed having spoken his last words.

Eddie put his hand on Bonny's knee. She pushed it away. She smiled at Eddie as though to say *really*!

He accompanied her to the funeral. The parents reclaimed their son. They didn't want Butt's birds pecking at him. They'd have gone to law.

Bonny and Eddie were admitted only to the third car in the procession to Kensal Green. They stood together later in the drawing room in Connaught Square. Bonny wore black: black net, black jacket, black hose. Alasdair Hogg-Tod grinned at Eddie as one might at a chimpanzee. He led Bonny away. His arm was three inches too low on her back. In the hall she felt his fingers at the top of her buttocks. He leaned her against the multi-locked front door.

It was a simple enough proposition: 'For every quid a quo.' He leered. 'We could, um, come to an accommodation.'

Bonny turned to the door, fought to open it.

She was anally raped by a blackman on her deathbed. That's the lore of The Mellow September, of Daph's sunset home behind the grisly laurels. And it's true. So is this:

When that sad stray dolphin (the one with the sick geography, the one that was fazed by the uniform labyrinth of the oceans) was pushed by the dawn tide onto the Hayling shore all the Voys, Jonjon and Sonny and Laddy, beat it with a shuttering plank, a cosh of heating pipe, a brick. They took it out on that dolphin. They've just walked round their grandma's new house. Dawn, after a party. They were only going to throw them in the sea, their weapons. They'd picked them up near the house which shone with newness. They beat the dolphin as if it was Mary – foreign, intrusive, washed up. It died with a smile. It stained the sand. It might have made a meal for a thousand mewling gulls. Jonjon wanted to put it in the jam's dinky hatchback and take it up Dave Ring in Fratton but Laddy's still no businessman and, besides, he enjoys the power the length of heating pipe gives him. Like a no-rent alchemist he turns mammal to meat to pulp that even a fishmonger so bent and so bereft of pride as Dave Ring will not touch it. Sonny kicked it. So Jonjon left them there. They left it there. Dog food.

The sky was soot and pearl, luminous murk, it needed a clean. The Voys mill through the womanly dunes whose shiv grass incises all the skin it touches. They booted the coarse sand's detritus, the packs and cans and wept-for toys. They put their arms around each other's shoulders. They trudged as one across the links where Sonny squatted to stool chocolate into the thirteenth hole – bad luck for the happy putter. They reached the road at Sinah Farm. Look north and you're looking at mud. When the moon has ordered out the water that's what's left.

Straggler channels, dead wet arteries, slowcoach ducts, mud; jellied, bulgy, sculpted mud. It's every grey you want to forget. If you're a bird with special adaptations you're in 7H. Otherwise try another harbour, another creek. It's no help being able to swim. Dump the Voys in it and that'll be the last of them . . . No, no. Let them live, let them walk the open road where the pack dogs roam. They walked the open road whose verges show dark roots where the killer wind rehearses. They went past the boats beached on wooden cradles above the ooze. You can tell the people who live in them are poor people – the horizontal smoke from their stovepipes is septum-grating, black particles gyro through it (they burn beach trash). The Voys hurled stones at that skiff whose balancing act on a buttock of slime is as wonderful as gravity itself. They jigged gaily down the path to the foot-ferry waiting by the slipway, it must have been the ozone that made them frisky.

Mad Bantu was on the boat too. They were astonished to see him, at this hour of day, on the first ferry of the day. Hayling wasn't Bantu's beat. And he hadn't been at the party. The little craft's engine roared at the ebb tide, fought against the lunar pull to sea. Bantu was talking to himself, the way he did now. Sonny and Laddy stuck at the prow and looked anywhere save at him. They looked at the mudscape gaseous enough to fuel a kingdom's farts, at the distant towers of Pompey aflare with molten dawn, at the trees crippled for life by the Spithead Bite, at the gulls making civil war over the sewage outfall. They looked anywhere save at Bantu: he's been working to earn his name.

He's a no-go body, a sicko survivalist. His drainpipes were gross – biscuit brown waffle-weave; their zipper was oxidised dayglo peppermint and ringed with dried waste. Through them he absent-mindedly stroked his cock which should have flopped with guilt and shame but which bucked tumid with his prodding and frotting. From between his incisors he pulled a brittle grey pubic hair and rubbed it between his fingers. Then he let the Bite take it, the keepsake of a night's triumph is also the tell-tale that traps. That lost hair (we'll never find it now) was evidence of Mad Bantu's assault on that bed of wheels. His glans had come out of her mouth with dentures round it like a ruff. The plasters

435

holding the milky tubes up her nostrils tore. The drip-needle slipped out and dangled in the draught causing a little saline puddle on the lino and a little bloody trickle on her immemorial forearm. She was almost bald, she was almost dead, her skin was piebald (parchment with mauve contusions), her incontinence was chronic and required a doggybag. Bad Bantu must have been mad to do what he did. This was outside his brief.

This was not what Mary had paid him to do, in fivers, in the gents at The Dead Villiers. No, this was above and beyond. Rough someone, but gently, OK. Gib a handbag, yes. Do the safe and the silver, Daph's pewter, the EPNS by all means. Smash locks, kill a dog, crack jambs, trash the office. Mary told him what was in order and what was not. He stood at the urinal sniffing Dettol, smegma, tobacco. Had he taken his starter fee in the bar where the jazzer played jocular sax, where good cheer was on tap it might have been different. But here in the jakes the coincidence of exposed penis – albeit exposed to the innocent end of pissing beer – with the exhortation to violence made an ill meld. He was unable to disassociate the brawn in his palm from the bother he was being hired to hawk.

He had always suffered a bent to literality. As a soldier he had been able to fire successive rounds through the cut-out head of a pop-up anthropoid but had failed in a Derry skirmish even to touch the trigger because he didn't recognise the masked man-of-violence as a human simulacrum of that one-dimensional Tidworth training target. He never made lance jack. And he had so wanted to succeed in the colours, in the khaki and face paint: it was his way, it had to be because the army stands whilst the navy floats, and he loathed the sailors who used his mother, he hated the bell-bottomed uncles, every one of them, every breakfast a new uncle from the briny. (His own trouser cuffs never exceeded 15 inches, they were a full foot short of Laddy's.) Other mitigations are:

1) Vivienne Souch, the deathbed case in question, very likely didn't notice. She was that far gone. She noticed nothing. She didn't notice when Daph took away her dog and had it put down. They'd been an item, Vivi and Pepsi. Lifeblood of The

Mellow September till the last month, till she accelerated into The Avenue's last bend and there was no brake fluid left.

2) If she did notice, if the line from rectum to respondent chamber of the brain *was* intact, she probably mistook it for yet another internal examination. Fact: all doctors are drunks and all drunks are clumsy no matter that they affect dainty. 'Dainty like you're bevvied, mind, not like you're an iron, ducky.' Ray Butt differentiates, Catterick, 12.6.52. Laughter.

3) She mistook what she saw entering her mouth beyond the filigree of milky tubes for an hallucination of a serpentine death's head. Fact: there were only two tubes, and they were not entwined. Such things multiply with flawed eyes, perpetual bed, Adriamycin, senility, dreams.

4) It wasn't necrophilia. No one can call it that. It may have been cheating at necrophilia, simulating it – but that's not the same. What was the same was the victim's ignorance, the impossibility of her having knowledge of the actions performed against her. Is her victimhood then mitigated? Is, indeed, she no longer a victim at all? Is sentience a condition of this state? Let's get round the table on this one some other time.

Bantu climbed from the ferry onto the slithey green boards of the landing pontoon at Eastney. Two men with a dozen puppies on string leashes were waiting. Hayling is where Pompey dumps its unwanted dogs that are not drowned or thrown from high windows. Hayling is the kind choice. In 1975 a puppy-man's rate was £1.75 per dog. Dogs not charged on the ferry. Pompey Yellow Pages for that year lists six. They worked at night, making their collections after the kiddies are tucked up, releasing their charges into society early the next day. The Voys negotiated the excitable dogs. The wind's weight put a gull on a treadmill. A ship's horn blew bumptious music. They kept their distance behind Bantu but he waited for them at the top of the bobbing walkway, bedlam-eyed, grinning, thrusting a finger under Laddy's nose.

'Sniff sniff, matey, sniff sniff – that's mature quim matey. Eh?' He laughed, saluted, double-quicked along the road past Eddie's poor cabin, towards Eastney Barracks and the luminous might of Pompey. 'Fol *de* rol,' exclaim the Voys in one voice.

Bantu, hearing, breaks into a reel with a hand crooked over his mad head. Just a couple of steps – he is in a hurry, he has a wad to fetch, a pony, crisp new Wellingtons. He had stipulated *crisp new* because they always give him *tired old* down the DHSS. Hear the pop pop pop of repeater fire on the range. See the losers on jankers sweating round the parade ground, rucksacked with stones. He's not going to let bad memories spoil his pay day. He gave up waiting for the D7 bus (fucking clippies) and stole a cycle left against the esplanade railways by a boy fisherman who was baiting a rod twenty feet below. Mary, wearing a sarong and hair to his shoulders, grunts into the intercom, greets him with a scowl. The flat at the Sallyport is a massif of cases and tea chests containing the accumulated gifts of one Belgian to another.

'I could murder', announces Bantu, causing Mary to slop coffee on a dustsheet, 'a bacon sarnie. Got any rashers? With lashings of sauce.' Smile.

'Caff,' says Mary, curt and dry, resenting the maniac's dramatic pause.

'Love to, matey, soon as you settle up.'

Mary returns, counts the money with deliberation, as though for an innumerate, laying each unfolded note on veneer.

'Nice . . . Good lad . . . Pleasure doing business – *if I may say so*. I done the dirty good and proper.'

Mary's nod was mock-graceful. Just so long as it discomfits Daph; just so long as it hurts the interfering bitch; just so long as it keeps her, his stepdaughter-in-common-law, off his back; just so long as the virgin harridan is otherwise preoccupied the day her mother moves house – that's all, a comprehensive programme for familial ease. Bruno Berg had taught him that truce is achieved through belligerence, pacts through actions. He showed Bantu the door, dressed, worked on a new breakthrough song waiting for the removal van, instructed the burly hefter and the Scots hefter on fragility, locked up for ever, led the way in his MGB, kept them in his mirror, crooned Albeau's 'Le Plaisir De Ma Connaissance' crossing the bridge to Hayling, noticed three police cars parked behind the grimy laurels in The Mellow September's driveway, stopped for a teacher and children to cross when the right of way was his, waved to the honest workman erecting the sign Ixelles Villa, second-geared it along the sandy track between yellow gorse walls, saw the sea, saw the dream house (or villa), saw the tall pantechnicon, saw May running towards him holding down her Cleopatra wig in the wind and moving as quickly as her age, her heels and her hobble skirt would allow. The house shone, gift-wrapped by the sun, packaged for two for eternity. He had arrived.

'Christ on the cross!' said the burly hefter at the wheel as May, multiply handicapped, raced towards the two vehicles.

'Scrag end, I'd call that,' replied the Scots hefter, 'dressed as gigot. The T is sometimes silent.'

May Butt's powder and slap (it would be imprecise to state 'her cheeks') were streaked with eyeliner, charcoal rivulets; a lachrymose delta was drying on them. She stands beside the open-top car, her head pitifully slumped towards her wired lie of a chest. She clutches Mary's arm. She sobs: 'There's been a murder.'

Mad Bantu (who was never pulled in to help with inquiries) spent the morning in a café, a department store, an amusement arcade. He ate three bacon sandwiches, bought one pair of jeans, won one teddybear. The dockyard workers and matloes to whom he offered his prize for sale in The Prentice Victualler at lunchtime told him: 'Fuck off nog.' He gave it to the new barmaid who had replaced the old barmaid who was now the stripper.

'Better wages, better work conditions,' rued the new barmaid, 'if you got the tits and the bottle.'

Bonny Hogg-Tod, née Vallender, had both, had been the barmaid, the (relatively) new barmaid hired when her predecessor had gone on stage in place of the OMO wife who'd reported for work one lunch with OMB[1] all over, lacerations and tears not to mention black and blue. When Bonny's predecessor started growing dorsal nipples the clientele was divided; when brown lesions appeared round and above the garter line there was a unanimous foot vote and they sought noon beaver at The Very Best Intent where the beer was pee and the sightlines

[1] Old man's back.

tragic. Bonny brought them back, in frames,[1] though they didn't know it was Bonny. She used the stage name Vallée (a strippery name). She used, too, panatellas, bottlenecks, cucumbers,[2] anything they threw on stage – within reason; within the bounds of capability and safety. Pineapples and spanners went straight back into the audience with the warning that *any more of that* . . . The punters who threw them risked the mob (average: eight pints per head per lunchtime). She was a seam of gold. Mine host: 24 stone Danny, the fat quean who used to deal proscribed drugs in pubs (p. 264); who is now fully licensed, as D.L.R. Garcia, above all three doors, to sell legit intoxication; who will buy on the house on his birthday, 29 Feb (a gimmick, but very genuine, reckons Messrs ——'s Tenancy Applications Committee, South Central Region); who makes up for his lack of missus with (according to that same committee) 'individualist character form and outgoing repartee'. He tells Bonny, every 13.50 when she comes off: 'You're my seam of gold darling.' And he hands her a twist of white, a little hit that grows by the week. He keeps her happy. If she's happy they're happy, three fifty plus every lunch-hour, happy, pissed and happy, munching crisps (pub peculiars, extra salt for extra thirst), peanuts (ditto). No messing with pub grub here (labour: demands fucking remuneration, I ask you). They swill.

At 13.30 all eyes turn to the stage at the end of this dark, barnlike, bevelled glass boozer. A pennant is stretched above it: 'Blighty's Best Does Pompey Proud'. The old slogan was used by the former (independent) brewery to exploit the fame the city derived from the League Championship winning team of 1948–49 and 49–50. It referred evidently to beer. The three hundred and fifty whistling, stamping, catcalling voyeurs who shake the building in their anticipatory impatience know very well it refers to their Vallée. They've sailed the seven seas (some of them), and there's none that can compare. Not the Bangkok snake artistes; not the cigarette smokers in Toulon; not the Day twins,

1 Collective noun for pocket billiards players.
2 A stall selling cucumbers, bananas, sticks of Pompey rock and barley sugar was positioned in the southernmost doorway, 'the one with the glazed tiles depicting the victualler's craft'.

change, glass – awe cannot stem throats or commerce),
has reigned to bursting point – she always knew wh...
spoke, she husked: 'The last miracle.' She slowly m...
right hand from the imaginary cross and lowers it to h...
Oh, they cheer, they bawl, they howl. Fat Dan at th...
all stops out. Vallée's painted labial lips pout. Marc...
leer hits every ear: 'She's faster than most/ And she...
coast.' Her timing is just so. Smack destroys nerv...
just. It lets her rest a while longer, lets her take it...
tell you: Fat Dan, who never touches the gear ('...
a share of the feed we throw to the animals wh...
do we ducky?'), sweats. She takes it that far...
on bongo there. Hi, Mickey! The song is ca...

That's Poor Eddie at the very back, fur...
throw. He abases himself by the very act...
of the dirtied flesh. He disgusts himself...
on his tod,[1] lurking. He's ashamed he...
to a halt. Yet he's so proud. It's his g...
who has the power over them. He...
what they all want to touch but d...
stage when she invites *you all ou*...
mouths a kiss and a 'tomorrow'...
door her. Back to graft. She wa...
as remote as that. Poor poor ...
never stop hoping, he'll live...
was meant to be. Even th...
Mary he says nothing...
uncertain about who he's...
bananas. Even ...man like ...onke...
they are like bananas.

[1] Tod Sloan was a jockey who overate... defeat he overran, was des...
wiz... the monkey'. Wonderful turn of phrase ... that's the English turf-clue...
... name is a synonym of *alone* due solely in the fo...or of its rhyme, but Today tel...
Eddie. 'It's not down to chance. Is it. Come on. It can't be.' The coincidence of tod
(rhyming slang) signifying *alone* and tod (German) meaning ... Donald
Hogg-Tod, understandably, Dudie ... Today ... death did not thus imply
loneliness that The Good Guy communicates ... vistas... of signs and may
have only a smattering of German let alone a knowledge of slang derived from English
for serving

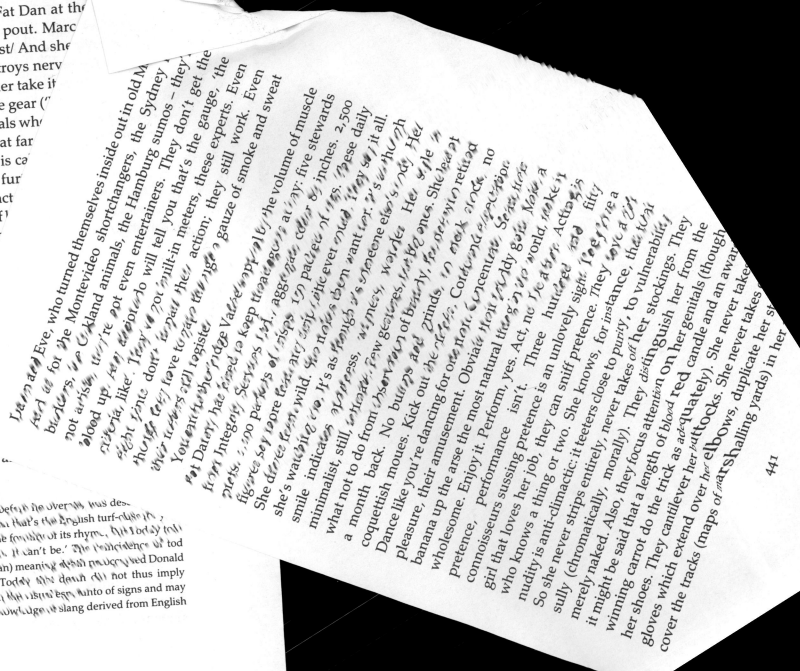

in Winchester Gaol were few, and conditions poor. [...] up for lost frying when he moved to Pompey, to 486. [...] for his former trade he fries tonight and every night [...] dripping that has to be smoking before he drops in the b[...] coley/cod/hake/huss from Dave Ring. An industrial [...] saved from scrap and refurbished by his own hand, domi[...] his room. Its smell dominates the house; he fries with his o[...] impasted as those of his room. Eddie casts a smoke-stung ey[...] open to relieve the heat. Thus the hall's walls are as grea[...] over the wall near the payphone.

This is where Old Man Dod writes the messages, in the [...] grease, with his forefinger, back to front. A lifetime in the [...] print, composing in hot metal, has left him almost blind, has [...] left him unable to read and write save back to front. In the [...] brightness of the matutinal back garden that gives onto the [...] allotments he holds a mirror to headlines: that's the way he's [...] used to seeing them, those are the only letters big enough for [...] him to see. Half a century's proximity to presses did not affli[...] his hearing. He's up from his armchair to answer the payph[...] just as soon it has rung. It's never for him; but no matte[...] enjoys his conversations with strangers in the gloom of [...] whose unshaded bulb hardly glimmers through its [...] grease and particles. These are his only conversa[...] makes friends with the strangers, recognises t[...] imagines their faces, asks them to visit – but [...] calling anyway and it's no trouble. He ne[...] inscribe their message even when he knows th[...] his invitation is a lie. He's the house's hist[...] temporaries from ten years back, he can [...] phoned for tenants he never actually sa[...] voice. And his ears, they got better [...] they never missed an outgoing call, [...] through the greasy ceiling with the [...] missed nothing.

He knows them by their fo[...] skiddy tiles and he's got their [...] The pedal revelation of cha[...] then Old Man Dod has

itsel[...]
is a constr[...]
string allowance. [...]
lets them scrap for it, [...]
down like hounds. There's [...]
garment always got torn. She weigh[...]
reach the back. It chugs through smoke and [...]
to catch it, bag it, make off with it, this souvenir of [...]
The tumbled knot of bodies scrabbling for the trophy bru[...]
missing the display of chocolate bars that goes in time to 'A[...]
Tears Go By'. Their beerbellies prone them so long they don't get
an eyeful of that languorous self-stroking which culminates in
their Vallée statued with her arms stretched as though she's on a
cross for her sins of immodesty and lubricity, getting what
Magdalene was meant to have got, what she would have got had
The Good Guy not given her a redeemer, a miracle man to carry
the can. Her armpits are hirsute as her pubes; their adjacence to
glove-tops give her auxiliary genitals. She entwines her shins,
her ankles, her high-strapped shoes. Her arms are still as ice.
Can they see the nails that pierce the palms? They can't. But
350 collaborators collude in silence when the music stops.
They know the form. First-timers learn stum, and soonish. They
cannot see the nails but their imaginations are mined, dredged
out of the slough. She educated the barked-at navvies, the yes-
sir matloes, the men whose uniforms deny them thought, who
are subjects of systems where imagination is a boss prerogative,
a far-off luxury (like caviar which only generals, and admirals,
have *earned* the right to), and thus derided. She shows them its
[be]auty without ever admitting that she's prising it out for them.
[...]straight arms, the hung head – that posture rings a bell.
[...]tart to see the nails, the cross; they are party to her
[...] And when silence has reigned (save for hawks, keg,

Dawn and Eve, who turned themselves inside out in old Macau. And as for the Montevideo shortchangers, the Sydney lard bladders, the Oakland animals, the Hamburg sumos – they're not artists, they're not even entertainers. They don't get the blood up. Any aficionado will tell you that's the gauge, 'the criteria, like'. They've got built-in meters, these experts. Even eight pints don't impair their action; they still work. Even though they have to gape through a gauze of smoke and sweat their meters still register.

You can further judge Vallée's appeal by the volume of muscle Fat Danny has hired to keep theatregoers at bay: five stewards from Integrity Services Ltd., aggregate collar 89 inches. 2,500 pints. 1,100 packets of crisps. 150 packets of cigs. These daily figures say more than any strip critic ever could. They say it all. She drives them wild. She makes them want her. It's as though she's watching too. It's as though it's someone else's body. Her smile indicates apartness, wryness, wonder. Her style is minimalist, still, intimate. Few gestures, but big ones. She learnt what not to do from observation of Brandy, the one who retired a month back. No bumps and grinds, no mock shock, no coquettish moues. Kick out the clichés. Confound expectation. Dance like you're dancing for one man. Concentrate. Share their pleasure, their amusement. Obviate their proddy guilt. Make a banana up the arse the most natural thing in the world, make it wholesome. Enjoy it. Perform, yes. Act, no. Do a turn. Acting is pretence, performance isn't. Three hundred and fifty connoisseurs sussing pretence is an unlovely sight. They love a girl that loves her job, they can sniff pretence. They love a girl who knows a thing or two. She knows, for instance, that total nudity is anti-climactic: it teeters close to purity, to vulnerability. So she never strips entirely, never takes off her stockings. They sully (chromatically, morally). They distinguish her from the merely naked. Also, they focus attention on her genitals (though it might be said that a length of blood red candle and an award-winning carrot do the trick as adequately). She never takes off her shoes. They cantilever her buttocks. She never takes off her gloves which extend over her elbows, duplicate her stockings, cover the tracks (maps of marshalling yards) in her arms – but she'd keep them on anyway for they (and the rest of her thermally incompetent clothes) are a uniform, they proclaim her status, they objectify and depersonalise her, they give her power. (Ask any jobsworth about his cap, his epaulettes, about reification. On the other hand don't ask him: he must seek multiple permissions before he can answer, and then the reply itself must be sanctioned in quadruplicate.) She is an artifice, she is a construct. Some clothes are expendable. She insists on a g-string allowance. She daily offers this item to her devotees. She lets them scrap for it, for the first right of inhalation. They're down like hounds. There's often a floor-level incident. The garment always got torn. She weights it some days so that it will reach the back. It chugs through smoke and motes. Arms stretch to catch it, bag it, make off with it, this souvenir of Blighty's Best. The tumbled knot of bodies scrabbling for the trophy brush risks missing the display of chocolate bars that goes in time to 'As Tears Go By'. Their beerbellies prone them so long they don't get an eyeful of that languorous self-stroking which culminates in their Vallée statued with her arms stretched as though she's on a cross for her sins of immodesty and lubricity, getting what Magdalene was meant to have got, what she would have got had The Good Guy not given her a redeemer, a miracle man to carry the can. Her armpits are hirsute as her pubes; their adjacence to glove-tops give her auxiliary genitals. She entwines her shins, her ankles, her high-strapped shoes. Her arms are still as ice. Can they see the nails that pierce the palms? They can't. But 350 collaborators collude in silence when the music stops. They know the form. First-timers learn stum, and soonish. They cannot see the nails but their imaginations are mined, dredged out of the slough. She educated the barked-at navvies, the yes-sir matloes, the men whose uniforms deny them thought, who are subjects of systems where imagination is a boss prerogative, a far-off luxury (like caviar which only generals, and admirals, have *earned* the right to), and thus derided. She shows them its beauty without ever admitting that she's prising it out for them. The straight arms, the hung head – that posture rings a bell. They start to see the nails, the cross; they are party to her allusion. And when silence has reigned (save for hawks, keg,

442

change, glass – awe cannot stem throats or commerce), when it has reigned to bursting point – she always knew when – she spoke, she husked: 'The last miracle.' She slowly moves her right hand from the imaginary cross and lowers it to her clitoris. Oh, they cheer, they bawl, they howl. Fat Dan at the PA pulls all stops out. Vallée's painted labial lips pout. Marc Bolan's sly leer hits every ear: 'She's faster than most/ And she lives on the coast.' Her timing is just so. Smack destroys nerves – doesn't it just. It lets her rest a while longer, lets her take it to the brink – I tell you: Fat Dan, who never touches the gear ('We don't ask for a share of the feed we throw to the animals when we go the zoo – do we ducky?'), sweats. She takes it that far. Bolan has Mickey on bongo there. Hi, Mickey! The song is called 'Hot Love'.

That's Poor Eddie at the very back, further than his girl can throw. He abases himself by the very act of entry to this church of the dirtied flesh. He disgusts himself by skulking in, all alone, on his tod,[1] lurking. He's ashamed he cannot bring the spectacle to a halt. Yet he's so proud. It's his girl they yell for, it's his girl who has the power over them. He is the one who's touched what they all want to touch but dare not: no one ever goes on stage when she invites *you all out there*, at the end, before she mouths a kiss and a 'tomorrow'. No one goes round to stage-door her. Back to graft. She was that calendar come to life. She's as remote as that. Poor poor Eddie wonders if it'll ever be: he'll never stop hoping, he'll live through every adulteration of what was meant to be. Even though he may, possibly, know about Mary he says nothing. Tact. Discretion. Uncertainty. He's uncertain about who he's seen go in and out. People are not bananas. Even banana-like people are more like people than they are like bananas.

---

[1] Tod Sloan was a jockey who overate, who, before he overate, was described as 'a wizzened monkey'. Wonderful turn of phrase, but that's the English turf-class for you. His name is a synonym of *alone* due, solely, to the fortuity of its rhyme. But Toddy told Eddie: 'It's not down to chance. Is it. Come on. It can't be.' The coincidence of tod (rhyming slang) signifying alone and tod (German) meaning death preoccupied Donald Hogg-Tod, understandably. Eddie convinced Toddy that death did not thus imply loneliness, that The Good Guy communicates in the visual esperanto of signs and may have only a smattering of German let alone a knowledge of slang derived from English horseracing.

They are definitely different, one from the next, the people who enter 486 Fratton Road. Poor Eddie is parked twenty yards down the street in a van he hasn't the licence to drive, the company vehicle he's entitled to, with legends on both sides: The Church Of The Best Ever Redemption. He's above the law on driving, he feels: Belgians can drive without having passed a test. He sticks within the limit, never exceeds 18 mph, signals in advance, slows to 10 mph to do so, prepares to park when he sees the sign saying Toronto Road, takes the last 400 yards nice and easy. 486 Fratton Road is the gabled slum where Bonny went to live after the man from Chasnev Properties Ltd came round the sixth time, demanding the three months back rent, walking through it like it was his (which it was, strictly), mentioning the bailiffs, the dogs, the lengths that have been gone to by other landlords, the illegitimate methods which Chasnev Properties Ltd would never have recourse to. Eddie loaded her into the van. He'd never seen so many coathangers; the folded people filled the back. He was often round, parked on double yellow, trying to help, see her settle in (it was a bedsit from a small ad). He'd lug her shopping any time she pay-called. He was always at The Church (you know the number). And if not, at home (ditto). He didn't mind carrying up the two flights. The greasy carpet didn't offend. He was happy to heft. Poor Eddie knew this sort of house (p. 380). He goes in often. He goes in as often as he watches from down the road, envious, curious, pining, lacking an excuse to visit. But he's often there, fetching, running errands. 'Don't tell me – sixty Bensedges, two pints hogonised,' chirps the cheery crone every time Eddie's entry rings the bell in the seedy little corner shop (the last such in Pompey now that Arth's is sold to self-service Halals). He nods and smiles and carries the usual back to 486. The privet's buntinged with polythene shreds. The garden's carpeted with soggy carpet; there are lino fins, ashes, rusting dustbins, a pram axle, ripped tights, a television's innards, dolls' clothes. The garden's a prologue to the house. And the house is an anthology of hardluck stories. Here's Boumphrey, ground floor front; here's Old Man Dod, ground floor rear. Bonny's at the top. She suffers the hardest luck of

444

all. She lost everyone. She lost more than Boumphrey, more than Dod.

Eddie always knew when Boumphrey was at home. Even before the smell gave him away. The incendiary flickering beyond the sheet he used as a curtain announced his presence. You could see it from the garden, you could see it from the other side of the privet if you didn't have the nous to look away when passing 486. Poor Eddie is carrying so much for Bonny (cigs, milk, cooking brandy for drinking, a yard of white sliced loaf, six six-packs) that he's grateful there's no front door lock. The temporaries traditionally forget their keys, kick the door open. It's such an old tradition that there's no jamb left to affix a catch to. And anyway the temporaries always leave after a week or two taking their keys with them so there's no point in doing repairs.

They leave, likely as not, because of Boumphrey. In his day Boumphrey was the finest fish fryer on the south coast, winner of countless fry-offs, a legend in frying circles. Now he's not even a former legend, his name means nothing to the new generation with their lighter batters and unsaturated oils. He hit the bottle when he failed to be crowned King Of Crispness for the third consecutive year at InterFry in 1961: it was the Yorkshire lobby that did for him. His wife left, took the lad with her. His business suffered. Especially on the cleanliness front. Health and Safety found rodent droppings. He drifted from job to job, chippie to chippie, a pan for hire. He was a dripping man who made his feelings known when he was required to fry in oil. His pride was his enemy. He was frying in Weymouth when he met his wife and the lad, on holiday for a week with the wife's new fella. He took the lad, a strapping future fryer of fifteen summers, on the piss. And after he'd taken him on the piss he took him home to his digs, took him to bed.

'Why?' asked the psychiatrist to whom he was remanded for reports.

'I hadn't seen him since he was eight . . . I wanted to get to know him.'

'You could have taken him to the zoo,' said the psychiatrist.

Four years; out after twenty-six months; frying opportunities

445

in Winchester Gaol were few, and conditions poor. He made up for lost frying when he moved to Pompey, to 486. Nostalgic for his former trade he fries tonight and every night in beef dripping that has to be smoking before he drops in the battered coley/cod/hake/huss from Dave Ring. An industrial fryer, saved from scrap and refurbished by his own hand, dominates his room. Its smell dominates the house; he fries with his door open to relieve the heat. Thus the hall's walls are as grease-impasted as those of his room. Eddie casts a smoke-stung eye over the wall near the payphone.

This is where Old Man Dod writes the messages, in the grease, with his forefinger, back to front. A lifetime in the print, composing in hot metal, has left him almost blind, has left him unable to read and write save back to front. In the brightness of the matutinal back garden that gives onto the allotments he holds a mirror to headlines: that's the way he's used to seeing them, those are the only letters big enough for him to see. Half a century's proximity to presses did not afflict his hearing. He's up from his armchair to answer the payphone just as soon it has rung. It's never for him; but no matter, he enjoys his conversations with strangers in the gloom of the hall whose unshaded bulb hardly glimmers through its coat of grease and particles. These are his only conversations. He makes friends with the strangers, recognises their voices, imagines their faces, asks them to visit – but only if they're calling anyway and it's no trouble. He never neglects to inscribe their message even when he knows their acceptance of his invitation is a lie. He's the house's historian, he can recall temporaries from ten years back, he can recall strangers who phoned for tenants he never actually saw. He never forgets a voice. And his ears, they got better with age and blindness, they never missed an outgoing call, they heard through walls, through the greasy ceiling with the paint-clogged lightrose. He missed nothing.

He knows them by their footfalls too. Three paces on the skiddy tiles and he's got them. Not just room number, either. The pedal revelation of character. It takes a practised ear, but then Old Man Dod has little else to occupy him: he can no longer read the walls papered with front pages he set. He has them to a t.

Poor Eddie the dogged, exploited suitor.

Bonny the inebriate trollop.

Fat Dan the fubsy quean – he's literally light on his feet, such amazing delicacy in a man of that build, it's always a give-away. Old Man Dod knows the type: shit under the fingernails, cock cheese behind the ears.

Mary the furtive fancy man, hurrying, looking over his shoulder, half dressed when he descends, straightening his apparel, smoothing his hair, pausing before he opens the front door, taking a big breath, never without his attaché case. Old Man Dod enjoys Mary's visits, takes brute comfort in their invariable pattern: the lovey-dovey, her pleading, his placation, her accusations, his: 'You don't getting yourself together what you expect. You don't getting off of that shit what you expect.' Then there are tears, redemption by squealing bedsprings, a minute's silence in honour of their deaths – and then more bull and cow. Old Man Dod's excited fists tremble, he rocks in his chair. An expert in these matters, he foresees a sticky end. He nods sagely whenever he considers it. His gums are jammed together in his version of a grin: yes, that's what he foresees for those two. Then the phone rings and he's up like a dog called to its bone, switching off the kettle, grabbing his teeth from an ashtray on the dresser, spitting phlegm, shuffling in his perished slippers.

He hears a new voice, a voice called Lou or Lew, a harsh curt voice, a voice abundant in phonemic mishaps (w for r, au for ōu etc.), a London voice, wivaht daht, a London number too.

'Two eight six,' repeats Old Man Dod, pausing to squint at his grease graffito,' – where's that then?'

'Wha'?' asks the voice.

'Not the same without the names,' says Old Man Dod. 'The admirals – RODney, FRObisher . . .'

'The wha'? Doosefayvuh – '

'G,U,L̄ – GULliver. Camden Town. S,P,E, SPEedwell – Hampstead . . .'

'Wivyuh. C,U,N this was. Wouldn' like to say wha' tha' were

447

shor' for . . . Nngrrrech! Now you tell 'er to wing Lou. Wight? Ayll. Ow. Ewe. Gohtha'? Goodclad.'

'L,I,V – LIVingstone. I'll wager you don't know where that was.' But Lou had rung off before Dod could tell him Norwood, before he could invite him to visit.

'Who's Lou?' asked Eddie, accusatorily, dropping the day's shopping on a formica table. 'There's a message for you – ring somebody called Lou. Who's Lou?'

Bonny, dressed in a towel, gazing at the allotment huts, watering her window box from a toothmug: *'Eddie!* . . . Oh pop those in the kitchenette would you be a love.' She returns to pelargonia.

He grudgingly transports the bags behind a nylon shower curtain. Unpacks noisily, rings the draining board. 'Who's Lou?'

'Business as a matter of fact. Not that it's any of yours. You don't own me Eddie. He's a man I'm seeing about a dog – if you really want to know. OK? Now I've got to have a kip. Yeh? See you soon Ed. Yeh? Oh – and thanks for the *victuals*.'

Kip meant a fix. The euphemism was an irony. Bonny's vein tipple inhibited sleep, kept her awake so that she could earn the next kip.

Poor Eddie's feet slump from one stairtread to its inferior. It's a downward step that signifies (to Old Man Dod's ears) an unequivocal blow dealt by blowsy Madame Life, up there in her room, to the pathetic ruffian who descends like a pegleg, furious in his impotence, resentful heels scuffing the treads. (Or maybe he's simply wary of the ice-like carpet. Boumphrey's frying tonight as every night.) Cheated Eddie winces whilst he writes Lou's number on his soiled cuff. A rolling bolster of slate blue smoke follows him out of the house.

He rings area code, numerical exchange, two further ciphers, then hangs up. He sits in the deserted office at The Church, lit by The Cross's bounced floods, flunking, and again. If he can inspire the ad hoc crosses whose shadows are cast against The Cross, if he can bring them from Göttingen, Adelaide, Uppsala, Findhorn, Glastonbury (no, not Glastonbury – the wobbliest old truck can do it in less than a morning from there), from Santa Cruz (more like it), Ibiza (now we're motoring) – if he can do all that he can do nine digits in easy batches, suffer the wait as the *pro*tagonist: he's the aggressor, the sonic intruder, surprise is his weapon.

'Lou's in the sauna. Sorreee. I'd take a message but I got doggy to feed. Try 'im later I'd advise. Byee.' The woman sounded friendly, wifely – and she was not lying, the family's pet's lusty bark was audible, insistent. A happy home, the hard-earned home of (Eddie judged by the wife's chirpy proletarianism) a self-made grafter enjoying the rewards of his toil, a businessman. The knowledge served to bate his jealous curiosity. The next day he was so tired after ministering to a minibusful of Iowan polyesters that he was disinclined to visit Bonny. He bought a chowmein takeaway from the Guozi next door but one to the launderette, ate it with a plastic spoon, watched his clothes froth and spin. The day after that he ran up the stairs of 486 with a gift bottle of Punt E Mes and a little something extra, a nice lardy cake from Stobb's of Cosham.

There was no answer. He rapped against the door again. Old Man Dod was out of his room with characteristic alacrity, calling up the stairs: 'Here, I say, I shouldn't bother knocking no more she's not going to answer she's gone away hasn't she.' Poor Eddie stood at the bottom of the stairs, his gifts dangling by his side. 'Went yesterday evening she did – I happened to hear her telephoning for a taxicab, going to the station she were. Can't help but overhear, living where I do like, with ears like mine. Twenty-year-old's, they say they are. Fancy a nice cup of tea?'

'The number,' said Eddie, pointing to the wall, 'there was a number for someone called Lou. You wrote his number. Where is it?'

'Oh yes. Right you are. Lou. Yes. Nice fella – but he didn't know about the admirals. I remember that . . . I think you'll find I wrote over it. Boumphrey there had several messages.'

Desperate Eddie spilled the contents of his blue polythene launderette bag onto his narrow, cot-like bed. He found the shirt. He identified the cuff. It was a testimonial to Omo's efficacy. There was not even an amorphous stain. Vanished.

'You tell me, love, you tell me,' said Fat Dan, despondently swilling gimlet. 'If I knew I'd be in there with the marines to get

449

her back. Sstoh! Fate's such a bitch and no mistake. One moment I'm the envy of every guv'nor from here to the West Pier at Brighton, next . . . well . . . Ooh, you should have seen the one the agency sent today. *Split* does *not* do it justice love. It looked like it had been run over. And as for the rest of it – ughch . . . Turn you into a vegan for life. No, she's a naughty girl our Bonny. If you see her you give her a spank from Danny and you tell her she's making a horrible dent in my takings. And that's after two days . . . God knows. I had my heart set on a new Jag come August. Reg: STR 1P.[1] She can write her own contract. She can come back on any conditions she wants.'

Bonny aka Vallée never again performed at The Prentice Victualler. He had a big heart, Fat Dan did – but business is business. That's what he has to tell her six months later when she shows, out of the blue, one sad morning, tapping on the bevelled glass, out there in the first sleet of winter. He looks up from the Blighty's Best ashtray he's wiping, scowls, yells to the silhouetted pest to scram (imperious flick of the wrist). She taps again, waves. He marches to the door, unbolts it, prepares to give whoever it is a piece of his hangover. Whoever is it? Fat Dan does not recognise her. He has to acquaint himself with the parts, juggle the features, figure the jigsaw – processes prosecuted in less than a blink, of course, but a blink that's stretched by incipient horror.

Her face had been peeled. The eyes in it were indignant, uncomprehending, locked in a terrible grief, the rare grief of the devenustated. She had the sort of looks she was told she'd never lose – a lie. Loss of beauty is like loss of a limb. It was more than that to Bonny: her beauty defined her; her looks were her livelihood; her prettiness lifted her, privileged her; her talent was her appearance; her face and her fortunes were glued together. Disfigurement was not only physical indignity, pain, wound. A scar is a dermal tumulus, a *perpetual* monument to the past, to an accident of birth, to a trip through a windscreen, whatever. A scar has a future: it amends the prospectus, it deprives Bonny of her power.

[1] That Pompey registration mark which would have come into being on 1 August 1975 was, in any case, proscribed by DVLC Swansea 'in case it should cause offence'.

Bonny's fans when her face was intact and her name was Vallée included harmless and hopeless specimens such as Crimper Pike who had eighteen convictions for cutting or attempting to cut women's hair as they stood in bus queues, sat on benches in Esplanade Gardens, waited to cross the road. They also included Lou Melchior (eight arrests, no convictions) who came to watch her twice before he drew up beside her in his Buick which was open topped, metallic lime, l.h.d. (a boon to UK crawlers, it places them that much closer to the kerb). He held up the g-string she had shed twenty minutes earlier and for which he had paid a navvy a tenner. He powersteered with a chunkily jewelled finger.

He held the g-string to his face and inhaled: 'I like it. I like it a lot.' Bonny turned round. Lou reversed.

'I wanna make you a pwopzition.'

She glared.

'Biz darlin, biz . . .' He glanced in the rearview mirror, across the street too. He pulled a transparent polythene bag from the streamlined glove compartment. Bonny gaped. She had never seen so much smack in all her junky life. 'Wanna talk then darlin?'

It was the gloves she wore. Lou, an old hand in The Flesh, saw through them as though they had been see-through. Cover-up? Get away. They're a give-away. He promised to double Fat Dan's money. He promised her all the cosy she could snort/smoke/send rushing through her veins to appease the greedy tyrant in her head.

In the summer of 1975, far from Pompey, far from Fretting Eddie, far from Fat Dan's cashflow crisis she appeared in these films: *Afternoon Swordsman*; *Dick's Dominion*; *Donkey Derby*; *Farmyard Of The Senses*; *Finger Food*; *The German Shepherd's Bush*; *Head Mistress*; *Lad Laps Lap*; *Meat And Two Vag*; *Mouthful Of Meat*; *My Packard, Your Garage*; *Penile Dementia*; *Penile Servitude*; *Pipe And Hose*; *Rectal Furlough*; *Tess Tossed Her Own*; *Yodelling On The Matterhorn*.

She didn't *act* in them. Acting is representation, analogy, illusion. Pornographic performance dispenses with illusion. It forgets (if it ever knew) that naturalism is artifice. They do not pretend, the couplers, who may be treblers (and sometimes trebles – but not in Lou's oeuvre, that sort of thing disgusted him, kiddies were sacred to him, never with kids). There is no distinction between that which they seem to do and that which they actually do. They do do. Thus they present rather than *re*present. The performer *is* the role. This is a state which many actors have aspired to, but were it applied to the legit canon every actor playing, say, Polonius would actually die: the electric carving knife thrust through the dutifully anachronistic room-divider would kill the player. The stage would become a form of public suicide for art's sake, as thrilling as Tyburn. And The Profession's endemic unemployment problem would be overcome. Yes, pornography does have lessons to teach besides the anatomical and the choreographic. It teaches the manufacturer that it is through Incremental Product Mutation that the consumer is hooked; the extra feature is the lure. The progress from one woman, to one woman plus one man, to one woman plus two men, to three women, six men, a horse, a cwt of wurst, a milking machine etc., is the model for the electric shaver which shaves, which is succeeded by the electric shaver which shaves and has sideburn trimming attachment, which is succeeded by one which possesses variable speeds, and that by the latest thing of the year before last with nostril hair clipper, clock etc. The Swiss Army's top brass are myopes with hair on their palms.

It teaches *its* manufacturers to make the workforce dependent: Bonny was already on a gram a day when she began to work for Lou Melchior, i.e. £55 per day before she could lift a cup without aching, before she could don workclothes without their scratching. (Nylon.) She was an employer's dream. Manipulable; engagingly prone to narcotic amnesia; responsive to both carrot and stick; obedient. It is the beau ideal of capitalistic enterprise. The product is universally popular, possibly addictive, of dubious legality thus admissive of outlandish price rises. Advertising costs: nil. Production costs: minimal. Tax: optional. Economic lessons apart it has something for everyone. It gives its opponents something to rail against.

The Founder: 'Adult! Adult? No no no! They got that wrong. That's the big lie. It's the opposite of adult. It was shown to me and I saw – though I had me eyes closed half the time – I saw, I know and I can tell you that though *they* may be adults, only may be, mind, what they're doing is infantile. It's grown-ups playing doctors and nurses. You show me yours and I'll show you mine. Infantile. It's regression. They regress in behaviour, got me? They regress in behaviour . . . But they haven't got the excuse of innocence. They're children in adults' bodies. Shameless. Ignorant – that's what innocence is. It's ignorance. It's one of The Good Guy's supreme achievements: to speed us through childhood, get us out of it quick. Advance into sentience. I know and I can tell you that The Good Guy does not give out chits to any Tom and Dick – sorry! – who fancies regressing; He does not sanction regression. Regression is blasphemy. It's going against the current on the Avenue Of Life. You got a paradox here: if it was just children and animals playing at mucky pups and showing off – well, then, *it would be more natural*. Really. More excusable. Yes. Because children and animals, in their temporary ignorance, in the throes of their infirmity, can't be expected to know no better. Pre-social, they are. Your nature film doesn't shy from showing the humping rhinoceri. Does it? No it's not the act itself in public it's the regression. Any other quest . . . Yes. Gent with the bobble hat.'

What does it teach the regressive adults themselves, these adults who have returned to the (pre) infantile state of pure appetite? It teaches them to ignore the functions of the mores they have learnt, to make moral trespass, to believe that anything is permitted. There are no limits to abandon. If you allow five men to ejaculate simultaneously on your face for an unseen audience of five million (before the tape is pirated, and many millions more thereafter) you are enshamed to break the bounds. Anything's all right by you, then, and posthumously. It teaches a special discernment: Bonny distinguished and recognised Bovril, Julio, Al, Alun and Tiger by their blood-distended cyclopean bulbs rather than by their vacuous faces and elaborate hair. Lou's perennials, bless 'em, they're regular as robots, The Five Postmen – they always deliver, always spew the money shot. And of course their faces are that way, they don't express themselves with their faces, they don't even need them, save as tongues and sinks. Bonny could distinguish though between these would-be animals and a genuine animal, an animal which does not have to try to be an animal.

Say hullo to Dusty. Covet his pelt. Listen to his rasping bark. Watch now as he bounds into the room. See the warm and happy smile he brings to Lou's face, a smile of paternal pride – but no, Lou's not his father, this dog is all dog. When Lou calls him 'my boy' or 'Dusty my son' the appellation should not be taken in earnest: the bestial miscegenation of Lou's world is barren. No starlet has ever emulated Pasiphaë, no bitch pupped to Lou in *them 'alcyon days* when he was a performer, before he broke into production. Look at Dusty snuffling in the deep pile carpet. See him leap into Lou's lap, a well-judged jump for a blind dog. Lou hugs him, pats him, ruffles his gleaming pelt, nuzzles his pointy ears. He fingers Dusty's rhinestone collar: 'Oo's a superstud then, oo's a superwover, oo's a big big boy, oo's a doggy-woger, oo's a lady's man then? Come on you wascal – own up!' Dusty might have been a veteran but he was still 'ot pwopty, he still had (Lou's vet's expert estimate) two, maybe three years of working life left to him. That's the sort of news his devotees wanted to hear. There were many of them. Despite the accident that had threatened to jeopardise his career he was among the biggest grossing dogs in Europe and, had he been able to travel, would surely have been the very biggest: 'I thought wiv this common market . . . kwawantine's cwiminal, inibits twade, dunt?' He had fan clubs in Hamburg, Valenciennes, Clermont-Ferrand. Festivals of his films had been held in Amsterdam and behind the central station in Copenhagen. When Lou strokes his tummy this dog who is a wolf's cousin sits up on his rear haunches and his nasty pink secret slides out from its hiding place in the fur, a warhead emerging from an Alsatian forest, a target for a taskforce of film stars past conscriptable age. A different genre of film to *The German Shepherd's Bush* whose story was a variation on Lou's casting-couch formula: a BBC TV producer (Bonny) is auditioning participants for a new Minorities Unit programme about the blind entitled 'Shades, Stick, Dog', when Dusty, playing a sighted guide dog, arrives in a PVC harness with his master

454

(Bovril). 'And it's not long before all three of them get down (!) to some hot doggy action. Soon they're joined by two gorgeous dancers who are just panting for it and Kevin the cameraman with the extra long lens.' The blurb, written by Lou himself, unaided, omits the information that only Bonny has congress with Dusty. This due to Lou having no other performer sufficiently trained, i.e. so enslaved by junk, so cowed by the threat of deprivation; he had, at that time, no other performer with the looks *and* the broken will.

Two of Dusty's former co-stars had died of overdoses, crying too loudly for help; the o.d., the o.g., is a trade disease, part of the job, accepted, one of those things. The magnificence of Lou's floral tributes was surpassed only by Dusty's: 'To a wonderful professional and a tremendous human being', signed with the print of a paw dipped in ink. Disease was not a trade disease. The ghost writer of Dusty's autobiographical memoir – not Reg Voice, one of his lesser brethren – put it thus: 'I was immune to the diseases that are attendant on my kind of stardom. They are not transmittable to dogs. The spirochaete – the slow assassin that corkscrewed through Lord Randolph Churchill, Boswell, most poets, Frederick Delius, my precursor Errol Flynn and millions more besides – might know me but could never enter me. And just as I required no prophylaxis so could my co-stars dispense with the chemical and mechanical apparatus of contra-ception; my seed can do nothing to you people, don't worry.' That was written after the success of *The Alsatian* and *Lorraine* and *The Things Girls Do With Sauerkraut*, when Dusty was making *Hot Dog, Sausage Dog* with Giulia Cicutto (butobarbitone, Tia Maria). Dusty's voice got it right, told the truth; but the truth is mutable, one year's truth is the next year's lie.

Six weeks after the final wrap on *Farmyard Of The Senses* – of which Bonny's only memory was the dog's dead eyes – Lou woke with his wife Sammi on one side of him and Dusty on the other. He patted Dusty. Dusty snapped at him, and had it not been for the protective cluster of rings he wore Lou might have lost a finger. The dog had never done that before. Nor had he refused to get up – he was a sporty sort, ever keen to go fetch during his pre-breakfast soiling of the nearby park. Then there was the vomiting, which was rum given his loss of appetite over the previous few days. *He wasn't himself.*

Timmy The Vet, DVM, MRCVS, diagnosed a virus, explained that the white blood cells release interleukin-1 which causes the hypothalamus to raise body temperature to a degree which the virus cannot bear. Natural defence. Nothing to worry about. Right as rain in a couple of days. Come the end of the week he was worse. He wasn't right as rain. Timmy The Vet was wrong. Dusty wouldn't eat. He hardly moved from the bed. When he did move he bumped into things: a lamp standard, a sofa, Lou's bamboo bar. Lou consulted his library: *Dog Problems And Problem Dogs; The Doggy In The Window And Other Traumas Of Canine Domestication; Your Pet Is A Person Too; The Pooch On The Couch.* Timmy The Vet made a house call. Dusty lay on the carpet like a fish on a riverbank. He looked that sick. Timmy reminded Lou that he wasn't simply a pet, that work related stress was increasingly prevalent in police dogs and dogs for the blind.

'An' no wonder,' said Lou ' – all that twaffic. All them cwims . . . Nngrrrech! All them quims. Follow? Yirh. That'll be it. Work lated stwess. My boy needs noliday.'

Dusty died in his master's arms, in a roadhouse's car park, on Thanet, one early dusk when the fall sky was mighty across the flatlands and the clouds were striations of pink and baby blue – an empyreal salute (they liked to think) to Dusty whose favourite ice-cream was cassata. Sammi ran in the Prospect Inn (archt: Oliver Hill, 1938, round, white, moderne). She phoned Mrs Giles to tell her to turn off the heating at their villa at Sandwich Bay; because of the tragedy they were going straight back Up The Smoke. But not before Lou, begrutten, flushed, puffy, had carried the warm corpse in its now oversized overcoat (an XXL garment on an S body) in his arms, in all tenderness, into the bar where they all stopped talking, as they would when a man puts a dead Alsatian on a naugahyde settle and blubs: 'King. He was a king.' Lou bought. The interrupted punters listened. To tales of the dog that rescued kiddies by jumping into canals/ twaffic/ the may'em of a crowd. To one about the dog that found the ball in the rough (Lou was up for the Woyal St George's). To that which recounted their meeting:

'Ow I found 'in wandrin, all alone like a doggy orphan.' Lou bought, paid, rang Timmy The Vet, disturbed him at home. 'Don' give me fuckin peop t' dinnah. You got fuckn' wetainah. Mate. Wan' pos'-mortem. While my lad's still warm. Wight?'

They sat in the waiting-room reading magazines for people with healthy pets. Timmy spared him the zip noise of an incised belly. He told them: 'You might as well go home. This is lab stuff.' They could hear Timmy The Vet scrubbing his hands, expostulating, plagued with fret.

Bits of their dog went round London. Prime cut, obviously, to Paterson at The Royal Veterinary, Royal College Street, NW1 – and thence, by bifurcated slices, to Wellcome and the School Of Tropical Medicine; to Reypens in Glasgow, to Jeeps at the Department Of Animal Oncology at Newcastle, to Rothampstead Research Station, Herts., and so on. But no doctor who treated humans got a slice. Nothing to Pompey, nothing to the perplexed sawbones in uniform who might – they had fine minds, they had fine samples, they hadn't been with the OMO wives to mitigate the fineness of their minds nor the scrutinies of their samples – have put two and two together. Nothing then to Dr David Sadgrove (p. 406), who might have made the link. Lou made it, himself, instinctively. He instinctively knew the source.

Blow torch and Stanley knife, they're what he took with him.

Fat Dan took her back as a barmaid. Her hair was died black. It was cut to cover her face. She wears sunglasses.

Lou had lied. He had said: 'There are thousands of chicks like you. All the slagettes and cumbabas . . . There was only one of him.' Then he lit the torch with a pocket lighter.

She flinched ever after at the sight of lighters, matches, the intimacy of shared flame; even a Dutch fuck frightened her. This is not an attribute a guv'nor seeks in his bar staff. Nor is an antipathy to the scent of aniseed, whose distillations Lou had rubbed on her to attract Dusty: think of Pernod sales. And her melted cheek, the cooked meat attached to her face – this was not punters' fancy. They had short memories, selective memories. In her perfection when junk had bloomed her face like a peach, blackberried her nipples, ravaged her inhibitions, allowed her to turn herself inside out for their delectation, they had craved Vallée, craved her gaping stockinged wound that ingested the leguminous tokens of themselves. Now she was Bonny, back behind the bar, an adjunct to a tap, a dermal freak rather than a lubricious one – and they pushed their sleevers elsewhere, held them up to Pauline (not, frankly, a work in oils, herself) or Patsy or Patsy's daughter Trish. Fat Dan had to archer her in a cost-cut. She was back at 486 Fratton Road. Time speeds when you're Old Dod's age, it seemed she'd only been gone a fortnight.

She signed on at the DHSS at Landport. The queue didn't give her face a second glance, her sort of face was par – shove a dimp in the corner of its mouth, make it fit in more. Cough. The building reeked of ash. She counted notes outside a Post Office. She counted pennies. She ached from lack. She scratched till she was sore, till she incised new tracks with her fretted nails.

She walked. She'd never walked before in all her life. Poverty transport, she despised it and herself for using it. She walked one night to the Hayling Ferry. She walked across the links and along the shore. She bounced on the freeway turf. She jumped in the bunkers like they were sandpits. The gorse clump. Her silhouette against the Solent stars, against the clear pure sky from a picture book. The dunes. The house on the dunes, the gerontophile's prize. The windows were rectilinear torches, brilliant panels suspended in the night. The house's shape was indiscernible. The gorse was barbed wire forged by nature. She went back towards the shore, approached the house from across the cutting dunes. She knelt in the sharp grass. On the other side of a picture window sat Mary, his legs over a chair's arm, his guitar in his lap. The room was rich with carpets, vases, stoutly carpentered wood. A troupe of flames in a fireplace built of mortared boulders. Bonny's tummy tightened, a ball of wool and lard filled her oesophagus, she trembled. She moved closer to the house, skirted the rhomboid of white sand that the window light casually colonised. Mary looked over his shoulder. He stretched out his large left hand. Onto this domestic stage teetered a pantomime dame, a cross-dressed senior citizen in a hat. Bonny had not seen May Butt before. And it wasn't a hat she wore but a geometrically cut wig. And if her make-up was theatrical, so what? She was making show for the night's unseen spectators. She bent over the chair to kiss the throat she had no right to, she bent over so far the hat of nun's hair threatened to fall on his chest. Bonny saw her man's hand reach between the dame's legs, she saw May Butt clasp it to her. This old woman was a parody of a young woman, a counterfeit of her former self, a fake whose allure was on life-support, a witch who might not have crossed the boundary of gender in her peruked pretence but had surely crossed that of age, and so *was* a TV – that's what Bonny would tell him. The veteran coquette ruffled Mary's hair and left the room with an exaggerated wiggle that might have been more convincing had she had her hips replaced: that was another thing Bonny would tell him. She crouched in shadow, at the end of the verandah. She listened to him, to the violent passage of his fingers on metal, to the coarsened voice that penetrated the invisible pane. The song, lubricious and minatory, might have been by Albeau. Bonny so wanted it to be for her, so wanted it to be Mary's teasing salute to the woman he could feel beyond light's empire, whom he knew to be listening to words that might be heard by the world but could be understood only by their addressee:

'I shall push my needle through your skin.

I shall stain you, I shall dye you

In remembrance of your sin.

It lasts for ever, my tattoo.'

He wanted her to bear his child! That was what he was saying in code, to her alone.

She waited for the last ferry. There were loud voices in the pub by the slipway, there were maudlin country songs of bad love, of too much heartache for one lifetime. Bonny hadn't enough money to buy herself a drink. And she hadn't the face to rely on being bought one. Not that she wanted pick-ups now. She watched the blueblack tide's silver rush. She leaned against a tarred sail-loft and stared beyond the lights of Pompey to the neon-lit Cross. She felt exultant, needed, spoken to, acknowledged, loved.

When she telephones Ixelles Villa the old woman she hates

459

answers, so she hangs up. Or Mary answers and, upon hearing her voice, hangs up. That'll be because the old woman she hates is in the room, filching his air, intruding, preventing him from talking to her, guarding him. She gauged his thwarted love for her by the length of time that passed before he regretfully hung up, by how long he dared listen to her giving love-phone, by how long he colluded. Every second was a precious sign, every second augmented his deceit. There was a pattern of his inhalation that she craved, two sniffs pursued by a breath that reached the pit of his lungs. He thus savoured her, luxuriated in her particular scent; he lingered over it, he drew it down the line, got it in his nostrils by the knack of synaesthetic reconstitution. That's what she believed. She didn't consider that he inhaled in exasperation. Nor did she consider the ambient smell around the phone at 486 Fratton Road. Boumphrey was increasingly neglectful of his dripping, he failed to strain out particulates of batter, fish, potato let alone renew the fat. Money problems. She was suffering them too: where once her floor had been abundantly carpeted with needles in steel parody of a pine wood now it was a rollered cake of lino, carpet, underlay – the materials fused and indistinguishable. She could no longer afford her prodigality with needles. She had to re-use. She had, too, to dilute her smack. She had to drink scrumpy.

Boumphrey suggested she put an OMO packet in his window which was visible from the street but she told him she had no old man. But the idea was a sound one and Boumphrey's offer generous. She settled on a packet of SURF (Sexy undies. Rimming. French.) but no one came so far north on Fratton Road for any of those and, besides, the nonce product placement was non-sense in the city of OMO.

She shoplifted, unambitiously. Such theft requires confidence and Bonny's confidence had disappeared with her facial features. Her characteristic expression now was furtive, imploring, as though pleading with the world that her disfigurement would go unnoticed: thus she drew attention to herself, thus she invalidated herself from a life of light fingers and voluminous clothes.

She wrote to her mother in Spain. No reply. She accepted subs from Eddie who loved her none the less for her sad looks and slyly believed that her undesirability to the general might favour the possibility of his consummating an act which could by now never match its multiple anticipations.

She told him soberly, as soberly as smack and scrumpy would allow: 'I'm not going to, Eddie love. You're not a dog are you.' Her face would quiver with lachrymal suppression: 'Sorry Eddie . . . you know how it is. It's not what we were made for.' She did not foresee a circumstance under which she'd change her mind. She'd have sworn then that she never would. It was a matter in which her will was impregnable, a token of pre-addiction, a link to The Garth and those times when plenty was the norm, when hers was the choice in everything. She sat in her room watching the allotment holders, reverencing the ordered banality of lives within limits, admiring their dogged toil, measuring the weeks in January Kings, feeling for them at the first frost, wishing she could celebrate small satisfactions with a Primus brew in a hut, wishing she could partake of humilities and predictability (p. 372). She knew she had stretched too far for all that. It didn't accord with her practice of begging a spoon of Boumphrey's lard, melting it in a pan on her Baby Belling, inserting a depressed syringe into the radial artery of her left forearm and filling it with blood which she squirts into the bubbling fat to fry as a skinless black pudding. Salt to taste. Sprinkle with Sarson's. That was not her exclusive diet. She ate sweets and crisps too, plus chocolate bars for nourishment. And scrumpy was fruit, a vital part of any regime. Toddy, to whom she talked, whose face she discerned in the crazed ceiling, whose presence above her she never doubted, had believed that alcohol was the ne plus ultra of veganism. She slumped supine on the matted candle-wick that reeked (to anyone but 486's inhabitants) of old frying, old dust. She slumped, and muttered in her widowhood, mulling over the past which had held so much, fearing to prospect the future which was surely thin beside it. (Compare the pile of pages beneath your left hand with that beneath your right.) She told Toddy that she was lonely, that she was poor. She had not been born to privations, she lacked the apparatus to endure them. She could vanquish them only by stepping back.

461

She observed the chainsmoking girl in front of her in the Post Office queue cash a Giro for £27.50p. Bonny cashed her own (£16) and hurried out into the gull-grey sleet of a Pompey Feb. The girl replied: 'Sfor the nipper. You get extra support if you got a nipper . . . An' you get a flat, you do. Gives you a head start on the housing a nipper does.'

She talked it over with her ex up there on the ceiling. It was a matter they had avoided during their curtailed years of duologue. There had been a covert assumption that procreation was to be postponed sine anno, that is till the time was ripe, when hedonism had palled. She told him she would love it, succour it, cherish it because it – the abstraction without sex or name, the beau ideal of babyhood, the cutesy bundle of gurgles and mirth – would be *theirs*, shared, entrusted to her womb and her terrestrial stewardship, but shared all the same, jointly authored by heaven and earth, by past and present, by yesterday's seed and today's egg, by the technologies of refrigeration and insemination. Poor Eddie gave her the fee for the last. 'I'll be a father to it,' he told her.

He patted her tummy signalling his claim in it. His lack had taught him the importance of the father to the child. He had pined for Guy, for the man in the photographs, the man in the maw of the beast. He invested the proto-child with manifold hopes. He had lifted Bonny and spun her round the day her pregnancy was confirmed. She had become pregnant so quickly, so easily, so painlessly ('just like going to the vet's'). He took that alacrity as an import of foetal viability, of a new dawn around the corner.

He prayed for mother and child. Ray Butt pronounced that St Christopher was the patron of mothers-to-be rather than of travellers for he gave an example in bearing, carrying, transporting: the river he crosses is an apt spatial symbol of the equally wet but temporal state of uterine habitation. 'I tell you what – more than likely this Christopher was a Christine but they told the story that way to . . . to externalise it eh? Get the sprog out of the belly plonk it on the shoulder. More of an image eh? It's our friends the Old Masters (p. 282) at it again, twisting the truth for the sake of a painting. If you got a Saint Christopher on the dashboard ditch it! I'm going to tell my sister I am – Saint Christine key rings for expectant mums. Hand em out at the clinic.'

Bonny attended The Church Of The Best Ever Redemption. She felt The Founder speak to her: all through the early spring of '76 he addressed the 'problem alleys' that lead into The Avenue Of Life. He warned her (it was her) of the scallywags of temptation who lurk in those alleys. He spoke, obfuscatingly, of 'The Pagan Hag', the black alley abortionist, whose archetype is Old Ma Cropper, who wants to seize foetuses for Satan, who seduces with a prospectus of freedom from nappy chores, of continued indulgence, of high times on the tiles. He railed against the institutionalised right to choose: 'Look up, breathe in. Doesn't a day like today make you want to thank The Good Guy that he didn't give *your* mother the right to choose. Doesn't it make you want to curse the pygmy usurpers of His will? To brand them? To give them eyes of different colours?' Bonny agreed.

A girl child stood in best gingham in the shadow of The Cross Of The World beside Ray Butt and talked into the microphone he handed her: 'When I was a bird I used to flap my wings and before I was a bird I was an elephant.' The congregation cheered.

Bonny knew her child, too, would be possessed of imaginative innocence. She prided herself on the ordinariness she had begun to achieve, on having tasted the exoticism of sobriety and stability. She was coming off junk. She was swelling to the point where Housing showed the friendly face of bureaudom.

She didn't mind holding hands with Eddie when they shopped for a cot. She shared his proud embarrassment when Sam the pram mechanic (p. 305) recognised him from a Southern Television documentary entitled 'Our Deep South'. He shook Eddie's hand with devotional frig. He mentioned his wife's connection with Daph. He asked after May. He offered them a celebrity discount, a generous 10% on a Pedigree with suspension that 'makes a DS's look frankly naive'; a generous 7.5% call it 8% on a buggy that's 'like riding on a soufflé'. The mention of May provoked Bonny, got her goat, got her demanding 15% and 12% respectively. From a chandler's in Old Pompey they bought a hammock – so Bonny and the babe within might sleep in the Haven On Earth's only bed whilst Eddie swung between the stout tarred crucks planning but never prosecuting a nocturnal raid on his coz below. The wavelets will lap.

'I want you, I beseech you,' yelled Ray Butt on Sunday 2 May 1976, 'to think about my mum. My May. She's a jewel. A real gem. Give her a moment of your time. You moan at Him for her. All right?'

Pompey was in mourning because So'ton had won the Cup Final the previous day by a goal deemed offside in all the pubs. Bonny listened to Eddie. He reiterated his hatred of the Saints' name.

He told her that May was ill, confined to a clinic at Hindhead with which Daph did contras. An asthmatic allergy to dune grasses said the doctors. *A through-ball from Jim McCalliog* said The Voys, i.e. an undetected foul: they reckoned Mary had been poisoning her. They knew the terms of her will. They didn't trust him, not after what he'd done to the band, not after what he'd already done to their granma. 'Ood wanta gogo dancer for a gran?' asked Laddy. 'E cheapened our family,' said Sonny. The Founder and his sons didn't regret a penny spent on her health care, they revered her beyond all price, she was *where they come from*. Eddie was inured to their complaints about Mary. In his stride. And their slicks of exasperation, he accepted them: people were like that, sizing up to the nears and dears. It was *the ideal* of family that he longed for, that he believed achievable, that might be attained with Bonny.

They came in family-handed, all of the Butts: Ray in his chair, Daph in her beige, Jonjon and Hankey, Sonny and Laddy. He heard them coming – the echoes in The Founder Bunker, the bite of the Voys' quarter irons, harsh murmurs' rasp. They stood before Poor Eddie Vallender in his subterranean office. They ignored niceties. He'd never seen them thus. They stood as for a family photo, titches to the edges, Daph to the right and Hankey to the left. Abstracted, they made an open pediment, with Butt the bust in its centre. They came to Eddie as supplicants to a regent. They had their teeth, their wheels, their suits, their unity of purpose. The combined lapels of the four males were forty-eight inches. Their teeth were shiny half moons. It was, of course, The Founder who stated their position. He concluded: 'We thought long and hard Ed. We thought long and hard before we consulted you Ed. But you are family. You are family. And you're the one in the family with the gift.'

'We want,' said Jonjon, looking about him, 'we want you to do him pyschic harm.'

Sonny leans over Eddie's desk: 'Mary's got it coming. Asked for it. Asn't he?'

Laddy: 'What he done to our gran. All down to greed. Not love. Greed. Poncing. Exploitation. He needs psychic harming.'

'Drift?' asked Jonjon. 'Get it?'

'With your gift . . .' leered Sonny, the enamelled flatterer, 'you'll find a way . . . A little dish of revenge.'

'I didn't hear that,' said the Founder.

'Putting matters straight then,' corrected Sonny, 'on Gran's behalf, on Aunt Daph's behalf. He's never done you no favours Ed has he now? Doesn't exactly come the faithful friend does he now? Our Mary . . . I can remember the night he was still Jean-Marie.'

Poor Eddie was sensitive to the threatening weight of their expectation. Their collective stare was imprecatory. They – with the evident exception of Ray Butt – stood. He sat. They had never thus previously acknowledged the authority that derived from his power. They were treating him as though he were shaman, capo, warrior (so he thought). It was as if The Church was recognising a Power greater than The Founder, greater than The Cross. The Church Of The Best Ever Redemption was admitting to the inequity of its Trinity.

But what is 'psychic harm'? What did The Founder's family expect of him? Bemused Eddie had no one to consult. Dr Clark W. Grover had died in 1974: the author of *Our Forgotten Bodies: A Forty Point Plan For Maximal Potential* tripped over a child's tricycle after three 'beefy' Manhattans at a Sunday bar-b-q in a neighbour's garden in Highland Park, Illinois, and fell in the pool. His cries for help were regarded as 'just another of Clark's jokes'. The author couldn't swim.

Dredgable Possibility admitted injury, sure: like all science it was bereft of integral good. 'Ill at will,' Eddie had told Chubb. Eddie consulted Laddy. They walked the ramparts of Fort Widley.

'What', asked Laddy, mocking, squeezing the bulb in his pocket to make the joke-shop carnation in his buttonhole spray water, 'do you think it means? It means psychic harm.'

Poor Eddie had, all his life, understood the comforting power of euphemism; Laddy walked on ahead of him, kicking clods into the dry moat a vertigo below. Poor Eddie looked at The Cross. The euphemism, the evasion, the happy-speak, was contained in the adjective. Harm. Unqualified harm. Eddie stared on the roofs of Flamebryte's lean-tos, on the warped armature of a Nissen, on the slack and filthy ropes looping across the lorry's top. He kicked a clod with his left foot which was as able as his right. Elderflowers made big dandruff on their leaves. Starlings. He hated Mary.

Bonny Vallender was fourteen weeks pregnant, ticking a checklist (Grapenuts, skimmed milk, no Omo, Mackeson, Marmite, silver foil) in Buyright, pondering by an aisle's end, Bic in mit, sloppy, daps, XXL T-shirt already, unmade-up, carrying a basket when she met Mary. Collided with Mary. His was a fecund trolley. Wires twined. They had not spoken. He had seen the face before. Her devenustation kind of roused him. He winked, he shopped, he pushed his trolley. Most of all he looked behind him. Bonny saw her then, that was the one time face to face, beside the meat counter where the flies bathed in blood. May zimmered a foot away, wig in air, frail as a corpse. She wore auburn. Her left thigh quivered. She had no bum, no breasts, no flesh. She didn't notice when Mary put his arm around her shoulder and smiled over his own shoulder at Bonny. She didn't notice when Mary feigned forgetfulness and strode back through the aisle of pulses, nodding to the beat of the easy shopping music. Bonny leant against a cream cracker display, red and white, Crawford's. He held up one finger. He gestured towards his now invisible consort, his bit, his woman

466

on a frame. He held up one finger: 'One year. I give her one year.' He grins the way Albeau did, the way he never unlearnt. He pats her baby, the posthumous gift that kicks: 'One year. But you get rid of that.'

Bonny aborted when the child was sixteen weeks old. It was a girl. It had been a girl. It would have been a girl. Daph's mechanics did a pro job. She was in and out overnight. Cash. False name. No immediate regrets. She walked across the night dunes again. She watched her man feed the zimmercase, watched him hold the spoon to her mouth. Week by week she saw the old bag grow to health. She was there, squatting in the couch grass, the night Old May stood straight again. She came in the room in a scoop-neck blouse and a flouncy skirt, the entire outfit in magenta. Bonny cried when Mary kissed her. May danced about. They danced to unseen sounds, they twisted, they waltzed.

Bonny, the firework maker's daughter, lies childless and emptied on her matted counterpane, sobbing at her loss, sobbing for her beloved tiny daughter. She had committed proxy suicide. She keened, she fretted, she wailed. She cursed the old woman who had entrapped her man, who blighted her future. She blamed May. She despised May's resilience, her capability to recover. The crone's had more than her share of this earth. She's greeded on years.

I saw them along about this time, Poor Eddie and Bitter Bonny. I'd spent a day in So'ton, assuring myself that Bevois Valley looked the way I thought it did. It didn't. But by the time that I had reached Pompey that street's banality had disappeared and my memorious version had triumphed again, it had regained the slummy, vertiginous magnificence my imagination had long ago granted it. I tried to pretend that I didn't notice Bonny's wound, the poreless skin, her animal eyes. I watched Eddie clean a frying pan with toilet roll. They seemed unsurprised to see me, cocooned in an oblivion that I couldn't understand. I don't know what rules they were playing to. They were unsurprised to see me go after a few minutes. They may already have been burdened with prospective guilt – whatever secret they shared it was a profound one, a shameful one, something which disgusted them but which had an autonomous power of its own.

Bonny had said one night to Eddie, had said this under the mask of frivolity, had presented it as a gag, had dissembled its enormity: 'If you were to sort out the May problem Eddie – you know what I'd do. I'd let you have me.' Eddie didn't reply: he didn't believe her. Bonny giggled.

Old Man Dod, listening at the door, nodded sagely. He was no end of help when the police came round.

Poor Eddie Vallender had understood in an instant the meaning of psychic harm. Bonny watched the idea grow just as she had watched her baby grow. The very presence of the possibility contaminated their shared world of chores and smalltalk. It was always there. When they caught each other's eye. Eddie had so wanted to be father to that rued child, had longed for the dutiful steadiness of paternity. An idea swells; it does not suffer miscarriage, it does not spontaneously abort, it has sufficient strength to avoid that fate; nor is it aborted by its begetters; they accept the prospect of fruition, the birth. Words turn into blood on the carpet and spleen on the walls.

Bonny whispered to him: 'You have given so much life. So much Eddie. Isn't it time you took some back. For yourself. For your own sake.'

He believed that the symmetry of the demands made on him was beyond coincidence. He was being asked to fire with right and left. He was the power sought by two sides to achieve a violent mediation. There was a reason for this. He was the one man who might work mirrored extinctions. He was a unique agent whose interests were not those of his supplicants. It was beyond coincidence to be so solicited. Poor Eddie discerned meanings, patterns, destiny-directives. Sniff, sniff – The Good Guy's shuffling with a wink, he's dealing off the bottom of the deck (p. 30), he's using Eddie the way Eddie's always been used. Eddie's quarry. Poor Eddie read the signs: the magpies, the blue cars all in a row, the four blind women, snatches of dusk conversation that precisely echo ones heard at dawn. He was in touch with more than Ray Butt had ever dreamed of. He could turn knowing that, say, the man behind him on the pavement was so engrossed in his folded newspaper that he would trip over a Pomeranian's stretched lead. He suffered delusions of scale, felt some days as though he was walking through a city that was subtly smaller than he was, that was, say, a 9/10 model of itself. In a cul de sac in Cosham he saw a house stretched across the short street's end like a stage flat. It was austere, symmetrical, flanked by identical Lombardy poplars. He experienced a suburban epiphany. He was looking at the end of The Avenue Of Life, and saw that it was as strange as only the banal can be. It was also very close. He looked up to The Cross.

He visited Geoff Dickinson, aka Pigfucker (p. 278). The drought had hit the farm. Poor Eddie told the soft-brained farmer that he'd arrange for rain. He had come for a gun: 'Self protection, Geoff.'

'Gandhi should have thought along them lines,' said Pigfucker, surprisingly.

'And I'm going to shoot those cussed gulls,' said Eddie, asserting his independence.

'Strip the feathers off and you can sell them down Dave Ring's as pigeon.'

Pigfucker led him to a cacophonous henhut where two .22s and a sawnoff lay hidden beneath the straw. He chose the sawnoff. Feathers were stuck to its stock. He dutifully admired the pigs.

Pigfucker grinned: 'Next week's bacon – such is life.'

Poor Eddie drove the vehicle he had stolen; the virgin drove the nicked Simca from the car park of The Danish Play, its ashtrays were full of butts. He had no driving licence but he could drive across the dunes, and that would be the least of his offences.

He thought of Bonny, he thought of his fate, he thought he knew who'd come for him. He had begun to understand.

He drove at night across Hayling, he overtook a dawdling PC in a Panda. He heard dogs howling at the sea. He turned off the metalled road near the end of the golf links. The lane to Ixelles Villa was by now well worn: two equal tracks of dusty baked earth, a strip of lanterns between them. The uniforms, the CID, the forensics in their van/lab will wear it down more. Later, that is. The next morning. Det-Inspector Smerdon will grimace: 'Like

469

an abattoir it is in there – someone's been playing silly buggers.' A rooky vomits. The house *is* an abattoir.

He stopped the Simca in the sand. He touches the cartridges in his pocket. He is doing this for his future. This is the messy condition upon which his glory is founded. His sanctity will be based on blood. This is the path of symmetry, the just and apt way. All this is necessary. The confluence of mutually antago- nistic desires is sited within *him*. The balance between the poles. He wore a hat. He tied a handkerchief across his face. He had no fear of being recognised, that was not why he went kitted that way. They were going to be unavailable to report on the identity of the killer. And he was not masked from shame. He simply sought the extra potency of facelessness. Without features he was fate. Hat and mask were crutches. The route to The Cross is hard, help along it comes in many shapes, many manifests. The house was lit, was loud with a song by Albeau: 'Quand J'Aurai Disparu'. Mary strummed his guitar to it. (Eddie understood the euphemism, of course. He appreciated the aptness.) He was propped up, too, by the intimacy he achieved with the weapon. The executioner snuggles up to it, caresses it, bends it to his will and immortal destiny. It is an extra limb, an instrument which prosecutes the soul's bidding. It is prosthetic like glasses or a zimmer. On which subject: here's May's zimmer.

She holds it as a shield, as though it is solid, as though it will protect her. Skulls snap with the noise of an army marching over nougat. Her wig went that way with the top of her head in it. The rest of her head was a crimson fountain.

Albeau sang on. Mary's brains slid down a wooden wall. The night was hot. The smell of contaminated blood is warm, metallic. A carpet goes red with a litre of AO-1. Waste! Mary could have sold it. The plateglass in the picture window is ten thousand icicles across the ensanguined floor.

Look at the old woman twitch.

He never knew Mary had so much gift gold in his teeth.

Eddie was dazed. But no more dazed than he had been since two squalid temporal plots combined to reveal the awful magnificence that would come to him.

He walked back to the car. A pack of former Pompey puppies

470

grown into wild dogs came roaring over a dune and he had to run. He gasped for breath. The car's wheels skidded. He beat his head against the steering wheel. The gun is on the seat beside him. The pack howled. The house on the dunes is still lit. Nothing has happened. It looks good as new, homely, polished. We can hear Albeau's voice. His son who was not his son cannot hear it. That is the difference. The couch grass waves in the breeze. The keen-nosed pack runs into the house for a feed. We can smell the sea as well as blood. And there are the lights of Pompey, there is The Cross, and here are the allotments at the back of Fratton Road.

That's where Poor Eddie lay. A virgin and a healer in a cabbage patch. He was there all the next day. Shivering, awaiting his fate, staring at the sun. He knew they'd come for him. He knew they'd find him. He didn't try to hide. Bonny saw him from her window. She no longer had any reason not to tell the Voys where he could be found. They'd been round twice already, weeping for their Gran.

'What does he think psychic harm means?' asked Laddy. 'I'd never have wished *that* on Mary . . . Funny sort, naughty boy, but you don't wish that on 'im. You ever meet Mary?'

Exculpated Bonny, mouth agape, nods with a shrug.

'He wasn't the sort you'd remember, not necessarily.'

It was getting on for 4 pm when she saw Eddie beyond the huts and hurdles and blinding cloches. He was writhing, holding his knees to his chest. She phoned The Church.

The Voys had no idea that they were colluding with Poor Eddie who believed himself a saint and a martyr. The Voys beat him with rakes and shovels. They did it for their Gran. They punctured his stomach with the tines of a gardening fork. He vomited blood on cabbages and marrows. He vomited blood on the seat of the hatchback in which they drove him from the allotments to The Church Of The Best Ever Redemption. He did not resist them. He made no fight.

At nightfall, Friday 20 August 1976, Sonny, Jonjon and Laddy bolted Poor Eddie Vallender to one of the ad hoc crosses that had been erected down the years at the foot of The Cross Of The World. They used screws, wire, nails, bolts – one bolt went through the line of life and two arteries and a delta of tendons and through the median nerve too. They mistook his compliance for an admission of his guilt. At midnight that makeshift Easter they appropriated from Flamebryte Ltd a lorry fitted with a winch. They hauled the cross that bore Poor Eddie 200 feet high onto the crux of The Cross Of The World. He swung on his personal armature against the concrete and bulbs and neon. He swayed as though he had wings. His world undulated beneath him. He was nearly dead when the Spithead Bite blew so hard that he was gusted up, lifted like a rag then dropped back against The Cross with such force that neon tubes snapped and little flames ran through the circuit.

The subsequent fire below in the premises of Flamebryte Ltd was visible all across the city of HoTLoVe and OMO, and, they say, from thirty miles out to sea. All the tars and all the tarts leaned from their windows to watch the most consummate display of fireworks that ever coloured our southern sky.

Here was Pompey's Pride. It lit Lucky Eddie in death. He was illumined in His glory. As He passed from one state to another, from present to future indefinite, He dreamed of a grand deposition, of meeting His mother at the base of The Cross. He never knew it was not to be. The good guy's greatest joke is to make us believe in him when he's not there at all, and his next best gag is the cruel lie about eternal reunion, about The Garden of Chums, The Bounteous Fellowship Cloister, Serenity Meadow, The Village With A Song In Its Heart – he's had us all. There was no one to greet Poor Eddie.

Never mind. It was a lovely show for those on this side. The Cross burnt hard and bright at its centre. They will never forget it – a pyrotechnical miracle that was akin to the magical mayo made when egg truck and oil tanker collide. That night was shrill with colour. It was bright enough to blind. Mineral light beat out the black. Darkness was defeated. The man I saw became a bird.

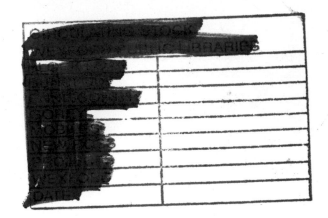